Also by Lew W. L. Salledyn

Scientific Fragments: Songs of Mourning

Fragments of the History of Assyria

Lew W. L. Salledyn
salledyn@gmail.com

Scapegrace and Misfit Press 2024

I replied, "My Lady, devoutly to the utmost that I can,
do I thank Him
who from the mortal world has removed me.
But tell me, what are the dusky marks [segni]
of this body, which there below on earth
make people fable about Cain?"

Dante, second canto of *Paradise*, translated by Charles Norton

Night would invade, but there the neighboring moon
(So call that opposite fair star) her aid
Timely interposes, and her monthly round
Still ending, still renewing, through mid-heav'n;
With borrowed light her countenance triform
Hence fills and empties to enlighten th' Earth
And in her pale dominion checks the night.

Milton, *Paradise Lost*, Book III

Nabû, the administrator of the universe, gave him [Nabû-na'id] the art of writing.

Excerpt of the inscription found on two clay cylinders possibly from Marad, dated to between the third and tenth years of the reign of Nabû-na'id.

Although I [Nabû-na'id] do not know the art of writing, I have read secret things.

Excerpt of the Verse Account of Nabû-na'id.

...In that time [of Cyrus] there was still in this sacred domain a human statue of solid gold 12 cubits high. I myself have not seen it, but the things told by the Chaldeans I tell. Darius the son of Hystaspes, though he plotted to take this statue, did not have the gall to seize it; Xerxes the son of Darius took it and killed the priest who forbid him from moving it... Now many others came to be rulers of this city of Babylon, adorners of its walls and holy places, of whom I shall craft memory in my Assyrian Accounts. *Among these were two women: ...Semiramis...and [five generations later] Nitocris.*

Excerpt of *The Histories* of Herodotus, Book 1 chapters 183-5. His *Assyrian Accounts* are otherwise unknown.

To Miranda and Rebecca, former students
whose lesson to me was their example.

To my comrades long ago at Umm el-Marra and
in the fishbowl of D-Level.

To my own eccentric family, human and not.

Contents

Chapter 1. Youthful Tales

"My mother used to tell me a story," Nabû-na'id confided. "Anzû, golden-maned like a lion but colorfully feathered like a bird, placed himself on the only path to a city, a path teetering atop a cliff which plunged into the river Purattu. He insisted that travelers answer a riddle. "What are you?" he would ask. One man responded, "I am a chicken." Anzû stared at him for a moment. Then, with a swipe of his taloned paw, he pitched him off the cliff. A second man responded, "I am a donkey." Again Anzû stared; again Anzû swept the man from the cliff. A third man responded, "I am a hat." Down the cliff he went. Then came a fourth man, who responded, "I am Anzû." Having foreseen this eventual answer, Anzû merely knocked the man from the cliff. The last man responded, "I am a man." For a moment a peaceful silence reigned while Anzû held the man's gaze. Then, with a swipe of his taloned paw, Anzû pitched him off the cliff. After this no more men came. Visitors abandoned the city whose inhabitants, if there were any, never left. Still, many years passed before Anzû himself departed, as mysteriously as he had arrived."

"Did not the last man answer the question properly?" Gubaru asked. "What was the proper answer?"

"Who is to say that there is anything to understand of Anzû?" Nabû-na'id replied.

"My mother used to tell me a story," Nabû-na'id confided a second time. "A man from Ḫarrānu was commanded by a god to abandon the land of his father. The god promised him a son and from that son, sons as many as are heaven's stars. The man, accompanied only by his wife, did as the god commanded. So keenly did this man listen for the god that he would hear nothing else, no bird song, no lowing cattle, neither the woman's weeping nor her laughter. Decade after decade did they toil westward, always silent lest the god should speak. In advanced old age the woman continued to gather food for the man, drew for him water, prepared their repast, bore him one shocking evening a son. The man was overjoyed; the god had at last fulfilled the first part of his promise. More years passed. While the boy and the woman would chatter like birds in each other's company, in the presence of the man, who was always straining to hear the god, they were respectfully silent. The man did not strain in vain. One day he heard distinctly the god's command. It bore no questioning, either of the god or of himself. He could not doubt that he had heard. The next morning, saying nothing, he set out with the boy. For three days he walked, eyes cast down. They climbed the promised mountain. On its barren, lifeless summit – not so much as a thicket – in the absolute silence of the breaking day, he sacrificed his son."

"Did the god ever speak to him again?" Gubaru asked. "What did he tell him?"

"Who is to say the god did not speak in the absolute silence of that morning?" Nabû-na'id replied.

"My mother used to tell me a story," Nabû-na'id confided a third time. "In the age of the sages, one of them, Adapa, broke the wing of the wind. The god Ea, his father, warned him that he would be held to account. When they bring you before these gods, flatter them, said Ea, but to these others speak truthfully. Above all, beware the food of death, *ša mūti* – do not eat it! Beware the drink of death, *ša mūti* – do not drink it! As his father predicted, the gods sent for the sage. He flattered those his father said to flatter; to those others he spoke truthfully. Enlil was pleased and offered him the food of life, heavens' food – *šamūti*. The sage would not eat. Enlil offered him the drink of life, heavens' drink – *šamūti*. The sage would not drink. Why have you chosen death over life? Enlil asked. The sage would not answer."

"Did his father mean to trick him?" Gubaru asked. "What end did that serve?"

"Who is to say that even a god can trick a sage?" Nabû-na'id replied.

The two boys, Nabû-na'id and Gubaru, rose from the dirt where they had been seated. Nabû-na'id was the older, by a few years, with eyes which seemed almost sand-colored. Already his posture was stooped and, in comparison to the other boy, he seemed somehow less full, though he was the taller of the two. "Let us play *pukku* and *mekkû*," he suggested. Gubaru, his dark, wavy hair partially covering his eyes, remained troubled. "Why do you answer my questions with questions?" he asked. "Do you not know the answers? Do you even understand your responses?" Nabû-na'id looked at him solemnly. "Let us play *pukku* and *mekkû*," he repeated, giving a tug to Gubaru's robe. "Someday, perhaps we will both understand." "Does your mother understand?" Gubaru asked. "That isn't the right question for my mother," Nabû-na'id replied. "My mother acts as the god wills, but has the god willed that she understand? If he has, then she does; if he has not, she is content with that too. My mother, as you know, is inscrutable. She has seen the Deep. It may not matter to her or to anyone whether she has understood it."

Gubaru looked at him strangely. "You are very like your mother," he said.

Nabû-na'id stared at him, then laughed, swiped at him and missed as Gubaru twisted out of the way. "Perhaps there is nothing to understand!" he shouted, running through the field toward a canal. Gubaru stood still for a moment and watched. He heard the peal of his friend's voice rise out of and then sink back into the swaying field of barley. "Come! Play!" Still he stood, as if lost in thought though thinking nothing. Then suddenly, without realizing that he had decided to, he raced after Nabû-na'id.

Some later time. His mother, dressed in sackcloth, covered in ash, walked past them, murmuring a prayer. For an instant they exchanged glances – hers sharp, penetrating, almost painful. And his? He did not know what his gaze was like. The instant passed; his mother did not stop. She was inscrutable.

"Where is your father?" Gubaru asked.

"If you mean Nabû-balaṭsu-iqbi, I am told that for now he is serving in Sardis. But I am not sure that a man such as he – a hunched-over, weak-eyed scribe – could have fathered me on a woman such as my mother. Perhaps instead I am the spawn of a *lillu*-demon... What did this man, this minor official, see in my mother – already old, already mourning, dragged here in captivity from beloved and ruined Ḫarrānu? What did she see in him, she who has seen the Deep? No, it was a *lillu*-demon, I think, who begot me on my mother. From my other father she took his access to the schools and to the court, small door though it was – she would need no more. And she took from him his titular deity, Nabû, the god of scribes, or if not, the scribe god, to give me wisdom, writing and prophecy. And yet I think it pained her to name me in praise of Nabû. That name, I am sure, cost her more dearly than any other importunity of my would-be father."

"You think that she would have named you for Sîn? Even if it was not a proper time to honor Sîn? Perhaps it was a new moon, and Sîn refused to look on us."

"For my mother, it is proper to honor Sîn at all times. That he looks away from us is further reason to exalt him. What are we that a god shouldn't tire of regarding us?" He paused. "Sîn has looked away from us since he deserted Ḫarrānu, since he gave the city to Nabû-apal-uṣur and the Umman Manda."

"Another man named in honor of Nabû," Gubaru observed in a teasing tone. "As is our present king. Perhaps the time of Sîn is past. Perhaps ours is the age of Nabû." Gubaru looked at him provocatively, but Nabû-na'id showed no reaction. "Are you wise, son of Nabû-balaṭsu-iqbi or, if you prefer, of a *lillu*-demon? Will mud tell you the secrets of faraway men, of distant men, past men and future men? Someday will you hold the Tablets of Destiny?"

"If ever I do," murmured Nabû-na'id, speaking slowly and almost in a whisper, "I shall read them by the light of the moon."

They were playing in the field, but they had lost the *pukku* and the *mekkû*. Nabû-na'id was nearly in tears. "If only I had left them in the shop! If only I had left them in the shop! Then we would have them for tomorrow!"

Gubaru was perplexed. "I have never seen you this upset, Nabû-na'id! Why are you so bothered?" But Nabû-na'id did not respond; he sat on the ground, clawing and clenching the dirt with his fingers. He rocked back and forth, while a tear slid down his clay-covered face. Standing awkwardly beside him, at a loss, Gubaru placed a hand on his shoulder. Nabû-na'id did not react. "Surely we can get another *pukku* and *mekkû*," Gubaru said. "The carpenter will build them for us."

"You are a boy," Nabû-na'id spat out, angrily. "My grief is not for the *pukku* and the *mekkû*. They are not what is lost."

"Then what is lost?" Gubaru demanded.

"Tomorrow. I have lost tomorrow."

Gubaru did not understand, so he stood in silence.

"You have lost it too," Nabû-na'id added.

The next morning, Gubaru ran up to Nabû-na'id. "You see!" he laughed. "Tomorrow was not lost after all!"

Nabû-na'id did not laugh with him.

They went to the field where they had lost the *pukku* and the *mekkû*. "Are we going to look for them again?" Gubaru asked.

"No." They walked together in silence, hearing only the crunch of sand and pebbles and dry vegetation beneath their feet. They were climbing a small hill. Nabû-na'id looked only at the ground.

After a while, still on the slope of the hill, he stopped, squatted, and signaled Gubaru to do likewise. He pointed at something in the dirt. "Have you ever wondered why we can't help but trample on these?"

Gubaru was surprised to see that he was pointing only at pottery sherds. "Well, because people throw their junk away."

"But look at all the sherds. Where are all the people carrying pieces of broken pottery beneath their robes, waiting for an opportune moment to dump them?" He looked Gubaru directly in the eyes, his own face strangely intense. "Look at all the sherds, Gubaru!" he repeated.

"Well, some of them have probably been here for a while."

"Yes!" Nabû-na'id said excitedly. "*But for how long?*"

"Can it be that I lost tomorrow and discovered yesterday?" Nabû-na'id wondered.

"A tablet!"

"Pieces of one, anyway."

"Where did you get it?

"My mother gave it to me. She said that it came from

Ḫarrānu, or near there."

"Can she read it?"

"I don't know. With my mother, anything is possible."

"Can you?"

"I have been trying since she gave it to me. Parts of it I understand. It involves a king – I don't know how to read his name. His city is Karkemiš, where the great battle with Muṣur was fought. But I think this is before then, perhaps long before. He is somehow involved in freeing a slave into a slave."

"That doesn't make any sense!"

Nabû-na'id looked pensively at the tablet, his brow furrowed.

"Doesn't it?" was all he said.

Adad-guppi looked at him and he at her. She was, as always, in sackcloth, her hair tangled and matted, smeared with ash like her face, her hands, her arms, her clothes. Her eyes were wild. They were always wild. "Why does it perplex you?" she murmured.

"Who is freed into slavery?"

"Who is not?" she said.

"Can you read, mother?"

"Has it ever struck you that there is a god who writes but not a god who reads?"

"What do you mean, mother? Surely if you can write, you can read."

"Writing is only the beginning of reading. Nabû, may he be exalted – perhaps HE has begun to read." She emphasized the pronoun and smiled; she still had most of her teeth, despite her age.

"And you?"

"Perhaps I have begun as well."

A sudden thought struck Nabû-na'id. "Can you write?"

"Everyone writes," she said.

"Who is this boy you are always with?" she asked him.

"Gubaru is my brother."

"I gave you no brother."

"You did not have to. I took one."

"Soon would be the *Akītu* festival in Ḫarrānu, the festival for Sîn," she said. Nabû-na'id and Gubaru stood before her. She eyed them slowly, as if measuring them – not idly, in terms of lengths and widths and weights – but in terms of future deeds whose need she foresaw. Her son met her gaze, as she knew he would. There was a sharpness, a wildness, to his eyes too – once you got past the lostness. And the other boy? He looked away, but she had already seen.

"Someday you must lead the god by his hand and return him to Ḫarrānu, to his temple, the Eḫulḫul," she declared to her son.

And to Gubaru: "You will help him."

"Perhaps Sîn is happy in Bābilim," Nabû-na'id suggested audaciously.

She had already turned her back on them and was walking toward the inner chamber. "He is not," she said over her shoulder, neither slowing nor turning.

"Why do you think Anzû killed the men?" Gubaru asked.

"In the story my mother used to tell me?"

"Yes."

"What are you, Gubaru?"

"Well, I am or will soon be a man. But that answer didn't satisfy Anzû."

"Perhaps. But if it didn't, why not?"

"I don't know. If it was a woman dressed up as a man, maybe that's why. Or maybe a slave pretending to be a free-man. But if the man really was a man..."

"If I asked you – who are you? – what would you say?"

"I would say I am Gubaru, of course."

"Why do you not say you are a man?"

Gubaru looked exasperated. "Because the question was who, not what."

"But what's the difference, Gubaru, between who and what? Why is what you are 'a man,' and not 'Gubaru'?"

"If you ask me what I am, you are asking to what I belong. This table – it belongs to a collection of things like it, things we call tables. What I am is always something I share with others. But if you ask me who I am, that is uniquely my own."

"But there are other Gubarus in the world, Gubaru. Perhaps someday you will meet one or be confused for one. Maybe it will become a great mystery: 'Was that Gubaru the same as this Gubaru?' people will ask. Then they will collect all the Gubarus and examine them. They will say: 'These are things we call Gubarus.' You will be just like the table."

Gubaru laughed. "You know that isn't true!"

"I am not sure if I know that. My name is not only my own. You pointed it out before: I am a Nabû-man, one of many – like Nabû-apal-uṣur and Nabû-kudurri-uṣur and my father. Perhaps that is the answer Anzû waited for. 'What are you?' 'I am a Nabû-man,' I'd say. But then I'd hasten to add: 'That's what I was assigned, anyway – what my parents called me. But in my heart of hearts, I am not a Nabû-man.'"

"Don't you think you'd already be falling from the cliff before you could say all that?" Gubaru asked, laughing again.

"Maybe. But you be Anzû. I've finished my statement. For some reason you haven't pitched me from the cliff. What happens next?"

Gubaru was silent for a moment as he thought. Then, with a mock-serious expression on his face and in an unnaturally deep voice, he intoned, "You have not answered my question. You first say that you are a Nabû-man, but then that you are not. My question was what you are, not what you are not. So, again, what are you?"

"Good, good... That is what Anzû would ask, I think – assuming he even cares about our answers.

"Why would he ask if he didn't care?"

"Have you never asked a question whose answer you didn't care about?"

Gubaru tossed his head. "I'd care about the answer if I was going to pitch someone off a cliff because of it," he declared.

"But that's another problem, it seems to me. Maybe the two occurrences are unrelated. Maybe there's no 'because.'"

"So he asks questions and pitches people off of cliffs, and there's no connection?"

"Right. Like me being a Nabû-man. I fell into that name. Or rather: I was pitched into it. Just like I was pitched into being a man, rather than a chicken or a demon. But what I am – that is a different question, an unrelated question."

Gubaru hesitated. "It may be that the question is unrelated to the action, at least in Anzû's mind," he acknowledged. "But can they be unrelated in our own?"

"What do you mean?"

"If you're about to be pitched from a cliff, shouldn't you know what you are?"

Nabû-na'id smiled, but in a strange, sorrowful way. "This is why we are friends, why we are brothers," he murmured. And then, looking Gubaru directly in the eyes: "What difference does it make whether I know the answer? As he tumbled down the cliff, did the chicken-man revisit the question or his answer? Did the donkey-man or the Anzû-man or even the man-man? Or was the question so totally forgotten that it might as well never have been asked, as soon as these men found no ground beneath their feet, as soon as the flame of terror flickered and burst and consumed them, like an exploding log?"

For a long time the two friends sat together in silence.

Then Nabû-na'id spoke very quietly, whether to himself or to Gubaru: "Or perhaps is it that we fall to our deaths like we drift into sleep, ever rounding the same thought which becomes clearer and more magical – but of course! there it is, there it is! – and we are asleep, we have understood everything or else we have relinquished understanding, it doesn't matter, we are asleep, we sleep..."

The god Enlil could not sleep. "What is that racket?" he demanded.

"The noise of mankind," the ghost of Geshtu-e responded.

"Unleash šuruppu-*disease among them. I will have my sleep."*

The god Enlil could not sleep. "What is that racket?" he demanded.

"The noise of mankind," the ghost of Geshtu-e responded.

"Unleash drought among them. I will have my sleep."

The god Enlil could not sleep. "What is that racket?" he demanded.

"The noise of mankind," the ghost of Geshtu-e responded.

"Flood the earth. Drown them. I will have my sleep."

"Do you know the tale of Izdubar?" Nabû-na'id asked.

"I don't think so."

"Izdubar was an ancient king. He was two-thirds god and one-third man. Never would he sleep. During the day he would play *pukku* and *mekkû* with all the young men; or he would wrestle them one by one, always winning. At night, he made love to every newly-wed woman in the city, the whole night long, while each of their husbands waited. The people cried out to the gods: 'We are tired, gods!' they said. 'Make Izdubar sleep, so we can sleep.'

"The gods heard the people. They decided to make Izdubar sleep. 'How should we do this?' Enlil asked Ea. 'Perhaps we could have a fly bite him? Or a meteor hit him on the head? What do you advise?'

"'Let me think about it,' Ea said, and he went down to Apsû, transformed into a fish, swam around in the sweet waters for a while. By the time he left the water, he had had an idea. He returned to the air and stood before Enlil. 'I have an idea,' he said. 'Let me handle it.' 'Do as you see fit,' Enlil commanded.

"The next day Izdubar was inspecting the walls of his city. In the shadow of the wall, partially concealed in a cleft, was a young cat. She was very tiny and easily fit in Izdubar's immense hand. Her fur was black and shiny and her head a little too small for her body. He brought her to his palace. She was not daunted by the fact that he was a king; she climbed his furniture, scratched his skin and whined at him when she was hungry. To his attendants' surprise, Izdubar did her bidding. Fascinated by her, he would follow her around. Sometimes he would pick her up and cradle her in his arms. Sometimes he would taunt her with a long blade of grass, which she would attack or pretend to attack. He forgot to play *pukku* and *mekkû* with the young men; they rested. At night he followed her in the dark; he forgot to make love to the newlyweds – their husbands did instead, but not the whole night long; they rested. 'Why do you play with the cat?' his advisors asked him. 'Why does she play with me?' he answered. One day the cat leapt onto Izdubar's lap as he sat on his throne. She yawned, curled into a tight ball, and went to sleep purring. Izdubar sat and watched her, stroking her gently. The day passed into evening, the evening into night. The cat still slept, content; Izdubar would not wake her. Night became morning; the cat did not waken but slept. Days and nights passed, the cat sleeping on Izdubar's lap beneath his watchful eyes. Weeks passed, and still the cat slept, and Izdubar would not stir. Years passed, Izdubar unmoving, the cat asleep on his lap, purring softly. 'Is he asleep?' the townspeople asked of Izdubar. 'Is he asleep?' Enlil asked of Ea."

Nabû-na'id stopped. Gubaru waited for him to continue, but he did not. "Well?" said Gubaru. "Was he asleep? What did Ea say?"

"Ea never said. I don't think Ea knew."

"Do you know the tale of Zisudris?" Nabû-na'id asked.

"I don't think so."

"He was the brother of Atraḫasīs."

"I didn't know Atraḫasīs had a brother."

"Why should Atraḫasīs not have a brother, brother? Let this one be called Zisudris. When Enlil decided to flood the earth, Ea defied him and warned mankind. He did it in this way. To the reed hut and to the walls he said: 'Listen to me! Never waver in your listening. Attend to every word! Tear apart this house and make instead a boat. Fill it with life, not things! Its roof should be like the vault of heaven – there must be no cracks! Its bitumen should be the finest – no water must leak through! Soon Enlil will release Anzû to tear the heavens with his talons. Your heaven must replace that heaven! Soon water will pour from the gashes in the sky; your bitumen must keep it out!' So spoke Ea to the reed hut and to the walls, but what could the reed hut or the walls do? Atraḫasīs and Zisudris had been within, however. They overheard. Atraḫasīs said to Zisudris: 'We must build a boat!' But Zisudris did not agree.

"Zisudris said to Atraḫasīs: 'Let us build a boat. Then what?

We survive with a few other living things. Enlil sleeps as is his wont. Eventually the gods miss the savory smell of sacrifice. We survivors burn for them some flesh and they come to it like flies. They let the waters recede; they repair the rifts in heaven. For a while, all is well – until Enlil tires again and we disturb his sleep. Then you and I must again tear down the reed hut and tear down the walls; we must again find the finest bitumen; we must again build a boat and shepherd a few of the living onto it. We must again endure the screeching of Anzû and the high-pitched squeal of the ripping sky. We must again bury ourselves in that boat and pretend that its roof is heaven. When at last we emerge from our coffins a second time and again make sacrifice, the gods buzzing to the burning flesh will no less be like flies than the first time. Always they will be as flies, no matter what we suffer and endure. Always will it be flies that reward us, just as it will always be flies that punish us – small, uncomprehending beings, nuisances.'

"'You must not say such things!' an astonished Atraḫasīs warned. But Zisudris refused to recant. He refused as well to help build the boat. He returned to his home. Several days passed. Then Atraḫasīs sought his brother. The boat was almost finished; he wished his brother to join him on it. He went to his brother's house and there he found Zisudris seated in the dirt. 'What are you doing?' he asked. Zisudris answered, 'I am writing.' 'Why?' 'To give an account of everything, to give the story and the history of the world before it was destroyed by flies,' Zisudris replied. 'Who will read it?' Atraḫasīs asked. 'I don't know. Perhaps no one.' 'Write it on the boat!' Atraḫasīs declared excitedly. 'Come! Hurry! The rains will soon be upon us. Come with me! Finish this with me on the boat!

"Zisudris looked at him, then pointed at his writing. 'This is my boat,' he said simply.

"Eventually Atraḫasīs left without his brother."

"What became of Zisudris and his writing?" Gubaru asked.

"Zisudris must have died. As for his writing – no one knows. According to my mother, there is a tradition that, before he drowned, Zisudris buried his writing in Sippar. Perhaps someday we will find it."

Gubaru looked puzzled. "But..." he began, "how could there be a tradition if the writing hasn't been found?"

"If a god tells you to kill the son he gave you, should you do it?" Gubaru asked.

But Nabû-na'id countered, "What does a god sound like? In what language does a god speak?"

"Set that problem aside," said Gubaru. "Let's assume the god has spoken to you – of that there's no doubt. He tells you to sacrifice your son, the one he promised you. Do you do it?"

"What is a god's to give is a god's to take away... Is that what I am supposed to say?"

"If you believe it."

"But isn't belief the problem? How would I know it was a god that I heard? How would I know that that god always spoke in words rather than in silences? Has it not struck you how silent the gods can be? Is that because they have nothing to say, or because silence is what they say and how they say it?"

"I don't understand what you mean."

"You know how we say that a wise person is a person whose ears are wide? My mother, for example – she has *uznin rapšatim*. Does that mean she hears especially well even what the gods choose to whisper? Or does it mean that she attends to their silences, hears those silences?"

"But the god has said, 'Sacrifice your son!' He has used words, words you heard distinctly. Why are you instead focusing on the silences?"

"Because silence always accompanies words. Because, if words are meaningful, silences are meaningful too. Because, in my life, it is usually the silence of the gods that deafens me; it is the silence of the gods that disturbs my sleep."

Nabû-na'id paused, then continued. "In that story about the man of Ḫarrānu, are you not struck by the absolute silence of the mountain top? The man doesn't hear his own breathing and hears nothing from his son. What is that silence? Could it be the god's invitation to protest, to scream? Could the god be provoking the man into interrupting his unbearable silence? Perhaps for the god no less than for the man this is a nightmare from which he dares to hope to be awakened. 'Make noise!' the god says with his silence. 'Awaken me!' And maybe the man who listens so keenly hears even this. But he thinks it better to keep the silence, even though it means killing his son."

"Why would the man think it better to keep the silence?"

"For fear that his protest would not mean; for fear that his scream would not waken. The man knows, or thinks he knows, that the silence of the god has meaning – though its meaning is terrible. But what if the voice, his voice, has no meaning at all? However shrill and loud the man's cry, what if the god cannot be awakened from his nightmare?" He paused again. "Is it not better for the god to think the man misunderstood or misheard his silence, than to know that for him, for the god, there is no escape, no waking? Has the man shown the god mercy – even love – by refusing to fail to waken him?"

Gubaru did not answer but looked at Nabû-na'id with bewilderment and alarm.

Some later time. "What if the god's silence is meaningless?" Gubaru asked.

Some later time. "What is the difference between the dream of a god and the world?" Gubaru asked.

The god Enlil could not sleep. "Why can I not sleep?" he demanded. But there was no answer, no ghost of a god who replied, no racket over which a response could be heard.

Gubaru stirred suddenly, opened his eyes, gave voice to a wordless gasp. Then: "Did you waken me?" he asked. "Why am I awake?"

Nabû-na'id replied that he had done nothing.

"Has a dream come to me?" Gubaru asked. "Nabû-na'id, I have seen a dream!"

"What was your dream, Gubaru?"

"I could run with the wild animals, effortlessly. I knew the haunts of the forest, including where gods and the henchmen of gods lurked. I understood their ways and could avoid what must be avoided. But then a hunter came. He told me about Izdubar, how he would not rest and would not let his people rest. 'Human beings must sleep!' the hunter declared. 'Come with me; force Izdubar to rest.' I followed the hunter. He took me to the city. I admired its walls, which I did not understand. And then I was before the throne. There sat Izdubar with a cat on his lap. The cat purred; Izdubar, looking off into a distance I could not see, stroked the cat rhythmically. The rest of the city was still and quiet; I saw no one; I heard nothing, only the purring of the cat. 'I am come," I announced. Izdubar made no response. Nothing changed; the purring continued, the stroking continued, the stillness and the quiet of the city continued. 'Why did you bring me here?' I asked the hunter, angrily. No one replied. I whirled around, but the hunter was not there. I whirled around again, but now I saw nothing; I was alone. But, from no place I could find, or else from all around me, I heard something. Purring. Soft, gentle, endless."

"Then you awoke?" Nabû-na'id asked.

"No. What woke me was the sound of my name."

Gubaru stirred suddenly, opened his eyes, gave voice to a wordless gasp. Then: "Did you waken me?" he asked. "Why am I awake?"

Nabû-na'id replied that he had done nothing.

"Has a dream come to me?" Gubaru asked. "Nabû-na'id, I have seen a second dream!"

"What was your dream, Gubaru?"

"I came to a tavern at the far edge of the world. The tavern-keeper, a woman, barred the door. I pounded on it. 'Who are you? Are you the hunter?' 'No,' I cried. 'I am a wanderer, come in search of Atraḫasīs, he who was given immortal life.' Reluctantly she opened the door, let me in. 'You cannot reach Atraḫasīs,' she said. 'The gods, it is true, made him immortal, as a reward for feeding them after the flood. But they placed a condition on that gift. He would be alone forever. Never could he be reached; not even the flies would visit him. It is said that Atraḫasīs was so eager not to die that he accepted the gift with its condition. Nothing more is known.'"

"'How is this much known?' I asked. The tavern-keeper smiled at me. 'It was written in the tablet of Zisudris,' she replied. 'Then the tablet has been found?' I exclaimed. 'Long ago, by the priests of Šamaš in Sippar,' she answered."

"I thought to myself, 'I must go to Sippar and see the tablet.' I turned to leave the tavern. The tavern-keeper was no longer there and the door was far behind me. I took a step toward it, but the door somehow became further away. I took another step, and now the door was almost out of sight. I stopped, not daring to move, and the door stayed where it was, far in the distance. Somehow I knew that even a single step more would remove the door from my sight."

"Then you awoke?" Nabû-na'id asked.

"No. What woke me was the sound of a name – Atraḫasīs."

Atraḫasīs wept but his cheeks did not feel his tears. Atraḫasīs shouted but his ears did not hear his words. Atraḫasīs could not think his own thoughts. Even the agony of bewilderment that was his existence was not his own. Far away flies buzzed in the savory smoke of a sacrifice. One fly did not say to another, 'Do you remember Atraḫasīs, who fed us when we were so hungry long ago?' The other fly did not reply to the first, 'What a trick we played on him! What a reward we gave him!' Instead, both flies simply buzzed in the savory smoke. Atraḫasīs they forgot completely.

Anzû had stolen the tablet and flown with it to the furthest mountain top. He alighted. Now, beneath the full moon, he would read what Zisudris had written. But what was written on the tablet could not be understood. He thought: Is this only a list of names, as many as are possible? He thought: Is this only a combination of signs, as many as are possible? He thought: Was Zisudris mad?

From the shadows cast by moonlight came a chortle, a howl, a guttural, gasping, wordless voice. Anzû looked up. There crouched Nabû, grinning toothlessly. "Nabû!" shouted Anzû, surprised. "How did you find me? What are you doing here?" But Nabû, still crouching, still grinning toothlessly, answered only with hisses and coughs and growls. Anzû bared his taloned paw. "Speak!" he demanded. Nabû scratched the ground with his clenched, claw-like hand. "Speak!" Anzû screamed. "Use words!" But in response he heard only scratchings in dirt and in a tongueless throat while Nabû, grinning toothlessly, drooled and squatted, scratching and scratching and only scratching the ground.

"When you said that everyone writes," Nabû-na'id asked his mother, "what did you mean?"

Adad-guppi looked at him. "When I look at you," she said,

"I see Nabû-na'id. I see my son. I see the one who will lead Sîn by his hand to the Eḫulḫul in Ḫarrānu. I also see a storyteller and story-interpreter, a boy who wonders about the meanings of the gods and for whom the loss of his *pukku* and *mekkû* endangers the coming of tomorrow."

She paused.

"When you look at me, do you see only a woman, only sackcloth, only ash? Or do you see your mother, do you see the vestments of mourning?"

"I see my mother, of course. I see her mourning Sîn's abandonment of Ḫarrānu." Nabû-na'id stopped, then added with emphasis, "I see *you*."

"But do you? Or rather, what would that mean? What is this "you" that you claim to see? How can it apply to others besides me? Where are its limits? When is it complete? When have you completely seen it?"

"I talked to Gubaru once about this – about what his name means, to what his name refers. About whether there's a difference between the question 'what?' and the question 'who?'. I don't think he understood. I'm not sure I understood."

"What would it mean to understand? Would understanding be an exhausting of *šumum*, of meaning and of the name? Would understanding be like overturning every covered face of a stone and revealing it once more to the sun? But to reveal one of the stone's faces, we always cover another… We say, for example, that a stone has a face, and by speaking in this way we understand something of the stone, while covering up something else."

"What do we cover up when we say a stone has a face?" Nabû-na'id asked.

"We cover up one of the most important aspects of a stone," she replied. "We cover up the absence of a face."

"So should we just speak literally, only saying what strictly speaking is true?"

She laughed. "If only we could. But that is not the way we encounter the world. Perhaps it is not the way gods encounter it either. We only ever know one thing as another. We never know it as itself. As itself, it is for us mute, invisible, formless. Perhaps it is not even there if as itself alone." She pointed at a grasshopper. "It is the same for the grasshopper. Do you think he sees the world as it is, while for us it is always veiled, whether in an excess or a shortage of meanings? It is veiled for him too. He does not see a grasshopper in any naked simplicity that we might attribute to grasshoppers. He sees a mate or a competitor or prey. Perhaps he sees his mother in mourning, though we cannot tell. In his world as in ours, one thing is known as another."

"What does this have to do with writing?"

"How is it different from writing? How is a grasshopper's reading of one thing as another different from your seeing an image in clay and understanding it to mean a word?"

"So even grasshoppers write?" Nabû-na'id, exasperated, asked.

"Everyone writes," she replied. "Even those who would prefer not to."

My mother used to tell me a story, he said, about a creature that emerged from the sea. He had two heads – the head of a fish and, above it, the head of a man. He had a fish's body, covered in silvery scales that sometimes seemed like mirrors. He had the tail of a fish, but below it, the legs and feet of a man. He did not have arms or hands, only fins. The name of this creature, the creature's voice said, was Uanna. Another time the creature's voice said his name was Adapa. He taught humankind everything that humankind has ever known; not one thing, my mother claimed, had been discovered since. He taught men and women to grow plants, build cities, make laws; he taught them to fashion statues but worship gods; he taught them to write, though how he wielded a reed stylus with fins is hard to understand. Perhaps he had no need for a stylus and impressed the signs with his fins. At first humankind wanted to worship him, but he said no: worship these statue-gods you've fashioned, clothe them, feed them, protect them from enemies. But as for myself, he said, I am not a god; as you see, I wear no clothes, only these mirror-scales which are also my skin; and not once, as you must have observed, have I eaten, though every day you prepare a feast for the statue-gods. I move myself, which statue-gods do not; and I require, indeed desire, no protection – unlike the gods. If only to prove that to you, let me teach you one last thing... And the last thing the fish-man taught humankind was to fish; the fish-man left behind fishermen.

Every night, after giving human beings their lessons, he returned to the water. But I have sometimes wondered whether the water was any more a home to him than the land; whether fish were any more a family to him than people. I have also wondered what he did in the waters – whether there as on land he taught fish to grow plants, build cities, make laws; to fashion statues but worship gods; to write or even to read. Or are the lessons beneficial to fish different from the lessons beneficial to humankind? Might he have taught fish something different from what we have learned? Have fish a need for cities, laws, statues and gods? But surely fish at least write? Or is it we who write while it is the fish who read?

You snicker, my friend, but what is there to laugh at? Has it not occurred to you that human beings strut about in a world they think themselves authors of, even while they can't even once read the world's writing? Perhaps fish have a different fate than ours. They have no need for fire, hence for metallurgy, hence for weapons; they have no need for cooked food and so do not disguise their victims; and perhaps they have no need for forgiveness, which would deliver them from gods and statues.

We look to the stars in heaven for our fate, and to sense how small we are beneath the inscrutable universe; but they look down rather than up, to the grains of sand which are even more numerous than the stars; moreover which endure both day and night and never are eclipsed. We human beings have the entire daytime to forget our smallness and write our greatness – but as for fish, do they not always have reminders strewn across the riverbed, strewn across every lake and every sea? Some say that writing enables us to forget, even seduces us into forgetting; but writing actually requires us to forget, if only how unfathomably small we are. We can't write the world if the stars are perpetually overhanging us; we need the oblivion of the day to embolden the avatars of ourselves we send bravely into the night. We need our fish-men in order for us to dare being fishermen.

Or Gubaru, is it the other way around?

My mother used to tell me a story, he said, about a Šumeran named Bilgames. She also used to tell me the great story of Gilgameš. There were many similarities between Bilgames and Gilgameš – their names, to begin with; their friendships with Enkidu; several of their adventures or aspects of their adventures. It was easy to suspect that Bilgames WAS Gilgameš, or else the other way around. But one thing stands out which truly distinguishes them, perhaps rendering them or rending them incompatible, irreducible to one another: the story of Gilgameš is somehow woven into a single story of several parts, parts which build on and complement each other; there is, furthermore, an arc to Gilgameš's great story. But the stories of Bilgames are not like that. There's no weave connecting them; there's no arc, no build-up, no denouement, no sustained question or problem and no eventual response. It's not even clear that the Bilgames in each story is the same Bilgames or a different Bilgames, or that this is in any way a concern. Every time someone tells me, "Oh,

Bilgames – that's just the Šumeran name for Gilgameš" or "Oh, Gilgameš – that's just the name we use for Bilgames" I recall this difference and it gives me pause. I can't simply agree. And then I wonder… This is what I wonder, Gubaru: not only whether Gilgameš and Bilgames are secretly the same, but – if they are not – to which are our stories more alike? Are we, you and I, like Bilgames, the focus or even just the tag for a collection of otherwise unrelated stories? Or is there an arc, a warp and woof, which makes of our stories one? But perhaps I am being too simplistic in thinking that either Bilgames and Gilgameš are one, or they are not. Maybe when Bilgames is translated into Akkadian, his tales weave together into one; but when Gilgameš is translated into Šumeran, they pull apart as separate strands. So the question may be, What are we in Akkadian? What are we in Šumeran? What are we on land? What are we in water? There is no question, What are we?

But, he said, grabbing Gubaru's sleeve and with urgency entering his voice, if that is so, then what are we?

My mother used to tell me that heaven and earth each created itself of its own accord. But then she would add that, created, each was an abyss. "I don't understand," said Gubaru. "How can they be created and still be an abyss?" "If they were created, I don't see how they could be an abyss," Nabû-na'id agreed. "But if they created themselves, how could they not be?"

A tablet, smaller than the palm of a hand, journeyed west to the coast. It boarded a ship and sailed southeast, usually within sight of land. At Ṣurru it disembarked and began the long inland journey. Some rivers it crossed; others it travelled. At times it followed centuries' old caravan routes; at times it followed newly constructed roads. The stars above did not dazzle it; the noon-day sun did not blind it. It feared no wild beast, no savage tribe, no military outpost and no bandit. Death was of no consequence to it. Time was of no consequence to it. Its destination was of no consequence to it – which perhaps is to question the possibility of its having a destination at all. Never did the tablet tire. Steadily, relentlessly, eastward and southward it travelled. Men looked at it, attentively or not: ignorant men, some with the disinterest of incomprehension, others with its fascination; learned men, some with the fascination of comprehension, others with its disinterest. Animals and bugs looked at it too, but their expressions were inscrutable. And one day a woman with wild eyes, dressed in sackcloth and covered in ash, looked at it. Her expression was like the animals' and the bugs' – but that was of no consequence to the tablet, which rested, whether briefly or forever, in the precinct sand, baking slowly, slowly being buried, where the woman threw it.

"My father has called me to Sardis," Nabû-na'id said to Gubaru. The two boys looked at each other in silence. Then Nabû-na'id added, "Come with me."

"I had the carpenter make them for you," Gubaru said to Nabû-na'id. "So that on the journey to Sardis you would not be without tomorrow."

* * * * *

From the [fragmentary] Assyrian Accounts of Herodotus

...including him. As to why he participated in the delegation, I have heard several accounts. Some say it was because he was unusually learned and it was expected his abilities would be useful in a foreign land. I find this hard to believe for one so young. For what could a youth know that would be of use on such a trip, that older scribes and

more experienced men would not know? Others say he was sent because of the influence his mother had with the king. This seems improbable to me – not because a captive should gain power with a king (for we know she did, and many others have as well, and further she had a role at the temple), but because she would surely have exerted her influence toward something less precarious and more certain. What was to come, after all, of such a delegation? Who could know? A third account says he was sent because an oracle demanded it. What the oracle was, to whom it was made, and how it involved the boy – of this I have heard yet more accounts. The two that seem most probable to me are these. (I think them probable based on what happened afterwards.) According to the first, the oracle demanded that a boy be sent to block the view of the sun; only in shadow could peace be brought to the land. The oracle was unusual – at least for Babylon – because it gave the boy's name quite precisely. The king consulted his sages but no one knew how the boy was to block the sun. They decided nonetheless to send him, on the assumption that he and a god would figure it out. According to the second, however, the oracle threatened actual danger to the king, to be averted only if the boy were sent away. The king at first wanted to kill the boy, but the oracle did not permit that. He must be sent to Sardis. Some of the sages comforted the king that a boy could not be expected to survive such a journey, especially in that season, so why kill what inevitably must die? In any event, the oracle was clear – it mentioned Sardis explicitly and, again unusually, the boy by name. And so – whether because of this oracle or the other one, or perhaps they both happened – the king sent Labynetus. Accompanying him were the same Labaxidinus, Rimax and Zerius who had come before, and one Gobryas.

It is said that the day they arrived in the Lydian court, the queen gave birth. The boy was that Croesus of whom I have written in the Histories. I will have more to say about him.

Chapter 2. A Scribe in Sardis

As he had imagined, his father was stooped, lean, bearded but gray, with squinting eyes. He didn't dress especially well, which made him stand out in the court, where everyone else dressed ornately in every sense: they wore the finest materials, richly dyed, and accompanied their clothing with extravagant jewelry wrought from metals and precious stones. Not his father, however; in any other setting he would be nondescript, but here he almost stood out.

Most of the time his father huddled with officials as well as the man from the Egibi House (who always wore a scarlet cap), often in one of the palace's internal courtyards or else in a gallery off such a courtyard. The officials, Nabû-na'id had quickly realized, were useful, but not clever and certainly not interesting. The Egibi man was a different matter. He worked toward something steadily, slyly, subtly. He was the kind of man better to have as an ally than an enemy – but perhaps best not to know at all. Certainly, one would never be confident that he was truly an ally. The ends he served were his own, and secret. Nabû-na'id did not doubt that his father knew this. He even suspected that his father enjoyed the challenge. It was a game to him, perhaps to both men, and the game was something like this: can I anticipate you better than you can anticipate me? Or rather: can I think your thoughts better than you can think mine? It was a game, Nabû-na'id realized one morning with sudden clarity, of reading.

As for himself – his father offered no explanation of why he had sent for him. Instead, his father made him work on scribal exercises, writing and computations; he made him study Luddan; otherwise he accompanied his father like a shadow and like a shadow he was insignificant.

"I am insignificant like a shadow."

"What do you expect?" Nabû-balaṭsu-iqbi responded. "You are a boy."

"I am on the threshold of manhood, and I am your son. Should not your son be more than a shadow?"

"You sound like a brat. Have you never thought what a shadow is? Do you think the world is changed by anything other than shadows? It is hard for me to believe you are your mother's son."

"I have no doubt I am my mother's son; it is a wonder, though, that you do not doubt that I am yours."

Nabû-balaṭsu-iqbi barked harshly. Somehow, without anything changing, the bark became a laugh.

"Do you know the *Namburbi* ritual? Do you know what it is?"

"It's what you do when you dig a well. You pour libations to Šamaš, the Anunnaki and your ancestors."

"Why?"

"In thanks for the water, I suppose."

"No. In repentance or appeasement or whatever you wish to call it. Because you have violated the realm of the dead."

"By digging in the earth?"

"By digging in the earth."

"Because that's where we bury the dead?"

"Because that's where the dead are."

"What is your point? That we honor shadows?"

"We honor them because we love them. And because we fear them. Doesn't that suggest shadows may be important in our lives?"

Nabû-na'id did not respond, but on his face was a crooked, even pained, smile.

"Do you know what reward the gods gave the greatest man who ever lived?" continued Nabû-balaṭsu-iqbi.

"Everlasting life?"

Nabû-balaṭsu-iqbi again laughed his disconcerting bark. "What kind of gift is that? But, yes, in a manner of speaking. The only difference between us and gods is that we die and they don't. So, yes, they gave him life everlasting, which is to say they made him into a god. But on one condition: he had to be the god of the dead. One of their jokes, I suppose."

"Why is it a joke?"

"Because – how can a god be the god of the dead? How is the god of the dead different from the dead? Why do the dead need a god? Why does a god need the dead? What can either do for the other?"

He stroked his beard. "It is my opinion," he said, "that when we dig a well, we secretly pray to the god of the dead. And we pray to him because –" He stopped.

"Because?"

"Because he's the only god who matters. The only god who we can touch and who can touch us. The only god who's – human."

"Why do you joust with the Egibi man?"

"Because I can't very well dance with the others."

"Because they are stupid?"

"Because they are thoughtless."

"Is the Egibi man not thoughtless?"

His father made a face. "In one way he is thoughtless, in another he is not. Unlike the others, he has questioned enough not to believe anything. In that way he's thoughtful. But not to believe anything is not thoughtful."

"Why?"

"Because –" His father groped for words. "Because – not to believe anything is just another way of believing."

Nabû-na'id thought about this while his father wrote. His father's hands moved with astonishing speed and deftness across the clay; they left in their wake a trail of wedges that, Nabû-na'id knew, somehow held meaning – stilled it, comforted it, succored it. It was like his father was a god, breathing and spitting life into mud. And yet his father could write without seeming to pay attention to what he was doing. He could at the same time carry on a conversation or mull his next move against the Egibi man. It is a strange god who gives life to dirt distractedly, absent-mindedly, mused Nabû-na'id. And the life thus engendered is at least as strange – mute, helpless, incomplete. Waiting to be read. But then Nabû-na'id remembered his thought of a previous morning, about his father's game with the Egibi man.

Eventually, he broke the silence. "How do you know?" he asked his father simply.

Weeks passed. Many times Nabû-na'id asked his father if he was a devotee of Sîn like his mother. Never would his father answer. Finally, while he was copying an ancient epic, without looking up, he changed the question. "Why will you not tell me if you are a devotee of Sîn like my mother?"

His father also did not look up from the tablet he was working on. "Because I do not know." They were silent. Then, gruffly, his father added, "Or perhaps because I really do worship only the god of the dead. I don't know that either."

"This game you play with the Egibi man – what is it for?"

His father grunted. "The Egibi man would say that everything's at stake."

"What would you say?"

His father yawned. "I doubt anything at all is at stake."

Nabû-na'id was surprised. "Why do you play?"

His father scratched himself and resumed his writing. He had composed several lines before he responded. "I'm not sure."

"You're not sure why you play, or you're not sure if anything is at stake?"

"Both."

They continued writing in silence, Nabû-na'id still practicing by copying the epic. His father finished his tablet. "Do you see this?" he asked, holding it up for Nabû-na'id to inspect.

"Yes."

"I'm going to bake it. After it cools, I will throw it from the city walls."

The two of them walked through Sardis together. His father had done as he promised. Nabû-na'id had not thought he would. "Why did you waste all of your effort?" he asked his father with dismay after watching him hurl the tablet.

"Perhaps I haven't," his father answered. "That's the thing about tablets. You can never be sure they'll be read – even if you give them straight to the messenger. But you can also never be sure they won't be read." His father looked into his eyes. "Even if you chuck them over a wall."

Nabû-na'id and Gubaru were together on the hill where they had lost the *pukku* and the *mekkû*. They were digging in the dirt, in silence. Their fingers were bleeding; constantly they were finding pieces of pottery, which they threw to the side, and then they continued to dig even more furiously. But the faster they dug, the more pottery they found, and the more their fingers bled. Gubaru was weeping, but they continued to dig in silence. "We must perform the *Namburbi*," Gubaru suddenly moaned. Nabû-na'id ignored him. "We must perform the *Namburbi*!"

Gubaru repeated desperately. Nabû-na'id dug harder, faster, ripping his fingers to the bone. Only more pottery! Pottery everywhere! In fact, pieces of pottery were now rising out of the hole that he was digging; they were piling up into a mound where the hole had been; the mound was growing, pottery sherds pouring down its sides. Nabû-na'id, fierce, reckless, horrified, tried to knock the mound out of the way so he could make his hole deeper. "We must perform the *Namburbi*!" he heard Gubaru intone somewhere behind him. The pottery sherds clung to his bleeding fingers, the mound still growing, all of his work hidden now beneath countless pieces of broken pottery. His fingers, sticky with blood, were becoming encrusted in pottery pieces. He was slowly being buried alive in pottery. He looked helplessly at the pottery and suddenly realized that on each sherd his blood had left wedge-shaped signs. Every time he knocked sherds away, they became covered in signs from his own blood. "We must find it!" he screamed, while Gubaru intoned, "We must perform the *Namburbi*!" "We must find it!" he screamed again, as sherds marked with his own blood swept over him. "...the *Namburbi*..." he heard Gubaru's voice say from far away, "...the *Namburbi*... the *Namburbi*..."

In the night black as pitch, he could not tell if his eyes were open, if he had woken or still slept.

At daylight, he looked at the *pukku* and the *mekkû* that Gubaru had given him before he left for Sardis. Then he took them and lay them on the ground. He got some water and some seeds. In privacy, he dug a hole in the dirt beside the *pukku* and the *mekkû*. "Šamaš, behold. Great Annunaki, behold. Dead ancestors, I have not forgotten you. May none of you want for water." He poured water into the hole. "May none of you hunger." He dropped seeds into the pooled water. "May the only god who is human not oversee parched ghosts; may he not oversee famished ghosts; may he not oversee sonless ghosts."

He then poured some water on the *pukku* and the *mekkû*. "May there yet be tomorrows for us all."

"What were you looking for?" his father asked.

"I don't know."

"What did the signs on the pottery sherds say?"

Nabû-na'id paused, astonished. "In the dream, it never occurred to me to read them."

His father looked at him with a mixture of curiosity and mockery.

"Well then, if you can't answer any of the important questions – who is the boy with the curious name, Gubaru?"

Nabû-na'id raised his head defiantly. "He is my brother."

Again his father looked at him with a mixture of curiosity and mockery. But something else mingled in his glance, something that Nabû-na'id had not seen before in him and could not recognize. For a while, his father was content to say nothing. It was only when Nabû-na'id rose to leave that his father spoke.

"I am glad you have a brother."

"Father, what did you write on the tablet that you threw over the wall?"

"Find it and find out," was his father's reply.

"Father, what did you write on the tablet that led to my coming here?"

"Find it and find out," was his father's reply.

"I have been here for more than a year, without knowing why you brought me here. I spend most of my time, like you, writing – but for me it is just copying, whereas you write new things. Is this the life I should know will be mine?"

They were outside in the dark of night, looking at the stars.

"You ask a lot if you want to know what life will be yours. That's a question for a priest, not for me."

"No it's not!" Nabû-na'id said angrily. "I am not asking you to foretell the future, I'm asking you to tell me what you've decided. Am I to stay here, just copying texts forever? Will that be my life?"

"I don't think I would say you are 'just' copying texts."

"I'm not writing anything new, like you."

"Nabû-na'id." It was rare for his father to address him by name. "I sympathize. But be more thoughtful and more careful. Are you sure that you can tell when you are 'just' copying a text, versus writing something new? Are you sure I can tell?"

"Of course you can tell, and so can I. Why do you make mysteries where there are none?" His father did not answer. After a while, Nabû-na'id added, grumbling, "You're like my mother."

"What an admission!" His father barked his awful laugh.

They stood under the stars – the moon was new – without speaking. Nabû-balaṭsu-iqbi was breathing heavily and every now and then made an annoying, clucking sound.

"Look at those stars," his father finally said. "Are they signs too? Do you and I know how to read depressions in mud, while priests know how to read stars and livers and patterns in water?"

"If it is as you say," his father continued, "that your being here is a question merely of my decision, if you think it is for me to decide what life will be yours, then how do the stars know what decision I will make? Or do you think the priests are lying and cannot read the stars?"

Nabû-na'id did not respond.

"If it's my decision," his father persisted, "am I writing a new text of your life, one that the stars will be bound to copy unless the priests are lying? Or is it I who am copying a text already to be found on a moonless night if I look hard enough? Which is it,

Nabû-na'id? Are you sure that you know? Can you be sure that I do?"

"I once told Gubaru that my true father was a *lillu*-demon," his son replied. "Maybe I only wished that. You and my mother are so alike, and so different. Both of you see and hear many of the same things. But she does not seem to doubt what she sees or hears."

"And I – ?" his father prompted.

"You seem only to doubt."

"Learn to read the stars," his father said abruptly. "I want you to learn to read the stars. There are a series of tablets, containing the wisdom and observations of thousands of years. I will give them to you to copy and to study. Make them yours. You will learn to read the stars; and then you will tell me, is your mother right, or am I? Tell me before I die. I should like to know."

The next morning, a new tablet awaited him, its opening line *Enuma Anu Sîn* – "When the heavens and the moon" or "When the gods Anu and Sîn." "There are over 100 different tablets in this series," his father remarked. "It is unusual to have access to them. How I have managed it I shall not tell you. But when you finish one tablet, let me know; I'll get you the next."

"I'm just to copy them?" Nabû-na'id asked.

"It has never been your task just to copy. Read them, understand them, make them yours – and yes, copy them."

His father paused. "Did you never read and think about the epics you've been copying for so long?"

"I knew those stories already. I sometimes talked about them with Gubaru."

His father sighed. "Did you? Were you surprised by the last tablet?"

Nabû-na'id responded quickly, without deliberation. "No,

not really. I considered it a different tradition. The epic really ended with the 11th tablet; in the 12th, we're just reminded of related stories about the hero, similar to the Šumeran stories of Bilgames. That's why his companion is alive again. It's also why his companion is just a servant, not a friend."

His father sighed a second time. "Of course that may be so, boring though it is. But what if you entertained the more interesting idea – that the last tablet really is a part of the whole? Indeed, what if it's the last part, the part that completes the whole?"

"How could it be? It's inconsistent and discontinuous with everything that came before. Would the hero have sought immortality if his companion hadn't died? Would he have found Uta-napištim? He came home a failure, doomed to die, having lost even the rejuvenating plant – and then in the next tablet, there he is, his companion is alive again, with no explanation? It doesn't make any sense!"

"But – *what if that's what happened*?"

"You know as well as I do – our lives are not like that." It surprised Nabû-na'id to hear himself sound so conventional and dogmatic. He knew that he had thought very different things before, but for some reason he couldn't think them now. It was something his father's presence stifled.

His father gave him a penetrating look. "No I don't, and neither do you," he said curtly. "Maybe our lives are pervaded with inconsistencies and discontinuities, just like that last tablet. Maybe that can only be seen from the outside, not from within. Or maybe lives that are continuous and consistent can end only in failure, and it's for the more radical life, the one that tolerates what cannot be explained, to find what it seeks."

Nabû-na'id stared dully at the ground.

"Learn to read the stars," his father repeated angrily, pointing at the first tablet of the *Enuma Anu Sîn*, and with his other hand, somewhat pathetically, waving at where the sky would be if a roof weren't in the way. "I'm sure you'll find no discontinuities or inconsistencies there. That, in any event, should please you... and won't tax you with too much to think about."

He walked away.

This particular set was written in wax, rather than clay, on a polyptych board lined with ivory. How it had ended up in Sardis wasn't clear to Nabû-na'id, but he bet his father had something to do with it. His father was strange in that way: on the one hand, a hunched-over scribe, physically unimposing. On the other hand, the things he set out to do ended up done. Nabû-na'id remembered speaking contemptuously of his father to Gubaru. He remembered suggesting that his father couldn't have fathered him, that it had to have been a lillu-demon – because what man could be equal to his mother? But as he spent more time with his father here in Sardis, he was beginning to appreciate how like a *lillu*-demon his father was – and how like his mother, too.

And so here he was in a foreign land with an astronomical series written in his native language, a series which, for some reason, his father expected him to study. Did his father make a copy of it from some palace or temple archive back in Bābilim, and then lug it all the way here? How was it that his father managed to have access to the baskets and chests of tablets, seemingly as easily here as if they were in Bābilim? Or was it that all these materials were disseminated across the four corners, the work not of his father but of countless nameless scribes and countless nameless administrators over the ages? But did an administrator really need an astronomical series?

Pondering these thoughts, Nabû-na'id admitted to himself, was a way of not having to struggle with the astronomical series. He always found them especially difficult to work through, though in another way they entranced him. The mathematics wasn't obvious to him, so he had to go slowly. But, working through the mathematics and the observations of stars going back generations and centuries, he was also filled with wonder: wonder that past men took the trouble to notice all these things and to record them – but for whom? And wonder as well that perhaps his father was serious about reading the stars. *Šiṭir šamē*, heavenly writing. Who wrote the heavens, he wondered? Was it on the same principle and in the same hope as those ancient observers who recorded what they had seen for a dimly imagined posterity? Or was it a mistake to imagine that what was readable had first to have been written?

Nabû-na'id thought about his own proclivity to write – or at least to copy. It wasn't clear that he wrote to someone or for someone – that a reader, or at least a reader different from himself, was at issue. No, the activity of writing was more complex than that, its motivations more obscure. It happened more than it was done. And that happening rather than doing pointed to something – to the uneasy, unsettled, ungrounded relationship between writing and reading. Reading always required a leap. It required inspiration, even possession. And if inspiration and possession, also abandonment. The inspired reader, the possessed reader, abandoned himself. Was it a surprise, then, that he found it easier to write than to read, though he knew few would agree with him? He sometimes even thought that, while writing had been invented – or at least existed – reading was still on its way, still far from arrived. The writing had made it to Sardis, but not the reading.

But look at the trouble he was going to, even right now, to avoid reading these tablets! He wondered if the ancient astronomers who recorded the *Enuma Anu Sîn* had written in order not to read. There, scrawled above their heads, was the *šiṭir šamē*, all the more imposing if authored by a god. What were they to do with it? They looked down, and in some form copied into clay or into wax what they took to be the signs poked into the sky. Less readers than writers, they were less writers than copyists. He thought of all the copying exercises he had done for his father and before that. When had he ceased to copy and begun to write? He couldn't say – he couldn't even say that he had, that he wasn't still a mere copyist. A divinatory series which he had read, somewhere, somewhen, came to mind: "If the liver is the mirror image of the sky" was its first line. Were the omens writ into a lamb's liver just another copying, some version of what the astronomers had done when they recorded rather than read the heavens? Were even the gods just copying from one place into another? Was the whole history of writing a history of copying done in lieu of reading, even perhaps to defer the – dare he say it? – impossibility of reading? Even what we think is a reading – perhaps that is just another re-inscription, another deferral – or maybe just an excuse to stop copying. There, that was it, he thought: what we call reading is in fact the excuse we give ourselves to stop copying.

And yet here he was, neither copying nor reading. And what after all was writing if reading was impossible? Maybe then there was neither reading nor writing, just copying. But there was also the reprieve, the gap – such as now – not the excuse to stop copying, but the excuse not to start. What a ridiculous figure he was, seated on his bench, a basket of tablets before him, not reading, not writing, not copying. Maybe this is why Izdubar sat so still, never stirring, a sleeping or dead cat purring or not purring on his lap. He was deferring… but everything is a deferral. Writing which is copying is a deferral of writing. Reading which is stopped-copying is a deferral of reading. Izdubar sat there, cat on his lap, deferring – deferring!

It took a while for Nabû-na'id to realize that the disturbed, disturbing laughter he now heard echoing in the room was his own.

If the Moon wanders with the Overseer, the days of the king will be short.

If the Moon chases the Swallow, jubilation will be sung.

If the Moon keeps company with the Farmhand, labor will bear fruit.

If the Moon confronts the Bull of Heaven, the king's victory will be short-lived.

If the Moon encounters the Great Twins, the king will see the god.

If the Moon is weighed on the Scales, the king will win or the king will lose – it will be decided.

Why should I believe these? Nabû-na'id wondered.

The first several tablets consisted only of pronouncements about the moon, all written in the same hypothetical style. *If the Moon* something, then a future consequence. Of course, extispicy texts had a similar form, but they also related omens. What Nabû-na'id was especially reminded of, however, were the great lists of laws, like those of the Assyrians, Hammurabi or Ur-Nammu. They too were written in this formulaic way. "If a son says to his father, 'you are not my father,' his father will sell him for silver." "If a woman says to her husband, 'you are not my husband,' she will throw herself from the bank of a river." "If a man steals silver, they will cut off his hand." A condition, when met, culminated in a determined future. The question for Nabû-na'id was this: if the laws and the omens have the same form, does that point to their hidden similarity? Or even their more hidden sameness?

Without looking up, he turned his head in the direction of Gubaru: "If laws and omens are secretly the same, does that mean laws are really omens, or that omens are really laws?"

Gubaru offered no answer.

His father would say he was being too quick. (He heard his father say it: "You are being too quick. You have found a likeness. Is there any difference?" To which Nabû-na'id, after pausing and thinking, would respond: "In the laws, the future and the present are usually connected at least by a shared human actor. If a man steals, it is his hand that gets cut off. But in the astronomical texts, it was different, the connection was less direct. Why are the days of the king short if the Moon wanders with the Overseer?")

"What have the Moon and the Overseer to do with the king?" he said aloud.

Neither Gubaru nor his father responded.

"Gubaru," he asked, "what do you think it means for the Moon to wander with the Overseer?"

Silence.

Nabû-na'id looked up. For a few moments, while focusing on the tablet and his own thoughts, he had forgotten the small cell where he worked, with its one window behind his back. Neither the window nor the walls had existed for him; the dirt in which he was seated cross-legged had not existed; in a certain sense, the tablet lying on the ground before him had not existed, at least not as a material object. Looking around him, the materiality of the world suddenly surged back, overwhelming him and making him small.

First he realized, and then he remembered, that he was alone.

He worked in the cell or, sometimes, in the yard, usually alone, for the months that followed. He learned – when he came across the star lists in later tablets – that names like "Overseer," "Swallow" and "Farmhand" referred to individual stars or groups of stars. They described places where the Moon could be found. But he wondered in what sense those were places, in what sense the Moon found himself in a cell. Or, as he stared out into the dark night, he wondered, "Am I too with the Overseer now? Am I even now confronting the Bull of Heaven? Are those my places too?" He wondered, "Am I like the Moon? Am I like the stars? Are they like me?" He wondered, "Are laws omens? Are omens laws?" Sometimes he spoke these thoughts aloud – if the room was empty. But for some reason that he himself did not understand, he never gave voice to these questions when he shared the room with another.

He imagined his father thought him a dull copyist, unmoved by what he copied.

"I have figured out something quite small," he told his father one day.

"Yes?"

"When the Moon wanders with the Overseer, the only season that happens in is winter. The days are short in winter. That's why the king's days are short too. All of our days are short."

"So the omen is true?"

Nabû-na'id smiled. "It is, if that's what we mean by 'the king's days are short.' But father, you and I both know that a reader of omens – or a king – might understand those words differently."

His father smiled back. "Yes. Yes, we do."

"I have thought some more about the Moon omens," he told his father a few days later.

"Yes?"

"The one that interests me the most right now is the Bull of Heaven one. It reminds me of the epic I was translating. When Gilgameš and Enkidu killed the Bull of Heaven, their triumph was short-lived. In fact, in some ways, it was their last triumph, at least together. After that, the gods punished them and Enkidu died."

"So?"

"So the omen suggests that a small victory may come with a greater loss. Perhaps a king like Gilgameš would be wise to forego the victory, in order to avoid something worse."

"But how do you know it's worse? Maybe that moment of triumph that Gilgameš and Enkidu shared was worth everything that came after."

"Not for Enkidu it wasn't! He died!"

His father looked at him with a curious expression on his face. "We all die. Death will conclude every triumph, however small or large, of our lives. Should we avoid acting – not meet the challenge of the gods – not challenge the gods – all in a vain hope that, in being so terribly small, they will overlook us and allow us to live our totally insignificant lives indefinitely?"

"Aren't you challenging the very purpose behind omens, father?"

"There's an extispicy text I read once. Let me tell it to you. 'If a liver has a lobe, a path, a palace gate and a gall bladder, and absorbed the *nidi kussim* into the finger besides, it is the omen of Luḫuššum – that a man during his life will die."

"How is that an omen? What it says we all know!"

"Like we know that days are short in winter? Perhaps what these omens say is both simple and obvious, and at the same time, hard and deep. Perhaps learning to read – whether the stars or a tablet or both – is always about seeing past the first layer into those that are beneath it."

"Until you get to the bottom?"

"Until you tire. Or – lose your nerve."

"That liver text you read me – which came first, the path and palace gate that a liver has, or the one that we have, that we see in the city, for example?"

"I'll answer that with a question. That moon text you read to me – which came first, the Moon's confrontation with the Bull of Heaven, or Gilgameš's?"

"Well, don't you think we learn stories like Gilgameš's, and then we understand the heavens in terms of them?"

"If that's the case, what role can the heavens have – or a liver – in describing our futures to us? They are only telling us what we told them. We would be better off consulting the hymns and poems and epics that inspired us."

That sat together in silence for a few moments. Then his father spoke again. "I wonder what you mean when you ask which came first?"

"I just mean – which happened before the other?"

"But will that explain anything at all, Nabû-na'id?"

Nabû-na'id had been working on the *Enuma Anu Sîn* tablets for several years. He read them and copied them by day, then studied the sky by night. He began to think of the Moon omens in the early tablets as not only predictive but mnemonic. Or maybe those were the same thing: he noticed that, if nothing else, the omens often reminded him of where to look for something in the sky. Perhaps the future is wound all about us, he thought, winding and winding in every direction, layer after layer, like a ball of string. It is always there to read, but the problem is that it is always too much to read. In a heaven too rich in stars, something must focus our gaze. That's what the omen texts did – they directed our gaze to the corner of the sky where, if we have understood, we could expect a particular event – whether the meeting of star with star or some small thread of our own future. The star catalogues that came later in the *Enuma Anu Sîn* accomplished a similar goal, but differently. The omens said – our two worlds reflect one another, in the dances of stars may be seen the dances of men, and vice versa. The catalogues said – a man once stood and saw this star climb to this height, and he measured it, and he recorded when it happened, all in the faith that he, or someone else – Nabû-na'id even – would both look for it and see it again. In the faith that stars, no less than men, had places and habits and rituals, from which they strayed only to return. In the faith that those places and habits and rituals could be captured in a mathematics which, generation after generation, adapted the eyes of men to the eyes of stars, that their glances might meet.

Those mathematical tablets had troubled Nabû-na'id, and with them the complicated descriptions of methods and procedures, whether mathematical, observational or calendrical. The last were most striking to him. If the worlds of men and stars bear so many secret affinities, why are they nonetheless ever falling out of sync? How did the human calendar drift free of the celestial one? Why couldn't they just be stuck together, like mud brick with bitumen?

The *Enuma Anu Sîn* contained many other types of observation – of atmospheric phenomena as they related to celestial ones; of when a given star first appeared and when it disappeared; of eclipses; and of stars whose cycle of return exceeded the lifespan of a man. It was given to no man to see such a star twice; instead every man relied on the tenuous belief that what he had seen was what another before him had described; and every man, in his heart, wondered if he was right. Belief and doubt – equally fragile, and very near one another. A strange and telling image of that near-kinship, for Nabû-na'id, was the meticulous measurement of shadows recorded in the *Enuma Anu Sîn*, their heights over the course of a day on a solstice or an equinox. He knew the usefulness of such measurements, and yet what he was touched by was not their usefulness but their tenacious fragility. He imagined men crawling in the dirt, exerting care to mark as precisely as possible the height of a shadow. I am doing this for future men, they said to themselves. I am doing this to unlock the secrets of the heavens. But those secrets are writ in shadows – even our own.

Sometimes he would imagine those men, perhaps as foreign to him as the Luddans were. Some must have lived long ago, perhaps even in the age, if not the court, of Gilgameš. Perhaps before then, too. What would he have made of them, or they of him? Here in Sardis Nabû-na'id was often struck by the strangeness of the Luddans, whose customs and behavior he often failed to predict or understand. He had little to do with them. He seldom altered his routine, working on his own with texts most of the day and staring at the heavens throughout much of the night. The city and its people were still foreign to him, though he had lived there many years. He could speak their tongue, but he could not taste with it. To be fair, he had barely tried. And yet surely wise men interested in the heavens existed among the Luddans, possibly even some who had studied the *Enuma Anu Sîn*. Were these his secret kin, a brotherhood which knew no boundaries in space or time, language or custom? Were he to squat on a hill and watch the morning star flirt with the breaking day, with a Luddan on one side, and an ancient astronomer, dead these thousand years, on the other, would they three understand each other? Was there a wordless but deep communion that existed when all those gazes met in a single point, far beyond them all, a point that they agreed to think a star?

He marveled at that thought and at a parallel one: the star that visits but once in the life of a man – I can share that with them: with men in foreign courts which I will never visit; with wise men who know to expect it; with ignorant men mute in doubtful astonishment; with the long dead and long forgotten, famished sonless ghosts; and with those generations to whom I will be among the long, perhaps famished, dead. This messenger, in his long and tireless circuit, shuttles among us all, on the condition only that he extort our message from us – our wordless wonder.

Lābu had summoned his father.

"What did the king want with you?"

"We 'Chaldeans'" – his father sneered at the word – "are renown for our prophetic skills. He wanted to know the future."

"Was this about the supplicants?"

His father stared at him. "What do you know about them?"

"Only what I have read in the stars," Nabû-na'id replied coyly. He then added, "And from a little gossip here and there." He smiled.

"Have the stars suggested anything to you?" his father asked very seriously.

"The omens I have read are not about supplicants but about guests – and about when to inquire why they have come. Has Lābu already asked them that?"

"No. He has deliberately not met them yet. He wanted to consult with me – and others – first."

"They're Iškuza, fleeing the Umman Manda?"

"Yes."

"But we don't know why they're fleeing."

"That is the question that so far has been carefully, even painfully, avoided."

"I have been thinking about the messages that men send each other – from afar. The messages, for example, that men who are now dead thrust with all their might and with their dying breath into the future, in the hope or even the faith that someone will receive the message. Like Zisudris, writing his tablet. Or scribes, hundreds of years ago, who recorded the stars. Or the poets. Sîn-leqi-unninni. Enheduanna. You, when you trusted your words to the tablet that eventually found me and brought me here. Perhaps you, too, when you threw the tablet over the wall."

His father said nothing but waited.

"The question is always – should I accept the message? Should I read it? What if it contains a curse? What if it destroys me? Or what if it's my salvation? You and I both know, father, that there is no escape from this bind. The only way to find out if you should read something is to read it. Of course you can always choose not to read it – but then you will not know if you should have. I say this because I can even now go read the stars, looking for an answer to the question Lābu has posed to you. But my reading the stars, regardless of what they tell me, is already an answer to that question."

His father sat still for a long time, looking in the direction of his son with half-closed eyes. Eventually, he said, "You have not passed these years in vain." He got up, stretching his stiff legs. "You have done well."

"Are you going to the king?" Nabû-na'id asked.

"Yes."

"What will you tell him?"

"That no one can do his reading for him." He smiled. "Not in so many words, of course."

"What have you heard?"

"The king gave them asylum."

"Did he ask them why they were fleeing the Umman Manda?"

"No. He gave them asylum without asking. He still has not asked. The court is supposedly in uproar."

"And what do you think?"

"I am glad," Gubaru said, "that he did not ask."

* * * * *

From the [fragmentary] Assyrian Accounts of Herodotus

...Cyaxares, the son of Phraortes, the son of Deioces, was then the ruler of Media. It was his grandfather, Deioces, who built the labyrinth from the inside. According to him, never should anyone have admittance to the king; above all, never must the king be seen. To that end, he concocted an elaborate ceremony, requiring that all business be transacted solely through messengers. A messenger would be sent into the labyrinth where eventually he would encounter another messenger; that second messenger would proceed deeper into the labyrinth until he encountered a third; and so on. Some say Deioces himself posed as a messenger, or simply was one; others that, long ago, Deioces, like a famished spider, had died at the center of his labyrinth, patiently awaiting his first message. In any event, a message would be sent into the labyrinth, then the inquirer would wait for a sign – whether a dream, or a falling star, or a stranger's word heard in passing, or things of that sort. When he thought he had received it, he would go away. So Deioces ruled – if he ruled. As for his son Phraortes, many said he was no son at all, but rather was a messenger from within the labyrinth who had escaped or decided to leave. Phraortes in any event permitted himself to be seen. He replaced his father's elaborate ceremony with one of his own, through which he would consult a god, always hidden behind a screen. Only the king could consult a god, Phraortes maintained; only the king dared look into a god's face; and it was only in a king's ear that a god would whisper an answer. Thus he made his decisions – or a god did.

Cyaxares, however, was quite unlike both father and grandfather. He gloried in being king. He gloried in being seen. He gloried in making decisions in full view and without consulting a god. Among those decisions was one regarding supplicants from Scythia. They appeared without explanation one morning and begged for asylum. "I will give you asylum," Cyaxares said, "on the condition that you hunt rare game for me and teach my boys to hunt and to use your famous bows." The Scythians, who were desperate and could refuse nothing, of course accepted. Later a Scythian leader arrived to demand their surrender. Cyaxares refused. "Do you know what they have done, what pollution you have brought into your land?" the Scythian asked. Cyaxares said that he did not care, so long as he ate rare game and had sons who were skilled hunters and archers. The Scythian leader cursed him. "You will no doubt get what you want," he said, and spat on the ground. Then he left.

The Scythian refugees kept their promise. They hunted rare game with admirable success; and several of the king's younger sons accompanied them on their hunts, to learn their ways and to master their bows. When after a time their hunts ceased to be successful, however, Cyaxares became enraged. He claimed his palace women could hunt better than a Scythian, and to prove his point, he ordered the Scythians to dress henceforth as women. For the Scythians this was a dreadful insult, not to be borne, and they determined that they would leave Media as soon as possible – but first they plotted their revenge. They begged leave to undertake one last hunt, even if dressed as women. Without giving it much thought, Cyaxares decided to let them, perhaps amused by the idea of men hunting in women's dress. And so they left, in the company of several of those sons of the king who had gone with them before. When the opportunity presented itself, however, they killed those sons, dressed them as if they were game, and returned to the court of Cyaxares. "We have had amazing success, though clothed as women," they said. "Here is game such as you have never tested before." Cyaxares was very pleased and a feast was prepared, of which he and all of his nobles partook. While they ate, the Scythians, disguised now as men, slipped away. They went to Lydia, to Sardis. There Alyattes, the son of Sadyattes, the son of Ardys, the son of Gyges, was then the ruler.

This is what Alyattes said to the Scythians. "Some of my advisors say not to let you in, for fear that you are evil or have done evil. Others of my advisors think you will be useful against the Mede from whom you have come. I do not know if you have done evil or are evil. I do not know if you will be useful against the Mede. But come, enter. Every wall must have a door; and it is only a door if people pass through it."

And so the Scythians fleeing the Medes came to Sardis. Not long after arrived Cyaxares and his men, having discovered the trick done to them. Of course they demanded that the Scythians be handed over. Alyattes refused. "Do you know what they have done, what pollution you have brought into your land?" Cyaxares demanded. Alyattes claimed not to. "I have not inquired," he said, "nor have they volunteered to tell me." When Cyaxares began to recount what the Scythians had done, however, Alyattes stopped him. "I will not hear evil spoken of my guests." "Your guests ARE evil," Cyaxares shouted, but Alyattes had turned away. So the two sides prepared for war.

It is said that Alyattes acted in a strange way then. Bringing his young son, who was then only five or six years old and was in fact the very same Croesus about whom I have already spoken, he called the Scythians before him and warned them that, on their account, a war would be fought. "I had an ancestor once who famously saw more than he should have. As a result he became a king, but in his own eyes an infidel and a traitor. Now, out of fear of the same condemnation, I am risking my kingdom, having deliberately not seen. Only you know what it is that I would look upon." "Do you wish us to tell you?" the Scythians asked. "No. I wish you and above all my son to understand how great and how dangerous is our duty to strangers. According to some of my wise men, it is no more possible to distinguish a fly from a god than a monster from a man. May you not be monsters, and may the gods not be flies." With that he took his son by the hand and led him away.

For the five years that followed, war raged between the Lydians and the Medes, with the Medes sometimes prevailing and sometimes the Lydians. As the war was a stalemate, Alyattes conferred again with his wise men to ask what could be done. Among these was Labynetus, the Babylonian, who had lived and worked for many years in Sardis and whose earlier advice about the Scythian refugees the king had followed. "It was you," Alyattes told him, "who convinced me it was best to shelter our guests, whether they be monsters or men, gods or flies. But it seems more likely to me now that they were flies and that we have endured five years of hardship and death for flies. What in your wisdom," he asked sarcastically, "do you counsel me now?"

"The war that has raged between the Lydians and the Medes has been as evenly matched as night and day," replied Labynetus. "Clearly what you require is that day yield to night, or night to day. That will happen soon. When it does, give me leave to negotiate a favorable peace for you." The king scoffed. "You are lucky that I am hospitable even to guests who disappoint me – so far," Alyattes threatened. "Remember my words," the unperturbed Labynetus responded, "and come for me when they are fulfilled. Neither of us will have long to wait." Indeed, Labynetus had every reason to feel confident. Having studied the stars and with access to ancient Babylonian records, he knew an eclipse of daylight was nigh; this same eclipse had also been predicted by Thales of Miletus, who told the Ionians the year in which it would occur. Sure enough, not long afterwards, in the midst of an evenly matched battle, the moon crossed before the sun and cast the day into night. Both sides were awed and put aside their fighting, instead becoming anxious for peace. Alyattes, no less awed for having been forewarned of the event, sent for Labynetus and immediately appointed him to negotiate on behalf of the Lydians. The Medes in turn asked Syennesis the Cilician to serve as intermediate. These decided that a lasting peace required strong ties, and so they proposed that Alyattes give his daughter, Aryenis, as bride to Astyages, son and heir of Cyaxares. Exerting themselves, they succeeded in persuading both sides. The two kings were brought together. Sharing a single knife, they slit each other's arms and licked each other's blood, and thus was

the pact sworn and the marriage arranged. It is said that the boy Croesus was present and that he cried, not at his father's bleeding, but when Cyaxares licked his father's blood. What became of the Scythian supplicants, I do not know.

Within the year, Cyaxares died, Astyages became king of Media and Aryenis bore him a child – a daughter, Mandane, who would be the mother of Cyrus.

* * * * *

Nabû-balaṭsu-iqbi called his son to him. "Nabû-na'id, at the request of King Lābu, I am to endeavor to negotiate an end to this war. I wish you to assist me."

"What will you have me do?"

"Take notes of my meetings with their negotiator – a man from Ḫume, I believe. That will be your official duty."

"And unofficially?"

"Tell me what you think."

Several weeks passed. "Our negotiations are at a dead-end," his father announced without emotion. "Soon, they will simply be at an end."

"You look tired, father."

His father smiled wanly. "I am. That man from the Egibi House – he would enjoy a challenge like this. But I hate it. I see only loss and death – and pettiness. What, who and how many will be sacrificed to the pride of kings?"

A few moments passed as Nabû-na'id thought in silence. "Can you really blame Waksatar, father? Some of the captured prisoners say he was tricked into eating the flesh of his sons. Had you been tricked into eating my flesh, would you not insist that the perpetrators be given to you for vengeance?"

"That is a different matter."

"How?"

"I am not, at least as yet, accustomed to the flesh of men."

"Neither was Waksatar!"

"Are you sure? He strikes me as having always been a man who eats men."

"Do you think it was a mistake to give refuge to the Iškuza?"

"Of course. But it was a necessary mistake."

"What do you mean, father?"

"We can either wall ourselves off forever and make of our city a tomb – or we can have windows and doors, through which strangers necessarily enter. And those strangers are perhaps as likely to bring evil as good. Who can say? Most of the time, those strangers will not matter, like most of the time the rest of us don't either. But only a fool would preclude the possibility of evil. The same fool would preclude the possibility of good."

"So it's better to have doors and windows, even if sometimes it is through them that suffering and death enter?"

His father looked profoundly sad. "Yes," he answered firmly. "It is better. Just barely, it is better."

"So we are at an impasse so long as we harbor the Iškuza?"

"Yes," Nabû-balaṭsu-iqbi replied.

"And the king will not relinquish them?"

"He fears the judgment of all-seeing Šamaš. The god of justice will punish those who give asylum only to take it away."

They sat together in silence. Then his father looked up. "Nabû-na'id, what is wrong? Why are you so pale?"

His son bit his lip and trembled. "I am not sure if I should tell you."

His father looked at him. "There is the decision of the host, to welcome or not to welcome. There is the decision of the guest, to enter or not to enter. They are both momentous." Then, quietly, softly, he added, "I have made mine."

"The guest must also worry, not only about the harm which may come to him, but the harm which he may bring."

"Yes. The host has a similar worry."

"How is it to be decided? How is it to be weighed?"

"It cannot be weighed. We only weigh what we can see and touch – but what you and I are talking about isn't there, isn't here, isn't anywhere, at least not yet. So it can't be weighed. It can only be decided."

"I don't know how to decide."

His father looked at him kindly. "No one does."

His son was standing before him. "You have decided?"

"Father, in a few weeks' time will come an event of use to us."

"What?"

"Sîn will displace Šamaš; for a brief period, we will be beneath his gaze alone."

"What are you saying?"

"I am saying, father, that the all-seeing Sun, the god of justice, will have his sight obstructed. Only the Moon and not the Sun will see what men do."

"What will you do?"

"I don't know," his father answered.

"What happens, do you think, if your father tells the king?" Gubaru asked.

"I think the Iškuza die, whether because the king kills them or Waksatar does, and the land returns to peace."

"Do they not deserve to die? They tricked a father into cannibalizing his sons – not to mention whatever they did in their homeland."

"I don't know. I am afraid to decide who deserves to live or to die. I believe my father is too. What they did to Waksatar is horrible – though there may be something already in Waksatar to match that horror. My father seems to think so."

Gubaru looked at him blankly. "What do you mean?"

"I don't know. According to my father, Waksatar was already a cannibal. I don't think he meant that literally, and it's not a small thing to assume a metaphorical cannibal is basically the same as a literal one. I doubt my father thinks it's small either, by the way."

Gubaru drew figures idly in the dirt. They were both squatting.

"If the Iškuza die," he began hesitatingly, "surely it is worth it? Think how many Luddans and Umman Manda have already died."

"By that logic, the Iškuza should have been handed over from the very beginning."

"Shouldn't they have been?"

"Would you live in a world, Gubaru, where there is no asylum for strangers, where there is no prospect of pardon? Isn't that the world that results? Those who do evil become evildoers; evildoers die; there is no escape."

"What is wrong with that world? Isn't it just?"

"Is it?" Nabû-na'id met Gubaru's gaze with an intensity and sadness that shocked Gubaru. Then he continued, almost in a whisper. "Who among us has done no evil?"

The two young men stared at each other. "I don't think I have done any evil," Gubaru said, "and I don't think you have either."

"Haven't I? I think I have cannibalized my father."

"What?!"

"My father is now responsible for deciding between the lives of Iškuza strangers and the lives of Luddan and Umman Manda strangers. The man I have come to know over the last many years will be tormented by that responsibility, even though he will also not run from it. But had I said nothing, that agony would not be his."

"No – it would only be yours."

"Is it not evil to pass on such a burden to another?"

"It wasn't your burden to bear. Nor is it your father's. He should simply pass it on to the king; it is a king's burden."

"I do not believe that and neither, I am sure, does my father. In passing my burden on to him, I am no less encumbered by it, though it is now shared; and should my father pass it on to the king, he will in no wise as a result be disburdened, either. He will bear responsibility for the king's decision, and he knows it."

"And so you too bear responsibility for your father's decision?"

"Yes."

"What is a decision that you can be responsible for someone else's?"

"I don't know."

Again they were silent. Gubaru resumed tracing figures in the dirt. Then, quietly, he asked, "Why did you tell your father?"

There was a long pause before Nabû-na'id answered. "Because – it was too much for me. Because – I trust his judgment more than my own." He stopped and looked intently at his friend. "If I am honest – because I thought that in involving him a weight would be lifted from me. But I now see and feel and know how wrong I was to think that."

"And were you wrong to tell your father?"

"I may have done evil to him, Gubaru, by telling him. I know that. But I am not sure that that means I was wrong."

"You say the Moon will block the Sun, that for a while Sîn will prevent Šamaš from seeing."

"Yes."

"And you questioned whether a justice without the possibility ever of pardon was truly just."

"I did."

"What if Sîn's obstruction of Šamaš's sight is just a way to make pardon possible? What if the gods agree with you – and so they have arranged, every now and then, that Šamaš *not* see?"

Nabû-na'id smiled unhappily. "Can we be pardoned in advance? Is an evil deed that we pre-meditatively schedule within a window of pardon still a pardonable deed?"

"A window of pardon..." Gubaru mused. "The Moon obstructs the sight of the Sun, and you call that a window?"

"What is it Gubaru? What has happened?"

Gubaru could not speak. Nabû-na'id, concerned for him, put his hand on his shoulder. "Take a breath, my friend. Take a breath. Then tell me when you are ready." As he spoke he was disconcerted by the wild look in Gubaru's eyes – a look that, to Nabû-na'id, communicated not only anguish but, disturbingly, sympathy.

"Your father –" Gubaru began.

Nabû-na'id felt his heart leap.

"Your father – he just died. He died, Nabû-na'id, right before me. He died."

Nabû-na'id's heart fell, and fell, and bottomlessly fell.

Now it was his friend who held his shoulder – who, now, was holding all of him, fiercely hugging him. Nabû-na'id said nothing.

Clutching him, Gubaru wept and, through his tears, tried to explain. "He was working, writing. He had sent for me. I didn't expect it. I came in, he rose, there was a sudden look of astonishment on his face, and he fell. That was all. That was all."

Still Nabû-na'id said nothing, as his friend held him, as he stared at the wall in front of him, which he suddenly realized was not and had never been real.

"He did not go to his fate," Gubaru murmured almost into his ear, still clutching him fiercely. "His fate came to him."

Still Nabû-na'id stared at the wall. It was not real. It had never been real.

Two weeks had passed. "I am sorry about your father," the red-haired man from Ḫume said. Nabû-na'id did not respond. "May you serve his ghost well – may his name never be forgotten from your lips – may the food you burn for him and the beer you pour for him keep him satiated."

"Until I am dead," Nabû-na'id said. "And perhaps after me, my sons will remember him, and after them, their sons. But my father's fate, like mine, like yours, will eventually be as a famished, forgotten ghost, anonymous among the hordes of forgotten, famished ghosts that lurk and wail and blow away in the Netherworld."

The man from Ḫume said nothing.

"Only I can remember him," Nabû-na'id said. "My sons, if I ever have any, will remember a name." A shadow passed across his face, though what cast it was within, not without. "Perhaps eventually that will be all that I remember too. Nabû spoke his life; now the word has been uttered, and in its wake ripples a silence without end."

Both men looked at the dirt and said nothing for a few moments. It was the man from Ḫume who broke the silence. "Why have I been asked here?" he inquired politely.

Nabû-na'id said nothing for a long while, staring only at the wall. The man from Ḫume was on the verge of repeating himself when the youth spoke, slowly, in a low voice, each word punctuated by a silence that communicated grief and struggle and exhaustion. "Tomorrow the day will become night. Šamaš will not see what men do. King Lābu will give the Iškuza to King Waksatar then."

"What do you mean, the day will become night?"

"You will see. When it happens, you will know."

"And at that moment Lābu will give up the Iškuza?"

"He will give them up, yes."

"Alive or dead?"

Nabû-na'id's voice, still low, became almost a monotone. "The last gift that their host will give them before he gives them up is death."

"Waksatar will not like that."

"He will not have them otherwise."

The man from Ḫume pursed his lips and thought. "I think I can prevail on him," he said in a slow drawl. "One way or another, I will send Lābu word by nightfall. Everything else, I assume, will be as your father and I negotiated?" Nabû-na'id's nod was barely perceptible. "Hmmm. Then the war will end. The Umman Manda and the Luddans will count themselves allies, friends and brothers." The man from Ḫume looked at him with something resembling care or sympathy. "We will have brought peace, you and I."

Šamaš could not see the Earth. Before him was the face of the Moon – a face that reflected his face, in all of its glory, in all of its light. "You blind me, Sîn!" Šamaš roared. "You blind me!"

"Why do you blame me, when it is your own image that you see?" Sîn replied.

Chapter 3. Matrimony and Madness in Bābilim

He had returned to Bābilim after over a decade spent in the company of foreigners – and of his father. For the first time in all those years he saw again his mother and was shocked at how little she had changed. Well past middle age, she was otherwise ageless, not discernably different in looks from when he had last seen her. Still she wore sackcloth and coated herself in ash; still her eyes were wild. Yet she remained honored by the king, as she had been by his predecessor and father, whose mourning she kept alongside her devotions to Sîn. He did not know if she mourned his own father, her husband. It was possible, even likely, that she had not seen Nabû-balaṭsu-iqbi in over twenty years; certainly Nabû-na'id had no memory of the two of them together. In fact, he could barely imagine it. How does one couple with a woman coated in ash? How was I brought forth from that? – he found himself thinking, before banishing the questions. Now the two of them were standing in a first-floor gallery of the palace waiting for the king.

Nabû-kudurri-uṣur entered briskly, trailed by only two attendants. Although his worn face, gray hair and beard suggested a man perhaps in his late fifties, his physical condition gave the impression of a younger man, still strong and energetic. Nabû-na'id was surprised to see that his mother made no obvious gesture of obeisance but instead simply introduced them: "Your Excellency, King of all Kings, King of the Four Corners, may I present at your request my son, Nabû-na'id, son of Nabû-balaṭsu-iqbi, returned at last from Sardis where he served you in the court of the Luddan king."

Nabû-na'id and Nabû-kudurri-uṣur examined one another, each meeting the other's gaze. "So you are the youth who brought me peace between the Luddans and the Umman Manda. That was very useful to me."

"My father brought you that peace; I only finished what he began."

"My brother Lābu tells me differently." The king looked at him from beneath half-closed eyes. "He tells me you are a prophet, and that peace was only possible because of your prophecy." The king waited for a response from Nabû-na'id, but he said nothing. "Your father, though a man I esteemed, was not a prophet."

"I am not a prophet," Nabû-na'id said firmly.

"You're not a lackey either, I see," countered the king sharply. Nabû-na'id again met his gaze but said nothing.

"Like your mother," the king resumed, with a slight nod to her. "And your father. You come from parents I respect, Nabû-na'id, parents who have done great service to me and to my father." The king looked directly at Adad-guppi. "And now you too have joined that tradition of doing me service. I am glad for it. And –" he paused for effect "I am grateful."

Nabû-na'id showed no reaction.

"You know," Nabû-kudurri-uṣur continued, "that now we have an alliance, we men of Bābilim, with both the Luddans and the Umman Manda. Lābu has sought my friendship, a wise thing for him to do, in part because of the role you – and your father – played. And Waksatar was my father's ally in the glorious sack of Ninua – to say nothing, forgive me, of your mother's hallowed city – and, yet more significantly, is the father of that remarkable woman, Ḫumati, my wife. We three now are united as family, as fathers and sons and brothers – and in my campaigns to the west, I no longer need concern myself with a threat from the north. That," he finished with emphasis, "is useful."

"My father, who was a good and far-seeing man, perhaps saw those benefits, your Excellency. But I am so far from a prophet that I cannot claim to have."

The king gave a shrill laugh. "You have much to learn about the court of Bābilim," he observed. "I have no other courtier who does not accept the credit that I bestow on him, whether rightly or wrongly."

"I am not a courtier," Nabû-na'id answered crisply.

"No you are not," the king murmured. "Like your father wasn't either. But that is useful too." The two men exchanged frank, appraising glances. "I could promise you whatever reward you should ask for," the king said. "But I, who am also not a prophet, nonetheless foresee that that is the wrong approach with you." Silence ensued. Nabû-na'id could hear the king breathing. "Has your mother told you about the oracle?"

"No," Nabû-na'id answered simply.

"I have received word from the god that you are to join my family."

Shock and bewilderment gripped Nabû-na'id. This he had not foreseen.

"One of my more interesting daughters, Niṭil-Kišar, is to be your wife. And you are to be at my side. I could use a prophet at hand." The king laughed his shrill laugh. "I could even use an honest man."

Nabû-na'id was in the shadows, watching from afar. The priest slit the lamb's throat, in one fluid motion flipped the animal on her back, slit open her belly and plunged his arms deep within. His face did not change, showing neither fascination nor pity; his eyes were not a fanatic's; his lips were marred by no stream of saliva betokening madness or zealotry. This was a deed that he did every day; he did it like those things that we all do every day – proficiently, almost automatically, often thoughtlessly.

But now the priest was his mother; it was her arms which were steeped in blood, as she pulled them from within the lamb, clutching the entrails in her fingers. "Let me see, let me see," she kept saying. "What has our lamb written?" She looked up and spotted Nabû-na'id in the shadows. "Everyone writes," she said directly to him, across the vast distance separating them, while blood dripped off of her arms, as high as her shoulders. He realized the animal was still alive, though she held its liver in her hands. "It is the omen of Luḫuššum," she announced. "Come see, come see!" she cried excitedly, beckoning him to her. "You know how to read!" He did not stir.

Then suddenly he was on the dais, beside the blood-stained altar. He was alone, but for the lamb. It was he who now held the liver, while the dying animal squirmed beneath him. The room was lit, but not where he was; and no matter how he moved, he could not escape the shadows – shadows which had become the color of blood. All of him was in shadow, blood-shadow; there was no escape to the light. "Is your mother right, or am I?" his father asked. "Tell me before I die. I should like to know." "I'm looking, father. I will know as soon as I read what this lamb has written." "But that isn't a lamb!" his father exclaimed. "Look!"

Nabû-na'id looked.

The two of them were outside, seated next to one another with their backs against a mud-brick wall which also cast shade over them. "What did you see?" Gubaru asked. He was now a member of the king's guard.

"I don't know. Maybe I woke before I could see. Or maybe what I saw woke me up. Whatever it was, I don't remember."

"Do you think a god gave you this dream?"

"A god, perhaps, or a ghost. Maybe Sîn. Maybe my father."

"In order to tell you what?" his friend inquired delicately.

Nabû-na'id reflected for a while, more bothered than he cared for Gubaru to know. Maybe dreams don't tell us anything, just like a landscape of immense beauty or immense horror is not there to communicate a message. One does not say, "I saw the waterfall – and understood" or "I saw the volcano erupt and destroy everything in its path – and understood." If a god or a ghost sent him the dream, perhaps it was to stand beside him and see it with him. Nothing more. Or perhaps it was to stand apart and to watch him watch the dream. Perhaps this god or ghost was cruel.

"I am meeting Niṭil-Kišar this afternoon," he said, changing the subject.

"Are you excited?"

"I don't know. I didn't seek this – marriage or a court life. I think I might be more like my father – a man content to live apart and study obscure things."

"But was your father really that way? He was always conspiring with or against the man from the Egibi House, and in the end was drawn into the peace negotiations too."

"He did those things despite himself."

"We all do things despite ourselves," Gubaru observed. "But then we become that."

Nabû-na'id let out a sharp laugh, a bark, and immediately remembered his father. Pain shot through him. "We become what we are in spite of ourselves?" he asked.

"I guess."

"Who is the 'ourself,' then, whom we spite?"

Gubaru looked a little cowed and didn't answer. Nabû-na'id relented. "I'm not mocking you, Gubaru. I think you may be right. That doesn't make my question go away, though."

"No, it doesn't."

"In my dream, am I the man far off in the shadows, who

abhors and fears the sacrifice for reasons that even he doesn't understand? Or am I the man on the dais, the participant, maybe even the sacrificer? Which one am I truly, which one do I spite or am I in spite of?"

Gubaru shrugged.

"How do I find out?" Nabû-na'id asked him.

"You look," he answered.

Niṭil-Kišar was a girl of fifteen or sixteen. She stood before him, veiled, accompanied by two attendants. The king was there, as was his mother. "This man will be your husband," the king said to the girl officiously. Nabû-na'id, not knowing what was expected of him, and put off by this terse, nameless introduction, took a half-step forward. Should I turn, put myself on display, play the comic? he wondered despairingly. Or bow and proceed with excessive majesty, as if not knowing that she is a pawn – and that I am?

He heard, seemingly magnified, the sound of a buzzing fly. It was as if all other sounds had ceased, and the room contained only mute figures and that buzzing. Effortlessly, almost despite himself, he spotted the fly midway between the girl and him, on the ground, spinning on its back. He took two paces toward it – and, he realized as an afterthought, toward the girl. Watching the fly and without looking up, he spoke. "I pity dying flies. In the prelude to their deaths, in the ferocity of their struggle to live, they tear themselves to pieces, limb by limb. Eventually they end on their backs, unable to flip over. That sound we hear is the song of their wings, no longer casting them into the air, but beating the dirt pointlessly, as they lie there, legless, hopeless. And then they wait, sometimes for days, every now and then yielding to panic and to fervor and beating the dirt with their useless wings. At last they give even that up and only look at the world, helpless to do anything, helpless even to not look. It seems

– horrid."

One of the two attendants snickered – then stopped abruptly beneath the cold gaze of the king. It was enough, however, to remind Nabû-na'id that he was supposedly wooing the king's daughter, and that this was presumably not the way to do it. He blushed but still did not look up.

"Perhaps there is a peace in that seeing," he heard a voice say. "Whether it beholds the pale blue of the sky or the heavens at night or, even now, our faces and bodies in strange perspective, or simply the beams of the roof. Perhaps in all of that or any of that lies revelation – for a fly."

It was the girl who spoke. He thought he detected something sharp, possibly satirical, in her voice.

"How would we distinguish the cruelest suffering from revelation?" he asked softly, ignoring his own sense that she was ridiculing him. He looked up and at her for the first time since he had stepped forward. She too had taken a step closer, and he could just see – or perhaps he only fancied seeing – the outline of her face behind the veil. She didn't respond to his question, however, apart from a twitch of her hand that he didn't know how to interpret but was inclined to consider as dismissive.

"What is it that possesses a being to rip itself apart from the inside?" he asked, surprised by his own sense of urgency.

A long silence followed. Then, in a whisper barely louder than a breath, intended for his ears alone, she answered, "Is that so hard to imagine?" It was a shockingly intimate response. He let a question express itself in his gaze, a gaze met in turn only by the faceless veil. He could not have said what his own question was.

The girl suddenly walked to the fire at the side of the room. With her sandaled foot she fearlessly kicked a burning ember from it towards the room's center, near Nabû-na'id. He watched it pulsating red and orange in the dirt, not far from the fly; he watched it as it gradually cooled.

Clearly, distinctly, to everyone in the room, the girl spoke. "Fire inhabits what it burns." Then she left, followed by her attendants.

The king cleared his throat. Nabû-na'id turned to him, but the king was regarding not him but his mother. Her face was blank, expressionless. "I think they shall do nicely together," the king declared, with what Nabû-na'id could only assume was a heavy dose of irony. Then, without looking at him, the king left. His mother, however, examined him keenly before unhurriedly following the king.

He was now alone in the room, or almost alone. For, after all, beside a cooling ember lay a dying fly. Did he really care about the fly? he wondered. And – was he really not alone, because the fly happened to be there? In fact, why, under these circumstances, had he talked of flies?

The answer to the first question was probably no; his loneliness convinced him that the answer to the second was also probably no. But he had little clue how to answer the third. Instead, he wondered about the limbless fly, spinning on its back in the dirt. Was it a mercy, for the fly, to have striven with such ferocity that it tore its own limbs off? Could a fly, having done that, rest in the comfort that it had exerted itself to the utmost? "Nothing more could be expected of me; I have left no stone unturned." Is that the view of a fly? – flies who lack the strength to overturn stones?

Or rather, does a fly exert itself without goal or object? Do its limbs rip free in a convulsion of effort and pain that for the fly has no discernible point, beyond a desire that hitherto, for a fly, had been one with the deed? For, Nabû-na'id found himself thinking, a fly does not desire to fly, but flies; it does not desire to walk but walks; and now, mysteriously, for the first and only time, deed and desire have been flung apart.

"Why did you speak to me of flies?" a voice inquired suddenly.

He had been lost in thought; he had not noticed the silent arrival of the girl, who now stood before him, only a few feet away, alone.

"Where are your attendants?"

"The thing about veils," she responded obliquely, "is that a person wearing one is much the same as another person wearing one." So speaking, she lifted her veil and revealed a thin face, more triangular than oval, with dark, curly hair, brown, intelligent eyes which hinted at gold, and the bare trace of a moustache around thin lips. On the arch of her left cheek were two dark moles, which reminded him of the few early stars which boldly shine even as night is just beginning to fall. Her chin was a little angular, almost too small for her face. "My attendants seem to have confused me with someone else," she continued.

Nabû-na'id smiled at what he took to be a show of spirit. "Thank you for letting me see your face," he said, as they glanced shyly at each other and then, more daringly, met and held each other's gaze. There was a spark in her eyes; there was life in them.

"Answer my question," she demanded imperiously.

"I can't. I don't know the answer."

She pursed her lips. "You're making quite the impression," she observed, with what Nabû-na'id thought was perhaps a playful tone. "Did you understand why I kicked the ember at you?"

"Oh – it was at me, not to me. I hadn't understood *that*. Why you did it, I'm sure I don't know; but this is what I understood by it: wood does not burn in fire, fire burns in wood. You can see that when you look at a burning log; the fire is inside of the log."

"Yes. The fire is a part of the log, even if it is also what consumes the log."

"But now, I suppose, we are speaking of flies and of ourselves, and not just logs," Nabû-na'id noted. "Maybe we are different things than flies and logs, though... And anyway, how do you understand that the log had to catch on fire first? If the fire was always a part of it."

"Poets aren't supposed to ask such detailed questions," she answered mockingly. "Nor are prophets. Besides –" she paused for a moment "– just because something is within us, it doesn't mean that it's within our power to activate it."

"That which is within – may not, precisely, be our own."

"Yes, poet."

"Why do you think I am a poet?"

"Because you wooed me with flies!" Then she corrected herself. "With a dying fly, rather."

Nabû-na'id looked at her for a moment and felt a grin growing across his face – he felt it catch fire and burn across his face, beyond his power, which in any event he would happily have yielded. "How else," he answered through his smile, "would I woo you, poet?"

She smiled back at him – he was virtually certain she did so despite herself. Then, quickly, she re-veiled. "Would it be lucky if my attendants have not noticed their mistake?" she inquired. "Or is that its own curse?" Nabû-na'id didn't answer. "You and I will be seeing more of each other," the girl said. "Wooing, we both know, is in our case both extraneous and irrelevant – perhaps as much as that fly over there is."

Nabû-na'id expected that she was going to add something. She did not but turned and left abruptly.

* * * * *

...In the Babylonian king's employ was Baltasar, an exile from the great city of Cadytis in the mountainous region of Syria, on the route to Egypt. This city, whose size and splendor once rivaled Sardis, had fallen a few years earlier; its king had been captured, his line extinguished and he blinded. The city's inhabitants, but for the very poorest, had been dispersed throughout the empire, many to Babylon. Of these was Baltasar, still a youth. Having been separated from his family – if they were even still alive – he had resorted to street thievery when he was caught in the act by a high-ranking official, one Aspenax by name. "Why should I not have this hand cut off?" he asked the boy, holding and shaking his arm by the elbow. "Would you cut off the hand of your own son?" the boy responded. "If he were a thief!" Aspenax answered. He was in the process of bringing the boy to the judges when one of his underlings approached him. "Your son has been captured for thieving," he whispered. "He is in our custody. What shall we do?" "Do the judges know?" Aspenax asked anxiously. "Not yet," was the reply. "Release him to me and keep this quiet." Once his subordinate had left, Baltasar, who had observed the exchange, again spoke to Aspenax. "Would you have my hand cut off, I who have no one and thieve for survival, while sparing your own son, whom you feed and house and clothe?" Aspenax, who was an upright man, could not justify sparing the one and not the other. At last he said, "So long as I stand beneath the sun, I will not have the hand of my son cut off." He then arranged for Baltasar to enter his household and raised him as a second son – much to the chagrin of his first.

In the years that followed, this Baltasar became well-known as a sage, especially as a dream-interpreter. In particular he had come to the attention of the king, over whom he exerted considerable influence. At the time, the Babylonians had been engaged for many years in besieging Tyre – and indeed when I visited Tyre the priests showed me the remains of a wall that, they said, the Babylonians had built during that siege. With no end in sight, however, the king was contemplating lifting the siege; with the troops thereby released, he was also contemplating a war with Egypt. His son-in-law, Neriklassor, strongly favored the latter, but he was hindered by Baltasar, whose prophecies of failure and devastation had thus far held the king back from an invasion. Neriklassor, thinking Baltasar an opportunist and a fraud, thought to eliminate him by proposing to the king that he test his sages. "A false sage is of no use to you," Neriklassor urged. "Kill the ones who lie and then your confidence in the advice of the others will be all the greater." The king was persuaded by his argument and accordingly devised a test for his sages.

Among those sages, besides Baltasar, was Labynetus. Because Labynetus was now also a son-in-law of the king, having a few years earlier married one of his daughters, Nitocris, and also because the king liked and trusted him, the king was anxious to exempt him from the trial. Labynetus refused. "You are contemplating evil," he told the king, "and if I cannot spare you from it, neither shall I spare myself." The king was angered by both the accusation and the obstinacy of Labynetus and resolved that his fate would be what it would be.

Thus the king, advised by Neriklassor, made trial of his sages. He summoned them as a group and announced that he wished for them to interpret a dream. Those who interpreted it truthfully he would honor; but those who did so falsely he would not spare. The sages inquired of him, "How will you know your dream has been interpreted truthfully? The unfolding of a dream, and its correlation with the events of our lives, can be subtle matters, and what may first seem false may later be revealed as true." The king smiled wickedly. "In this I shall know the truth without doubt; and the obfuscations of a fearful sage will be known by me as well." The sages of course were not comforted by this response, perhaps in the case of some of them because they knew themselves to be false, while others may honestly have believed what the first sage had said. Nonetheless they had little choice but to resign themselves to this trial and to whatever it would bring.

"Tell us your dream," they said. "Ah!" the king replied. "That is where the trial begins. You must interpret my dream without my telling it to you." In great consternation, the sages talked excitedly among themselves before one of them came forward. "It cannot be done, your Excellency. What you ask is the work of a god, not of a sage." "I will give you some time to make it your work," was the king's reply. "How long?" "That too will be your work to determine." With this their audience ended.

In the days that followed, the honest sages consulted what means they had in an effort to divine a response to the king, while many of the dishonest endeavored to slip away. Meanwhile, after six or seven days, the king's patience came to an end, and he summoned his official Aspenax to him. "At dawn tomorrow collect the sages throughout Babylon. They will give me an answer, and if they are wrong, you and your men are to kill them." Aspenax of course was horrified at the danger facing Baltasar, whom he regarded and had made his son, and so he warned him that night to flee. But Baltasar would not. "I will not abandon my god who will not abandon me," he declared. Indeed, far from fleeing, and to the great despair of his father, he sought instead an audience with the king that very night. While he waited in the king's antechambers, he was surprised to encounter Labynetus, who had also requested an audience. "Do you know what comes in the morrow?" he asked Labynetus. "None may know the king's dream," Labynetus responded, "but few there are who don't know tomorrow's secret." "Why have you not fled? Do you know the dream?" Baltasar inquired. "I do not know the dream. I am come to convince the king that he is contemplating evil." Labynetus inspected Baltasar. "And you, do you know the dream?" Baltasar responded that he did not but that his god would deliver him.

The king called the two of them together before him. "Tell me my dream," he said to them. "We have not come for that," Labynetus responded. "Tell me anyway," the king commanded. The two men stood silently in front of the king, before finally Baltasar spoke. "In your dream you see a great statue in your own likeness, a statue as tall as a temple. The top of the statue, its head, is made of gold, then beneath that, the neck and the shoulders are silver; and further down still it turns to bronze, then iron, then stone and finally clay, which the feet are made of." The king smiled smugly. "And what would this dream portend?" "That your golden reign will soon give way to something lesser – to silver; and from there it will continue inexorably to decline, until at last it is reduced to mud." This response angered the king but, hiding that, he turned to Labynetus. "Is this your answer too?"

"It is," Labynetus replied, "and it is not. My answer is that you had no dream, and thus what you would have us interpret is nothing. But nothing can be interpreted variously; in nothing all interpretations culminate; and among those is that which Baltasar spoke truthfully to you – that you are, even now, beholding an image of yourself, and it is in your hands what it will be made of, which is the same as what you will be made of. At hand, your Excellency, is your own choice – would you cast yourself in gold or in mud? For ridding your kingdom of your best servants is as throwing gold into a river; what you will replace it with will be less valuable, until at last it has no value at all."

The king was deeply disturbed by Labynetus's answer, especially because Labynetus was right – he had had no dream. It was in this that he had laid his trap for the false sages. He was inclined therefore to spare Labynetus, who had spoken truthfully; but could he spare Labynetus and not Baltasar, whose answer Labynetus had affirmed? Having had no dream, there was no dream of a statue, and thus Baltasar had spoken falsely; yet, if Labynetus was right, to kill Baltasar would risk making Baltasar's interpretation true and would, as a result, be a sort of fashioning of his own statue. Neither he nor Neriklassor had foreseen such complexities. The king was at once irked and impressed. He contemplated the two men for a long time in silence, marveling as well that neither Baltasar nor Labynetus betrayed any fear.

At last the king answered. "Henceforth shall you both be honored above all my other advisors, for you have spoken well and served me truthfully." He then dismissed them, summoned Aspenax and rescinded his order for the morrow.

* * * * *

"That was fool-hardy," Niṭil-Kišar said. "My father is unpredictable. When he offered to exempt you, you should have accepted. And afterwards, when you were warned to flee, you should have fled. As for the other sage, to link your fate to his was madness." She looked at him coolly, but he sensed something close to rage burning beneath the surface. Fire, he recalled, inhabits what it burns. "You are lucky to be alive," she concluded.

"I know, Niṭ" he acknowledged patiently.

"If you know, then why did you play this game? This was a trap – and if you were not the intended target, certainly you would still have been a delightful bonus."

"Why do you think the whole thing was a trap?"

"Eradicating the king's sages – purging his advisors – hmm..." She pretended to be genuinely puzzled. "Who could benefit from leaving my father more isolated, more beholden to the few remaining voices with access to his ear?" Then she let slip the mask: "Who indeed! We may think a king all-powerful – but his arm is not his own, his eyes are not his own, and eventually he is not his own."

Nabû-na'id considered his wife's words. He thought vaguely of Atraḫasīs, but instead asked, "You fear that the king will be ruled by his proxies?"

"Of course! They see and act for him. Without them he is helpless and blind – little better than that fly you wooed me with.

His instruments could make him their instrument."

"Perhaps, then, that is the benefit of an unpredictable king; unpredictability is protection against being instrumentalized."

"Or it is a sign of how removed from the world my father has already become."

"Do you think of him as your father or as the king?" Nabû-na'id asked gently.

"In my life, my father has always been king, and the king has always been my father. I do not know what a father is who isn't king; or what a king is who isn't my father."

Nabû-na'id wrapped his arms around his wife. They were both seated, somewhat eccentrically, on the ground, he with his back against the wall, she with her back against him. "If there is no one who will speak honestly with your father, then he is lost. Perhaps then we all are. The way I acted – it was to try to keep that possibility in abeyance."

"Out of loyalty to my father?"

Nabû-na'id did not answer but kissed the back of his wife's neck.

"Out of loyalty to me?"

Nabû-na'id continued to kiss her neck. She twisted to face him, her eyes glaring and aflame, her face flushed with anger.

"Do not get yourself killed on my behalf!"

"I would not, if I could at all help it," he protested. "I do not look forward to my days as a ghost… and I'm well aware that in your anger you would not be above denying me sacrifices, starving and parching me into repentance." He laughed.

"You're right," she agreed, curling into his arms. "I would not be above that. If you are stupid enough to get yourself killed, know that I'll starve and parch your ghost – just out of pique." She looked into his eyes, and he saw, as he often did, a way that her eyes could dance, while his own eyes, following hers, would dance too. She kissed him. "Your eyes are dancing," she said.

"No, yours are," he murmured, kissing her.

"I see our brother's hand in this," she said abruptly, pulling away.

"Nergal-šar-uṣur?"

"Who else?"

"He is ambitious," Nabû-na'id conceded. "Not very bright, but ambitious. But for now he is stymied. The sage and I – we have the king's ear. For now."

"What will you whisper in his ear?" she whispered into his.

"I have already done my whispering!" he laughed. "Gubaru and I will go to Ṣurru, to end that bloody siege – if Sîn will let us."

She straightened her elbows and held herself at arm's length from him. "And I am to stay behind?"

"Yes. I thought we could wrap you in veil after veil, consign you to the most central room of an inner palace, surround that with an outer palace, and then that palace with fortifying walls, and those walls with more walls, and add as well legions of attendants to guard you, lest you connive to sneak away to do your mischief." Nabû-na'id adopted a mock self-satisfied expression. "But while I'm arranging that, I thought you could tag along."

"You are a very good instrument," she said, smiling.

"Yes, your highness," he replied. "You know, there's a story I heard when I lived in Sardis, about a man who suffered a great misfortune."

"What was that?"

"He fell in love with his own wife."

Niṭil-Kišar looked up at him, her eyebrow raised. "That's a sorry state of affairs," she murmured, nuzzling against his chest.

"It led to the downfall of his kingdom, his betrayal by his guard and friend, and his death… But, though that's how the story was told, I don't think it was really because he fell in love with his wife that he was unfortunate."

"What do you think?"

"I think some of the riches in our lives are only within, while the rest are only without. The internal ones make the others, and everything else, seem like nothing. This man, this king, was used to being admired and envied for his external riches. Perhaps this envy and admiration even constituted a great deal of their value to him. When he fell in love with his own wife, he couldn't imagine how to value that if others didn't value it too – even though it was necessarily denied them. Especially, in fact, because it was so denied."

"So his mistake was in trying to reveal a treasure that not only couldn't be shared, but couldn't be witnessed?"

"Something like that. Maybe his first mistake was to value loving his wife."

"What do you mean?" Niṭil-Kišar asked sharply.

"I mean – something other than what you think I mean. Let us value grain and bricks and houses and fields. We can take their measures, so we can value them. But perhaps there are those things whose measures cannot be taken, and that are therefore outside of value. I would even suggest" – he gave his wife a friendly squeeze – "that those are the best things."

"I like this idea better," Niṭil-Kišar commented. "But in our marriage contract, don't I recall a bride price?"

Nabû-na'id sighed. "I can think what I like; it doesn't mean the conventions of the world will change. The bride-price was no indication of your value; let it have been a token, a gesture, an acknowledgement of an undeserved gift…"

"… to the tune of a few shekels of silver and the odd ox, I suppose?" She finished his sentence for him, perhaps not quite as he intended, while looking challengingly and playfully into his eyes.

"Aren't you aggravating," he observed dryly. "And you

know nothing about the going rate for a king's daughter if you think a few shekels of silver and the odd ox will measure up." She made a face at him, which he tried to imitate back at her. "But I'm trying to be serious. The things I'm talking about can't be valued, maybe because they're not really things. They're not removable or separable from the relations that they're in. It's not that they can't be shared; it's that they're only shared. But that doesn't mean they're shared with anyone. Part of the gift is the wonder of its being shared, not by everyone, but specifically by you and me, for example. Do you understand what I mean?"

"I think so, poet," she murmured.

"I'm not sure if any of this means it can't be witnessed... But I doubt it can be proven. Those who witness it may suspect it's there, may even devoutly believe it's there – but they can't prove it's there. You and I are witnesses to what we share; Gubaru witnesses it too, I think; you witness what Gubaru and I share; but if called before the judges, what would any of us say? 'Give me the strongest oath and I shall swear it.' But doesn't that oath seem strangely superfluous, like taking an oath that you truly meant your previous oath and would mean this one too?"

"I don't see what you mean."

"Maybe I'm confusing myself. Maybe I'm only trying to say that this secret which you and I share, which we cannot bring into the open – it exists so long as we trust it, so long as we don't demand that it show itself in the full light of day. That demand implicitly would be an expression of disbelief, but belief is a necessary and irreplaceable ingredient in what this is."

"Why do you call it a secret?"

"Because there is nothing more secret! Neither you nor I can make what I am talking about appear as itself in the world; and there is no observer, hidden behind a door, who can intercept the message passing between us – because the passing between *is* the message."

Niṭil-Kišar mulled his words thoughtfully. "You've chosen an optimistic reading. Others are possible."

"What are you thinking?"

"There could be no message. Our faith – or should I say your faith? – could be misplaced. And the danger represented by that surreptitious observer you speak of is that he observe *that*. He could see that there is no message, or even – though this is a different thing – that the message is blank. Maybe in this story you heard in Sardis that's why everything unraveled. The king sought to share something that couldn't be shared, and the reason it couldn't be shared was *it wasn't there*. Maybe every kingdom totters over that same abyss – maybe everything human does."

Nabû-na'id examined her intently. "I don't deny that what you say could be so, Niṭ" he said quietly. "There have been times in my life when I have thought that it was."

"It's also why you're wrong about measurement," Niṭil-Kišar continued. "Everything is measurable. That's because measurement is a species of invention, a flight of the imagination as much as anything else. You said we could measure grain and fields and houses, and that's why those things can be valued. But what we measure in each case is only some aspect of any of those things. Think of all the life in a field, think of every cricket, every grain of dirt, every dewdrop, think of the moon reflected in each dewdrop… Can we really take the measure of that?"

"No," Nabû-na'id said despite himself.

"But –" his wife clutched him emphatically "– the answer is *also* yes, because we *do* measure the field. To think that we limit measurement to some special class of measurable things is to misunderstand measurement. It is like thinking that poetry can apply only to gods and to beauty, but not to love or to flowers or even to ugliness."

"Measurement is a kind of poetry?" Nabû-na'id asked, his

words tumbling slowly out of his mouth one after another.

"Of course. And hence so is valuation. Maybe not the best kind of poetry, the most interesting or challenging or beautiful – but it is undoubtedly poetry."

"I shrink from what you're saying," Nabû-na'id spoke softly, "even if it's true."

Niṭil-Kišar, regarding him with sympathy, stroked his cheek with her hand. "It is possible we measure what isn't there, and that every poem is an ode to nothing," she observed not unkindly. "But it is also possible that it is – otherwise." She paused. "And maybe there is a way that nothing is our most tender gift." A tear slid down her cheek. Very gently, he brushed it away.

* * * * *

From the [fragmentary] Assyrian Accounts of Herodotus

...As I have already had occasion to mention, on my return from Egypt I visited Tyre especially to consult the priests about the worship of Heracles. But while I was there they also showed me the walls that the Babylonians had abandoned when they lifted their siege, a little more than a century before. Rather than remove the walls themselves, the Tyrians left most of them in place and to this day make an offering there on the last night before each new Moon, when only the Moon's smallest sliver can be seen. They do this in honor of Artemis of the Stranger, as they call her, who saved them from destruction by the Babylonians only at the last possible instant, by prevailing on Nitocris, Queen of Babylon, in a dream. For, say the Tyrians, their own situation had become desperate, both because of starvation and a plague that had broken out in the city. The city's fall was imminent, and the Queen of Babylon had come to witness it. Instead, however, Artemis visited her and, through a dream, commanded that she relent.

While I am sure that Nitocris was not then Queen of Babylon, despite what the Phoenicians say – for Amytis, the daughter of Cyaxares, was still alive and, in any event, her husband ruled and not she; and it was that king, as I have already noted, who first contemplated lifting the siege as part of his plan to invade Egypt, though it would be many years later before he did *invade Egypt – still, that Artemis should have intervened through the king's daughter (for so Nitocris was) does not seem improbable to me, at least given the little that mortals know of the cares, loyalties or even duties of gods. After all, but for the intervention of a god, why should the Babylonians have relented, when the annihilation of the city and its people were at last within their grasp?*

* * * * *

He and the other sage, Belet-ṣeri-dannat, wearing a blue robe and cap, stood before Nabû-kudurri-uṣur in a back room of the palace. "Why have you called us before you, your Excellency?" he asked.

"I want your advice." The king inspected them in silence for a few moments. "My wife Ḫumati is unhappy."

"Has she told you why?" Belet-ṣeri-dannat asked.

"She says that she misses her homeland – Manda."

"And do you think that really is why she is unhappy?" pursued Belet-ṣeri-dannat fearlessly.

The king looked at this foreign sage strangely. "Are you married?"

"No."

"But you are," the king noted, looking this time at Nabû-na'id.

"As you well know," Nabû-na'id answered.

"If Niṭil-Kišar told you she was unhappy, would you believe the reason she gave?"

"I would trust her not to be trying to deceive me."

"But would you believe the reason she gave?"

"I don't know. When are we confident that we understand our own unhappiness?"

"I am unhappy," the king declared imperiously, "because my wife is unhappy." He looked challengingly at Nabû-na'id, who returned his gaze but said nothing. Silence settled uncomfortably upon the three men.

"When you say that your wife misses her homeland," Belet-ṣeri-dannat began anew, "what exactly does she miss? Her family? The people? The customs? The language? The mountains? The flowers?"

"I brought many of her family members here. She is surrounded by Umman Manda; she encounters her people, her customs and her language daily. So what can she miss?" The king sounded both perplexed and irritated. "Am I to bring the mountains to her, and their flowers? That would be madness."

"Perhaps she can be distracted," suggested Belet-ṣeri-dannat. "Perhaps her nostalgia is just boredom. Perhaps –" he paused. "Perhaps she wants a child."

"It is not guesswork that I want," the king declared angrily. "Consult stars, dreams, livers, flowing water, birds – I do not care what you consult. But find out what must be done to make my wife happy."

Nabû-na'id stood outside, examining the stars, wearing only a light cloak over his normal robes despite the cold. Niṭil-Kišar, wrapped in a heavier cloak, joined him. "They are much the same as those we saw in Ṣurru," she said. "Are they not?"

"Yes."

"I think to myself of how long and hard we journeyed; I think how strange the people of Ṣurru seemed to me, how odd their language, how unfamiliar their customs. And yet overhead are the same stars directing their destinies as ours."

"Perhaps."

"Only perhaps?"

"We see different things in the stars than they do. We call that collection over there by one name – because it reminds us of a bull. They call that collection by a different name, and they include that faint, almost blue star far to the left." He pointed at the blue star, even though it was too dark for the gesture to be helpful. "It makes me wonder in what sense the stars are the same for them and for us, and in what sense they are different."

"You surprise me. I had expected you would challenge me for saying the stars direct destinies, not for saying they were the same."

He could feel more than see that she was smiling at him. She continued, "After all, I have married the strangest of astrologers, one who doesn't believe in astrology. Even though his prophecies are true." She murmured the last words.

"One of what you call my prophecies came true. One. Because it was made true. You do not know much about that and would be wise not to look very hard."

"Why?"

"Because it is very painful to me. Because perhaps it would become painful for you too. You might discover that all this while you have been married to a monster you mistook for a man."

She put her hand on his shoulder and stood beside him in silence for a while. "Does Gubaru know?" she whispered after a while.

"He was there," he answered both brusquely and evasively.

A long time passed in silence – long enough to be aware of the stars' passages across the sky. "Even the stars do not rest," Niṭil-Kišar abruptly observed with a sigh.

"No," he agreed.

“Are you looking for something in particular?” she asked.

“No, not really. I am letting my thoughts wander. The king has asked something of me, and it seemed to me to demand wandering thoughts, even more than stars. But my thoughts aren’t wandering in any clear direction – I would need the skills of a bird interpreter to make sense of them, as they flutter in chaos every which way.”

“Maybe your thoughts are falling stars, not birds. Maybe if you thought about them that way, you would understand.”

Nabû-na’id felt a shock of astonishment, enough to turn in the direction of his wife and hold her closer to him, unseen face to unseen face. “How is it that so often you know my mind?” he whispered almost fiercely.

She didn’t answer, but he could feel her breath on his face and, as before, her smile, though in the darkness the one was as invisible as the other.

“I was thinking about how we see the stars,” Nabû-na’id continued, “and about how prophecy can work. And my thought was – the truth is not in the stars, but in the relationships we make with the stars, in the stories that we read in them and in the stories that we don’t. A person from Bābilim sees a bull where a Ṣurran sees a snail; and who can doubt that the influence that a bull exerts in the world and in our lives is different – not necessarily better or worse, but different – from a snail’s? That was what I was thinking; and then you said, ‘Where you see a flock of birds, try seeing instead a falling star’ – and I felt shock and gratitude.”

She placed her head on his chest and they held one another. “Do you think that in a flock of birds can also be found a falling star?” she asked after a while. “Like in that story you once told me, of Anzû. Pluck away all of his feathers, you said, and the surprise is that he is a man. Is Anzû, ultimately, only a man, or can he still be Anzû, even if a man lies beneath his feathers?”

"Must we choose between bird flocks and stars, between snails and bulls, between the traditions of Ṣurru and those of Bābilim? Is that what you're asking?"

"Something like that."

"I've wondered that too. In some moods, when I feel lighter and stronger and more playful, I think we can choose – 'today,' I hear an excited voice within me say, 'I shall live under a snail and see where that leads!' But there are darker moods, moods that shroud me perpetually in shadow, when that other view seems the hope of a child, too young or unobservant to have yet realized the patterns of choice that have governed his life already, even when he thought he was being whimsical. In those moments, I think to myself – to pretend you see a snail, when in fact you see a bull, is only to lie."

"But in fact you don't see a bull, you see stars," his wife corrected.

"Maybe," Nabû-na'id answered grudgingly.

"You haven't answered my other question."

"You didn't really ask it."

"But you know what it is."

"Yes. You want to know what the king asked of me."

"Well done, Anzû-man."

"He wants to know how to make Ḫumati happy."

Niṭil-Kišar burst into laughter.

The king had ordered an enormous statue to be made of his wife, all in gold and dressed in the finest, most colorful textiles. It stood within the city, looking towards Manda. It was said that the back of the head could be seen even from far outside the walls, since it towered above them, though neither Gubaru nor Nabû-na'id had yet had occasion to leave the city to confirm that. For now, they stood some distance away from the statue among a small crowd of onlookers and watched as the craftsmen put finishing touches to the image. They were carefully painting her eyes.

"It is extraordinary," Gubaru observed. "Nowhere has a king's wife been more honored. It will be a wonder of the world."

"It seems to me that it will not be the right wonder," Nabû-na'id commented obscurely.

"What do you mean?"

In lieu of answering, Nabû-na'id hailed another man, dressed in the fine costume and ornaments of court. "Belet-ṣeri-dannat, was this your doing?"

The other man, short with sharp eyebrows and an owl-beak nose, shrugged meaningfully. "My God does not permit the worship of idols. This image will lead only to evil."

"What is your god's objection to idols?" Nabû-na'id asked with genuine curiosity.

"Why don't you ask Him?" the short man responded enigmatically.

"My god is not your god," Nabû-na'id rejoined with a smile.

But the man answered gravely, "There is only one God." Then he gave a slight bow and continued on his way. Nabû-na'id watched him with interest until he turned out of sight.

"A fanatic?" Gubaru asked.

"No more than the rest of us, I think. Say, Gubaru, I have a question for you."

"What?"

"Do you think we can count gods?"

The two men exchanged frank looks, Gubaru searching his friend's face for a sign of how this question was intended.

"Why not?"

"Is a number an idol of a god? If I have counted a god, have I made an idol of him?"

"What are you talking about? Šamaš is clearly not Sîn, as you and your mother surely would contend before anyone else; and if they are not the same, they are two. But I don't see how that makes an idol of them."

"When I write the name of Sîn, have I made an idol with those signs, the dinger and the EN and the ZU?" Nabû-na'id continued, still on his own track of thought. "Isn't that an image of the god, in a certain sense, and hence an idol? But I could just as easily write "dinger 30," since 30 is the number of Sîn. So if one set of signs is an idol, the other set is too, right?"

"But none of those resemble the god! I don't know how to read, but surely the god doesn't look like the pigeon tracks on a clay tablet."

"Doesn't he? I wonder… But maybe the better question is – does an idol that represents the god also have to look like the god?" Nabû-na'id picked up a random stone from the street. "Why can this stone not serve to remind me of Sîn? Why can I not make it my idol, or even understand that the god has given me this stone to represent him by?"

"Well then, if that is so, what's not potentially an idol? The very name of the god would be an idol!" Gubaru declared testily.

Nabû-na'id thought for a moment. "You may be right, as so often, my friend," he said eventually. "If, as Belet-ṣeri-dannat would have it, I am not to have an idol of my god, I may well be compelled to worship a nameless god, or at least a god whose name I cannot – can never – know." With the peculiar intensity which his friend recognized all too well and had seen since their boyhoods together, Nabû-na'id looked directly at Gubaru and said meaningfully. "I think a god who does not permit idols will have to be nameless and uncountable!"

Gubaru felt bewildered. Why was this a concern to Nabû-na'id? "But there *are* idols of the gods! They're permitted!" he protested.

"Yes, yes." Nabû-na'id waved his hand in front of his face

dismissively. "But should they be?" He pointed at the queen's statue. "Like our friend, I foresee trouble here. Not evil, perhaps, but trouble."

"Why?"

"Because, no matter how exact the likeness, how fine the materials or how grand the scale, that image can only disappoint the queen."

"Why?"

"Because it can only emphasize their differences. Even what's best about it does this. The queen is not a giant; she is not made of gold; and no matter what tower she climbs, she cannot see her homeland. That image, intended to exalt and comfort her, will inevitably come to trouble her, because it is too unfaithful to what she is." He mused for a moment, and then he added, "And also because it is too faithful to what she cannot be."

"What do you mean?"

"The statue is as blind as she is – neither can see Manda. The statue is as immobile as she is – neither can visit Manda. The statue is too much a token of the king's pride and power. And perhaps she feels herself to be the same."

"He should not have ordered it built, then?"

"I would not have advised it. Someone else must have his ear." He took Gubaru by the elbow and nudged him forward, as they resumed their walk. "The problem with idols is that they can only fall short, for being too like us and too different," he said.

A letter once read by Nabû-na'id, even then over a millennium old:

Speak to Sîn-iddinam, thus speaks Ḫammurapi.

The goddesses of Emutbalum that are your responsibility – the troops under Inuḫ-samar's charge will bring them to you safely. When they have reached you, from among the troops under your authority assign some that they may bring the goddesses safely to their dwellings.

Nabû-na'id rose from a dream, unsettled. But the words that he had seen while dreaming did not simply evaporate in wakefulness. He could still see them, written as moon-cast shadows on the wall. He could only read them.

What was written was not that a god exists who is without idol. Nor that an idol exists who is without god. What was written was this:

Mimma ilī kalîšunu ṣalmum	Even gods, all of them, [are] an idol.
Ilum ištēn ṣalmum ilim	Each god [is] an idol of god.

He looked again at the wall.

Lā ilum ištēn	No god [is] one.
Mimma ilim ul ištēn	Even god [is] not one.

He looked again.

Mimma šarrātim kalîšina ṣalmum	Even queens, all of them, [are] an idol.
Ilū šarrātum atta	Gods, queens, you.

Nabû-na'id rose from a dream, unsettled. But he was comforted by the soft light of the moon and the meaningless play of shadows against the wall.

Niṭil-Kišar was again pregnant. She had been pregnant several times but only one child had survived beyond his first year – their son Bel-šar-uṣur, on whom she doted, though Nabû-na'id himself remained distant from him. "Let him survive infancy, then I shall dare to love him," his father had seemed to think; then, "Let him survive his toddlerdom, then I shall dare to love him." And now, "Let him survive a decade, then I shall know it is safe to love him." This was how her husband appeared to Niṭil-Kišar's critical and angry eye. But she had never spoken to him about it. In her heart it was she whom she condemned. "Lamaštu plagues me," she said in secret to herself. "He would not be blamed if he took another wife, a wife who was not cursed. I would not blame him."

This pregnancy too was difficult; Niṭil-Kišar was often sick, and for the most part she remained confined, attended regularly by Nabû-na'id and occasionally by his mother. He was with her this morning.

"I am bored," she said.

"Shall I build you a statue?" responded Nabû-na'id playfully. She smiled weakly and he regretted the joke.

He tried again. "Shall I tell you a story?"

"One of your mother's stories, you mean?"

"Well… It's not always clear to me which stories are hers and which ones are mine. Or where one of hers ends and one of mine begins."

"You can tell me a story, but first let me make a request."

"Yes?"

"Teach me to read and to write."

Nabû-na'id looked at her but said nothing.

"Are you unwilling?" she asked.

"No. I was just thinking."

"About what?"

"Oh, something trivial, in a sense. I was thinking – how can I teach someone to read and to write?"

"Just do to me what your teachers did to you."

Nabû-na'id smiled. "You don't really want that. My first teachers had me copy tablets endlessly and would beat my hands with sticks when I fell short of their expectations. And often I could not read what I was writing." *Perhaps I still can't*, he thought to himself.

"So teach me to read first, then to write. And don't beat me."

"All right." He thought some more, all the while holding her hand. She was lying on the bed, a blanket decorated with butterfly images drawn around her body and her head propped against the wall. He was seated next to her.

"I have three suggestions," he finally said. "First, tell me the sort of thing you'd like to read – whether hymns, or tales from the past, or laws. We'll choose something and read it together."

"Ok. I'll give it thought."

"Second, let's limit ourselves to what we write in clay and stone. For now, let's not worry too much about the short-lived, ink-stained papyrus and parchment that flutter about."

She shrugged. "And your third suggestion?"

"Ask my mother to teach you as well. I am sure that she knows how to read; and if I'm right, she probably figured it out on her own. She may be a better teacher than I can be. So ask her too."

"Do you think she would help me? I have never known what she made of me."

"Nor have I – of you or of me. But I think she would help you, though I could not say what it is that makes me think that."

"All right. Now you can tell me a story," his wife said with an almost child-like simplicity.

Nabû-na'id collected his thoughts, then began. "There was once a king of a land called Suḫu. He was surrounded by greater kings and he watched these greater kings gobble up kingdoms like his own. His advisors warned him that his kingdom would soon be threatened, and they urged him to try to play one great king against another. 'Only then will you avoid the fate of your neighbors,' they claimed. But this king had watched those very neighbors play precisely that game, and so he was not very encouraged. 'Let us go into the mountains,' he said abruptly one morning, and soon afterwards they did. He and an entourage of leading figures from the land plus picked men from his army headed northeast into the mountains. 'Why are we doing this?' court officials asked the king. 'I am looking for something,' he told them. 'What?' demanded the officials. 'A gift for my people, one that, whatever our fates, will be an example for the future.' But then his court officials wanted to know what it would be an example of. Is he going to conquer some other land, they whispered among themselves, and bring down to Suḫu their treasures, their women and their children? 'What is your plan?' they asked him. 'I don't know,' he replied. 'I don't even know what I am looking for. But I trust that my god will make it clear to me when I have found it.'

"As you can imagine, there was a lot of grumbling among the court officials. 'Our king is mad,' they said. 'Here we are, a small, surrounded kingdom, and he sets off into the mountains – he might as well be chasing Anzû!' The king was aware of this criticism but chose to ignore it. They proceeded slowly through the mountains, seldom encountering anyone and skirting any towns along the way. The king waited patiently for guidance from his god, and lo, one day it came. The Moon passed in front of the sun, twisting, distorting and eventually obscuring it, and the day gave way to night when it shouldn't have. The king took this to mean that he had arrived at wherever he was going. When light returned, he investigated the area carefully, and he discovered a hive of bees, something that he and his people had never seen before. 'Can this be what my god sent me in search of?' he wondered. 'It must be,' he decided.

"A man of the hills lived nearby, and he came to the king's attention because he understood bees. The king asked the man to teach him what he knew, and so the man tried to do that. He showed the king the large bee that stayed in the hive and to whom all the other bees were loyal. 'That bee is a king,' the king thought, and for the most part he pitied it, since it never left its palace, never alighted on the petals of a flower, never hovered beneath the blue sky. The man also showed the king how to listen to the bees and how to read them, to find out where they had foraged successfully. 'I did not know bees talked with one another, much less wrote to each other,' the king exclaimed, but the man of the hills did not seem surprised. 'How else will they get their little kingdom to work,' he said to the king, 'if they don't talk to each other? It stands to reason that they must. Look at how many of them there are – more than I can count, maybe as many as there are stars. It'd be chaos if they didn't talk to each other.' Then the man showed the king how to collect honey from the hive. 'You can eat this,' he told the king. 'If you're sick, it sometimes makes you better. You can also put it on wounds, and it helps them heal. And you can make it into a drink like beer.' And he showed the king how to do all of these things.

"The king said, 'I must bring these bees back to my people. Can you help me do that?' The man of the hills answered that it would be easy – 'You just have to bring the big bee that you call king down with you. The rest will follow.' And so the king of the land of Suḫu arranged to do that. He gave gifts to the bee king, and he had a special carrier prepared, made of precious wood ornately carved, and he extended every other dignity he could think of to the bee king. 'I invite you, your Excellency, to my land,' he said to the bee king. And then they headed south, the bee king and the king of the land of Suḫu travelling together, while at a distance the courtiers mocked their ruler, whom they said had gone mad. And when they returned to their land, the king showed his gardeners what the man of the hills had shown him; and he continued to do great honor to the bee king, and ordained that all must do likewise; and his people learned how to harvest honey, and they learned the uses of honey, and they made honey-beer, as the king called it.

"For almost twenty years the people of Suḫu prospered, in part because of the king's gift. And then one year the king of Aššur came; he easily defeated the king of Suḫu, captured him and killed him; he enslaved the land. But the king of Aššur never remarked the bees, and the people of Suḫu were careful never to reveal to him this their secret treasure. And so, he never taxed it and he never took it from them. Even in the worst of times, they prospered from honey, which they called the gift of the sun; and even when they had forgotten that great king who had brought to them the bees, they still prospered, they still benefited from and enjoyed that gift."

"So the king was forgotten?" Niṭil-Kišar asked.

"His name was forgotten," Nabû-na'id responded. "But perhaps there's a more enduring type of remembrance, in the traditions that he learned from the man of the hills and passed on to his own people, which they in turn have passed on generation by generation; and perhaps even in the joy a man feels when his lips taste the sweetness of honey – maybe that's a type of remembrance too."

"Then why did you tell me the story as you did, rather than just give me some honey?" his wife asked with a smile.

"That second story would have pleased you less, I think. But by telling you the story as I did, now other stories are possible because of it. Now you will listen to hear whether a passing bee has anything to tell you, and when your tongue savors honey, you will remember a forgotten king and perhaps, as with the bee, listen for something there too."

"And how did you learn this story yourself? Did a passing bee tell you?"

"But of course!" he answered.

They were seated side-by-side on a bench in a second-floor room. Most of the room was bright from the windows on all sides. Before them was a basket full of tablets. Lying on the bench beside them was a wax board and a stylus.

"Before we begin tradition requires that I make you swear an oath not to reveal the secrets you will learn," Nabû-na'id began.

Niṭil-Kišar laughed. "In short you would have me swear the oath that you are about to break?"

Her husband frowned, his face solemn. "I don't know. Can there be teaching without the revelation of a secret? Perhaps what binds teacher and student is precisely the broken oath, the sense the student has that the oath was broken for him."

"Or her," his wife added.

"Or her," Nabû-na'id acknowledged. "In fact I wonder a little how writing became the work mostly of men. It isn't clear to me that that was always so. The oldest tablets of Šumeru and some of the oldest of Akkadê describe that goddess of writing, Nisaba, for whom we named our daughter; Nabû's ascendancy seems more recent. And then the scribe of the underworld is also a woman."

"Maybe it's because men are barren – and therefore, out of jealousy or spite, they stole writing from women," Niṭil-Kišar suggested.

Her husband took the suggestion more seriously than she had intended. He stroked his beard and hmmed. After a while, he agreed. "That makes some sense to me," he said. "It's probably also why we have laws that allow a man to divorce a barren wife but not the other way around. Because all men are barren. What would become of marriage if women could divorce their barren men?"

His wife laughed a second time. "Maybe that's what a king's harem really is – the secret sanctuary of women who want company with the unbarren."

Nabû-na'id acted like he hadn't heard this. "Why is there a scribe of the Underworld, and why is that scribe a woman?" he wondered.

"Perhaps each realm – the realm of the Underworld, the realm of the World and the realm of the Overworld – had its scribe, had its mother-scribe, had its scribe-mother. That was when writing was alive and the writer gave birth to something alive. But then men took writing over and killed it and called what they had killed creation. Writing once writhed and wriggled and wailed like a newborn, but now it is always still-born."

"Is it?" her husband responded. "We speak of tablets like they're one of us. We speak of them as having a mouth, as having words, as being killed, as being re-born. In court cases, tablets like human beings stand as witnesses. Like us they are made of clay – or like them, we are. Does that suggest that even now, somehow, a living tablet manages to be born?"

"You speak of tablets," his wife answered. "I speak of writing. Maybe you barren men every now and then manage to labor a tablet into life – and you hold its ruddy form before us and say, "See, I can give birth too!" But all about you is the writing of women, writing not at all confined to a tablet or even a slab of diorite. You think you're here to teach me how to write, but perhaps, as so often the case, it's the other way around."

"You'll teach me?" Nabû-na'id asked, arching his eyebrows.

She leaned forward, grabbed the top of his robe and kissed him. "I'll do my best," she said teasingly, "despite the obvious shortcomings."

A woman stood with a lapis lazuli tablet in her hands and, as a stylus, a sheaf of barley. But how can a sheaf of barley inscribe lapis lazuli? Perhaps that was why Nabû, ever silent, sneered.

"The tablet is already inscribed," she explained aloud, "just like the stars in heaven." She brushed the tablet with her barley sheaf. "I use my stylus to protect the stone from dust." Then she sat in the dirt, cross-legged, and in her hands were beads of many different colors, shapes and sizes. She began to string them together. Around her the dirt began to sprout; the grays and browns became green, then golden; mud turned to plant; and as the necklace grew she, seated as she was, disappeared beneath the towering spires of grain which bent and flowed in the wind.

Watching this, the god became angry – or so it seemed his face indicated. Perhaps it was the colors which angered him, in his gray-shaded world of dust and dirt, where even stone is only dust and dirt.

"You think everything is only dust and dirt," she observed without looking at him. "But I am interested in what is inscribed, whether on this lapis lazuli tablet or in the stars of heaven or even here in this field. All of this you think is only dust and dirt; but I say, what is only dust and dirt is also all of this."

The silent, sullen god said nothing. Was not their task to write, not speak?

"What have I been doing if not writing?" she said aloud. The necklace had grown. Now it encompassed the field as if taking its measure, while the beads glittered and twinkled like stars. Or were they stars? "Your writing is death," she said to Nabû. "Mine is life."

"Quelle différence?" the god might have replied, had he spoken.

"Yes, exactly," she affirmed. "Quelle différance!" She started to scramble to her feet, somehow hugging the field and the stars and the necklace all to her body, making of them some kind of garment. "I must go," she stated, almost apologetically. "I am being summoned. I have been asked," she said importantly, "to help teach a woman to write. But, using my stylus here –" she brandished the sheaf of barley – "I shall only teach her to brush away the dirt and the mud to reveal

what is already written, what is written in stone, in gems, in the flesh, even on the very earth in those furrows others call canals."

The silent god looked at her, still angry but serious too.

"You think that I will teach her, then, that writing is just the revelation of emptiness?" The woman laughed. "Oh you men! All you see is emptiness or fullness, emptiness as the fulfillment of fullness or vice versa, death as the fulfillment of life or vice versa."

The god's face expressed a challenge.

"Do I see something different? Perhaps not," answered Nisaba. "What I see," she continued, "is differently." And she gathered to her body the field, which had become many fields glimmering gold under the reflecting Sun, and the stars, which were shining together with the reflecting Moon, and the necklace on which all was strung, each adorning the other, and skipped lightly away. Nabû, squatting now in the dirt, scratched at it with his long fingernails, then stared for a long time at what he had scratched, silent.

Niṭil-Kišar woke. Nabû-na'id was asleep beside her. They were on their roof, where it was cooler to sleep in the summer, so the darkness wasn't total – the stars overhead were like tiny holes in the darkness, pinpricks. She wondered if they were inscribed or even were a kind of inscription – holes wrought in the canopy of heaven much like the wedges impressed into clay. What did they say? Could they be read? "Nabû-na'id," she whispered. He didn't stir. She touched him, and still he didn't stir, so she shook him. She felt his body waken, she could almost feel his eyes open, she could almost hear him blinking. "Can you read the stars?" she asked, almost urgently. He didn't at first respond; she could sense his bewilderment, his uncertainness that he was awake and why and what her question meant. Finally, haltingly, he spoke.

"If you mean, can I predict the future based on the stars, then yes, you know I can. I foretold that eclipse."

"That is not what I mean."

"What other kind of star-reading is there?" he asked, not rhetorically but genuinely. Some vague remembrance of *šiṭir šamē*, heavenly writing, stirred within him but it was too elusive for him to grasp.

"I don't know. Like reading the blades of grass in a field, or the jewels in a necklace."

"What do you mean?"

"I don't know," she repeated. Then, after a moment, she almost mumbled, "Reading that affirms. Reading that lives, rather than dies."

She felt him turn so his body faced hers, though they couldn't see each other. Only the stars were visible; no Moon could be seen, no Moon could see. She felt his hand find and then rest on her hip and she also felt, though this was harder to explain, that he was staring into her eyes, or staring into the darkness that he imagined were her eyes.

"Any reading that doesn't live isn't reading," he said. "But most of us don't read. Most of what happens isn't alive."

"But what if it is?" she whispered back. "What if you are too quick to see all that's dead rather than all that's alive?"

"Is this about me, then?" he asked.

"Maybe. You are teaching me to read and to write. You are my Nabû, you are my Nisaba."

His lips broke into a smile that again she could sense though she could not see it. "I have sometimes wondered," he almost drawled, "whether Nabû isn't a deranged god, whether he's even capable of speech or can only write. I have sometimes wondered whether it wouldn't be better to leave his duties to Nisaba – to let writing find its place alongside the seed-planting in the furrows, alongside the harvest as it stretches toward the Sun. Although we then cut it down, or else watch it wither into death."

"Maybe that is only to say that writing shouldn't last forever, that it should have its own time to flourish and then it should recede and give way to something else."

"Well, that will be the case, no matter what. It will wither, recede, give way. It just doesn't have a time proper to it. Our clay practice-tablets may last longer than our epics or our hymns. Once it's written, we yield it to another time, neither ours nor its own."

She snuggled into him, found his ear, whispered into it: "You always like having the last word. That's the time YOU lay claim to. The last."

Once again he had been called before Nabû-kudurri-uṣur. He was not surprised to be led to the same back room as before and to find that Belet-ṣeri-dannat, again dressed in blue with a blue cap, had been summoned as well. They exchanged curt nods. Belet-ṣeri-dannat whispered to him, "Do you know what the king wants of us?" Nabû-na'id shrugged. "I doubt even he knows." He immediately regretted this confidence, though the comment did not seem to offend or surprise Belet-ṣeri-dannat.

The king entered, alone. He looked at them briefly. Without preamble, he began.

"My wife does not like the statue," he said, his voice in pitiable contrast to his extravagant royal robes and crown.

Neither sage offered any comment.

"What am I to do?"

The two sages looked at the ground.

"She is still unhappy."

All three men stood in silence for some time. Nabû-kudurri-uṣur's patience, seldom in great supply, was soon exhausted. "You are my advisors! Advise me!"

Somewhat to his surprise, Nabû-na'id heard himself answer impulsively. ""What the eagle can't find, send the bee to seek."

"Excuse me?" said the king.

Nabû-na'id cleared his throat. "Introduce her to the kingdom of bees."

"What?" The king's tone indicated incredulity and anger. "Would you dare toy with your king?"

"I am not toying with you, your Excellency," Nabû-na'id responded with an evenness he did not particularly feel. "I was thinking of a king from an earlier time, who became engrossed with beekeeping. As he became immersed in the affairs of the bees, he was less troubled by his own, which seemed to him not very different in type or scale from those of the bees. That perspective helped him rule better and more wisely – and not just rule but live that way too. Perhaps bees could give your wife something similar, something to fascinate her and take her mind off her troubles, while perhaps also making those troubles seem smaller."

"What became of this king?" Nabû-kudurri-uṣur demanded.

"Eventually he went to his fates, like his predecessors before him. But we can hardly judge a life on that circumstance."

"So, after a long and successful reign, he died of old age?"

"Not exactly. He was relatively old when he died, but the king of Assyria hastened him along."

"His kingdom was conquered?"

"All but the bees," Nabû-na'id responded a little glibly.

"And you think this was wisdom and good rule? I expected better of you, Nabû-na'id. I expected that you'd at least take me seriously, and not risk your life by trivializing my problems and insulting my intelligence. I have burned people alive for less."

"I meant no insult, your Excellency, and was trivializing nothing. My advice was offered in good faith."

"That is for me to decide," the king uttered ominously.

Belet-ṣeri-dannat cleared his throat. "I think my esteemed colleague has advised you well," he said simply. Nabû-na'id felt a rush of surprise and gratitude, while the king glared at the second sage. "Your wife is home-sick, is she not?" the sage asked, then proceeded without waiting for an answer. "She comes from the mountains, from a region where bees are commonly cultivated. Bringing bees to her is the same as bringing a small part of her homeland to her."

The king offered no reaction but stared at both men inscrutably.

"You could do more than bring just the bees down," Belet-ṣeri-dannat continued. "You could bring some of the flowering plants down too. Perhaps even the trees."

"I am to build her a garden?" inquired the king.

"If you cannot bring her back to her land, bring her land back to her."

There was a long silence. Then the king said, "I will think about it," and dismissed them.

When the two sages were by themselves, Nabû-na'id touched Belet-ṣeri-dannat lightly on the shoulder. "Thank you," was all he said. Belet-ṣeri-dannat shrugged. "God sent you once to assist me; this time, may He be praised, He sent me to assist you." He paused. "In the tradition of my people, God refused to stay in our midst, certain that otherwise we and our stiff-necked ways would provoke Him to destroy us. 'How are we to find where we are going, if you do not lead us?' my people asked God. He directed them to a land of bees and honey. "You deserve to be abandoned, and I will abandon you,' was God's message to my people; 'but,' he promised with the bees and the honey, 'not forever.'"

"So you do not think my advice was foolish?"

"It was perhaps foolish to give it, but it was not foolish advice. Not that the king heard."

"No. He heard a construction project. Soon it will be that statue who is not lonely for her homeland."

* * * * *

From the [fragmentary] Assyrian Accounts of Herodotus

...The king's madness was prolonged, lasting, it is said, seven years. During this time he relinquished his rule, not so much by design as simply in practice, to his son-in-law Neriklassor, and this was to have serious consequences when the king died. For Neriklassor took advantage of his position to cultivate loyalties among court officials and generals and so, when the king's son ascended to the throne, he inherited a kingdom which, before he died, was no longer even his father's. Soon thereafter, the son was eliminated and Neriklassor made his in name what was already his in deed. But this happened after the king's madness; for shortly before he died the king recovered from his madness, but not in time to recover from its consequences.

The king's madness was of this form. He had dedicated himself to refashioning large parts of Babylon into an image of his wife's homeland, Media. Thus were the renowned gardens constructed and filled with animals as well as flowers, trees and even insects, all imported from Media with the bemused assistance of Astyages, then Media's king as well as Amytis's brother. The Babylonian king became obsessed that the likeness of the gardens to his wife's homeland be perfect. He even had towers built to serve as mountains on which to grow his wife's beloved forests. Yet never was she satisfied, and when she would point out even the smallest of short-comings – famously the color and texture of the dirt, and the variety of the earthworms – the observation would thrust the king into despair. For, he thought, what excuse have I, who am the most powerful man on earth, to fail in this simple endeavor, merely to realize Media in Babylon?

At what point the king lost his mind is a question best left to philosophers, or perhaps, to geometers. For when does a succession of points, each lying as close as you wish to its neighbor, suddenly blaze forth as instead a line? And when do the small increments of eccentricity and obsession at last tally as madness? A time was reached, in any event, when the king, despite his wife's objections, insisted that Media lay perfectly within Babylon; indeed, he insisted it was no likeness but Media itself which Babylon now contained. But his madness did not stop there. He would demand expeditions be assembled that he might hunt in the mountains of Media, and the people of Babylon would be treated to the spectacle of the king and his richly dressed entourage hunting game on terraced buildings which the king believed were mountains. There was in particular a beast, the namaxum, *whether real or fantastical I do not know, which legend placed in the Median forests, and when the king heard of this, he was determined to find it. And so for days at a time he and his nobles would comb Babylon – though the king thought it Media – looking for the* namaxum, *the king wholly oblivious to the absurdity of the endeavor. Over time, this beast took on particular importance to him, and he became adamant that his wife's happiness would at last be complete only when he had brought her this prized game, which he became determined to capture alive.*

Then one morning the king was found by himself in one of the terraced gardens, naked and on all fours. "What has happened, your Excellency?" the courtier who found him demanded. The king answered, "I have found the namaxum, *which I am. Tell my wife!" And as the king calmly chewed a tuft of grass, the look on his face was one of perfect and insurmountable joy.*

* * * * *

"Perhaps the king is the *mušḫuššu*," Nabû-na'id pointed out. "Or the *kusarikku*. Is it madness to acknowledge that a man is more – or less – than meets the eye?"

Belet-ṣeri-dannat sighed. Gubaru, however, was too agitated not to speak. "That's ridiculous! The king is mad! There's no position of reasonableness which can make that go away. He's naked, eating grass! He's not performing the work and duties of a king."

"But what are those duties, that they aren't themselves mad?" Nabû-na'id asked quietly, in marked contrast to his friend's exuberance.

"What is mad about hearing cases and making judgments? Or about setting wages, prices and interest rates? Would you call campaigning to extend the empire and to protect it mad?"

"Perhaps I would! Why is it more mad for a king to think himself a beast, than for him to think that justice lies within his grasp, that he alone can set the value of a man's work or of time itself, or that there is this thing called empire that can be extended and protected? You don't think of these as species of madness only because you are familiar with them – but why should familiarity exclude madness? Or rather, why not confess to ourselves that our worlds are organized in mad ways? Everyone says the king is mad right now – but if he ordered a courtier to kill you, almost certainly the courtier would. Why is that not mad?"

Belet-ṣeri-dannat interposed himself. "I think you are saying only what wise men among my people have long said. A king who thinks the power is his own, and not God's, is mad. A king who worships an idol and calls it a god is mad. And so too for any man, whether king or slave. In this sense, most people are mad."

"But how do you know that the one god whom you believe in isn't himself a manifestation of madness?" Nabû-na'id asked. "You and I have discussed that story of old, similar to the one my mother used to tell me, about the man from Uru (or Ḫarrānu, as my mother said) who abandoned everything to do as his god demanded, all in the promise that he would eventually have a son. But when he had that son, the very same god demanded that he kill him! Wouldn't it be mad to follow that god? Or, worse, doesn't that suggest even gods go mad?"

"You have never understood that tale," Belet-ṣeri-dannat complained. "The account you know is mistaken. The father did not kill the son; he was prepared to, but at the last minute, a ram was substituted for the boy. God was just testing the father."

"There is no ram in the account my mother told me; and the man comes down from the mountain alone. But –" Nabû-na'id clutched Belet-ṣeri-dannat's shoulder emphatically, "*– it makes no difference.* If the boy came down from the mountain, it was as a son who had been sacrificed. It was as a ghost, even if he was alive. And maybe the same is true of the father. Whatever grace may have been extended came and could only come too late. And that is to say nothing of the ram, if there was one."

"What is there to say of the ram?" Gubaru asked.

"Everything. Nothing," Nabû-na'id answered enigmatically. "Everything, because the ram, if there was one, could not speak for himself, because he was a ram and because he was killed. Nothing, because who dares to speak in the place of a sacrifice?"

"I don't understand what your complaint is about the ram," Belet-ṣeri-dannat said.

"Has not this god betrayed the ram, in order to get out of betraying the man and his son? Should that comfort us?"

"It is only a ram," Belet-ṣeri-dannat responded with a shrug.

"All three of us have talked in the past about our duty to strangers. You are alone in the desert. Out of nowhere a stranger appears. You offer the stranger everything you have – food, water and shelter – never asking who and certainly not what he is. At last you have satisfied his hunger, his thirst and his need for rest. He begins to unwind the robes in which he has been bundled, sheltered and hidden. And lo, only now do you realize – he is not a man! He is a woman or a cat or a fly or the *mušḫuššu* or the *kusarikku*. Perhaps he is even a ram. If we take seriously our responsibility to the stranger, including the stranger whose face is hidden – as we must expect in a land of toilsome sun and biting, wind-driven sand – must we not bear in mind that that stranger may not be us?"

"There are limits," Belet-ṣeri-dannat said, "to what we owe."

"But by your own account, contained within those limits is the debt of a father's only son! How can we owe *that* but have no obligation to the stranger who, we have only now discovered, was all along secretly a ram?"

"But rams do not come dressed in clothing, seeking shelter from a sandstorm. Rams do not speak."

"Neither do infants. My son, when he was born, only wailed; and he was naked, not even clothed in the fur that most animals have the decency to cover themselves with."

"But now he is clothed! Now he speaks!"

"And so presumably did the man's son. Why would this god of yours, who alone can preserve us from madness – why would this god demand the boy's sacrifice when he is most clearly marked as human, least animal-like – unless that divide we are so accustomed to, between human beings and animals, is itself the accomplishment of madness? Why else? Why else?" Nabû-na'id's voice was raised and he spoke with passion. Gubaru was taken aback and thought to intervene, if only to calm his friend down. Before he could do anything, however, Belet-ṣeri-dannat responded antagonistically, almost contemptuously.

"You have, I'm sure, never sacrificed an animal?"

"I have sacrificed animals *and* men," Nabû-na'id retorted. He stood up abruptly, a look of anger on his face. Twice he opened his mouth to speak, his face contorted with rage, but not only that – with pain too. But he did not speak. Instead he left – abruptly. At a loss, Gubaru hurried after him.

They sat in unlit silence. The day had long since dimmed and only a wick of light remained. "You remember that story I told you about Izdubar and the black cat?"

"Yes," Gubaru answered.

"Do you think it is believable?"

"That a mighty king would be tamed by a black cat, foregoing adventure and fame and instead sitting forever with that cat purring on his lap? No, I don't think it is believable."

"Yet you do not question that a king might go mad, strip naked and eat grass?"

"I see that before me."

"But why do you not see a cat before you?"

Gubaru looked around helplessly. "There is no cat before me," he said, bewildered.

"A petitioner comes to the king," Nabû-na'id pressed on. "Why is that petitioner more important than a cat that happens to sit on the king's lap? Why should the king stir and disrupt the cat, just so he can deal with whatever the petitioner wants?"

"Because the petitioner is a human being, not a cat."

"But can't a cat, in her own way, petition us? Can she not request food from us and warmth and comfort and play? Why are those less important if coming from a cat than from a human being?"

"Because cats are less important than human beings. Because it is not our duty to give cats food, warmth, comfort and play. Because we human beings owe each other things like justice and honor, of which a cat has no conception."

"So when the man from Uru, if it wasn't Ḫarrānu, dragged the ram to his makeshift mountain altar as a substitute for his son, the ram –"

"– felt fear," Gubaru interrupted. "But it did not feel wronged. It did not consider itself unjustly treated."

"Are you sure?" Nabû-na'id inquired slowly, skeptically.

"Yes."

"How can you possibly be sure?" Nabû-na'id wondered in

disbelief.

"When have you heard a ram, or a cat for that matter, say 'This is unjust!'"

"I'm not sure I don't hear that when they bleat or meow. And I'm even less sure that I don't see that in their eyes and in their faces."

"Why is this so important to you?" Gubaru whispered fiercely.

Nabû-na'id for a long while didn't respond. Then, in a low voice, he spoke. "I live in a haunted world, like my father did and, in a different way, like my mother does. 'Everyone writes,' my mother once said. If that is true, we are surrounded by messages, from those we love, from strangers, from men, from animals, from the living and from the dead. From everyone. To whom do we listen? Whose messages do we examine? How do we decide, not knowing, of course, what each message says? I have no answers, Gubaru. I have no answers. But I answer all the time, with silence and evasion and obtuseness as much as with an articulated 'you' or 'not you' or with a 'yes,' 'no' or 'maybe.' I have no answers and I answer all the time, even by not answering. You might think a king is the one beset without deliverance by petitioners; that it is for a king to crack beneath this endless strain; that perhaps for a king we can understand what the appeal of nakedness and simple tufts of grass might be. But there are no kings, Gubaru, and we are all kings, and there is none who is not surrounded by petitioners, none who does not petition."

"Surely you are imagining these petitions," Gubaru said. "Surely the requests that you think the dead accost you with, or a cat or a ram, surely those aren't really there."

"Or an Iškuza," Nabû-na'id added, as if in agreement. "Or my father. Or the battered slave I saw in the marketplace. Or the battered donkey, its hide grooved with ribs. Surely none of those are really there," he finished in a whisper.

"Right!" Gubaru affirmed.

The two men again sat together in silence. It was only broken when Nabû-na'id reached over and touched Gubaru's knee. "You do not understand what you say, my friend." And then he got up and left.

He sat with his daughter cuddled into his arm. He was absurdly fond of the child, showing a fascination and an attachment which Niṭil-Kišar had not observed in him toward their son. It both pleased and angered her. He had been telling her about the conversation, and she heard herself say, "If you had to choose between our son and a ram, don't tell me you'd choose the ram?" she asked.

"No. I would choose him. But I don't know why."

"Would you know why if it was our daughter instead?"

He looked at her levelly, anger not far from the surface.

"That is beneath you, Niṭ" he said.

"You would choose them because they are your children."

"Our children," he corrected. "But that's a description, not an answer."

"Because you – love them."

"Yes. But why do I love this little one here and not another?" Nabû-na'id wondered innocently, oblivious to the searching look his wife gave him.

After a while, she asked, "Does the fate of the ram really torment you? Or is it like the fly?"

Nabû-na'id didn't answer. Niṭil-Kišar looked at him and answered for him. "You don't know." He nodded. "That's what torments you. You don't know if you really care." She made a face at him. "You and your torments! Such strange torments, too."

"And yet you understand," he said.

"Perhaps I do, perhaps I don't," she answered. "Perhaps if it were for me to save you or a ram, I would save the ram. And if I did, perhaps I would not know if I did it to make a point to you, or because something of the ram or in the ram spoke to me, or because I didn't care about you or the ram." Nabû-na'id smiled. "You think I'm kidding," she observed, eyebrows arched.

"No," he answered, "I do not."

The girl started to cry and her mother came to her, took her from her father without ceremony, and soon began nursing her. Nabû-na'id watched, his face revealing a thoughtful absorption.

"There may be an intimacy in killing," his wife said matter-of-factly, looking down at the child at her breast. "We kill to connect ourselves to the gods; we kill to eat; we kill to make ourselves into something, a something that in some way includes what we've killed. We become what we kill and it becomes us. I think –" she raised her eyes and stared directly into the eyes of her husband, "– that you are too quick to forget the ways in which death is not only a taking away but also a giving, a gift. I suggested as much when we first –" she cleared her throat "– courted. I suggested to you that a fly delimbed and helpless on the floor might stare for the first time into the heavens and find there his first and only revelation."

Nabû-na'id returned her gaze with admiration, improbably ornamented with a sense of insurmountable distance which both intensified and made bittersweet their fellowship. "When, as I understand it out of pity, I flip the struggling fly onto the stubs that remain of his legs, since this seems to be what he is struggling towards, then I have denied him revelation."

"It's possible," she said. "It's also possible that you have acted for yourself, not the fly; that you have righted the fly in order to leave him and to forget him. Righting the fly may be your favored form of sacrifice."

"The fly twirling on its back, the ram caught in the thorn

bush, the sacrificial lamb, the son on the mountain – each of these poses to us a question that is also a demand, insistent, absolutely unavoidable. Everything one does is an answer. One is always answering these demands, with every step, every breath."

"Yes," she said. "Whether one notices or not. Perhaps we are often the last to hear the answers we give."

"I have moments when I would throw myself to the ground, bathe myself in dust and ash like my mother, give bodily expression to what the ghost within me feels – inexhaustible mourning, writhing, excruciating pain."

"Yes," she said.

"And an overwhelming desire for pardon – which is so close to a desire to be permitted to not know and a desire to forget. So close, so terribly close…"

"Yes," she said.

With the girl still at her breast, she continued to meet her husband's gaze evenly, calmly, almost unblinkingly – forgiving and condemning him all at once.

"I read this," she said to him. "Perhaps it was a prayer or a song long ago." She recited:

Say I may wait for you.
I wait. I waited. I can wait more.
Say I may wait for you – tell me this at least.
I look to the Sun. The Day is far declined.
The Sun engraves my shadow in light.
Soon the Moon will engrave my shadow in darkness.
Still, say I may wait for you – tell me this at last,
So I who wait and waited can wait more.

"What do you think?" she asked.

"Who is being waited for?"

"It says – you."

"But who is this you?"

"It doesn't say."

"It's a you who doesn't ever appear, except in a hoped for, seemingly disembodied command – a command, moreover, to wait."

"Yes."

"Did you write this, Niṭil-Kišar?"

"I read it."

"But did you write it? Did you make it up?

She looked frankly into his eyes. "You have told me that your mother once said that everyone writes. And she herself has told me that too. So, if everyone writes, surely I have written something, whether or not it is this."

"I have a corollary to your mother's claim," she continued.

"Yes?"

"Everyone waits."

Across the mountains of Manda roamed the beast. "What are you?" a grasshopper wondered nervously. "I don't know." "Do you eat grasshoppers?" "Only accidentally, when they are camouflaged amid tufts of grass." The beast smiled – its lips forming an enormous mouth which seemed always to have two expressions at once, the second an ironic version of the first. "Why do you roam the mountains?" the grasshopper continued to inquire. "What else is there to do?" responded the beast, its prehensile lips seemingly articulating both sounds and the gaps between sounds. "Why are you naked?" asked the grasshopper. "Am I? How can you tell?" To this the grasshopper had no response. Eventually he began to hop away. The beast stretched its gigantic neck toward the grasshopper, and lo! The beast was chewing a tuft of grass.

Westward roamed the beast, descending the mountains of Manda. "What are you?" a bee wondered nervously. "I don't know." "Do you eat bees?" "Only accidentally, when I confuse them with the bloom of flowers." The beast smiled – its lips forming an enormous mouth which seemed always to have two expressions at once, the second an ironic version of the first. "Why do you roam westward, descending the mountains?" the bee continued to inquire. "What else is there to do?" responded the beast, its prehensile lips seemingly articulating both sounds and the gaps between sounds. "Could you not roam eastward and ascend the mountains?" asked the bee. "Am I not doing that already, just in reverse?" To this the bee had no response. Eventually, he flew a short distance away, alighting on a petal. But then the beast stretched its gigantic neck toward the bee, and lo! The beast was chewing a bloom of flowers.

Southward roamed the beast, along the riverbank. "What are you?" a water-strider called out nervously from the shallows. "I don't know." "Do you eat water-striders?" "Only accidentally, when I take a deep draught of water." The beast smiled – its lips forming an enormous mouth which seemed always to have two expressions at once, the second an ironic version of the first. "Why do you roam southward, along the riverbank?" the water-strider continued to inquire. "What else is there to do?" responded the beast, its prehensile lips seemingly articulating both sounds and the gaps between sounds. "Do you only drink water, or do you clean and purify yourself in it?" asked the water-strider. "What is cleaner and more purifying about water than dust?" To this the water-strider had no response. Eventually, he skipped a short distance away, pausing atop a small pool. But then the beast stretched its gigantic neck toward the water-strider, and lo! The beast was drinking a deep draught of water.

Into Bābilim roamed the beast. "What are you?" he demanded of a fly. "I am the king of Bābilim," answered the fly. "Do you hunt beasts?" the beast inquired. "Only accidentally, while seeking better game." The beast smiled – its lips forming an enormous mouth which seemed always to have two expressions at once, the second an ironic version of the first. "Why do you roam aimlessly in your city?" "What else is there to do," responded the king, "but to roam these mountains, ford these rivers, and make the world my own?" "But does not the world lose distinctness in becoming your own?" "If only it were so simple!" cried the fly. He buzzed a short distance away. Then the beast stretched its gigantic neck toward the fly, and lo! Was it a kiss that the fly and the beast exchanged?

Chapter 4. Fathers and Sons

Speak to Nabû-kudurri-uṣur, king of Šumeru and Akkadê, king of the universe, thus speaks Nergal-šar-uṣur.

May Šamaš and Marduk keep you alive forever for my sake.

I write concerning your health. Send me news that you prosper.

I have investigated the matter of concern to you. Your son is well. Soon I will come to Bābilim and make report to you. Shall I bring your son with me?

Send me your wishes and news of your well-being, over which too often I have trembled, that I may instead rejoice.

Be well forever for my sake.

Speak to Nergal-šar-uṣur, thus speaks the king.

Bring me my son!

Belet-ṣeri-dannat and Nabû-na'id huddled together in a corner of an otherwise deserted palace room. "It were better had the king never awakened from his madness," observed Belet-ṣeri-dannat. "He will die seeing with blighted eyes what under his enchantment had seemed beautiful."

"He does not understand his position," Nabû-na'id stated. "In that, he is still, as you put it, enchanted."

"Nergal-šar-uṣur wastes no opportunity to remind him of his recent, prolonged frailty. Perhaps that's his way of being merciful. It is a wonder that he has not simply killed the king."

"What threat is the king, a weakened old man only recently recovered from madness? Nergal-šar-uṣur can perhaps afford patience."

"Awil-Marduk cannot."

"No. Awil-Marduk cannot."

Nabû-kudurri-uṣur stood before him. They were alone in a modest, private chamber of the king, a place Nabû-na'id had never been before.

"Your Excellency," Nabû-na'id said with a deep bow. "You have requested my presence?"

The old king looked at him warily. His years of madness had reduced him to a shadow of his former strength. His beard, which during his madness had become gnarled and matted with grime and shit, had had to be shaved away, leaving behind a naked face embarrassing in a grown man and much more in a king. He had become excessively thin, and his body was covered in bruises. His hands trembled. His hair was dirty and gray, and he had lost most of his teeth.

"I remember you," he said uncertainly.

Nabû-na'id met the king's gaze matter-of-factly but said nothing.

"You were never a courtier. Or a prophet." The king made a smile so grotesque that at first Nabû-na'id could not recognize what he was attempting.

"I shock you," the king observed.

"You are much changed from the man who gave me his daughter – the greatest gift of my life," Nabû-na'id responded.

"Yes, I am much changed."

The two men stood in silence before one another – a silence surprising for being calm, even agreeable.

"I know my kingdom is no longer mine."

Nabû-na'id said nothing.

"Is it too late for it to be my heir's – my son by Ḫumati?" The king's question, immediately followed by his feeble clarification, was accompanied by a look so plaintive and fragile that for a moment Nabû-na'id was overwhelmed by pity – a pity which the question's naivete could only compound.

"Would you really wish that upon him, your Excellency?" Nabû-na'id answered evasively.

"What becomes of him if I don't?"

Nabû-na'id was at a loss for a response.

For the first time in their long history together, the king touched him, placing his hand, brittle and weak, on his son-in-law's shoulder. "Please answer me. Please tell me what you think."

Nabû-na'id looked him directly in the eyes. "You are right to fear for your heir. So long as you live and allow Nergal-šar-uṣur to pretend he is your proxy, you and he are safe. But when you die, your son and Ḫumati's will no longer be safe."

"What can I do?" It was not a king who asked, but a pathetic old man.

"I have thought of only one possibility. You will not like it. Your son will like it less."

"What is it?"

"Adopt Nergal-šar-uṣur as your oldest son. Make him your heir. Formalize in law what already exists in deed."

"Nergal-šar-uṣur is already my heir?"

"Yes, your Excellency. Whether you want it or not, he is your heir. And your son is not."

"My son will revile me. He will curse my tomb."

"Perhaps. But this may be a way for him to live."

A tear trickled down the old man's face. "I, a king once mighty, will be forgotten."

"Not so long as my ash- and dust-covered mother lives," Nabû-na'id responded. "Not so long as your daughter lives. Not so long as I live." He took the king's hand in his own. "You gave me the greatest gift of my life," he repeated. "I will not forget."

“Let me congratulate you, if congratulations are in order,” Nabû-na’id said.

“Yes, thank you,” replied Nergal-šar-uṣur. “The king has honored me greatly.” He paused and leaned closer to Nabû-na’id. “Of course, I am sorry for the – turmoil – that this has caused the king and his family. I would not have – wanted that. Still, it is – wise – don’t you think?”

“I hope there is wisdom in it,” Nabû-na’id answered.

“Yes, indeed. I would never speak ill of the boy, but Awil-Marduk has shown – what shall we say? – disturbing tendencies. You must have remarked them. A fancy perhaps all too – familial. And a wantonness, a lack of – restraint. Of judgment. The boy may not have the temperament. I shall take my responsibilities as an older brother seriously, of course. Help him. Guide him. But the king has acted – wisely – surely you agree? – to remove the – temptations – of the throne from one so – let us say – young.”

Nabû-na’id fought back the anger that the halting, winking way this man talked provoked in him. “The throne would be no gift for Awil-Marduk, though he is hardly a boy” he pointed out. “I’m not sure the throne is ever really a gift at all. Should you someday find yourself upon it, bear that in mind. May you treat it well, of course, but may it also treat you well.”

“If that day comes, may it be long in the future, my friend,” Nergal-šar-uṣur proclaimed, slapping him on the back. “May we long have the happiness to serve the wisdom of our current king!”

“I poured a libation to my father,” Nabû-na’id announced to his wife. “I summoned his image in my mind. I held his gaze. I spoke to him. I heard the tone and timbre of his voice, but not words. And then I poured beer into a hole I dug in the dirt and invited him to drink; in my mind, the hole was a cup, and I offered it to him."

"I have seen you do this every morning since our marriage," Niṭil-Kišar observed. "Why only now are you explaining it to me?"

"I may have had a vision," Nabû-na'id stated flatly.

"A vision? You, my non-believing astrologer-poet, have had a vision? How remarkable."

"It is a vision versions of which I have had before. I am at a sacrifice. First I observe it, eventually I take part in it."

"That is unlike you."

"Yes."

"And it bothered you?"

"I can never see what it is that I am sacrificing, but I think I know."

"What," she asked, then hesitated, then resumed, "is it?"

"Men."

"Oh." They were both silent.

"In my vision, the omen I read in the extispicy is the omen of Gilgameš," Nabû-na'id said at last.

"Meaning?"

He handed her a small tablet and pointed to the relevant description.

"The omen of Gilgameš, who ruled the land," she read aloud. "There will be a ŠU king of the land." She paused. "What is a ŠU king?"

"I don't know."

"Perhaps you should find out."

"I think Awil-Marduk is trying to maneuver himself into a position to claim the throne when your father dies," Nabû-na'id announced abruptly.

"I think so too."

"I don't know how to stop him."

"It is not for you to stop him."

"I have – basically – promised your father that I will endeavor to protect his son. And the only way I see to do that is to keep him from ambition's path. But he is setting out on that path anyway – and it leads only one place."

Niṭil-Kišar said nothing.

"Nergal-šar-uṣur will not hesitate to kill him."

She turned to him, and he swore he saw the blaze beneath her eyes, the fire inside of her. "The fate of my father's son is not your concern. Have you not noticed you have a son of your own? Concern yourself with him. Concern yourself with Bel-šar-uṣur."

The old king had summoned him again. He had gone to the chambers and waited. After a time, the king entered, but he said nothing. So the two men stood in silence. Eventually the king sat down – not on one of his ornate chairs but on the floor. He scratched at the floor with his fingers and eventually with a piece of mosaic, until he had gouged a hole deep enough to dip his hand into. All this he did in silence. Then with his now-meager, always trembling hand, he grabbed a clawful of dirt, lifted it above his head and sprinkled it over his hair. This he did over and over again, saying nothing. The scene was pathetic – not only because a king was bathing himself in dirt, but because all the strength of the king amounted each time only to a thimbleful of dirt. Thimble by thimble, with his tremoring claws, he begrimed himself, never breaking the silence.

Nabû-na'id, who had continued to stand and to watch, stirred himself. He walked to the king and wordlessly sat down beside him. The king appeared not to notice. Still his ruined hands wept dirt where once his crown had stood.

Nabû-na'id waited. Then, to his own surprise, he put his hand over the king's as it scooped once more its pathetic bounty of dirt. “Father,” he said gently. The king did not look at him or respond. “Father,” he repeated, “it falls to no man to bury himself. It is a gift for which we must rely on others.” Gently he displaced the king’s hand from the hole and replaced it with his own. This time it was he who gathered the dirt. When he had filled his cupped hand, he stood, straightened and over the sitting king poured the dirt. Tears silently streamed down the old man’s face.

“I must now perform the *Namburbi*, father.” Again in his cupped hand he gathered water from one of the fountains along the walls of the room. He brought the water to the hole in the ground.

“Šamaš,” he intoned, “behold. Great Annunaki, behold. Dead ancestors, I have not forgotten you. May none of you want for water.” He poured the water into the hole. “May none of you hunger.” With his knife he cut himself, then allowed drops of his own rich blood to fall and mix in the pooled water. “May the only god who is human not oversee parched ghosts; may he not oversee famished ghosts; may he not oversee sonless ghosts.” He then returned to the fountain, washed his wound and bound it, and then again collected water in his cupped hands. He brought the water to the king and poured it on his head. “May there yet be tomorrows,” he prayed aloud, “for us all.”

Niṭil-Kišar stood with her back to him as he told her. When he finished, she offered no response. He waited, but she said nothing and didn’t turn. Finally he approached her, only to put his arms around her. He realized she was crying.

“He is hated by both Awil-Marduk and Ḫumati,” she said in a low voice. “They do not understand or believe him.”

“I know.” He continued to hold her. She continued to cry.

“He is becoming only a father to me, and not a king. But his being king and not king – reveals to me the man beneath it all –

gives me glances of the man, or whatever he is, beneath it all. Neither king nor father. A man with a secret name that even he doesn't know."

Nabû-na'id could say nothing.

She turned and faced him, no longer crying but with the tracks of tears still clearly staining her face. "Must we only ever wait?" she asked entreatingly.

Nabû-na'id had repeatedly seen Awil-Marduk and Belet-ṣeri-dannat confer, but whenever he approached they stopped and separated. He did and did not know what this meant; and what he knew obliged him, he thought, to know what he didn't. If only on behalf of the king. After all, the king had acted on his advice, and in doing so, had compounded his own and his family's suffering. He had perhaps even sacrificed what was most precious to him – whether that was his son or his wife, Nabû-na'id did not know. He also did not know toward what end this suffering was tending or even if there was an end to it. In piercing moments of anxiety that did not and could not last, he feared that the events he had set into motion would instead succeed only in bringing about the very result – even if not end – that he and through him, the king, had sought to avoid.

Belet-ṣeri-dannat was in the marketplace. Nabû-na'id hailed him: "I have not seen much of you lately, my old friend."

"It has been a while," Belet-ṣeri-dannat observed non-committally.

Nabû-na'id looked at him frankly. "You are avoiding me."

"Yes," Belet-ṣeri-dannat answered with equal frankness.

"Why?"

"That I cannot say."

"Yet you trust me enough to tell me you do not trust me."

"Your own perspicacious analysis suggests that this is not about whether I trust you. In fact I do."

"But you cannot tell me what this is about?"

"No. But consider, Nabû-na'id, that what you do not know it may be good for you not to know."

"It may be so. But consider, Belet-ṣeri-dannat, that what you do not know it may be good for you to know – it may even change everything."

"That may be so too," the man with the owl-beak nose acknowledged.

"We are at an impasse," he added after a moment.

"How do we proceed from here?" Nabû-na'id asked.

"You know as well as I do, my friend," Belet-ṣeri-dannat replied, "that at impasses one does not proceed. One either turns back – or waits."

The two men looked at each other, not unkindly. Nabû-na'id leaned forward, his hand on the other man's shoulder, and stated softly, "Know that I shall wait."

Bel-šar-uṣur was a teen-ager. Already he was taller than his father, with better posture and the promise that, before long, he would fill out more than his father had. Beneath thick brows his eyes were, like Nabû-na'id's, hazel, and he had a single mole on the arch of his left cheek, reminiscent, like his chin, of his mother. Right now, Nabû-na'id was trying to interest him in a tale of Anzû which, Nabû-na'id claimed, his mother had once told him. He had become more sensitive to the ways in which he neglected the boy, picking up, if still somewhat obtusely, on some of his wife's comments. The boy had shown no interest in writing or reading – unlike his precocious younger sister – but perhaps he would at least like and think about stories. Nabû-na'id tried to convince himself this was as good a place to start as anywhere; he tried to convince himself as well that the boy reminded him of a young Gubaru. In his heart, though, he did not believe it. In his heart he condemned himself. "If some god demanded that I sacrifice this boy on a mountain top, would I have to imagine him as a ram before I could stir my indignation?" he wondered, with a coldness and a possible injustice toward his own heart which he may or may not have deserved.

Gubaru, agitated, burst upon them. He ignored the boy and with both hands on Nabû-na'id's shoulders shook him. "What is this I have heard?" he nearly shouted. "They say you are Nergal-šar-uṣur's man, manipulating the king to his heir's ends! How can this be?"

Shocked, Nabû-na'id squirmed free of Gubaru's arms and signaled his son to leave. When the boy was out of earshot, he remonstrated angrily with his friend. "How could you possibly believe that of me?"

"Everyone believes it of you! Tell me it is wrong. Please. I will believe you if you tell me."

"You should believe me even if I don't."

"Will you tell me anyway?"

"Gubaru," Nabû-na'id said, heart-broken and walking away, "I already have."

The moon was full. He had retreated beneath its glare, wandering the dark alleys of Bābilim. He did not know where he was taking himself until he arrived there: the statue of Ḫumati, foreboding more than glamorous under the veil of night and in the soft moonlight. Her painted eyes, to him the statue's most interesting aspect, were now sunken pits, notable only as patches of greater darkness on the darkness that would be a face.

He sat down cross-legged in the dirt before it. He let his mind go, to continue travelling what back alleys it would, to arrive before what idol it would. What he should think about: his advice to the king, his unwanted involvement in palace machinations, his potential manipulation by Nergal-šar-uṣur or by someone of his party or – perhaps worse – by someone unknown and with his own agenda. In short, his entailment. His entanglement. As in a web. He was caught in a spider's web, into which he had flown unseeing. He was a fly.

He thought therefore about flies.

What was a web to a fly? Some ravel in space, some unseaming, in which a fly could be caught and lost forever. But it was a surprise, always a surprise. No fly leaves a web to tell other flies about it. Each time its own discovery. No rumors, no myths. One fly does not say to another – 'Have you heard about those ripples in space where motion ceases, where you lie and wait or twist and turn, but always in vain?' The other fly does not say – 'Space? What is that?' No, always a surprise. The rare fly that breaks free of the web falls to the ground, its limbs and wings knotted together by invisible threads that could just as well be a part of the fly as have come from the web. For does a fly distinguish himself from a web? 'I cannot move from here,' says the fly, 'but is that limitation my own or something imposed on me? Is it intrinsic or extrinsic?' Are these questions for a fly?

Why do webs catch flies? What is it about a web that accounts for its success in capturing flies? Why is it mostly emptiness? What is it that spiders understand about flies that accounts for the form they give to webs? He mused about this for a few minutes, wondering if it didn't suggest that there's something about a fly that a spider knows better than a fly. Perhaps, he thought, a web is nothing less than a spider's portrait of a fly. 'Let me show you what you are,' the spider murmurs, adding *sub voce* 'to me.' One catches one's prey with a mirror, but always a distorting mirror. There are no others.

And if it were so? Does that make a web an idol too, a representation of the fly, a spider's representation? And the fly might be a god… (The thought was invasive, and he shooed it away. But then he beckoned it back.) He asked again: and if it were so? If gods can appear as fish, for example, why not as flies?

But if as flies, is a fly no less a representation of a god than a web is of a fly? Or is a web by transitivity also the representation of a god? Does a spider's cunning extend so far as to understand even gods, at least to trap them? Or is there nothing to understand here, an arbitrariness which announces that a web, even if it is a portrait of you, need nonetheless be faithful to nothing about you, nothing at all, except perhaps that you are nothing...

Nabû-na'id felt his thoughts stick, one by one; felt himself entangled, confused, entrapped. Enwebbed. But it was strange, this immobility imposed on him by a falling without cease. For (and he looked at the statue) if we find our foundation in understanding this as an image of Ḫumati (and not, for example, as an image of a king's power or of a king's anxiety or of a king's desire), what forbids us from asking in turn what Ḫumati herself is an image of?

By an almost invisible thread he connected these musings and questions to the omen from the sacrifice in his dream: "The omen of Gilgameš, who ruled the land: there will be a ŠU king of the land." What is a ŠU king? The sign was not the one usually used to indicate the syllabic value šu, assuming that was even the value intended here. It could perhaps be some strange logogram. Belet-ṣeri-dannat had opined that it was a rare symbol used discreetly to mean "despotic," its rarity being allied to its discretion. Another scribe had suggested it meant "universal." The portent, then of a despotic king or of a universal king? Were those different types of kings or the same king? What in fact was a universal king?

Niṭil-Kišar had made a third suggestion. "Why not let it have its face value?" she had asked. Then it would mean simply "that king": "There will be that king of the land." There will be a king, the omen might be saying, of such familiarity that he need not be named. We know who we are talking about – "that king," we say, with a meaningful lifting of the eyebrows. Or was it rather singularity than familiarity that the "that" announced – a king so singular that he can only be pointed out, no name being sufficient to name him? "That one," an onlooker might dare to whisper, or simply, finger extended, "That." But perhaps that becomes "King That," then. Maybe the unusual sign for šu was a way of indicating an unusual use of the corresponding word, normally a pronoun or an adjective, here a noun, maybe even a proper noun. There will be a king, the omen might be saying, of such singularity that he will be only improperly named. And yet there was no determinative signaling the use of šu as a name here. That was hardly decisive, however.

What if the omen invited all of these readings – invited even the suspicion that all of these readings were secretly the same reading? The despotic king is the universal king is the most familiar king is the most singular king. Is it possible to think all of those at the same time, of the same thing?

And then a small, ironic voice whispered in the back of his head: Is it possible to think this while seated cross-legged before the statue of Ḫumati, while wondering also what Ḫumati is a statue of?

The thought startled Nabû-na'id, strangely and confusedly alarming him. He rose as from a dream, unsettled. In the play of reflected and reflecting moonlight, in the perpetual dance of shadows, he found no comfort. Time ended. Space ended.

Have I left the web, he wondered, or do the shadows only create the illusion of my motion, as they wax and wane?

Where is the lair of a spider, he wondered, if not shadow, which is neither simply darkness nor simply light?

Is not the fly's last vision his own eightfold reflection in the eyes of the spider?

A hand, a claw, gripped him strongly from behind. "I have found you!" The voice was Gubaru's. "I spent the night looking for you. Praise Marduk I have found you!"

Nabû-na'id stirred. He was still before the statue. Morning was breaking. He did not know how it had arrived. He did not know if he had been dreaming or in a trance. Much less did he know whether he had been trapped and eaten, or yet lived. If time and space ended, how did they begin?

He was in the familiar back room. He was, familiarly, uncertain why he was there. The wait was unusually long. They had summoned him when he was beside his daughter's bed, singing her into sleep. Their request brooked neither refusal nor delay. He handed off the singing duties to Niṭil-Kišar, made a face at her, and hurriedly followed the messenger. But what was the hurry for? To wait here indefinitely? Or had they forgotten about him?

No, they had not.

A servant he didn't recognize finally led him into another room – in fact, to his surprise, the throne room. But the king sat not on the throne but to the side, in the dirt. He did not look up when Nabû-na'id entered. Had he, it wouldn't have mattered; Nabû-na'id's eyes were quickly directed instead at the youthful man, perhaps in his mid-to-late twenties, dressed in an ornate golden robe and standing in the center of the room before the throne. Awil-Marduk.

"Your Excellency," Nabû-na'id said, turning and directing his words toward the seated king.

"So you are the prophet," observed Awil-Marduk.

"Your Excellency," Nabû-na'id repeated, still addressing himself to the prostrate king. There was no response. "Father," he said gently.

"That man whom you've treated like a toy and a tool is by no means your father!" Awil-Marduk angrily declared.

Nabû-na'id turned and faced him. "Are you sure," he asked coolly, articulating each word carefully, "you can tell when a man is treated as a toy or a tool instead of as a father?"

Awil-Marduk struck him. "I know you are Nergal-šar-uṣur's tool," he stated.

"I am not," Nabû-na'id replied calmly, as blood trickled through his beard from his mouth to his chin.

"I know it was you who tricked my father into replacing me with that bastard."

"I didn't trick your father into that. I convinced him of it. For, among other reasons, your sake."

Awil-Marduk struck him again. "Notice that I am not a decrepit old man, not a man easily fooled," he shouted.

"Aren't you?" Nabû-na'id retorted and was hit across the face a third time.

"You will pay for what you have done to me," Awil-Marduk hissed, "and for what you have done to my father."

"I have done my best for the king who is your father – and who has made himself mine. And I have even done my best for you."

"Do you think I am a child, or a madman, that you can simply lie betrayal into friendship and day into night?"

Nabû-na'id was struck dumb by the turn of phrase – by the circumstances of his own life when day and night had converged, and by his own unwillingness to deny that friendship and betrayal lie close, beside or even within one another.

"I can see your confession writ across your face," Awil-Marduk announced triumphantly.

"How unfortunate, then, that you cannot read," answered Nabû-na'id.

Awil-Marduk hit him a fourth time. "You will die," he said.

"No," came a voice from the floor, "he will not. So long as I am king, he will not."

He looked up at an owl-beaked nose.

"How long have I been here?" he asked Belet-ṣeri-dannat.

"Seven days."

"How is Niṭil-Kišar?"

Belet-ṣeri-dannat smiled. "I'm sure she's concerned, but what she expresses is something quite a bit more – fiery. I have been to see her. In the company of your mother, of course. And Gubaru."

"Thank you, my friend."

"You may not wish to thank me. Or call me 'friend.' That you are here is in no small part due to me."

"I rather thought so," Nabû-na'id remarked. "And yet I am thankful to a man who shows my wife kindness. And my mother."

"You do not know that I was kind."

Nabû-na'id looked long and intently into the face of the other man. "I think I do."

"Are you not going to ask me what part I played in your current predicament?"

"No."

"Do you think you know already?"

"More or less. As much as I want to know."

Belet-ṣeri-dannat laughed. "You must have great faith in that god of yours, a faith like mine!"

"Faith? I doubt it. You won't understand this, I don't think, but I feel like I am trapped in a web and falling endlessly, the two together. That is my crisis. I know no solution, and my faith, if I have any, is inadequate. And what is inadequate faith but not-faith? This might also surprise you, Belet-ṣeri-dannat – my crisis began, not with my arrest, but some nights before, in front of that statue that has troubled us both all these many years."

Belet-ṣeri-dannat sat down cross-legged in the grime of the cell, alongside Nabû-na'id. "I have only a short time with you; do you wish to spend it speaking of statues?"

"Statues and idols. What else is there to speak of? I'm here because Awil-Marduk takes me for Nergal-šar-uṣur's idol or even puppet. I'm not; but that doesn't mean I'm not an idol or puppet, only that I'm not my brother-in-law's. Either of them."

Belet-ṣeri-dannat thought in silence for a while. "You're saying you're not Nergal-šar-uṣur's tool. Good. I did not believe you were. Keep saying that. But the rest – is wisely kept to yourself."

"That I'm a tool, but of what I don't know? Of what! I don't even know there is a what, Belet-ṣeri-dannat. That is my falling; that is my entanglement."

"You are the tool of God, as am I."

"Then you are his image; then you are his idol. Have you not broken his commandment?"

"We are prohibited from making a graven image of Him. I am not gravened. And I did not make myself."

"Are you sure you're not gravened? And are you sure that he made you in his image, rather than that you or your fathers made him in yours?"

"Be careful," Belet-ṣeri-dannat hissed. "My friendship to you is not without limit. My duty is first to my God – in fact, to God. If you do not believe me, then consider that it is in His service that I have acted as I have, even knowing the risk that I have put you in. You are here in part because of my duty to God. So be careful. I will warn you only this once. Do not push your questions – questions which I hear as sacrilege – too far. I will disown you before I disown God."

"You have bound me," Nabû-na'id observed, not without

interest. "This cell is my mountain top."

"If I have bound you, it is in the hope I may unbind you."

"Does faith permit such hope, my friend?"

Belet-ṣeri-dannat did not respond or look at him. But he also did not leave. And so they sat in silence beside one another, if not precisely together. When the jailer came, it was to witness so strange a scene – two men, one a prisoner, one his visitor, seated side by side in dirt, in silence. Belet-ṣeri-dannat rose when the man arrived, brushed dirt from his blue robe and straightened it, exchanged a not unfriendly glance with Nabû-na'id, and left.

It was sometime later when Nabû-na'id noticed the tablet he had left behind.

To Nabû-na'id, thus Niṭil-Kišar.

May Šamaš and Marduk and your beloved Sîn preserve you, that you may see again your children, and I you, if only to curse you to your face for your foolishness.

Your children, your mother and I – we are well. Gubaru and the messenger are providing for us.

Should you die, you will thirst, you will hunger! Never will I quench the one or sate the other. Do not forget.

I intend to speak to my father.

On the back side of the tablet:

Do not die. I am unsure if even I can remember to forget you for the rest of my days. Perhaps I do not want to know.

He scrounged dirt from the floor and used most of the water allowed him to wet it. Then he molded the mud into a tablet and scratched out a rudimentary message:

Nabû-na'id, who cannot speak, writes; may you read, Niṭil-Kišar.

I do not know if Sîn is more dear to me or Nabû. I have even begun to wonder if they aren't in secret the same god. The specularity of the Moon is the condition of this and of all messages.

No one, not even a god, is more dear to me than you. May they forgive me for admitting it. May you.

Do not speak with your father. It will serve no purpose but will risk both him and you. Be patient. So long as I do not stir, the spider will feel no urge to visit.

It was several days before Belet-ṣeri-dannat visited again. The news he brought was unwelcome. The king was ill. Awil-Marduk had been re-instated as principal heir, an accomplishment all the easier because Nergal-šar-uṣur was campaigning far to the west. But word had already been sent to him; tablets daily raced the sun to greet him; and though losing race after race, day after day, a time would come when they would earn their rest before the sun did and would loll in the thrill of victory. One day, not far distant. After that, the consequences were not entirely unpredictable.

Nabû-na'id gave Belet-ṣeri-dannat the tablet he had made. "Be careful. It is not baked. You may have some difficulty hiding it."

"Hiding it? I shall not hide it. These men here do not fear mud."

"May some of them have the fortune to survive the error of their ways."

When Belet-ṣeri-dannat had left, another tablet was left behind in his stead.

To Nabû-na'id, thus Niṭil-Kišar.

My father who is also a king longs to be forgotten. He begs me to forget him. He begs me to beg you to forget him. Everyone else, he observes, already has.

Yet, he tells me that he has not forgotten you.

Perhaps we shall see, you and I and our children, the heavens of

Ṣurru again, or even the court of Muṣur; maybe Ḫarrānu beckons you back, or Sardis. I cannot read the stars. These tablets I can read without you, but not the stars.

Nabû-na'id, who cannot speak, writes; may you read, Niṭil-Kišar.

At first I found it strange to write you a tablet when we live in the same city and perhaps even now lie only a brisk walk apart.

But I think you and I have always written to each other, a fly here, a burning ember there. We write in death or in the dying, but quickly forget that as we become enamored with the message borne by and of so woeful a messenger. In the background, then, the fly died, forgotten, the room empty and dark and cold. Beside the fly an ember burned out. But for us, those husks hid and conveyed life; they were ways we infected each other with life and shuttled life between us.

In the end, you only read without me – even the stars. If I know that, I read it with you. When nothing became a tender gift.

A tablet was beside him when he awoke in the morning.

Read Nabû-na'id, Niṭil-Kišar writes.

You make the Moon into a mirror, forgetting that the dirt and spit you called a tablet is a mirror too. But perhaps that is your point.

According to our messenger, a single god, the only god, shaped man out of mud and breathed life into him. He called him "Mud." "Mud" was an image and a likeness of that god. But in what sense? In being dirt and water and air? In drying, ossifying, and eventually breaking what hitherto would bend? In ultimately eroding into nondescript particles of dirt, to mix in the sand or in the nearest stream bed or to be dispersed by a gust of summer wind?

What kind of mirror is your moon or your tablet or this god? What kind of mirror are we?

Nabû-na'id awoke with a start.

In the pitch blackness, a voice that he recognized told him to be quiet. "The king has died," the voice said in a whisper. "You must flee."

A hand touched him – from a different direction than the voice had come from. Two people, then. He thought he recognized the touch. He allowed himself to be guided by the hand that touched him. The two of them traced the wall until they came to the door, where the voice was. Assembled in this way, they left in a single file, each clinging to the robe of the person in front of him. They proceeded very slowly.

Nabû-na'id wondered why there were no guards, but he said nothing. He could feel, and dared not disrupt, the intensity and concentration of the other two.

Their escape was painstaking and interminable. It was with shock and foreboding that suddenly Nabû-na'id saw stars, and the moon, and, not very distant, the statue of Ḫumati, imposing all the more for being a shadow cast among shadows.

In the open, Gubaru hugged him impulsively. He hugged him back. "There is no time for that. We must get him out of the city." The voice was Belet-ṣeri-dannat's.

"My family?" Nabû-na'id asked.

"Safe. You will see them soon enough. Now be quiet and hurry."

And so they hurried in silence, passing the inner and outer walls not through the grand gates but in the channel of the river, aboard the folding circular boats that the peasants had used since time began. They parted ways as the promise of sunrise gathered at the horizon, Belet-ṣeri-dannat to return to Bābilim, Nabû-na'id and Gubaru to continue onward – to Upija, a town north of Bābilim on the edge of the Mandan wall.

But they paused, Gubaru and he, when the sun finally broke the horizon. Together they did the *Namburbi* ritual, for Nabû-balaṭsu-iqbi and for Nabû-kudurri-uṣur. "This is not normally how we remember the dead," Gubaru observed, perplexed. "This is how I do," was Nabû-na'id's simple response. "With what right I do not know."

He performed the ritual a third time, but he did not tell Gubaru why.

He did it for the fly.

* * * * *

From the [fragmentary] Assyrian Accounts of Herodotus

...death followed shortly afterwards. A period of uncertainty ensued. The king's son, Amelmarduk, was promptly crowned, but the court was divided in its loyalties between him and Neriklassor, the king's son-in-law and, during his madness, for all intents and purposes his regent. At the time of the king's death, Neriklassor was off campaigning to the west and hence was both away from the city and in command of an army. Indeed, the absence of Neriklassor precisely when the king died was considered by some as more than a little suspicious, and rumors circulated, perhaps instigated by some of Neriklassor's supporters, that the new king was a parricide. If this were true, I do not know why Amelmarduk would nonetheless have entrusted his rival with military power – unless he really was inattentive, foolish and, as some say, impulsive. For then he might not have planned what in fact did not end well for him. In any event, I do not know where the truth lies, but I favor the opinion shared with me by an elderly priest of Babylonian Apollo. He said that the king was wretched and died of a broken heart, unable to reconcile himself to a world whose blemishes his madness had rather polished and made ornate. Death from a heart broken by a world seen, as for the first time, without its varnish might happen to any man, and indeed does. Perhaps contributing as well was the earlier death of his wife Amytis,

the two having never overcome an estrangement initiated by his madness – if his madness was not initiated by it.

Amelmarduk's support largely lay – so the priest told me – among a cadre of highly competent functionaries who administered the empire efficiently regardless of who ruled, and sometimes even in spite of that person. It is worthy of reflection that, despite their manifest abilities, such allies are of little value to a king whose rule is precarious. It does not appear, however, that Amelmarduk appreciated this distinction, the fineness of which may easily be overlooked when a regime is stable, and by those who do not distinguish between the functioning of government and its ceremony. In any event, among these men was that same Baltasar of whom I have written, and it was he who convinced Amelmarduk to release the Judean king from his captivity of over thirty years. This move, as well as the undue influence of Baltasar, a foreigner, on the king, had the benefit for Amelmarduk of rallying to his support the few thousand Judean exiles then living in Babylon – but at the cost of alienating the powerful religious establishment, many members of which were already inclined toward Neriklassor. They feared the king would be swayed toward the heretical practices openly espoused by Baltasar and associated as well with the Judean king. Shortly thereafter, Amelmarduk's ill-timed declaration of debt relief deprived the temples of a major tax for the New Year's festival, a move that again curried favor among the weak at the mere expense of angering the strong. In particular, some in the temples believed or pretended to believe that the debt relief was a deliberate action aimed at weakening the religious establishment ultimately in order to prepare the way for the worship of a single, heathen god.

Amelmarduk's final blunder was to attempt a land reform. His father had grown his army by rewarding soldiers with land. He was in turn rewarded with their loyalty and with a problem: men who are fighting cannot farm, and men who are farming cannot fight. The city needed both soldiers and grain. The earlier king therefore had facilitated large-scale rental of property, much of it arranged through a merchant house called the Egibatila, which began by managing but often ended by owning the property of the absent veterans. Amelmarduk's plan was to confiscate the land that the Egibatila had acquired and to use it to assemble his own army. This naturally had the consequence of angering the Egibatila, whose head, already a close ally of Neriklassor, accordingly began seeking common ground with the temples. Amelmarduk's confiscations were no less alienating to the retired veterans who thought the land should have been returned to them. Meanwhile, there were the people who already rented the land, often on three- or four-year contracts; it was unclear to whom they owed their payments, or even whether their contracts would be honored. Naturally, unscrupulous men took advantage of this confusion, whether to collect payments not owed them or to dispossess tenant farmers of the land they had cultivated through their toil. In one fell swoop, Amelmarduk thus completed the alienation of the most important institutions in Babylonian society, including in the end even the poor who originally had favored him. He also lost the support of the functionaries, largely because they found his decisions and actions unpredictable, inefficient and demonstrative, minimally of impatience, but more likely of an incapacity to follow a long-term plan. It is, I think, on these bases that Amelmarduk came to be remembered later as lawless and outrageous, though his faults had as much to do with his relative youth and inexperience.

Neriklassor meanwhile, being well informed of the chaos Amelmarduk was wreaking in Babylon, and in no hurry to save the young king from himself, instead dallied in his return to the city. Indeed, rather than heading directly home, he proceeded north and, through prior arrangement, had a friendly tete-à-tete in the western city of Beroea with none other than Croesus, then the prince and day-to-day co-ruler of Lydia. (Alyattes, though still alive, shared much of the regular administration with his son.) What the two discussed is not known, and indeed some say the meeting never took place; but, whether it did or not, news that the two had met and were apparently on terms of the warmest friendship was soon widely spread throughout the empire, and especially in Babylon. Thereafter, Neriklassor did not have to ask for what he wanted; and when, as Neriklassor drew near the city, an ambitious nobleman took it upon himself to deliver that unasked-for gift, Amelmarduk's days came to an end. The nobleman had the misfortune to survive his own deed, as the city officials and even the young king's guard were uncertain whether to act appalled; and so it fell to a somewhat exasperated Neriklassor to reward the enterprising man with condemnation, torture and eventual execution as a regicide, all the while honoring his misfortunate predecessor with an extravagant funeral and much rending of hair and garments.

By a curious coincidence, Neriklassor had been officially in power only a short time before Alyattes died and Croesus, too, sat alone upon a throne. The burial of his father, much of which the latter had prepared in advance, was yet more extraordinary than the lavish mourning by which Neriklassor and the Babylonians marked the passing of their own king. But I have already described it in my Histories.

* * * * *

An old woman, dressed in sackcloth, covered in ash, walked past him, murmuring a prayer. Belet-ṣeri-dannat called out to her. "Am I right," he asked, "that you are the mother of Nabû-na'id?"

She looked at him with wild eyes that startled him. "Yes," she said simply.

"I am his friend."

"You are the heretic who worships only one god."

"I worship only one god amid heretics who falsely believe there are others."

"Yes," she said, flashing a gap-filled smile. She came closer and said in a conspiratorial whisper, "The image of God is the face of the Moon."

"It is we who are the image of God," he replied. "There is no other image."

"There are only images of God," she answered sternly. "And the Moon is the image of that."

Belet-ṣeri-dannat marveled that he was having a conversation such as this with a woman – even if the most famous, the most eccentric woman in Bābilim. Truly she was Nabû-na'id's mother. And he her son.

"Why are you in mourning?" he inquired.

"Is it not true that today there are more dead than yesterday? Why are you not in mourning?"

"Because it is also true that today there are more living than yesterday."

"Is that true?" she wondered. "I doubt it. If it is, it will not last." Again she leaned forward and whispered, "I carry the weight of kings, of dead kings. It is I who keep their ritual. Nabû-apal-uṣur. Nabû-kudurri-uṣur. Awil-Marduk. Their names are become light ironies. Nothing to laugh at. Nabû-apal-uṣur destroyed my city, Ḫarrānu. I mourn my city and the departure of the God from it. I mourn them all, destroyed and destroyer. But I will see the day of my God's return. My son will lead him by the hand into the rebuilt temple, the Eḫulḫul."

"It was about your son that I wished to speak to you. Where is he?"

She looked at him circumspectly.

"He is out of danger," Belet-ṣeri-dannat explained. "Nergal-šar-uṣur is grateful to him, wants to reward him. I am trying to find out where he is, so I can send him a message and recall him."

"Where would you go if you were he?" the old woman asked. It was an annoying question.

"As far away as I could get, while Awil-Marduk reigned. But

that doesn't exactly narrow the field."

"It's also not how my son thinks," Adad-guppi observed. "He was travelling with his wife, his son, his daughter. And that other boy went with them too. His childhood friend. Gubaru." She paused. "I suppose he's no longer a boy," she mused.

"I know he was travelling with all of them. But how does that help me find him?"

"You should ask yourself what it is he would want to show them," the old woman replied.

Belet-ṣeri-dannat felt disappointed. He sighed. "I take it, then, that you don't know where he is?" he asked.

"It makes no difference to me where he is, only where he would go – whether he did or not."

The man with the owl-beak nose looked at her frankly. "You are at least as confusing as your son is," he announced. He bowed slightly. "I am grateful for what help you could give me," he observed, making little effort to disguise the sarcasm. He started to leave.

She placed her old woman's hand on his bicep and stopped him. "I am right about the Moon." She looked piercingly into his eyes. "Ask your god if I am not." She released him.

He had taken no more than ten steps when a sudden thought occurred to him. He turned and called out to her. "Why do you mourn both the destroyed and the destroyer?"

She stared at him in a silence that grew uncomfortably long. At last he said, "Did you hear me?" but she answered almost at the same moment, so that they talked over each other. "What else is possible?" was her reply.

The young man – a youth probably in his late teens – looked familiar. It took Belet-ṣeri-dannat a moment to place him. Suddenly it came to him. "Bel-šar-uṣur!" he yelled. The youth halted and wheeled around in one graceful motion, then looked at him without recognition. "You probably don't remember me," Belet-ṣeri-dannat began. "I am a friend of your father's. When I last saw you, it was maybe two or three years ago. Before you left Bābilim." The youth nodded but said nothing. "I am looking for your father." Belet-ṣeri-dannat continued. "I take it he has returned to Bābilim?"

The youth shook his head.

"Does your father not know that he can come back to Bābilim?" Belet-ṣeri-dannat asked in some surprise.

"Oh he knows." The youth gave him a weird, uncomfortable smile. "He just doesn't care."

The older man stared at the youth for a moment. He was at a loss. Finally he roused himself. "What is he doing?" he asked.

"He is digging holes," the youth answered.

They were seated opposite one another, having just finished a meal together. The youth was clearly gratified to have dined one-on-one with an important figure from the court. "So you came to Bābilim with Gubaru?" Belet-ṣeri-dannat repeated.

"Yes. I was stir-crazy, as you can imagine, and my father needed supplies anyway, so he sent Gubaru here to get them. I tagged along. At first he didn't want to let me go, but Gubaru reminded him that the two of them had made a similar but longer journey when younger even than me – all the way to Sardis. You probably know that that's where my father became famous."

"Yes, I've heard he did something remarkable in Sardis."

"Anyway, I'm not a weak little boy anymore. I am a man. Gubaru was not much older than me when he became a father for the first time, and he says I am stronger than he was then."

Belet-ṣeri-dannat examined the youth cursorily. He was certainly well-built and probably quite strong. But he did not say that. "It sounds like Gubaru is fond of you," he noted instead.

"No it isn't that." The youth responded too quickly – defensively, in fact. He lacked his father's subtlety. "Gubaru sees what I am, what I'm capable of. My parents still think of me as what I was."

"Hmm." This was not an avenue of inquiry that much interested Belet-ṣeri-dannat. "Tell me about your travels, when you first left Bābilim."

"We met up in Upija. My father liked it there. He called the town 'the gate of Bābilim, the gate of the gate of the god.' He would joke about whether there was a gate of the gate of the gate of the god. The sort of thing he finds funny. And he enjoyed strolling along the river. But we didn't stay – it was too dangerous. We headed north and west. Toward Ḫarrānu."

"Ah! I had wondered about Ḫarrānu. Your grandmother told me to think of places your father would want to show you. It had occurred to me that surely Ḫarrānu was one of those."

The youth looked mildly scornful. "We never made it to Ḫarrānu. Just off the road to Ḫalab, my father discovered some decrepit mudbrick ruins. And he forced us to stop, to stay there. There was an old bee-hive village not far away – he paid the villagers to give us food and water and some other supplies. But it was beside the ruins that we actually pitched our tents. We just stayed out in the open like that. And my father started digging holes."

"Why did he do that?"

"I don't know. It never made sense to me. He said he was looking for the *pukku* and *mekkû*, that he was like Gilgameš. 'Do you remember the sherds, do you remember the sherds?' he'd yell excitedly at Gubaru. He claimed that tomorrow is to be found only by discovering yesterday. All of it made as much sense as a king eating tufts of grass."

Belet-ṣeri-dannat cocked an eyebrow. "So you think your father is mad?"

Bel-šar-uṣur shifted uncomfortably. To disparage his father made him feel like he was free – but only so long as the disparagement never broke the surface, never announced itself directly. "No," he said, drawing out the word. "No, he's not mad. Forgive me for implying it. He is – but you must know this – he is eccentric. It's his eccentricity that I don't understand. I wish he'd be practical."

"A reasonable thing to wish for," the older man murmured. "But sometimes we are directed to something greater than the practical. I have felt it in my own life. I know your father has. Perhaps someday you will too."

"You're the one who believes only in a single god, right?" Bel-šar-uṣur asked with a sense of daring.

"I believe in the only God there is."

"So you're like my grandmother, then. She believes only in Sîn. I mean, she'll never say that, of course – not in so many words. But all the other gods are for her just manifestations of Sîn. Is it Sîn that you believe in too?"

"No. Your grandmother was granted a great revelation. She has unhappily twisted it into idolatry. Such are the risks of revelation. We are fragile vessels in which to contain them."

"We are vessels?" the youth asked.

"Figuratively speaking, yes."

"Like statues?"

Belet-ṣeri-dannat paused, pursed his lips, and then, after some thought, broke into a smile. "So you are your father's son after all!" The youth looked conflicted, both gratified and alarmed. Belet-ṣeri-dannat changed the subject. "When your father was digging holes in the middle of nowhere, what did he find?"

"Not much, as far as I could tell. They found a few old walls, the outlines of a house. In a corner, a pot with a baby's skeleton inside – but they accidentally broke it when they were digging and only found the pieces. That seemed to bother my father a lot. And my mother. The two of them did a ritual afterwards, and they wept."

"Did they find anything else?"

"They found a beautiful plaque with a carving of a horse on it. They found a single tablet. There were pottery sherds everywhere, of course. And a cluster of stones that my father insisted was a floor, although I don't know how he could tell."

"Hmm," grunted Belet-ṣeri-dannat, not particularly interested.

"And the weirdest thing they found was – a hole. Right where you'd expect an extension of a mudbrick and stone wall, there was a big gap, and then the wall resumed. My father puzzled over it for a long time. He finally decided that some later people came and dug a pit, removed the stones, and used them for building something else."

"How curious," Belet-ṣeri-dannat murmured, again without much interest. But then, to his surprise, the flame suddenly caught and he discovered in himself a strange curiosity.

"Your father dug a pit to uncover the past," he observed, "and in uncovering the past he discovered a pit that robbers dug to remove the past. I can imagine your father being very struck by that."

"Yes, he was. I didn't understand what was so exciting about literally finding nothing."

"That's what was so exciting," Belet-ṣeri-dannat announced, feeling a small exhilaration himself. "Literally finding nothing." He recalled one of their earliest meetings, Nabû-na'id and he, when Nabû-na'id had expounded on the meaning of nothing. Nothing is, he had said in so many words, but what is not.

The odd look the youth was giving him stirred him abruptly from his reminisces.

"Some things are so totally forgotten that you won't even

find nothing," Belet-ṣeri-dannat stated in explanation. "That's what your father would have been thinking. I'm sure of it."

Nothing in the youth's eyes suggested that he understood. The older man looked past them, past the youth altogether, and suddenly realized for the first time that the sun would soon be setting. "You should get on your way," he announced. "I'm sorry I've kept you so long."

"I've been honored by your attention," the youth answered politely.

"Will you be going back to your father soon? Can I give you a message to bring to him?"

"Give it to Gubaru. He will head back shortly. For myself, I have decided to stay on in Bābilim."

To Nabû-na'id, thus Belet-ṣeri-dannat.

May the god keep you well and alive.

I have met with your son, who told me of the hole you found in your hole. I am sure that between us we would find much to say about nothing.

You know it is safe for you to return. Your influence here would be helpful. Not least with your son, who I see is both ambitious and inexperienced. Your spark every now and then flashes in him – but it is not nothing which he craves.

If it's not political influence or influence over your son which will lure you, then consider that I miss your company, misguided heretic though you are. It was on my account that you were nearly destroyed. It was also on my account that you were not. Does that mean you owe me something or nothing?

"You're the son of Nabû-na'id," the stranger said. He was young, not much older than Bel-šar-uṣur. What was most remarkable about him were not his looks but his smell, the sheer strength of his perfume.

"Yes," Bel-šar-uṣur responded, before asking snarkily, "With the son of whom do I have the pleasure of speaking?"

The other man laughed. "I am Itti-Marduk-balaṭu. My father is Nabû-aḫḫe-iddina, head of the House of Egibi. It was my father's uncle who was working in Sardis with your – well, I guess he was your grandfather. Do you know about that?"

"Not much. My father's mentioned a few things here and there. What were your uncle and my grandfather doing?"

Again the man laughed. "Probably something hideously boring that they pretended was terribly important! 'Argue over a grain of barley,' my uncle used to say, 'and if you win, an empire may be born.' That's probably what you have to tell yourself when you spend your life arguing over grains of barley."

"Based on what my father's told me, it would surprise me if my grandfather argued over grains of barley. Or cared much about empires being born."

"It may be so. My uncle thought he was canny and uncanny all at once. Smart and strange, always striking his own course and seemingly not too interested in the normal rewards of men. A man to be respected precisely because you couldn't take his measure – and for that reason also a man to keep at a distance."

"My father says he was a great man."

"Perhaps he was. But, my new friend, you shouldn't lose sight of a difficult but insurmountable fact."

"What's that?"

"Already almost no one remembers your grandfather. And very soon, no one will."

"So long as I live –" Bel-šar-uṣur began.

"No," the other man interrupted. "You remember his name, not the man. Who can you think of who remembers the man?"

Bel-šar-uṣur paused and thought. "My father. Gubaru. My grandmother. The king of Luddu." He paused. "Your uncle," he added cleverly.

"No, not my uncle. He's dead too. As is the old king of Luddu; his son now sits on that throne. And how old is your grandmother? One might think she succeeded where Gilgameš failed!"

"What is your point?" Bel-šar-uṣur asked challengingly. What had seemed a light-hearted conversation had become, it seemed, hostile and threatening.

Itti-Marduk-balaṭu looked at him for a moment probingly. Then suddenly he laughed again. "I'm sorry, I see I've made you uncomfortable. I was just making small talk, trying to impress you with my knowledge of your remarkable family. That's all. You and your family are much spoken of in the House of Egibi."

"I am? That I doubt."

"You underestimate yourself, my new friend. Anyone can see you're an up-and-comer, well-traveled already for one so young, and on such friendly terms with important people – was that Belet-ṣeri-dannat I saw you with the other day? And you are, of course, of royal lineage. That's not nothing!" He gave Bel-šar-uṣur a slap on the back. "I'm sure I'm not the only one who would be delighted to count you a friend! And perhaps time will show that it is not a terrible thing to count me a friend as well."

Bel-šar-uṣur didn't know how to respond. The awkward silence didn't seem to bother Itti-Marduk-balaṭu, however. "Tell you what," he said. "Why don't I introduce you to my father?"

To Nabû-na'id, thus Belet-ṣeri-dannat.

May you be well and alive, and may the god keep you so.

I had hoped to hear from you, but perhaps messengers are hard to come by for hole-diggers in the middle of nowhere. May the instructions Gubaru gave allow this message to find you – a futile wish, I know, to commit to writing.

The House of Egibi has taken a considerable interest in your son. I have endeavored to keep an eye on him, but my influence wanes as another's waxes.

I find myself wondering about sparrows. Surely their songs amount to very little. And yet there are those who listen to them keenly. Whatever do they listen for?

Nabû-na'id sat in a tent with Gubaru, Niṭil-Kišar and their daughter, Mikum-Nisaba.

The dog sat at his side – a puppy with mostly charcoal gray fur, except for a splash of white on the back of his head and neck, and white boots on his legs from his paws to his elbows. Nabû-na'id had found the dog when they first arrived over a year before. The nearby villagers considered dogs nuisances; typically they rounded them up and stoned them. For whatever reason, however, Nabû-na'id had intervened and prevented that fate – for this dog, not for all dogs. He had called the dog "Fly." "It's a strange name to give a dog," his daughter had commented. "Like calling me 'Boy' or calling a bird 'Fish.' Why is this dog a fly?" Nabû-na'id told her to ask her mother – she would know. So the girl had looked to Niṭil-Kišar, who didn't bother to wait for the question to be repeated. "It's your father's way of convincing himself that concerns he has long spoken about exist in his heart as well as in his words." "What does that mean?" the girl had asked. "I am sure that neither your mother nor I am certain that it *does* mean," Nabû-na'id had answered. The girl gave him a pitiable look. "I know!" he had exclaimed happily. "I am confusing you. I should have called you 'Fly' too, and then everything would be simple: for you are one with my heart, like your mother." And he had held her, kissed her forehead and formally introduced her to Fly. "I am not sure I would like being called 'Fly,'" she had said.

But a year had passed for all of them. The dog was almost full grown. Their daughter was around a decade old. His beard and his wife's long hair both showed ribbons of gray. Gubaru looked more youthful, his hair still as dark as it had ever been, his face unlined, his eyes expressing an openness that had characterized him all the years of his life. Those years, many of them spent in military service, seemed to have taken little toll on him, physically or emotionally.

"We shall have to go back to Bābilim, I think," Nabû-na'id began. "This letter from Belet-ṣeri-dannat is worrisome."

"Why is it worrisome, father?"

"This House of Egibi that's mentioned in it – it is a sort of labyrinth, once entered, hard to leave; best not entered," her father answered gruffly. "What monsters lie within, I do not know and do not wish to know."

"The members of that house are all very respected," Gubaru objected.

"Certainly. You can't have a monster-concealing labyrinth in the middle of a great city without being respected," Nabû-na'id answered matter-of-factly. Gubaru's furrowed brow suggested the answer was less than satisfying.

"Poet," Niṭil-Kišar interposed. "Enough with the House of Egibi. It is no less made of mud and stone than any other. Admit that even you tire of digging holes and instead long for Bābilim. Let us go home. It would not be a horrible thing for Bel-šar-uṣur to know that, for once, we followed his lead, for once realized that his course was the better one for us all."

Nabû-na'id examined his wife closely. "You're comfortable with him becoming entangled in the Egibi House?" he asked.

"No," admitted Niṭil-Kišar. "But however he strikes out on his own will leave me with some discomfort. And you too. Let it be the discomfort of mere parents, not romantic poets. Consider that –" she stopped.

"Consider that what?"

"Consider that a gift. For Bel-šar-uṣur."

The husband and wife exchanged a long glance. Eventually

Nabû-na'id's eyes fell to the floor.

"You are right," he said. "Let us go and be reunited with Bel-šar-uṣur, whom we all miss." Then he smiled. "In the meanwhile, let me tell you a story that I heard from a traveler at the crossroads – or perhaps it was my mother who once told it to me long ago." Nabû-na'id winked at his daughter. "It's about labyrinths."

No sooner had Mikum-Nisaba heard this than she settled down into a posture of happy expectancy. She loved her father's stories; often she would mull and tease at them for days on end, pondering and re-pondering every detail. Niṭil-Kišar's eyes revealed something more complicated – something tired and worried, besides but not displacing an appreciation for this art they shared between them of shuttling secrets to and fro in plain sight. Even Gubaru had a look of pleased anticipation; his friend's stories had always mesmerized him, even if they culminated, as they usually did, in a confusion or mystification which he could never sort into clarity. The dog, meanwhile, gnawed contentedly on Nabû-na'id's sleeve.

"There are actually two different versions of the tale that I've heard. Once I've told them to you, tell me which one you think is the right one." Mikum-Nisaba nodded her acceptance of this charge with great seriousness.

"Once in an ancient city a *šēdu*-like monster was born. Like all *šēdu*, it was part man, part ox and part eagle, but instead of having a human head on an ox's body with eagle wings, it had an ox's head on a human body and a long bird-tail and talons instead of fingers. Or so people said. No one knows the origin of this *šēdu* or why it was deformed in this way, unlike all the other *šēdu*. Some say the boy – for he was a boy – was the secret child of the king, and that the latter, out of love, refused to destroy him. Instead he hid him away. He had a great labyrinth built beneath the city, and he made of this a subterranean palace for the boy. But, palace notwithstanding, if we put ourselves in the place of that monster –" Nabû-na'id gave his daughter a serious look "– we must image that he was terribly lonely, wandering his underground palace by himself, never encountering other beings like him. And the beings he did encounter, he destroyed, much like Fly here is doing to my sleeve. Perhaps, then, not out of anger but out of excessive enthusiasm and even playfulness; or perhaps this strange *šēdu* monster no more understood why, or even that, he destroyed those beings than Fly here understands what he is doing to my sleeve."

He paused. "But perhaps it is I who do not understand what he is doing to my sleeve," he heard himself wonder aloud in a subdued voice.

He resumed. "While the king lived, he would periodically send slaves and captives into the monster's labyrinth. They never returned and the king never asked what became of them. No one knew precisely why he did this, perhaps least of all himself, and after a while it became part of the city's ritual observances. Even after the king died, they would send at regular intervals victims – for everyone by then acknowledged that that was what they were – into the *šēdu*'s lair.

"There was a young prince, however, who wanted to end this observance. 'It's barbaric,' he told anyone who would listen. 'If you wish to end it,' responded the priests, 'you'll have to go down into the labyrinth, kill the *šēdu*, and then somehow find your way back out again. Otherwise, for as long as the *šēdu* lives, we will keep the observance.' 'How do you know the *šēdu* is alive even now?' the prince asked. 'He must be,' they replied. 'What else has become of our victims?' So the prince decided to go into the labyrinth and kill the *šēdu*.

"The next morning he departed, to much fanfare – weeping from those who loved him, otherwise a sense of celebration and excitement that something new for once was happening. They took him to the great gates; he opened the door; he saw the enormous stone staircase descending into the earth and into darkness. He started down. They closed the door. His torch illuminated only a small globe around him, and its flames seemed weak, like already they were tiring from pointlessly, hopelessly beating back the pitch blackness.

"He had only gone down a few steps when he heard something. His hair prickled, his heart raced, he drew his sword. It was the sound of breathing. He took a few more steps, and he heard a voice, a woman's voice. 'Prince!' the voice said. 'I am the priestess Ennindaba. I have come to prevent you from doing this.' 'How did you get here?' he asked. 'I came yesterday and stayed the night,' she replied. 'Were you not frightened?' 'Yes,' she answered simply. 'Then why did you do it?' 'I have already told you,' she answered. 'To prevent you from doing this, from killing the *šēdu*.' At this point she had come close enough to enter the fringes of his globe of light, and he could see her frail, slight form. 'I must kill the *šēdu*,' he answered. 'It's what I have come for.' 'Then you do not know what you have come for,' she said. 'Has it not occurred to you that the *šēdu* died long ago, of starvation or madness or loneliness? Has it not occurred to you that all the victims who have been sent down suffered similar fates? Or even that, if any of them survived, they became the *šēdu*?' 'How could they become the *šēdu*?' he asked. 'We may be what a place makes us. The *šēdu* may be less a hybrid of man, bull and eagle than it is this place, this labyrinth, this unholy grave.' The prince thought for a moment. 'Doesn't that mean, then, that you and I are both the *šēdu*?' The priestess laughed shrilly, a nervous, exhausted, unhappy laugh. 'If it is so, all the more reason for us to leave.'

"The prince thought some more. 'How can I leave? How can I show my face again to the sun?' The priestess now was only a step away. She lightly touched his sleeve. 'Tell them the truth,' she said. 'Tell them the *šēdu* is dead. And then seal the door to this palace and curse it – curse anyone unwise enough to break the seal and enter.' Still she held his sleeve tenaciously, urgently. He looked at her hand and in the dance of flames and shadow thought he saw instead a claw there. 'It shall be as you say,' he announced. They turned and climbed the stairs together. He pounded the door; when it was opened, he was momentarily blinded by the sunlight and the towering shadow of the chief priest. 'Is it done?' the priest demanded. 'As the priestess Ennindaba is my witness,' the prince replied, 'the *šēdu* is dead.' The priest looked startled, seeing the priestess for the first time. 'How is it possible? She cannot possibly be alive!' 'But I am,' Ennindaba answered simply, coming forward, her robes wrapped tightly around her, exposing only the forehead of her bowed form – otherwise not a shred of skin, not even a knuckle. 'And the prince has spoken the truth. The *šēdu* is dead.'

"That night the sounds of celebration, music, laughter, stomping and dancing feet, all resonated through the floor and echoed deep within the underlying labyrinth. What lost, forgotten victims still remained wandering in darkness, looking for the *šēdu* who they were, looking as well for a way out, were surely tormented by the sound. But perhaps even then they were comforted too."

He stopped and looked about him. His daughter's expression was rapt. Gubaru's was less so. "Perhaps this is not the best story for a child," he began clumsily, gesturing, also clumsily, at Mikum-Nisaba. The girl stopped him. "When I was very little, I overheard the mudbrick in my room speaking about me," she said. "They pitied me. One mudbrick said to the other, 'That thing doesn't even have a name.'" She paused and was silent for a moment. "Nothing will ever bother me more than that." Gubaru looked alarmed. "It must have been a dream!" he exclaimed. "And if it was?" the girl answered. Gubaru was at a loss. "But you *do* have a name – you're Mikum-Nisaba," he protested. Then he added, somewhat absurdly, "The mudbrick didn't know what they were talking about." "What if we all have the same name, Gubaru, and it's '*šēdu*.' Isn't that the point of your story, father?" But before Nabû-na'id could answer, Niṭil-Kišar spoke. "What was the other version of this tale that you heard?" she asked sharply.

"It starts much like the first version. The *šēdu* is in the labyrinth, victims are sent to him periodically, a young prince comes along. He gets to the stairs as before; he descends them into darkness; he hears breathing. It is the priestess, Ennindaba. She gives him an enormous ball of thread. 'Tie it to the door,' she says, 'and then unfurl it as you travel in the labyrinth. Otherwise you will never find your way back.' He does as she instructs and then proceeds into the labyrinth with his torch and his sword. He's constantly having to choose whether to go straight or to turn right or to turn left; he is grateful for the thread. Meanwhile, he hears nothing and sees no evidence of the *šēdu*. But after a while, he notices a taut string on the ground, stretching behind and in front of him as far as he can make out. 'Is it my thread?' he wonders. He follows it. He hasn't gone a very great distance when he notices a second thread, just like the first. 'Is it my thread?' he wonders again. 'Am I going in circles?' He turns around and follows the thread that he is holding. But again he hasn't gone very far before, lo, he sees yet another thread like the others, taut and stretching indefinitely forward and backward. Now it is with immense difficulty that he manages to stave off his sense of panic. 'If I follow only the thread in my hand, furling it as I go, I will come to my starting point, regardless of what these other threads do,' he tells himself. And this is what he does. He continues to follow the thread in his hand backward. He continues to discover more and more strings on the ground. Meanwhile the threads proliferate; now there are hundreds; now there are thousands; and never does he come to the end of his own thread. Eventually he realizes that the *šēdu* was never a monster, a hybrid of ox, eagle and man; those were just the first twines of a *šēdu* coming to be. In other words, he realizes that this labyrinth with its multiplying threads *is* the *šēdu*. And so he sits down, he gives up, and he instead imagines what it would have been like had he turned back when he met the priestess and simply left the labyrinth then, declaring a victory where only declaration was possible." He stopped.

"So there really was only one version of the story," Mikum-Nisaba murmured. "No," Niṭil-Kišar said abruptly. "That's one possible reading, not the only possible one. It's why this man here, this poet, in his wisdom, gave us a choice about which story was right." From her tone and from her words, Nabû-na'id realized that she was angry at him.

Just then, in a particularly ferocious assault on his sleeve, the dog accidentally bit him.

Speak to Bel-šar-uṣur, thus speaks his father.

Your mother, your sister and Gubaru have all convinced me that we would be wise to follow your lead and return to Bābilim. So I am setting aside my habitual recalcitrance and my fascination with dust. This letter will be in advance of us, I hope, not by much. Await our return and may all be well with you.

Chapter 5. Labyrinths, What They Capture or Contain

I who, not knowing, had no thought of kingship for myself.

He had been in Bābilim only a few days when Nergal-šar-uṣur summoned him. He stood before the familiar throne and for the blink of an eye saw the ghost of Nabû-kudurri-uṣur. In that instant he endeavored to meet the ghost's gaze, but he could find no eyes into which to peer, only darkness, whether of holes or shadows he could not tell. The image evaporated no sooner than it had materialized, and gradually the new king, coarse, solid, embodied, came into view. "Your Excellency," Nabû-na'id managed to say, drawing the words as from a recess where ghosts could not be seen.

"Nabû-na'id!" the new king exclaimed, and then again, "Nabû-na'id! I am so – pleased you have found your way – back to Bābilim." The new king was short and stocky, his eyes perpetually squinting.

"It is good to be back."

"I am sorry – you had to – leave. I know, of course – the circumstances. And, of course, what – led to them. I am sorry for those too."

Nabû-na'id bowed in acknowledgement.

The king continued. "Sorry – and grateful. Your – assistance in these – matters, even several years ago – when the king made me his – heir – your assistance in all of – that – I recognized then. And still do. All the more – extraordinary – because you didn't ask for – anything."

Nabû-na'id could think of nothing to say. He said nothing.

"Our father valued – you – as a man who would speak – frankly – with him."

"I am honored if he did. So I endeavored, within the limits of the possible."

"Within the limits...?" the king raised an eyebrow. Nabû-na'id waved his hand dismissively. "I did my best," he clarified.

"When you proposed – me – as his – heir, were you speaking – frankly – to him?"

Nabû-na'id paused and considered the question. "If you mean, did I have an ulterior motive that I hid from the king, I do not think that I did."

"Why did you – oppose – the, um – Awil-Marduk?"

Nabû-na'id chose his words carefully. "I saw no way for him to rule safely," he replied.

Nergal-šar-uṣur smiled. "Yes! He was – headstrong – fickle. Maybe just – young. But such a rule is – dangerous. Especially in these times. With the growing – powers – around us."

Again Nabû-na'id could think of nothing he wished to say. He felt uncomfortable as the king beamed at him – uncomfortable as the king misunderstood him, with his own complicity. He felt uncomfortable even by how much he was annoyed by the king's idiosyncratic, halting manner of speaking.

"I would like you to do for me what you did – for him. For the king." Nergal-šar-uṣur paused as he dimly realized that he needed to be more explicit. "For Nabû-kudurri-uṣur."

"Meaning what, exactly?" Nabû-na'id asked.

"I want to trust you to speak – frankly – with me," answered the new king.

Nabû-na'id was silent for a long time. At last, with a slight bow, he said, "I will try, your Excellency."

The king appeared perturbed by the length of the silence, even if it culminated in a qualified assent. A questioning look flit across his face – and then, seemingly, was forgotten. The two men embraced. "There is much to – discuss," the king said. "The western front is – precarious. We must be – vigilant." The king waved his hand. "But that is for – another day. For now, I am – glad – to have you back – in Bābilim – at my side." They embraced again before the king walked Nabû-na'id to the door of the chamber. "I will send for you – when you are – needed."

Nabû-na'id found no satisfaction and no comfort in the interview or in his current standing with the king. He would have liked to find in Bābilim an anonymity which he had relinquished when he left Sardis all those years ago, and which he had only briefly re-found while digging holes in the west. But he also sensed his position was precarious. Nergal-šar-uṣur was apparently grateful to him and not threatened – but that would likely change. Gratitude is, for a king, innately threatening. Moreover, it was a gratitude based on a misunderstanding. Should Nergal-šar-uṣur come to suspect the deeper motives underlying Nabû-na'id's role in his adoption as heir, no good would come. But this left Nabû-na'id feeling more constrained, 'honored' as it were by a role which meant little to him, but which in all probability he could not safely relinquish. Certainly he could not cavalierly relinquish it.

He was still within sight of the palace when he caught sight of Belet-ṣeri-dannat – probably, he reflected, not by chance. They hailed one another.

"Nabû-na'id! Welcome back to Bābilim!"

"It is good to see you, my friend." He drew Belet-ṣeri-dannat closer and said in a low voice, "Thank you for keeping an eye out for my son."

"It's no problem. Have you disentangled him from the House of Egibi?"

Nabû-na'id frowned and shook his head.

"You intend to, I assume?"

"Perhaps. If I can. That house bears little attraction for me."

"For your son, it is like honey," the owl-beaked man observed. Nabû-na'id shrugged, a gesture that led Belet-ṣeri-dannat to inspect him more closely. "You and he are not so alike, I see."

"Perhaps not. But surely that is not why you waited for me to return from my audience with the king." The two men exchanged frank looks.

"Yes, I did wait for you," Belet-ṣeri-dannat admitted. "I wanted to find out where things stood between you and Nergal-šar-uṣur."

"They stand apparently well. For now."

"Good. That could be useful."

It was Nabû-na'id's turn to inspect his friend more closely. "I imagine," he stated, "that your influence with Awil-Marduk has put you on rather shaky ground with our new king."

"Yes."

"In fact, it's a wonder you have been allowed to stay at court. He might have exiled you – or worse."

"He hasn't made up his mind whether I was serving Awil-Marduk or restraining a youth prone to excesses. Best-case scenario, I suppose, is that I continue in my current state – tolerated, with no influence or access to speak of."

"That is not a terrible fate. I even find it desirable. Enviable."

"You and I are not very alike on this point either, then.

"No, perhaps not."

"If other scenarios come into play…" Belet-ṣeri-dannat let his implication drift off toward the horizon.

"Of course I will do what I can for you, my friend," Nabû-na'id promised. "But" he added a moment later, after some thought, "I am surprised you would seek my support when you have the support of your god."

"You are I are but tools of the God," Belet-ṣeri-dannat

responded, his eyes looking to the ground.

"It would seem that I am to be everyone's tool," Nabû-na'id grumbled.

Fly was sniffing a beetle. The insect was frozen in position, its abdomen sticking upward toward the sky. "What is he doing?" the girl asked, holding her father's hand. She had her mother's curls but her hair wasn't as dark. Like her mother, her brown eyes had sparks of gold and laughter. She wore a simple, pale-colored robe embroidered with flower images. Her father didn't immediately respond to her question. "Leave the beetle alone," he said instead to the dog. The dog stared intently at the beetle some more and then tore himself away.

"Was he just trying to say hi to the beetle?" the girl asked. "You know, the way he says hi to other dogs?"

"You mean by sniffing the beetle's nose and the beetle's bum, wagging his tale the whole time?" the father replied.

"Yes. Was that what he was doing?"

"But his tail wasn't wagging," observed the father.

"True," the girl agreed pensively. She wondered what the beetle was to the dog – whether the beetle was a beetle to the dog, as it was to her, or if it was something else. She wondered as well what a dog was to a dog – why Fly's tail wagged when he saw a dog but didn't wag when he saw a beetle. And then she wondered what a dog was to a beetle, what she was to a beetle. "What do beetles think we are?" she asked her father.

Her father laughed. "How would I know? We'd have to ask a beetle!"

"How do we do that?" she immediately replied, eager and smiling.

Her father was silent for a moment, thoughtful. "I'm not sure," he said. "Do you have any ideas?"

Still holding hands, the two of them continued walking

down the street, past all the red-painted doors, their sandaled feet crunching broken-up mudbrick. Fly, who had been running ahead, came back to check on them.

"If we just went up to a beetle and said, 'How do you think of us?'," the girl responded hesitantly, "that would be like Fly trying to sniff the beetle's nose and bum. That would work if the beetle were a dog, just as us questioning the beetle would work if the beetle were a human. But the beetle isn't a dog or a human." She paused, and then added triumphantly, "What we should do is watch how beetles greet each other, and then…" She trailed off.

"Will beetles agree that what they're meeting is another beetle, just because that's how it looks to us?" her father asked seriously. "And what if what we have to do is not watch how beetles greet each other, but listen to how they greet each other, or smell how they greet each other, or taste how they greet each other?"

"Oh, you're making this too difficult!" the girl announced, pouting and feeling frustrated.

"But maybe it really is difficult," her father responded reasonably.

They trudged along together, at some sort of impasse, one of them frustrated and the other smiling but also uneasy. After a while, the girl picked up the conversation. "Even if we could learn how beetles recognize each other and greet each other, that doesn't really get us any closer to understanding how they think about us. Or how they feel about us, which may be a different thing."

"Or it may not be different," her father suggested.

"Yeah," the girl said glumly. She kicked a stone and then asked, "Father, what do you think I am?"

Nabû-na'id and Fly were walking about the city. He was looking for two people, his mother and his son. But he was also hoping that he would not find them and that instead he and Fly would be left alone to enjoy each other's company. Sometimes he chose the way, sometimes Fly did; and whoever chose, the other yielded, perhaps on the premise – at least it was Nabû-na'id's – that something dictated the choice. For him the game often became trying to understand what. What was it that directed Fly's gaze in the world? Or perhaps, instead of his gaze, his sniff. How did Fly make sense of all the hustle and bustle, all the sound and fury, of Bābilim – its shouting vendors and pushing slaves and bleating animals? But, at least as interesting, how did he also make sense of Bābilim's silences – its bricks, its walls, its towers? Were they silent to him? What were the odors, as much of those silences as of that cacophony, that Fly, perhaps, knew and he did not?

What did Fly think about?

Often as not, Fly's choice would lead to a mound of dung or to rancid meat on the path or to another dog. These are not enlightened choices, one might say; never did they culminate in contemplation of the great statue of Ḫumati, or of the endlessly flowing river, or of the massive walls which contain as well as exclude – much less of the sun or of the moon or of the heavens generally. A dog does not appear to confront the possibility of god in the mystery of sunlight. But Fly might rejoin, how do you know my choices are not, as you put it, enlightened? How much, in fact, do you understand of a mound of dung or of rancid meat or of other dogs? How much have you ever tried to appreciate them? Can you be certain that there is less mystery in a pile of shit than in all the stars of heaven? Less of the divine too? Come and smell; taste it; find out. And next time I shall endeavor to understand whatever it is that you see in the stars, cold and distant though they seem.

Someone was tugging at his robe. "Lost in thought, I see," Gubaru noted. "As usual." Nabû-na'id blinked and tried to recast his mind into a mold more welcoming of his friend. But is it welcoming to shunt encounters through prescribed channels, to cast one's mind into this shape for that person, and that shape for this one? Or is that just a more sophisticated form of a wall, which simultaneously denies one person entrance and another exit? Was it possible his friend could no longer touch him, that he, recast into one mold after another, had become – how had his wife described it? Was he as mud, knowing no form for himself but that in which he was dried, ossified and friable? And yet, can no concession be made to that other being who confronts you, not even the concession of trying to speak what you believe is a common language? (But why do you believe it?)

Someone was still tugging at his robe. "Extremely lost in thought, I see," Gubaru repeated. Fly had doubled back and stood near Nabû-na'id, uncertain how to respond to what might be an assault. Nabû-na'id signaled that all was well, and Fly, contentedly believing him, resumed his investigations. He then turned to Gubaru. "I'm sorry," he said. "I was lost in thought."

"What brings you out to this part of town?"

"I was looking for my son, among others," Nabû-na'id answered honestly.

"Ah. No wonder you were lost in thought." Gubaru gave him a friendly slap on the back. "My children cause me no end of trouble, even now when they are grown."

Nabû-na'id paused for a moment, thinking about Gubaru's children. He especially liked the middle boy, Kayvan, who reminded him of Gubaru at the same age: guileless, honest to a fault, somehow both open and resilient. "How is Kayvan?" he asked.

"Ah! He is a hard worker, that one. With his older brother married, and me with more military responsibilities, I have come to rely more on him. It will be a shame when he too marries and starts his own household – I shall miss him, and not only for the work that I trust him to do and to do well."

"You should send him to me sometime. When he was little, I used to like telling him stories. He always thought about them with such – directness, such clarity. Like you when we were young."

"Perhaps, then, by 'directness,' you mean 'lack of sophistication.'"

Nabû-na'id winced. "No," he said. "I'm not teasing you or making fun of you. Directness is much more rare and much more important than sophistication. It's one of the reasons I trust you – you and Niṭ. Both of you sometimes show me where I have played even myself false." Fly came over to check on him, so he pat him absent-mindedly. "I think I see a similar quality in your son. It's something I honor not only because of its rarity but because so often I lack it."

Gubaru smiled, visibly pleased. "I am proud of him."

"You should be. It is too bad – " He stopped.

"What?"

"It is too bad that he and Bel-šar-uṣur have never become close, like me and you."

"Ah, well… You have a fine son yourself, you know. Strong and sophisticated, more experienced than many his age, and already circulating among men of importance here in Bābilim."

"Yes, I know. It's what I worry about. I wish he were attracted to – something else."

"What?"

"I'm not sure. I wish he mulled over details the way you and I did when we were growing up. I wish make-believe stories gripped him in a way that they don't, precisely because for him, 'make-believe' means 'unreal.' I wish he saw how much of what he takes to be real is make-believe. I wish – in short – that he had learned to read and to write."

"You wish he were a poet!"

Nabû-na'id reflected for a moment. "Yes. Yes, I do. Instead I fear he will be drawn into a tapestry of prestige and power without ever knowing it's a tapestry."

"But maybe it's not. Maybe he sees that more clearly than you."

"What do you mean, my friend?"

"I mean – isn't it the case that you see everything as a variety of tapestry? And if everything is, maybe that means that for all intents and purposes, nothing is; or at least, that the tapestry-ness can be overlooked, and maybe ought to be."

Nabû-na'id smiled a gentle smile. "As so often, you speak wisely my friend. I am not sure if I can take your words to heart, but I will endeavor to understand what that would mean."

"You are always endeavoring to understand!" Gubaru exclaimed energetically. He thumped his chest with his hand. "Feel! See where that goes instead."

Nabû-na'id looked at him, at his eagerly helpful expression, and he envied a man who could feel without simultaneously kneading that feeling into thought. Simultaneously and reflexively.

Gubaru put his arm around Nabû-na'id's shoulders and steered him to the right. "Now, let's go find your son. I think I know where he would be around now." Nabû-na'id whistled for Fly, and the three started on their way.

Itti-Marduk-balaṭu, strongly perfumed as usual, and Bel-šar-uṣur were returning from an interview that they had conducted – really, that Itti-Marduk-balaṭu had conducted – at a private home in the northern part of the city. "I don't see that we accomplished anything," Bel-šar-uṣur stated, feeling frustrated. He was always hearing about how powerful and influential the

House of Egibi was; and yet, all he ever did was tag along on these seemingly pointless visits that Itti-Marduk-balaṭu made. The conversations that he would witness were of two kinds. The first revolved around arcane details: interest rates, dates, the manner of repayment, the type of measure that would be used, the precise location of a field, a review of tablets, lists of witnesses. He didn't doubt that some of this mattered, but to his mind it was only appropriate that it should matter to someone else – not him. The other type of conversation was stranger still; there, nothing ever was directly said; everything was spoken as if in code, with a pleasantry somehow acquiring the meaning of menace, and a request transforming before his eyes into a command. And yet he was at a loss how to explain why he took the conversations to imply something other than, and beyond, their literal meaning. He was no less at a loss how it was that Itti-Marduk-balaṭu was able to command words to do such tricks for him.

"You don't see the accomplishment," Itti-Marduk-balaṭu answered, "because you're looking too directly for it. You need to look for it out of the corner of your eyes. Everything in the end is accomplished peripherally."

"That's the kind of thing I'd expect my father to say, not a down-to-earth businessman."

"Your father may be eccentric, as everyone knows. But he has a remarkable track record for getting things done. So maybe where he and I see things similarly – always out of the corners of our eyes – it's because we both see them clearly."

"What has my father done that so impresses you?"

"What has he not done? He's the son of a nobody – forgive me for saying so, but you know it's true – who somehow has managed to wield incredible influence with kings, both foreign and our own. Do you not realize that it was your father who talked Nabû-kudurri-uṣur into picking our current king as his heir?"

"I've heard such things. But people say my father was just the tool of Nergal-šar-uṣur."

"One of the tricks you'll learn over time is that, when seen through one's peripheral vision, it's often the saw that pulls the arm."

"Again you sound like my father!"

"What a compliment! I sound like the man who rules our kings."

"Why do you say that? My father has no interest in rule. He'd rather dig holes in the middle of nowhere."

"And yet, somehow or other, kings do his bidding."

"If he has such influence with kings, why didn't Nabû-kudurri-uṣur make him his heir, instead of Nergal-šar-uṣur? He was no less a son-in-law, moreover married to a daughter whom everyone knew the king liked better."

"Use your peripheral vision. The king is only the second-most powerful man in the land."

"Really? That's a new one. Who, pray tell, is the most powerful?"

"Whoever advises the king. Whoever tells the king what's real and what's not. Whoever thinks for the king and decides for the king."

"And that's my father?"

"So the House of Egibi believes. But" Itti-Marduk-balaṭu stopped and pointed, "why don't you ask him yourself?" His father, Gubaru and the dog were wandering in front of them.

"Not now," Bel-šar-uṣur said heatedly. "I don't want to talk to him right now."

"But you could introduce us!"

"Not now," Bel-šar-uṣur repeated emphatically. "Besides, he doesn't like you."

"Me?" Itti-Marduk-balaṭu said, inflecting his voice in mock surprise. "How shocking!"

They watched as Nabû-na'id, Gubaru and the dog continued walking, the two men deep in conversation and the dog periodically dallying here or there before catching up with them for a check-in.

"If the most powerful man is the advisor to the king, as you say," Bel-šar-uṣur began, "why would my father not have had himself made king, and then kept his own counsel?"

"It's a good question. Since your father hasn't done it, I'll assume it's at least very difficult and maybe impossible. But perhaps it's also undesirable. Think about it: a king, for all his power, is enormously constrained. He has to hear court cases, perform ritual duties, go on campaign. As much as he may choose to do one thing or another, he also inherits a bunch of tasks that only he can perform, whatever he thinks of them. And then there's all the detail work. Have you read any of Ḫammurapi's letters?"

"No, I'm not much of a reader."

"Ḫammurapi used to concern himself with even the details of chisel manufacturing! And maybe he did that so he could keep his own counsel – but that's the point: for a king to keep his own counsel, he has to do everything. And it's more than doubtful that anyone can. Of course, he can try, like Ḫammurapi apparently did – sending letters all over the country to keep track of everything from chisel manufacturing to calendar revision. But all of his life, then, is claimed by such minutiae, and even then he still has to delegate. He is, after all, sending letters to someone. He can't be in all places at all times. So he says, "Do this – or else!" And he hopes the letter's recipient takes it all seriously and doesn't play games – because if he does play games, what is the king to do? He'll find out from a letter, which he'll have to decide to trust, and then his options are limited. Almost certainly they will boil down to writing another letter."

"So kings are letter-writers?"

"The ones who try to keep their own counsel. Not that they really succeed, of course. After all, even Ḫammurapi probably relied on someone to do his reading and writing for him, a scribe to tell him what the mysterious clay tablets portended. But can such a king, even a micromanager like Ḫammurapi, really be sure that it isn't his scribe who rules? Surely there is a reason your father trained as a scribe… Just like the king beholden to his diviner must hope the diviner practices his craft truthfully, so must he hope that his scribe does too – practices it truthfully but also practices it with subtlety and discernment. For that king relies on his scribe to distinguish the rhetorical from the real question – and on this an empire may depend."

"You exaggerate. There's a level of common-sense that cuts through all of this, a baseline that the deceitful or devious or even careless use of words can't burrow beyond."

"Sure. But where is it?" Itti-Marduk-balaṭu gave a greasy smile.

"Plus," Bel-šar-uṣur continued, "kings can put to death their advisors, even on a whim. And even if that advisor is the one supposedly thinking for him."

"Yes, yes… It happens. There's often no greater threat to a kingdom than when a king thinks he can think for himself."

Bel-šar-uṣur said nothing. He felt uncomfortable, like sedition was just beneath the surface and he was being tricked into digging through the floor. But, despite himself, he also sensed something deeper at stake, something that he resisted even formulating to himself – something having to do with whether, beneath the floor, there was anything at all. It was a characteristic of his jittery thought to refuse to let such a question crystallize, even so much as to be suspected. Maybe it's what made his thought jittery in the first place. His companion, on the other hand, believed that this was a crystal he knew well and could handle deftly; and in this he was certainly the less perspicacious of the two.

Itti-Marduk-balaṭu pointed to Nabû-na'id and Gubaru, who remained within sight, though farther away now, and were still deep in conversation. "What does your father see in that one? What do they talk about?"

"What, you mean Gubaru?"

"Yeah. He seems a bit of an oaf. What does your father see in him?"

"They've been friends all of their lives. My father trusts and respects Gubaru."

"Really? I wonder if there isn't something else going on."

"What do you mean?"

"If a man who controls kings chooses to hang out with an oaf, he probably has a reason for it, something not at the surface – something you need your peripheral vision to see."

"So you don't believe that they could just be friends?"

"Of course they could be friends," Itti-Marduk-balaṭu rejoined, again smiling greasily. "But for what are they friends?"

They found his mother.

It had been several years since Nabû-na'id had encountered her in person. When he left Bābilim, they communicated – rarely – by letter. Moreover, by letters of the most eccentric kind. At one point his mother had sent him a single-line note: "Shall there be enough ash in the world for the mourning to come?" she had written. The letter was neither addressed nor signed; how it had found him, he could not explain. But he had no doubt she had sent it, though he could only wonder why. "In our mourning, we as well as the dead become ash. The world shall never want for ash," he had written back. Months passed before the next enigmatic message. "This tablet is of dirt mixed with ash. In it is my life and my death. Are they distinguishable? Such are all tablets." His response: "Such is all writing – and what is not writing?" A few words committed to mud, burned into stone and handed to a bewildered messenger; give it to the wild-eyed woman who bathes in dust and ash and dresses in sackcloth, he might as well have said; what it contains she already knows, but give it to her anyway. But those were never his instructions, only his thoughts. Few were the messengers curious about the message they bore. Fewer still those who wondered if they had managed to deliver it. And yet, Nabû-na'id thought, who is there who is not a messenger? Who is there who is not a message? It is our delicate incuriosity about what we are and about what we represent that enables us to eat, to breathe, to act and to endure. Every message carries a sentence of death for the messenger – and is it not perhaps wise of a messenger to leave this fate, always unavoidable, also always unconfirmed?

Their reunion was not of a sentimental nature.

"Ḫarrānu still awaits its temple; Eḫulḫul still awaits its god; the god still awaits your hand," she announced. She gave her son a piercing stare – but all her stares were piercing. "Even the Moon will not last forever. And I certainly shall not."

Nabû-na'id returned her gaze. He thought: in her eyes is a reflection of my image and in mine, a reflection of hers. And in my reflected image in her eyes is a tiny reflection of her image in my eyes. And so it goes, reflection after reflection, impossibly small and ever smaller. Does that not go on forever? In other words, is forever something to come or is it all about us, in every glance we meet?

"Maybe forever doesn't last," he answered.

She opened her mouth into a smile filled with gaps. Holes in a hole, her son thought. "All the more reason to hurry," was her reply. She turned and started to shuffle away.

"Mother!" he heard himself say, although he had no idea what would follow. She paused, her back to him. They were silent, she waiting, he wondering what it was that he wished to say or would say.

"I received letters from you," he said. "Perhaps not all that you sent, but some."

Still without turning to face him, she bowed her head in acknowledgment but said nothing.

"And I met this dog, whom I call Fly."

"It is a strange name," she commented after a moment.

"Because he is a dog and not a fly?"

"No. Because it tells us nothing further about the fly. It is like a god's name: 'Sky' or 'Lord.' But what man is called "Man" much less "Woman" or "Dog" or "Fly"? Our names, human names, are invocations, requests, declarations. Who were our last three kings? 'May Nergal guard the king,' 'The man of Marduk,' and 'May Nabû guard my son.' Who are you? In the human realm, what we are named, and what we are, is in relation to the gods. You make no such assertion on behalf of your dog whom you call Fly. You make no such request. Because he is only a fly, which is to say a dog? Or because he has no need of the gods? Or because you have no need?"

"There is another option, mother. It may be that there is nothing so divine as a fly."

"Do you mean a fly that flies" – she gestured its flight in erratic jerks of her ancient finger, "or a fly that howls? Or do you mean, as I take you to mean, that mirroring, that reflecting, which can make of a fly both a dog and a god, not to mention anything else, including a fly?"

Nabû-na'id thought for a moment.

"Would we ground ourselves in names anchored to a god? Is that really grounding? Surely there is a reason, mother, that your devotion has always been to Sîn, that it is the god of the Moon that you would have me return to Eḫulḫul – and yet I am named for the god of scribes, the god of writing, Nabû. Is there a secret here, mother, which unites the one with the other, as I have united a fly with a dog? Or is it rather that their would-be union is a chase, each reflecting the other while never catching up with him?"

His mother turned to face him fully. "You want ground," she said. She crouched, picked up dirt from the street in her bird-claw hands, and sprinkled it on her own head. "I bathe in it." She glared at him unblinkingly. "As for Nabû and Sîn – perhaps they are, as you suggest, one. Does that mean they do not write to each other? They only write to each other." She turned again and started walking away. But Nabû-na'id could still hear, or perhaps overhear, murmuring that came from her retreating figure: "Everything that happens – what is it but one chasing after the other with a message?"

Nabû-na'id continued to stare after her, even when she had disappeared from sight. He seemed to be trapped. Stuck. Unable to move. It was Gubaru who finally nudged him, touched his elbow, urged him on. "I do not understand you or your mother," he said simply. "And I wonder what sense she makes of me, if she even sees me – and what sense she makes of my name."

The last comment stirred Nabû-na'id. He looked up at his friend probingly. "Not to mention of that which has no name," he added. Then he allowed himself, gratefully, to be led away. The dog, whose name Nabû-na'id had made Fly, whether as imposition or gift or both, soon followed.

* * * * *

From the [fragmentary] Assyrian Accounts of Herodotus

...Over these ten generations it had grown in stature, wealth and power, becoming either an indispensable ally or intractable foe to the Babylonian kings. But it had begun much more modestly simply as a house of grain merchants. How it got its name – the Egibatila – is an

interesting story. The name is in the language of a people who called themselves "The Black-Headed Ones" and who rivalled even the Egyptians in their antiquity. But the people themselves had long before disappeared, even while their language endured, albeit almost exclusively in writing, which the Black-Headed Ones may have invented if the Egyptians did not. For the Egyptians say that it was an invention of an ancient sage of theirs, who feared that the rites of the ever-growing dead could only be forgotten. So he created writing as a tool of remembrance – which is why they consider writing sacred. Aesop's parable about this is well-known; and whether, as the story goes, the jackal writes in order to remember the dead, or as permission to forget them, I leave others to decide.

The Assyrian account, however, says it was the Black-Headed Ones, and not the Egyptians, who first invented writing. This is how they say it happened. There was a woman, a tavern-keeper, whose name was Kubaba or, some say, Kugba. She kept a tavern by a river where, by leave of the king, fisherman fished. According to the king's promise, the fishermen would give a third of their fish to the king, a third to the temple, and would keep the third fraction for themselves. But every time the fishermen returned to the shore, the king's officers took their whole catch; and when the fishermen protested, the officers could not remember what the king had decreed, or so they said. This kind of thing happened for quite a while, until one night Kubaba had a dream. In the dream a fish spoke to her. "Rescue me from the catch," the fish said, "and I will give you kingship over the land." But Kubaba, when she awoke, did nothing; for it did not seem likely to her that a fish could give her kingship, and even if it did, she doubted that she wanted it. But the second night she had a second dream. Again a fish spoke to her. "Rescue me from the catch," the fish said, "and I will restore uprightness to the land." But Kubaba, when she awoke, again did nothing; for she was a tavern-keeper and had seen much of the ways of men, and she doubted whether the land could ever be upright. And so having done nothing, that third night she went to sleep and that third night she dreamt her third dream. "Rescue me from the catch," the fish said, "or else." Now when she awoke Kubaba was at a loss; she did not know what "or else" could possibly mean or what harm could come from a fish, much less from a fish in need of rescue. But she resolved to do as she had been told, since, if nothing else, it seemed clear that a god was speaking to her, if it wasn't a fish. So she hurried to the shore just as the fishermen were returning with their catch. She witnessed the king's officers confiscating the catch, and she heard the protests of the fishermen who were left with nothing. As the king's officers left, a single fish flopped free and lay in the dirt. Kubaba grabbed it, but the fishermen saw her and demanded that she give the fish to them – their only compensation for all their work. Kubaba refused and instead threw the fish back in the river. But then she invited the fishermen to her tavern, and she fed them, gave them beer to drink and thanked them for their fishing.

That night in her dream came the fish. The fish said that his name was Abgal and that because she had saved him, he would help her restore uprightness to the land. He instructed her to go with the fishermen and have an audience with the king. When the king stipulated the conditions of their fishing, the fish told Kubaba to make three figurines out of mud: one like the crown of the king, one like the temple building, and one like a boat. These, the fish explained, would represent that one share of the catch would go to the king, one share to the temple, and one share to the fishermen. Then, said the fish, make a large, hollow, envelope out of clay and in the shape of a fish, put the three figurines inside, seal it, and bake it. Then, if there was a dispute, in front of the officers the fish- envelope could be produced and broken, the figurines revealed, and the shares settled. And so the next day she did as she was told: she went to the king with the fishermen, she made the figurines and the fish-shaped envelope, and the events transpired just as the dream-fish had predicted. When there was a dispute about the catch, the envelope was produced and broken, the figurines were revealed, the officers were chastened, and the fishermen were allowed to keep one-third of their catch.

This practice prevailed for some time, with good effect. But there was a corrupt official of the king who insisted on confiscating half of the fish and giving the other half to the temple. When the fishermen produced their fish-envelope, the official broke it, but he deliberately discarded the boat-shaped token, and so he said that the envelope proved that he was right: half of the catch would go to the king and half to the temple. Nothing was left for the fishermen. After the official and his officers had left, the fishermen went to Kubaba's tavern. What should we do? they asked. She said she didn't know. But she fed them and she gave them beer to drink and that night she had a dream. The fish Abgal re-appeared, and this is what he told her to do: carve images of a crown, a temple building and a boat, he said, on the outside of the unbaked fish-envelope, then bake it. That way the outside would confirm what was stored on the inside. When she awoke, she did as the fish had described. She went with the fishermen to the king and there demonstrated this new technique to them all, and they were satisfied. Again this new practice prevailed for some time, and peace reigned; and after a while, because it was easier, they ceased to make the tokens which they placed inside the fish-envelope and instead relied only on the drawings that were carved on the fish-envelope's surface.

But again there was a corrupt official of the king who insisted on confiscating half of the fish and giving the other half to the temple. And this official, when shown the drawing of the boat, said that it was clearly just a crack in the clay, and that it signified nothing. And so, he said, the envelope proved that he was right: half of the catch would go to the king and half to the temple. Nothing was left for the fishermen. After the official and his officers had left, the fishermen went to Kubaba's tavern. What should we do? they asked. She said she didn't know. But she fed them and she gave them beer to drink and that night she had a dream. The fish Abgal re-appeared, and he guided her in adding extra impressions on the outside of the fish-envelope to prove that the images were purposeful and not merely cracks. And when she awoke, she did what had been described to her, and the king and the fishermen were satisfied, and for a while peace reigned.

But over and over the same pattern recurred: a corrupt official would dispute the reading of the envelope, which would require that the system of signs on its outside become more complicated. And eventually it required that there also be more fish-envelopes, or as they called them, tablets. For they needed tablets to serve as a list of all their signs. So tablets as well as signs proliferated, each time resolving a prior reading dispute but becoming in turn the cause of a future one. And Kubaba as well as the fishermen found it all very tiresome. For sure enough, yet another corrupt official would always arise and claim too great a share of the fish, and the fishermen, after protesting to no avail, would yet again come to Kubaba's tavern and ask what to do, and she would yet again feed them and give them beer to drink and say that she did not know. "This is a curse," she said aloud to herself one evening, after giving succor to the fishermen. "This is like a swarm of gnats or a plague – a plague of tablets and signs, always proliferating, always serving as their own poison and remedy, with no end in sight. I have been cursed for helping that fish and I am cursed for helping these men." That night she dreamt, and the fish Abgal once more came to her. He did not instruct her on how to further complicate the signs, however. Instead he said, "To restore uprightness to the land, I will give you kingship over it." That was all. And when in the morning the fishermen came to her and asked what she had determined they should do, she could only tell them that she did not know. "Perhaps we should try talking this out yet again with the king," she suggested wearily. So she and the fishermen went to the king; but when she offered no improvement to the writing system, the king dismissed them summarily. This enraged the fishermen, and impulsively, as one, they suddenly rose up, slaughtered the king and his men, and put Kubaba on the throne. And so she became king – by inventing writing, acting uprightly and generously, and listening to fish. And it is said that she ruled wisely, and after her death was worshipped as a god and perhaps became one. For she is the same as the one the Lydians called Kuvava; and we Greeks know her as Kubele. Perhaps Abgal was the ancient name for Attis, or possibly Agdistis.

This is how the Assyrians say their land's ancestors, the Black-Headed Ones, invented writing, even before the Egyptians; and it was from the language of the Black-Headed Ones, a language that was then used only for writing and had been so for thousands of years, that the house, the Egibatila, got its name. For this name means "Sîn" – which is their name for the god of the moon – "you give (or gave), let live." What Sîn gave, some say was a child; others a ram. The story goes like this: an old man and his wife were childless. The god Sîn came to the old woman in a dream, and he told her that if she would prophesy in Babylon, if she would dress in sackcloth and dirt and ashes, then he would give her a child. In the morning, the old woman told the dream to her husband, but he only laughed. "At your age, a child! Besides, what would a god want with you?" This embittered the old woman as it did the god, and that night he again came to her in a dream. "Ignore your fool husband! Prophesy in Babylon!" The woman awoke, and while her husband still slept, she stole away to Babylon, a journey of many days. When she arrived, she dressed in sackcloth, dirt and ash and endeavored to prophesy. But she did not know what to say. She could only repeat, "The god has sent me to prophesy, I have come to prophesy" – but she had no idea what her prophecy was. On this the god was silent. And so the people laughed at her like her husband had laughed at her. Still she persisted, day after day, prophesying an undisclosed prophecy.

Her husband meanwhile was looking for her, and it occurred to him that she might have been mad enough to go to Babylon. And so there he went and, after several weeks – for Babylon is immense – he found her. He demanded that she return with him, but she refused; and so one night he bound her, gagged her and dragged her away. When they reached their old home many days later, he had no sooner undone her bindings than a baby leapt from her womb. Both of them were astonished, but the man's astonishment soon turned to anger. "You have made me a cuckold in my old age!" he shouted. And he grabbed the child and rushed toward the mountain, there to leave the child exposed on its summit. The child's mother wept but, after her captive journey, was too weak to follow. When the husband came down from the mountain, he came down alone. But barely had he arrived home when a ram with a dirty, ash-colored coat came following after him, and on its back, the child. And so the woman prayed to Sîn, and she said, "You gave; now let live" and this became the child's name. What could the husband do but relent? For was it not clear that a god was involved? And so the child lived and grew up and himself became father to offspring as numerous as the stars, until one of them founded the Egibatila and named it in commemoration of his ancestor. What became of the ram is not told.

The fortunes of this house were like those of its ancestor – success being torn from the very teeth of defeat, like the rescued babe. While it is true that Amelmarduk alienated them with his various, poorly-considered reforms, it is also true – or so I believe – that those reforms were partially retaliation for the support the Egibatila had given Neriklassor during the reign of his father. For they had even transferred some of the living king's personal property into accounts bearing Neriklassor's name – a practice which, I am told, was extremely unorthodox, if only because it circumvented the inheritance of the king's sons. I was shown tablets from the Egibatila archive that, the priests said, demonstrated this transfer, though of course I could not read them. Assuming that Amelmarduk knew about this – and it seems likely to me that he did, based on his subsequent conduct – then his actions, while reckless, may well have been directed at weakening or even punishing the Egibatila, if he could, and that this was not merely their incidental consequence. For where did the power lie? In the hands of a man called king or in the documents preserved if not manufactured by the Egibatila, declaring the possessors of the world and the intentions of the dead? Did it lie with the living voice or with the dead tablet? Had Amelmarduk endured on the throne, it is likely that his answer to this question would have been much to the woe of the Egibatila. But he did not. For him there was no ram.

* * * * *

"What do you see in this Itti-Marduk-balaṭu?" Nabû-na'id asked gently. They were seated side by side on a bench in a courtyard by their house, Nabû-na'id in his wrinkled gown and his son in more extravagant clothing, richly dyed and ornamented with jewels. Surprisingly, despite his youth, Bel-šar-uṣur's hair was already showing signs of gray.

"What kind of question is that?" Bel-šar-uṣur responded.

His father made a guttural sound. "I don't know," he admitted. "I don't really know much about that house, apart from what I saw of its agent in Sardis all those years ago. But I will confess I mistrust it – if only because their aims seem so small to me, and yet their pursuit of them so dogged. I wonder sometimes if they aren't mad."

"YOU wonder if THEY aren't mad?" His son barely held back a scoff. Then he added in a murmur, "It is not they who spend their time digging holes in the middle of nowhere."

His father looked at him strangely for a moment, then, somewhat uneasily, laughed. "Yes, you're right, I am the last person perhaps to make such judgments. I must look as mad to them as they do to me."

"But you don't," his son said quietly. "You don't look mad to them. They respect you."

Nabû-na'id could not hide his surprise. "Really!"

"Itti-Marduk-balaṭu says that you have been the true power behind kings, that Nabû-kudurri-uṣur did your bidding and that Nergal-šar-uṣur does it now." Bel-šar-uṣur could not help but accompany this statement with a note of challenge – and of pride.

His father looked alarmed. "It's nonsense!" he exclaimed. "Why would they think such things?" It was more exclamation than question. "Why would they say such things?" This was more question than exclamation. He looked earnestly at his son. "Why would they say such things?" he repeated seriously.

His son, turning toward him, examined him with unusual earnestness. "Why did Nabû-kudurri-uṣur honor you so? Why did he give you my mother as wife? Why have you never told me?"

Nabû-na'id sighed and took a slow, long, deep breath. "When I was young," he said speaking quietly, "my father had me learn, not only how to read and write, but how to read the heavens. Because of that I foresaw something that was of use to the king. It helped forge peace between Luddu and Manda, a peace that was useful. That is all."

"What did you foresee?"

"I foresaw an eclipse."

His son was, for a moment, stunned. "How did that bring peace?" he asked after a moment.

Nabû-na'id looked at his son for a long time, saying nothing. Finally, he decided. "I have rarely spoken about this with anyone except Gubaru, who was with me at the time," he said. "Not even your mother. It is very painful to me." He paused for a long time. Finally, with a pronounced intake of breath, he resumed. "Because of that eclipse, an outrageous deed was committed against guests, one that would not have been allowed under normal circumstances. And I bear responsibility for that deed."

"Were they –?"

"Yes."

"Why?"

His father exhaled audibly. "Why did I – participate in it?"

His son nodded. "Because it seemed to me that it was the course of lesser harm. But I don't know that that is true. I don't know if it was the course of lesser harm, and I don't know that that really was why I chose it."

"But it led to something better, it led to peace."

"Yes."

"So you were right to choose as you did."

"I don't think it's that simple. I suspect there are men whose ghosts would agree that it isn't. Or wasn't."

His son was quiet for a moment. "You make everything harder than it has to be," he announced at last. "Difficult choices must be made. But you make them more difficult, even when they're done. It is foolish."

His father bowed his head slightly. "Perhaps." His son started to speak but Nabû-na'id spoke over him. "It is more foolish, I am certain, to make them simpler than they are," he said.

"Itti-Marduk-balaṭu says that some knots should just be cut with knives. To untangle them otherwise is either impossible or not worth your time. So long as you know what you're doing, I don't see that he's wrong."

"Yes, that is the mentality of his house. They sleep well at night. I do not."

"What does this have to do with sleeping?"

His father snorted. "It has everything to do with sleeping," he said, "but enough for now. If you carry on with Itti-Marduk-balaṭu, at least bear in mind that what he says about knots applies to you too."

"You think he'd cut me like a knot?"

"Sure. I doubt it would represent a difficulty for him."

It was his son's turn to snort. "What can you really say? You don't even know him."

"True. I may be wrong. But bear this warning in mind. I

suspect that there is much that Itti-Marduk-balaṭu and I see similarly – but we have drawn very different conclusions. Conclusions perhaps based not on the weight of evidence so much as on the world we would live in, even if it is not the world that exists. So think about that. Think about the choices that one must make for a world to come."

"But that's precisely where you differ from Itti-Marduk-balaṭu. He's all about the real world. He doesn't worry about this world of yours to come. He acts according to the demands of the world as it actually exists."

Again his father gave him a prolonged look. "That world, Bel-šar-uṣur, is and has always been an illusion."

"Then what in the name of Apsû do you think the real world is?"

"I don't know. Something inaccessible to us, but also something that in a sense we bring into being."

"Then you agree with Itti-Marduk-balaṭu. He says that part of living in the real world is recognizing that we make our own reality, and taking advantage of that."

"Yes, he thinks he can control that. He thinks the real world is accessible to him as his own creation. It's partly the arrogance of youth and partly the arrogance of his house. But many other men believe similarly. And more than anything it is a desire whose force is in direct proportion to the unattainability of its object."

"Do you call him arrogant only because he has reached a conclusion that you haven't dared?" Bel-šar-uṣur stared at his father fiercely before continuing. "Is it his willingness to act in this world that goads you to insult him? Is it your envy?"

Nabû-na'id held back from answering. He doubted his son could hear right now the most honest answer, an answer issuing out of bewilderment and doubt. He also sensed the possibility that here honesty could do harm, could foreseeably be misinterpreted as a definitive answer. "I have only knots to offer my son," he thought to himself, "and right now he is enamored only with cutting them." The thought briefly whipped up a flash of anger at his son – brightly and intensely burning, quickly smothered. Another, smaller fire burned within him against the House of Egibi, and this he let burn.

"If we are authors of the world in which we live," he finally said, "that in no way means we are its masters. Far from it."

"But enough of authorship!" Bel-šar-uṣur exclaimed, pressing his advantage. "Enough of this abstract mumbo-jumbo. If you aren't the secret puppet-master of kings, then what are you? Are you anything? Is supposedly authoring the world just your deceitful way of avoiding acting in it?"

"I think I permitted myself to speak to my father in such a way," Nabû-na'id said quietly, "once or twice." Father and son looked at each other. "I regretted it. I regret it to this day."

"Am I to be sorry that I am speaking to you, for once, honestly?"

"No, if you are also listening to me honestly."

"I think it is you who do not listen honestly."

"So I gathered. Your friend Itti-Marduk-balaṭu seems the more honest to you, and the more clear-sighted."

"Because he is."

"No he is not. But I will not convince you of that. You shall have to convince yourself. I hope you do – and not at a terrible price. A price such as I paid, for example." Nabû-na'id got up, stretched his legs, dusted dirt from his robe. "I am returning home. You are welcome to walk with me if you like."

"I'll come later," Bel-šar-uṣur answered curtly.

"All right." Nabû-na'id whistled, waited a moment, and whistled again. Soon the dog came bounding towards him. "Let's go Fly," he said.

His daughter, seated at a table when he entered the room, looked up briefly. "Where did you go with Fly?" she asked.

"Oh, wherever the whim took us, sometimes with him in the lead, sometimes me. I was also looking for your brother."

"Did you find him?" she asked without again looking up.

"Yes." The answer came out flatter than he intended; and he thought he saw his daughter make a note of that. "We talked for a while. He'll be along soon enough."

"Hmmm," was his daughter's response.

"What are you up to?" he asked.

"Nothing I'm supposed to be doing. I've been –" She paused and looked slightly embarrassed. "I'm trying to write something."

"Oh?" Nabû-na'id was genuinely interested. "Of what sort?"

"I'm not sure what to call it. It's not a hymn, it's not a letter – not really. It's not even true."

"Describe it to me."

Her embarrassment faded away and instead she looked eager. "Here. See for yourself." She handed him a tablet.

She watched him as he read in silence, an unusual habit of his that she was practicing herself. Some people claimed to find it disconcerting that he never gave voice to the words. She remembered a conversation her father had had with Gubaru. "Do you hear the words in your head?" Gubaru had asked. "I don't know," he had answered. "I cannot tell whether I hear them or see them." This had puzzled Gubaru. "How can you not tell?" Her father had given him an amused look, and she remembered his answer very distinctly: "Is it stranger to hear what no one else can hear, see what no one else can see, or not be able to tell the difference?"

She realized he had stopped reading and was looking at her.

She met his gaze.

"Why did you say this is not a letter?" he asked gently.

"Because it's intended for someone who can never read it, someone who's dead," she answered.

"That's what makes it a letter."

"But she can't respond!"

Her father tilted his head to one side and looked thoughtful. "I don't know. I don't know," he said twice. "Who is to say she cannot?"

"But Enḫeduanna's been dead for thousands of years!"

"Yes, that's a long time to hold your peace. She must be bursting." He smiled, and she smiled back. "What do you think she would answer you, if she could?"

"I think she would write a poem."

"Then let her. Think of yourself as a stylus, and let her write through you, with you. When she is done, read what she has written."

"How will I know if it came from her, instead of just me making it up?"

"You won't. But then, are you sure you know when it's just you making stuff up?"

They sat together in silence for a while. Nabû-na'id recalled hymns of Enḫeduanna that he had heard since his childhood. It was said that she wrote the words but also made the tunes; and he wondered for the first time whether tunes could be written like words, whether they could be pressed into clay and told to endure. Or do tunes only survive when breath fills their sail and passes them gently from lip to lip? He started to sing. After a few moments, his daughter joined him.

Sometime later, Bel-šar-uṣur arrived, entered, interrupted their singing. "What are you doing?" he asked with the slightest hint of mockery.

"We are listening to Enḫeduanna," his sister replied.

The priestess cocked her head, listened intently. From far far away, from a crack in the mud wall of the cella, from beyond that crack something small and slow and almost silent, almost imperceptible, too subtle ever to be called perception or imagination or inside or outside or true or false or real or fake – the slightest thread of music – or else it was silence – a thread thinner than a spider's – if it was a thread at all. This was how the Moon god spoke to her. She called them loud silences; she called them the company of solitude. She took them within her, and she magnified them like all she was was a reflector of sound, sound building within her, simplicity and silence unfolding itself, building itself out of what it was not, faithful to what it was, building itself out of her, from her, with her, in her, building into her throat and into her mouth and into her tongue and into her lips and, past her teeth, bursting into song. Each time a birth, in anguish and delight.

And then she would gather it all up again, and with her delicate hands she would knead it, gently, relentlessly smaller, massaging it into tightness, compactness, folding and refolding it, never relenting but with exquisite tenderness refusing to yield, always pushing it back and letting it fall back towards smallness and slowness and silence, falling and falling and falling into falling, and always her delicate hands gently pushing it further and further away, far far away, so slow and silent and small now, so simple, there it is, finally, it is in the crack, a mere crack, in mud.

Or was it she who was born out of mud and returned to it, she who was nursed into sound and kneaded into silence, she who flit only from crack to crack?

If she were now in the crack, would not her empty cella be but another crack?

Is this what I am, an emptiness coursing through clay and leaving behind only its path which is itself emptiness?

Then: from far far away, from a crack in the mud wall of the cella, from beyond that crack, something small and slow and almost silent, almost imperceptible, too subtle ever to be called perception or imagination or inside or outside or true or false or real or fake – the slightest thread of music – or else it was silence. And as this came barreling towards her the priestess loosed her questions and let them flee, and she braced herself, caught as it were by a single thread of the spider, if there was a thread, if there was a spider, caught and waiting for what was to come. This was perhaps how the Moon god spoke to her, wrapping her in a shroud of invisible threads, drawing her close and closer and serenading her with soft clicks of his rhythmically blinking eyes, all eight of them, each one showing her a version of herself. And the doubt, once panicked, now tired: will this be able to unfold within me, will this silence find its way to my lips, or at last have we, the silence and I, been overtaken by silence?

* * * * *

Years passed.

* * * * *

Gubaru and Kayvan were at the door.

"Enter! Enter!" Niṭil-Kišar insisted, surprised. Mikum-Nisaba, little more than a teenager, quickly covered her face with a dark veil, which made of her face almost a flower on the white stalk of her robes. Fly rushed to the door, tail wagging. The men entered, Gubaru abashed, his son even more so, and were bustled to the center of the house, where they sat down. There were no attendants – an eccentricity of Nabû-na'id's home that Gubaru was used to. Only after Niṭil-Kišar had offered them refreshment did anyone speak. "You honor our house," she said. "You will always honor our house, you who have been so dear a friend to my husband and to us all. What may we do for you?"

Gubaru found his voice with difficulty. "I am sorry so to disturb you and your daughter," he began. "Kayvan, my son, had told me news that disturbed me, and I thought it important to bring it immediately to Nabû-na'id's attention. But I see he is not here."

"He will be back before long," Niṭil-Kišar assured him. "Do you wish to wait? You are welcome."

Gubaru looked at his son and realized he was blushing; he followed his son's gaze to the dark eyes of Mikum-Nisaba, the only part of her face that could be seen. The eyes were both mirthful and challenging, in spirit even more than color much like her mother's eyes, though the latter's veil did not hide the creases that years and experience had given them. And yet, her creased and weary eyes, Gubaru thought, were strangely the more compelling.

"No," Gubaru answered. "That would perhaps be – unnecessary." He was going to say 'unwise' but stopped himself just in time. "Do you know where I can find him?"

"I do not."

They were silent for a moment. Niṭil-Kišar vacillated between the delicacy that a hostess owes her guests and her curiosity and spiritedness. She made up her mind. "Gubaru, if you wish to confide in me, I can pass on your message to Nabû-na'id. You know, as I do, that we two" – she indicated Gubaru and herself – "are his most trusted confidantes."

Gubaru bowed slightly. "That my friend should trust me as much as he trusts you is a great honor to me. May it be so. But this message is not mine to deliver; it is Kayvan's."

"Ah," said Niṭil-Kišar. She turned to Kayvan. "You may do as you are comfortable, my son."

The boy blushed more intensely. Gubaru saw amusement flash across Niṭil-Kišar's eyes – and he shared in it for a moment, before touching his son on the elbow. "I imagine you would be more comfortable talking to Nabû-na'id? It is as you wish."

Kayvan gave his father a helpless look.

"Shall we go find Nabû-na'id?" Gubaru repeated kindly.

"Yes," the youth said, the words escaping as from a strangled man.

And so they rose and left, Mikum-Nisaba's dancing eyes following Kayvan all the while. She was exhilarated by a power she suddenly sensed – the power of touching someone with her gaze, the power of knowing that Kayvan felt her gaze even as he turned from her and walked away, stumbling, barely able to reach the door beneath her amused and confident stare.

When they had left, Niṭil-Kišar swept her own veil off. She turned to her daughter, carefully unveiled her and then, with a sigh, rested her hands on her daughter's shoulders. The two looked at each other in silence, the mother seemingly searching for something, her look sifting through her daughter's eyes like sand. Near the surface: mirth, challenge, a youthful delight in strength. But beneath it? Was there sorrow, anxiety, a knowledge of frailty?

Saying nothing, she gently kissed her daughter's forehead, her eyelids, her lips. "What, I wonder, will you give voice to?" she asked and turned away.

Nabû-na'id was walking with Belet-ṣeri-dannat along the inside wall. "There are days, my friend, when these walls do not seem defensive to me; they are not here to keep things out but to keep things in. To keep me in. And on those days I long to return to that hole I was digging in the middle of nowhere, unbothered by the concerns of petty and powerful men."

"It is an easily understandable longing," Belet-ṣeri-dannat observed.

"And you? Do you not ever long to leave, to return to the land of your fathers?"

"That day will come. My God has promised it to me. But only when I am old. Until then, I am to remain here."

"Do you find that hard?"

"I don't find it anything," Belet-ṣeri-dannat answered with a shrug. "Most of my world is gray, still and without relief; only when my God chooses to speak to me does it acquire color, shape and motion. It has always been thus, even when I was a boy. My father – the father of my childhood – used to tell me that I was already an old man as a child, as a little child."

"And yet you were also a thief."

"When I came here, yes; but even that was an old man's trick. A boy learns to survive on the street by ceasing to be a boy."

"What became of your brother? I mean, the brother of your childhood here, your adopted father's son."

"He's an official in the provinces somewhere, some sort of overseer or governor. I've never really bothered with him. I'm sure we'll both be happy if we never encounter each other again."

Nabû-na'id made an unspecific guttural noise and they walked a few steps together in silence.

It was Belet-ṣeri-dannat who broke the silence. "How go the king's campaigns?" he asked eagerly.

"Word from Ḫume has been good so far. As you know, last year Pirindu's king was put to flight but escaped. If I know my brother-in-law, he will pursue and bring an end to the matter this year. So long as there is time for fighting, he will fight. Even to no purpose."

"Did you advise him otherwise?"

"I have not advised him. He may once have thought he wanted a neutral man, but by now he's seen he can go far without one."

"Far, yes. Forever, no."

"It doesn't matter to me. I just wish his underlings would cease to consult with me too."

"What do they consult about?"

Nabû-na'id cocked an eyebrow and examined his friend. "You miss it all, don't you? For all your religious fervor, despite that grayness, stillness and shapelessness you spoke of earlier – you miss court life. How can that be?"

Belet-ṣeri-dannat grimaced. "Perhaps I do," he admitted grudgingly. "So?"

"A god speaks to you, and yet you miss the court!"

"The God speaks to me," Belet-ṣeri-dannat corrected. "At His whim. Whether I am lonely or busy or interested or bored. But of late, for a long while now, I have only been lonely and bored, and God has said nothing to me."

"Perhaps your god is saying something different to you, in a different way."

"No."

"You can be sure?"

"Yes. And don't ask me how."

"I won't. I know you don't know. Which may mean that you're wrong but doesn't preclude that you're right."

Belet-ṣeri-dannat's smile was pained. "I am right," he said stubbornly.

Gubaru hailed him. "Belet-ṣeri-dannat! Have you seen Nabû-na'id?"

"I was talking with him earlier."

Gubaru drew closer, a young man in tow. "Do you know where he went?"

"I do not."

Nabû-na'id entered the house. Niṭil-Kišar was seated in the center of the room, waiting for him. The sound of Mikum-Nisaba's singing voice could be heard coming from a back room.

"Gubaru came here looking for you," Niṭil-Kišar announced.

"Here? He came here?"

"Yes," she answered solemnly.

"What did he want?" he asked quietly, half to himself.

"It was his son – Kayvan, I think – who wanted to speak with you."

The two of them exchanged glances. "That's odd," Nabû-na'id remarked. "It must be important."

"Yes." She continued to look at him intensely.

After a moment, he said truthfully, "I don't know what this is about, Niṭil-Kišar."

"What do you think it's about?"

He sighed. "The same as you, my dear. The same as you." He turned towards the door. "If Gubaru returns, you'll know where to send him?"

"Yes."

"Ok." He started to leave but after only a few steps stopped. "Fly!" he yelled. "Fly!" A few moments later the dog came into sight at the street corner. "Come along," Nabû-na'id invited. "I could use some company."

"What an honor it is to have you here," Itti-Marduk-balaṭu proclaimed.

"I am looking for my son. Is he here?" Nabû-na'id found himself struck by the strength of the man's perfume.

"Bel-šar-uṣur? He was around earlier. Perhaps he still is. I'll send someone to find out." He gestured to one of the slaves. "Go see if you can find Bel-šar-uṣur," he commanded the man, without taking his eyes off Nabû-na'id. "My father would be delighted to make your acquaintance, after all these years. Shall I call him?"

"No."

Itti-Marduk-balaṭu smiled greasily. "You have never much liked our house, have you?"

"No. I have never much liked your house."

"Why?"

"That," Nabû-na'id answered, "is a good question. Your reputation, of course, precedes you, but I don't know if it's true."

"You have a reputation too, you know."

"Mostly a tapestry of hyperbole and misunderstandings. Perhaps," he conceded, "like your house's reputation."

"Indeed." The two men stood for a moment in silence, a silence that on Nabû-na'id's end was awkward, even while his counterpart seemed perfectly at ease.

"What does my son do here?" Nabû-na'id asked.

"Oh, odds and ends. Mostly he helps conduct negotiations. He's quite useful to us."

"I would have thought for negotiations a scribe would be more useful."

"Of course, scribes are useful too. Given your own background, I'm surprised your son isn't more of one. But no matter, he still has quite a lot of value to the house."

Nabû-na'id grit his teeth.

"While we wait, I hope you'll forgive my idle curiosity," Itti-Marduk-balaṭu began. "In our house your actions in Sardis all those years ago are really quite legendary – except no one really knows what you did. Not that people haven't had theories! I don't suppose you would take a moment to enlighten me?"

"No."

Itti-Marduk-balaṭu twisted his face into a mask of

exaggerated disappointment. “Well, I’m not surprised. Bel-šar-uṣur, of course, has told us a few things,” he paused, “– but I suppose it’s not my place to press you, a guest in my house, on such matters.”

Nabû-na’id stared ahead of him like a statue. “Bel-šar-uṣur wasn’t there either,” was all he said.

“Well, I guess I’ll have to save the little mystery for another day. I’m sure I’ll figure it out eventually. It’s the business of our house to get to the bottom of things. We seldom fail.”

“Perhaps there are more ways of failing than you realize,” Nabû-na’id observed.

“That’s only true if you fail to make your goal clear to yourself. No one has ever accused the House of Egibi of lacking clarity of vision.”

“Has it never occurred to you that such clarity might itself be a failure?”

Itti-Marduk-balaṭu laughed. “If so, it’s an indispensable one,” he said. Then he signaled to a slave, a different one than before. “Any sign of Bel-šar-uṣur?” he asked, again without looking away from Nabû-na’id.

“No, he left some time ago,” the slave answered.

“Ah. Too bad. I fear we’ve been wasting our time.” He bowed his head slightly. “My father will be sorry yet again to miss the opportunity of making your acquaintance.”

“Hmmph,” Nabû-na’id responded.

“Of course, when Bel-šar-uṣur returns, I’ll tell him you came here for him.”

“I’m sure you will.” Nabû-na’id whistled. “Come along, Fly.”

Together they strolled in silence for some time. Then Nabû-na’id sighed and spoke. “Well, Fly, I seem to have just lost a battle of wits, and I haven’t the foggiest idea what it was about.”

Fly wagged his tail encouragingly.

"That's probably why I lost," Nabû-na'id conceded. "Unclear vision."

Fly, by wagging his tail, allowed that that could be so.

"Or maybe that house grounds itself by making everything a game of which it's the master. You can be perfectly right in knowing there's no game, but by their rules, that means you lose. Which also means, in a certain sense, there was in fact a game."

That analysis seemed quite possible to Fly, so he wagged his tail.

"Once men learn that little trick – well, they end up with a House and no World. That's what I think. They end up saying 'The acuity of my vision defines what is real, and I am the ground that I stand on.' That's what they say, or at least think, and then they belittle all those silly folks who need a different ground, whether it's the priests or the king or their fathers. But they, these sophisticates who think they are game-masters because they alone know that nothing matters – they're the simpletons, the ones who've taken everything for granted, including that something in fact does matter."

"That's very much how we dogs have seen it," Fly's wagging tail seemed to say.

"Unless of course they're right."

Fly expressed his disdain for such a possibility by rushing off to smell and eat a fresh pile of manure, tail wagging all the while.

Nabû-na'id squatted to the ground and, leaning backwards against the side of a building, watched as Fly eagerly ate. Almost instantly he forgot what he had been ruminating about and in an idle blankness watched the dog. When the latter was done, he meandered his way back to Nabû-na'id and, wagging his tail, eagerly began licking his face. Nabû-na'id could smell the manure on his breath, but he made no effort to stop Fly. Instead, when Fly began to let up, he buried his own face into the dog's furry chest. "I am not sure if I know how to speak with you seriously," he confessed. "I am sure I don't know how to listen. Forgive me, Fly."

Judging by the way the dog wagged his tail, perhaps he did.

He was still squatting, with his head held against the dog and his beard smelling of manure, when his son found him. He was in his young twenties and loomed over his father like a demon, the sun at his back. "What are you doing? You're making a scene, sitting here in the dust, groveling to a dog."

Nabû-na'id looked up, squinting. "Am I?"

"Yes! People will know you for your mother's son."

"I *am* my mother's son," Nabû-na'id pointed out. "I'm not ashamed to be known that way."

"Do you think it's in your interest to be considered mad?"

Nabû-na'id didn't respond immediately as he collected his thoughts. His son didn't wait. "You know most people think she's mad."

"Really, most? Do you mean in Bābilim or throughout the four corners of the world?"

Bel-šar-uṣur sneered.

"Let's take a step back," Nabû-na'id said to his son. "You asked if I act like this because it's in my interest. That's the thinking of the House of Egibi. It doesn't have to be your thinking. A man doesn't have to conduct his life pretending it's a great big game with a single goal defined as winning. We can be more to each other and more to ourselves than game pieces."

Bel-šar-uṣur squatted beside his father. "Say what you like," he whispered. "But I know what you really are."

Nabû-na'id, who had been leaning against a building, abruptly rocked forward. "What do you think that is?"

Bel-šar-uṣur smiled. "If you must play this game even with me, your own son, very well. But you'll see that I can play too.

Whether or not you spy on me." He stood up, turned and with long, determined strides quickly walked away.

Gubaru hailed him. "Have you seen your father? We've been looking for him all day."

Bel-šar-uṣur barely stopped. "The last time I saw him, he was seated in the dirt talking to a dog." He brushed past them.

"When?" Gubaru called after him. "Where?"

But Bel-šar-uṣur didn't respond.

Niṭil-Kišar kissed him, then drew away. "Your beard smells like manure."

"Er… yes," Nabû-na'id acknowledged.

"Did you find him? Or did Gubaru find you? What's going on?"

"I still haven't found Gubaru. I did talk with our son, but it didn't go well."

"What happened?"

For an instant, Nabû-na'id's face gave a greater expression to his bewilderment than any speech could. Then he sighed and hunted for words. "I'm in an impossible position with him," he began. "He is openly contemptuous of me – such as I never was with my own father. I can imagine few other fathers tolerating it. But at the same time, he also seems to think I'm some great master spider secretly controlling with my invisible threads every twitch and jerk that happens in Bābilim. So I'm a contemptible insect – who controls the world. And when I tell him I don't control the world, he half-believes me and thinks that all I am, then, is a contemptible insect; but the other half of him thinks that I just don't trust him enough to let him in on the secret. Which makes me contemptible in another way."

"Am I to take it that you're *not* a spider?" Niṭil-Kišar asked, drawing away in mock disdain.

Nabû-na'id gave another long and tired sigh and pulled her closer to him – but not so close as to offend her with his beard. "The gods know what I am." He looked earnestly at his wife. "How did it come to this between me and our son? To what have I been blind, Niṭ?"

Niṭil-Kišar gave him a vexed look. "You have always shared your heart with me and with Mikum-Nisaba." She held his gaze and then said carefully, articulating every word, "But not with Bel-šar-uṣur."

At first he didn't respond. He looked at the ground, and it was as if from the ground that he drew the words which followed, slowly and falteringly, like they were very heavy and his grasp kept slipping. "When I tell you what is in my heart – you let it resonate within you. And when you answer I hear a chord that's part you, part me." He spoke softly. "Something that's both foreign and recognizable, and something that in turn resonates within me. I won't say all those chords are beautiful. They are not. But I trust that they are there, even – even! – when I cannot be sure I hear them." He paused for a long time. "With Mikum-Nisaba it's similar." Another pause, and then only in a whisper: "But with our son, I strike a note and all I hear is it dying far off in the distance. No chord resonates back toward me."

She said nothing.

"Is it that he doesn't respond, that my notes find nothing inside of him against which to strike? Or is it that I am deaf?"

With her hands she combed his hair off his forehead and smoothed it over his temples and ears. "It's both," she said simply. She held his face away from her and looked into his eyes. "You're no spider. You're a fly on your back, most of your legs ripped off because you've struggled with such hopeless ferocity. Mikum-Nisaba and I, we're a little smarter as flies go; we haven't allowed ourselves to be flipped on our backs, and we have all our legs. But because you can see us and see something of yourself in us you feel a real and true kinship that makes you less lonely and your plight easier to bear."

"And Bel-šar-uṣur?"

"Oh, he's the one nearest you. Since you're on your back and looking up, you can't see him. But he's lying not far from you at all, also on his back, not yet as delimbed as his father but on his way. And all these years he's heard you call out to me and to Mikum-Nisaba, and he's heard you reminisce with us about your days of flight – but when you speak of such things with him, not seeing that he too is on his back until forever ends, you treat him cruelly without knowing it. And he responds in kind."

"How did we end up like this?"

She shrugged.

"Let me ask you a question like he would ask," said Nabû-na'id.

"A good thing to attempt," she murmured.

"What use is your allegory? Am I to go to him and say, 'Son, it's come to my attention we're both doomed flies, and that's why there's so much tension between us…'?"

Niṭil-Kišar laughed. "It's what you would say to me!" she pointed out. "And to Mikum-Nisaba." She pursed her lips. "But yes, you'll need to find a different path to our son."

"Any advice?"

"Of a non-allegorical kind?"

"Yes."

"No," she answered.

Rumor spread like a grassfire, the flames at times barely burning and seldom leaping high. And yet in its wake almost every inch of ground was covered in a waste of ash. Was it true? Who could say? The messengers brought tablets of mud, but the mud did not speak. A man must be fetched – to speak for mud.

Of course the messenger himself could speak; he could say

what it was that he had heard from the previous messenger; and that previous messenger could say what it was that he had heard from the messenger before that; and perhaps there really was, long before these other messengers, a first or almost-first messenger who had received the message from the ruler's own dying breath. But that breath had never been enough, and so even that first messenger – if he ever existed – was entrusted clay, and only afterwards, the ruler's dying breath. Breath is always a gift to clay. Clay always precedes it – is molded and sculpted if only to receive in its cracks and crevices the breath it will contain. And clay always outlasts it, as from those cracks and crevices the breath withdraws, scatters, flees. The breath can say, in a fumbling, awe-struck whisper: "I am dead!" But no messenger can understand such a message. "Of course you're not!" the messenger whispers back, encouragingly. More urgent now, the breath, in a hiss: "I am dead!" And the messenger: "You'll be fine!" And the breath, now in a howl: "I am dead!" And the messenger, with a friendly smile: "Hush now and get some sleep." And so the breath instead surges or streams or trickles toward the mud, down and through its carved channels. The breath with its dying breath infuses the mud with spaces for its dying breath. "I am dead," the tablet reads; and the messenger peels it from the ruler's cold, now clay-like hands, shocked that the fellow took such a terrible turn, and heads off on his relay.

"Can it be true?" Belet-ṣeri-dannat demanded, his eyes flashing with excitement.

"Of course it can be true. But that doesn't mean it is true."

"They say the omens at the New Year's Festival were not good. And then he left the city so abruptly, so strangely."

"Who knows what that means."

"Have you seen the tablet?"

"Not yet."

"Do you think the messenger can't be trusted?"

"We'll see what the tablet says."

"And if it is true?"

"You don't need my help to answer that question, my friend."

"Are you going to the palace?"

"Of course."

"May I come with you?"

"Yes."

Through the chaotic throng, Gubaru grabbed his arm.

"Nabû-na'id! We MUST speak!"

"Even now?"

"Especially now!"

Nabû-na'id disengaged himself from Belet-ṣeri-dannat. "Wait for me at the palace," he said. Then he turned to his old friend and to his son, Kayvan, who was with him.

"What is it?" he asked, looking quizzically first at Gubaru, then at the youth. "What is your message for me?"

Kayvan told him.

"Bel-šar-uṣur!" his father roared. His son wheeled around, stunned to be roared at, and saw his father racing towards him. Before he could blink, Nabû-na'id had grabbed him by his shoulders, lifted him from the ground and pinned him against a wall. "Is it true? Is it true what I have heard?"

"What have you heard?" Bel-šar-uṣur answered uncertainly, squirming in his father's grasp.

"Have Nergal-šar-uṣur's estates been transferred to your name? Did you accept them before witnesses? Do the tablets bear your seal?"

"How could that be? Of course not. I – I was just part of a transaction, something Itti-Marduk-balaṭu arranged, as a favor for the House of Egibi. But it was a – a mere formality. I took an oath in front of witnesses and sealed it with my seal, but it didn't – it didn't matter. I was given nothing, nothing changed hands."

"There was a tablet. That's never nothing. Did you read it?"

His son looked sheepish. "No."

"But you still swore the oath? Not knowing what you were swearing for? Are you such a fool?"

Bel-šar-uṣur grew pale. "Why are you belittling me? What concern is it of yours?"

"You don't know what the tablet says, but it bears your seal. Witnesses will come forward. They don't care if you read the tablet, they only have to say you swore. And you did. And you don't know what for."

"People do this all the time. What's the big deal?"

"What's the big deal? Can you really not imagine how claiming the estates of a king immediately after he has died will look? Must I spell it out for you?"

Bel-šar-uṣur bit his lip as dawning comprehension – and apprehension – slowly spread across his face.

"That's right," his father said, his voice suddenly very quiet. "Labaši-Marduk's handlers will kill you. They'll have to." Then, for some reason, still gripping his son by his shoulders, seeing fear and anger in his son's face, he nonetheless found himself most struck by the mole on the arch of his son's left cheek.

"I need to speak to the head of the house. To Nabû-aḫḫe-iddina. Tell him Nabû-na'id has come."

He waited for a very long time.

Only as dusk was settling did the old man come. "Ah," he said. "Nabû-na'id. You finally honor me with a meeting." On his right stood his son Itti-Marduk-balaṭu.

"I do nothing of the kind. I honor you not at all. I have come for the tablet you tricked my son into signing."

"I am sure we have tricked your son into nothing. That is not the way of the House."

"Let me see the tablet."

"Of course, as a courtesy to an honored guest, I am happy to show you the tablet." With a slight inclination of his head he sent his son scurrying for the tablet.

"How long have you known about Nergal-šar-uṣur's death?" Nabû-na'id asked.

"A few days. It is the business of our House to know. Being aware of something a few days before everyone else – even something as small as that can be advantageous."

"Advantageous for what? What do you care if Labaši-Marduk rules?"

"Ah," the old man said. "That dear little thing? It's hard to imagine a boy so young as he will ever rule. What a trying time this must be for him."

Itti-Marduk-balaṭu appeared with the tablet and handed it to his father. His father gestured toward Nabû-na'id. "Give it to him, our honored guest. I am sure he would be careful not to break it, since there are no witnesses. A tablet broken without witnesses would help no one."

Itti-Marduk-balaṭu handed the tablet to Nabû-na'id. He read it and then, for a while, simply stared at it.

"I had heard you could read silently," Nabû-aḫḫe-iddina observed. "What a marvelous skill."

"How could you transfer estates belonging to Nergal-šar-uṣur to my son? How could that happen without a sale?" Nabû-na'id asked quietly.

"Well, there are a few other tablets your son was – party – to. I can get them for you. In fact –" he gave a slight wave to his son, "get them for our honored guest here." Itti-Marduk-balaṭu promptly departed. "While we wait, I can brief you on their content. Your son – let me compliment you on such a bright, ambitious young man – has laid claim to our former king's estates as a direct blood descendant of his grandfather Nabû-kudurri-uṣur, whose estates, after all, they once were. But, as you no doubt realize, Bel-šar-uṣur is not just a direct descendant; he is the oldest living male and hence, he claims, the rightful heir. Labaši-Marduk, of course, is another grandson, but a much younger one. I suppose the two of them and their partisans will have to duke it out." The old man looked evenly at Nabû-na'id and then, without inflection, added, "We can only pray they have the wisdom to do it before the judges. For it is a rare occasion indeed when all-seeing justice finds its view obstructed, wouldn't you say?"

Itti-Marduk-balaṭu arrived with more tablets and, at a gesture from his father, handed them to Nabû-na'id. Nabû-na'id again read them in silence. When he was done, he gave a hoarse laugh.

"You have made my unwitting son either a king or a dead man. Not that there's much difference between the two. As a king you'll play him like the toy he's let himself be; and as a dead man he is no concern of yours."

"Such harsh words! We may understand something of your son that you do not. Certainly we respect him highly in our House. Should he prevail in the disputes to come, I am sure we will be in good hands." The old man smiled a ghastly grin. "Perhaps you too would be wise to have greater faith in so enterprising a young man." He paused and, with a face crafted as of stone, stared coldly at Nabû-na'id. Then, seemingly as an afterthought, without the slightest inflection, he added, "And in his allies. No doubt, he will be in great need of them."

* * * * *

...he had only just begun when he came down with the fever which rendered him, some said mad, others prophetic. At one point in his agitation he insisted that on the wall before him was written his death: "The writing is on the wall! The writing on the wall! On the wall! Writing!" he kept exclaiming. And sometimes he said the wall was writing. But of course the wall was a wall, and no one else could see any writing on it. Only with great effort did they succeed in calming him; and by morning he was dead – which perhaps means that he read the wall properly. For in Babylon walls are held in high significance, and not just for their defensive value. A great hero of theirs, it is said, sought life everlasting, trekking to the last corners of the earth in search of it. But he failed. With time, while surveying the walls of one of their cities, Orekh, he reconciled himself to that failure. This is the immortality of man, he proclaimed: walls that, at his command, had been built, even if of mud; walls that protected and magnified his city, which was also his immortality; walls that both separated inside from outside and joined them. And one day, he said, these walls will disintegrate into the dust that made them, and of that dust, and of the dust which the city will then be too, and of the dust to which worms and maggots will have reduced even him, out of all that dust, gathered together in heaps and piles, a hill will rise, and grass will grow on it, and shepherds will graze their flocks there. So he said; and he said that that was what a wall was; and to prove it, he wrote something – some say an account of his life, others a prayer or a hymn, if any of these are different – and he buried it in the wall. But what was written has never been found. Perhaps, in the manner of a prophet, it was this writing, whatever it said, that Neriklassor saw.

And so in the fourth year of his reign, on the Syrian frontier far to the northwest of Babylon, Neriklassor had died, as Croesus' seer had predicted. When the news reached Babylon, the city was cast into turmoil. For the king's son was only a young boy, perhaps six or seven years old, and in no position to rule. And yet the faction that adhered to him quickly proclaimed him king, as the rightful heir of his father – a gesture undertaken, they said, out of loyalty, even though it assured the boy's destruction and the end of the king's line. For what else could result? The boy could not defend himself, nor could he fail to be a threat to whomever ruled, whether a man ostensibly his regent or an opponent. If the ghost of swift-footed Achilles was comforted by word of the exploits of his still-living son, how much worse for the ghost of a king to be served by a loyalty that blindly bequeathed only doom to his heir? For the kingdom's elite, and not least the members of the Egibatila, opposed the boy-king, either for fear that his reign would resemble the brief but disastrous one of Amelmarduk, or because they lacked influence with the boy or his handlers. And some say as well that fear of Lydia, on the one hand, and on the other, of the rising power of the Medes and of Persia – for Cyrus was already king of Persia and would soon be king of the Medes – led many to oppose the rule of a child when what was needed was the strength of a man.

Thus a second faction emerged and rallied behind the oldest male descendant in the Chaldean line still living. For recall that Neriklassor was not of this line, but his wife, the daughter of the former king, was; as was Labynetus's wife Nitocris. Each of these women had a single son, one being the boy-king Lapsimarduk, and the other, Nitocris's son and Labynetus's, Balsazor, who was much older. And it was this man Balsazor whom a faction supported as the rightful heir and true king.

Here it would seem that Labynetus outwitted everyone. For, with the Egibatila, he conspired against Lapsimarduk, and indeed, it is said, together they arranged the murder of the child, thus clearing the path for Balsazor. But even though the boy was too weak to protect himself, or even to survive, the faction gathered around him was anything but weak; and having no alternative candidate to support, they nonetheless still refused to support Balsazor, who despite being older than Lapsimarduk, was nonetheless far from an experienced man and, some thought, too much the creature of the Egibatila. And so the kingdom tottered on the brink of civil war, a prospect eagerly awaited by its northern neighbors. And here Labynetus revealed his cunning and got the better even of the Egibatila – a betrayal long in coming, some believe, for such unnatural allies, given the mistrust and antipathy between the two parties going back even to the boyhood of Labynetus in Sardis. For Labynetus proposed a compromise candidate as king: a man known to be unambitious, and already elderly – in his fifties or sixties; a reclusive scholar, though not inexperienced in the ways of governance; and by marriage related to both fallen kings, one his father-in-law, the other his brother-in-law, and whose son, when more mature and prepared for rule, would continue the Chaldean line.

In short, it was Labynetus whom Labynetus proposed, and thus snatched for himself, and from his very own son's already outstretched hands, the kingship.

* * * * *

"I am become the *šēdu*," Nabû-na'id whispered to Niṭil-Kišar. "Beware."

And then, as she held his head against her chest and stroked his hair, Nabû-na'id wept. "Beware, beware," he kept repeating.

Chapter 6. Fathers and Daughters

Once there was a gap-toothed, wire-haired, shepherd's runt with a wandering eye who met a foreign lackey and either ran off with him or was carried off. To his home they went, a forgettable man and a forgettable woman – to a home in a faraway outpost with a heaped-up rubble-pile that some called a wall. But through a strange and unlikely set of circumstances, a chieftain who called himself a king got involved and then another – and soon ships were launched to recover the girl and above all to recover her virtue, the kings in huts (now ennobled as palaces) meanwhile imagining gold, trade routes, courage and the songs men would sing. They also imagined men (but they never imagined their faces), and these men were willing to die for honor, friendship and virtue – and for a woman. But was that woman the woman they had come for? Who had they come for? Gradually, unbeknownst to anyone, that woman was re-invented, re-clothed and re-born; her garments became embroidered, her beauty legendary, her parentage divine. Now she was a queen in need of rescue, not a moley, angle-headed, gummy shepherd's runt. Her abductor was a prince, and the ships launched in her defense became ten thousand. These ten thousand ships then beached on a shore of a startled village behind a midden heap; and gradually the midden heap became a formidable wall, and the village a kingdom. Amidst all these transformations, day after day, mirabile dictu, *the village-kingdom withstood the attacks of what even then was becoming an age's worth of heroes; it withstood their raids which were glorified as battles; above all it withstood their jeering. In part because theirs was a futile assault of a village in order to take an imagined kingdom, the invaders always failed; and that failure stirred their rage until they hopelessly confused their power of siege simply with their power to kill and to die. Meanwhile the weak endured the strong out of mute hopelessness and impossibility – defenses more formidable than their wall. The girl herself was raped and killed in a raid in the seventh year, but no one noticed; and the village – but even the villagers started to believe it was a kingdom – was finally destroyed by fire in the tenth year, when, among a dozen or perhaps a thousand dozens of similar scenes, a ten-year-old orphan, gap-toothed, wire-haired, wandering eye, trying to escape the flames, was slaughtered in bleating panic like a lamb. Gold and trade routes were not found; no queen was found; courage, honor, friendship, virtue – of these there was a little; but what endures and will endure now and for what of time remains are the songs. Songs that praise the courage of the men who killed the orphan while besieging the kingdom that did not exist for a woman who was not beautiful enough.*

Were it for naught, it would not have been done; that it was done must mean it was not for naught.

* * * * *

He recalled a conversation he had had with Niṭil-Kišar long ago, when he was still more a scribe's son than a king's. "My mother used to tell me a story," he had begun, as he usually did, "about a queen named Naqi'a. She was the wife of Sîn-aḫḫī-erība and the mother of Aššur-aḫa-iddina, both of whom she survived. According to my mother, she ruled a region of the kingdom around Laḫira, after Bābilim had been destroyed by her husband. How it was destroyed, though, was at her urging. It was she who had the idea to flood the city, using the canals of the city against it. No less was it she who oversaw its rebuilding during the reign of her son. Perhaps like the gods she thought of a flood as the best way both to destroy and to create; perhaps like the gods her sleep had been disturbed by the boisterous banter of Bābilim, by the city's babel. More likely, though, by their tiresome revolts.

Like that Luddan king I once told you about, her husband had the fortune or misfortune of being in love with her, and under her influence he chose his youngest son – the son he had by her – as his and his kingdom's heir. It cost him his life, as two of his sons, including the former crown prince, conspired against him and murdered him in the temple of Sîn in Ninua. But his own chosen heir, Naqi'a's son, waged war against his brothers, avenged his father, and attained the throne promised him, at the cost only of a father, two brothers, and a paranoia which would engulf him for the rest of his days. How many times did omens force him into brief abdications of his throne to substitute kings, whose fates Aššur-aḫa-iddina made sure were fulfilled! And yet it was he, alone of the kings of Aššur, who conquered Muṣur, the land of the pharaohs – and he did this, it is known, with the blessing of Sîn. For he was passing through Ḫarrānu when that god declared an omen to him, that he would conquer all the world. This he did. But it is unclear to me whether the god was blessing or cursing him. Later a lowly slave-girl, also in Ḫarrānu, proclaimed herself a divine messenger and prophesied the destruction of the name and seed of Sîn-aḫḫī-erība. Revolt followed; Aššur-aḫa-iddina prevailed, though at the cost of most of his officials, whom he massacred out of mistrust, and of his sanity too. Muṣur took advantage and also revolted, and as Aššur-aḫa-iddina travelled there, he took sick and died – where else but at Ḫarrānu?

"My mother also claims, though she says this is secret knowledge, that Naqi'a like my mother was a devotee of Sîn, that her homeland, again like my mother, was Ḫarrānu, and that my mother is her direct descendant. As a result, says my mother, I belong to the royal line of Aššur, and I am at once of the name and seed of Sîn-aḫḫī-erība and of women more devoted to Sîn than to their husbands or sons."

"So yours is a cursed history of Aššur not of Bābilim?" Niṭil-

Kišar had asked, half-mockingly.

"The one is no less mistaken than the other," he had replied. "Perhaps mine is rather more a history of mothers than cursed fathers, or of wives instead of cursed husbands, or of daughters instead of cursed sons. Or perhaps my history, insofar as it is mine at all, is actually of women's single-minded devotion to Sîn, come what may to the men who tag along."

His mother stood before him in a private chamber of the palace. A very old woman now, she was in many ways remarkably unchanged. Still her garments were of mourning; still she bathed in dust and ash. Her gray hair had thinned some; her wrinkles had deepened; she was more bent over; but she still saw and heard; she still chewed her own food and walked on her own; she still prophesied and kept the rites of dead kings.

"*Šar pûḫi*," she said to him.

He raised an eyebrow.

"*Šar pûḫi*," she repeated. "You know the tradition?"

"Of course. When evil looms for a king – when, for example, Sîn, he who alone dares to block the sight of the Sun, himself retreats and disappears – a substitute is found, becomes king, rules as king, lives as king and, at the appointed time, dies as king. Prophecies that demand the appointment of a *šar pûḫi* never fail; they fulfill themselves."

"*Šar pûḫi*," she repeated a third time. "That's what you are."

"Mother," he answered tiredly, "that's what all kings are. All kings are substitute kings, stand-ins for a supposed real king who will appear again when the danger has passed. This is the heartbeat of kingship, this is its throbbing secret – that all kings are substitutes for that real king, maybe that ŠU king who may never come and may, for all we know, never have been. Substitute king, *šar pûḫi* – of course that's what I am."

His mother smiled, her grin wide but more gapped than

before. "Then hurry!" she urged.

"Hurry?"

"Restore Eḫulḫul, restore Ḫarrānu, before the ŠU king comes for you. Lead Sîn back to his temple, back to his city – lead him back by his hand, before he retreats and disappears. Before he abandons you."

"Before the ŠU king comes, not to replace me, not to claim his throne, but simply to lead me away."

"Yes. Before that."

"Does it bother you, Mother, that I shall be destroyed?"

"The god's temple has been destroyed. His city has been destroyed. I have kissed the hands that destroyed them. Are you the god's temple? Are you the god's city?" She leaned closer to him. "Life the gods kept for themselves. You remember? Life they kept for themselves."

"I remember," he murmured. "Gilgameš learned that from a tavern keeper, but he didn't believe her, not at first."

His mother clutched his wrist. "Life the gods kept for themselves," she repeated, "but to us they gave afterlives. We don't get to live, we live-after. In clay. In walls and tablets and temples and cities. That is our excess of life that we never had, our overlife, our afterlife. In clay, like I am always in clay; in dust like I am always in dust. Sîn is the god of that."

Nabû-na'id thought for a moment, his mother still clutching his wrist. "Sîn is the god of reflections, of specters, of substitutes. He is the god of all of us who are substitute kings. All of us, kings and non-kings alike, are substitute kings."

"Yes," his mother said solemnly, her eyes dancing madly at the same time. A moment later she released his wrist from her claw-like grip.

"Restore Eḫulḫul, restore Ḫarrānu," she resaid. "Hurry."

He had been sitting alone on his throne. It seemed ridiculous to him, and so he got up and sat in the dirt beside it. Any less ridiculous, was it? No, but there he sat. He was thinking about the omen of Gilgameš, which he had dreamed all those years ago. Had that dream foretold his own fate? Had he misread it? The ŠU king – King That – was it he?

Why was this Gilgameš's omen? Because he had striven more than any other man and failed more than any other man, and reconciled himself to that failure, and tried thereafter to rule wisely? Or because he hadn't failed but had succeeded in the only way a man can – by dying, by becoming king of the dead when what he sought was to live forever?

Which of these options best fit his case? Was he the broken man endeavoring nonetheless to rule well? Or was he the butt of the gods' jokes, the one given immortal death when he sought immortal life? Or were these really not two cases but one, different perspectives on a single, unified, whole man?

A single, unified, whole man broken into bits, like the pottery sherds that over time pile up as hills and mountains – that become, over time, the only ground there is beneath our feet.

He remembered another tale he used to tell, of a king he called Izdubar who found a black cat and was enchanted by her. As he sat beside his throne, all alone, he tried to conjure that cat or at least to conjure her muted purring, the way her claws painfully kneaded his flesh, the warmth and weight of her body as she slept on his lap and the smell of her breath. He held her there, this tenuously drawn memory or creation or being of fragments, he held her there though she was not there, and sitting alone on his throne of dirt with a ghost on his lap he helplessly wished that he could weep. But he could not.

King That, keeper of the dead.

They walked slowly down the street, Fly and Nabû-na'id. Under their feet crunched the debris of the city – pottery sherds, broken mudbrick, food waste and human waste from each house as they passed. Dogs and pigs rooted about, gobbling what they could find, sometimes something living, sometimes something dead, sometimes something else. For the most part, people ignored the animals, but every now and then a dog or a pig would cross some invisible line and a person would charge them, shouting and brandishing a stick. The animals would move on, not especially bothered. The house doors, most of them red, were often open in the morning, in part to help cool down the house, in part to let light in, since only rarely did a house have windows on the first floor. Most of the dogs and pigs knew better than to enter – as did most of the people. Rest assured a door was open only if someone was waiting inside. At the threshold there were also often figurines, frequently dog statues but sometimes demons, and these did a good or at least an adequate job of checking would-be intruders. The second story windows were also open, again for the light and the still-cool morning air, and pigeons sometimes perched on their sills, eying the passersby warily and prepared suddenly to panic and flap en masse into the air, where an initial chaos of wings would gradually soothe itself into circling birds and eventually resettle on the sills. A cat in the shadows might watch them, motionless, intent, for now lazy. People, mostly men, bustled about and, no matter where you were in the city, you would hear more than one language and see the costumes and colors of far-off lands. Some people tried to sell things right there in the street, though others would open shop along the wharves and a few main avenues instead. The canals were never far distant, the big ones with bridges or ferries for crossing. The water in them slid along languidly more than it flowed, birds sometimes drinking or bathing or pecking invisible insects from the air. On the water's surface you could see the reflection of the sun and sometimes of the houses nearby – slightly ruffled as the water slid past – and the shadows of insects, otherwise not visible, betrayed them on the canal floor. Take the water away, and most of the insects would disappear, too – but first the birds, then the dogs and the pigs, and eventually the people would soon follow them to wherever the insects had gone. And of course all the green plants, the grasses and reeds and date palms, would brown and yellow and fade into a backdrop that became once more more dirt than life. The houses, too: they would crumble, they were always already crumbling, but once the water left, no one would stay to repair them, and there would be no mud to repair them with. Only the streets would thrive once the water left, and then only for a while. No street thrives untraveled.

The houses were made of square mudbrick, each side the length of an adult forearm. The floors were stamped dirt, but sometimes a person with time on their hands would collect stones and make the floor cobbled. Under the dirt or the cobblestones lay the family's dead – generations past but also future generations cut short: the still-born babe buried in a jar, the infant or toddler succumbed to disease or malnourishment or the sting of a scorpion. Both babe and toddler were buried alongside grandparents, great-grandparents, and generations even further back than these. Figurines were buried too, often at the threshold. Some care had to be taken not to bury the figurines with the people, that is, not to unearth the people. Let the people, let the dead, let the past, stay earthed. In that earth, stamped into that dirt, were the family's history, the family's ghosts and the family's failed hopes, alongside small statues that never decayed to bone but sometimes, like the bones themselves, decayed past bone to dust. The very dust which, combined with water and grass and the heat of the sun, would become a future mudbrick, the wall born of the floor. Sometimes Nabû-na'id imagined messages passing between the figurines and the dead, perhaps carried by crawling insects, by worms or beetles, or by the slow spread of water underground or even by the offerings that the living poured for the dead. Sometimes he even imagined the sympathy which a statue could have for the dead – the desire to protect, to defend fiercely, these fragile beings who turn to dust so quickly; and he imagined as well the comfort that a dead child might feel knowing a dog lay near, guarding the entrance. Or perhaps the comfort came from knowing that it was a statue which stood guard? And did any of them derive comfort from the sound and pressure of feet walking above them, the babel of human voices, the trickle of light that seeped down the cracks in the floor? Or is oblivion the fate of all beneath the ground? One looks into the eyes of a statue and sees blankness – not even one's reflection. And dust doesn't even have eyes, so it doesn't even have blankness. It's blanker than that.

How is it, wondered Nabû-na'id, that I stroll with my living dog past these houses of mudbrick, and torment myself with what lies beneath their floors? How is it that I more easily imagine the insects turning flesh to dust, and the statues keeping watch, than the ways of the living within, not underneath, the walls? There Fly trots, inspecting who knows what in a street throbbing with life, but I, king of it all, only wonder about messages rolled like dung by beetles between corpses and inert figurines. It is I who belong in the ground, who should molder there and await a response to all that I ever managed to gather up into what I at least call a message.

He pointed to the ants. "Have you ever thought how alike we and the ants are?"

His son looked in the direction indicated but said nothing.

The ants were streaming back and forth along a narrow column, the procession at once orderly and purposeful. They disappeared from view in the shrubbery a few paces away.

"Have you?" His father repeated.

"No," Bel-šar-uṣur answered sullenly.

"If you are to be king, you shall have to think about how we are all like the ants."

"Yesterday it was flies."

"Yes, that too."

"And before long, it will be dogs and cats. And why not the *mušḫuššu* or the *kusarikku* too?"

"Yes, that's right. That's the way to go."

"Is this a joke?"

It was his father's turn not to respond.

"If you want to prepare me for the kingship, let me attend your deliberations. Give me a voice at the councils. Let me learn to be a general. But enough with flies and ants and your fetish for the obscure and the insignificant."

His father acted as if he hadn't heard. "What interests me about the ants," he observed, "is how imaginative they are – and how unimaginative they are. So fine a column as they have made over there, divided into two lanes with those going on one side and those returning on the other – and if you look closely (which you haven't), you'll see most of the returning ants are carrying something in their jaws, I think perhaps the young of a different nest – all of it suggests imagination, especially (if I am right) the carrying away of the eggs from the other nest. They imagine the order to which they adhere, and the purpose which they serve. They imagine what those eggs will become. Food, perhaps. Or maybe foster children or even slaves. All of it imagined, as each one says to himself, 'I shall go to that particular place where there is a certain thing, and I shall bring it back here.' Pure poetry. Even more poetic if they think "here" is home… It is a wonder that we aren't more commonly mesmerized by such astonishing creativity."

Bel-šar-uṣur was silent. After a while, his father resumed.

"But for all this imaginative prowess, does anyone ever break rank? There they go from one place to another, in a terribly straight line – and to the right and the left, and above them and beneath them – the entire world! Endless in every direction. It would seem that their vivid imagination, the one giving them order and purpose, is also what distracts them from imagining any other possibility. You look at them and it's almost a sense of pity that they inspire, alongside the wonder. Ants are capable of such great things – and yet that greatness is achieved precisely by an absolute blindness, an absolute lack of imagination, regarding a world almost endlessly rich in possibilities. What invites our respect also invites our pity. They are such accomplished, handicapped beings. So terribly handicapped, so terribly accomplished. Just look at them!" He pointed excitedly. "That such puny beings take themselves seriously is at once comical and inspiring – and all the while, the source of their strength is their absolute weakness. So impressed by the rich world they've made their own, they paradoxically can't begin to imagine the richness of the world."

"They're ants. They know nothing of the world," Bel-šar-uṣur said dismissively.

"Yes, exactly my point," his father answered.

"Then why are you wasting our time speaking of ants?"

His father raised his eyebrows. "Oh, I thought I already said why. Because –" he looked directly at his son "– you are an ant. Like your father, my boy, like your father. Just an ant."

"You are the king of Bābilim. Why is your first concern to marry your daughter off to a commoner?" an exasperated Belet-ṣeri-dannat demanded.

Nabû-na'id gave him an impatient and, at the same time, ironic look. "Really. Is that how it seems to you that I have spent my time? I passed the summer not campaigning in Ḫume, despite all appearances and the inexorable royal propaganda, but in reality husband-hunting among barbarian peasants. And, here in Bābilim, when I have done my ritual duty before gods I no longer recognize, no doubt it was in order to better examine the local bumpkins. And in your view, I take it, when I have heard sorry dispute after sorry dispute, each time snatching at what shred of wisdom remains in these pitiful lives of ours, it was in the hope that a suitable commoner would appear before me, a man I could properly disgrace my daughter with? What a strange man and even more strange king am I."

"I don't deny you've done your royal part. But marrying your daughter to a commoner is not an option for a king. You must keep your daughter for the hand of someone else, someone whose friendship is almost as valuable as his threat is dangerous. Kirsus, perhaps; or Ištumegu; or that upstart Kuraš."

"You are foolish to think any of the three will hold back because of a marriage tie. These are men who eat men, their brothers, their fathers and their friends. And you would have me be like them."

"Of course not!"

"You would have me eat my daughter. You would have me sacrifice her at a profane, political altar. I will not."

"It is not a question of sacrifice or of – eating. It is a question of reality. As you well know. Or am I deluding myself, and it wasn't you who all those years ago secured our border with the Luddans and the Umman Manda through a dynastic marriage?"

"It wasn't me."

"You can't possibly deny it!"

"That man – who I rather like from afar – was a stargazer and a poet and, above all, a youth unequal to his circumstances.

But that man also is no more."

"You are he!"

Nabû-na'id stared evenly at Belet-ṣeri-dannat, his eyes, as they ever were nowadays, at once distant and tinged with irony. "Are you still a street-thief?" he asked quietly.

"I no longer thieve; but I am the man that boy became."

"But the boy is no more."

"I am that boy, grown up."

"No, no… At best you are the figure of that boy. That's all. The boy slipped away, from his captor-father, from his jealous brother, from himself not least of all. He now wanders all by himself in his utter lonesomeness, an exile in a foreign land, perpetually hungry and invisible to all." He stared ahead of him. "We are all of us killers of boys."

Belet-ṣeri-dannat put his hand on Nabû-na'id's arm and for a moment said nothing. "God demands us to make sacrifices that we can bear only with His help," he finally observed.

Nabû-na'id tolerated the hand on his arm and continued to look away.

"Do you not realize that the truer horror is how much we bear without God's help? How much that ought to be unbearable is nonetheless bearable, in fact is easily bearable, is thoughtlessly bearable… Perhaps there is nothing so awful that it could be borne only with the help of God. An unbearable possibility – but look, I bear it, no god in sight."

"Those are words of despair."

"Are they? And what of your counsel to whore my daughter to some power-hungry prince? Which of us is the more despairing?"

"And marrying her to a commoner would be different? It's only whoring if it's a prince?"

Nabû-na'id slapped him across the face. Then, looking down, speaking slowly and articulating each word carefully, he stated, "I have every reason to believe that Kayvan and Mikum-Nisaba would be good to each other. If I did not," he continued to articulate slowly and carefully, "I would not permit her to marry." He looked up at Belet-ṣeri-dannat, who returned his gaze angrily. "Now get out."

"Will she marry him?" Niṭil-Kišar asked.

"I don't know. The court, even my friend Belet-ṣeri-dannat, wants to save her for a political marriage. They are doing everything they can to throw obstacles in the way."

"And you?"

"What do I want?"

"Yes."

"I want what's best for her, Niṭ. If I only knew what that was. The life of court – as you know, I hate it. It is hard for me to imagine it could be good for her. But I may have a responsibility to try to imagine just that – a responsibility not to the state, but to her. And so far I can't get myself to." He took a breath and looked at his wife. "What do you think?" he asked in a low voice.

"I like Kayvan, for all his shyness. I think he is like his father – deep-feeling even if not deep-thinking, reliable, fair. He will not understand much of what she says, but there will be many times, even without knowing it, that he will understand what she feels. That is not nothing."

"Is it enough?"

"Who is to say?"

"It has worked out for us, hasn't it?"

Niṭil-Kišar smiled, but there was something sad as well as joyous in the smile. "Sometimes," she said.

"Do you know how I courted your mother?"

"You spoke of flies," she said. "And she kicked a burning ember at you."

"Yes."

"But you didn't really court. It was arranged by the king. Whether either of you wanted it."

"The second part is true. But that doesn't mean I didn't court your mother, or that she didn't court me. Do you know how she disguised herself, slipped away, so we could talk in private – the one and only time we ever had that opportunity before we married?"

"No, she never told me that."

"Perhaps she didn't want to scandalize you. Your mother understood even as a girl that knives always cut two ways."

"What do you mean?"

"A veil protects a woman's modesty, controls and limits how she can present herself to the world; but it also preserves her anonymity – which of course becomes an opportunity to present herself to the world differently."

His daughter thought for a moment, then laughed. "She switched places with someone, didn't she?"

Nabû-na'id smiled, both at his daughter's laughter and at the memory. "Yes. So I misspoke when I said she disguised herself. She escaped, as it were, by not disguising herself, which in a certain context was disguise enough."

"Why are you telling me this?" Mikum-Nisaba got to the point.

"I am inclined to arrange a marriage for you with Kayvan, a man I have come to know and respect, the son of a man I have known my whole life and who, after your mother, I count my closest friend. By the standards of the world, it is not an advantageous marriage. Now especially, you could be married instead to a prince in some foreign land –"

"The fate of Ḫumati," his daughter said with a mixture of disdain and pity.

"– or to virtually any noble in our own land. Would that be

better for you – I am doubtful. A man who will treat you well and seriously, who will respect you and whom you can trust – that is ultimately what I seek, and that I think I have found in Kayvan."

"But of course I will do as you wish," Mikum-Nisaba murmured, her head bowed.

"I know you will." He stopped for a moment. "But perhaps you should discuss with your mother –" the suggestion emerged with an unexpected and almost endearing awkwardness "– how to confuse attendants and, er… satisfy your own mind." He paused, then added, "To the degree that you can in such matters, which is a small degree."

"You're saying…?" Her eyes had a mischievous glint.

"Get advice from your mother." He grinned sheepishly. "That is all that I am saying."

They were in one of the palace's smaller rooms, he and Gubaru. He longed for the strolls he used to take of old, he and Gubaru and Fly, wandering willy-nilly through the city and discussing whatever came into their heads. It was only with great difficulty that a king could undertake such a stroll, under circumstances which basically undid the stroll's appeal. In his own mind, this restriction was an example of what he called his veil, through which he would, he imagined, sometimes with an almost claustrophobic panic, henceforth forever see the world.

Although there were chairs in the room, they were seated on the ground beside each other, their backs to the wall. Fly was there too, lazily lying on his side.

Gubaru was uncomfortable. His fidgeting said as much as his words, and his words were simple: "I am uncomfortable."

"I am not surprised."

"It is very unorthodox."

"They should meet and know each other a little before we

sentence them to a life together."

"But it is unsupervised!"

"Do you trust your son?"

"Yes!" he said with pride.

"And I my daughter." There was pride in Nabû-na'id's voice too.

"It would be scandalous if anyone ever found out."

"Yes, I suppose," Nabû-na'id agreed. "Let us hope no one does." They sat in silence for a moment before Nabû-na'id added, "It will be scandalous in any event."

Gubaru didn't respond at first, instead continuing his fidgeting. At last he began, "We are friends since childhood. But I am nothing more than an old military man who's good nowadays for only the odd task here and there. My son is like me – what he appears and nothing more. Why –"

Nabû-na'id interrupted him. "There is no one who is only as he appears and nothing more. Would that it were otherwise!"

Gubaru looked at him strangely but resisted the urge to dispute him. He continued, "Why would you want your daughter to marry my son? She could be a queen! Is it as a favor to me that you do this? As a favor to my son?"

"I can speak for myself that being given a king's daughter in marriage is no simple favor. It has landed me in prison, imperiled my life and in some ways ruined it. Though Niṭil-Kišar has been the greatest gift of my life too – alongside you, my friend. No, it isn't as a favor to you or your son that I pursue this marriage. I can marry her to men who see her as a steppingstone to the throne, a dreary life for her and a threat to me and especially to Bel-šar-uṣur. Or I can send her away to a foreign land, never see her again, and comfort myself that in so doing I secure a border and an ally. As if brother never killed brother, or uncle nephew." He paused for a long time, staring fiercely at the ground. Then, looking up at Gubaru: "Is it so strange to want something different than that for my daughter?"

"No," Gubaru answered softly, "it is not so strange."

Nabû-na'id, as if he hadn't heard, continued intensely, "Is it mad for me to look for a husband who might also become Mikum-Nisaba's friend?"

"No," Gubaru again answered softly, "it is not mad."

"But perhaps it is! Look at what I have become, Gubaru! I am a king with blood on his hands, a man who followed as his thread through the labyrinth not best or worst but better or worse – as it seemed to me – and it has led here, to this corner, with blood on my hands. Around the next corner, what will I find? Who would dare be the friend of a *šēdu* in its lair? Who would the *šēdu* dare befriend? Is there a way to deliver those I love from the labyrinth where, because of me, they find themselves?"

Gubaru had no answer.

"Your son is not what he appears, Gubaru. He is the light of day seen through a crack in the wall. He is, I hope, my daughter's escape." Then, hunching forward and speaking to the ground, in a ragged whisper, he added more to himself than Gubaru, "Or he is another thread in the labyrinth."

"Where have you been?" Bel-šar-uṣur demanded.

"Out," she answered simply.

"Unattended?"

"Of course not."

"Then where are your attendants?"

"They shall be in shortly. They came with me to the gate, then I sent them on an errand. Surely you don't object to my travelling from our gate to our door unattended?" Her voice conveyed a fraction of the ironic contempt that her eyes expressed.

"You are not your own. You think you are, but you are not.

You are destined for a king's harem – and any breach in decorum could compromise that."

"I wonder what a breach in decorum looks like, what kind of wall decorum is that it can be breached."

"I'm serious!"

"You think you are, but you don't know what you're talking about. I'm not destined for a king's harem, Sîn be praised." She said it matter-of-factly.

Her brother cocked his eyebrow. "Of course you are," he said.

"Nope." She shook her head.

"For what are you destined then?" he asked carefully.

She laughed provocatively. "You haven't heard?"

"I've heard nothing."

"Well, then," she teased, "perhaps nothing has really transpired, if that's what you've heard."

"What are you talking about?" he demanded, an edge to his voice.

"Clearly I'm talking about nothing, or else you would have heard – something." She gave him a haughty look. "Now stop bullying me. Surely the prince of Bābilim has more important things to do."

He stalked out, angry.

He had not gone very far when he saw Kayvan walking before him. And suddenly he was struck by a wild idea.

"Father, I think Mikum-Nisaba may be – carrying on."

Nabû-na'id paused for a moment, and then, without looking up, continued working on his clay tablet. "Oh?" he said without much interest.

"I mean, I think she might be carrying on – with a man. With Kayvan, Gubaru's son."

Again Nabû-na'id paused, for longer this time. He still

didn't look up, however. "Surely her attendants wouldn't let that kind of thing go on," he stated matter-of-factly.

"I'm serious, father! If I'm right, you won't be able to arrange a marriage for her. No prince or king will take a damaged woman."

"Do you have reason to think your sister is damaged?"

"I told you," Bel-šar-uṣur exclaimed, exasperated, "I think she's carrying on with Kayvan!"

Nabû-na'id at last looked up. "And that's damaging how?" he wondered with deliberate blandness.

Bel-šar-uṣur just glared at him. "A king's daughter marrying a nobody… Of course that wouldn't bother you, what was I thinking? You'd have no objection if she married Fly!"

"To that," he answered slowly, "I would object. Even if he's otherwise an excellent companion, I doubt Fly would be a decent husband for her. But is there reason to doubt Kayvan would be? He strikes me as a good man, even a man you could wisely learn from. Do you have reason to think otherwise?"

The two men looked at each other in silence for a while, the father's expression nonchalant and otherwise inscrutable, the son's fuming. After a while, Nabû-na'id returned his attention to his tablet. His son left.

Anzû bared his taloned paw. "Speak!" he demanded. Nabû scratched the ground with his clenched, claw-like hand. "Speak!" Anzû screamed. "Use words!" But in response he heard only scratchings in dirt and in a tongueless throat while Nabû, grinning toothlessly, drooled and squatted, scratching and scratching and only scratching the ground.

* * * * *

From the [fragmentary] Assyrian Accounts of Herodotus

...With the marriage impending, Balsazor set aside his opposition and reconciled himself to his father's choice. Indeed, as a gesture of reconciliation, the king's son invited Kauphon, the son of Gobryas, to hunt with him – just as he did according to the other account. "What are we hunting for?" Kauphon, who was an accomplished spearman, asked. "Whatever game we find!" Balsazor answered. "Who knows? Perhaps we will encounter a namaxum *or even a* siddu," *he exclaimed, laughing and slapping Kauphon on the back. So they went together on the hunt. They had gone only a little way when Balsazor asked Kauphon, "Have you ever hunted the* namaxum?" *"Of course not," the young man answered. "No one has ever hunted the* namaxum. *It is a beast of myth, not a beast of the wild." "And yet our old king thought he had found one and was one," murmured Balsazor. They went a little way further. "Have you ever hunted the* siddu?" *Balsazor asked Kauphon. "Of course not," the young man answered again, this time with a nervous laugh, before repeating himself: "No one has ever hunted the* siddu. *Like the other one, it is a beast of myth, not a beast of the wild." "And yet our current king says he is one," murmured Balsazor. After that they continued in silence until, late in the day, they roused a lion. Then the two men fought the lion; Balsazor threw his javelin but missed while Kauphon bravely stood his ground and speared him expertly from close range. "Bravo!" Balsazor congratulated Kauphon as he picked up his misthrown javelin. "You are clearly a man of strength and courage. And look! Your reward is that you have killed a* namaxum, *even though you thought it was a myth." "But it is a lion that I killed!" Kauphon responded in confusion. "No, look at it more closely," Balsazor urged. "You killed a* namaxum, *even though you thought it was a lion." "But it IS a lion," Kauphon insisted. "How can you tell?" Balsazor asked.*

"Could not a namaxum *look like a lion," he continued, "just as a* siddu *can look like a man?" Then Balsazor drove his javelin into Kauphon. The stunned youth fell to the ground in agony. Balsazor, setting his foot against the fallen man's chest, wrenched his weapon free and then, leaning over the dying youth, whispered, "Now the question is, has a man just killed a* siddu *or has a* siddu *just killed a man?"*

This is the account, I am told, that has been passed down in the Egibatila all these generations, and that they say was first spoken – though I find this hard to believe – by the lips of Balsazor. Certainly the other and not this one was the official account. And while the one is scandalous and the other not, perhaps such a detail too much diverts the eye – for the accounts agree on the principal facts, both that Balsazor's javelin missed the lion and that it struck instead his companion. It is this last, whether or not embroidered with scandal, which is surely the chief fact, the one for which Kauphon died. Perhaps to judge whether those events, known at most to two men and perhaps not even them, were purposeful or accidental – and to think that this matters – is no less extraordinary than to distinguish man and siddu, *lion and* namaxum.

* * * * *

Nabû-na'id told Gubaru himself. Then they wept, side by side. Who was father, who was friend – no man could say.

Nabû-na'id and Niṭil-Kišar together told Mikum-Nisaba. The girl responded with silence, a shocked expression on her suddenly pale face. Then abruptly she turned and with hurried steps retreated to her quarters. Her mother followed.

Mother and daughter said nothing. But when Mikum-Nisaba bathed herself, her mother helped her, washing her back and her long, dark hair. Without being asked, her mother gave her the fragrant oil, and she anointed herself. Then, silently, her mother brought her the royal white robe, and in it the girl covered her naked, sweet-smelling body. Together, wordlessly, they made ready her dowry. When she draped around her neck the precious lapis beads, it was her mother who tied the clasp in back. Then the girl started toward the door. "Not yet," her mother said, breaking the silence. She went into a back room that connected to her own chambers, then returned a moment later. She held something in her hand. "You must have this as well," she said, giving it to her daughter. It was a cylinder seal, one which long before Niṭil-Kišar had had specially made for Mikum-Nisaba.

When they at last opened the door to the courtyard, the moonlight streamed into the room. Nabû-na'id stood up – he had been waiting, seated against the wall. Fly also stirred – he had been waiting too. For a long time, no one spoke, as the moonlight streamed into the room, filled it, overflowed.

"I am ready for my marriage now," Mikum-Nisaba said quietly.

Nabû-na'id's expression betrayed his helplessness and pity.

"Marry me," the girl said distinctly, "to the Moon." And then at last her self-control snapped. Crumpling into her mother's arms, she sobbed. Nabû-na'id, broken-hearted, watched from far, far away.

She wrote in the clay. Then she rolled her seal, named for the image it impressed, Ea-in-a-boat, over the writing. She wrote on top of that. Again she rolled her seal, Ea-in-a-boat, over the writing. The words obliterated the image; the image obliterated the words.

She did this all morning, all afternoon.

"If everyone writes," she thought, "that does not mean nothing is lost." Again she wrote. Again she rolled her seal, Ea-in-a-boat, over the writing.

"Lost without a trace," she added.

She spoke her thoughts to her mother.

Her beautiful eyes, more worn and tired, burning less bright, full of sorrow and protest, resignation and courage, held her daughter's gaze.

"We cannot know if anything is lost without trace," she said simply. "That it is, or that it is not."

Her father taught her the *Namburbi* ritual, the ritual by which he – no one else – honored the dead. "Even now, after all these years, it is not merely that I would provide food and water for my father's ghost. Far more important is that it is the moment when I would remember him, when I would offer myself to him that he may live through me."

Mikum-Nisaba touched her father's shoulder. "How can you tell that you're remembering him and not forgetting him?" she asked quietly.

After a long silence, he answered. "You can't."

"I will do no *Namburbi* ritual," she said.

Ea set sail; the Lord of the Earth set sail; Ea, the God of the Waters, set sail for the Underworld. He was the God of Wisdom.

A storm buffeted him; windswept debris like flies swarmed him; huge hailstones like attacking turtles battered him. He was the God of Wisdom.

The waters nipped like puppies at his boat's keel; the waves bit his boat's stern like wolves; his bow was devoured by lions. He was the God of the Waters.

The strips of his sail shook like reeds on the shore; his mast snapped like a stylus; he sank through the waters and settled into the clay like a sign. He was the Lord of the Earth.

"She wishes to be a priestess of Sîn."

"We haven't consecrated a priestess of Sîn in a thousand years," the temple official said.

"It is what she wants. It is what I want. Make it happen." Nabû-na'id tried to sound imperious.

The official gave him a calculating look. "We can't just make up a rite, your Excellency, as I'm certain you realize. This is not simply a question of our own preferences or desires. This is a question of the gods."

"Surely you concede that once we consecrated priestesses to Sîn?"

"There is reason to think so, yes – but we have no tradition anymore. We don't know how to do it."

"Then search the archives!"

"Of course we are happy to do so. It is undoubtedly the task of years."

Nabû-na'id was silent for a moment. Then, without much hope, he suggested, "Why not just do something like we do for the other priestesses?"

"If that is your wish, then why not have your daughter serve Ištar instead? That is the traditional role for a king's daughter, and it is a tradition that we know well and that has served us well all these many years."

"And it can't be adapted toward the service of Sîn?"

The man looked at him with a shocked, or else ironic, expression. "Of course," he asked, "you do not think it is merely a matter of substituting names?"

In the assembly of the gods, Enlil slept – do not disturb him! Ea, his place was empty; Nabû, his place was empty too; Šamaš was blinded; the naked Ištar hung from a meat hook; Sîn shined in his throne; beneath his gaze, playing in the dirt, Nabû.

"Who are you?" the king demanded.

"I am Nabû-zer-lišir, the scribe. I am tasked with the excavation of the temple foundations, the Egipar in Uru, in advance of its restoration."

"Oh," Nabû-na'id responded disinterestedly.

The scribe was visibly discouraged by the king's tone and took a step back.

"Yes?" Nabû-na'id prompted.

"I have found something. An inscription. I think it merits your attention."

"Why do you think that?"

"It is an inscription from the time of Nabû-kudurri-uṣur."

"That is hardly surprising."

"No, not that Nabû-kudurri-uṣur. The one before him."

Nabû-na'id opened his mouth and closed it. Eventually he re-opened it. "How old do you think it is?"

"I don't know. It is from long ago – many hundreds of years ago."

"What does it describe?"

"It is a stele of an *entu* priestess."

Nabû-na'id's jaw went slack. "A priestess of which god?" he asked, enunciating each word slowly and with care.

"Sîn. It is the stele of an *entu* priestess of Sîn."

"Well?" Nabû-na'id asked.

"Well what?" she answered.

"Do you think it is just a coincidence?"

"I don't know," she said. "I don't know what you mean by 'just a coincidence.'"

"We wish to consecrate our daughter to Sîn, but no one knows how. Then a stele shows up from hundreds of years ago, from the time of an ancient king whose name happens to have been the same as your father's, and the stele describes precisely the rites we are in search of. 'Just a coincidence' means that none of this has meaning, even though it appears to."

"It *means* that none of this has meaning," Niṭil-Kišar repeated.

"You know what I mean!" he declared energetically.

"Do I?"

He sighed and was silent for a moment. "Let us say you found a soft clay tablet that a bird had trod on – you had watched as the bird did so. Then, when you picked up the tablet, you saw that each of the footsteps of the bird could be read as a sign, that the tablet as a whole was legible. What would you conclude?"

Niṭil-Kišar didn't at first answer.

"I mean, wouldn't it at least make you wonder if a god or a ghost spoke to you through that bird?"

"Through that bird's footprints, you mean," Niṭil-Kišar corrected softly.

"Very well. But wouldn't it make you wonder?"

"Yes," she admitted. "That is among the things I would wonder."

The two remained quiet for a while. Then, somewhat grudgingly, Nabû-na'id pursued his wife's answer. "What else would you wonder?"

Again, she didn't respond at first but sat tight-lipped, her hands lying on her lap and curled into fists. "I would wonder what you wonder," she finally began. "I would wonder if what I greatly desired to believe was true. Has Sîn at last spoken to me? Has he relinquished his dreadful silence and given me a clear message? Has he been here all along, singing on the branch of the tree, tormenting worms, leaving messages for me with every footstep though I failed to see? I would wonder that, yes, of course, I would wonder that." She paused. "But I would also wonder other things. I would wonder if it was the bird, and not the god, who spoke to me. I would also wonder why she chose to write rather than to sing."

Nabû-na'id shrugged, conceding the possibility and the question without being very interested.

Niṭil-Kišar took a deep breath. "I would wonder," she continued, "whether the seeming-meaning of a bird's footprints in clay weren't the condition of possibility for meaning as such."

This time Nabû-na'id's response was not a shrug but absolute stillness. "What do you –" he hesitated, "mean?"

She let out a smothered half-laugh, by no means a happy thing. "You told me that your mother once said that everyone writes. Everyone would include birds. Perhaps, then, birds leave messages for us in the dirt, as some of our diviners say they do in their flights through the sky. Perhaps flowing water leaves messages, as do the dancing branches of a tree, the gory entrails of the sacrifice, the passages of the stars through the heavens. But isn't there the other side to your mother's saying, the side that suggests that all along writing has been nothing but scratches in the dirt?"

"But we read..." Nabû-na'id began.

"Surely we can read scratches in dirt whether they are meaningful or not. You are the one who taught me that, the astrologer who doesn't believe in astrology. Just because we confront the world as meaningful doesn't mean that it is."

Nabû-na'id was silent for a long time before responding, slowly, in a low voice. "Don't you ever need it to be?" he asked, each word punctuated and almost strangled. He continued in this staccatoed form. "Can you endure the world if it is otherwise?"

Niṭil-Kišar smiled wanly. "Like you, I fear I may be able to endure the world – no matter what."

They sat together in silence, Nabû-na'id fidgeting and uncomfortable. "I feel so tired," he said at last. "I feel like I have acted so often according to what seemed best – and despite those efforts, which I made in good faith, terrible things have occurred, terrible things for which I bear responsibility. Maybe that is evidence that a sign is only a scratch in the dirt, and our intentions are only signs. But –" he looked imploringly at his wife, "– I am so tired!" As if exhaustion were explanation.

"I know," she said.

"I need a thrush on a branch to be more than a thrush on a branch."

"I know," she said. "You want the bird to be a god or a god's messenger."

Nabû-na'id stared at her for a moment. "Yes. Does that make sense?"

She shrugged, and he resumed more softly. "I need Ea to return from his trip to the Underworld, to resume his place among the gods, to have benefited from his trials – out of which his wisdom was born."

She waited for him to continue.

"Like Gilgameš. Like Ištar. From the Underworld let them all, let all of us, again summit the heavens. Let Kayvan's death not be in vain; let it mean. Let our daughter's grief not be in vain; let Gubaru's grief not be in vain. Let us wake from our death-sleep refreshed, restored, revived. Let everything mean!"

His wife held her peace, but to herself she thought: do we wish loss to mean, is that what we really want? Or do we wish it not to mean, to be forgettable, forgotten, the nothing that it already is?

Meanwhile, Nabû-na'id repeated himself. "From the Underworld let us again summit the heavens. Let the circle that is half-done be completed."

Niṭil-Kišar reached out and touched his hand but said nothing.

"Say something," her husband almost begged. "Please."

She regarded him with pity, with love and with revulsion,

from up close and from far away. Then in response she whispered sadly, "Half a circle is not a circle – not even half of one."

Her husband looked stricken and clasped her hand tightly before suddenly releasing it and taking a few steps away.

"But it may be! It may be! Who are we to discount that possibility?"

"We can't. But neither can we count on it."

"But, Niṭil-Kišar," he stated imploringly, one more time, "I'm tired! I'm so tired!"

Gilgameš never slept – not until the day his journey ended. "Stay awake just a little longer, and you shall have eternal life," Uta-napištim promised. But he saw Gilgameš blinking his eyes tiredly, he saw the hero suppress a yawn. "Stay awake just a little longer, and additionally you shall have eternal youth," Uta-napištim promised. But he saw Gilgameš now close one eye to let it rest, he saw the hero now close the other eye to let it rest. "Stay awake just a little longer, and Enkidu shall be restored to you," Uta-napištim promised. But already Gilgameš was striding tirelessly in his dream, already the hero had set off on his journey.

Did he want a thrush on a branch to be a thrush on a branch, or did he want that thrush to be a messenger from god? Was that not the problem that she had forced him to confess? A problem he knew well; one he had confessed many times before. Why must he confess it once more? Why did his confessions not take root, why did they not endure?

Let a thrush mean, he had insisted. Let Kayvan's death mean. But was he prepared for that? Might that death mean, for example – "You killed me. Had you left well enough alone, had you left me out of your plans, I would still be alive. My life was a perfectly fine life without you – and now it is over because of you." Might it not mean that? Indeed, if his death were *also* to mean "I, Sîn, have a plan; each of you are signs that I press into clay to deliver my message, and perhaps some day I shall disclose to you what you have spelled" – would that efface or overwrite the other message, the dreadful one he was fleeing?

Would it not be better for a thrush simply to be a thrush and a death a death?

She seemed to be suggesting other possibilities, too: a thrush as the message of a thrush. As a scream of protest, too. Was that not her implication, that the possibility of meaning is that mad scream, that inarticulate howl, provoked by what is meaningless? Perhaps each of us has a howl uniquely our own, our one true name that even we do not know… but we stand on the edge of the world and launch it like a javelin past all borders, a shriek that is our name, a shriek demanding meaning because the shrieker recognizes there is none. Or maybe shrieker and shriek are the same.

And what exactly was he shrieking anyway? Was it really about meaning or its absence? Look more closely, listen harder – widen the ears. Did he not seek a particular meaning – absolution, grace, forgiveness, something like that? A meaning that was not quite a forgetting, but almost; permission to forget, perhaps: yes, you have done wrong; yes, you have harmed others, even those you love; but you may forget now, it doesn't matter anymore.

It doesn't matter anymore. Another, a higher, meaning will take its place. For if it didn't – if that thrush only had its single chance atop the branch, a chance that he, Nabû-na'id, had taken from it and destroyed – then how can it be permissible to forget that? A thrush that is only a thrush, a thrush that is the only thrush, lost forever: nothing can contain that if it doesn't mean. That loss falls away and falls away, forever and ever; nothing can contain it if it doesn't mean. Meaning constrains, meaning makes palatable what otherwise exceeds all limits. "Turn into a fly, that I may swallow you," the god says; "turn into meaning, that I may swallow you," the god says, or the man says, or perhaps even the fly says. (What does the thrush say?)

And he? What was it that he was saying, he the exalter of Nabû? Would he traipse between permission to forget and desire to mean? A permission which can never be fully exercised, lest it erase the meaning which makes the permission possible…

And the thrush? What *does* the thrush say? Who is there to grant the permission to forget, or the permission to almost forget, if the thrush isn't there to do so? Who speaks for the thrush and says what the thrush would say? Who dares? He, the killer of thrushes – would he speak for them, pronounce on their behalf his own forgiveness? But if not he, who?

And by what right had he transformed Kayvan into a thrush?

Mikum-Nisaba pressed her seal into the clay, then with her stylus wrote over it. Then she pressed her seal again into the clay, obliterating the signs, before again overwriting the image with her stylus. Why do I do this? she wondered. Why do I not leave the clay untouched, signless, rather than endeavoring to impress cacophony into what cannot hold cacophony?

For clay is always silent. Clay does not shout, chatter or whisper. Sink into clay and you sink into a world where widening one's ears catches nothing; there is no wisdom when sunk in clay. It doesn't exist. Such a world is not even deaf. For clay is always silent – so silent that for clay there is not even silence.

(Yet she can hear her reed press into clay; she can hear her seal roll over clay. Do those not count? Are those not perhaps the gasps and utterances of clay for the world?)

(Yet here is her tablet, in her hand, the recipient of cacophony: and it says nothing. If you do not believe me, listen.)

She looked at the tablet in her hands. How is it that I read this? she wondered. Do I not see what is not there? She smiled at her own tortured thought – bittersweetly she smiled.

Reading requires that you see what is not there. Spaces that make signs. Spaces that separate signs. Meanings that are not intended. Meanings that are. This sign (she made a sign in the clay) – it can mean UTU, the Šumeran name of Šamaš. It can mean BABBAR, part of the sign for silver. It can mean the sound ud or ut or uṭ or even u. It can also mean the sound tam. What else can it mean? Who is to say that every now and then, feeling rebellious, it doesn't insist on meaning something else? "Scribal error" people say – but why do they rule out the ambition of a renegade sign? ('Today,' the sign says, 'I shall mean Sîn, not Šamaš. I wonder,' the sign wonders, 'if anyone will notice?') (But signs don't feel, they don't insist, they have no ambition and they never rebel.) (But does the invocation of error really explain the appearance of a wayward sign?)

Reading requires seeing what is not there. Even if what is not there is also there. We have no way of distinguishing a blank that is there from our own blindness. We could not read if we were not blind.

(Was she sure that she knew what she meant?)

(She was not.)

Gubaru had sat in the gate, wrenching his garments, tearing the flesh of his arms, his chest, his face. "My son! My son!" he had cried. "Kayvan!"

One rat had said to another rat: "Poor fellow!"

"Yes, poor fellow!" the second rat had agreed.

"His son has probably been eaten," the first rat had said.

"Most likely," the second rat had agreed.

"Now he will have to live like we do – marking what is not there by not speaking."

"Yes, that is what he will have to do," the second rat had agreed.

"He will have to live like a rat, squeaking and not speaking, surrounded by all those absences that we mark with our silence."

"So he will," the second rat had agreed.

"Surely that is what he is doing now," the first rat had concluded.

(But I did not really overhear this conversation. Rats, we all know, do not speak.)

Nabû-na'id had joined Gubaru in the gate, had wrenched his own garments, had torn his own flesh. He had wept, but he had called out no names. It was for a father to call out names and to call them back.

But then, the fly observed, mysteriously something changed. No longer was one man in the gate; no longer did the other man join him. Grief abated, it seemed. Something transpired. To the fly it was mysterious. He had heard men talk of it, but what it was he did not understand. What happened they called "time." How it happened, how it accomplished what it accomplished – the fly did not know. To the fly it was a mystery.

(But who can be surprised at the ignorance of a fly?)

"We have found a way to marry you to the Moon," Nabû-na'id announced quietly.

Mikum-Nisaba's face was like a mask, its expression unchanged and unchangeable.

"Is it still what you want?" he asked.

"What way have you found?" she in turn asked, avoiding his

question.

"Long ago – hundreds of years ago – there lived a king with the same name as your grandfather. When we were restoring the foundations of Sîn's main temple, the Egipar in Uru, we found one of this king's steles. On it was a relief showing an *entu* priestess of Sîn, and beside the relief was text describing her rites. That's what we've found."

"May I see it?"

"We haven't removed it from the foundations yet. When we do, I'll have copies made."

"May I see it where it is? That's what I want."

"It's at the Egipar in Uru," he responded. She just looked at him. "We would have to travel there," he explained. Still, she just looked at him. They looked at each other. After a long pause, he answered, "Yes, you may."

"Will you become a priestess of Sîn?" Bel-šar-uṣur asked.

She did not answer him. She did not look at him.

"You're going to Uru?" he persisted.

Her response was the same.

"It is better that way," he said cruelly.

Nabû-na'id, Niṭil-Kišar and Mikum-Nisaba travelled to Uru. The three walked together to the Egipar, mother and daughter holding hands. It was with evident surprise that Nabû-zer-lišir greeted them when they arrived. "We wish to see the stele," Nabû-na'id declared. "The one you told me about." Nabû-zer-lišir brought them to it and, without ceremony, began to read it to them.

"Stop," Nabû-na'id commanded. "I can read." Then he added, responding to Nabû-zer-lišir's questioning gaze, "All of us can read."

Then, side by side, in silence, father, mother and daughter

stood before the inscription.

"How was the stele lost all these years?" Mikum-Nisaba eventually asked quietly. "And why is it so low?"

Nabû-zer-lišir wasn't sure if he was supposed to respond. A glance from Nabû-na'id clarified the matter.

"Over time, dirt and debris collect around buildings. They gradually raise the floor. People start building on the remains of earlier times, though they often don't realize it."

"Like all those pottery sherds," Mikum-Nisaba observed to her father.

"Yes," he answered. "Every day we crush beneath our feet the memories of the past."

"We should preserve those memories," Mikum-Nisaba said.

"It's not clear what memories you could reawaken with only a pottery sherd," Nabû-zer-lišir pointed out. "But with a stele, or any inscription really – it is as if you have conquered time."

Though she, like Mikum-Nisaba, was veiled, Nabû-na'id heard his wife draw her breath, as if about to say something; but she said nothing.

"I can imagine how a floor would gradually be raised with time, no one particularly noticing. But how was the stele lost? You haven't answered that." Mikum-Nisaba persisted.

"It must have fallen down," Nabû-zer-lišir responded. "Face-down."

"Why was it not righted?"

Nabû-zer-lišir looked uncomfortable. "I don't know."

Niṭil-Kišar touched her daughter's sleeve gently. "You're asking a lot of our friend here," she murmured. "You're asking him to explain why it is and how it is that we forget."

"But a toppled stele? How can that be forgotten?"

"There are worse things, far worse things, far more impossible things, that we forget," her mother answered.

They were talking in their chambers.

"He called it 'reawakening.' I liked that; it made sense to me. We should reawaken every toppled stele, every forgotten votive statue, every last sherd of pottery. We should let the past come alive again."

"Which is it that you want?" her mother asked gently. "To reawaken the past, or to revivify it? You've said both, but they're different."

"They don't have to be different," Mikum-Nisaba answered stubbornly.

"Would you leave no shred of the past to its slumbers?" Niṭil-Kišar asked, a little playfully.

"No. Reawaken everything!"

Her mother made a face. "For myself, I am more and more inclined to leave the sherds to their dreaming, and with them the statues and the forgotten inscriptions and all the names."

"I will awaken them all," her daughter declared.

"Some things ought to be forgotten," Niṭil-Kišar said to Nabû-na'id. "They need to be."

"Yes," he agreed.

"Without forgetting we would have no emptiness to move around in. There would be no articulation of sound, no space separating one written sign from another. There would be no breath. We would suffocate, all of us."

"I agree."

"Our daughter wants to unforget all forgetting, to reawaken all that slumbers."

"She would be Gilgameš!" Nabû-na'id said with a smile. "She would force her own wakefulness on the world."

"I would rather she let it sleep."

"Along with Enlil, the drowsy godhead." Nabû-na'id often called Enlil "the drowsy godhead," like an epithet.

Niṭil-Kišar squinted at him. "She thinks she can remember Kayvan back into existence. That's what she wants."

Nabû-na'id suddenly looked sad. "I know. She is young. She thinks all loss can somehow be recovered." He paused and looked at his wife. "Should we disabuse her of that hope?"

"It's a false hope," Niṭil-Kišar answered.

"Yes."

"And it is not even something we should hope for. She won't understand this, but you and I both know it. We need a world which includes the forgotten. It isn't just that we must endeavor not to forget. We must also remember to forget."

Nabû-na'id was pensive but silent.

"What is it?" his wife asked.

"We need something else, too. Or I do. An elusive term in between." He abruptly stopped and then, as if gathering strength, continued. "A term in between remembering and forgetting. People have called it different things. Forgiveness, pardon, grace. Whatever the name, it is not a mere forgetting – for we do that all the time. Even those of us who have done horrible things – much of every day is passed not remembering, not thinking about them. They are, if not absolutely forgotten, then mostly forgotten. But forgiveness must be something else. Or, perhaps I am only saying –" his face became distorted, pained, almost pleading "– that I need it to be something else." He stopped and was silent for a long time, his face frozen in that same mask of pain and pleading. "But neither could it be a simple remembering. It is from that remembering that I would be delivered! It is what I often desire to run from, to flee, as if it were not carried with me." Again he was silent for a long time, while Niṭil-Kišar studied the ground. "So it has to be between the two," he concluded. "If there is a between the two."

"It sounds to me like you want to start over," Niṭil-Kišar said quietly.

"Yes." With a strange and touching simplicity, the two of them looked at each other. "Very often," confided Nabû-na'id, "I fear that, so long as I live, I shall have no atonement; and that after I die, atonement too is no more."

Both became pensive and silence settled between them without either noticing. Then, abruptly, Niṭil-Kišar rose, approached Nabû-na'id and knelt before him. Into her hands she scooped dirt from the ground and then, lifting herself, she poured it over her husband's astonished head. "My husband," she said – but it sounded very much like "My death" – "it falls to no man to bury himself. It is a gift for which we must rely on others." He continued to stare at her in bewilderment. "It is the omen of Luḫuššum, you fool. That a man in his lifetime will die." She paused and stared intensely into his eyes. "Now, dead man, go live."

Izdubar stirred. He opened his eyes, moved his legs. The beautiful cat on his lap purred softly. "I shall have to get up soon," he said to her. "I am being called to life." He looked at her delicate lips, partially lined with fur; he looked at the white badge of fur on her chest; he scratched the fur beneath her chin. Her eyes remained tightly closed, even as she stretched, or seemed to stretch, her neck the better to be scratched. So he scratched it and, very gently, he stroked her fur, trying to impress it forever into his memory. Meanwhile, softly, she purred. "I shall have to leave you soon," he said to her. "I am being called to life."

He started to rise – and stopped. A tear slipped down his cheek.

"But not yet," he added, sitting down again. "I'm not ready to leave you yet."

And the black cat, ever so softly, barely audibly, purred.

(In the background, a ferret scuttled across the room.)

"Why have you chosen death over life?" Enlil asked a second time.

The sage would not answer.

"Is it because you feel guilt for having broken the wing of the wind?"

The sage would not answer.

"Or is it because you feel guilty for endeavoring to cajole your way into our good graces?"

The sage would not answer.

"Or is it because you have foolishly put your trust in the trickster god Ea over me, even if he is your father?"

The sage would not answer.

"How dare you not answer me?" Enlil demanded furiously.

"Ah, finally a question I can answer," the sage said with composure. "For I did not choose death over life. A god cannot know this, but a man knows it: to choose one is to choose the other."

(A ferret scuttled back the other way.)

Šamaš and Sîn could not see one another. "Where have you gone, Sîn?" cried Šamaš. "I am hiding behind the world," Sîn's voice replied, "but where are you?" "Where I always am, keeping watch over the world." "Ah, so you are become now the halo of the world," Sîn's voice observed. "I don't know what you could possibly mean," answered Šamaš. "I am as I have always been." "Very well," agreed Sîn's voice. "In any event you will not be a halo for long."

It was as Sîn's voice predicted. The world lost its halo and the sun, the god of justice, could again see the face of the moon.

"Mikum-Nisaba, wake up." She opened her eyes. "Come, look." Her father said, beckoning her outside. It was somewhere between night and morning, the 13th day of Ululu.

She got up and joined him in the pale moonlight. "What is happening?" she asked, puzzled. "Why is the Moon darkening?"

"It is a mystery," her father answered somberly. "Or perhaps it is a question."

"What do you mean?"

"You already asked the question – but you asked it of me. Perhaps you should ask it of the Moon."

"I should ask the Moon why it is darkening?"

"Yes."

Mikum-Nisaba didn't say anything for a moment. "Why should I ask a question of an entity that can't respond – or at least won't respond?"

"Those are different claims. First you have to decide which it is. Can it not respond, or will it not respond? But perhaps there is something else you have to decide beforehand."

"What's that?"

"If the Moon were to respond, would you know how to hear it?"

"Obviously not," his daughter replied almost immediately.

"Why is that obvious?"

"Because there is no one who can hear the Moon, no one who ever has, no one who ever will."

"And yet you might become the priestess of Sîn, if you ever make up your mind…" He let the implication fade away with his words.

"Is that what this is about?" she demanded after a long pause.

"What's the 'this'?" Nabû-na'id asked.

"Our conversation."

"Yours and mine? Or yours and the Moon's?"

"I am not having a conversation with the Moon."

"And yet its face has darkened, even in the little time that we've been talking."

"That's not a conversation. What I see is different from what I hear."

"Not too long ago, however, while we were in Uru, did you not hear the words of a dead king and see the life of an *entu* priestess who died 5 centuries ago?"

"I didn't hear any words, I read them."

"Why, Mikum-Nisaba, is the Moon darkening?"

She stared at her father for a long while, her eyes blank and unblinking. Then, very calmly, she turned and looked at the Moon, watching as the half-circle of darkness crept across its face until at last it was completely veiled, but for a peeking sliver; then watching as, ever so slowly, it began to unveil. But it did not finish. Still partially veiled, it set during the morning watch.

Mikum-Nisaba shuddered under its cold, obstructed gaze. She wondered: can I endure a coldness passing through no veil?

Is it for weariness that you are pale?
The weariness of climbing heaven?
Is it for loneliness that you are cold?
The loneliness of gazing from afar?

"What is this?" she inquired.

"It's part of a series of tablets called the *Enuma Anu Enlil*. Mostly they discuss omens based on the phenomena in the heavens."

Mikum-Nisaba darted a glance at her father. "Are these the texts you read in Sardis?" she asked excitedly.

"No. They're similar, but I was working off a different set of tablets, the *Enuma Anu Sîn*."

"Oh."

"I wasn't sure whether to show this to you or not. I decided

I had a responsibility to offer it to you. But you may refuse."

"What would I be refusing?"

"You could refuse to read the tablet. But of course, if you refuse to read it, you won't know what it is that you've refused."

"And I can't refuse it after having read it?"

The expression on her father's face was well-meaning and frank. "You can try."

"Well, that's what I'll do then. I'll read it and, if necessary, refuse what I've read."

She reached for the first tablet, but her father grabbed her arm and stopped her. "Mikum-Nisaba," he said softly, "I'm not sure how much you've heard about what I did in Sardis, when I wasn't much older than you are now. I believe that I have only ever told your brother, though I know he's told others. So perhaps you have heard a few things. But the important point is that, having read something, I was no longer able to refuse it. It forced me into a position of decision and responsibility, no matter what. And this may do the same to you."

Mikum-Nisaba opened and then closed her mouth. "What did you read in Sardis?" she asked.

Her father sighed. "I read that the Moon would, for a while, block the all-seeing gaze of the sun. I read that Sîn would avert the eyes of Justice."

"So?"

"So – I set in motion, and then watched over with my own blighted eyes, what should not have been done in the light of day, in a world overseen by Justice."

Mikum-Nisaba looked at the ground. "Why?" a small, trembling voice inquired.

Her father released her arm, which he had been holding since she reached for the tablet. "It seemed to me that worse suffering would be averted."

"Were you right?"

"I don't know. I will never know. It is possible that there is no answer."

They sat in silence for a moment, before Nabû-na'id added, "My life changed in that moment forever, and set me on a path that I have found lonesome, painful and sometimes evil. But that path also brought me to your mother, and to you – and to your brother. To this day, I do not know if that text I read in my youth was a blessing or a curse."

"And so you have put me in that position? To risk a blessing that may instead be a curse?"

"Perhaps it will be both. Perhaps that is what it has been for me."

"But why have you put me in this position?"

He looked straight into her eyes. "Because we are always in this position, and you might as well know it," he answered coldly. He rose and started to stride from the room. "You don't have to read the tablets. I am not even sure that I would advise that you do." He left.

She sat in the room with the tablets.

If in the month of Ululu, the moon sets during the morning watch while eclipsed: it is the desire of Sîn that he have an entu *priestess.*

"The Moon is darkening for me," she whispered. Then, softly, she sang:

Is it for weariness that you are pale?
The weariness of climbing heaven?
Is it for loneliness that you are cold?
The loneliness of gazing from afar?
Am I to wander companionless beside you?

When the song ended, she wept.

The installation ceremony had ended and the priestess of

Sîn had retired to the palace her father had built for her in Uru. He had escorted her there and, at the threshold, had re-named her. "Henceforth you are En-nigaldi-Nanna." Then he pointed to the door post, on which there was an inscription. "Read it aloud," he said.

For an instant, she thought: shall I refuse to read, or shall I be reckless in reading? She blinked.

"I built anew the house of En-nigaldi-Nanna, my daughter, the priestess of Sîn," she read. "I purified my daughter and offered her to Sîn. May En-nigaldi-Nanna the daughter, the beloved of my heart, be strong before all; and may her word prevail."

"Beloved of my heart, priestess, desire of the god of the Moon," her father said, "may your word prevail."

I am your priestess now, she wrote. *Fill me with songs of praise. May it not be for naught that all this has been done; that it has been done must mean it was not for naught. Fill me with your cold, cold light; let me warm it into songs of praise. Fill me fill me fill me – may it not be for naught. Fill me that I may sing your praise.*

And then, very carefully, with her seal Ea-in-a-boat, she obliterated her message.

Chapter 7. Facing Statues

In the shadow of the temple of Šamaš, the Ebabbar, amidst the fill of the excavated foundation, lay a ruined, almost obliterated statue. The head was half smashed; and the half that remained was so scoured by time – as much by gentle breezes and the rare rain, by collisions with dust and gnats and emptiness, as by violence – that the face, if ever it had one, was almost gone. Nabû-zer-lišir, only recently transferred to Sippar, dug carefully around the statue, often with his bare hands. Sometimes he dared only to blow the dirt away with his breath, for fear of damaging further what was already more rock than statue. Statues come from rock and return to it. His care was directed in part by the hope of finding an inscription, something which would tell him what was missing, what was effaced, what was lost – something which would identify not the rock but the statue, something which would give the worn and shattered visage a name.

Eventually he found it.

Nabû-na'id examined the wreck. This is what it means to be remembered, he thought. Here lies a monument with which one of our most heralded kings thought to immortalize himself. Did he foresee the years of ignominy, the defacement, the humble obliteration that made of his likeness mere fill in a foundation? Some illiterate worker looked upon him one day and saw no sneer of cold command, no haughty might, nothing even to inspire envy or revenge. He saw a stone plug, useful for a wall. And who is to say that the educated scribe who suspected that meaning lay hidden in this ruin saw more clearly than that worker? Where should one's sight end: at the rock or at the statue? And is it possible to see them both, both statue and rock, what would point to a man and what would point beyond him?

The face was gone – almost gone. But who is to say, he thought, that it was a face, much less that it is a face? A few signs scrawled near the base: with what right, with what power, do they claim the rock as their own? With what right, with what power, do they make it a statue, give it a face, give the face a name? Madness! Madness! The scribe (he continued thinking) tells me it is Šarru-kēn; I have seen the signs myself; and now the question is: do I agree, do I accede, do I let this poor rock become a poor king, among the greatest of our history? Or do I hush the scribe, tell him to leave the rock in place, undisturbed, peacefully forgotten, returning to what it always already almost was? Shall I bathe this king in dust as I did a living king long ago? Shall my gift be one of burial or remembrance, or are those the same? Is my duty to the king or to the rock?

Madness! Madness! I don't know where my sight should end, whether at the rock or at the statue. I don't know if there is a should any more than if there is an end.

He drew his hand slowly across the almost-face, letting his fingers flow over the hollow of an eye, a cheek's curve and the curls of the beard and then into the crags and pits of fragmentation, where statue ended and stone began. "Šarru-kēn," he whispered. "True King, Legitimate King. Your son was Naram-Sîn, the Beloved of Sîn – as my daughter is now. But is not this stone also your progeny, your imperfect likeness, your desire stamped for a moment onto the world? And look what it has amounted to! A different likeness of you endured – the signs carved into the base that spell your name. Why did you order a statue crafted? Why were those signs not enough? Did you really think a statue would make a better likeness of you than the signs that spelled your name? Surely you realized that a statue invites defacement. Perhaps it was Gutians overrunning the walls, and not the accidents of time, which shattered your face. Or perhaps it was an angry son. But rare is the son who reads, rarer still the Gutian: more likely, then, that your name, rather than your image, would endure in safety, which is to say, in secret. Immortality – what is that but a sign no one can read anymore, one mistaken for a rock's fissure or the cracking of overheated clay? So perhaps it is the fate of signs as well as statues to return to, or be mistaken for, rock and mud; perhaps our immortality is always at the sake of our identity. Did you know this, King of the World, King of the Four Corners? And what now would you ask of me, your twofold heir – recipient of your kingdom and of this your stone and all-too-pitiful statue?"

And the stone said, the statue replied –

The Lord of the Earth stirred in the mud; the God of the Waters emerged from the Deep; over the face of the waters blew the God of Wisdom; from the Underworld blessed Ea found his way.

And the stone said, the statue replied –

From the dirt rose Nabû; Sîn shined in his throne; from the meat hook they lifted Ištar; Šamaš blinked and could see; all made ready the throne of Ea. But Enlil slept, amidst the commotion slept he, in the assembly of the gods slept Enlil – do not disturb him!

And the stone said, the statue replied –

But listen as he might, the side of his face pressed to the stone, Nabû-na'id heard nothing, neither sound nor breath tickled his ear. Listen as he might, the side of his face pressed to the statue, Nabû-na'id heard nothing, neither sound nor breath tickled his ear. Listen as he might, the side of his face pressed to the face of the statue, Nabû-na'id heard nothing, neither sound nor breath tickled his ear.

Then Nabû-na'id's face grew taut and rigid and cold; then his face was shattered and worn; then Nabû-na'id, King of the World, King of the Four Corners, King of Bābilim, became stone. And a voice spoke.

Enlil was sleeping. A ferret bustled around the room; all about was the drone of flies. The thrones were empty, every one but the last: and there lay curled a black ball, a cat asleep, her eyes tightly closed, purring softly.

This is the tablet of Zisudris that Gubaru dreamed in a dream I gave him long ago, a voice announced. This is where the fate of Atraḫasīs buried alive forever is set down. But it was the fate of Zisudris too, who gave himself to the flood and settled like water-logged timber into the mud. It was the fate of Gubaru in the dream, buried alive in a tavern whose door he could not reach. Was it a door he reached when he awoke? And it is your fate, whether here in Sippar at the gate of the temple of Šamaš or in the heart of Bābilim. One will come who will deface you – and preserve you. One will come for whom you are anything but yourself. Your sacrifices are to him, their sweet savor his, the bellows of the victim his; and your reward is to be preserved by the one who forgets you.

But, a voice continued, what is his fate but the same? This statue which is a rock which is a tablet is his fate no less than yours no less than Gubaru's no less than Atraḫasīs's no less than Zisudris's no less than Šarru-kēn's. Whose fate is it not? That droning you hear is the laughter of the flies who are the gods who your sacrifices rescued: but do you think the fate of the gods who are flies any different than your fate? And are there gods who are not flies? What am I, you might wonder? I am Nabû, I am Sîn, I am the writing god, I am the mirror god, neither Leviathan nor whirlwind can contain me, and what is there that does not contain me? I too am a fly. The tablet of Zisudris precedes even me; I am no less written than all.

So a voice said, but Nabû-na'id did not hear, for he had become a statue, his eyes glazed, his cheeks smoothed, the curls of his beard rigid. A statue, which is only a stone, cannot hear. Its ears only resemble ears and are not ears. A statue of a man only resembles a man and is not a man. And what resembles a man but is not one, moreover with ears that are in fact only the likenesses of ears and not ears, cannot hear, not even a voice that is not there.

Again he did not respond. "How would you have me proceed, Your Excellency?" Nabû-zer-lišir asked a third time.

Nabû-na'id blinked, then stirred. His face was still pressed to the stone. For a moment he looked uncomprehendingly at the scribe. Then, with immense effort, he cleared his throat and a distant, gravelly sound awakened in his ears. He redoubled his effort and slowly the gravel slid into place, one chunk beside another, until at least, dimly, from far away, his ears made out a solid word.

"Carefully."

To Mikum-Nisaba I write, thus I, your father, I.

I consecrated you the priestess of Sîn, but it is I he plagues, casting dreams upon me day and night, taxing me to distinguish his whispering from the gentlest breeze coursing through the blades of grass. A statue of Šarru-kēn was found, he the father of Enḫeduanna to whom once you wrote – and perhaps for whom you wrote as well, none of us shall ever know – and then we sang her words together, you and I. A moment which will live in joy in my heart, when we were together though the words were another's. Are they not always another's?

This statue of Šarru-kēn is a sort of tablet too, a tablet telling the history of the world – what of it has been kept. It faithfully records the droning of our god-flies and faithfully forgets them; in it I read myself, as a crack which may also be a sign, as a terribly small dent in a shattered visage. Which caused which, I wonder, the dent the shattering or the shattering the dent? Or is it too hopeful to imagine them related?

I think to myself: this king, Šarru-kēn, who gave his daughter away as a priestess to Sîn– was it with misgivings, with a sense of loss, with despair? Was it instead pride he felt? Or did it not matter to him beyond what peace it brought him with the temple? Did an eclipse goad him, cajole him, trick him into this sacrifice? Did he make it confidently?

And I think of Enḫeduanna, wed to a far distant being whose light is cold. I think of her alone in her priestly chambers. She pecks at the holy food set down for her. She smooths her robes. She examines yet again every single crack in the wall, and she dreads lest a whisper issue from one of them – like I dread these whisperings which lurk on the periphery of my sensation, maybe the periphery of my imagination, maybe the periphery of my sanity – there they lurk. But I hope – or rather, perhaps she hopes, however dreadfully, for this contact, this communion, if only to horrify her out of her solitude.

Has the god visited you, beloved of my heart, my daughter? Dare I ask a question so intimate? But is there anything intimate about the importunity of a god? A god, like the rest of us, is but a fly, but a fly, like us, all of us, flies. Has your word prevailed, or the god's? Buzzing buzzing buzzing, your word, his word, after a while who can tell buzzing apart from silence? One concentrates on the crack; and on the fear that is also a desire that a whisper come – let it come! Trembling, taut with nervous excitement, with concentration, solitude and despair, what one hears, even if it is silence, does it not sound like a whisper?

So I wonder about that girl of long ago, Enḫeduanna, who united us with her song. What a brave, what a remarkable human being to turn silence into song! And to give it to us. Perhaps I shall write songs too, songs which I will imagine come from you in your cella, even if they come as well from a crack in a wall – my wall, your wall, who can tell.

You needn't worry, child – I shall not send this to you, as you did not send Enḫeduanna your letter. That does not mean it will not be sent; only that it shall not be I who sends it – and, may the gods help me (and with them the flies, always the flies), it will not be to you that it is sent. I have already burdened you with too much. I burden my children with gifts and watch them from afar, individual pack animals toiling in solitude through the desert. And were I to curse my children? What then?

Your brother, for example. What of your brother? What of your brother? Is your fate worse than his?

Speak to Bel-šar-uṣur, thus speaks Nabû-na'id.

You are right that you should be more involved in governance. Come to me in Sippar, and together we can return to Bābilim when our work here is done. I shall hereafter keep you at my side and prepare you as well as I can.

Speak to Belet-ṣeri-dannat, thus speaks Nabû-na'id, the king.

I shall want your assistance henceforth in advising my son. Join me in Sippar; henceforth you will travel with us.

Scribe: read no further. Give this tablet directly to Belet-ṣeri-dannat. Belet-ṣeri-dannat: Forgive the tone of peremptory command, old friend. I need you.

Nabû-na'id, who cannot speak, writes; may you read, Niṭil-Kišar.

I am unsure when I will return to Bābilim. I am in the grip of a statue; I do not understand its hold on me. When I return, I shall discuss it with you.

I have thought more about your proposal regarding the canals. I am confused by your goals; everything you describe is double-edged. In one light, it may bewilder and delay the Umman Manda, when they come (as they will); in another light, it will hasten their arrival. It made me think of Naqi'a, whom we discussed long ago; and I wonder, are you to be confused with her? Even a straight line can be a labyrinth – and vice versa. I sense something less straightforward than you've admitted and wonder (a second time): must she be devious even with me? Why? That is a question, not a reproach – and maybe more a question for me than for you. In the meanwhile, I leave the matter in your hands, I who am gripped by a statue. When I return, should this statue release me, I shall assign an official and troops to answer to you.

To En-nigaldi-Nanna, thus write I, Nabû-na'id.

You are much on my mind, daughter, beloved of my heart. I have even written you letters that I have not sent for fear that their tone – but can a letter, can these bird tracks in mud, capture a tone? – might disturb you. I have thought more than once of our discussion of Enḫeduanna, when you wrote her that letter, and when we sang her hymns together. She is an inspiration to me, that one; and I remind you of her in the hope that she will inspire you too, as perhaps will memory of that time together that we shared.

I am in Sippar, where we found a statue, badly damaged, of Enḫeduanna's father Šarru-kēn. Or we say, anyway, that it is the statue which is damaged; but perhaps it was the man who was damaged, and a damaged man which the statue faithfully represented. If so, the question is not how to fix the statue, but how to fix the man? Assuredly, though, it is far too late for that. I shall do what I can for the statue, then.

May this find you well, in heart as well as health.

It was the four of them, and the statue: Nabû-na'id, his son Bel-šar-uṣur, his advisor Belet-ṣeri-dannat and the scribe Nabû-zer-lišir. And a statue of a man's fractured visage (so Nabû-na'id thought of it) or (as others saw it) a fractured statue.

"I wish you to oversee two projects," Nabû-na'id explained to the scribe. "I wish you to restore the face" (*ha ha! But how? But how?* he thought); "and I wish you to direct the making of a second statue – of me. We shall put them together in the temple; let mine be votive, an image of me making an offering." (*Which is to say of me trying not to forget; and of me, through this image, giving myself permission to forget. I shall let the statue remember, it shall hold the place of remembering for me…*) (Nabû-na'id chuckled weirdly.) "And the offerings will be to this king here, or to his statue" (*who can say?*). "We'll talk about the specific nature of those offerings closer to the time." Nabû-na'id looked expectantly at the scribe, who nodded if only to show that he had comprehended.

Bel-šar-uṣur spoke up. "Does a king not have better things to do than concern himself with damaged statues?" His look, as so often, was brazen, challenging. Nabû-na'id instead gazed at the earth and left the response to Belet-ṣeri-dannat.

"A king must look to the past no less than the present and the future. In this a king is no different than any other man, though his responsibilities are heavier."

"A statue," Bel-šar-uṣur observed acidly, "is not the past."

"A statue," Belet-ṣeri-dannat responded in the same tone, "is a way of reminding ourselves of our responsibility to the past."

(*And what of our responsibility to statues, even to rocks? What is a statue but a rock which aspires to a face? I too aspire to a face.*) Nabû-na'id grinned, again weirdly. The exchange between his son and Belet-ṣeri-dannat was continuing, but he had ceased to follow it. "We shall have to discuss," he said, interrupting he knew not what, "how to give this poor rock here a face." He smiled pleasantly at them all. "Do any of you have suggestions?"

Bel-šar-uṣur looked disgusted. "Find a sculptor, obviously" he muttered. "Let him do it."

"Let him do what?" Nabû-na'id inquired sweetly.

"Let him fix what was smashed – carve a face."

"I'm not sure those are the same," his father observed, "and I am not at all sure that to do either would be to give the rock a face." He paused. "But that is what I want to do."

Belet-ṣeri-dannat examined his old friend for a moment, letting his eyes linger over the aged face and finally bringing them to rest on Nabû-na'id's eyes. "What you want may not be in our power to provide."

"How right you are!" Nabû-na'id answered. "It *may* not." The two men held each other's gaze. "But what if it is?"

Bel-šar-uṣur stomped his foot. "The Umman Manda grow stronger and brigands threaten our western and southern trade routes – and we are discussing *faces*? Hire a sculptor and be done with it!"

"Of course that's what we shall do," his father said quickly, almost as soon as his son finished speaking. "But you must learn the difference between knowing *what* to do and knowing *how* to do it. Especially –" he gave a short, weird laugh – "especially when what you're doing is impossible."

"Your son thinks you're going mad, like his grandfather."

"He's long thought that. Not that I'm going mad, but that I am mad."

"Is he right?"

Nabû-na'id looked long and hard at Belet-ṣeri-dannat. "I suppose you have to ask," he muttered grudgingly, more to himself than his friend. "Well, what do you think?" he asked.

"I think," Belet-ṣeri-dannat began, drawing out the last word into a lingering sigh, "that you have always been eccentric and thoughtful – if those aren't the same thing – but that as king you now run the risk of having nothing to oppose and to channel those eccentricities."

Nabû-na'id was silent for a moment before responding. "Quite the opposite, my friend, quite the opposite," he said.

"Say more."

"I am opposed at every step. I am channeled at every step. Opposing me is the impossibility of restoring a face to a statue of a man who had none. Channeling me is the necessity of nonetheless doing so."

"Why is it a necessity?"

"Have we not already had too many faceless leaders? Would you not wish a king to have a face?"

Belet-ṣeri-dannat stared at him. "This is why your son fears for your sanity."

"My son does not *fear* for my sanity, he dismisses it. Even as we speak he is wearing away and fracturing his own face. He is disfiguring himself, and yet I am the one who is mad!" Angrily, he took a step away, then whistled for Fly.

"What do you mean?" Belet-ṣeri-dannat inquired.

Nabû-na'id ignored him for the moment and whistled again for the dog. He waited until the dog came trotting into view.

"My son has given himself a mask for so long that he does not realize that his face has eroded beneath it and perhaps because of it. That is the fate of kings. It is my fate no less. And look at what became of Šarru-kēn."

"You're confusing a man with his image."

"No I'm not. I'm reading an image for what it tells me of the man."

"But Šarru-kēn didn't really look like that. Of course not. He wouldn't have survived. It is the statue that is fractured; the man wasn't."

"The statue reveals the truth of the man. It is like the Tablet of Destinies – if we dare read it."

"If that's so, then it is the truth of every man, or at least of every man so unfortunate as to have a statue made of him. Surely you recognize that that will be the eventual fate of your own statue, the one you've commissioned."

Nabû-na'id looked triumphant. "My point exactly." He squatted beside the dog, who was lying in the corner, and began petting him. "I'm not sure about everything, though. Women – women have found other possibilities. You might be wrong to exclude men from those possibilities too."

Belet-ṣeri-dannat looked lost. "What do you mean?"

"Well, Enḫeduanna, after all, managed to sing. Perhaps men can learn to sing and to compose song. Perhaps it is possible for men to be other than statues." Nabû-na'id saw that Belet-ṣeri-dannat's expression was still one of bewilderment. He sighed and explained heavy-handedly, as if talking to a child, "I'm being optimistic. I would have thought you'd approve." He let his sarcasm fade, then continued, "Perhaps the truth of every man is not limited to statues, as you say it is. Perhaps we have within us the strength to write poetry and to give it to song, like that remarkable girl Enḫeduanna, a girl far greater than her father. That's all I mean."

Belet-ṣeri-dannat said nothing.

"But you're right to be skeptical," Nabû-na'id continued. "Not least because these decrepit statues in which our fates are probably available to be read are themselves, in some strange and twisted sense, already poems, maybe even songs – of the silent variety, of course." He pet the dog distractedly, then brought his face near the dog's. Fly sniffed it and then, satisfied, licked it.

"There is hope for me yet," Nabû-na'id murmured. "I dread the day when Fly treats my face like a statue – scentless and unlickable. It is coming, but I have passed today's test. Today, Fly tells me, I still have something that could be a face." Rising, he looked wearily at Belet-ṣeri-dannat. "As for tomorrow, we'll see."

"If you're so afraid of losing your face –" Belet-ṣeri-dannat began.

"There's no if," Nabû-na'id interrupted. "I *will* lose my face – if I ever had one. And I fear it."

"And only the dog will know?"

"I didn't say that. But I am confident the dog will know."

"Will anyone else?"

"Niṭil-Kišar, certainly – and she would know what she saw. Gubaru, without knowing what he saw but vaguely, instinctively, sensing what he did not see. Possibly Mikum-Nisaba."

"Will I know?"

Nabû-na'id looked at him frankly. "The man I once knew, the fanatic who more than once plunged precipitously into the valley of the shadow of death – perhaps he would have known. But, my old friend, you are, like me, much changed. I'm not sure if you can tell death's shadow from all the other shadows which flit about us. Or rather, I suspect that you think you can."

"And that means that, unlike your family and close friends and even mere dogs, I shall fail to notice when you became faceless?"

"I never said dogs in general would notice. I said Fly, I expect, would notice."

"But I would not?"

"Probably not."

"Why not?"

"You don't need me to tell you," Nabû-na'id answered quietly.

Belet-ṣeri-dannat nodded sadly. "Because you need a face to see a face," he said slowly. "And the faceless do not see the faceless." He lifted his head and looked fiercely at the king. "Is that what I have become in your eyes?"

"What does it matter what you have become in my eyes?" Nabû-na'id responded. "See what the dog thinks of you." He gestured at Fly. "See what Fly thinks of you."

"No." Belet-ṣeri-dannat answered simply. "You're inconsistent," he added after a moment. "Sometimes you say you have a face which you are in danger of losing. Sometimes you imply you don't have a face. Which is it?"

"I don't know. Maybe it's that we all have the potential for faces. We are born with the possibility of a face. And, over the course of our lives, that possibility diminishes – steadily, perhaps inexorably. When we die, we are buried not with a face but with a death mask confused for a face."

"Too simple," Belet-ṣeri-dannat almost barked. "Every moment of our lives we have what could be a face, what could be a mask. Their possible confusion persists from birth to death and never abates."

Nabû-na'id looked at him curiously. "Perhaps you are not as changed as I thought," he murmured. Then, stepping forward, he clutched his friend by the shoulders and kissed his cheeks. "How glad I am to see you again!"

Who are you? I asked.

The lean ibis head bearing on its crown the cusped moon answered that some called him Sîn, when seen from the front, and others Nabû, when seen from the side, but that he was best known as Thoth and that he was a god of writing. Having spoken, using his beak as a stylus, he recorded something on the tablet that he held in his hand.

What have you recorded? I asked.

I would like to say everything, the lean ibis head responded. But that is not possible – certainly not for a god of writing. Again he bent over his tablet and wrote with his beaked mouth.

What do you mean? I asked.

That is precisely the problem, he answered – and wrote.

Why do you keep writing? I asked.

I am a god of writing. What else am I to do? Again he inscribed something in his tablet.

Why am I here? I asked.

Did you not come in search of a face? he inquired, not looking up from his writing.

Yes.

Come closer.

I approached the scribbling god. All the while he sewed signs into his tablet with his beak.

Closer.

I approached more closely.

Closer.

I was now a finger's length from the god's bent and pounding head. As I neared, his beak-writing became for some reason ever more furious, and no doubt accidentally, the cusped moon on his crown rhythmically hammered the top of my head. I could see the tablet in his hands, and every time he lifted his head, I could see the signs that he wrote. But I did not recognize the signs. They could as easily be the footprints of birds, I thought. Perhaps they were not signs.

He stopped writing – if that was what he was doing – and looked up, looked at me, into me, through me. I could not understand what it was that confronted me. I could make no sense of his beak or his eyes or the rest of what would be a face. In fact, I could not tell if he had a face or if he did not. I could not tell if it was a face that I was looking at. If not a face, what? I did not know.

Gently, putting his tablet aside, he cupped my head in his hands. He brought his beak forward, as if to kiss my forehead. And then, like a tattoo artist but fiercely, he began to write my face.

(But this that I have written is not entirely true. I do not

understand why I have misled you, much less why I am confessing now. For what I have attributed to Thoth as spoken words he did not in fact speak. What I took him to say he said with gestures, not words; and hence developed my suspicion, perhaps exaggerated, that the god did not know how to talk.)

(Dare I confess my other suspicion? That the god did not know how to write? That his few dots, zigzags and lines were but the imitation of writing, or even, perhaps, the imitations of footprints – of bird prints and animal prints and even the prints left by hermit crabs as they scuttle across submerged sands? And yet I submitted to his writing of my face. I was curious. Perhaps – this has occurred to me too – perhaps I was even desperate.)

* * * * *

From the [fragmentary] Assyrian Accounts of Herodotus

...Labynetus's obsession with Sargon was widely spoken of, the priests say, and by many was condemned. In part this had to do with the manner in which Labynetus worshipped the ancient king, not only as a god but as part of the cult of the Moon. Some considered this impious; Labynetus claimed, however, that such worship was anciently attested, and my priestly sources grudgingly admit that there is some truth in this. But, they add, it was precisely the impiety of Sargon and his sons that was responsible for the later troubles of his empire, which culminated in its collapse and utter destruction, as I shall describe. And so they still consider Labynetus's conduct to have been sacrilegious and yet another reason for the punishment the gods brought to bear against him and his line, when they anointed Cyrus true king of Babylon. His fate proves his sacrilege, they say, as Sargon's did before him. It is possible. But – and this is an old man who speaks – have we not seen good men punished by envious gods, and bad men rewarded? Or a good man who reaps the dues of evil wrought by an

ancient ancestor, while a bad man reaps the rewards earned through an ancestor's struggle and sacrifice? Is this not evidence that to the gods we are not what we are to ourselves? In our own eyes we are points; in theirs, lines; or, if in our eyes we are lines, yet to theirs we are circles, triangles, squares; or again, where we are to ourselves shapes, we are to them solids. The gods perceive a dimension more of us than we do. The old man I have become wonders who is the more deceived, gods or men. An even older man, however, wonders instead if the gods see a dimension less *than men, who are and have ever been only individual points, incapable of stringing themselves together even into something as paltry as a line, much less a figure or a solid. But the oldest man I have yet become suspects instead that gods are not geometers at all but voids, as it were the dust in which a point or a line may be drawn – dust that is helpful for seeing what is not a point but an image of a point, dust then that does not affect the point, is not needed by it and thus is irrelevant to the point as it really is. Add to this that the dust is not even dust and you will understand.*

But let us say for now that Sargon was not a point, line, figure or solid, just as the stars and their motions through the heavens are not, though we understand something of them through geometry. Who then was Sargon? So long ago did he live, I am told, that his name is older than Egypt's. The story goes that he was the son of a priestess of the Moon, herself the daughter of the king. Impregnated by the god, she gave birth in secret and, whether out of fear or because a god told her to, abandoned the baby in a reed basket that she placed in the river. A man named Akkes, gardener of the king, found the basket and in it the child, and together with his wife raised the boy as his own. As the years passed Sargon grew into a youth of great strength, speed and stature, famed as well for his courage and judgment. That he could not be the son of a mere gardener all acknowledged; though whether he was the son of a god, a hero or a king no one could say.

There arrived a day when Sargon was helping his seeming father Akkes tend the king's lands. A royal hunt drew nigh and over the course of it a lion was wounded but not killed. The enraged animal turned on its tormenter and was on the verge of destroying him when Sargon, drawn by the commotion, arrived, rescued the youth and with the latter's own misthrown javelin killed the beast. It turned out that the youth was none other than the youngest and most beloved son of the king, whose name was Ursabes; the city which he ruled was called Kis. His son's rescue of course brought Sargon to the attention of Ursabes, who, unbeknownst to either of them, was also Sargon's grandfather. Though the king was determined to richly reward him, he was nonetheless troubled by Sargon's name; for in their language, Sargon means "true king" or "just king," and to invite a man so-named into political life seemed to Ursabes an unwise proposition. Therefore he instead decreed only that Sargon be the companion and cupbearer of the prince whom he had rescued. Yet this ended up having the opposite effect than the king intended; for over the course of the years, all three of his older sons died, either in battle or of sickness; and at last the youngest son became his heir and was required at court. Sargon of course arrived with him and so was exposed regularly to court life, where he became not only experienced but respected, as much for his deliberation and wisdom as for his courage and strength. Even the king, despite his apprehensions, came to value Sargon's counsel and as the years wore on kept him more at his own side than at his son's. Indeed, he kept Sargon at his side more than he kept his son and heir there.

But then Ursabes was visited by a recurring dream, one that disturbed him deeply. In the dream, a great hero – who had conquered monsters and visited the Underworld, and whose city was called Orekh – visited Ursabes. "Beware of the cupbearer," the hero said, "for in his cup he pours both remedy and poison. It is he who shall tear down my walls, walls that I built by my own hands and with the strength of a god to assure my immortality – and he will tear them down! And if my walls, what of yours?" So the hero in the dream said. Night after night came the same dream, and the king became frightened. He told no one, however – except his son. Around the same time, Sargon too had a dream. One night, a second night, three nights he had the dream. So bothered was he by the dream that he endeavored not to sleep and over time grew sickly and weak. His friend the prince observed his pallor and asked him about it. "It is because my sleep is troubled," Sargon explained. "It is because in my dreams I fight fiercely against a god-like opponent, and though I prevail, I awaken exhausted from the struggle." "Tell me your dream," the prince urged. So Sargon recounted his dream to the prince. "In my dream," he said, "a great hero of old comes to me, and we wrestle in the doorways, and then in the streets. I set my leg and bend my knee and with great strength I hurl him at his walls, the very ones he built by his own hands and with the strength of a god, and at the impact the walls crumble and fall. I rush up to my opponent, but beneath the debris of the wall I find no man, only dust and clay."

The prince, hearing the dreams of both his father and his friend, immediately recognized their import, not least because Sargon was his own cupbearer. He was uncertain what to do, torn between his loyalty to the man who gave him his life and to the one who saved it. At last he decided on the following course. He approached his father and told him that he had a matter of immense importance to share, but that he could do so only if his father swore a mighty oath. "What must I swear?" his father asked. "You must give me a man's life that I ask for and swear not to raise a weapon against him." "That is an odd request, but this matter is important, you say, and you are my only remaining son, whom I trust and love. Therefore do I swear as you request of me." And the king then swore the oath demanded of him. When he had finished, his son related the dream of Sargon. The king immediately saw its relevance. "We must kill this cupbearer before he brings harm to our land!" he exclaimed. His son stopped him. "That I forbid," his son proclaimed daringly, "for it is Sargon's life that you must give to me; it is against Sargon that you have sworn not to raise your weapon."

The king acceded to his son's demand out of respect for his oath, but his heart was far from easy. Moreover, he continued to be visited by the same dream, and if anything, the hero in it was the more urgent in his warnings. "And if my walls, what of yours?" he repeated, before one night adding, "What can a king bequeath to his heir without walls?" Without telling his son, the king therefore decided to consult with one of his advisors, a man well-known for his sagacity. When he had described his dreams to this man and had disclosed what the prince had told him of Sargon's dreams, the advisor, considering the matter clear cut, immediately urged that Sargon be sent away. "One does not keep scorpions by one's bed," he observed. "Where should I send him, that he can do me no harm?" the king asked. "There is only one place to send him where he can do no harm," the sage replied, "and we both know where that is." "My oath precludes that possibility," the king answered. "Your oath prevents you from raising a weapon against this man; it does not prevent you from sending him where another might." With that, the sage advised the following: "Entrust a written message to Sargon and have him deliver it to your friend, King Zages of Orekh. And let the message be simple: in it demand the execution of the messenger. Thereby will you be delivered of blood guilt as well as of Sargon." The king reluctantly agreed that this was the best course and made preparations accordingly. The message he wrote urged King Zages that, by force of an omen received by Ursabes, whoever bore this message to him must be killed – and that both their kingdoms depended upon it.

So off to Orekh, to King Zages, Sargon went, himself bearing the message of his own doom – much as Homer relates of Bellerophon in the Iliad. *But when Sargon arrived at Orekh, so astonished was he by its famous walls that he desired to investigate them more closely. At the main gate of the city, after he announced who he was, for what he had come and by whom he was sent, he then declared his admiration of the walls. "May I be permitted," he asked, "to pace out the walls, to study the foundation terrace and inspect the brickwork?" "What of your message?" the guard asked. "Can it not be delivered to the king on my behalf?" The guard agreed that it could and hailed a palace messenger to take receipt of the tablet and deliver it. Meanwhile Sargon examined the upper walls, whose facing gleamed like copper; he gazed at the lower course, with nowhere its equal; he mounted the stone stairway, there from days of old; and he wondered at the kiln-fired brick, its perfect dimensions and its strength drawn as if by the hands of a god from the lowliest mud. And when he had satisfied himself, he returned home to Kis.*

Of course Ursabes was shocked by Sargon's return. "Was the message delivered?" he asked. "It was," said Sargon, "and I had the opportunity as well to explore Orekh's miraculous walls." "Did you deliver the message in person?" the king asked. "No," confessed Sargon, "it was given to a palace messenger, and it was he who delivered it." Ursabes immediately realized his mistake, but he hid his displeasure and instead thanked Sargon for fulfilling his task. "You have done admirably," he said. "I may make use of you in a similar role in the future." Several days passed before, one night, Sargon was again visited by a dream. In the dream, a goddess, the Babylonian Aphrodite, came to him. She instructed him to follow her, which he did; and at her indication, he hid in the brush by a vernal pool. Much to his surprise, the king Ursabes came to the pool, undressed, and began to bathe. Then, to Sargon's astonishment, the goddess joined the king in the pool, splashed him and played with him, then drew him beneath the waters. The king never returned, and eventually Sargon woke from a dream which had become endless contemplation of still waters at the surface of a pool. He was much bothered by this dream, and since it involved the king, he felt obliged to tell Ursabes. Of course, when he did so, the king was terrified beyond belief, though he hid it. Instead, he thanked Sargon for this disclosure, whose meaning (he said) he could not begin to comprehend, and sent him on his way. But later in the same day he summoned Sargon, again with a message for him to bear to the king of Orekh. "It is essential that you hand this to him in person," Ursabes insisted. In the tablet, he again urged King Zages, on account of omens portending evil for them both, to kill the messenger, after first confirming that he was Sargon, and to return the man's head to Kis by a different messenger.

So Sargon set off on his way, but he had barely left when he encountered the prince whose life he had saved. "Where are you off to?" the prince inquired. "Your father has again sent me to Orekh with an urgent message, one that I am to deliver in person," replied Sargon. "May I join you?" the prince asked. "Of course! I should be glad of the company." And so the two travelled together to Orekh. But just as the great walls of that city were rising distantly into view, Sargon grew weak and feverish. He endeavored to press on but could barely stand. "You must rest," the prince said, leading his friend to a road-side tavern. "But the message is urgent," Sargon insisted. "I have promised your father the king to deliver it as quickly as possible, and in person." "I will deliver the message for you," the prince replied. "Surely whatever my father would entrust to you he would entrust to his only son." And so the prince left Sargon in the care of a woman who kept the tavern and himself proceeded with all due speed to Orekh. When he arrived, he announced himself as the prince of Kis, come to see King Zages in person with an urgent message. King Zages greeted him and received the tablet. Once its content had been made known to him, he was much troubled. "Your father gave this to you to deliver?" he asked. "I am indeed delivering it for my father," the prince replied. "And you are Sargon?" But the prince thought the king was asking him if he was a true king, meaning also a just or upright king, which is what the name "Sargon" signifies; and perhaps this is indeed what the king asked, not realizing "Sargon" was a name. The prince, though perplexed by such a question, answered, "I swear that I shall be." This answer was no less perplexing to King Zages, and he was uncertain how to proceed. "And who are you now?" he asked. "I am the man who will be a true king," the prince answered. King Zages looked at him sadly. "I fear not," he said, "for omens are terrible things, and the gods as fickle as flies." And he gave order as the tablet of Ursabes instructed.

Meanwhile, Sargon's condition improved and the following day he went to Orekh in search of his friend. When he arrived, he announced that he had come to confirm the delivery of the king's urgent message of the day before. "Yes, it was delivered," a palace attendant confirmed. "And has the messenger, the prince of Kis, been sent back already?" Sargon asked. "Yes," the attendant answered, "we have sent our must trustworthy messenger back with him, as your king demanded." Sargon, initially surprised that the prince was no longer there, understood this to reflect the importance of the message and of King Zages's response. Accordingly, he himself set off to return to Kis.

When the messenger from Orekh arrived, Ursabes happened to be in his bath. The messenger handed off the sack with the prince's head to a palace attendant, who brought it to the king without opening it. "This sack has arrived, sent with great urgency from Orekh's king," the attendant announced. "What shall I do with it?" "Bring it here," the king announced from his bath, "then leave me, all of you" he said, referring as well to his domestic servants. So he was left alone with the sack. With a sense both of melancholy and relief, he reached in and pulled the head out by its hair. When to his shock and horror he saw the gruesome face of his own son, he fainted dead-away and thus drowned in his bath. As fate would have it, he was there discovered by the very counselor who had first suggested the course of action the king had followed. This counselor, at first mystified why the king was drowned in his bath holding the head of his son, found a tablet that had accompanied the sack and, reading it, and realizing as a result at least partially what had transpired, destroyed first the tablet then himself in anguish. Thus was the palace left to discover a mystery without solution: the remains of a destroyed tablet scattered across the floor beside a blood-soaked sack, a counselor slain by his own hand, a decapitated prince, and a dead, drowned king. It was to the chaos of this scene that Sargon arrived. Understanding only that his friend the prince was dead and that he had been slaughtered through what could only be considered the perfidy of King Zages, he immediately raised and led an army, after much trial sacked Orekh and destroyed the very walls he had once admired, and returning in triumph was selected by the city elders king of Kis.

So this astonishing story was told to me by the priests. I was much troubled by it, though for a long time I could not think why. But finally it occurred to me, in time enough to ask the priests before my return from Babylon. "If that is what happened," I asked, "and all who knew of the king's two letters to Zages died, how is it that this story has been told? How is it that this mystery without solution has been solved?" My question was greeted with a long and unsettling silence, before at last a very ancient priest signaled to me to approach him. I approached, and with every step he beckoned me closer, until I could see the spittle on his lips and in the corners of his mouth and could feel his breath against my face. Into my ear this is what he whispered: "Some say the story was revealed to a prophet, perhaps in a dream." Then he stopped and I started to draw away, unsatisfied. But his claw-like hands gripped the back of my head and again drew me closer. "That is what some say," he whispered. "For my part, I believe what my father told me, and what his father told him, generation after generation." Again he stopped, but this time I waited, listening to his breath and feeling it in my ear, smelling his long-unwashed body, with his gnarled hands still entwined in the hair of my head. At last I heard the intake of breath that promised the revelation to come. The whisper was even quieter now, barely audible – I could not be sure I heard. But this is what I believe he said: "For my part, I imagine that Sargon knew how to read."

* * * * *

"Mother! How did you ever get here?"

"What does it matter, but that I am here?" the ancient woman responded. Still she wore rags and bathed in dirt – still, after all these years.

Nabû-na'id signaled for an attendant to bring a chair. One hurriedly did. "Bring some water – and beer," Nabû-na'id commanded. A second attendant hurried off. Meanwhile, Adad-guppi, almost a century old, sat down.

"Why have you come, Mother?"

"I wish to put off my mourning," she answered simply.

"Then do so."

She stared at him with her fierce, wild eyes. "How can I? How can I?" she almost shrieked. "How can I when you have yet to guide Sîn by hand to his temple in Ḫarrānu?"

Nabû-na'id held her gaze but said nothing.

"I do not wish to die in mourning," his mother added. "I have mourned almost my entire life. Shall my life only have been mourning?"

"You have mourned as long as I have known you," Nabû-na'id murmured. "But does that mean your life has only been mourning?"

"Yes," the old woman replied. "Yes. My every action I have done in mourning, my every word I have spoken in grief, my every breath has been a sigh of loss."

"And nothing else?"

"My sorrow is that there is nothing else."

They looked at each other for a moment in silence. The attendant arrived with water and beer. Adad-guppi ignored the water but without embarrassment drained the goblet of beer.

"Why do you obsess over the face of a statue?" she asked, wiping her mouth crudely with the back of her archaic hand.

"How do you know that that's what I do?"

"All of Bābilim speaks of it. They speak of our king turned

to stone in Sippar, our king who has made himself into a statue so that he can converse with statues."

"Ah," said Nabû-na'id with a smile both amused and sad. "Perhaps my duty to this statue is similar to yours to the god."

"It is not," his mother declared definitively. "You are not in mourning, as I am. Your every deed has not been dictated by it, as mine have been. You do not work to fulfill your duty, as I do. This," she continued, shaking her frail, skin-draped finger-bone at him, "is mere indulgence, mere reverie."

"You can tell just at a glance?" asked Nabû-na'id coldly.

"My glance is more penetrating than most," she answered.

"Yes, so it has often been." Again silence settled between them.

"I was thinking," his mother began anew, "as I was laboring from Bābilim to here. It is said you are troubled by the statue of Šarru-kēn because his face is smashed. It is said you are uncertain how to restore the face."

"Something like that," Nabû-na'id agreed.

"Is it that, or is it *like* that?" his mother asked sharply.

"It is *like* that. I am unsure whether there was ever a face to be restored."

"Of course there was."

"If so, then I am unsure if it was Šarru-kēn's or the statue's."

"There is no difference."

"Well, then, mother, you may happily join my cadre of advisors, who see things much as you do," Nabû-na'id commented acerbically.

"Why do you think there is such a sharp divide between a man and a statue, or even a stone?" his mother demanded. "Why are you paralyzed by whether there was ever a face? Do you not realize that a face is only a tapestry of scars, clefts wrought by time and by injury, quickly if by weapons and slowly if by tears? You would not deny a river its channel, why would you deny a man or a statue or a stone its face?"

"To restore a face is to take a face away, to hide it, even to erase it. I do not take that lightly."

"But what ever do you think a face is, if it isn't what is perpetually being erased, hidden and taken away? These scars that make my eyes, my nose, my mouth and my ears – you don't honestly think they are simply mine, do you? They were given to me, and not only by friends."

"And so I too am to give a stone ennobled into a statue of Šarru-kēn the scars that others call a face?"

"Of course, you foolish boy, of course."

Nabû-na'id smiled to hear himself called a boy. "Mother, how is it that we have lived so long, you and I, when for us life is so burdensome?" he asked quietly.

"I do not know how *you* live," his mother answered, emphasizing the pronoun, "when even a statue torments you. But *I* live to see, with my own eyes, the Moon again rise over Ḫarrānu, even if that moonrise signals the last of my days."

Nabû-na'id sighed. "Do you not know that Ḫarrānu is surrounded by Umman Manda? To restore the Eḫulḫul, to return Sîn to his temple, would mean war – a war that I am far from sure we could win."

"Ye of little faith," his mother chided. "I have dreamed that the time is nigh when the Umman Manda will have problems of his own. Sîn has favored me with those dreams, perhaps to bolster my spirits in the wake of my own son's almost blunted purpose."

"What have your dreams foretold?"

"You shall see for yourself."

Nabû-na'id laughed. "What, would a dream be like a tablet, to be shuttled from one reader to the next?"

"What is there that is not like a tablet?" his mother asked, before abruptly rising and turning in the direction from which she came.

"Where are you going?"

"Back."

"To Bābilim?"

"Where else? Ḫarrānu, you have told me, is not yet available."

"Why do you dawdle in Sippar?" It was Marduk who spoke, though his face was expressionless, his body without gesture. Sîn stood at his side, radiant.

"I am restoring, carving, scarring and creating a face. When I am done, I shall leave."

"It is no face you carve," the expressionless, gestureless god announced. "You well know what that statue is; it is the Tablet of Destinies. You have lingered with it enough, scrawled what you will across it, and now I have come to reclaim it." With awful, jerking motions, the god lifted one arm, then the other, as if to receive the Tablet. The arms were held too far apart and were uneven with each other. Sîn, meanwhile, remained at his side, silent, radiant.

Nabû-na'id found in his hands the statue of Šarru-kēn. He raised it, held it out to the god. Marduk's arms jerked ineffectually, as if striving to come closer, and Nabû-na'id stretched forward with the statue, endeavoring to deliver it to where the god's arms already were. He pressed the base of the statue into the right hand of Marduk, and then freeing his own hand, used it to manipulate the god's left hand around the other side of the base. Then he let go. He knew what would happen, though he was strangely helpless to avert it.

The statue tumbled from Marduk's useless hands, crashed to the ground, shattered.

With jerking motions, the god withdrew first one arm, then the other, until they rested stiffly at his side. Sîn, meanwhile, remained silent, radiant.

"No matter. My son shall write another," said the god,

expressionless, gestureless.

"It was the Tablet of Destinies!" Nabû-na'id cried out in despair.

"So it was. No matter. My son shall write another," repeated the god, without intonation. "You must turn your attention to other things." Then, grotesquely, the god endeavored to kick a fragment of the statue to the side. His foot caught on the fragment – the fragment was stronger than his kick – and as a result he fell face-forward.

"What other things must I turn my attention to?" Nabû-na'id asked the prostrate god. The god did not answer but lay there, helpless, face to the ground. Nabû-na'id remembered the fly, long ago, tumbled on its back, uselessly striving to climb into the heavens with feet that found no purchase in the sky. "The fly with which I wooed Niṭil-Kišar," he whispered to himself. "A bouquet made from another's suffering."

"I am not suffering," the god's muffled voice proclaimed from the ground, into which he spoke.

"Why do you not rise?"

"I am fine where I am."

Sîn, meanwhile, shone silent radiance.

"What other things must I turn my attention to?" Nabû-na'id repeated.

"You know," the muffled voice answered into the dirt, the god's body surreally still. "Carry bricks on your horse, build the Eḫulḫul and establish the dwelling of Sîn, the great lord, in its midst."

"But how am I to return –" he looked up at the silent, radiant god, "– Sîn to Ḫarrānu when it is surrounded by the Umman Manda?"

"The Umman Manda whom you mention, he, his country and the kings who march at his side will cease to exist," the prostrate god replied, speaking to the dirt. "Let the brood feed on its parent; let the prince of Anšan devour his grandfather; let Kuraš eat the Umman Manda."

Nabû-na'id looked quizzically at the back of the feeble god. "If

Anšan should overpower the Umman Manda, would that truly bode any better for my kingdom?"

"Trust me," Marduk answered simply.

"Trust a god who writhes helplessly in the dirt, like a worm?"

"I am not helpless." The god's body twitched ineffectually several times. "I choose to lie here like this. It is what I want."

"Why would a god wish to lie prone in the dirt?"

"Gods are mysterious beings. You cannot understand our ways."

"So you say. But what I see is a god who lacks the strength to hold a statue, who cannot coordinate his hands and feet, who has the dexterity of a corpse. I see a god who destroyed the Tablet of Destinies out of sheer clumsiness. I see a god whose advice I cannot wisely leave unquestioned."

"Why not?" the muffled, inflectionless voice replied pathetically.

"What kind of advocate could you be?" Nabû-na'id demanded.

"As good as any other," the inflectionless voice spoke into the dirt.

"You can't even rise!"

The god twitched uselessly several times. "I could if I wanted to," said his voice.

"You are a bug!"

"I am a god!" the monotone declared.

"Bug!"

"God!" But then Marduk coughed violently, having inadvertently breathed dirt into his nose and mouth. From Sîn, meanwhile, shone silence radiant.

Then, abruptly, a certainty gripped Nabû-na'id, a certainty he could neither doubt nor explain. Marduk, he suddenly knew, was only a puppet, and Sîn was his puppet-master. Sîn had delivered the puppet to Nabû-na'id's feet and his command was clear: destroy the god, squash the bug, proclaim the reign of Sîn. And in echo he heard the prostrate god declare, inflectionlessly, "Destroy me, squash me, proclaim the reign of Sîn." And Sîn stood silent, shining radiantly.

Nabû-na'id hovered over the helpless god, raised his foot, prepared to stomp him –

But his limbs jerked ineffectually, he could not coordinate his legs, he fell face-first into the dirt.

"So the giver-of-faces has returned," Niṭil-Kišar observed without rising. "Welcome back to Bābilim, the gate of the gods."

"I am glad to see you," Nabû-na'id said quietly.

"Did you succeed?"

"In giving Šarru-kēn a face? Who can say? The statue has a new and different scar, anyway, one which effaces several that were earlier." He paused. "You never told me why you chose not to come with me."

"That is true; I did not."

They were both silent for a few moments. "Were you lonely here, with Mikum-Nisaba in Uru and me in Sippar?"

"I was ok. I saw our son a few times and made a trip to visit our priestess-daughter. And I worked on my canal project, which you in your letter associated with Naqi'a. You have not forgotten your promise?"

"To assign an official and work crew to carry out your orders?"

"Yes."

"No, I have not forgotten."

"It will be done?"

"It will be done." He paused, then added, "You haven't really explained that project to me."

"No," she agreed. "I have not." There was another awkward silence. She volunteered nothing; he asked nothing, beyond the question he had suggested but not asked. Eventually, weakly, she suggested, "You have your preparations to make, should the Umman Manda come…"

He looked at her silently for a moment, holding her gaze until she turned away. "I no longer think it will be the Umman

Manda," he volunteered, "at least not in the form that we have known him. That young upstart Kuraš –" Nabû-na'id stopped for a moment, collected his thoughts. "His future is bright like the sun," he concluded simply, "at least for a while."

"What makes you think so? I've heard little about him."

"My mother told me. And I had a dream. And you know what was most convincing about my dream? The sense that lingered with me afterwards – that Kuraš was like the men I encountered long ago in Luddu, the men who, only thinly disguised, eat each other's flesh."

"He's a cannibal?" she asked, arching an eyebrow.

"Figuratively speaking, yes – and that's the most dangerous kind. But another way of putting it is – in my dream, I sensed that Kuraš is... more alive... than the rest of us. Certainly, than me."

"That bodes well for him, then."

"It bodes well for a conqueror, anyway." He stopped again, and then added, "I came home because I realized that whatever I gave that statue of Šarru-kēn would not be a face. Or if it was, it wouldn't matter. And that's because I sensed something else about this Kuraš fellow, this young upstart. I sensed that he's the new face of Šarru-kēn."

"Destined, then, to rule Akkadê once more?"

"No doubt."

"Will you resist?"

"When the time comes, in some small degree." He looked at his wife, then added, "It is a sign of our doddering empire that its doddering king should be gripped by a statue more than he is by the growing shadow of a gathering enemy. Kuraš, if he is indeed the new face of Šarru-kēn, looks to a future when he shall rule the world as his predecessor did. This is in part why he is more alive than the rest of us; he overflows into the future. But not indefinitely... He doesn't foresee his own defaced statue as building fill thousands of years from now. And he doesn't see beyond that, either. He doesn't see himself, as I am beginning to see myself, from the perspective of a forever that has already happened."

"Ah," said Niṭil-Kišar, "I am beginning to understand. He is more alive than you are, but you are more dead than he."

Nabû-na'id smiled sadly. "Voilà, my advantage."

* * * * *

From the [fragmentary] Assyrian Accounts of Herodotus

...Of Nitocris's waterworks, of their genius and their folly, I have already written in my Histories.

* * * * *

Read Nabû-na'id, thus writes En-nigaldi-Nanna, a priestess of Sîn, and Mikum-Nisaba, a king's daughter and a scribe's.

I have been imagining you with this statue, which has so tightly gripped you – as if you were the statue, to be held and handled, and it the man, active, reflective, empowered. And who is to say it is not? Are there not objects that capture our glance and refuse to release it, sometimes because what our glance encompasses it cannot fathom, other times because their demand of us is incessant and unyielding? Maybe those are not two different instances, but one. What is the difference, do you think, between what is beyond our ken, before which our understanding collapses, and an endlessly unfurling duty relentlessly extorted from us? I think of the black cat on Izdubar's lap, in those stories you used to tell. He does not dare to rise and unsettle her; his duty to her unrolls like a royal carpet plummeting down an endless flight of stairs. May he sit forever! That's what I say today, but tomorrow – I make no promise about what I shall say tomorrow. But is this plummeting carpet really a different experience than the first that I described, when our glance is torn from us because it pursues a horizon that's always retreating? I think I remember Šarru-kēn describing his conquest all the way to the sea, where land ends and water begins and never again ends. Perhaps that was when he became a statue, as his gaze chased after the horizon forever. Maybe these are the same, these two instances, the cat on our lap and the indefinite sea – moments when we are confronted with the world all around us, but this time in its mystery and impossibility.

In any event, in these moments it is either the world that confronts us, or we who confront the world. Either the statue grips you, or you the statue. But I'm making myself dizzy and can no longer tell who is who. Perhaps that's what it means to be gripped by a statue, or to fall forever down a flight of stairs. (But am I a carpet now, I who before beheld the unwinding carpet?)

This is a different matter now – or the same – I am not sure. As I am not sure what it would mean were the god to visit me. I hope I should notice! But I begin to suspect that it is possible I would not. Is one any the lonelier for awaiting a god's possible visit than – for not awaiting it? It will not seem as strange to you as it does to me, but what I miss right now, more than you and more than my mother, is Fly. I miss the dog. Perhaps that is because, a few days ago, an attendant brought me a small, broken statue – a figurine really – of a dog. "Where did this come from?" I asked. "It was left with the offerings." "For me?" "For you or for the god." Does it matter, I wondered, if it was for me or for the god, since now I am the god's? Whether he deign visit me or not; whether I deign notice his visit or not. I, like a god, am not without my pride. I accepted the figurine as mine, anyway; let the god protest if he likes. And so now I have a small clay dog with a broken foot. You trouble yourself with restoring faces – I would prefer to think of it as a re-awakening, a re-vivifying, but no matter. I am to trouble myself with something much harder, surely: supplying a foot to a statue. Harder because, for a dog, a foot must be not only what you stand on, but what you run with. Faces can be unperturbed, but not feet. If you don't believe me, ask Fly.

Your encounter with the statue of a shattered face, and mine with the broken-footed dog figurine, has given me an idea – that I shall share this sanctuary (if that is what it is) with those vestiges of the past which for whatever reason the dirt yields. Statues, figurines, steles, even sherds of broken pottery, the same as we stomp under our feet. A pot in which an unsurpassable grief and a child's bones have been sealed – only to be accidentally broken and released. All these shall find a place, however temporary, here with me in the god's empty house. I require of these my visitors only that they be forgotten; and that they sleep. They shall sleep here – and perhaps, someday, as I once imagined, I will conjure all my strength, my creativity and my longing into re-awakening them once more. Or, like Izdubar, perhaps I shall be the better host if instead I leave them to sleep forever on my lap.

He nodded at Belet-ṣeri-dannat and Nabû-zer-lišir and greeted his son. "Bel-šar-uṣur, has Belet-ṣeri-dannat brought you up to speed?"

"Yes," his son replied. "I know about mother's river project, as well as your plans for the Eḫulḫul and for the western campaigns."

"Good. I'll discuss that in more detail with you in a moment. Nabû-zer-lišir," he said, turning to the scribe, "I have been impressed with your work restoring the Eulmaš and with the –" he paused, then continued quickly, "– statue of Šarru-kēn. I wish you next to go to Akkadê. As you may know, during the restoration of Ištar's temple there, evidence was found of an ancient palace. I think it is the palace of Naram-Sîn."

"Šarru-kēn's son?" the scribe asked with evident interest.

"So it is said. He reigned, if I'm not mistaken, over three thousand years ago. I wish to bring his foundations back into the light."

"Very well."

"Show the same care as you did in Sippar and with Nabû-kudurri-uṣur's stele in Uru, and stay in touch with me, especially if you find anything that you have reason to know might interest me."

"Very well."

"Then go now; the palace scribes know of the project and will help you gather what resources you need."

With a bow the scribe left.

"Now, Bel-šar-uṣur, you will be king sooner rather than later, I suspect. We need to help prepare you. Let's set aside your mother's project, which is in her more-than-capable hands. As for mine, what are the steps we must take in order to realize them?"

"We shall have to make ready the army and prepare a campaign to the north and west – to drive the Umman Manda away, secure Ḫarrānu, then proceed from there south into Amurru."

"But would that be wise? Short of obliterating the Umman Manda, we would leave an embittered foe on our flank."

"Then we shall have to obliterate him."

"An ambitious, maybe foolhardy task. Let me propose something else as a lesson for a young man who will soon take the reins of kingship."

Bel-šar-uṣur gave his father an impatient and irritated glace. "Shall we restore more statues in preparation?" he asked sarcastically.

"No," his father answered, ignoring his son's tone. "We shall begin by writing letters."

"Letters?"

"To Kirsus in Luddu. And to Kuraš in Anšan."

"And what shall our letters say?"

"To Kirsus we shall remind him of those moments when our

paths have already crossed – much to the advantage of his land. We shall propose an alliance, against the Umman Manda and, if Kirsus is wise, against Kuraš as well."

"What concern do you have with Kuraš and his little kingdom – really his band of ruffians?" Bel-šar-uṣur asked. "He's a nobody."

"I too was a nobody, the son of nobody," Nabû-na'id observed, "that is to say, the son of a mad woman from Ḫarrānu and an eccentric scribe who passed his days more or less as an exile in foreign courts. That you are somebody, being my son, though I am, or was, myself nobody the son of nobody, should give you pause... And if you took statues more seriously, that would give you pause too. Šarru-kēn, they say, was the son of a gardener."

"And no doubt this Kuraš will be Šarru-kēn's second coming!" Bel-šar-uṣur declared mockingly.

Belet-ṣeri-dannat spoke up. "He may well be. Your father is right to be wary of him. Kirsus looks the more formidable, but word has it that Kirsus is mostly a fool. A wise king is rightfully more anxious about lean and hungry men like Kuraš than men born into luxury, pampered and fat. Surely you would agree?"

"Very well, very well – perhaps I am too quick to mock. What shall you write this terribly dangerous upstart, father?"

"Only that I have observed his poor treatment by the Umman Manda and am hopeful that my mighty neighbor Ištumegu comes to his senses before his grandson's commendable patience is exhausted. For the gods, it is said, do not blame the abused man who defends himself."

"That's a new view of the gods, coming from you," Bel-šar-uṣur commented acerbically.

"What people say of the gods is not necessarily the same as my view of them."

"So what do you imagine this little note of commiseration

will accomplish?"

"In the short-term, not much. In the longer term, perhaps it will help open the path to Ḫarrānu, so that I can fulfill what is my duty either to a god or my mother and rebuild the Eḫulḫul."

"And, in the longest term, thereby secure Ḫattu," his son added.

"Ḫattu," Nabû-na'id remarked, looking evenly at his son, "will be secured – for a while. That is all."

"Perhaps that is all – in your reign. But in a reign to come, perhaps we shall see the empire of Šarru-kēn not only reborn but enlarged and stretching from one end of the earth to the other."

Nabû-na'id exchanged glances with Belet-ṣeri-dannat. The latter spoke. "If I am not mistaken, that is precisely what your father foresees."

"For once, then," Bel-šar-uṣur announced triumphantly, "we, father and son, are on the same page. I am glad you have turned your attention back to the true responsibilities of rulership; let our actions be inspired by Šarru-kēn, not by a statue!" He gave his father's upper arm a companionable slap. "Now, let's discuss your plans for Amurru."

Chapter 8. The New Year's Festival

"Well, what do you think?"

"I think he's matured a lot in the last year," Belet-ṣeri-dannat admitted. He was once again wearing his customary blue with his customary cap. "He's been paying much better attention to detail, he's been more subtle, his rapport with the troops is good, even his rapport with the administrators is good."

"How is his rapport with you?"

"I think it's gotten better – grudgingly, on his part. He resented me for a long time, perhaps pegging me as some sort of minder. But it seems to me that, even if he doesn't trust my person, he trusts my advice. And" Belet-ṣeri-dannat smiled wryly, "I have the advantage, in his eyes, of at least being practical, unlike some."

Nabû-na'id grimaced. "I take it you haven't found occasion to discuss your god with him, then."

"My god is God, the one and the only. If He should require it of me, then even Bel-šar-uṣur would hear of Him from me."

"And yet," Nabû-na'id quietly observed, "it has been some time since god has spoken to you, has it not?"

Belet-ṣeri-dannat froze for a moment, then, with obvious and even dutiful effort, relaxed. "I am in no position to judge God, not his timing nor his company."

"You do not fear that perhaps you have lost the way?"

Belet-ṣeri-dannat looked at him without answering.

"I know it is a painful question," Nabû-na'id acknowledged, speaking softly. "I pose it not as your king, nor out of mockery. I pose it as your friend."

"I know," Belet-ṣeri-dannat answered. "Or at least –" he again smiled wryly "– I think I know." He paused. "I have to trust that God would correct me had I gone astray."

"But what would that correction look like? Or sound like?"

"I will know it if I see it. Or hear it."

"Do you never doubt your eyes or your ears? Do you never worry that your sight or your hearing could fail you? Or perhaps already have?"

"God will supplement me where I fall short."

"And within your innermost heart you have no misgiving?"

"The Law is inscribed in my heart, by the finger of God."

They sat beside one another in silence. After a while, Nabû-na'id again spoke. "I am sorry to pester you. My own encounters with the divine – which is not your divine –"

"There is only one divine," interrupted his friend.

"– have not inspired a faith so exalted as yours," Nabû-na'id continued, ignoring the interruption. "A faith, perhaps, but not an exalted one. On the difference, you and I should talk some time. But I wonder, sometimes, that your faith can be so exalted while your concerns and actions are so worldly. You seem to have a greater tolerance and, if I'm not mistaken, even a greater interest, in this competitive, conniving, often trivial world of ours than I do, even though your understanding of the divine, and of your relationship to the divine, is so much –" he searched for a word "– *grander* than mine. I confess that it confuses me."

"Is it truly as strange as you make out that I engage with the world and with men – the world which God made, the men who are His likeness – while not thinking that God is a fly?"

A laugh erupted from Nabû-na'id like a bark. "Put that way," he admitted, "perhaps not. And yet, this world with which you engage – does it not strike you as a fly's world? Your god, how could he concern himself with so petty, ugly and cruel a world? A world in which even good men are transformed into monsters."

"Perhaps that is why he concerns himself with it," Belet-ṣeri-dannat pronounced sanctimoniously.

"Then he is a god of flies."

"No, God is God of all, of flies and of leviathans and of everything in between."

Nabû-na'id pursed his lips in thought for a moment. "Seen from a particular light," he observed, "there is no in between and even flies are leviathans." He waited a moment, then added, "And, of course, vice versa: surely, to a god, even a leviathan is a mere fly." He paused. "Although..." he began, a glint of almost child-like curiosity in his eyes, "do you think a god can experience wonder, even if looking at his own creations? Could a leviathan, or even a fly, amaze him? Do you think we amaze him?"

Belet-ṣeri-dannat made a face, then proceeded with a tone of thickening sarcasm. "Is it for me to declare God awe-stricken? How could it be? God, our Book says, feels wrath, satisfaction, even jealousy. But amazement? While we're at it, should we not add sublimity to the traits either denied God or, if not, inexplicable in him? With enough effort, then, perhaps we can happily reduce God from the uncanny to the merely paradoxical, and you and I can ponder how best to make a statue of Him. But wait – it is as if I have forgotten – my God forbids idols. Perhaps He has a reason? And perhaps idols are as like to be crafted in words as in wood, stone or gold."

"And yet you admit your book describes God as angry, satisfied and jealous."

"So it does. But those are not words, but allegories. Or rather, they are neither words nor allegories, but like allegories."

"And yet they look and sound so like words."

"So they do." Silence settled between them again, somewhat uncomfortably, Nabû-na'id pondering the necessity of words which at best aspire to allegory. He said nothing however, and it was instead his friend who spoke. "Is this why you have called me here, to discuss the characteristics of God, his capacity for wonder, sublimity, even – if we dare ask – irony?"

Nabû-na'id looked at him frankly and sighed. "No, my friend. I wish it were. Such discussions may not be practical – whatever practical means – but they seem to cut closer to the bone than the dutiful conversations that are habitual between a king and his advisers. If I were to talk about chisel manufacture, after all," he noted with a bitter laugh, "no one would complain."

"So what is it that you called me here for?" Belet-ṣeri-dannat persisted.

"Oh, that." Nabû-na'id waved his hand dismissively. "I was wondering if in your judgment Bel-šar-uṣur is ready to govern. For," he murmured, watching his friend closely, "I should like to go away."

Nabû-na'id, Gubaru and Fly were walking together outside the city walls. "How rare it is, nowadays, to take a stroll with you," Gubaru observed.

"You forget; I am 'inspecting the battlements,'" Nabû-na'id announced in a grand and mocking tone.

"But of course," responded Gubaru, echoing the mockery.

"Your point, however, is not irrelevant to one of the reasons why I asked you to accompany my inspection." They walked together for a few steps while Gubaru waited for his friend to say more. Fly, meanwhile, ran off ahead and frolicked.

Nabû-na'id drew a deep breath. "I want to go away. In fact, I want to run away. And I'd like you to come with me, as one of my military advisors and head of my personal guard."

"Where will you go?"

"First, to the west, to Ammananu. The city has risen up; my departure will be on the pretext of settling that matter."

"And then?"

"I don't know. Beyond. Perhaps I'll set out in search of Humbaba or Uta-napištim."

"And I'm to be your Enkidu? I doubt I'd be wise to accept such a proposition."

"I was mostly kidding," Nabû-na'id admitted, "although whether you'd be wise or not to play the role of Enkidu remains a more subtle question. Still, I am not in search of a great name, for myself, for you, for anyone. To be honest, I'd like to be left alone. But that's a wish no king sees fulfilled."

"Probably not."

"Definitely not. A king runs away, and half the court comes with him. That's a strange flight, hardly what your typical runaway – or this one – has in mind. But so be it; nothing else right now is possible."

"Will your son accompany you?" Gubaru was careful never to mention Bel-šar-uṣur by name.

"No."

"If he will not go, then I am willing to."

Nabû-na'id stopped, grabbed Gubaru by the arm and asked him point-blank, "Will you forever be my son's enemy?"

"I will never be the friend of the man who killed my own son," Gubaru answered, holding Nabû-na'id's gaze.

"Does that mean you will be his enemy?"

"Not if I can avoid it – and him."

They stared at each other in silence. Eventually Nabû-na'id released his friend's arm, turned and started to walk again. Gubaru continued with him.

"If you come with me, you'll avoid him. It will be harder if you stay. I'll leave him in charge of Bābilim."

Alarm spread across Gubaru's face. "Is that wise?" he asked anxiously.

"Wiser to do so now, while I live and can rein him in, than

later. It also seems to me that he has grown a lot in the last few years, become accustomed to more responsibilities, handled himself better. I put him under the guidance of Belet-ṣeri-dannat some time ago, which at least separated the problem of learning to be a king from the problem of being my son. It has also lessened the influence of the Egibi House."

"Lessened."

"Yes, lessened. They still have my son's ear, but I think he is less their plaything than before. The little trick they pulled on him – which could have cost him his life and did cost Labaši-Marduk's his – has made him more wary."

"It made him a prince, and you a king."

"Curses, both."

"Does your son see them that way?"

"I doubt it. Not yet at least. Perhaps someday he will become sufficiently discerning, or wise, or tired, or old, or whatever it is that reveals or transforms blessings into curses."

Fly rejoined them and the three walked together in a companionable silence.

"Will Niṭil-Kišar come?" Gubaru asked.

"If she wishes to. If I can convince her to. She has become very taken with her river project and spends much of her time consulting with scribes or inspecting it in person. She also visits our daughter in Uru regularly. She may not want to leave all that behind. And to be honest, if she doesn't come, that's a further leash on –" he paused briefly "– our son. I trust her judgment as much as, or better than, my own. And her relationship with him is – warmer – than mine."

"It sounds like you don't expect that she will come."

"No, I don't."

"How long do you imagine being away?"

"I don't know. As long as I can get away with. But possibly I underestimate my own propensity for homesickness."

"Were you homesick when we were together in Luddu? As boys?"

"Yes and no. As my relationship with my father grew stronger, less so."

"He was a good man."

"Are there such things?" Nabû-na'id asked bitterly.

"Yes," Gubaru answered without hesitation.

Nabû-na'id looked closely at his friend. "There is at least one," he said after a moment.

Again they walked together in a companionable silence.

"When would you leave?"

"The New Year's Festival begins the day after tomorrow; to disrupt that would be chaotic and possibly catastrophic. As soon as it is done, we'll march to Ammananu –"

"Is the delay serious, do you think? It'll be at least two weeks." Gubaru interrupted.

"No. The army generals already know the plan and it gives us more time to get everything ready. Plus, I'm not worried about Ammananu. I'd like to put an end to their revolt quickly and bloodlessly, if it can be done. As long ago we managed, you and I and Niṭil-Kišar, in Ṣurru."

"As I recall, mainly Niṭil-Kišar."

"Yes, mainly Niṭil-Kišar."

"Where exactly is Ammananu? Is it far?"

"As I said, it's west, in a mountain range just beyond Ḫattu. Under good conditions, I think we could be there in two- or three-weeks' march. If we propagandize the march well, they might capitulate to our reputation before we even arrive. That in any event is my hope, and I have some ideas how to facilitate it."

"And after that – 'beyond'?"

"Yes. After that, beyond."

"But you will have to return in a year's time, I imagine, if only for the New Year's Festival."

Fly, who had been off investigating a drainage ditch, came loping back, muddy, stinky and seemingly well-satisfied. He waited for Nabû-na'id to lean down and let himself be sniffed. Nabû-na'id did it almost absent-mindedly. After suitable inspection, Fly gave his face a quick lick and headed back towards the drainage ditch. "There is hope for me yet," murmured the king. He turned his attention back to Gubaru.

"I'll respect this year's festival, since it's almost upon us. But I don't know what I'll do next year."

Gubaru looked stunned. "Are you serious?" he demanded.

"We'll see if I'm serious or not. Perhaps even I don't know."

Gubaru touched his friend's sleeve – the king's sleeve. "Be careful what you say, however you mean it. Marduk may be listening."

"Indeed, he may be. Or perhaps he is even now lying face-first on the ground, unable to rise."

Gubaru's face looked anguished. "Be careful!" he repeated, still gripping the sleeve. "Marduk may be listening!"

Nabû-na'id's eyes narrowed. "Gubaru," he began, "have you ever wondered why, in our festival, Marduk must be rescued by Nabû? And if it's Nabû who's the hero of the occasion, why is it that it's Marduk whom we celebrate?"

But Gubaru couldn't answer. He could only repeat, eyes wild with alarm, "Be careful! Be careful! Marduk may be listening!"

From the finest mountain cedar, from lapis lazuli, from gold, the craftsmen wrought their images. The puppets' bodies were of cedar, exquisitely carved to reveal not only the smooth flow of muscle just beneath the surface but even more remarkably the soft texture of the skin. The nails of the hands and feet were of the finest, most delicately inlaid gold, as was the face – the latter so subtly shaped that the puppets' expressions changed continually in the light, whether of the sun or of the flickering flame, or perhaps even their own light. The eyes were amethyst and the ears, the enormous ears, were lapis lazuli. Jarringly, the teeth were ebony, though usually concealed behind coral lips. Their wigs were woven from the hair of priestesses and kings, while the eyelashes and eyebrows were the gift of a baby's head. By way of strings as fine as those in spider webs, the arms at the shoulders and the elbow, the hands, the fingers, the legs at the waist and at the knee, the feet, the toes, the neck, the jaw, the coral lips, the eyebrows, even the eyelids made of shell, moved according to another's will.

For each puppet, a male and a female, three garments were prepared: one of prized linen, the gift from Muṣur's king; one of wool, shorn from the finest, unblemished sheep of the palace; and the last mere sackcloth woven from the tangled hair of feral goats captured for the purpose. Each garment was stained crimson with a dye produced from snails and brought to the capital by special caravan all the way from Ṣurru. The linen garment was further embroidered with gold; the trim of the wool one was of a fine indigo dye, again prepared and brought from Ṣurru; as for the sackcloth, once stained crimson, it was roughly rubbed in dirt and ash, and in the process torn.

Two crowns were also prepared: one of horn, silver and gold – a god's crown; the other of densely-matted felt interlaced with gems – a king's.

Who were the puppets? Adorned in linen from Muṣur and crowned in horn, they were gods; arrayed in wool and crowned in felt, they were royalty, king and queen; clothed in sackcloth, bareheaded, sandal-less, they were but a man, but a woman.

Having been fashioned and dressed in the attire of gods, for now they waited, their faces expectant and proud. Their role was to wait and to witness. More, much more, would be asked of them later.

It was the third day of the Akītu festival.

On the fourth day of the Akītu festival, the priest began, "When on high," and the puppets rose as one. "There was as yet no name, nor yet a name below. Apsû, the first one, the Begetter, and Tiamat, the Maker who bore all, flowed together, into one another they flowed, with no pasture to separate them, no bed of reeds to conceal them, nor was a single god manifest, nor a single name pronounced, nor a single destiny decreed. The gods were born within them, and within them their names."

The puppets swiveled their heads, one to the right, one to the left, so that their enormous lapis lazuli ears could better catch the divine names. First they heard "Laḫmu" and "Laḫamu," then "Anšar" and "Kišar," then "Anu" and "Nudimmud." And the puppets wondered – were these the names of different gods, or the different names of a single god? And what was "Apsû," what was "Tiamat"? Yet the puppets said nothing; their coral lips were still.

Not so the name-given gods. They spoke, they shouted, their clamor reverberated within Tiamat; in her belly they bellowed and bawled, in Anduruna, home of the gods, their home, their play was boisterous, their play was raucous. Apsû could not calm them, could not lull them, could not quiet them; and Tiamat would not try. However grievous their behavior, however bad their ways, no reproof of the child-gods escaped her; no sound, no word, no name escaped her.

Not so Apsû; from deep within, from his cavernous being, a wind stirred, a wind gathered, a wind erupted; and on the wings of the wind streamed words. "By day I cannot rest; by night I cannot sleep. These godlings, their ways I shall abolish; they I shall disperse; peace I shall impose," Apsû thundered. "Peace I shall impose – and with it sleep."

The puppets nodded at one another, and one mimed to the other, raising its baby-hair eyebrows, pursing its coral lips, "sleep," and the other fluttered its eyelid-shells, closed them, slumped to the ground, let its head droop to one side like a dew-logged flower, grew still, slept – until Tiamat screamed, until Tiamat shouted, until Tiamat shrieked, "How dare we let perish what we ourselves created!" – and the puppet drifting into sleep was jolted awake, leapt up, its eyes wide, its face pale; and beside it the other puppet trembled, the other puppet bit its lip, the other puppet stared blankly straight ahead.

Not only the puppets but Ea heard the shriek; Ea alone of the gods heard the shriek; over the din and clamor and racket of his fellows, Ea heard the shriek of Tiamat. Surreptitiously, he listened – and the puppets listened too – as vizier Mummu the Maker whispered into the ear of Apsû, "Put an end to their rowdy ways, put an end to their blaring riots, let poor Tiamat sleep!" Apsû nodded, was pleased, his face lit up; ecstatically Apsû and Mummu the Maker hugged, ecstatically they kissed; and Ea the witness, troubled, frightened, horrified, slunk away. Hands at their faces, their mouths ajar, aghast, the puppets exchanged shocked glances, their limbs twitching in wild, helpless, noiseless gestures.

But mighty Ea, conniving, clever and wise, spun a spell; he stilled the waters and poured sleep gently over the revelers; the boisterous gods he drenched quietly in sleep. Silence reigned. Apsû rested, Mummu the Maker rested, Tiamat rested; slowly, softly, tenderly, they gave themselves to sleep. Then, alone in all the silent world stood Ea. He wasted not a moment. To his father he went, to Apsû; he held him down; him he slew; Apsû Ea slew. Then, unfastening his father's brilliant cloak, his father's resilient belt, his father's radiant crown, Ea wore these himself.

(The puppets turned one to the other; each doffed its crown, then whirled, its crimson robe rising, opening, like a flower greeting the morning sun. Then each restored its crown to its place, bowed, and again gave its attention to the story-telling priest.)

In their stead, across slain Apsû, Ea bound Mummu the Maker, grasped by a nose-rope, then let loose a roar of triumph. Only then did Ea rest; costumed as his father Ea rested; very quietly in his private quarters Ea gave himself to rest. And in the stillness, before the other gods had awakened, he decreed, only in a whisper – so softly spoken that the puppets had to lean in, hold their breath, turn their enormous ears, one to the left, one to the right, toward the speaker – in a whisper he decreed, "These my quarters shall be called 'Apsû.'" There he welcomed his lover Damkina; in magnificence, in the gallery of destinies, in the chamber of designs, he welcomed her. First he created and she bore Bel, sage of the gods; then, hero of the gods, Marduk she bore and he created. Twins they were, the sage and the hero, created, born and suckled in pure Apsû, their father's home. Bel, the wise one, the clever one, never opened his eyes, never parted his lips; forever was he listening with his wide, his perfect ears; but his brother Marduk, proud, strong, heroic – four were his eyes, four his ears, from his lips blazed fire, his limbs were perfect, his height unsurpassed, his strength outstanding. Anu, perceiving him, cried out –

"Mariutu, Mariutu" chanted the puppets in unison. "Son, majesty, highness, sun of the gods!"

From his head rays of light tore forth; in his clenched fists writhed the winds; his mantle was the mantle of ten gods. "Son," Anu cried –

"Let the winds play!" the puppets chanted in unison.

And so Marduk fashioned dust for the winds, and they seized it joyfully and lofted it on high, into the sky the winds whirled, the whirlwind carried dust into the sky.

The commotion of the winds unsettled Tiamat; the gusting winds disturbed the gods; winds tossed and heaved them all. Qingu, deputy of the gods, approached Tiamat –

"Come, mother, do you not love us?" the puppets sang together.

"Come, mother, do you not love us?" repeated Qingu. "First Apsû was slain, Apsû whom you loved was slain, Apsû your lover was slain; but you said nothing. Now the winds are riled up, through your belly they twist and shriek, and no god can sleep. Will you again say nothing? Are you not a mother? You lurch uncomfortably, you stagger, you list; and your children cannot sleep! What about us? Remove this burden that we may rest; loose the battle-cry and gain vengeance! Destroy the destroyers, annihilate them, return them to nothing!"

So he rallied Tiamat and pleased her. And of herself she created, then she bore, first a pair of giant snakes, javelin-fanged, venom coursing in the place of blood; then two dragons helmeted with piercing rays of light. Around them she stationed the horned serpent, the mušḫuššu-dragon, the laḫmu-hero, the ugallu-demon, the rabid dog, the scorpion-man, the umu-demon, the fish-man, the bull-man, the šēdu and the awful, the relentless, the scavenging fly. Eleven others she made, more fearsome even than the first; and all she armed with weapons indomitable and with fearlessness. Over these and over all the gods she named Qingu chief, and upon a throne she placed him, saying, "My spell is cast, now shall reign your commands, your will and your whims. You alone shall be my lover; by my spell you are greatest of the gods." Then into his hands she pressed the Tablet of Destinies. "Clutch this to your chest always; only then will your word endure unchanged, only then will it be law!"

"Only then will your word endure unchanged, only then will it be law!" echoed the puppets excitedly.

Qingu rose majestically and from his lips issued destinies for each of the gods. When he finished, to them all he ordained, "What springs from your mouths shall smother fire, your spit shall be venom to the enemy, your glares shall strike him like lightning!" Anšar, meanwhile, overheard, became distraught. He bit his lip, fidgeted with his fingers, paced up and down; his liver erupted, his heart raced, his belly was in turmoil. "Ea!" he roared, but his voice broke, his voice cracked, his roar was quite feeble. Yet wily Ea heard him, approached, listened attentively, grew fearful. "But it is you who fix the fates unfathomably, you who create and who destroy!" Ea declared. "What they have done cannot be done! What can I do to undo what cannot be done?" To him responded Anšar, to the slayer of Apsû Anšar answered, the wily one Anšar chided, "Gather strength like a god, cultivate courage like a god, be like a god! Raise your arm against Tiamat!" But Ea looked askance, he twisted his mouth in dread, his agitation contorted his face. "What cannot be done cannot be undone," he insisted, withdrawing to his quarters.

"What cannot be done cannot be undone," repeated the puppets somberly.

Then Anšar summoned Anu, his son. "Here is the indomitable kašušu weapon, a warrior's weapon, its strength invincible, too great to behold, unfaceable. Take it, confront Tiamat, before the weapon force her to hear your words, your words and mine. What she has done cannot be done; tell her, for fear of the weapon, to undo it." Anu set out, Anu left as his father directed, Anu went toward Tiamat. But with every step the kašušu weapon grew smaller, with every step his confidence waned, the words in his heart grew jumbled and meaningless with each successive step. At last he could find no words and see no weapon, his confidence was gone, he turned back. Tiamat was too great. He stood before his speechless father, who tore his garments in despair, gnashed his teeth, beheld both Anu and Ea with disgust.

But Ea was not dismayed, Ea in his wisdom knew the way, from his secret chambers Ea called out. "Marduk the Hero, Hero Marduk, approach Anšar, stand before him, learn the task he asks of you and fulfill it." Marduk's heart was filled with joy, it danced to his father's words. He kissed Ea's lips and set off to Anšar. "Anšar," he said –

"Break your silence, part your lips, release to me your heart's desire," the puppets chanted.

"Anšar," Marduk repeated, "break your silence, part your lips, release to me your heart's desire."

"Hero Marduk, have you been fooled?" asked Anšar. "Has a trickster whispered deceitfully into your ears? Do you not understand that it is Tiamat, of womankind, bold, fearless, unconquerable, against whom you advance?"

"I am not fooled, no trickery has entered my ears; to me, Marduk the Hero, Tiamat matters not. Rejoice, Creator! Soon your foot will rest on the neck of your enemy."

"Soon on the neck of his enemy Anšar will rest his foot," the puppets intoned, each lifting its foot, one the right, one the left, in expectation of the victory.

"Then go!" Anšar replied joyfully. "Take the storm chariot and

ride against our foe!"

From the shadows came a voice, one since ancient times never before heard, words issued from lips hitherto inseparable. "If Hero Marduk is to defeat Tiamat, if we all are to be saved by Marduk the Hero, convene the assembly, name for him a special fate, give to him the utterance of fates. Never shall his creations be changed, never shall the words of Hero Marduk, my brother, my twin, be altered!" The god who spoke, his eyes were closed, never had he opened them; but he heard all, Bel, sage of the gods, heard everything, Bel, twin of Marduk, was all-hearing.

Anšar nodded. To Kakka his vizier he commanded, "Escort Laḫmu and Laḫamu here; escort before me the gods my fathers; bring here all the gods together, to eat fine bread and to drink finer wine, to celebrate and to be joyous, and then to name for Marduk their champion, for Hero Marduk, the fate he deserves, the fate deserved by the destroyer of Tiamat. For, tell them, she has risen against us. Against us she has made a pair of giant snakes, javelin-fanged, venom coursing in the place of blood; then two dragons helmeted with piercing rays of light. Around them she has stationed the horned serpent, the mušḫuššu-dragon, the laḫmu-hero, the ugallu-demon, the rabid dog, the scorpion-man, the umu-demon, the fish-man, the bull-man, the šēdu and the awful, the relentless, the scavenging fly. Eleven others she has made, more fearsome even than the first; and all she has armed with weapons indomitable and with fearlessness, and over them, and over all the gods, she has named Qingu chief. Tell them this, and tell them that only Marduk dares defend us, only Marduk the Hero will be our champion, only Hero Marduk will protect us from destruction. For Nudimmud, though I sent him, would not go; and Anu, though he went, could not face her. Only Marduk, his heart dancing with joy, came forward, exulting to confront Tiamat, of his own free will daring to challenge she who is unconquerable, fearless and bold, she of womankind! That he succeed, he asks that you name for him a special fate, give to him the utterance of fates. Never shall his creations be changed, never shall the words of Hero Marduk be altered! Make haste, come here, hurry; quickly name your destiny for him so that he may leave to defend you from your foe." So spoke Anšar to his vizier Kakka. Immediately Kakka left, found his way to Laḫmu and Laḫamu, stood before the gods his fathers. And he told them, thus spoke he:

"I am the messenger of your son, Great Anšar, who has sent these his words through me: 'Tiamat has risen against us. Against us she has made a pair of giant snakes, javelin-fanged, venom coursing in the place of blood; then two dragons helmeted with piercing rays of light. Around them she has stationed the horned serpent, the mušḫuššu-dragon, the laḫmu-hero, the ugallu-demon, the rabid dog, the scorpion-man, the umu-demon, the fish-man, the bull-man, the šēdu and the awful, the relentless, the scavenging fly. Eleven others she has made, more fearsome even than the first; and all she has armed with weapons indomitable and with fearlessness, and over them, and over all the gods, she has named Qingu chief. Only Marduk dares defend us, only Marduk the Hero will be our champion, only Hero Marduk will protect us from destruction. For Nudimmud, though he was sent, would not go; and Anu, though he went, could not face her. Only Marduk, his heart dancing with joy, came forward, exulting to confront Tiamat, of his own free will daring to challenge she who is unconquerable, fearless and bold, she of womankind! That he succeed, he asks that you name for him a special fate, give to him the utterance of fates. Never shall his creations be changed, never shall the words of Hero Marduk be altered! Make haste, come here, hurry; quickly name your destiny for him so that he may leave to defend you from your foe.' So spoke Anšar to me, and I to you, and Anšar through me to you; now decide."

"Now decide," muttered the puppets, their brows furrowed by thought and dismay.

All who heard grew pale, from the gods in assembly came moans, despair and disbelief, from Laḫmu and Laḫamu cries issued forth.

"Our destruction so nigh and we unaware! Let us go at once, let us feast with Anšar, kiss the faces of our fellow gods, fill our hearts once again with fragile, carefree joy; let us name for Marduk a special fate, to him the utterance of fates!" And so they left, joining Anšar's feast, the fine bread and the finer wine, celebrating and being joyous. They named for Marduk their champion, for Hero Marduk, the fate he deserved, the fate deserved by the destroyer of Tiamat; they gave to him – he did not seize it – sovereignty over all, over everything. For him the stars would vanish at a word, for his word alone would they reappear. His was the command of destruction, his the order of creation. Marduk they called king, and these they gave to him as gifts: a shrine, a scepter, a throne, a weapon indomitable; they gave to him his destiny, to utter destinies; their master they made him, instructing him in obedience and peace; and at their word they sent him to kill Tiamat, to cut her from life, to breach her and destroy her: "You are as a mite, who eats his mother from within in order to be born; now go, lord, master, hero, save us from she who bears us."

"Save us from she who bears us," repeated the puppets, "great lord, master, hero, mite."

Marduk lifted the weapon indomitable, rose from his throne, raised his scepter, took leave of his shrine. In the storm chariot he set off against Tiamat, light tearing forth from his head, the winds writhing in his clenched fist, his mantle the mantle of ten gods, and in his wake the dust-carrying whirlwind. The commotion unsettled his mother; her belly was roiled, her stomach churned; turmoil grew within Tiamat. The steeds of the storm chariot trampled her innards; 'Slaughter' and 'Merciless' and 'Destruction' and 'Panic' trampled her innards. On his right marched Mêlée and Confusion; on his left, Discord and Chaos; they stomped, they kicked, they flattened their mother's guts. In his teeth Marduk bit a spell; on his lips were poison remedies. All about him swarmed the gods, trodding Tiamat's tummy.

But as he drew near, confusion gripped him; drawing near, his will weakened, bent and crumpled; drawn near, words became noise and he could discern no meaning. The gods about him slackened, began to disperse. Marduk Tiamat mocked; Hero Marduk she bullied; Marduk the Hero Tiamat taunted. From her lips she cast a lie; from her teeth she spat a falsehood; from her tongue unrolled a spell. But he could not tell, her words were as noise, discernment had left him – until she spoke his name. Marduk was bewildered, conquered, lost, the champion defeated, the hero overcome – until Tiamat called his name, until from her lips, her teeth, her tongue, "Marduk" escaped, until his mother named him. Then the Lord gathered strength, raised high his weapon indomitable, rallied the winds to his side.

"What has become of compassion?" he thundered. "Since when do you let perish what you yourself created? Is sleep so important, is noise so unbearable, that you reject those you bore? You have done what cannot be done; I, Marduk the Hero, Hero Marduk, am come to make you undo it."

"Marduk is come to make you undo it," chanted the puppets excitedly.

Tiamat heard, grew enraged, became wild. Tiamat screamed, Tiamat shouted, Tiamat shrieked! The puppets flinched, stepped back, raised their hands to their ears. Tiamat's gut trembled to its depths; the puppets became unsteady, struggled to stand. From her mouth Tiamat hurled incantations, spells and curses, thick as flies; and the puppets swatted at them ineffectually. But not so Marduk! He caught them in his net, he swirled them in his net, he entrapped them in his net. Then he cast the winds in the face of Tiamat; the whirlwind, the dust-carrying whirlwind, he threw at Tiamat's face. But she opened wide her mouth and sucked the winds into her belly. Round and fat it grew, Tiamat's wind-distended belly, when suddenly, with his javelin, Marduk pierced her. Tiamat popped! Then Marduk slit her in two, split open her heart, stood atop her and was born.

No sooner born than he built the world, with her corpse he built the world, with the corpse of Tiamat Marduk built the world. One half of her he draped overhead as sky; one half he plopped underfoot as ground. Her waters he collected in pools, as lakes and seas; her eyes he set in the heavens as sun and moon; her breasts and udder became mountains; her skin became deserts; each hair he crafted into a single tree; from her nostrils poured the rivers Purattu and Idiqlat. Her monster army he dismembered; he made the scorpion from the scorpion-man, the fish from the fish-man, the bull from the bull-man. He released the serpent and the awful, the relentless, the scavenging fly. Of Qingu he took no account; effortlessly, heedlessly, distractedly, he plucked the Tablet of Destinies from his hands and shoved him to the ground.

Then streaking across the heavens Marduk sought a temple. The secret chambers of Nudimmud, the Apsû, he razed, and in its stead, dimension for dimension, he raised the Ešarra, the perfect shrine, center of Anu's cult, Enlil's and Ea's. For each god he made a pedestal, that none might rest his feet in dirt. Over their heads he placed canopies of stars; and each canopy he wove together with a story and called a constellation. Twelve there were, one for each month; and together they marked the year. Tiamat's moon eye he called jewel-of-night and gave it command to glower over the land and to wink slowly at Šamaš, the sun, the jewel-of-day, her other eye, measurer of the year. And in the drift of the canopies when they caught the wind, in their flapping, flagging and billowing between the eyes of Tiamat, he ordained the account of the future, prophesy, warning and instruction. There did he write the rules of cult; there did he establish the rites of the gods.

Only then did he turn back, only then did he give thought to his homecoming. Snatching in one hand the Tablet of Destinies, to be read aloud before the gods for the first time, and in the other hand, leading his captives by a nose-rope, their weapons smashed, their feet tied, their images engraved on the gate of Apsû, Marduk the Hero gave thought to his homecoming and turned back. "May this never be forgotten, my deeds today! May they stand as a sign forever, unforgettable!" he cried out rapturously. The other gods came forth to greet him: Laḫmu and

Laḫamu came forth, kissed his cheeks and did obeisance; Anšar came forth, kissed his lips and did obeisance; Anu and Ea came forth, offered gifts and did obeisance. All the gods, the Igigi and the Anunnaki, assembled before him, prostrated themselves and delighted to kiss his feet. So great was Marduk, so grateful were the gods his subjects! Eagerly they rushed to undress him, to remove his garments grimy with dust and battle-sweat. With cypress water they sprinkled his body, with rose water they cleaned him. Then they dressed him, wrapping him in the finest garment, the garment of the king of the gods, beautiful to behold, and on his head they placed aura and crown, dazzling, blinding, too great for beholding.

(In harmony with the priest's words, the puppets undressed one another and stood naked before the audience; then, carefully, the one on the right dressed the one on the left in the same costume as before; and the one on the left dressed the one on the right, also in the same costume. Finally, in perfect synchrony, the two puppets placed the divine crowns on each other's heads.)

Now did Marduk choose to speak; now did the Hero choose to talk with the gods; now did the King address his subjects. "For you have I raised Ešarra over the Apsû; before it do I make the dwelling of my kingship, where you shall come for rest, for blessed sleep, whether when you rise from the Apsû or when you descend from the heavens. And to this place before Ešarra I give a name: I call it the Gate of the Gods, I call it Bab Ili, I call it Bābilim – your home, the home of gods when they desire sleep. May it forever be your place of rest!" (Hearing this, the puppets jumped up and down.)

"But tell them," a confident voice declared, a voice coming from the shadow, a voice heard but once before, "tell them who shall care for them while they slumber, who shall feed them, honor them, protect them, for so long as they sleep, even should they sleep forever."

Marduk rejoiced at his brother's words; Marduk's heart danced to hear his twin's voice; Marduk was overjoyed that Bel's mind and his were one. Loudly he proclaimed to the assembled gods: "It is in my heart to accomplish miracles, to please you with impossible magnificence. Wait, and you shall see." (Elated, the puppets twittered impatiently at one another.) Then Hero Marduk signaled Ea to come forward.

"Father, the miracle in my heart is this. Blood and bones I will mix together, and from them I shall make man. Man it will be who serves the gods, who tends them in their leisure and their sleep, even should that last forever!"

"It is a wise plan," wily Ea declared. "It only wants blood, it only wants bones. But perhaps – this is an idea – Qingu's penance will supply them, he who upheaved the gods in the name of sleep! Call the gods to assembly; invite them to judge the case of the one who rose against them; then, when they convict him, let him be given up, given on high, given to destruction; and from him I shall craft for you these men you speak of."

Marduk approved this plan, gathered the gods in assembly, instructed them kindly: "I call on you," the Hero declared, "to judge the case of the one who rose against you; then, when you convict him, let him be given up, given on high, given to destruction; and from him I shall accomplish a miracle, please you with impossible magnificence! – I shall craft men, who will tend you in your leisure and your sleep, even should that last forever! Thus shall the peace you dwell in come from he who disturbed it."

The great gods listened respectfully, stirring among themselves and murmuring like pebbles dragged by waves up and down a strand. At last one stepped forward, one stood up, one emerged from the mass of the Igigi: "Qingu it was who rose against us, riled Tiamat and commanded her army. Let him bear the punishment!" Then was Qingu bound, wrapped in his bindings like a caterpillar, and brought before Ea. (The puppets became animated; their behavior became anxious, their faces more so.) Summarily, indifferently, prosaically, Ea slashed the god; with proficiency, automatically, almost thoughtlessly, wily Ea sacrificed Qingu. (The puppets as one stumbled and fell to the ground.) "The fate and omen of Luḫuššum," muttered Ea, then – impossible to describe! – he pooled the warm, dead blood into a jar he crafted from the warm dead flesh, from the warm dead bones of the dead god. "Now go forth and toil for the gods," he said to man thus crafted, "Now go forth and, free from toil, sleep" he said to the gods. All this did Nudimmud enact through the miracle of Marduk, through the impossible magnificence he bestowed.

(The puppets rose from the ground, dressed now in the costume of royalty, wearing a king's crown and a queen's, and, in their astonishment blinking, pale, at a loss for words.)

Now did the Anunnaki step forward and raise their voices for Marduk to hear. "What of Bab Ili, what of Bābilim, this place of rest you have promised us? What good is this freedom you have given us, without that shelter too, where sleep will pass undisturbed, even should it last forever?" Marduk, hearing this, beamed, light streamed from his face, his eyes and his teeth shone brilliantly. "How glad I am to hear your request, so close to my heart – the request to build great Bābilim! I give you leave to do it; bend your backs, strain your muscles, pack mudbricks one by one. Do this and only this for one year, then for two; raise high the walls, raise high the shrines, raise high the ziggurat of Bābilim. Then will it become the gate of the gods! Then at last will you earn your rest and only then will sleep claim you, perhaps – who knows? – forever."

"Who knows forever?" the puppets echoed haltingly.

The Annunaki bent their backs, strained their muscles, packed mudbricks one by one. For a year they shoveled and molded and piled, their bodies drenched in dust and sweat, with dirt in their eyes, their nose, their teeth, their ears, and beneath their fingernails; for a second year they did the same, toiling relentlessly day and night – never did they rest! And slowly Bābilim rose from the mud, like a flower uncurling from a seed, uncertain, hesitant, reaching at first frailly toward the sun, then with greater confidence, picking up speed, shooting higher with an audacity of delight, straining presumptuously for the kiss of the sun. So Bābilim rose and flowered – on the backs of gods worked to exhaustion. And when they had finished, the gods assembled in the city; before Marduk they stood; before their Hero, their Lord, their King, the assembled gods stood. "Behold Bab-Ili!" Marduk crowed triumphantly – and the gods, dazed, beheld it as for the first time, though it was they who made it. "Let us be merry!" Marduk shouted. "Let us feast, let us make the taqribtu offering, let us name every decree, fix every design, establish forever the stations of heaven and earth!"

At these words, the assembled gods buckled at the knees; at these words, their heads drooped in exhaustion. "Great Marduk!" they called out. "We have toiled without rest for two years; the first year we shoveled and molded and piled, and our bodies were drenched in dust and sweat, with dirt in our eyes, our nose, our teeth, our ears and beneath our fingernails; and the second year it was the same! Relentlessly we toiled day and night – never did we rest! But now, we beg of you only sleep, in this great city, the city you gave us for our rest – let us sleep!" Marduk, listening kindly, was inclined in his heart to grant their request, his answer was at the gate of his lips when, for only the third time, for the very last time, Bel, his eyes still shut – never have they been opened! – Bel spoke up, Bel spoke in the place of his brother. "Marduk, Hero, Lord, King, read to us, for the first time, the Tablet of Destinies; then, and only then, shall we sleep; then shall we only sleep."

So spoke Bel, and his words rang in Marduk's ears; all four ears rang with the words of wisdom wrung from Bel's seldom-parted lips, Bel who was all-hearing, Bel who chose not to see. Marduk assented; he granted the request of his brother, his twin, and with his mighty hand he raised the Tablet of Destinies before his eyes, and with a mighty voice he gave utterance to its contents:

"NAMES," he intoned, his eyes glittering. "Asarluḫi, Marduk, Marukka, Marutukku, Meršakušu, Lugal-Dimmer-Ankia, Bel, Nari-Lugal-Dimmer-Ankia, Asarluḫi, Asarluḫi as Namtila, Asarluḫi as

Namru, Asare, Asar-Alim, Asar-Alim-Nuna, Tutu, Tutu as Zi-Ukkina, Tutu as Ziku, Tutu as Agaku, Tutu as Tuku, Šazu, Šazu as Zisi, Šazu as Suḫrim, Šazu as Suḫgurim, Šazu as Zaḫrim, Šazu as Zaḫgurim, Enbilulu, Enbilulu as Epadun, Enbilulu as Gugal, Enbilulu as Ḫegal, Sirsir, Sirsir as Malaḫ, Gil, Gilima, Agilima, Zulum, Mummu the Maker, Mummu the Maker as Zulum-Ummu, Giš-Numum-Ab, Lugal-Ab-Dubur, Pagal-Guena, Lugal-Durmaḫ, Aranuna, Dumu-Duku, Lugal-Duku, Lugal-Šuanna, Iruga, Irqingu, Kinma, E-Sizkur, Gibil, Addu, Ašaru, Neberu, Enkurkur."

He turned the tablet over.

"NAMES," he intoned. "Asarluḫi, Marduk, Marukka, Marutukku, Meršakušu, Lugal-Dimmer-Ankia, Bel, Nari-Lugal-Dimmer-Ankia, Asarluḫi, Asarluḫi as Namtila, Asarluḫi as Namru, Asare, Asar-Alim, Asar-Alim-Nuna, Tutu, Tutu as Zi-Ukkina, Tutu as Ziku, Tutu as Agaku, Tutu as Tuku, Šazu, Šazu as Zisi, Šazu as Suḫrim, Šazu as Suḫgurim, Šazu as Zaḫrim, Šazu as Zaḫgurim, Enbilulu, Enbilulu as Epadun, Enbilulu as Gugal, Enbilulu as Ḫegal, Sirsir, Sirsir as Malaḫ, Gil, Gilima, Agilima, Zulum, Mummu the Maker, Mummu the Maker as Zulum-Ummu, Giš-Numum-Ab, Lugal-Ab-Dubur, Pagal-Guena, Lugal-Durmaḫ, Aranuna, Dumu-Duku, Lugal-Duku, Lugal-Šuanna, Iruga, Irqingu, Kinma, E-Sizkur, Gibil, Addu, Ašaru, Neberu, Enkurkur."

He turned the tablet over.

"NAMES," he intoned. "Asarluḫi, Marduk, Marukka, Marutukku, Meršakušu, Lugal-Dimmer-Ankia, Bel, Nari-Lugal-Dimmer-Ankia, Asarluḫi, Asarluḫi as Namtila, Asarluḫi as Namru, Asare, Asar-Alim, Asar-Alim-Nuna, Tutu, Tutu as Zi-Ukkina, Tutu as Ziku, Tutu as Agaku, Tutu as Tuku, Šazu, Šazu as Zisi, Šazu as Suḫrim, Šazu as Suḫgurim, Šazu as Zaḫrim, Šazu as Zaḫgurim, Enbilulu, Enbilulu as Epadun, Enbilulu as Gugal, Enbilulu as Ḫegal, Sirsir, Sirsir as Malaḫ, Gil, Gilima, Agilima, Zulum, Mummu the Maker, Mummu the Maker as Zulum-Ummu, Giš-Numum-Ab, Lugal-Ab-Dubur, Pagal-Guena, Lugal-Durmaḫ, Aranuna, Dumu-

Duku, Lugal-Duku, Lugal-Šuanna, Iruga, Irqingu, Kinma, E-Sizkur, Gibil, Addu, Ašaru, Neberu, Enkurkur."

He turned the tablet over.

"NAMES," he intoned. "Asarluḫi, Marduk, Marukka, Marutukku…"

The puppets listened, first standing, then seated, then resting one against the other; quietly the puppets nestled into sleep. The gods listened, first standing, then seated, then resting one against another; quietly they nestled into sleep. Whether Bel slept or not, who could tell? His eyes were always closed. Marduk read, transfixed, delighted; before his eyes unfurled the names; from his lips they unfurled; the names, or words, or whatnot, forever flowed from his eyes to his lips, as he turned the tablet over, and over, and over, never stopping.

These instructions, secret from ancient times, recited before him, the scribe recorded; the scribe set them down to be read by he who reads, by she who reads, by it who reads. May Marduk's people, in remembrance of he who conquered Tiamat and seized kingship, sing the song of Marduk; may they call upon him who created them; may they but sing his name.

It was the end of the fourth day of the Akītu festival; at last the priest grew silent.

Dawn had broken. The puppets stirred, still in their royal dress. The plaza before the Esagila was empty; the temple of Marduk was empty; the puppets were alone before Marduk's temple in Bābilim. They waited. A puppet has no idea how long it waits.

A procession approached. Far in advance, at its head – Marduk! The puppets looked at one another, grasped each other's hands, then turned again to examine the coming god more closely. Their shell-eyelids drew together; only a sliver of amethyst shown through; the puppets squinted. Was it Marduk who led the procession, or the high priest? The garb was the god's; the form was the man's; the face belonged to both. Which then led the procession? The question was too great for a puppet.

Far behind the Marduk-Man followed another, regal in his garments and his bearing. In his hand the scepter; on his head the royal crown. The king! The king who was a god among men, here following a god-man. In a cluster about him were the temple's other priests, somber and alert, their nervous excitement palpable even to a puppet, being so like the taut strings by which they themselves were plucked.

The Marduk-Man reached the altar and turned. Immediately, in synchrony with the turn, a priest grabbed the king's golden bracelet, brutally tore it off and cast it in the dirt. (The puppets, in utter surprise, gasped, almost squealed.) Another yanked the royal pendant free from the king's neck, breaking its chain and letting it too fall in the dust. A third grabbed the king's right foot and cut loose its sandal, not untying it; then the left sandal too. (As of their own accord, the sandals fell off the puppets' feet.) Had their eyes been keen enough, the puppets would have seen blood on the feet of the king, and on his neck, and on his wrist. (They themselves did not bleed.)

Barefoot now, the king continued to advance toward the Marduk-Man. A priest rushed forward and knocked the crown from the king's head, which snapped back painfully. (The puppets knocked each other's crowns off.) Another priest grabbed the scepter from the king's hand and unceremoniously snapped it in two against the king's shoulder, jarring him. Still, however, the king advanced, blood trickling from his feet, neck and wrists, his head bruised, empty-handed, barefoot. Now a priest came forward, stood in front of the king, their noses almost touching, his posture aggressive, threatening; then he seized the king's robe at the neck and ripped it open and apart, from the neck to the feet. (The puppets faced each other, clutched each other's garments, ripped them in two.) The king stumbled forward, his royal dress now rags, his nakedness more exposed than covered. The puppets, seeing clearly now the king's injuries, seeing him dishonored, seeing him threatened, could not hold back their tears – tears of concern and apprehension and sympathy.

At last the king stood before the Marduk-Man and the other priests fell back. They looked at each other, one in the garb of a god, the other beaten, bleeding, almost naked – his bearing, however, still royal. The tension built, the strings grew taut, even the puppets shivered, as king and Marduk-Man confronted one another, as king and Marduk-Man faced each other. Then, suddenly, furiously, the Marduk-Man slapped the king's face – a groan was heard – the king dropped to his knees.

The Marduk-Man spoke, his deep voice loud and bold. "Have you sinned, king of men? Have you in any way neglected me, my magnificence or my might?"

The king did not answer. The pause grew lengthy – only to the puppets was it not unseemly – and the priests surrounding the king twitched anxiously. (The puppets did not.)

The Marduk-Man spoke again, uncertainty entering his voice still loud and very nearly bold. "Have you sinned, king of men? Have you in any way neglected me, my magnificence of my might?"

The king rose, clearly surprising the Marduk-Man, who stumbled back. "If I have, may I be forgiven," the king said clearly. "If I have not, may I be forgiven anyway."

All was silence before the altar. The puppets, now in rags, stared breathlessly, no limb of wood creaking, no shell-eyelid clicking, even their jarring ebony teeth not chattering.

Marduk-Man and king, both standing, both unsettled, again confronted one another. This second confrontation was in no way like the first. In the first the Marduk-Man reigned imperious; in the first, what came came inexorably, as necessity. But not so now: anxiety, possibility, and strangely, most shocking of all, tenderness – these stood, somehow were born, in the space and silence between two faces.

Who dares to let silence last forever? The Marduk-Man spoke at last. "Fear not the words that escape the lips of Marduk, for their escape he contrived. Fear not to call the name of Marduk, should you know it. Trust to Marduk your prayers, your power and the greatness of your reign."

A priest then handed the king's fallen crown, rescued from the dust, to the Marduk-Man, and the Marduk-Man placed it on the king. A second priest furnished a scepter, new, more splendid even than its predecessor, and gave it to the Marduk-Man, who in turn placed it in the hand of the king. The bracelet, the pendant and the sandals he did not replace. Again king and Marduk-Man looked at each other. Then, as suddenly, as furiously as before, the Marduk-Man slapped the king's face. This time no groan was heard; the king did not flinch or stagger; much less did he fall to the ground.

The Marduk-Man turned, left, entered the temple alone, and disappeared. The king watched his departure and did not stir.

It was the fifth day of the Akītu festival.

The puppets were alone in their chamber, still wearing the rags that were once royal, still crown-less and sandal-less, still stunned by the events of the day.

A vision came to them, a vision like a dream, a dream come to the sleepless.

Alone, Marduk was entering his temple. Behind him could be seen the king, watching, not stirring. Marduk, alone, was now in the Esagila. But suddenly there were gods about him, gods who grabbed him from behind, gods who tackled him from the front. Six gods held down one arm, six gods the other; a god's hands covered each of his four eyes, each of his four ears. His legs were bound; his hands were bound, Marduk was bound, captured by the enemy gods! Though he could not see, though he could not hear, bound as he was, his lips, Marduk's lips were not motionless. "Tiamat!" he cried out. And in response, perhaps, a voice or, perhaps, a gust of wind, "Nothing," it said, perhaps, or perhaps it said nothing. The bound god waited, uncertain. Was it a response? Was it a voice? Was it the wind? Was it a name? Was it nothing? Then, tremulously, feebly, the god's voice: "Whose name is that? Mine or another's?" No answer; or was that an answer? Marduk fell silent.

The vision ended.

The puppets, paralyzed by shock, stood wordless. Time passed – but a puppet has no idea how long it waits.

Then together, as if on cue, the puppets, still wordless, removed each other's rags and carefully clothed themselves in their last garments, their torn and muddied sackcloth. They would greet the dawn of the sixth day in the garments of mourning – the garments of man.

Commotion filled the city – shrieks and wails, the sounds of fighting, smoke. Bands of priests opposed one another, shaking weapons, screaming insults, darting back and forth from rank to rank. Who defended Marduk, who the enemy gods – who could tell? Who was who? Who was only who? Meanwhile, onlookers assembled into small crowds, only to disperse in panic if priests drew near. And rushing to and fro, from every lip and throat, the bass notes of an unfolding chaos, words: "Marduk is captured! Marduk is prisoner! Marduk! Marduk! Marduk!" So often was "Marduk" spoken that it ceased to be a name; so often was it spoken that it ceased to be a word; so often was it spoken – noise, only noise.

The puppets, dressed in their torn, their ash-streaked sackcloth, sandal-less, bareheaded, hair disheveled, stood alone in the center of the plaza before the Esagila. How they had gotten there, why they had placed themselves there, no one could say. But for them, there lay no path to safety; always one band or another of maddened priests cut them off from refuge or from rescue. And who – onlooker, priest or puppet – could distinguish friend from foe? Who was who? Who was only who? The puppets were bewildered, terrified; in their look, agitation; their faces were pale; their ebony teeth – oh so jarring! – chattered helplessly. They clung to one another. And every time a band of priests surged toward them, one would shrink in fear – thinking the band an enemy – and the other would stretch out in hopeful expectation – thinking the band an ally. Their motions cancelled; confusion paralyzed them.

And the king – where was the king?

The king was nowhere.

Now the bands of priests were swelling, drawing closer, merging into one another; and the circle around the puppets tightened. Accompanying the shouts and challenges, javelins and flaming torches shook in the air like tambourines; and then, suddenly, one was lofted through the air, a javelin spiraling through its perfect arc. But it fell short; it missed the opposing priest; but only barely did it miss the puppets caught between. They yelped, clung yet more closely to each other. An answering javelin was loosed; it too fell short; it too almost grazed the helpless, mourning puppets. And now followed a barrage of javelins, like a rainstorm unleashed by a few tentative drops and grown bold; and all fell short, but not of the puppets. The puppets were buffeted by javelins, stunned and dented and bruised by javelins whose targets always lay beyond – whose targets they were not.

Then there were no more javelins to be thrown; like a desert rainstorm, the onslaught ended as abruptly as it began; the injured puppets, huddled together, almost indistinguishable the one from the other, a mass mostly of rent goat-hair and ash and battered cedar, moaned in disbelieving relief and began to stir apart, weeping and crawling blindly in the dirt.

But now a torch was thrown; a torch arced high in the air; and it had not landed before more torches were thrown, from both sides; the air became brilliant with fire, with lightning and falling stars. In the chaos no one saw, no one knew, which torch ignited the puppets' sackcloth; no one knew, no one saw, whether it was the torch of friend or foe, had these ever been distinguished. For who was who, and who was only who? The puppets themselves could not have said, so great was the anarchy and confusion; but even had they known, it was never for them to say. For the puppets burned. First the goat-hair sackcloth and their royal, their holy wigs, and their eyelashes and eyebrows of baby-hair; then the very threads by which their bodies moved, their spider-web spirits; then the cedar and finally the ebony, their jarring black teeth grown still. All burned. The litter of javelins and torches burned too; the fire became furious, outrageous; and in the heat the precious metals first were scarred, then sweated into melt, which ran into the dust and the dirt and joined there amethyst and lapis lazuli, shells and coral, all grown charred and black like coal, all grown purposeless, the remnants of what was no more.

Then, the gangs of priests having dispersed suddenly, unaccountably, leaving only the stillness that follows a ferocious and senseless storm, leaving only embers cooling and already cooled, leaving only the settling dusk and the terror of encroaching darkness, a whisper: "The king – the king is at the river!" Could it be true? But listen, here it is again, more persistent, more assured: "The king – the king is at the river!" And again, grown bold, almost loud: "The king is at the river!" Crowds of people surged toward the river; individuals, the young especially, raced past them in the lead; and mingling among them priests, from which factions none could say – not even the priests. All went to the river's banks, where it was said – first in a whisper, but now in heady proclamation – the king would be found.

And there he was, the king, the very one the god had abused and sanctified, dressed no longer in his ruined robes but in his gleaming, glorious battle gear, a mace in one hand, his new scepter in the other. There on the bank of the river was the king. He stood on a raised, ornate platform that had somehow materialized since morning. Before him – wonder to behold! – a procession of ships! Ships whose flags announced their origins: Uru, Eridu, Uruk, Nippur, Kiš, Marad, Borsippa, Kutha and Sippar, and many more. The ancient cities! The holy cities! And high on their decks, overseeing their ship's progress, the exertion of their sailors and the tumult of the shore-bound mob, dressed in their sacred regalia, were the gods. Sîn was there on the first ship, and after him Ea, Enlil, Ištar, Ninlil, Zababa, Anu – all the great gods had come – until last of all came Nabû, on the final ship. All were there; and the heroes Gilgameš and Etana were in their company too. (But Izdubar – Izdubar was not there.)

And the people on the shore saw to their astonishment that the gods were statues; but they saw as well that this did not rattle the king. Rather, he stood simultaneously with awe and confidence to await and welcome the gods. Sîn was first to reach the bank. The king called out in prayerful greeting and took him by the hand, which he kissed; and, still holding the hand, he bent and kissed the god's foot; and then, by the hand, he led him onto the platform and placed him in honor on his right side. Thus did he greet each of the other gods; and in honor he led them and placed them behind Sîn. Last of them all he welcomed Nabû, whose hand he kissed, then his foot; but Nabû he did not place behind Sîn with all the other gods; Nabû he placed on his left side. Now were the gods assembled beside the king on the platform. Dusk had long since settled, stars had punctured the sky, darkness could not much longer be held at bay. The king spoke:

"Let us honor our guests with wine and with burnt offerings, that they may refresh themselves after their journey. Then let us prepare their beds that they may sleep. Come morning the gods and I will deliver our deliverer; come morning, Marduk will be freed! But now our duties are the host's: let the wine be brought and the meat! Then let the beds be prepared and finally let silence reign. Let silence reign lest we disturb the sleep of the gods!"

The king's words were fulfilled. Wine flowed and meat was burned; beds were brought. Then the people, all who had gathered about in excitement, trepidation and wonder – all of them slipped away, ever so silently, on tip-toes they slipped away. As never before the city fell silent, so the gods could sleep.

So ended the sixth day of the Akītu festival.

"The gods have awakened." So the rumor went. Like a grass fire, it smoldered more than it flamed as it made its way through the city. Gradually it kindled the city into wakefulness. Uninstructed and

unsummoned, people gathered before the platform on the riverbank, where tents and beds had been placed that the gods might sleep after their journey. For now nothing stirred within the tents; there was no sound, no motion, nothing to see – and yet none doubted that the gods had awakened. Onlookers, not breaking the silence, not so much as touching it, merely waited. Their crowd grew, but with an astonishing grace and a more astonishing quiet. The people waited. The gods had awakened and, when they willed it, they would show themselves.

Suddenly the king appeared on the platform. From where he had come – how he had arrived – no one could say. He was dressed as before, in his glorious, his resplendent battle gear; but in lieu of a mace, he held a clay tablet; in lieu of a scepter he held a stylus. He stood alone on the platform, beside the closed tents where the gods had slept, facing neither the tents nor the people, and looking off into the distance, westward, not moving. The silence of the people quivered and in a few places snapped, only immediately to reseal itself. Gradually a surmise took seed among the people; ever so gradually it began to blossom. Perhaps the king had become a statue like the gods? So thought one onlooker; soon all thought it; but no one said a word. However great their agitation, the people dared neither to stir nor to speak. They barely dared to breathe. For a long while nothing happened – nothing but the sunrise.

Then, suddenly, the crown prince was beside his father. As before, eyes intently watching the dais nonetheless failed to see his arrival and his source. He was simply absent one moment, there the next. Such are the ways of royalty, so close are they to the gods. Bel-šar-uṣur was, like his father, dressed in battle gear; and it was he now who held the king's mace and the royal scepter. His father took no notice of him. He, whether man or statue, was looking west. All at once, as if a veil had simply been lifted, the people as a body understood what it was that he was watching. The Sun had risen at his back; before him was the setting Moon. It was the Moon which had cast its spell on him, which had mesmerized and frozen him. But not so his son: Bel-šar-uṣur looked elsewhere – he looked upon the people.

The moon disappeared at the horizon. The king that instant turned. "Sîn has given his instructions," he said calmly, his voice carrying effortlessly over the quiet stillness. "Nabû is ready; the gods, his cohort, are ready." The tents opened at his words; framed in the entry of each was a god in statue – and nearest the king was Sîn on his right, Nabû on his left. "Let us make way for the gods!" the king continued in his disconcerting calmness. "They shall lead us to the Esagila, to the deliverance of Marduk our deliverer!"

The crowds parted, instinctively knowing what path the gods would follow. Priests appeared from within the tents; and in pairs they lifted each statue onto their shoulders, and from there onto horse-drawn chariots. One by one, the gods in their chariots processed through the divided crowd, Nabû in the lead, followed closely by Sîn, then the rest of the gods, until last of all was Ea. After him came the king and behind him his son. The king began to sing; his son joined him, and then all the people:

"Here comes he from afar
The son who will rescue his father.
Here comes he from afar
Nabû the glory of Marduk!
At his side come gods from afar
Siblings who will rescue their brother.
Here come they from afar
behind Nabû the glory of Marduk!
At their sides come gods from afar
Parents who will rescue their child
Here come they from afar
Led by Nabû the glory of Marduk!"

The procession halted before the steps of the Esagila, the chariots of Nabû and Sîn drawn beside one another and flanked by all the other chariots. The gods, with the aid of the attending priests, dismounted. The people, meanwhile, held back and formed a crescent around the assembled gods and their now-empty chariots. The king and his son hurried forward to the head of the procession. When they arrived, they, like all before them, were astonished by what they saw: the people, the king, the prince, and the gods, all were astonished. An enormous gate barred the way; the Esagila had been fortified. When, no one could say; how, no one could say. The enemy gods – had they been forewarned of the coming assault? But who would tell them? Who would betray the rescue of Marduk, who would betray the people's salvation?

The king raised a hand. This unexpected turn of events had not rattled him; he could be seen conferring with his son, then addressing both Nabû and Sîn; his manner was confident, commanding. The king was not rattled. He raised his hand. "Listen!" he ordered the people. Though already silence reigned, it somehow deepened, and the people eagerly, desperately listened. They heard their own heartbeat, their own pulse, their own breathing – then gradually, ever so faintly, something else. They strained to hear what it was; their breathing stopped, their pulse, their heart – and then, in an instant, it was clear to all: from within the temple came the sounds of struggle. Their import was obvious; breath, pulse and beating heart rushed back joyously, like messengers with good news. For Marduk, captured these three days, had not submitted! Marduk, three days a prisoner, had not despaired! Even now after three days Marduk fought the evil gods, strove for his freedom and his city!

But how to get past the enormous gate, to join the fray in aid of Marduk? The young prince, impetuous, trusting too much to his strength, rushed against it, tried with all of his might first to pull back its bar, then, when that failed, to smash it with his mace. To no avail; one heard only the hollow sound of failure echoing against the stony silence of the gods, bemused and irritated all at once. The people were disconcerted, but not the king. He called the prince back to him, reprimanded him, reined him in. Then the king stopped, knelt on one knee, and against the other knee, wrote something on the tablet he carried. Whatever he wrote took some time. He refused to be hurried, even as all the people could feel the growing impatience of the crown prince, who had stormed the gate but failed.

When the king had finished, he brought the tablet before Nabû and gave it to him, while taking from the statue's hands a second tablet. The statue received the king's tablet but did not read it; but the king read the god's tablet in a bewildering silence. Then he turned and faced the assembled gods – Sîn on his left, Nabû on his right, the rest of the gods before him. He addressed them, speaking calmly and quietly; and his words carried to the people.

"Nabû," he announced, "has given me a spell, written in mud and air, to vanquish the gate also in the end but of mud and air." The king paused, but the gods said nothing. "Unless any of you object, I shall cast Nabû's spell at the gate; may it prevail!" The king paused a second time, but no god voiced an objection. After waiting a suitable time, the king turned, walked determinedly to the gate and stood before it. All was silence, anticipation and dread. If Nabû's spell did not prevail, if the king failed, what then? Meanwhile, the king stood still before the gate, his back to the people and the gods. What he did could not be seen; he appeared motionless. If he spoke, no one heard. For a long while thus he stood; and the anxiety of the people grew, intensified. Was this failure? The crown-prince could be seen fidgeting; his impatience was apparent; at any moment, imminently, he would again attack the gate with his own unleashed ferocity, though already it had proven powerless.

As if sensing the breaking point of his son's impatience – as if sensing the anxiety of the people had grown too great to bear – the king suddenly acted. It was a small act, even a carefree act. In one fluid gesture, he turned back toward the people and tossed the tablet over his shoulder and at the gate. When the tablet struck the gate, it collapsed in a hushed explosion of billowing dust. The king, however, even as the dust engulfed him, never looked back. He proceeded calmly to his prior position beside Nabû and Sîn. He bowed to each, first Nabû, then Sîn; only then did he turn to inspect the demolished gate, which Nabû's spell had vanquished. Then he stepped aside, out of the path of the gods.

In pairs, the priestly attendants lifted the gods' statues on their shoulders. Then, with a roar – which the crowd also immediately joined – they rushed up the stairs of the Esagila, Nabû in the lead, and disappeared within. The king and his son stayed behind and, alongside the assembled people, they waited. The sounds of struggle within intensified, grew louder and more chaotic – and, with the suddenness of death, ended. The deepest silence yet now fell on the scene and its audience, and it lingered unendurably, seemingly forever. The crown prince again was fidgeting, impatient, swinging his mace as if against ghosts in the air; the people quivered like an over-strung bow. Only the king remained unperturbed, as if even an indefinite wait could not concern him.

But the wait was not indefinite, not forever. Just as the sun reached its zenith, Nabû appeared at the doorway, in silence. Then, beside him, stood Marduk. The people, overwhelmed, let loose a scream of joy and triumph, and the seventh day of the Akītu festival gave way, from afternoon through evening and late into the night, to celebration, feasting and dance. Nabû had saved Marduk, the king, the city, all of them; the god of writing had rescued Bābilim.

The gods were assembled in the Hall of Destinies, the Ubšu Ukkina, each solemn statue in its rightful place. Enlil did not sleep; Ea's place was not empty; Šamaš was not blind; Ištar was neither naked nor hanging from a meat hook; Sîn shined in his throne; but beneath his gaze Nabû did not play in the dirt. Rather, in the Hall of Destinies, all the gods stood rigidly in their proper places, the places assigned to them for as long as men could remember, though by whom the assignment was made, and how – on this, tradition and men together were silent.

They were there to decree the destiny of Marduk, to name for him a special fate. The king would come, as the king came every year, and would implore the gods, calling them by name, to join their powers to Marduk's, to grant him supremacy, to submit to him, lest the events of the festival play out forever, lest the uncertainty, turmoil and anguish of the past three days never be vanquished absolutely. So would the king speak, and the gods, as they did every year, would deliberate. Their stone heads would huddle together, but no words would escape their stone lips; their deliberations, though before all, were silent, secret – but the king would understand, and the priests would. After a time, the priests would murmur a few words to the king, and the king would speak out loud and bold: "The gods have joined their powers to Marduk's! They grant him supremacy! For the space of a year they submit to him!" Relief would wash over the people; for a year they could trust to the fixity of the world, to its anchorage in the god. It would not drift away down the river or be caught like dust in the wind. Then the people would roar; like lions and thundering storms they would roar, rowdily and endlessly, and all the trials and tribulations of the last several days would be swept away, like twigs, leaves, dirt and insects in a maelstrom.

But this year it transpired differently – only a little, but the difference was noted, the difference left no one who was not unsettled. The king made his speech, calling each god by name. The gods huddled together, no word escaping their lips. The priests came and murmured a few words to the king. The king nodded in agreement, opened his mouth to speak – and closed it again, the words unspoken. He gestured excitedly at Nabû, then approached him. The king kissed the god's hand, then his foot; he did obeisance. When he rose, he accepted the tablet that the god held forth in his hand. Then he turned and faced the people and with them the priests. He read to them the contents of the tablet.

"What cannot be heard, much less spoken, may yet be legible.

The gods' deliberations have ended. They grant for a year that only Marduk shall grant; in his submission to their supremacy they submit to his; in all things they acknowledge in him their mirror image, their reflection, as already he acknowledges in them. So writes the scribe, the savior of Marduk – Nabû. So writes he by the light of the Moon." The king paused. Stunned bewilderment could be read, but only read, on the silent faces of the priests. Then, with an expansive smile, the king called out, loud and bold, "The gods have joined their powers to Marduk's! They grant him supremacy! For the space of a year they submit to him!"

The people cheered; they roared like lions and thundering storms.

It was the eighth day of the Akītu festival.

"Will you come?" Nabû-na'id asked.

"No," answered Niṭil-Kišar, "I shall stay behind, to tend to my water project and visit our daughter – and to advise our head-strong son, if possible."

Nabû-na'id did not speak for a moment, though she read in his face that he was both unsurprised and disappointed. "I'm sorry," she said, touching his hand.

"I know." Again he fell silent, though he held her hand even when she tried, half-heartedly, to withdraw it. "It may be a long time before I return," he observed finally. Then he leaned towards her and whispered conspiratorially: "I think I'm going to run away!" He winked.

She smiled at him. "You had better," she responded playfully. "I cannot imagine the priests aren't in uproar, after what you did during the *Akītu* festival. Your absence might give them opportunity to lick their wounds."

"Or to let them fester." He looked probingly at her. "You're not surprised that I may not return – for a long time?"

"No." She returned his gaze; hers was equally probing. She read the unstated question and answered it: "Yes," she said. "I'm disappointed. I will miss you."

"But you will not come."

"No."

He sighed. "I knew to expect this – but I confess, a part of me was hoping you would again join me and Gubaru on a westward journey, as we did all those many years ago, shortly after we were married. At the time, I let you come not because I foresaw how valuable you would be, but because I foresaw how much I would miss you. And because I knew I hadn't the power not to let you come." He smiled, and she smiled. "Every day on that journey I would lie beside you in our tent, under the uncountable stars, and rejoice. I would think: I am in this position, married to you and beside you and above all befriended by you, because in Luddu I set an atrocity into motion. And I would think: I cannot therefore regret it. I would lie beside you, and I would wonder: is this the reward for evil? But those were, for me, hopeful times. We were together on a project of peace, to end the siege of Ṣurru. Atonement seemed possible; a life of good deeds was still before me. And so I would lie beside you wondering not only if this was the reward for evil, but whether it wasn't instead proof of grace… And, as I've been planning this new westward journey, I confess that a part of me longed for that experience again, even if it was but an evocation, a phantom, of those earlier times. A part of me hoped you would come with me and convince me that grace, even now, was possible."

"Grace, it seems to me, is not something one can be convinced of, that it is or that it is not," she said.

He just looked at her, still holding her hand. "No," he eventually murmured. "Of course not."

"Did you fail to be reborn when I buried you?" she asked. "Why, death," – which also sounded like "husband" – "have you not gone to live?"

"Ah," he answered, "when you didn't pronounce but

performed the omen of Luḫuššum on me..." He looked at the ground. He still had not released her hand. "I think, Niṭil-Kišar, that I have forgotten how to live."

She looked at him, her expression at once severe and mocking. "Oh fiddlesticks!" she said. "Oh, poor Nabû-na'id, king of the world!" She laughed sharply. "Enough of this. Enough nonsense. It is not worthy of you."

Nabû-na'id's face betrayed shock for a moment, but then gradually evolved into a grin. "Yes, I suppose you're right," he admitted. "If one is to pretend toward meaning, one can nonetheless do better than melodrama."

"'To pretend toward meaning' is even what I object to," his wife declared, barely before he had finished speaking. "It assumes the consolation of meaning without risking anything, least of all meaning. You pretend *toward* meaning, so meaning exists, it's there; but your own approach to it is pretense, a feint, a feigning. That's what I mean – consolation without risk. If you doubt meaning, then mean it. If you don't doubt it, then mean."

Her husband shrugged. "You are probably right to criticize me. My despair may be too comfortable, too – in your words – consoling. Very well. Damnation is the last refuge of the damned. After that comes something worse. Very well. But –" He stopped.

"But what?" Niṭil-Kišar prompted.

"I'm not sure. I was thinking of the puppets in the *Akītu* festival. And then I had a thought: who is not a puppet in the *Akītu* festival? And it left me thinking something vague – about the necessity of linking meaning with pretending."

"Are you sure that the link is a necessity? Does meaning require pretending, or does that just cover up meaning's fragility, not only its delicacy but its inevitable rupture and disappearance, and even the way it's claimed into something else *as* something else? We don't have to pretend in order to mean... 'Pretending' is just an illusion which emerges after the fact, the aftertaste which lingers when meaning itself has gone."

"Because then at least we can still imagine that the real thing, meaning outside of pretending, would endure forever and unchanging?"

"Yes."

"I sense you and I are within a hair's breadth of agreeing."

"We have almost always been within a hair's breadth of each other. Seldom further. Never closer."

He looked at her earnestly and drew her close. "Come with me," he said.

"You're shaking," she observed.

"Come with me."

She returned his earnest gaze. "You're shaking," she repeated.

"Yes, I am shaking. Come with me."

She allowed herself to be held but did not respond for a long time. Then, finally, she kissed his forehead, gently separated herself from him, and ever-so-softly, ever-so-simply said no.

"I don't know if I will see you again," he said to her.

"It doesn't matter if you see me again," Adad-Guppi replied. "What matters is if I see Ḫarrānu again. What matters is if you lead Sîn by his hand back to the Eḫulḫul, before I die."

"And if I do it after you die?"

"You will have broken your word to me. You will have broken Sîn's word to me."

"And the god bears no responsibility for his broken word?"

"Words are strange entities – too strong to be broken by gods, all-too-easily broken by men."

"Strange indeed," Nabû-na'id murmured, as silence settled between them. After a while, it appeared his mother had forgotten that he was there. If she was forgetful, though, it wasn't because of her uncountable age. (Was she 100? He doubted whether even she knew.) If she was forgetful, it was because, in the shadow of her deepest concerns, anything else – whether son or king – was forgettable. He did not blame her.

She stirred suddenly. "I witnessed what you did at the *Akītu* festival. I saw and I understood."

"What did you understand?"

"You are preparing the way for Sîn."

"Yes."

She looked at him with her still-wild eyes, eyes that had made no concession to age, whether in seeing or being seen.

"I approve," she said, with an almost toothless smile. Then she added, urgently, "Only hurry!"

Chapter 9. Ṣalmu

To En-nigaldi-Nanna thus writes Nabû-na'id.

I have struggled how to begin this letter, daughter, beloved of my heart. To which name should I write? That is what I wondered. Shall this letter be to Mikum-Nisaba, who would sit on my lap when we told each other stories or sang together? Or shall it be to the priestess En-nigaldi-Nanna? Evidently I decided the latter, but I am not sure why. It is also not clear to me that the two names refer to the same person or evoke the same relationship between the two of us. But evidently I decided; the letter is addressed; and I don't know how I came to that particular name, any more than I know how I gave you either name in the first place. A baby once squirmed in my arms, and I recall thinking, "How shall I address you? By what name?" Why did I not instead wonder, "What is your name?" Or even, "Do you have a name?" But those were not my thoughts; my thoughts were of the name I would give you, the name that would be a gift from me to you. When you became a priestess I gave you a second name. Why? You have never asked. Perhaps I shall never tell. But, like the first name, I can only wonder – was this a gift or an imposition? Is either name how you call yourself? Do even you know how you call yourself, when you call yourself most intimately?

That's perhaps the rub. Every one of the most intimate conversations I've had with myself has been a surprise. I have not known they were coming; and the name I called myself in the course of them – if I called myself anything at all – would surely have been born in the modest circumstances of a conversation that never announced its intention to be intimate. Perhaps it is so for all of us.

When I visited you right before leaving on this campaign, I was much struck by your "palace." It seemed so austere and lonely; and at the same time there was something rich about it. I had not expected to find you surrounded by dog figurines, on shelves, in nooks and crannies, on the floor. I had not expected to find statues of Šulgi and Gudea, much less of Enḫeduanna. I had not expected that you would catalogue them all, keep notes about them, speculate as to their ages and origins. Is that all you do, or had I looked more closely would I have found transcripts of your conversations with these statues, accounts of the games you have played together or of the adventures you have shared – or even of the ways a dog figurine with a broken foot can console and be consoled by a priestess awaiting her god? Have I driven my daughter into some lonely form of lunacy, I wondered, or have I spurred her to discover another dimension to our world, the one which we share with statues and with ghosts? Are you rallying those statues and ghosts into wakefulness or are you joining them in their sleep?

Those were thoughts that pooled here and there in my mind, while we talked of other things, you and I in what perhaps – who can ever know? – was our last meeting face-to-face. (But are not these letters in some way more face-to-face than those other encounters, those other confrontations?) You wanted to know why I had acted as I did at the Akītu festival, especially on the eighth day; and how things had transpired afterwards. Did I give expression to what was most surprising? I know I made some fumbling attempt or other. On the eighth day, I had intercepted one message and replaced it with another – we should never forget (but we can only forget) that this is always possible with messages, even this very message you are reading now, if you are reading it. On that eighth day, I had given Marduk and his priests reason to look over their shoulders at the rising Moon. The foundations of the world should have trembled, at least for all those who have spent any amount of time inspecting them. The people – they I could get to roar, without knowing what they roared at. But surely the priests knew that the earth had shifted.

And they did, of course, and I'm sure not a single one liked it. But four days of the festival remained; and in those four days, the priests concerned themselves not with taking the contours of the newly shifted land, nor in wondering how it was that the ground beneath their feet could move in the first place. No. What the priests concerned themselves with was smoothing things over. *They concerned themselves with making sure days nine through twelve went off successfully. The cosmic order may be in disarray, but the festival – the festival!* That *must go off as well as possible, and we'll worry about the rest later. So I read them anyway; and I confess I was surprised, though as I write now I am less and less surprised, not surprised at all really. In the end, their concerns are foreseeable. Some I shall attract to my side with the allure of continued prominence and power; some I shall repel precisely because they sense their prominence and power threatened. But that the world beneath their feet should and could move – who takes that seriously? Do I, even? They are not believers in Marduk but in something else, something that remains unmoved; perhaps I, too, am a believer in that something else. But I doubt any of us knows what that something else is, much less whether it is worthy of belief.*

Perhaps we only need the belief, regardless of its worthiness. I doubt you haven't thought something similar, dear priestess-daughter of mine.

After seeing you, but before my departure, I took leave as well of your brother. I am sure that we do not, for the most part, understand each other – and that is horrible and exasperating, a lot of the time, but also a good thing. We can surprise each other. For my part, I had expected him to be focused only on practicalities – how we shall stay in communication, when to make decisions on his own versus to seek my counsel, things like that. So I was much surprised when he brought up the rēḫātu. *"What about the* rēḫātu*?" he asked. "What about it?" I responded. He smiled at me wryly. "Forgive my inexperience," he began, "but in my limited observation it has never appeared that the* *divine statues actually eat the food we offer them. What then shall we do with the food?" I confess I had not considered this problem. Traditionally, the food, having been offered to the gods and having been by them – or rather, by their statues – either declined or spiritually assimilated, is brought to the king. It falls to him to eat the sanctified meal reserved for the gods. All this, I'm sure, you know well – unless Sîn is an uncommonly voracious god-statue. Is he? Do you place his evening meal before him, only to discover crumbs by morning? Have you never suspected mice? If a mouse eats the meal of a god, could that not be the sign that the mouse is the god? And if a king eats the meal of a mouse, could that not be the sign that he is a mouse?*

But of course I did not say such things to your brother. The thought of the sanctified meals travelling vast distances under the hot sun to wherever I happened to be, in order for me to consume them – fell short of being appealing. "You should eat them," I said. "You will be acting as king." "I will be acting as king," he agreed, "but I shall not be *king. Surely there's all the difference in the world between acting and being a king." "Is there?" I queried, but he ignored me. "Besides," he continued, "what will the priests say?" I sighed and admitted that I didn't know. "We shall have to consult them." Consult them we did. At first they were resolute in their opposition to anyone but me eating the* rēḫātu, *but I managed to persuade them. "Should I die on campaign," I said, "it could be weeks before the city knows of it. Meanwhile, the* rēḫātu *will be sent out, only to decay and probably be lost, to our ignominy and possibly to the gods' wrath. Better to split the* rēḫātu *between us. That way, should I die, nonetheless they shall find their way to a king – to my son, who unbeknownst to anyone, least of all himself, will have been in a mere instant transformed from acting the king to being the king." So it was agreed; and I managed to reduce by half the rancid food which, besides perhaps sickening me, will leash me forever to Bābilim. Should you need me, my beloved daughter, you shall have only to follow the breadcrumbs.*

I confess, though, that in some strange way your brother's attention to detail about the rēḫātu *heartened me. Perhaps, in time, statues will call even to him. Whether that is a blessing or a curse – I leave that undecided. Quite probably it is both.*

For you, what is it? Do you know? Does your "palace" full of statues bring you joy or dread? Is it they who transform your abode into a home, or is it they who forbid that transformation? Do you surround yourself with statues, await the god, and consider yourself honored by your fate, or do you weep and gnash your teeth and spit my name into the dirt?

Shall I end this letter, then, by begging your forgiveness? But for what? For giving you a name? For something else? Would either of us know? So let me end it instead with my regards – to you and to the statues.

Nabû-na'id lay in his tent. For a third day he was delirious, and for a third day Gubaru tended him. Dispatches were sent daily – to Bel-šar-uṣur, to Niṭil-Kišar, to the people of Bābilim. Both in the camp and in the city, word spread: this was the king's punishment. This was the king's reward for his sacrilege during the *Akītu* festival. Marduk's vengeance had not been long in coming – but long enough. The god had waited for the king to leave on campaign. The god had waited so that the king would be without home and family when driven mad by fever and suffering. Homeless, his wife and children elsewhere, his magnificent city far behind him, to the east, where the sun rises: but the king was headed west, where the sun sets. Marduk's meaning could not be clearer.

So people murmured, nodding wisely, most of them not sorry for the king. No, they were not sorry but, in a certain way, even glad. For had this not once again confirmed Marduk's power, his reach, his peerlessness? Was not the king's sickness its own miniature version of the *Akītu* festival, with Marduk briefly eclipsed, only to re-assert himself in all his force and fury? That the king was pitiable – well, it was true. But few pitied him. They took comfort instead that the world had a ground, and that ground they knew by the name of Marduk.

Not so Gubaru, however. As he tended his childhood friend, he was oblivious to these swirling rumors and reprimands, these cannibalizing vaunts draped in moral rectitude. Nor did their possibility ever occur to him, as neither did a connection between the king's illness and the *Akītu* festival. He had warned Nabû-na'id at one point to beware of how he spoke about Marduk. Despite that warning, it never occurred to him, these many weeks later, to draw a connection. But perhaps there was something natural in that omission. After all, his son had been killed – and his son was a good man, no one doubted it. Here now was the king being crushed by the god – and the king, too, was a good man, Gubaru did not doubt.

Strange though it sounds, the very man who counseled pious care in the invocation and treatment of the gods never thought to relate a man's fate to that treatment. Indeed, Gubaru had ceased to seek explanation from the world, whether of its generosity or caprice. In some fashion which he never made explicit to himself, Gubaru did not expect that the world, or the god at its bottom, could rise to generosity or caprice, however much it appeared otherwise. He was like a man abandoned to the storm, in the grips of the maelstrom – and who kept his head above water to breathe without wondering why, simply because he could; and, when he could no longer, the same man let his head sink beneath the waves without recrimination or protest and without wondering why. Whether there was a time in his life when he had been otherwise, when he had despaired or hoped, when he had insisted that good be rewarded and evil punished – who could say? Not he, or at least no longer he.

Yet he was pious, you say? Yes, very; and in its trapping his piety was of the most traditional and unexceptional sort. But were you to look more closely, you would see that his was in fact a very strange piety, the rarest kind – a piety which, as if by some remarkable oversight, had forgotten to attempt to explain the world by its own terms.

It was this man who tended the king, the latter being to him not only a king but a boyhood friend. Gubaru still saw that boy in the lined face, much of it veiled by a beard, lying beaded with sweat before him. He recalled stories which Nabû-na'id told him, while they sat cross-legged beside one another – stories which Nabû-na'id always attributed to his mother. And he would always end the stories by goading Gubaru into a question, one which he would answer only with another question. It used to frustrate Gubaru but perhaps even in this could be found some trace, whether as seed or as condition, of his peculiar piety. For what is the difference between the man who asks questions which he has never learned to try to answer, on the one hand, and on the other, the man who over time forsakes questions altogether? Perhaps one of these men is more honest.

That is not to say, however, that Gubaru believed Nabû-na'id, even as a boy, only pretended to ask questions; Gubaru in fact never doubted his friend's pursuit of those questions. At some point, perhaps when they were in Luddu together, it had struck him, however, that pursuing a question was not the same as endeavoring to answer it. He had said as much to Nabû-na'id, who had seemed intrigued by the comment. "You may be right," Nabû-na'id had replied all those years ago. "It may even be that pursuing a question is better – wiser – more honest – than answering it. But then…" he had trailed off. "But then what?" Gubaru had asked. Nabû-na'id had given him a wild look, so like his mother's, and then, very quietly, had almost whispered: "Dare I ask what I mean by better, wiser, more honest? And what if those three words don't play nice with each other?" "What do you mean?" "What if wiser is not better, and more honest is not wise?" his friend had said with an ironic smile.

Perhaps in this moment too lay a trace of a seed or of a condition of Gubaru's peculiar piety. Meanwhile, remembering these and other occasions shared between them, and some as well not shared, he tended his friend, listened to his babel, pitied his suffering, loved him, all without hope and without despair.

In the corner of the tent lay the dog, panting and waiting.

Nabû-na'id, eyes closed, twisted on the ground, suddenly cried out: "Flies! Fleas! Gnats!"

Gubaru sponged his face. The king opened his eyes, strained his head upward and gripped Gubaru's hands. "Killing men like insects," he said, whispering urgently, "– it is too much to compare that to the extermination of insects. But Gubaru!"

"Yes?" his friend prompted.

"Killing insects like men – that is too much too! And killing insects like insects – too much! Too much! It's all too much!"

The king's head fell back to the ground. He closed his eyes.

A day passed and a night. Nabû-na'id, eyes closed, twisted on the ground, suddenly cried out: "Light!" Gubaru, who had been napping near the king's side, woke with a start. "What? What is it?" he asked. His friend again gripped him, strained to lift his head, his eyes opened wide. "Gubaru!" he whispered urgently. "Light comes from the stars – it whirls all around us, invisible – we breathe it. Gubaru, we breathe light!" Then his head fell back to the ground and he closed his eyes.

Gubaru felt warm breath on his face. He opened his eyes. The king, despite his weakness, had somehow half-raised himself and was leaning over his friend. Their faces were almost touching. "Don't worry, Enkidu," whispered Nabû-na'id gently.

"I am watching your nose for worms. I will not let worms fall out of your nose Enkidu. You can sleep while I keep watch."

Gubaru did not know what to do, so he closed his eyes and pretended to sleep. He counted to sixty, then he opened his eyes again. The king had fallen back to the ground where he lay twisted with fever, his eyes closed.

Before the temple, in the plaza, beneath him, he saw lit torches. They were useless; the balcony was easily visible, and the light of day was only beginning to dim. Still, there were the torches, flickering, full of empty purpose. All the people below were carrying torches, but it could not be to see. Some sort of sign, then, or at least a gesture. He could not understand.

'Well done.' Somehow he knew that that was exactly what the people below thought. They were congratulating themselves. 'Well done. We have given ourselves light by which to see.' [But you don't need that extra light to see, he protested.] 'And our solemnity, our silent awe here holding our torches – it is very fitting for the occasion.' [But what occasion is this? he wondered.]

The extra light, the unneeded light, made them all cold. It stirred the breeze against them, it darkened the periphery and brought it nearer – the periphery where night stood distantly waiting. And it crowded the people together, somehow made the group more compact, smaller, more fragile beneath the flickering flames that their very own hands uselessly held aloft. When the shadow finally falls, he thought, even familiar faces will leer distorted and monstrous, the silhouettes of those agile flames. Yet, he suddenly understood, the flames didn't only make the crowd compact, small and fragile, but also, somehow, it made it one, a unity. Soon, he speculated, will they not clasp each other's free hands and sing?

Would any of this be possible without the useless flames holding at bay a night still far, far off?

A figure on the balcony stepped forward, past him, almost

through him. In no way did the figure acknowledge him. Where he came from was unclear.

"The king is dead," the figure announced to the crowd. [He thought: "But I am the king!"]

Meanwhile, below: silence first, long and lingering, as the torches swayed and their flames flickered. Then, a lonely and awkward smattering of – what was it? Could it be applause? Yes. Applause trickled, gathered, burst forth – and there was stomping of feet – from somewhere, cheers, whistles, whoops – and then out of this thunder laced in flame something struck triumphantly, with unimaginable violence, force and loudness: laughter! Laughter laughter laughter growing building cresting laughter self-consuming laughter stomping cheers applause laughter. Again! Again! Laughter! Flames dancing, flames writing invisible letters against the far-off night, flames laughing.

Fly licked the king's face. Nabû-na'id opened his eyes, at a loss. Only slowly did comprehension dawn. "There is hope for me yet," he murmured. "How it can be, I do not know. But there is hope for me yet." He closed his eyes, smiling slightly, and rested. The fever had broken.

Speak to Niṭil-Kišar, thus speaks Gubaru.

May Šamaš and Marduk keep you alive forever for my sake. Send word that you are well, that I may please your husband with good news and be happy myself.

As you will have heard from the official dispatches, Nabû-na'id's health has greatly improved. He is eating and able to move about, albeit only a little. He remains very weak. Within a few weeks' time, however, I do not doubt that he will again be able to travel.

He asked after you, and I mentioned your wish that he return to Bābilim. He was adamant that he would not. Instead, he has decided to proceed south. Why, for what purpose, I do not know.

He has urged me to invite you in turn to come here, but he has said that you needn't respond to that request. Your response, he said, has already been given. He knows your answer.

I will remain by his side, as I promised you and as I promised myself.

Speak to Nabû-na'id the king thus speaks Bel-šar-uṣur the prince-regent.

May Šamaš and Marduk keep you alive. The city rejoices at your renewed health.

I shall instruct the temple to resume sending you one-half of the rēḫātu. *Please pass on the itinerary you plan to follow, once it is decided upon, that the* rēḫātu *may be sent to the right place – that it not be lost in the desert.*

"I was sick," Nabû-na'id said to the dog. "I was lying on my back, useless; in my writhing I had torn off all my limbs, and at last I reconciled myself to stare at the sky and wait. But then a man came, a stranger, and out of misguided kindness he flipped me onto my stomach, so that, though I was limbless, I could fly. In so doing, he denied me the sight of heaven and forced me to stare at the ground. With great difficulty, in immense pain, I wriggled myself back onto my back, but the man returned. Again, out of kindness, he flipped me over and encouraged me to fly, though my wings were no longer strong and I could not imagine where to go. I fluttered my wings weakly a few times, made a show of trying, and waited for him to leave so that I could again reconcile myself to my end beneath the awesome sky. But the man hovered over me; I sensed his shadow upon me; had I been on my back, I would have seen him, not the sky; and he was no different, I told myself, than the dirt at which I now stared. Dirt above me and below; it was as if I were buried. I cried out, but only a buzz escaped me – a buzz that of course the man misinterpreted. "You are frustrated," he said, "in your attempt to fly. Here, let me help you." And so he lifted me aloft and carried me, first to this land, then to that, all the way to the shores of the upper sea, then to the shores of the lower; from his hand I beheld the world entire, but not the sky. I beheld men of every size and shape; men like me with no limbs and useless wings; men who were striped and tailed; men who lived in water. Meanwhile, the man who carried me never rested, and so I never rested; he never ate, so I never ate; he never drank, so I never drank. I grew jittery from exhaustion, gaunt from hunger and parched from thirst; yet I saw the world and its inhabitants, only at the small price of being denied the sky – the Moon, the Sun, the stars, the endless blue of day and black of night. And I forgot these things, as I forgot the taste of food and drink and the sweet relief of sleep..."

Fly, who may or may not have been listening attentively, rolled onto his back, his teeth bared in a gruesome grin. He squirmed playfully. Nabû-na'id looked at him in amusement.

"Shall I scratch your belly?" he asked. "Or shall I flip you on your stomach, that you may fly?"

The dog didn't answer.

"Are you, even now, beholding the sky?" Nabû-na'id asked, this time with a strange urgency.

Again the dog did not answer, but his eyes peered down his nose at Nabû-na'id rather than at the sky.

"Are you not inspired by sun and moon and stars? Does not the endless expanse of blue or of black trouble you?"

Whether by way of reply or simply coincidentally, Fly growled playfully and squirmed some more. Nabû-na'id, reaching forward, scratched his belly, then wrapped his fist in the sleeve of his robe and offered it to the dog. The dog immediately flipped over and pounced, gnawing and tugging at the sleeve, grunting, wagging his tail happily.

"You ask too much of a dog," a voice said behind him.

Nabû-na'id, though not recognizing the voice, did not turn around or even, at first, respond. He continued to play with the dog, every now and then urging caution whenever Fly began to get carried away. "Careful," he would say. "I am your friend, not your enemy." And he would pull back his arm from the dog, unwrap the sleeve, examine the indentations from the dog's teeth, none of which had yet broken the skin. "Careful," he would repeat, either to himself or the dog, before re-wrapping his arm and offering it to the dog. Fly was quick to resume the game, with a barely restrained ferocity that at times allowed Nabû-na'id to lift him from the ground, simply by raising his arm to which the dog remained latched by his teeth, all the while growling intensely. More than once, this led Nabû-na'id to laugh.

"It isn't that I ask too much of a dog," he said to the voice behind him. "It's that too often I ask the wrong things. The fault is probably mine."

There was no response from the voice behind him. Perhaps it had gone. Nabû-na'id did not care. He continued to play with Fly until one or the other of them tired, whether of the game or the exertion. The dog sat down, then curled up. Nabû-na'id, king of the world, king of the four corners, sat down beside him. He too curled up, and before very long, man and dog were asleep.

The black cat, eyes closed, still purred ever-so-softly, barely audibly, as Izdubar pet her. He was, for a moment, content; and as he pet her, he wondered – might this last forever? Shall I hope for that or despair? Would that life be as meaningful as any other? More meaningful? Less? Did it matter?

Behind him, meanwhile, he could hear the pitter-patter of an exploring ferret's feet. He closed his eyes, listening to that and to the soft purring, while he stroked the cat slowly and rhythmically. Gratitude surged through him – but also, as if embroidering it, the suspicion, terribly faint, barely there at all, of boredom. He refused to examine it, to confirm it or disprove it; and instead he loosed his mind, let it wander, scatter, disperse into – was it sleep?

* * * * *

From the [fragmentary] Assyrian Accounts of Herodotus

...The western campaign of Labynetus was said to be very brutal; the revolt was put down mercilessly. That, anyway, is what is said; and confirming it was a border stele I saw and which, though I could not read it myself, was read to me.

(I should say a word about their script. It is famously complex, harder, I am told, even than that of the Egyptians. For one thing, though it began, supposedly, by depicting the images of things – just as the Egyptian script still does – now the signs resemble really nothing at all, except perhaps the footprints of birds in sand, sand moreover which not just one bird but entire flocks have trampled in every direction. I asked the priests to show me the beginnings and endings of their letters, but I could make no sense of what they said, for I could see no clear boundaries between their signs. It is possible, it seems to me, that they have no letters and even, strange though it sounds, that this is not writing. For, far from being an aid to memory, it requires prodigious memory. It is one thing for a travelling bard to recite the poems of Homer, aided by meter and alliteration and other tricks of the trade, but another for the same bard to somehow recollect hundreds upon hundreds of arbitrary signs, each with, as far as I could tell, multiple, innumerable meanings. That multiplicity of meanings – is it different from senselessness? The bard recounts how Zeus stole the wits of Glaukus when he exchanged gold for bronze, and who is there who does not understand what this means? But a Babylonian scribe scribbles footprints in clay and the reader must choose the proper meaning out of seemingly endless possibilities. Can that be writing? It

occurred to me that the Babylonian priests and scribes I encountered were privy to some grand and ancient joke, passed down to the elect generation by generation, like the Eleusinian Mysteries. "We shall pretend *that these mean," they say to one another of the signs, "and who will know differently?" But perhaps it is only my frustration which speaks, that I could not learn to read for myself those things whose witnesses live no more. For what I have here written cannot be true; and yet their script is so complicated it needs must be so.)*

The border stele which was read to me recounted massacres and piles of bodies devoured by birds, blood flowing across the land like rivers. Perhaps it was just as described, the priest admitted to me; but when I was a boy, he continued, I heard stories from a man who said he had gone on that campaign, and what he told was something different and strange. Their march, according to him, was unusual for its leisure, and the cities along the way opened their gates of their own accord. Not so much as a single battle was fought, he claimed. Instead, Labynetus, being anxious to put down the insurrection quickly and easily, endeavored to trick the rebels into submission through the deceit of words and false testimony (so the priest said); he suborned the enemy messengers and spies, as well as sundry witnesses, to paint a ghastly picture of the Babylonians' progress; he raised stele after stele memorializing ghoulish but also phantom deeds; and in short he cast the shadow of a monster that he might be greeted a man. And so it was, when at last he reached the stronghold in the mountains. When they beheld a man, moreover one even-tempered, reasonable and not unkind, so relieved were they to encounter what was akin to themselves that, with a single word, they delivered their city, their allies and their people to a harsher, yet not merciless, servitude.

That is what the priest claimed. But I have heard other stories too, stories more in accord with the border stele which was read to me. In fact, the subsequent illness of Labynetus, from which he nearly died, has been explained to me in terms of the unthinkable carnage that some say preceded it. The mountains of corpses, the deluge of blood, the flesh-eating birds (vultures, not sandpipers) – all transpired as the stele claimed, and Labynetus, beholding such desolation enacted at his command, by his word, ceased to recognize himself. The shadow was a man's, but only the shadow; the man himself was a monster. Not being able to endure this, the king sank into fever and debility and would have died, but for the love and care – some say of his childhood friend Gobryas, though others say it was the queen, his wife Nitocris, who cared for him. Thus are men who are monsters still loved – unaccountably.

I have also heard that this tale too is untrue, and that the illness of Labynetus had nothing to do with the savagery of his western campaign, but rather with a god's vengeance for an act of sacrilege in Babylon. For, according to many priests, and especially those found in the ancient city itself – the priests there being much more hostile to the ancient king, or to his memory, than those found in the periphery, and especially in the northwest where Labynetus is even revered – Labynetus (so say the better part of the priests in Babylon) was a heretic who worshipped the Moon – or else, some say, the god of writing – as the supreme god in their pantheon, and who subverted the city's religious festivals towards that end as well. Indeed, it was for this reason that the city fell to Cyrus, because it had grown impious under the direction of the heretical king; and it was for this reason that so many, and especially the priests, greeted Cyrus as Babylon's liberator, all the more when he acted quickly to restore the city's ancient practices. To blame Labynetus's illness on the savagery of war is madness, these people say, because all war is savage, and yet the gods often favor it and indeed its savagery; the gods punish men first and foremost for their treatment of the gods, not their treatment of men.

How to understand these conflicting accounts is not immediately clear, of course, nor is it really clear that the accounts are all necessarily in conflict. Might not a king be punished both by a god and by himself, at the same time and yet for different things – by the god for his treatment of gods, by the man for his treatment of men? And is it not also possible that neither god nor man cared enough about any of these acts to cause illness, and that the king instead became sick just by chance? After all, though I dare not speak of all gods, and I cannot speak of all men, I am convinced that there are some gods, and some men, who are untouched by any deed. (So speaks the old man I keep becoming.)

Let us say – for certainly I do not know – that Labynetus indeed did, for whatever reason, worship the god of writing as supreme. Or the Moon, if they are different gods. (For, as far as I can tell, Labynetus associated the one with the other, though whether this was an eccentricity of his or a long-established custom is unclear to me.) Why might he have done this, especially in a land whose script is so arcane, impenetrable, even (as I already suggested seriously and flippantly, perhaps ironically) meaningless? Is it because, through the power of writing, he could create an image of war to enable the reality of peace? Could he use writing as in the account of Sargon that I've already told – or in Homer's account of Bellerophon – to make distant men, men distant in space or in time, his instruments? Yet the tale of Sargon suggests the danger of that attempt: writing is faithless. Once orphaned from its parent, it is like those street urchins we find in the large cities – tools of those near at hand and more powerful than they, usually subverted to the pettiest tasks, thievery for example. Is this not the connection between writing and the Moon: does not writing wax and wane, is it not often eclipsed, is not its light faint and borrowed from another? And in it, in the light of the Moon, there is no warmth.

Would Labynetus not know this? Would he extol the Moon and writing out of the misapprehension that he at least could command them? But who does not think this who writes? Here I am, Herodotus of Halicarnassus, committing words to the page to commemorate deeds and men and above all problems, lest otherwise they be forgotten. I must believe I can cast a spell on these scribbles which enjoins them to dance only to my music. But the very things I write tell me it cannot be so. Is it not appalling, to commit words to a page in order to stave off forgetting, if committing those words to the page requires forgetting in the first place?

I am a storyteller grown old in his art and now fearful that it never was his art to begin with. My confidence would be greater, I am sure, if I could read the script of the Babylonians; it would be greater still were I assured that there was anyone – even just one person – who could read it. Lacking that assurance, even my own letters, these street urchins who have long served my beck and call, begin to look unfamiliar. Where I once saw an alpha now perhaps it is the head of an ox I see; where I once saw a beta, is that not its stable? Our alphabet becomes an ox's house, an animal's stable. I fear the coming day when I no longer recognize the letters as mine – or as urchin, ox or stable – or as anything at all. Indeed I fear the coming day when written Greek is as alien as Babylonian writing or even the writing, if it is writing, traced by the innumerable feet of birds flocking on beaches and, for now, just beyond the reach of the waves. Is that not the day when one, as for the first time or the last, sees one's shadow and does not know it? Monster, is it? Man? Me? Has it always been so?

There is no need for atrocity, for the savagery of war, to sink into debility, fever, madness. Or, if it be the case, to sink out of it.

* * * * *

Nabû-na'id, Gubaru and Fly were walking together on the outskirts of the camp. The king, although his strength had not fully returned – perhaps it never would – was yet strong enough for these walks if done slowly, and he insisted upon them. "No thing is so valuable to me as my walks," he had told Gubaru once, "as I also value those I share them with, or who share them with me."

(But what does it mean to share a walk? Gubaru had thought clumsily, letting the question tumble around for a while before it settled in the dirt and was forgotten. Yet, like a lost ball, might it not eventually be refound?)

They hadn't spoken for a while as instead they watched Fly eagerly investigate their surroundings. Their silence was companionable, shared rather than imposed. Had he thought of it, Gubaru might have wondered no less what it meant to share silence as to share a walk; but he did not think of it and instead took simple pleasure in the sounds of pebbles and dirt crunched beneath their sandals, and in the breeze that occasionally swept past and through them. He liked watching the dog. It did not occur to him, as it would to Nabû-na'id, to wonder why.

"Let's go that way," Nabû-na'id suddenly said, pointing vaguely to the south. Gubaru stopped, turned and started in the direction indicated. "No, not now," his friend added. "With the army."

"You mean to renew the campaign in Amurru? Are you ready? Are you strong enough?"

"I mean to go south. Renewing the campaign in Amurru and beyond – that is an excuse. In fact, it is a translation of my desire to go south into words that generals and administrators can understand. But it's not a good translation, however necessary. I want to go south. Or rather, I want to go *that way* –" (he waved his arm again vaguely toward the south) "– it's like a hymn or a poem. It expresses something deeper, more subtle and also more turbulent, than the words it employs. But bureaucrats don't understand such things. 'Renewing the campaign in Amurru' – for them there's no meter, no alliteration, no form, just content, just what they take to be a bald meaning. But Gubaru –!" Nabû-na'id turned and clutched his friend's sleeve with some urgency, "*I want to go that way*" he said, again waving his arm weakly toward the south.

"Why?" Gubaru asked.

"Why does Fly traipse from here to there?" the king responded, pointing to the dog as he did his rounds. "Might there not be something inscrutable within him that directs his outward flight? What of the bird or the fly or the ant, or even the flower stretching toward the sun? What directs them? Are they too renewing their campaigns in Amurru?" The king laughed sharply, disconcertingly.

"But –" began Gubaru, then stopped.

"But what?"

"You are not a dog, a bird, a fly, an ant or a flower. You are a king."

"Even to you, is that what I am?"

Gubaru was silent for a moment. "You are my friend from childhood," he said slowly. "But you are also the king, even to me."

Nabû-na'id trudged forward somberly, kicked a stone, followed it, kicked it again. "Of course," he said almost to himself. Then, louder: "Of course." He stopped in front of the now-resting stone and again spoke aloud, though more to himself than Gubaru. "I put on a costume and expect my friends to know that I remain beneath it, somehow untouched. But I am not untouched. Why would I think I was untouched? Why would I believe that was possible?" He looked at Gubaru intensely.

"Is that a question for me?" Gubaru asked, confused.

"No, it's a question for me! Or do you have the same question?"

Again Gubaru looked confused. "I don't know what you mean," he answered.

"Me neither," Nabû-na'id said, then laughed again in the same sharp and disconcerting way as before. "I want to go *that way*," he repeated, waving his hand weakly once more towards the south, "out of a mystical faith which even I don't believe that I can escape my shadow by so doing; that I can disrobe, cast away my scepter and my crown, stand naked not even before the god, but before nothing, and say – 'Here I am, as I am, as I really am, naked, shadowless, alone. Here I am.' But wherever I go, I go clothed, accompanied not only by a shadow but by men, most of them strangers who know only my costume. The costume that I also am."

Gubaru said nothing.

"But if I am also that costume," Nabû-na'id said abruptly, perking up, "why does Fly bite my sleeve?"

Gubaru was at a loss. "I don't understand."

"To you I am both childhood friend and king. But what am I to Fly? Does he see me more truly?"

Gubaru shrugged. "It seems doubtful that the dog sees you better than I do."

"Sees me, hears me, smells me, tastes me…" Nabû-na'id mused, again mostly to himself. "The dog knows dimensions of me that you don't," he said louder to Gubaru. "And you know dimensions of me that the dog doesn't. I wonder…" He trailed off.

"Yes?"

"I wonder what dimensions of me are known to others and not to myself. I wonder, if I stood naked, shadowless and alone before nothing at all, would even I recognize myself? Would there be a myself for me to recognize?" He touched Gubaru on the shoulder, and the latter stopped and faced him. "What of a puppet is not his costume?" Nabû-na'id asked his friend.

Bewilderment spread across Gubaru's face. He stuttered inarticulately at first before finally an intelligible protest burst from his lips: "You are a king and my friend. You are not and have never been a puppet!"

As if in agreement, Fly came frolicking back to them and nipped at Nabû-na'id's sleeve. The king looked at Gubaru and Fly in silence for a moment, then laughed for a third time – this time more richly than before, without sharpness, though disconcerting still, at least to Gubaru. In it he heard pleasure and joy and gratitude – but, burrowed deep within it, he heard sorrow too. And, though he did not understand it, he recognized it as somehow familiar, as somehow something he felt too.

Nabû-na'id, who cannot speak, writes; may you read, Niṭil-Kišar.

Here again I find myself writing you as I did those years ago when Awil-Marduk had imprisoned me. Then we were perhaps within shouting distance; and now, even were I to climb the tallest mountain and call for you, you would not hear. But that we write to each other – that we have always written to each other, beginning with the dying fly and burning ember, or the dying ember and the burning fly – does that not indicate something deeper and more unsettling? Even when we looked into each other's eyes or gave ourselves to love-making, were we not yet too far from one another to call out and be heard? Have we not always had to write? But why should that be?

It is a mistake to think we choose to write – that, in writing one another, we simply express a preference. We yield to writing, you and I; it is imposed on us irrefusably. If we would touch one another, it will be by way of the alienated letter, set free like a messenger bird to find, perhaps, its destination; or, better, like a waif slipped into a reed basket and sent floating down the river, in the hope that by some miracle it will survive, flourish and someday, impossibly, recognize its kin. Writing is the truth of speech, I think; the truth even of the most intimate caress. To touch you I do not become myself but another. Every touch, then, is a little death – hence the orphan in the basket.

And what of idols? Are they not a form of writing? When your father ill-advisedly cast an enormous image of his wife and his love against the sky, looking homeward, what was that if not, quite simply, a note? One which, alas, she read better than he – for this gesture of endearment, far from comforting her, only reminded her of her homelessness, even while it implied, probably falsely, that a home remained for her elsewhere. So do we learn, then, that what writing escapes us we may be the last to read. Writing is not ours. Or at least it is not mine.

As you know, we struck south, no doubt guided by concerns of state which I will leave my underlings to articulate and justify. I do not know what has pushed me in this direction, and I was equally uncertain how (or whether) I would know to stop. Surely we have all had moments when, having gotten ourselves into motion, the prospect of ceasing has become inconceivable – somehow we will walk forever, or even twirl forever. (I am thinking of my childhood, when I would endlessly swing myself in a tight circle, charmed because it was the world rather than me which seemed to move; and the end would come not from my volition but from collapse when, unbalanced, I would tumble to the very ground whose position I had ceased to be able to judge. Sweet was the assurance then that the ground did not, in fact, move; that it was steady as always; that my disorientation had been the accomplishment of my own bewildering motion, a perverse delight which I had inflicted upon myself perhaps for the thrill of being rescued from it.) (But have I been rescued?)

We struck south, but we are stopped now, near a place called Teima. What led me to command a halt, with all the dignity, wisdom and strategic purpose of a great king, Bābilim's latest if not her last? It was the name the locals gave to their Moon god, whom, my mother would be glad to know, they worship as supreme and honor with an enormous statue carved of the whitest stone I have ever seen, one whose glare in the sun is like the Moon's. And they call it, the god and the statue, Ṣalmu. *Yes,* Ṣalmu. *Some of the elite travelling with me thought this very funny. "These hicks worship as a god a statue that they call Statue!" they said, laughing, slapping each other's shoulders and knocking into one another as if the amusement of it all had set them to boiling. "Probably our traders long ago introduced them to the god and gave them a statue to worship – and they thought the statue was the god!" So the sophisticates laughed, too well-educated to be thoughtful, and thus the unwitting butt of their own joke. But I knew, anyway, that the time had come to stop, that the time had come for my twirling to end and for me to fall to the earth.*

And so here have I fallen, before a statue or a god or a statue-god or a god-statue of God the Statue or Statue the God. If only our daughter were with me: priestess of the Moon and hostess of statues, perhaps in this place her wanderings too would find their end.

To Belet-ṣeri-dannat, thus Nabû-na'id, the king.

I received your report. I too am troubled – but certainly not shocked – that the influence of the House of Egibi rises. Better for you, however, to retain Bel-šar-uṣur's trust, and hence a position of influence with him, than to jeopardize that by acting as my creature, reporting on him behind his back and otherwise spying. You must stop that. Trust can never be earned, only given; but mistrust can be earned. We must trust Bel-šar-uṣur and hope he trusts us. Be frank with him, even about those things you wrote to me; and if you cannot find his ear, as a last resort, consult with Niṭil-Kišar – but do it openly, that you not compromise her and thereby deprive Bel-šar-uṣur of his wisest advisor.

As you may have heard, we have halted near a city far to the southwest, in Arabi, actually – the city of Teima. It is a land surrounded by desert where one might wander for generations. That I believe. Whether the wandering culminates in the fulfilment of a promise, or rather keeps in abeyance such fulfilment so that the promise may endure as a promise – on that, as you know, we disagree. Is a promise better kept for being fulfilled? Isn't that fulfillment the end of a promise, the end of its keeping? Promises are like flames around which we huddle, under a cold sky whose darkness the flames exaggerate; and we are wise to keep the flames burning rather than to throw ourselves into them. But perhaps it is too much to ask a man to keep a promise forever, rather than see it realized; perhaps in this men are not different from flies, who can dance around the flame only so long before, whether in exhilaration, longing or despair – or all of these

– they plunge into the very heart of the flame to burn and die in a glory too great for them.

We have stopped here, I already wrote, but I am not convinced that it has brought either an end to my wandering or deliverance from the burden of carrying about a promise. I think of that tabernacle you say your people hauled through a desert much like this – perhaps this very desert – and what did they shroud within that holy ark if not a promise? Better to huddle around that ark under a cold and dark sky than to open it. But is it too late not to open it? When precisely has a fly not neared a flame but entered one? Does a flame truly have an edge?

Yes, yes, I am thinking of that god you describe as yours, who made idols to himself and called them men, then refused men the right to make idols of him. I am thinking as well of those puppets with the miserable fates during the Akītu festival. Sometimes they are dressed as gods, other times as royalty, still other times merely as men. Of which are they the true image? Is one of those forms their true form? Or is it a mistake, a desire or even a dream to imagine that there exists such a thing as a true form? Are the puppets destroyed, burned like the flame-enamored fly, because they fail to be what they represent, even what in a certain sense they are? Perhaps that is what happens to your god's idol-maker: the idol falls so terribly short of what it would model – or else so greatly exceeds it – that it is kindled into fire by the failed, hence frictive comparison. Or else it just sits around, forgotten and gathering dust, until someone needs a doorstop or a roof beam or some kindling. Why then does your god object to so innocuous and pathetic a thing as an idol?

But I should desist; this has been cause of more than one violent argument between us. I am thinking about it only because of the peculiarity of what I have found here. It is a land that worships the god of the Moon as supreme; but what they call him – in our language, though perhaps it doesn't mean this in theirs – is "Statue." I cannot help but linger over this – what is it? A coincidence? Proof that the locals are hillbillies? Or might it be a sign? That is what I wonder: might it be a sign? Or even if it isn't a sign – might it be read?

We bring the statues of the gods into the city during the Akītu festival. We gather them from all over the land, mount them on boats, regale them, honor them and celebrate them. We call the god of writing Nabû. We call the Moon god Sîn. Each god has its own proper name, and not one of those proper names is Statue. And my question is simply – why not? Is it perhaps that we wish not to remind ourselves that we are worshipping first and foremost a carved rock or a piece of wood or fashioned metal? Or is it that the name Statue is too unambitious – it aspires to too little – for surely a statue can represent a statue, but our statues dare to represent gods! But then, isn't the name superfluous? Why utter it? The statue is right there before us, representing what it represents, being what it is, perhaps even being what it represents or representing what it is. Why, in addition to all its finery, its exquisitely dyed robes and the glittering hand-carved jewelry, must it be crowned with a name? A name other than the name it already has, "statue"?

Perhaps such questions will grind your own desert wanderings to a halt, as they have mine; or perhaps I should enshrine them in a tabernacle and carry on. But for now, that is beyond me. For now, I am here – I, the man named Nabû-na'id, the man not named Man. Again I think of that tabernacle and wonder at its secrecy, at the curtains which veil its content, even if that content is nothing at all. (You would say it is not.) Perhaps the greatest secret is not what the curtains veil, but the curtains themselves; perhaps the secret has always been in plain sight. And I think: what is a name but a curtain or a veil?

As you know, I was able to see Niṭil-Kišar's face for the first time only because she was veiled.

A guard announced the functionary's arrival. Nabû-na'id waved his hand distractedly. "Let him in," he sighed. "Well?" he said when the man stood before him. "What do you want?"

"The generals have been expecting you since mid-day; they sent me to determine if your plans had changed or if you had other orders for them."

"Ah," Nabû-na'id responded gruffly. "I suppose it would not suffice to explain to them that I had forgotten, that they have been wasting these precious moments of their lives waiting for a man who for whatever reason could not be troubled to think about them."

The functionary took a step back but said nothing. Nabû-na'id narrowed his eyes, then stroked his beard.

"In fact," he admitted, "I *did* forget, but only because..." He paused and gestured feebly at nothing in particular. "Only because," he resumed, "I have been writing letters." The functionary took another step back. "Important matters," Nabû-na'id added. "Of state – of course." Then, somewhat grotesquely, the king smiled.

"Of course," the functionary repeated. "Shall I tell them...?"

"Tell them I will come shortly – I have one more letter to write, a brief one. Also tell them that I am sorry I forgot. It is easy to lose track of the passage of time," he observed, "while writing letters."

"Oh," the man said and started to turn.

"That is because," Nabû-na'id continued imperiously, his voice growing louder, "when one writes, one is between times, not in them."

The functionary stared blankly at him. After a moment of silence reigned between the two of them, he asked whether that was all. "Shall I return to the generals and convey your message?"

Again the king smiled grotesquely. "By all means, by all means... if you can." The man started to leave. He was barely out the door when Nabû-na'id again called out to him.

"Have you ever considered how much a kingdom requires

letters? I doubt there could be such a thing as a kingdom, without letters and letter-writers and letter-carriers."

"Not a very big kingdom, anyway," the man said.

Nabû-na'id looked at him sternly. "Not any kingdom at all," he corrected. "Not even an ant hill. What do you think it is that keeps ants so infernally busy? There's a king deep within the mound, busily scratching out letter after letter and handing them to his messengers. It is they we see streaming in and out of the mound, always in commotion, endeavoring to deliver their messages."

The functionary looked at the ground. "As you say, your highness."

"Surely it is hopeless, wouldn't you agree?" the king asked through his grotesque and unsettling smile.

"I would not know," the functionary answered, still looking at the ground.

"Of course not. Of course not. There is no one who knows. I wonder if the ant messengers have formed opinions on the matter, however."

The functionary waited, shuffling his feet and not looking up. Nabû-na'id inspected him closely. "You have spoken with me before, yes?"

"Yes, your highness."

"Well, we shall have to have another of these chats again sometime. For now, off you go. Be my messenger; announce that I shall come, that I have been delayed by writing state-enabling letters. But, my friend," the king concluded, almost intimately, "let's not mention the ants, shall we?"

He began one last letter. *Speak to Bel-šar-uṣur, thus writes the king his father*, he wrote, then continued. *We have provisionally established ourselves near the city of Teima and will soon prepare more permanent arrangements. The strategic value of this location speaks for itself, but if you have questions, interview the officials with whom I am sending this message. They are well-informed about the trade routes that we command from this vantage, as well as about those vassals who, should they stir, are within easy reach from here. Henceforth anything requiring my personal attention – legal cases, military decisions, diplomatic correspondence, cultic matters – anything at all, per your discretion – let them be sent here.*

He set the letter down and prepared to rise, but then stopped and took up the letter again. He added a final line: *That includes, of course, the* rēḫātu.

Then, still holding the letter and the reed stylus, he stared abstractly at the wall.

He was standing with his father on a tell near Bābilim. It was a place he and Gubaru had frequented regularly in their childhood; and it was the place where they had lost the pukku *and* mekkû. *"Ah," said Nabû-balaṭsu-iqbi. "This is where you lost tomorrow."*

"It is one of the places where I lost tomorrow. I've lost it so many times since then. When you died, when I betrayed the secret of the eclipse, when I took the kingship, when I gave my daughter to the Moon. Perhaps I have come to Arabi in search of tomorrows."

His father toed the dirt with his sandal. "I doubt you will succeed."

"You're here aren't you?" challenged Nabû-na'id.

"Is this Arabi? I thought we were on that tell near Bābilim where you and your friend played."

"Does it matter where we are?"

"It was you who indicated that it did."

Nabû-na'id didn't respond for a moment, then muttered under his breath, "Very well."

Then a long silence followed during which his father continued to toe the dirt with his sandal. "There are a lot of sherds," he observed.

"Yes," agreed his son. "As a child, I thought I had exchanged

tomorrow for yesterday, here on this tell. I had lost the pukku *and* mekkû, *but my eyes had been opened to all the sherds, to what they hinted of the past, even to the writing which one might find buried in the sand, whether as a tablet or a scratch on a sherd."* *He leaned over and picked up a sherd.*

"Sherd of the tell," he said, "why do you torment me?"

The sherd did not answer.

"What would it say if it could speak?" Nabû-na'id asked his father.

"I found a tablet once," Nabû-balaṭsu-iqbi responded, "on which was written the response of a sherd. A man asked, 'Why are you hostile to me?' and the sherd purportedly replied, 'I am the spike of a thorn bush – don't you dare step on me. I am the sting of a scorpion – don't you dare touch me.'"

"That's not an answer to the man's question," Nabû-na'id observed.

"No, it isn't. But it suggests an answer."

"Which is?"

"The man torments the sherd as much as the sherd torments the man."

"It can't be helped. You know that. Everywhere we step there are sherds; we can only step on sherds."

"Is that true in Arabi too?"

"I have not seen a single sherd," Nabû-na'id replied, "and yet it is also true there."

"Ah," his father replied with a sigh. "I suppose sherds eventually become dust – but that only means each particle of dust is a little sherd. And what, I wonder, becomes of that dust-sherd, what over time does it become?" He paused and looked at his son sympathetically. "Is it any comfort," he finally asked, "to you to know that at least another man besides yourself was once tormented by sherds?"

Nabû-na'id thought for a moment before saying anything. "Perhaps the sherd you quoted was just a belligerent sherd," he proposed, not answering his father's question. "Maybe men don't torment sherds, but sherds, some of them anyway, are full of bluster, trying to pretend to be what they're not, aspiring to a self-importance that doesn't belong to mud. Or if not sherds in general, then this sherd, the one who answered the man in the tablet."

"And yet you have been torn and stung by sherds, have you not?"

Nabû-na'id, who had been holding and fingering the sherd all the while, cocked his arm and threw it as far from him as he could. "Be gone, sherd!" he yelled.

"But there is another at your feet," Nabû-balaṭsu-iqbi pointed out, "right there."

Nabû-na'id picked it up and threw it far away.

"And another," repeated his father, pointing.

Nabû-na'id picked it up and threw it far away.

"And another," repeated his father, pointing.

Nabû-na'id picked it up –

"Will you be coming soon to speak with the generals?" the functionary asked, the same one as before, and Nabû-na'id woke with a start. He was still staring at the wall, though for some time it had not been a wall, but something else.

"Well, Fly, I shall have to go talk to those generals. I doubt they'll be put off for much longer, though of course they'll take their anger out on the messenger rather than on me. I wonder what exactly our functionary friend will say. 'The king has gone mad and speaks of ants.' 'The king was daydreaming.' 'The king is old and was sleeping again.' Is it so horrible a thing to sleep, Fly? You pass much of your time sleeping, do you not? Do you regret it? Is your life wasted for the amount of time you have passed in sleep?"

The dog ignored him, and so he continued. "Gilgameš slept, couldn't keep his eyes open, and lost immortality as a result. He slept again and lost a return to youthfulness. Because of his sleeping, the consolation prize, the achievement of his life, was a mere wall, which he had always already achieved, from the very beginning, before he set out to wander the earth, struggling and suffering all the while. The wall was there when he was born; if anything, he damaged it over the course of his life. Yet it was also the achievement of his life – a wall and a story inscribed on it and in it. The wall outlasted him, but it gradually gave itself and is always giving itself back to the earth. Not even walls are walls – not forever. And even when they are walls they are not walls, in a sense – for they are dirt too. If we were very small – if you were a fly rather than only being named one – we might never see the wall and only see the dirt. Such is the achievement of a man's life. But maybe the story is misunderstood. (Misunderstanding a story is how it is given back to the earth, don't you think?) Maybe, rather than being conquered by sleep, Gilgameš received sleep as a gift. To live forever is to lose everyone who does not. It is to see every grain of dust in what aspires to be a wall. But to sleep keeps open a promise: perhaps I will be a child again, and play on the tell; perhaps I will see my father again, though he is dead; perhaps it will again be possible for my longings to be satisfied by a wall. If Gilgameš knew this, was he not the wisest of men? He feigned sleep or gave himself to sleep – though sleep, I said before, was the gift – to avoid having to refuse a lesser gift." He paused, then grunted, "Yeah, that's Adapa's tale too. Better that the gods think a man weak or foolish than that they suspect he is too wise to receive or prize their gifts."

The dog bumped Nabû-na'id's hand with his head, and the king scratched his ears. "Should I be careful what I say about the gods, Fly? Or are you reminding me that there are more pressing matters than these vain speculations of mine? There is of course the matter of you! That your ears be scratched! That you be played with! Is that not so, boy?" Nabû-na'id knelt down and lowered his face even with the dog's. "Is there hope for me yet, boy?" he inquired in a tone suddenly somber. Fly smelled his beard, then licked his face. "So there is, still," the king muttered, his tone at once relieved and ironic. He burrowed his face in the dog's fur. "Thank you Fly," he murmured into the fur. Then he straightened and took a step back, before again addressing the dog.

"I shall have to go talk to those generals," he repeated. "And I have yet to write a letter to Mikum-Nisaba. Or is it En-nigaldi-Nanna to whom I should write? Maybe that's why I have put off the letter – once again I no longer know to what name I should address it." He paused and examined the dog intently. "Do you object to being called 'Fly?' he asked. The dog wagged his tail. "Fly – is that name ok with you?" The dog again wagged his tail, coming closer. "Fly – is that your name?" The dog nipped playfully at Nabû-na'id, who responded by giving him his sleeve to tug on.

"If you slept all the time, would you be different from a statue? Or is there a way to incite even a statue into a playful nip or a game of tug-of-war?"

The dog growled determinedly while pulling at the sleeve, but Nabû-na'id was unsure whether the growl was in answer to his question, or if it was, which question, or even what it meant.

"Are divine statues just sleeping gods, curled into their names like blankets?" asked the king, while the dog, clenching Nabû-na'id's sleeve in his teeth, tried to drag him forward. Nabû-na'id, laughing, fought back, lifting the dog off the ground by raising his arm and trusting to Fly's obstinacy not to let go.

The functionary appeared at the door. "Your excellency…"

"Can't you see that I am busy?" the king exclaimed heatedly. Then he lowered the dog to the ground, bent towards it and growled. Fly arched his lower back, lifting his wagging tail into the air, and barked playfully. And the king barked back.

"Take the city," he ordered. "Do what must be done. We will make this our base. We will make this our home."

The generals looked at one another. "Teima will certainly be ours," one of them said, "but a siege could take many months or longer."

"Very well."

"A significant fraction of the army will have to stay behind," the same general noted.

"The army that is here already – I will keep all of it here."

A spontaneous murmur broke out among the generals as they again exchanged glances. "You won't take a contingent back with you?" their self-appointed spokesperson asked.

Nabû-na'id pointedly inspected the general who spoke, and then, without a word, inspected each of the other generals in turn. Only when he had finished did he speak. "I am not going back," he said simply. "I intend to stay here."

"But – !" exclaimed a different general. "What about the *Akītu* festival? It cannot be conducted without the king!"

Nabû-na'id stared at him. "I am not returning to Bābilim," he repeated, speaking slowly and making eye contact with each of them one after the other. "Do what must be done to take Teima. I will reside here for as long as I see fit." He stood up and started to leave. "That is all," he announced as he turned.

* * * * *

From the [fragmentary] Assyrian Accounts of Herodotus

...At the command of Labynetus the city was taken. Large numbers of people were slaughtered or deported. Whether this was a departure from his regular practice or not – whether the acts of cruelty and the

lack of mercy shown on this campaign were unusual for this king or standard – whether they even took place, or were instead a veil created by words, hiding something better or something worse – I, Herodotus of Halicarnassus, who have dedicated myself to inquire into the deeds of men of yore, lest they be forgotten and lest, in forgetting them, we forget ourselves – I who thought he could discern the past curled behind the living words which escape men's lips – I who have endeavored to peek behind the accounts purportedly inscribed into stone or clay – I who have dedicated myself to record in writing the results of my inquiries that they may appear to all beneath the clear light of day – I do not know.

Chapter 10. Reign of Absence

From the Babylonian Royal Chronicle:
Fourth regnal year: The king lived in Teima; in Akkadê were the prince, his officers and his army. The month of Nisanu arrived but the king did not return to Bābilim. Nabû did not enter the city. Bel did not come out. No god left his sanctuary. There was no Akītu festival. Offerings were still presented, in the Esagila and the Ezida, to Bābilim's gods and to Borsippa's, as if the times were normal.

For my daughter do I impress these signs into clay, that she may read them. That you may read them – you my daughter or whoever you are.

Little in your account startled me. Of course I am anathema among Marduk's priests, for going off script last year and refusing the script this year. Everything, you see, is prescribed – everything is written in advance. The priests understand this much at least; what they don't understand is that even what is prescribed is prescribed.

What do I mean? I mutter that question to myself all the time, repeating it until the words cease to be words, cease to be anything. Sometimes an orderly will surprise me in the act of pacing up and down and muttering, while Fly watches me from a corner or nips at my sandals. But when an orderly surprises me, he averts his eyes; what he says, he says behind my back, behind the back of a mad king who has exiled himself and whom he calls by my name. And so it matters no more to me what he says than what the priests of Marduk say.

Even what is prescribed is prescribed, I wrote. I am thinking of the crown of Šamaš. What battles had to be fought over that crown! A crown that no one but me and a few priests would truly see. Of course anyone who looked at it would see it – but the it that they would see would be the it that they expected. Which may have little to do with the it before them. This is one way that even what is prescribed is prescribed.

The question was quite simply whether the sun god's crown had horns. I maintained that it did not, the priests that it did. They invoked tradition; they brought to bear tablets hundreds of years in age; they proved that in ancient times the sun god's crown had horns. For so was it written.

But I am a scholar too, perhaps a better scholar than they. I too invoked tradition; I too brought to bear tablets, tablets much older than theirs; and I proved that in even more ancient times the sun god's crown carried two crescent moons – a waxing and a waning moon, each mirroring the other. It is prescribed, I said; and my prescription predates yours.

Perhaps if I had stopped there I would have carried the day without much turmoil. But I could not help myself. I added: "Long ago, the crescent moons were misread. They were mistaken for horns. Your tradition has always been an error."

But even then, even as I saw the priests' fury building, I did not stop. "Comfort yourselves," I said, "that your error was at least prescribed – for who can truly say that the image of a crescent moon is not the image of a horn?" I tried to look at them kindly. "Even what is prescribed," I observed sagely, and maybe a little tendentiously, "is prescribed." This little witticism of mine, however true, was not well-received; and it occurred to me that, had it not been necessary for me to serve in the looming Akītu festival, these men might have ripped me to shreds with their bare hands, and joyously.

That realization was enough to check my pontificating impulse. I did not tell them, as I might have, that beneath every layer of text is another layer; nor that the fresh mud that even now I have molded into this tablet has yet a hundred times, a thousand times, served to carry the emptiness of signs from one place to another.

No, I simply commanded them to be sure that the horns – or rather the crescents – were carved more distinctly in the crown, "to avoid confusion," I said. "Lest people think they're horns." And so they were: I knew it, the priests knew it, no one else knew it. But already engraved upon the coming Akītu festival was our antagonism and contest, before I said a single word on that infamous eighth day. So it was that even then I was following a script. Just not theirs.

To Belet-ṣeri-dannat, thus Nabû-na'id, the king, your friend.

Very well, let them murmur of sacrilege. I perform their festival, and they accuse me; I avoid their festival, and they accuse me. It does not occur to them that I too must answer to the god and not just to them.

Yes, I wrote "the god," but it is doubtful I mean yours.

The work on the Eḫulḫul must proceed apace, whatever they mutter – for Kuraš's intrigues will soon enough flame forth and then he will not long be occupied with Ištumegu. Nor is it possible that my mother will long be alive. This is a promise she has exacted from me since my earliest days – and her faith, in me or her god or whatever her faith is in – has somehow fallen within our power to fulfill. It is too much for my heart, or what is left of it, to turn away from that promise and that opportunity; though my turn towards it instead is also not without misgivings.

And for yourself, have you not told me that the city of Ḫarrānu figures greatly in the tales of your patriarchs? The wandering man of Uru – did he not rest there? Did he not bury his father there? Was it not to Ḫarrānu that his sons and his sons' sons came for their wives? Surely I have not misremembered that the house of God, the gate of Heaven, is, you say, on the road to Ḫarrānu?

Appease your heart and your conscience, then; honor your god in honoring mine. In honoring Ḫarrānu, honor your people's path, they who lingered there and returned there more than once. Were they not welcomed, were their camels not watered, did they not fall in love with their wives, all in Ḫarrānu? Then make this project yours as it is mine, even if they are ours differently – and dispel from your mind that rebellious and sanctimonious chatter which can speak as little to your heart as it does to mine.

These priests who imagine themselves defenders of tradition, though they lack the courage and above all the conviction to lift a finger – if they ask, tell them this. Say to them, "Ea did not fashion Vizier Mummu and Anu did not know the name of Adapa. It is we who mold bricks and lay foundations, we who brighten walls with gypsum and bitumen. It is we who know names and teach them to the gods. It is for man to build a god's dwelling in Ḫarrānu; it is for man to name it Eḫulḫul; it is for man to take the god's hands and lead him to his home. Thus is it now; thus has it always been. Until Eḫulḫul rises again on the strength of man's obstinacy and dedication, what place among us is there for the god? Let the land mourn until we build that space, carving it from mud and ash and the sweat of our brows and the anguish of our hearts – let the land mourn until then. And until then there will be no Akītu festival because, until then, no old year will have ended, no new year begun."

And yes, they will call this sacrilege, they who know their tradition less well than I, they whose faith is passed down like tattered clothing rather than being born, as it must be, from their too weak and tattered hearts.

There. I have written it. Or it has been written. But from where did it come? Did it originate in me? Is it I who think that faith can be born only from a heart that is too weak, a heart that is in tatters? We have always heard otherwise. Faith, we have always heard, is the character of a strong heart, a heart able to leap where all others stumble. Is a leaping heart one that flutters, or is that a stumbling heart? What does it matter, if I can no longer distinguish leaps from stumbles, tattered garments from the most ornate? But why can't even a heart be naked? Is that too a prescription?

(Why, Fly, did I call you Fly? Is that your tattered garb, one that I dressed you in? Was your own garment not enough? Or was it your nakedness that compelled me to cover you in this hide, hide you in this covering – this name? What would have become of the two of us, what would have been possible between us, if you had not been Fly? And if you had had no name? Would that have been possible?)

(Fly, what have you to do with faith, what have you to do with my too weak and tattered heart?)

(Let me confess something to you, Fly. I look at you, and I think you are the expression of the entire cosmos. But a time will come when you are dead – yes, you, Fly. And then the cosmos will be the expression of the entirety of you. So it is for all of us; everything culminates in each of us, and each of us culminates in everything – like those children's toys found in tree-rich lands, seesaws they're called – which no pair of children is patient enough to balance forever, but which instead is ever breaking its poise by leaning now to this side, now to that. Now to the everything expressed in the one; now to the one expressed in the everything. The thought comforts me and for that reason I mistrust it. It makes everything fit; nothing is left over; the world is at least revealed as beautiful. But my suspicions lie elsewhere; that there is no real fit; that too much is left over and left unaccounted and lost, even; that "beautiful" is just our way of declaring balance or victory, when all that is before us is desolation – less than desolation.)

(So have I come to this oasis in the desert. It is like a fruit of a desert, the accomplishment of all of the desert's striving. But just as easily could we see the desert as the promise of the fruit, what it germinates and sprouts into. Shall we see promise in this, Fly, or despair? What do you see, or smell, or sense? But the question doesn't interest you, as far as I can tell – not so much as that spot there where you have rolled, where you have left a message. But for whom? Do you ever wonder for whom, Fly?)

(I wonder it, Fly. I wonder even as I lob these messages at you. For whom and to whom do I lob them? Is this the final fluttering of a too weak heart before it leaps the precipice and, poorly fledged bird that it is, plummets? Or is it that leap of daring, protest and demand which soars toward a relationship with the other – in this case not with a god but with you, Fly! – *on the only possible terms*: faith?)

(Could it be both, Fly? How distinct is falling from flying?)

Read Nabû-zer-lišir, thus writes Nabû-na'id.

Your excavation of the foundation of the Eḫulḫul must not be rushed, even should it take forever. The intrigues of Kuraš for now give us a freehand; that they will not last forever is certain, but for as long as they do, dig – and if you find a foundation, if there is a foundation, stop. And if not, dig.

Gubaru and he were walking together in the city conjured at his word out of another's defeat and destruction here in the desert's oasis. The city was built entirely of white stone – blindingly white stone.

"My mother used to tell me a story," he began.

Gubaru smiled. "It has been a long time since you spoke those words to me. And yet the words themselves bring back those distant times – bring them near."

"Near enough almost to touch," Nabû-na'id agreed, "and yet insurmountably far as well."

"Why must it be insurmountable?" Gubaru asked. "Can we not, even for a moment, be those boys again?"

"Those boys are gone, lost, dead."

"It may be so, but can we not still be them, even only for a little while?"

"Can we be dead boys?" Nabû-na'id asked almost with a

sneer. "Can we be the boys who died for us to become what we are, whom in a certain sense we killed?"

His friend kicked a stone and said nothing, out of a sense that he was being foolish and that his foolishness had annoyed Nabû-na'id.

"My mother used to tell me a story," Nabû-na'id repeated.

Gubaru interrupted again. "Why begin the story that way, so evocative of what we were and, you say, can never again be?" he asked angrily, surprised by his own anger.

"I am quoting."

"But why?"

"It is always possible to quote."

"Ok, but why *this* quote, why *this* beginning?"

Nabû-na'id breathed a heavy sigh. "Out of irony, perhaps; even out of cruelty, to you – and to me. Or maybe because I'm not convinced that I'm right and you're wrong. Maybe, like you, and despite myself, I still believe I can be that boy again."

They walked together in silence for a long while. Then, out of the blue, Nabû-na'id spoke again. "Or maybe I even believe that I *am* that boy, still."

Gubaru said nothing in response as they continued walking side-by-side. Then he felt his friend's hand on his arm, so he stopped and turned to face him.

"To have a relationship with that boy," Nabû-na'id began, his eyes expressing unusual emotion, "who, in some sense, I am, and in another sense, am not – does even that relation depend on faith?" Gubaru simply stared at him mutely. "If I have no faith, what am I? I'm stitched together but not by faith – by something else. What is it? And would it be better if my rapport with that boy weren't such a patchwork?"

Nabû-na'id continued to stare into the eyes of his boyhood friend and still held his arm. "What am I stitched together by?" he repeated. "Is it only words? Is there nothing else?"

Gubaru said nothing.

"Are words the invention of faith or is faith the invention of words? Do words substitute for faith – and is anything else possible?"

"These questions are too abstract for me, my friend," Gubaru said gently. "As you know." He cleared his throat and then began to speak again, but more slowly. "Let us set aside these questions of faith and words, these problems which so puzzle you about what communion there is between men and within them. For I can be of no help. I have never been of any help in these questions, all these many years which we have passed in each other's company." He cleared his throat a second time. "For simplicity's sake, or just for mine, perhaps you would be so kind as to recall that boy you used to tell stories to, even if he's only a ghost now – a boy who was often bewildered by those stories as even now I often am too. And, recalling him, why not tell me this story you were about to recount, this story you say you once heard from your mother?"

A moment passed as if Gubaru had said nothing and then, abruptly, Nabû-na'id let go of his arm, turned and started walking again.

"My mother used to tell me a story," he began a third time, as Gubaru caught up with him. "It was about Ḫarrānu and the Eḫulḫul and about a girl whose dedication to the god began on the eve of his abandonment of them all."

"I thought your mother was no longer a girl then – that she was middle-aged."

"This is a story about a girl, not about my mother. Or maybe it's a story about my mother as a girl, even if she was also no longer that girl." They walked for a few moments in silence.

"This girl was visited by Sîn in a dream," resumed Nabû-na'id. "The god called her by name. 'Here I am,' she answered. The god said, 'I am leaving you now. Say that you will wait for me.' The girl answered, 'I will wait for you.' The god continued, 'I may not come.' 'I will wait for you whether you come or not,' the girl responded. 'Do you not fear wasting your life waiting for a god who has forgotten you?' 'Yes,' the girl admitted, 'I am afraid of that.' 'Then why are you willing nonetheless to wait?' the god asked. 'I am not a god,' she said simply. 'I can only wait.' At this the god laughed. 'Then I give you permission. You may wait for me.' These were his last words. After that he vanished; after that, he abandoned her."

"And the girl has waited?"

"Yes."

"And what happened? Did the god come?"

"Who is to say? Might it not be better if he did not?"

Gubaru frowned. "Why would that be better?"

"Is it not better to wait for something than simply to wait?"

Gubaru didn't answer. A few moments later, Nabû-na'id added, "Are we not better served by an absent god than one who is present? Imagine if Marduk stood before you and you gave him the Tablet of Destinies and he dropped it. What would you think?"

"Marduk would not drop the Tablet of Destinies," Gubaru said with assurance.

"But if he did?" persisted Nabû-na'id.

"It is inconceivable."

"Perhaps it is. But might it be inconceivable only because Marduk is and has forever been absent?"

"Be careful what you say! Marduk may be listening!" Gubaru warned agitatedly.

"My god is not Marduk but Sîn – an absent god – a god whose light is not his own and has no warmth. And his absence has been a great gift to me and to my mother. She wishes me to restore the Eḫulḫul in Ḫarrānu, then lead the god by his hand back to his home. I shall only partially fulfill her wish. I shall restore the temple – already we are working on it – but what I shall lead into it by the hand will not be the god, but the statue of the god."

"The god is within the statue."

"So it is said. I believe the statue marks the god's absence – and I am grateful." Then Nabû-na'id laughed harshly. Gubaru did not know what his laughter meant.

Read Nabû-zer-lišir, thus writes Nabû-na'id.

I am aware that you are plenty busy overseeing the excavation and, we hope, eventually the restoration of the Eḫulḫul. Your busyness is a reward for your competence – for your exacting attention to detail. And now I propose to reward you further.

Here in Arabi I have come across a peculiar Moon cult which traces its origins forever backwards, to a time before all other times. They claim that their tradition alone was unbroken by the Flood and that their divine statue was never submerged – not fully. The world may have been destroyed, they say, but their statue was not. And so they say that their statue is older even than the world.

The statue that I am speaking of is dedicated to the Moon. Indeed, they worship the Moon as the supreme god, as the hypostasis of all gods. But they worship him, as I wrote, peculiarly; they reverence him in his guise as a statue. They even call him "Statue," using our word, our language.

You may know that the crown of Šamaš, so long believed to have horns, in fact carries atop it two crescent moons facing each other. So even our tradition recognizes a link between the two gods, though, through some ancient mistake, we give priority to the Sun. Here in Arabi, their older, their most old tradition reveals the truth: for theirs is a statue of the Moon eclipsing the Sun. Only an annulus or rather halo of the Sun glimmers behind the smooth, obliterating whiteness of the Moon. I wonder in fact if that halo, through misunderstanding, didn't in our tradition migrate upwards, break and become instead crescents, then horns, no longer overwriting the sun but crowning it.

The task that your diligence has earned is two-fold. First, in your excavations, take care lest you miss in the ancient foundations of the Eḫulḫul similar iconography. Should you find anything, you are to send me word at once.

Second, the messenger carrying this letter has been given a model of the statue as it exists here, carved from the same desert stone, as well as a tablet recording its precise dimensions. You are to oversee the construction of a replica as exact as possible – a small detail of soldiers will arrive with quarried desert rock for that purpose. Choose only the finest artisan and oversee everything yourself. I charge you with this, and not the priests, because I sense a dedication in you to the past, and especially to what is absent, which greatly exceeds theirs and, perhaps with the exception of my daughter's, all but mine.

You must not fail. When Ḫarrānu's temple is completed, it will be as a dwelling for the God in this his most ancient guise – as Statue.

In his dream he was in Sardis. He was walking down a hallway in the palace to warn his father of the coming eclipse. Always his father's door was at the end of the hallway; always he could just see it; always, however many steps he took, it never drew nearer. Meanwhile, behind his back, the eclipse was already beginning. He could sense the brightness of the day receding, curling up, tightening into darkness. He could feel the day, if it was still day, growing cold. He walked faster, towards his father's door, but he could make no headway. In desperation he started running, but to no avail. The hallway was growing quite dark now; there was almost no time to warn his father that an eclipse was coming. At random he turned, opened a door.

* * * * *

From the Babylonian Royal Chronicle:
Fifth regnal year: The king lived in Teima; in Akkadê were the prince, his officers and his army. The month of Nisanu arrived but the king did not return to Bābilim. Nabû did not enter the city. Bel did not come out. No god left his sanctuary. There was no Akītu festival. Offerings were still presented, in the Esagila and the Ezida, to Bābilim's gods and to Borsippa's, as if the times were normal.

"Has it not occurred to you, Gubaru, that this is the Cedar Forest?"

Gubaru opened his eyes wide and stared about him in disbelief. He then turned his stare on Nabû-na'id. "There is not a cedar tree in sight," he said somewhat reproachfully.

"There is nothing *we* call a cedar in sight, yes; but maybe some of those scraggly trees over there are what Gilgameš considered a cedar."

"He describes them as immense."

"Relative to what? Or perhaps he was exaggerating."

"Why not just take his words at their face value?"

Nabû-na'id laughed. "Words don't have faces!" he said with the simplicity of a child. "They have edges. Words never quite fit but you'll forget that unless you're near an edge. That's when words get really interesting, from their margins or, if it's conceivable, from the interstices."

Gubaru furrowed his brow. "What interstices? What is it that words don't fit?"

Nabû-na'id frowned. "That is the question, isn't it? That is the question." He lurched forward a few steps, as if off balance. Gubaru steadied him. "I simply don't know," Nabû-na'id said.

They continued walking, Fly periodically rallying around them and then disappearing again, not with the speed and impetuosity of his youth but with the measured pace, wiliness and dignity of a dog not far removed from being elderly. A breeze picked up.

"Have you ever wondered," Nabû-na'id began, "why Enkidu was so intent that Gilgameš kill Humbaba? Gilgameš seemed inclined to mercy, but Enkidu persuaded him otherwise. He convinced Gilgameš to kill Humbaba so that his name would be remembered forever."

"Is that not reason enough?" Gubaru asked.

"To commit an atrocity so that your name will be remembered?"

"Killing Humbaba was not an atrocity."

"If that was not an atrocity, is it not nonetheless atrocious to persuade a man to be merciless?"

"Not if you believe you are right."

"When is it right to be merciless? It is a question I have often asked." He paused and then smiled a humorless, painful smile. "From my deeds, you might even think I have an answer."

"You don't?"

He shook his head, but he said nothing, instead bending over to pet Fly, who had drawn near. Only after Fly had loped off again did he resume. "Anyway, why would Enkidu care about a name being remembered? He was a wild man spurred to enter the city not for the sake of fame or remembrance but because of the accounts of Gilgameš's outrageous behavior. He also urged that they not embark upon the Cedar Mountain expedition and that they leave Humbaba alone. So why, all of a sudden, is it he who cares about his friend's enduring name, even to the point of urging the slaughter of a defenseless, pleading foe?"

Gubaru thought for a moment before answering. "Perhaps he realized that a man's name is the only thing of his that may endure."

"But is it? Names no more have faces than other words; names are no less edged. 'Gilgameš' undoubtedly means something different now than it did then, just like 'cedar' might."

"The core of the word – of the name – endures. The rest is like embroidery. It's ok if it changes."

Nabû-na'id laughed again. "Why would you think there is a core?"

Gubaru didn't answer.

"Besides – and maybe this is relevant to that question – we don't remember Gilgameš because he slew Humbaba. Whatever it is we remember and associate with that name begins not with his heroic successes, but his even more heroic failure. But that only means one, horrible thing."

"What is the horrible thing that it means?" Gubaru asked wearily.

"It means Humbaba's death was superfluous. It means Enkidu's atrocious persuasion was – pointless."

Gubaru frowned but said nothing.

"There's another thing, too," Nabû-na'id added. "It means that embroidered now to Enkidu's name is his advocacy of mercilessness."

"It is not the core of Enkidu," Gubaru said gruffly.

"How glad I would be, were I certain you were right!" Nabû-na'id spoke with an unusual and almost youthful exuberance. Gubaru examined him closely, uncertain if his friend was being ironic or expressing something more genuine.

"When Enkidu died, Gilgameš made all of the city go into mourning; even the wild animals mourned; he himself rent his garments and tore out his hair and bathed in dust and ash. But he did not say to Enkidu, 'Your name, I promise, will live forever!' Instead, he had an enormous statue of Enkidu built, his chest made of gold, his beard of lapis lazuli, his eyes of amethyst. But his friend, while he lived, did not have a chest of gold; his beard was not of lapis lazuli; his eyes were not amethysts." He paused and looked intently at his friend. "Has none of this ever bothered you?"

"No," answered Gubaru.

"Well, it has obviously bothered me. I have thought: Gilgameš at first wanted to honor his friend by preserving his body. He tried to pretend to himself that his friend was merely sleeping. But then the body began to decay and it smelled and a worm fell out of Enkidu's nose. Gilgameš suddenly and painfully understood that the body was only a sign, like those which I inscribe in clay; and that this sign no longer meant what he thought it meant. So he tried to build something that would instead endure, something made of metals that don't decay. The problem was, the statue didn't look like his friend! It turned out that decay, fragility, ephemerality, change – all of these had always been a part of his friend, an aspect of him. Being faithful to that meant recognizing in his friend a perpetual stranger too. Recognizing a stranger! It's almost nonsensical. The statue became a mark of Enkidu's absence – but a mark of an absence that was *always there*."

"I can't pretend to understand you," Gubaru confessed. "It seems much simpler to me than you make it. Can't he just have loved his friend? Must this be so complicated? Wasn't it that love which he was commemorating with the statue?"

Nabû-na'id smiled, and then asked very quietly, "Why was the love not enough on its own?"

The black cat was curled on Izdubar's lap, sleeping softly and purring softly and otherwise not stirring. Izdubar called to her but she did not respond. He imagined her stretching her paws like she used to, or arching her back, or licking her hind leg, or yawning. He imagined her plaintive meows, her little screams which he always translated as "Don't forget about me, don't forget about me!" – precisely at those moments when he was actively remembering her, when he was setting food aside for her. But many years had passed since he had seen or heard her do such things. Many years had passed since she had done anything but sleep on his lap, purring softly. He could not in fact tell even whether she was purring – whether the noise he heard was hers or whether he heard noise at all. Many years had passed, neither of them stirring.

Why had he become motionless? Out of fear of disturbing her sleep? And yet, not a moment ago, he had called out to her. Not very loudly, as it happens – very timidly, very quietly. Barely audibly had he called out to her. He would soon gather his courage and try again, this time louder – perhaps. But what was it that he wanted from her when he called out?

Well, a response of course. He wanted a response. But was it worth the risk? Was it better to preserve the cat sleeping forever with the always deferred promise of eventual awakening? Or was it better to call out and risk revealing that promise as broken, perhaps broken long ago, perhaps broken from the very beginning?

His compromise – to become motionless and call out ever so softly, so that, should she not respond, it was possible that she had not heard – what was that but to feign sleep perpetually, to feign death perpetually? But what else was possible? And which was it: feigning sleep or feigning death?

(There was another risk, perhaps as frightening as the first, or more frightening. The first risk was that he would receive no response. The cat would not respond, because she couldn't or because she chose not to. Because, for example, she was dead. Or he was. The second risk, however, was that he would not recognize as a response whatever it was he received.)

(It occurred to him that these two risks might not in the end be different.)

"So Gilgameš fled into the wilderness after Enkidu's death. What it was that he was fleeing – I doubt even he knew. The decaying images of his decaying friend, perhaps. Or his friend's absence, especially in those places where Enkidu could normally be found. Gilgameš struck out into the wilderness just fleeing, madly fleeing, blindly fleeing, like a man in panic who doesn't care where he flees so long as he escapes. But how could Gilgameš escape? What he fled he carried with him."

"What was that, would you say?" Gubaru asked.

"It was many things, in many complicated ways. He fled from death and from fear of death. But he also fled from Enkidu."

"Why flee from what cannot follow?"

"There was an Enkidu who was a part of him. Gilgameš not only fled this Enkidu, but he tried to cast it out and forget it and kill it – and all the while grieving for it."

"What are you talking about?" Gubaru asked incredulously.

"It's what is impossible about mourning. We become a last refuge of the other who has died; and, over and over again, we deny him that refuge, we turn away from him, we refuse him – like a sick man that the city turns away for fear of infection. 'I did not love you so much,' we say, 'that I would love myself less than you.' 'You must go elsewhere,' we say. But we know that there is nowhere else for him. Still, he must go elsewhere. No more will we carry him."

"There is no place for ghosts but the netherworld."

"On the contrary, they follow us everywhere. They are us. We are inhabited by ghosts. But Gilgameš didn't know that at first, so he ran away. But everywhere he went, Enkidu followed – moaning 'Don't forget about me, don't forget about me!' So Gilgameš did the next obvious thing."

"Which was?"

"He disguised himself. He let his hair grow, he ceased to bathe, he wore the hides of animals. He hoped Enkidu would cease to recognize him. He even hoped to repel Enkidu."

"What do you mean?"

"Enkidu, you will recall, rescued wild animals from hunters, freeing them from traps. Gilgameš tried to repel Enkidu by instead killing animals indiscriminately, purposelessly. He even went further: he killed a lion and he said, 'I have killed Enkidu, even though I thought it was a lion.' But then there were more lions, there were other beasts – everywhere there was Enkidu. He killed them all; and yet there Enkidu was, everywhere. That's why the Moon god intervened."

"I did not know Sîn had involved himself."

"He does – in the tales we tell in the north. Perhaps not in all versions. In our version, Sîn intervenes. He tells Gilgameš to offer recompense, to beg forgiveness."

"Of Enkidu?"

"No. Of all the animals he has killed. 'Of each of them,' the Moon god says, 'make a clay image. Carry it with you until you are no more.'"

"Gilgameš did that?"

"Yes."

"To what purpose?"

"He carried the images so that he wouldn't forget. But what were those images but permission to forget as well? He could be faithful and unfaithful at once. He could remember to forget and forget to remember. This was the gift of the Moon."

"But what about Enkidu? Did he make an image of him too?"

"They were all images of Enkidu – just not only of Enkidu. Every one of them."

On the first night, the ghost said, "I do not know if I was killed by a *šēdu* or if I was a *šēdu* who was killed. Help me." Gubaru did not respond; he slept.

On the second night, the ghost said, "I do not know what I

was or that I was. Help me." Gubaru did not respond; but he did not sleep.

On the third night, the ghost said, "I do not know how I was called. I do not know if I had a name. Help me." Gubaru opened his mouth to respond; he opened it wide; a word, a name, tumbled from deep within the cavern of his mouth to the very tip of his tongue. But it would not go further; it would not come forth.

"I could not say his name," Gubaru told Nabû-na'id, his voice toneless but his expression anguished. "It was there but I could not say it; it just lingered on my tongue, past the walls of my teeth and jutting almost past my lips – but, like a bird afraid to fledge, it would not fly. I could not say it, I could not jar it loose or toss it into the air. And then, after a moment, I was no longer sure it was even there. It had gone back into its cave, into darkness, so deep I doubted it could ever be recalled. Another moment passed, and suddenly I was no longer sure it had been there in the first place; I was no longer sure if my mouth had ever opened, had ever, even once, been open; I was no longer sure whether there had ever been such a thing as speech, or a voice, or a name."

"You have been bewitched," Nabû-na'id announced calmly.

"How do I unbewitch myself?" Gubaru demanded.

"What you have just described is your unbewitching."

Gubaru looked despairingly at Nabû-na'id. "Do not do this to me," he said, his eyes fierce and glistening with tears. "Do not do this to me."

A look of shock spread across Nabû-na'id's face. He clutched Gubaru to him, hugged him and whispered into his ear, "I am sorry, I am sorry, I am sorry." Then he pushed Gubaru far enough away that they could see each other's faces. "His name," Nabû-na'id said clearly, "was Kayvan."

"Kayvan," Gubaru repeated like a child. "Kayvan."

"His name is Kayvan. Tell him when he comes. You will be able to."

"Your name is Kayvan," Gubaru told the ghost.

"How can you be sure?" the ghost asked.

"Because it is the name I gave you."

"But that is past and no longer exists. Like me."

"No. It is the name I gave you, and I am giving it to you again now, and I will give it to you every time I see you."

"And if it isn't my real name?"

"Then please accept it as a gift. Please accept it as the best I can do."

Enkidu strode up to Gilgameš. His chest was gold, his beard was lapis lazuli, his eyes were amethysts. In his belt he carried innumerable clay figurines of animals. Gilgameš opened his mouth in awe. "I do not know what to call you," he said. "I recognize my friend, and I do not."

"Has it not always been so?" a voice asked. "Did the two of you not wrestle in doorways because you recognized each other and did not? Was not that the fastness of your friendship?"

"Imagine what one door post says to another," a second voice suggested. "I recognize you and I do not."

"Together you make a door," a third voice said, "which of course both opens and closes."

* * * * *

From the Babylonian Royal Chronicle:

Sixth regnal year: The king lived in Teima; in Akkadê were the prince, his officers and his army. The month of Nisanu arrived but the king did not return to Bābilim. Nabû did not enter the city. Bel did not come out. No god left his sanctuary. There was no Akītu festival. Offerings were still presented, in the Esagila and the Ezida, to Bābilim's gods and to Borsippa's, as if the times were normal.

Speak to Nabû-na'id the king, thus speaks Bel-šar-uṣur the prince-regent.

I pass on glad news. Our Mandan enemy Ištumegu has fallen; Kuraš has prevailed. Now we have an ally on that front and our hands are free. No power is equal to our own, unless you are awed by the Luddan, whose wealth, I think, overvalues his might.

To Nabû-na'id, thus Belet-ṣeri-dannat.

May the god keep you well and alive.

You have heard no doubt of Ištumegu's fall. His kingdom is now Kuraš's. Others may soon follow. The court here is cocky and believes Ištumegu's loss is our gain. If only they could read the stars! If only they could see past their own glittering garments and the strength of walls built by the hands of others. I fear that Bel-šar-uṣur is too much in the thrall of our imagined power and fails to imagine Kuraš's. Or the power of which Kuraš is but a sign.

So at last the weed has overtaken the garden, and our time is dwindling: if we would rid ourselves of it, now may be our last chance. And yet you have long foreseen this weed's growth; you have even cultivated it; and so I suspect you have no intention to weed the weed. Why that is, I do not pretend to understand. Is it the fatalism of the last king of Bābilim, the last man of his era? Or is it the optimism of a man who bears the standards of a new age? I have never known how to think of you, whether you are obsolete or cutting edge, whether your despair isn't tomorrow's lone and fragile form of hope.

I know you will say that all gardens begin from weeds. But surely not all flowers are equally beautiful before the Lord? Just as a father loves one son or daughter more than the rest – blesses one and curses the other. Can you deny it? And if you cannot, can you face it?

For, as you must know, the time has come to decide. About Kuraš, about your son, about Bābilim. Or will you remain forever in the desert, keeping the promise of your promised land by refusing to stir yourself? Is a promise worth a kingdom? Can you be sure it is a promise you preserve, and not some sort of self-condemnation, some sort of punishment for being the man circumstances made you?

Bear in mind: Kuraš is wily and ruthless. He has overturned and unmanned his own grandfather. What will he do to you, to your wife and children, above all to your memory? You may object to this appeal; you may consider it coarse; you may be insulted that I invoke your own concerns alongside the concerns of state. But I no longer know what motivates you; I no longer know where you look for direction in your life and rule. Your son is easier for me to understand; he looks to what he imagines is power. But you look, if anything, to what you imagine is powerless. Or perhaps not even that.

How is that we two old men, prophets both, worshippers of a single god, cannot agree on the god, cannot agree on the direction, cannot but pose riddles to one another while the world we strive to believe in totters, awaiting – what is it? Our word? Our silence? But it is not my word that matters, not my silence.

How I wish I could see you and speak to you and not have to commit these ramblings to clay. Ramblings which, I see now, have escaped me, loose and in disarray, as if from a pillaged land. That is what I feel myself to be or to be becoming: a sacked city, walls torn down, buildings destroyed, streets filled with wailing refugees. How can this be what I am? What am I anymore, I who once survived on the streets and whispered the words of God into the ears of kings?

But I ramble, these words escape me, flee me, as I am told rats do from a sinking ship. I am sinking. Come to Bābilim – if not for your state, if not for your family, if not for yourself, then for me! Or send for me! Let me die in the land promised my people, the people whom God has favored with his love and anger.

To Belet-ṣeri-dannat, thus writes Nabû-na'id, king, friend.

Let me tell you of the fate of a locust, and of the empty spaces in clay that Gilgameš accepted as his immortality.

For I cannot write to you now of Kuraš. He is young and eager and perhaps he is the spirit of the world, which I have never been and never wished to be. Or perhaps he is the world's young spirit, and I its old one. Or he is the spirit who inhabits the world, while I am the one who haunts it. Let it be, I say. Let it be. He will come, and if not he, then another like him. The only defense is to become him, to be him better than him – but that defense leaves nothing left to defend. No, let be, let be, I say.

But I do not say it. I write it. Kuraš's power to taint my memory is less than you think, as is my power to preserve it. We entrust our memories, what we remember and how we are remembered, to blankness, to emptiness – and what becomes of them there no one can foresee. Not even we two who are, after a fashion, prophets. We yield our memories to what is not there, and in that odd space they wrestle, joust, become entangled, transform into something else, and always alongside all of this, they disappear too. Does Kuraš believe that he can control what is not there? Of course he does; all men like him believe that.

Gilgameš was a man like him – once. But Gilgameš died a different man. He grew old as the world's spirit also grew old; he who once inhabited himself ended by haunting himself, by being beside himself. He strove for immortality; but it either escaped him or he released it. He strove for renewed youth, but preferred in the end the joys of bathing in a vernal pool, even though he was old and tired – or especially because he was old and tired. So he lost that renewed youth, if he did not give it up. And he came home, at last, and surveyed his walls made of mud, and wrote tablets made of mud, and hid those mud tablets in his mud walls, and he thought: I too am made of mud.

What enlivens me is what is captured in that mud, the emptiness which courses through the mud. The emptiness inside the walls – the people, the city, those are but the frills of the more important and more predominant emptiness. And the emptiness in the tablet, the blanks that the stylus imposes on and in the mud. The stylus says: hold these – for now. And whether that emptiness will stay or not, who can say? For it is the mud holding it which gradually disappears. I cannot have – or I have not chosen – life immortal, or the return of youth. I choose this emptiness that I am and that I bequeath, that even now I am writing in clay in the hopes that the future for this emptiness will last – a while.

For we are mud, mud ennobled just a little bit by emptiness! The signs we carry are but spaces, voids, impressed upon us and in us. That alone distinguishes us from the rest of mud – for a time. The young Gilgameš, the man who was more than Kuraš's equal, did not know this. The old Gilgameš, the man who was more than my equal, did.

Do you understand, my friend, this emptiness that I am endeavoring to share with you, however fragilely, knit for now in the mud that I am sending to you? I do not send it in sorrow or despair – not simply. Greater would my sorrow be, greater my despair, were I of Kuraš's ilk, but I am no longer, I am not, I never was. What I understand, what Gilgameš understood, this young prince of Anšan could no more endure than he could carry forever a snowflake. But it will never come to that, for a man such as he has no patience for a single, singular flake of snow.

As for the locust, this wondrous, beautiful, enormous insect, such as I have seldom seen – I did not notice it until I heard the crunch of my sandal. I pulled up, and there it was, mortally injured but alive, perhaps suffering, bathed in the juices that once stirred only within it. Did I weep for the locust? Did I crush it out of a peculiar sense of mercy? Or did I walk away, troubled but soon forgetting – only to return the next day to find it as it was before, but dead now, ungrieved – or rather grieved but briefly – mostly forgotten, already, but now and then, here and there, a brief spark like the flash of a firefly, unpredictable, yes, the locust, I remember – but it goes out, this spark, each time perhaps forever. Even when entrusted, as here, to this emptiness.

Come if you like; die in the land, in the mud, promised your people. If I must, I shall dig a hole for you, a hole in mud just for you.

To Nabû-na'id, thus Belet-ṣeri-dannat.

May the god keep you well and alive. May my God – my God – do this for you, and for me.

For you are mistaken that it is emptiness which courses through our mud. That we are mud, I don't deny; but that we are filled only with nothing – on this you are wrong, terribly wrong. What fills us is the breath of God. You have mistaken what cannot be seen for what is not there.

After all, what would stir mud if it only contained emptiness? How would our limbs of clay move one after the other, and not only that, but along a straight line, with a purpose, towards an end? Have you seen the mud deposited on the bank of a river do this? On its own, that mud is inert; but let the wind pick it up and move it, let God's breath fill it with life and striving, and only then will we see an image of ourselves. We are dust storms, we are whirlwinds – and the air that moves us is God's air. That voice we hear, like the moans of wind gushing and echoing through a cave, is not simply our voice. It is God's voice, the voice God has given us when he kissed our lips and breathed himself into us.

This is not nothing. It is the opposite of nothing. I tell you this, I call out to you, I whisper this into your ear from far, far away out of friendship, that you not die having never heard the God who was always beside you and in you and with you.

If you write to me now, your letter will not find me. For I accept your invitation. At last will I leave the land of my exile, to live and die in what God has, since ancient times, promised me and mine.

I am coming.

I am writing you this last letter, Belet-ṣeri-dannat, though it shall never find you.

What moves mud is its emptiness, its lack which, from a different perspective, we call longing. Mud stirs precisely because there is nothing in it. Were it full and complete and whole, what would entice it away from what it is? "Here I am," it would say, if it could speak. "Here I am, and I need go nowhere else. Here I am." But not even this would it say. For we need emptiness to speak, we need nothing to form the borders of our words and our places and ourselves. Without that emptiness, there is no here, no I and no am. Mud either contains nothing, and that's what stirs it, the nothing within; or mud contains nothing, it is not stirred at all, because there is nothing within – not even nothing. Such mud, then, would be completely full: unmoved, unmovable, stagnant. Sometimes I think it is mud such as this that the gods are made of; and maybe that's why I do not worship them, but instead Sîn and Nabû, those other gods – if they are gods at all – who, like us, cradle nothing with that tenderness a mother can't help but bestow even upon a still-born child.

I am sending this letter in search of you, like that fly which pestered the cow all the way to Muṣur. It will buzz to Bābilim and sniff for you and retrace your steps and its own until it finds you, should that time ever come, which I doubt. We are old men, you and I; old friends who have argued the same argument for as long as we have known one another; we pester each other and are little more than flies. Those stings we give one another, even as they provoke pain and anger and the devastating, destroying slap – I understand them to be gifts too. Gifts of love.

"I am to take this to Bābilim?"

"Yes."

"But its recipient is no longer in Bābilim?"

"That is almost certainly the case."

"But then – to whom should I give it?"

"Its recipient will have left traces, tracks – let us hope anyway. Follow those, and through them, follow him. Follow him as long as you must, always striving to deliver this message."

"And if I do not find him?"

"How can you know that you have failed to find him? You are either looking for him, or with him. Those are the options."

"But you say he is an old man. Perhaps he will have died, especially if he has undertaken so long and arduous a journey."

"You are either looking for him, or with him," Nabû-na'id repeated. "Those are the only options."

He kissed his wife and each child, then his wife again. "I do not know that I shall ever return," the messenger said.

"How can that be?" she asked.

"The king has given me a message that he enjoins me to deliver, no matter what. But whether it can be delivered – even the king acknowledges it is doubtful."

"Make a reasonable effort," his wife advised. "Act in good faith. But if, after a time, you have not succeeded, then come home."

"What is a reasonable effort?" the messenger asked. "How can I act in good faith if, after a time, I come home?"

His wife kissed his lips a third time. "You have your faith to keep with the king," she said. "But it is not the only faith you must keep."

* * * * *

From the Babylonian Royal Chronicle:
Seventh regnal year: The king lived in Teima; in Akkadê were the prince, his officers and his army. The month of Nisanu arrived but the

king did not return to Bābilim. Nabû did not enter the city. Bel did not come out. No god left his sanctuary. There was no Akītu festival. Offerings were still presented, in the Esagila and the Ezida, to Bābilim's gods and to Borsippa's, as if the times were normal.

Speak to Nabû-na'id, king of the four corners, king of the world, thus speaks Nabû-zer-lišir.

I excavated the Eulmaš; I found its foundations and restored it. So too the palace of Naram-Sîn in Akkadê. Its foundations I brought to the light and restored his works to grandeur. But now I have dug, and my men have dug, for many years in Ḫarrānu; layer after layer of the Eḫulḫul we have exposed; and still I cannot be certain we have found its foundations. For it was built only of mudbrick and appears to be very ancient; and I do not trust myself to distinguish ancient mudbrick from mere mud. So it is possible that we dug through the foundations and are now digging only a hole in the earth; or it is possible that this is the most ancient structure in the world, made either of mudbrick or simply of mud, by hands for which we will never have names.

So I seek direction. Should I keep digging, even though I no longer trust that I could recognize a foundation even were I to come upon one? Or shall I stop, lay a firm and recognizable foundation of bricks stamped with your name, and rebuild this temple while there is yet a chance that your mother will see it?

As for the statue – we have completed it. The stone you sent is almost indistinguishable from the moon; and in the statue, the moon from the sun, which it eclipses. For now we have placed it before the Eḫulḫul, pending the term of our excavations. Even profane eyes can see it. Should we build a temple for it, until the Eḫulḫul is ready?

Read Nabû-zer-lišir, thus writes Nabû-na'id.

Dig. Dig forever if you must. Only if you find a foundation may you stop.

The secret of the statue is hidden in plain sight; it does not matter whether profane eyes see it or not, for they cannot see what they see. No temple is necessary, for the statue is its own temple.

I am sending my mother before it.

This is the hole he promised to dig for me, mused the ghost. A hole without bottom.

Yes, Adad-guppi replied angrily. Such is the kingship of my son. He can't stop restoring a face, or digging a grave, or excavating a foundation. Every task he begins he cannot end. Such is my son's kingship and his entire life.

You are bitter, observed the ghost.

Of course I am! I have passed the whole of my life in mourning; I am like the fly born at dusk who strives only to see the dawn. But my son has boarded the windows; or, if he's not done that, he's commanded the sun not to rise. Just so that I might die in darkness, as I have lived.

But your son cannot command the sun – I know this, since I am a ghost. And it is not boards which block your sight of the sun; it is the Moon. It has always been the Moon, the very Moon you await.

It is not so! the old woman cried.

But look!

I will not look! I await the dawn when my son shall fulfill his promise to me, and lead Sîn by the hand back to his restored temple. Back here, the place of my birth.

But look! You do not need to await the dawn. The Moon itself is bright enough; you can see by the light of the Moon.

No! It is not so! I know what Sîn's return will look like – and it is not this, it is not this!

But look!

There is nothing to see. It is a hole, a hole without bottom, a hole he will dig forever– never stopping to place even your bones there. You will not rest, as I have not rested. This is his gift to us: to tantalize us with a promise that will never be fulfilled, precisely because he insists on continuously fulfilling it.

The ghost pursed his lips. Yes, that is true of your son. He is afraid of promises.

No! Not afraid. He is a keeper of promises, a hoarder of promises. And because of that my life will only have been mourning, from first to last; and because of that your bones will never rest – and you will starve and thirst forever!

Because my grave will always be unfinished.

Because your grave will always be empty. Like my life.

But my grave is not empty. The breath of God swirls within it. Nabû-na'id digs forever only to make space for it – always more and more space, so great is the breath of God. What looks like emptiness is God. What looks like darkness is the very Moon you seek.

Adad-guppi spat. You are a young ghost, she said. You are not yet riveted by the pangs of hunger and thirst. But you will be! Then will you moan, as I am moaning; and your grief and your mourning will begin.

Even were I to moan, it would be the breath of my God moving within me.

But look! she said. Look at yourself. There is nothing there, nothing to contain this god's breath, nothing within which that breath can be.

It is not so! The ghost cried.

But look!

No – there is nothing to see.

It is a hole, a hole without bottom.

[*A messenger arrives*]

Messenger: I am come with a message, clay engraved with emptiness, which I must deliver to its recipient, or else ever travel in search of him.

Adad-guppi: Who is the recipient?

Messenger: It says right here. [He points at the spaces carved into the clay.]

Adad-guppi: But look for yourself. They're still digging the hole.

Messenger: It says right here.

Adad-guppi: There is no bottom.

Messenger: All I have to do is read the emptiness (it says it right here) – then I will know to whom I should deliver this.

Adad-guppi: Right here. (She points at the pit where the Eḫulḫul once stood.)

Messenger: Yes.

Adad-guppi: Well, then you'll just have to wait. Like me. Like a ghost.

Messenger: How long, do you think?

Adad-guppi: Until they find a bottom.

Messenger: When will that be?

Adad-guppi: At dawn.

Messenger: What a relief! My travels are near their end. I'll go to that inn I passed, take a drink and rest – and then I will return here at dawn.

Adad-guppi: Very well.

[*The messenger leaves.*]

"Bring a shovel!" yells the ghost after him, but no one hears.

* * * * *

From the [fragmentary] Assyrian Accounts of Herodotus

...All this time Labynetus remained in the desert, while on one side Cyrus's power grew, and on another side Croesus'. Still the king would not stir from his self-imposed exile. It is said that word of the eccentric king reached Solon while in the court of Croesus. "What do you make

of it?" Croesus asked "He could rule the world and rival even me in wealth; and instead he lives among barbarians in some small desert oasis. Does he think Cyrus will not nibble at his kingdom? Does he think I will not? What manner of fool must this king be!"

"He is probably a very foolish man," answered Solon, "or else a very wise one. It is possible even that he is both. I am sorry that on my way from Egypt I did not know to visit him in the desert."

"So that you could find out if he is wise or foolish?"

"Yes. Or both."

"But why would you ever call this man wise? He shall lose his kingdom to Cyrus or me or an ambitious son."

"Perhaps he shall. I was only thinking, maybe this man knows that it is better to be dead than alive. And seeing that the gods forbid that we end our own lives, he has done the next best thing and removed himself there where he hopes little will befall him."

"But a life where little befalls one is a poor life – a boring life. Look at all my riches: do you think I would have acquired any of this without effort, without risk, without daring to pass through my garden gate?"

"Yes, you are indeed very rich; and with luck you will die soon, while still at the height of your fortune."

Croesus laughed incredulously. "You wish me, your host, to die soon?"

"I only wish you the luck that you should die soon, before a jealous god takes from you everything which, through the favor of some other god, you have acquired."

"Should I join this fool in the desert then?"

"If he is a fool, perhaps not. If, on the other hand, he is wise and will have you, why not? If he is both a fool and wise, then you must like the rest of us take your chances."

"How can a man be both wise and a fool?"

"Foolishness often breeds wisdom. What better advisor for a king, for example, than he who has foolishly lost his own kingdom?"

"But that is a man who is a fool, then wise. I want to know how a man can be both wise and a fool."

"I yielded my voice to the written laws and fled my city that they might remain unchanged and speak in my stead. Is that not both wise and foolish?"

"It is only peculiar."

"What would you say of men who honored their mother by becoming her oxen, pulling her in a chariot forty-five stades and at the end dying of exhaustion?"

"They were fools."

"Of course they were; but were they not also the wisest of men, and among the luckiest and most blessed too?"

"Blessed?" Croesus laughed heartily. "Solon, my friend, look around you, then tell me what man on all the earth is most blessed."

Solon looked about him slowly, deliberately and without expression. "Well?" prodded Croesus. "What man on all the earth is most blessed? Surely not this Assyrian king!"

"I was thinking, Tellus the Athenian. As for that strange king, I can say nothing of him – at least so long as he lives. But Tellus happily is dead, and with any luck so will the Assyrian king soon be, and you and I as well. Until then, however, let us not forget to entreat the gods to set aside even some small fraction of Tellus's blessedness for us. For he lived in a good city with good laws; and he raised good sons and saw them raise their sons likewise; and he died gloriously protecting the city in battle and was buried at public expense on the very ground where he fell. No man, in my judgment, can be called more blessed, unless perhaps those sons who became their mother's oxen."

Again incredulous, but also angry, Croesus swept his arm around the room. "And this is not blessedness?" he demanded.

Solon again looked about him slowly and deliberately. "No it is not."

"Then go wherever you find blessedness, in the desert or the garbage heap; but so-called wisdom such as yours has worn out its

welcome here. Be gone; go there where the greatest blessedness lies."

"I will certainly leave; but it is for the gods, and not me, to lead me to my grave."

And so Solon left Sardis.

* * * * *

From the Babylonian Royal Chronicle:
Eighth regnal year: The king lived in Teima; in Akkadê were the prince, his officers and his army. The month of Nisanu arrived but the king did not return to Bābilim. Nabû did not enter the city. Bel did not come out. No god left his sanctuary. There was no Akītu festival. Offerings were still presented, in the Esagila and the Ezida, to Bābilim's gods and to Borsippa's, as if the times were normal.

Nabû-na'id and Fly were walking together alone, alone together, when the old, extremely ugly man approached them. Fly eagerly advanced and, surprisingly, the man dropped to his knees and the two sniffed each other. Nabû-na'id only watched and waited; the old man and Fly were in no hurry. He had noticed that despite his eagerness, Fly had not bounded to meet the man. He was noticing more and more that, like him, Fly was aged.

"This dog is aged," the ugly stranger said – in Luddan, moreover in a high, sing-songy pitch. "His joints hurt him, his eyesight is failing, even his hearing is not what it used to be."

"That is true," Nabû-na'id replied, also in Luddan. It did not seem to surprise the stranger that Nabû-na'id could speak his language. "I wonder how you know it, however," Nabû-na'id continued. "You can see he doesn't move as fluidly as he used to; perhaps you saw how misted are his eyes; but when did you test his hearing?"

"I didn't have to. It came up on its own," said the stranger, still squeaking. Apparently this was his normal voice.

"Ah." For some reason, Nabû-na'id was not surprised.

"Actually, I imagine that for him it is the world which is getting darker and more silent. I imagine that he misses the days of brightness, when the world chattered incessantly. But – " the old man scratched his ear vigorously " – what I am describing, it's easiest for most humans to understand as encroaching blindness and deafness. Humans think the world stays the same and only they change."

"But dogs think otherwise?"

"Who is to say, who besides a dog, but – why shouldn't they? You and I believe in sight and hearing; dogs perhaps do not. They see, they hear, what they do we understand in terms of sight and hearing – but that is not, perhaps, how dogs understand it."

"So for a dog there is no such thing as deafness and blindness?"

"Perhaps not."

"But when they meet other dogs, and those dogs describe a bright and loud world, even while Fly here experiences a darkening and ever more silent one, how do they make sense of that?"

The old man laughed. "You and I are alike!" he squeaked. "You'd be astonished how many people fail to notice that dogs have much to tell one another!"

Despite himself, Nabû-na'id smiled. "Yes, in that we are alike." He paused. "I have heard tales of young dogs guiding older, blind dogs. Doesn't that suggest that they are aware of something like blindness, something like sight?"

"Perhaps the young dog is only trying to share his world of light and sound. It suggests the two dogs are aware, or at least suspect, that their worlds are different; it suggests they are also hopeful that their worlds can in some sense be shared, though perhaps not completely. All this –" he smacked his lips bizarrely, then continued in his high, sing-songy voice " – seems clear. That doesn't mean, however, that they believe in blindness and deafness like we do."

"Ah," Nabû-na'id said again. For some reason, he liked this odd, ugly, old man. "His name is Fly," he volunteered without knowing why.

"That is what you call him."

"Isn't that what a name is – how we call others?"

"That is one thing a name is." The old man was silent.

Nabû-na'id waited, but when it was clear the old man would say no more, he prompted him. "What else would you say a name is?"

"It's how we don't call others."

"What do you mean?"

"A stranger arrives at the gate. 'Wear this,' we say to him, 'so that we can know you.' So we drape the stranger in a costume, pretend that is what he is. That's what a name is. It's a way of preventing strangers from ever passing through the gate. We always leave strangers outside the gate."

"But surely even a costumed, named stranger who passes through the gate remains still, in some important way, a stranger."

"Oh, of course," the old man agreed, nodding vigorously and smacking his lips bizarrely again. "But there are always more costumes, more names available."

"If you are trying to tell me that the name I have given Fly is an imposition – I already know that. I have often wondered how he calls himself, or even whether he does."

"Have you asked him?"

Nabû-na'id paused. "I suppose I have. But I have not understood his response, if there was one."

"Yes –" and suddenly the old man laughed, in fact he squealed. "That's always the rub!" Then he drew very close to

Nabû-na'id, tugging on the sleeve of his garment and bringing his face so near Nabû-na'id's that they could smell each other's fetid breath. "Perhaps even "Fly" must drape himself in costumes in order to hear himself! But perhaps, for a dog who believes neither in sight nor in hearing, a costume or a succession of costumes is also simply what he is."

"Who are you?" Nabû-na'id asked at a later time.

"I am ... of Sardis."

"I'm sorry, you are – who? – of Sardis?"

"I am ... of Sardis."

"I still didn't catch your name."

"I am ... of Sardis."

Nabû-na'id stared at him blankly.

"And you?" the old man asked.

"I am Nobody the son of Nobody."

This answer satisfied the old man.

And at a still later time: "What do you do?"

The old man smacked his lips. "I write."

"What do you write?"

"I write tales about animals. I weave costumes for animals. I disguise animals. When I am done, I deposit what I have accomplished in the library of the king, mainly for insects to nibble on, and occasionally to be read."

"Does Kirsus read your work?"

"The king is more likely to nibble on my work."

Nabû-na'id laughed. "Is Kirsus, then, a fly?"

The old man smiled an almost toothless smile. "Who isn't, for the most part, a fly? Even the gods are, for the most part, flies. Someday, perhaps, Kirsus will understand this."

"Am I to understand, then, that you write tales also about men who are flies, weave costumes for them, disguise them?"

"It's a good question. I hear people repeat what they say are my tales – but I don't recognize them. These tales I hear repeated have animals behave like men – they have us confront animals as if their human aspects were familiar; in fact they have us confront men thinly disguised as animals. But my tales would not make animals into men. I would have men recognize even a costumed animal as a stranger; or at least I would have them suspect that they've left that particular, naked animal at the gate. Where they can find a version of themselves as well. But mostly the tales people tell me as if they were my own are tales of men covering their nakedness with animal skins and thinking they are thus clothed, no longer naked."

"Can you give me an example of one of your tales – not what people say, but what you write?"

"*A man and a son were leading a mule loaded with goods into town. As they approached, some townsfolk made fun of them because they did not ride the mule. So the man put his son on the mule. But they'd only gone a little further when more townsfolk came, and this time they mocked the boy for riding while his father walked. So the boy came off the mule and the old man mounted. Again they had gone but a little distance before they were ridiculed by yet more townsfolk: why doesn't the mule carry both of you, they asked? So both the old man and his son got on the mule, alongside all their goods. But at this the mule would go no further. She would not say why. They beat her with a stick and kicked her, but the mule did not change her mind. The townsfolk formed a circle around them and laughed, and the more they laughed the more the man and his son beat the mule. But the mule did not change her mind, and the mule did not speak.*"

The old man stopped talking. Finally, Nabû-na'id asked, "Is that the end?"

"Yes," squealed the man.

"Tell me another."

"*On the Cedar Mountain there are monkeys. They chatter with each other and play games. When the lions come, they chatter and throw feces at them. When the wild ox comes, they chatter and dare one another to approach. When a monkey stranger comes, they chatter and drive it off. As for the serpent, when it comes, if the birds see it first, they sing their serpent songs; but if the monkeys see it first, they laugh their serpent laughs.*

"When the human comes, the monkeys have learned to be silent. Neither do they chatter nor do they laugh and in their eyes are stories they will never tell."

Again the old man stopped talking.

Nabû-na'id paused and thought for a while. "There is a story I often think about," he said eventually. "It is about a father and his son and their god and a ram and a mountain top. Have you ever heard such a story, or perhaps told one?"

"I have not."

"Well, we could imagine many things. We could imagine the father setting off in silence for the mountain, and a step behind him the boy burdened with kindling. Behind them, a mother, bewildered, anguish in her face, but silent. They walk for three days. They climb the mountain which has long hovered before them, at first only imperceptibly drawing near and then, when it seems close, always being yet further off. But on that third day, as if by a miracle, they have reached the mountain's summit. The boy drops his burden of wood, glad to relieve his sore back of its weight. But then his father binds him, and he raises in both hands his knife over the boy's chest and before the boy's terrified eyes. His hands plunge. Then he burns the offering. Watching unobserved the whole time was a ram concealed by some bushes; what the ram saw, what the ram heard, even what the ram smelled, was experienced by the ram as unspeakable.

"Only later did the man observe the ram. When the ram saw himself seen, he turned his back and hurried away. But the man

– for, after all, it is hardly clear whether he was anymore a father, not simply because his son was dead but because it was he who had killed his son – this man, beside the charred offering that was once his son, with the still lingering smell of burned fat, this man began muttering to himself. 'God shall provide, my son,' he said to himself; and he imagined the ram caught by its horns in a thicket. He imagined his hands clutching the knife and raised over the chest of his son, he imagined his son's terrified eyes, he imagined looking up and seeing the ram. 'God has provided a ram, my son,' the man imagines himself murmuring. 'The gift which God has demanded from us he has given to us to give back to him.' Then the man laughs and laughs, transforming his memory of the butchery of his son into the butchery of a ram, all for the glory of God. He comforts himself knowing that though God is satisfied with a sacrificed ram, there is nothing great about sacrificing a ram.

"Such a man, we can well imagine, never leaves that mountain top."

The stranger from Luddu looked thoughtful. "You wonder about the testimony of animals," he finally stated. "You wonder about what they have witnessed, what they would tell or perhaps do tell."

"Yes."

"What report would the ram give of what he had seen, the ram who hurried off and was not caught by his horns in a thicket?"

"I don't know. Is there perhaps not wisdom in the silence of that ram, in burying the horror within himself and in not sharing it?"

"Or perhaps he buried the horror within men. Perhaps for that ram men, or at least that man, are those beings which honor the silent invisible with their most precious gifts, all the while not knowing what the silent invisible is, whether it's there, whether they even believe in it. Perhaps, for a ram, a man is that being who sacrifices what he most loves *in order to believe*. Man is the one who memorializes the dead by hiding them, by burying them or transforming them to smoke."

"And rams are different?"

"Undoubtedly... but I am not sure in what way."

"I wonder if a ram is like a dog. I wonder, where there is neither blindness nor deafness, whether there can be an invisible, whose absence and silence become the signs of the divine."

The old man made no squeak or squeal in reply.

"I don't know about rams," Nabû-na'id continued after a while, "but with Fly here, I think he notices and responds to absences, less so – perhaps not at all – to lacks. But I think the human conception of the divine comes from both, from our sense of lack as well as our sense of absence. It's not only the silence and invisibility of god which weighs heavily on us, but what he does not say and the ways in which he is not seen."

The old man chuckled in a high-pitched, ascending scale. For a moment Nabû-na'id wondered if the laugh had ever ended or if it had simply trespassed into a realm which surpassed the acuity of his own hearing. He arched his eyebrow at Fly and looked to see whether the dog was responding to anything beyond his own ken – but Fly gave no such indication. His glance at Fly had not escaped the old man's notice, however.

"You wonder whether you've missed something which Fly has not?" the old man inquired in his exaggerated lilt.

"Yes."

"Ironic," the man murmured. "How would you tell?"

"From the response of my dog, from his face."

"And so you think he has a face?"

Nabû-na'id looked intensely at the ugly old man. "As much as you do," he replied. "As much as I do."

"Ironic," the man murmured again. He smacked his lips.

Then he told another tale.

"The stories of the Flood always speak of the human survivors and of the human dead. They speak of how man awaited the verdict of birds; and the verdict he believed was the one the bird did not deliver, because the bird did not return. 'This means,' thought the man, 'that the bird has found a place of rest.' It did not occur to the man that the bird, like many a man, flew ever toward the horizon, perhaps in the hope of finding that desired place of rest, or perhaps because she was hypnotized by her own motion and the lulling rhythm of her wings, or perhaps because she, like man, aspired to greatness – and greatness is always past the horizon. In any event, he read the lack of her return as a positive absence; it was as if he read her silence as affirmation when it could as easily have been negation; it was as if he read what was expressionless in her as a confident countenance; and certainly, not once, not ever, did he imagine her somewhere beyond his horizon, plummeting into the endless waters and drowning beside the innumerable, water-logged dragonflies."

* * * * *

From the [fragmentary] Assyrian Accounts of Herodotus

...That Aesop was in the court of Croesus at the very time when Solon visited is not undisputed. Some say, in fact, that he had already been thrown from the cliffs of Delphi – though these do not deny that it was Croesus who sent him to Delphi, only he did it earlier, they say, before Solon came to Sardis. But could not the same doubts be raised about Solon? How old a man must he have been, to have somehow visited Croesus near the end of his reign and still returned to Athens, there to resist, albeit futilely, the rise of Peisistratos and finally to die in Cyprus? What are these but apocryphal tales which I've told, hidden away things all the easier to hide because they never were? All the easier – and all the harder too.

For what is my evidence but the words of men? Could I but interview the birds, surely they saw a great deal; and dogs, swine and sheep, of course; and even the worms and flies. But I have known only to speak to men – and women – sometimes even slaves and children. I believe I have been faithful in recording what I have heard, or at least my judgments of what I have heard. On occasion I have even found the testimony of the dead, and I have recorded that too: what was written on a tomb, for example. If I know what the dead say, still, however, I do not know what the birds say.

(There are those who say of the dead that they become as birds in the Underworld. The Assyrians say this. The dead become as birds, dressed in feathers, but they stumble in darkness and cannot fly.)

So let us say, then, that Aesop and Solon did not meet in Sardis, as I have reported here; let us say that one or the other was already dead, or that both were. What prevents us from amending our tale so that the conversation they evidently did not have in Sardis they instead had in the Underworld, perhaps wearing the pelts of birds? Surely such a report is composed of words which someone might speak, or words which might be found committed, anonymously, to stone or pottery or cloth, or even clay, as with those signs which look so like the footprints of birds (and would that not be appropriate?). Must I merely find the words in order to justify their inclusion here? That is but the task of diligence, since the words exist here or there, now or later. The words exist, I claim – but I don't know what that means – and so let us focus instead on the task of diligence. It will be for you to judge whether I have duly performed it.

(But how will you know? Am I not even now speaking to you from the dead? Perhaps these *are the words of a feathered shadow.)*

Now I wonder – but my mind is straying, it is the straying mind of an old man soon to be put out to pasture – I wonder nonetheless whether we can report not only from what we are but from what we become, what we will become. Have I heard the testimony of birds and not known it? Ought you, reader, not to be asking these questions too as you read these words which were formerly mine but which, if they are still mine, are yet no longer a man's? And who are you, reader, right now but a dream, a vision, air incapable of holding shape or color? Think how mutable are we all. Perhaps this was something Aesop understood which better allowed him to hear the sounds and silences of animals, even plants. Perhaps he listened to the stem knowing that sooner or later it would be the leaf; and to the leaf knowing that sooner or later it would be the lamb. And he listened as himself a stem, a leaf, a lamb. If Solon told him, as he told Croesus, the tale of Kleobis and Biton – of how they drew their mother to the festival in an ox-cart, for all the world as if they were oxen – perhaps Aesop would have wondered whether in some sense they were in fact oxen, if only in learning the weight of their load and the endurance demanded by the road and the silence of exhaustion and suffering, all while anticipating the soundness of the sleep which awaited them.

But if Aesop and Solon had met in Sardis, as I maintain, rather than in the Underworld, which is also possible, what they said to one another, including about Labynetus and his strange exile to the desert, and whether Solon encouraged Aesop's visit there or not – of all this, of all those possible words, no record has been found.

Chapter 11. Empty Traces

Speak to Nabû-na'id the king, thus speaks Bel-šar-uṣur the prince-regent.

Kuraš, king of Anšan, now styles himself a greater king, king of the land of Parsua. Even those campaigns we did at your order last year alongside Kirsus, king of Luddu, seem not to have curtailed his ambition. He still acts provocatively, bullying our traders and skirmishing with the Luddans at sundry outposts. Has the time come to crush this insect, or shall we leave the task to Kirsus? But if we leave it to Kirsus, do we not risk creating a more dangerous foe in the Luddan? Is not Kirsus more to be feared than little, upstart Kuraš, however grandly he titles himself? There is word that Kirsus, who counts not only you but the king of Muṣur as his brothers, now seeks brotherhood also with a group of Aḫḫiyawa who call themselves Lakadama. These are unknown men.

Speak to Kirsus, king of Luddu, thus speaks Bel-šar-uṣur, prince-regent of Bābilim, son of Nabû-na'id, king of Bābilim.

May Šamaš and Marduk keep you alive and prospering.

The king my father is monitoring the activities of Kuraš, king of Anšan who calls himself king of Parsua. Keep us informed of his actions! Keep us informed of your intentions! Allies work best who conceal least.

Speak to Kuraš, king of Parsua, thus speaks Bel-šar-uṣur, prince-regent of Bābilim, son of Nabû-na'id, king of Bābilim.

May Šamaš and Marduk keep you alive and prospering.

I will convey your complaints against Kirsus, king of Luddu, to

Nabû-na'id, king of Bābilim, my father, and he will decide.

Speak to Bel-šar-uṣur, prince-regent of Bābilim and son of its absent king, Nabû-na'id the far-off one, who am I.

Your dispatches have arrived, along with the rancid rēḫātu. *Perhaps there is a mode of prophecy to be discovered in the tunnels and squirmings of maggots in the food of the gods – the food the gods have rejected and sent instead to me, a mark, no doubt, of their high favor. I wonder what the state of the food is which the gods of Kuraš give him, or Kirsus's gods. Knowing that would we not know enough? The fate of kingdoms may yet hinge on maggots. Perhaps this is as it should be. Moreover, even in this is there ambiguity. What is the greater sign of the gods' favor: fresh succulent meat or meat writhing with maggots? Something dead or something teeming with life? We should have to know something of the tastes of gods to answer, including whether life or death is more to their liking.*

But you, my clear-headed son, are not long patient with an absent, desert-entombed king's musings on insects. Though do not maggots become flies, and are not gods sometimes flies? And it was you, not me, who called Kuraš an insect... We need only discover whether it is a good thing to be an insect in the eyes of the gods.

I shall write Kirsus and tell him not to proceed without consulting the gods.

Speak to Kirsus, king of Luddu, thus speaks Nabû-na'id, king of Bābilim.

May Sîn and Nabû watch over you. May that be a good thing.

My son sends me disturbing news. Maggots writhe in royal, in holy meat. What does it mean? Is such meat rich or poor? It is rich – in maggots. To be rich in maggots, is that to be wealthy, to be prosperous? Are you wealthy and prosperous, dear brother, king of Luddu? Will your wealth attract maggots? Do maggots feed on the living or on the dead?

A bothersome insect buzzes about – so my son warns. Take heed before you swat at him, at Kuraš, king of Anšan, king of Parsua, king. Do not underestimate insects. Walk among your land's crops and see how many leaves have escaped their gnawing. Perhaps not a single one will you find. Think with what patience the mightiest wild bull endures the flies even in his eyes. Imagine that day which assuredly will come when our kingdoms, yours and mine, are but dust. And yet, look closely – see, there hovers the immortal fly, as impressed by dust as by mudbrick or gold. Take heed, then, before you swat at him. Consult the gods (who themselves are sometimes flies) and be sure to understand their buzzing.

This is the advice of your ally, your brother, the king of Bābilim, host of Teima, Nabû-na'id.

Speak to Nabû-aḫḫe-iddina, man of the house of Egibi, thus speaks Kirsus, king of Luddu.

Who is king of Bābilim? Is it the son or the father? Does father imitate father?

Speak to Kirsus, king of Luddu, thus speaks Nabû-aḫḫe-iddina, man of the house of Egibi.

Who is king of Bābilim? It is the tradition of our house to ask this question at the break of every day. So have we greeted the rising sun for five generations. We ask again at noon, and at dusk, and it is our last question before we sleep.

Is it the son or the father? Again this is a question my house traditionally does not neglect to ask. When it has been the son, who has known before the House of Egibi? But when it has been the father, sometimes even we have been fooled. Put otherwise: since the days of your infancy, when Nabû-na'id was but a youth in the court of your father, he taught our house never to underestimate him; and that he is king today is a reminder that we have nevertheless at least once underestimated him.

Does father imitate father? Which father is meant? Does Nabû-na'id imitate the dusty scribe, the mud-carver, the reader of arcana, the almost-forgotten Nabû-balaṭsu-iqbi? My house has not forgotten that father. But perhaps you mean his more famous father, the father of his wife. Then you are asking, does Nabû-na'id graze tufts of grass in his desert seclusion, as did Nabû-kudurri-uṣur in his famous gardens? But this father is much closer to being forgotten by my house. Perhaps he has already been forgotten.

In any event, if there are tufts of grass in Teima, and if Nabû-na'id amuses himself by chewing them, it will be the work of the House of Egibi to understand what on earth for.

Why have you come to me in a dream?

I could not write.

Why is that?

Lacking a body, I could make no imprint in clay. You need a body to make the space which would enclose the emptiness by which we mean.

She laughed. What are you if you lack a body? she asked. Are you not only emptiness then?

Why have you come to me in a dream?

I told you last night.

You did and you did not.

I told you I could not write.

Yes, I recall. You did not, however, tell me what you would have written.

Nothing.

You would have written nothing?

It's all there is to write.

Why have you come to me in a dream, now for three consecutive nights?

Are you sure it is not you who have come to me in a dream?

In your dream or in mine?

How am I to say?

Do the dead dream?

He laughed. Can emptiness dream? he asked.

Only emptiness can dream, she answered. The dead, they are not even empty.

"Grandmother," exclaimed Mikum-Nisaba, now called En-nigaldi-Nanna. "Why have you come?"

The old, the ancient woman, dressed in sackcloth, covered in ash, wild-eyed, stood in the entry and examined the room, every surface of which was cluttered with figurines, some hand-sized, some as large as a person, some whole, some broken. There were seemingly as many as there are ants in a colony. "You are perhaps odder even than me," the old woman murmured. "How am I to walk to you, across this cemetery of figures?"

"It does not matter if you break them," the priestess replied. "Some can be restored; the rest I will keep, even if broken. Why have you come?"

The old woman scuttled forward, knocking over and breaking some of the smaller figurines without apparent concern. En-nigaldi-Nanna met her half way, swept a couch clear of several small statues of animals and men, a few of them breaking in the process, and sat down with her grandmother. The old woman clutched her hand. "Perhaps, ancient as I am, I have more in common with these statues than with the living."

"Some are very old," En-nigaldi-Nanna murmured. She pointed at one of them, a man praying, carved in diorite. "If the inscription is to be believed, that is about 1500 years old, and the stone itself comes from Magan."

The old woman stood up, approached it, fingered it, and drew her trembling, claw-like hand slowly across its face, almost like she was trying to tear it. "Older even than me, then," Adad-guppi observed. "But I do not know where my stone comes from." Abruptly and purposefully she knocked the statue over. If she were younger, stronger, the act might have seemed violent, but instead it hovered between being violent and pathetic.

En-nigaldi-Nanna showed no reaction. "Perhaps your stone comes from Ḫarrānu," she suggested, smiling.

"Perhaps it comes from the Moon," her grandmother countered, not smiling.

After a long silence, En-nigaldi-Nanna again asked, "Why have you come?"

"I have received a message."

"A letter?"

"Something like a letter – a dream."

"And?"

"I would like to know if the God has spoken to you."

"What was the content of this message?" En-nigaldi-Nanna asked evasively.

"Nothing."

En-nigaldi-Nanna arched an eyebrow. "You have come a long way for nothing," she said.

"What is there that we do that isn't for nothing," the old woman replied resignedly. "Has the God spoken to you?"

"I never know if he has or if he has not."

The old woman was silent, expressionless – and then, after a moment, giggled weirdly. "I will soon return to Ḫarrānu. Even if the foundation of the Eḫulḫul has not been found, even if the temple has not been rebuilt – I must go." She looked En-nigaldi-Nanna directly in the eye. "Will the God go there with me?"

"Is it not for my father to lead the God by hand back to his temple?"

The old woman sniffed. "Will the God go there with me?" she repeated.

"From whom did your message of nothing come?" the priestess responded. "Was it not from the God?"

"It was from a lowly, already forgotten scribe... A scribe who can no longer write."

In her head, a voice: I have never been able to write.

There is only writing, she replied.

"Does the scribe have a name?"

"There was a time when he did, but the name was no name."

"What do you mean?"

"Nabû spoke his life... but Nabû doesn't speak."

The priestess paused. "Ah," she said. "Nabû-balaṭsu-iqbi."

The old woman said nothing.

"Why has the message of this scribe, my father's father, brought you here?"

"Because you are the priestess of Sîn – as, in a certain way, am I. We are more kin than mother and son, more kin than wife and husband. For it is not only that we have dedicated our lives to the God; it is that the God has accepted our lives, which are then no longer our own. Belonging to the God we belong to each other; and who is to say, in contemplating the mirror of the Moon, it is not your face which I see or my face which you see?"

En-nigaldi-Nanna offered no answer.

The old woman touched the priestess's face and turned it toward her own. "Look closely. This is your face, which you are seeing almost certainly for the last time. Now tell me – I who am called to that bottomless pit which my son digs for the God – I who shall soon fall and not cease from falling – I whose days of writing near their end – tell me: will the God go there with me?"

"To Ḫarrānu? To Eḫulḫul? Or to the pit without bottom, the hole without foundation?"

The old woman's wild eyes lit up, danced in their orbits. "Maybe it is my son's gift – or maybe it is the God's – to show me that, as your face is a mirror of mine and mine of yours, so is that pit a mirror of the temple. It is not just the presence of the Moon which we worship; we worship this God also for his absence."

"If that is so," En-nigaldi-Nanna began carefully, "why does it matter whether the god will go there with you?"

The old, the ancient, woman abruptly sat down beside the priestess. She pointed at a crack in the wall. "If His voice entered, it would enter there, perhaps. It would curl itself into your ear, enter you, fill you, become you; and then, slowly, it would uncoil and flow out your other ear, and you would feel only the slightest tickle – maybe not even that – and perhaps the God's voice would leave by that crack over there" – she pointed at the opposite wall – and perhaps that would be the only time in all of your life when the God would speak with you." Adad-guppi leaned forward. "The question is," she said, her voice brittle with age, "was what entered you something – or was it nothing? Were you filled with the fullness of the God? Or were you filled with His emptiness?"

"I have sometimes wondered something similar," the priestess replied. "I have wondered if it weren't my task to listen to the silence of the god." She paused, then murmured, "Perhaps Nabû is not the only god who refuses to speak. Or can't speak." She looked at the old woman intently. "As you well know, grandmother, my face is your reflection – and it isn't. There is no mirror so perfect, not even Sîn's, that it doesn't distort what it also reflects. There is no fidelity that isn't also unfaithful. There is no piety that isn't itself sacrilege."

The old woman slapped her. "You are too much your father's daughter, and too little the God's, if you believe that."

"If that is so, my father is too much his mother's son. Or why else would you have come?" The priestess stared defiantly at her grandmother. "What sanction could I give your journey, what promise could I confirm on the god's behalf? Why does your faith need my pledge? If it is time to return to Ḫarrānu, if it is time to guide the god by hand into his temple, even if the temple is not there, or even if the temple is only in your heart, you will have to do so on your own. You will have to hold in your hand, by yourself, the god's hand, though you cannot feel it, though you cannot feel Him. And whether that will be a faith in Him or in yourself I cannot say – or even whether it isn't just madness." She touched Adad-guppi's hand. "Grandmother, what you have waited for all these years, the task you laid at my father's feet when he was only a boy, is no longer necessary. It never was necessary."

The old woman looked at her. "Are these your words or the God's?" she asked severely.

"Who can tell to whom words belong?" the priestess replied.

Then, the old, the ancient woman, wild-eyed, began to weep – perhaps in sorrow, perhaps in joy. "Is this the end of mourning?" she asked. "Is this the end of mourning?"

To Nabû-na'id, king of Bābilim and father, thus the priestess En-nigaldi-Nanna.

The most loyal servant of Sîn and of long forgotten kings has set aside her sackcloth and bathed herself, not in dust or ash, but in clear, cool water. Dressed in my finest robes, Muṣur's linen stained crimson and embroidered with gold, she has with faltering steps and slow set off by herself to Ḫarrānu, she who is a hundred years old or older. Travelling only when the Moon is visible, she retires and rests when it is not. Always she holds beside her her right hand outstretched toward the Moon, and it is by this hand that she leads the god; and in her left she holds a figurine I gave her, a disk of smooth ivory with an enormous crack across its entire face, like a moon which is at once whole and broken. Nabû-zer-lišir sent it to me from his excavations of Eḫulḫul. He cannot tell if it is the product of a craftsman or of time; nor can he tell if it was once an offering to the god. Perhaps it is instead an offering from the god. Perhaps it once was intended to mean;

perhaps it never was intended to mean.

Is this not the beginning of a New Year, king, father? Are we at last to celebrate the festival?

To Niṭil-Kišar, my mother, thus I, Mikum-Nisaba.

Adad-guppi visited me – yes, somehow, she visited me, walking all the way here despite her hundred years. There is more life in that old woman than there is in me; or there is more death in me, anyway, I who live between these walls and eagerly welcome the forgotten relics of forgotten men. And, perhaps, of forgotten women too. Will Adad-guppi be forgotten, mother? Will you? Are the two of you not alike in being excessively alive, albeit very differently alive? Will people someday speak of you and write of you – there was a queen called Niṭil-Kišar who for reasons of her own constructed immense waterworks around the great city of Bābilim – who, then, like the capricious gods, brought a flood to the earth and transformed a city into an ark. Why, mother? Do you know?

I could ask as much of my grandmother and receive as inscrutable an answer as you likely will give me. She came to me seeking what she knew I could not give her. Why then did she come? Did she come to you as well? Are we as avatars of her missing son, her only human link to him? Or has his time passed, and it was I and perhaps you as well whom she sought, for something we might understand which he could not? But what was it that I was to understand? Do you know?

In any event, I did not understand her message, and so instead I gave her a message of my own, made her an instrument of my message, even as she was also the message's recipient. This I learned from my father: pay attention to the messenger, it may only be the messenger to whom the message is delivered. So I made Adad-guppi the messenger of a message for her. I doubt that either father or I is particularly sanguine that even messengers get the messages which they carry, however. And yet, still, I am writing you. Why? Do you know?

What was my message to Adad-guppi of which she was the

messenger, in a certain sense to herself, in a certain sense, I now realize, to you as well? I can tell you what I wrote, but that is perhaps not quite the same as telling you the message itself. What I wrote, what my writing was, was this: I dressed grandmother in my finest robes, linen from Muṣur stained crimson and embroidered with gold, and I gave her what might only have been a rock but might equally have been a talisman. I said, "Does this not resemble the Moon, both when it is full and when it is broken, whether waxing or waning? Does it not augur well for the Moon's return as well as for its absence?" And grandmother nodded but said nothing. "Understand yourself now as an Akītu puppet," I said to her. "You are dressed as one. You carry what is at once new and old in your hand. And you are connected by an invisible thread to the god. Or you are not. Either your motions are your own or his. Puppets know no more about this than you." So I said to her, and then I directed her, an ancient woman, to begin the long, the impossibly long, journey to Ḫarrānu.

Why? Do you know?

Speak to my brother Nabû-na'id, king of Bābilim, thus his brother Kirsus, King of Luddu.

May your gods Sîn and Nabû keep you healthy and well, and may your kingship last forever.

I am tiring of the antics of the king of Anšan who calls himself the king of Parsua. As you advised I have consulted the gods, who mock this upstart and promise the destruction of his so-called "great kingdom" if I cross the Halys. And yet if I cross the river, is not my brother-in-law waiting on the other side, ready to resume his kingship which Kuraš unlawfully took from him? How foolish it was of the upstart to leave Ištumegu alive. It is a mistake a true king would not make.

We are brothers; and the king of Muṣur is my brother too. Let us join forces and cross the Halys and restore Ištumegu and be done with this bothersome fly. Do not waste time in your reply but order your troops promptly to meet mine; the campaign season will soon be upon us, and then winter, which is not a season for war.

Speak to Kirsus, king of Luddu, thus speaks Nabû-na'id, king of Bābilim.

May Sîn and Nabû watch over you. May that be a good thing.
How can you tell when the gods are mocking?
Why must three armies be combined to crush a fly?
Why is winter not a season for war?

Speak to Bel-šar-uṣur, prince-regent of Bābilim, thus speaks Kirsus, king of Luddu.

May Šamaš and Marduk keep you alive and prospering.

Time is short, and your father's reply, which found me only after a month of waiting, makes no sense to me. He asks about the humor of the gods, and about how many armies are needed to crush a fly, and about the season for war. But I need to know whether your army will join mine and destroy once and for all Kuraš who calls himself king of Parsua. The oracles are good and I will not waste them. Read for yourself the words of your father, which I am sending with this message, and tell me whether they accord with my wish that Bābilim add its strength to mine to crush Kuraš.

Speak to Nabû-na'id the king, thus speaks Bel-šar-uṣur the prince-regent.

Kirsus, king of Luddu, does not understand your reply to his request. Should I send the army to join his? Answer clearly and quickly.

Speak to Bel-šar-uṣur the prince-regent of Bābilim, thus speaks Nabû-aḫḫe-iddina, man of the house of Egibi.

Await your father's response. Kirsus is reckless; your father is not; and our house does not believe Kuraš is either. Think how Ištumegu fell, how his generals mutinied on the field of battle. Do you believe Kuraš had no hand in that? Then he is a lucky man, a man the gods favor. But my house has seldom found such an assumption useful. More useful is to consider that Kuraš is not a lucky man but a well-prepared man. And a devious one.

Speak to Kuraš, king of Parsua, thus speaks Nabû-aḫḫe-iddina, man of the house of Egibi.

We doubt the king of Bābilim will join his brother Kirsus, king of Luddu.

Mother, why have you come to me in a dream?

I am writing one last account.

Why is that?

Because the time will soon come when I will no longer be able to.

He laughed. When has any of us been able to write? he asked. Though I have seen secret things, I do not know the art of writing.

Mother, why have you come to me in a dream?

I told you last night.

You did and you did not.

I told you I was writing one last account.

Yes, I recall. You did not, however, tell me what your account was of.

Nothing. My life. Both.

Can it be both?

Yes.

Mother, why have you come to me in a dream, now for three consecutive nights?

Are you sure it is not you who have come to me in a dream?

In your dream or in mine?

How am I to say?

Have you finished your account?

I have only one last bit of emptiness to carve into rock.

He laughed. What will that emptiness say? he asked.

How alike the dreaming are to the dead, she answered. The dead, however, do not even dream.

To Mikum-Nisaba, my daughter, thus I, Niṭil-Kišar

Adad-guppi did not come to visit me. As far as I know, only you were chosen. For what I cannot say. But you have chosen her as well, to bear a message – and I wonder if it is any clearer to you than to her, or to any of us, what that message is. Is it that she has always been the puppet of a god, and it is for her to embrace her puppetry? You wrote that she has more life in her than you, but how alive are puppets? What kind of life will one have led if one led a puppet's life? One might perhaps worry that you made your grandmother bear a taunting message to herself, or a message which provoked her to consider her own life's futility, when it's too late. But perhaps it isn't too late, or perhaps it's always too late and always has been too late.

But it also occurred to me that in dressing her like an Akītu puppet you were promising not a death but a birth. The end of one year and the beginning of the new. The end of mourning would be, it seems, a flowering, a blossoming forth into promise. How like you, who would recover and preserve all that has been lost, as if preservation and recovery were not at odds, as they are. Or rather – never forget that what ushers in the new is a puppet, that is to say, something not simply alive – though not simply dead, either.

Will Adad-guppi be remembered? Will I? What does it mean to be remembered? Has Gilgameš been remembered? At the end of his travels he sank himself into the Apsû, just as eons before, when floodwaters threatened, Utu-napištim had claimed he himself would. And sure enough, once the snake had stolen Gilgameš's plant of rejuvenation, what happened but floodwaters rose against him for twenty double leagues? What was left for him to do? He instructed the boatman to inspect the walls of Uruk, whose enormous square shape evoked Utu-napištim's ark. What instructions did Gilgameš give the boatman? It is not recorded but I think I know. I think he said, "Look for leaks."

And so, yes, perhaps I will be remembered as the addled architect of immense waterworks around Bābilim, perhaps I will be confused as well with your grandmother, perhaps our names will be corrupted and our deeds exaggerated or minimized – it is very nearly all the same. At some point to be remembered will have nothing to do with me. The point is not far off.

Meanwhile, my waterworks amount to little more than a test, one that I imagine will be overlooked from the beginning. For I want to know – How watertight are the walls? How sound is the ship? Is it ready for the flood to come?

(I am realizing that, like my daughter, I would pair preservation and recovery. Like my daughter I would seek, not immortality, but longevity in stone and mud. You would preserve and restore the past, in the form of statues; I would yield myself as a past to be preserved and restored, in the form of a city, perhaps ultimately in the form only of that city's name. Like Gilgameš.)

* * * * *

From the Babylonian Royal Chronicle:
Ninth regnal year: The king lived in Teima; in Akkadê were the prince, his officers and his army. The month of Nisanu arrived but the king did not return to Bābilim. Nabû did not enter the city. Bel did not come out. No god left his sanctuary. There was no Akītu festival. Offerings were still presented, in the Esagila and the Ezida, to Bābilim's gods and to Borsippa's, as if the times were normal…

Nabû-na'id, all alone, writes; read, my love and friend, Niṭil-Kišar.

The great wild bull is lying down, he is lying down.

The great wild bull is lying down, never to rise again.

So do I recall the lines of the poem, when Bilgames died – not as a man, but as a bull; not domesticated, but wild. Bilgames died, and his death was the occasion for pebbles to see the stars. How they frolicked and laughed, these long-submerged pebbles: to see the stars and the Sun and the Moon! Was it not worth the death of a bull or a man or a name? Who would I not let die, to see pebbles dance!

Except I have not seen pebbles dance. Drain the Purattu – bury a bull or a man or a name in the river's bed – keep watch. Not a pebble stirs: not during the day; not during the night. If they squint at the stars, I have not seen it; nor if they gaze at the Sun God in wonder; nor if they rejoice at the Moon. I have missed it all. A wind will sometimes gust and lift, not pebbles, but dust: is that the long-promised dance, the laughter, the chatter that I await from stone? This is what Belet-ṣeri-dannat and I used to argue about, but where is that prophet now? Is he whirlwind or is he dust – or is he yet coming, making his way slowly, inexorably, back to me, after all this time? "I have been lost in the wilderness," he will say. "A few years is but a short-time to be lost in the wilderness." Nipping at his heels the messenger I sent.

I dug a hole for him – I had a hole dug – perhaps they are still digging. This is my way of commanding stones to dance, in honor of those I love and of those I lose. And of messengers.

Never to rise again.

Never is such a long time, though not quite long enough. Because never too shall end, of this I am certain. In the meanwhile, the fly on its back who stared at the heavens – like the pebbles are said to have stared – that fly has ceased to stir. Its struggles are over, and whether it is contemplating (and if so, what?) at last in peace, or is dead, I cannot tell. Shall I press my ear to the chest of a fly? Shall I try to feel its faint breath? If I hear nothing, if I feel nothing, what does that prove?

Never, ever to rise again.

For I feel nothing, let me say that – or rather, write it. I feel nothing. Neither Fly's breath nor my own. I put my ear to my own chest and hear nothing. My flesh is cold to the touch; there is a worm even now gnawing my nose. I feel nothing, and I cannot tell whether that stillness is mine or another's. Whose death is this, I wonder. Whose death?

The day has come at last when Fly will no longer lick my face; that judgment which he renewed every day, that there is hope for me yet, is at last in abeyance, lost in abeyance forever. And I think: let the autumn wind gust and catch leaves and twirl them like tumbleweed, if only it recalls Fly racing in the riverbed – whatever his judgment. Let that be one of his afterlives, the way he lives in the windswept leaves; let it bring a smile to my face, and let that smile be another of his afterlives – whatever his judgment. I see him race even now through the arroyo, and I wonder: will there be a day when I race alongside him? As grievous as that day may seem to others (let us be honest, very few), will it not be an expression of unbounded joy that then surges like rising water through sand and pebbles, a joy that is neither simply mine, nor simply his, nor simply anyone's? Joy pouring through the desert and bringing it, however briefly, to life. Whatever his judgment.

Stones don't dance to see the Sun or the stars or the Moon. They dance for water, like children and old men do after a drought. They dance for life. Bilgames was buried in the riverbed so that we all, men and pebbles alike, could rejoice when the water returned, cleansing us of dirt and wickedness, renewing us, allowing us to forget and to grow skyward once more.

Fly died. I held him in my arms and I wept over him. But my tears were not strong enough.

* * * * *

Out of the quarried desert rock from Teima, the rock she called Moon-rock, his mother made a stele. "If Sîn will not come to me," she muttered, "I shall at least write him a message." On it she caused there to be carving. "If Nabû will not come to me," she muttered, "I shall at least scratch on a rock as if it were a message."

Had there been an Akītu festival, on this the third day: the revelation of the puppets.

(Nabû sat on the ground, clawing it with his talons. In the background, Sîn. A child wailed, naked, alone, lying in the dirt beside Nabû. Neither god responded. The old woman was bewildered. "I am having a vision," she thought. "How do I call their attention to the baby?" she thought. "It is I who must attend the baby," she thought. Still she did not stir. Unstirring, she was, like the majestic Moon, still. "Go to the babe," a voice did not say, and so she did not hear it. "I am having a vision," she thought again. "That is why there are no words.")

(And yet in a vision would I hear a wailing baby?)

(She thought of Izdubar with the black cat on his lap. Did Izdubar hear purring or only imagine it? How can one tell?)

What would my message read? she asked herself, all the while ignoring the wailing babe. (For it was most probably a vision.) She allowed her ancient fingers to slide across the smooth surface of her Moon-rock, caressing it no less and no more than tracing where signs would be were an emptiness found for them. Perhaps, she thought, if my vision were an eagle's, I would see even beneath my weak fingers a trail through the rock has in fact been carved. Yet, I am 104 and my eyesight is clear, my mind excellent: and I see no such trail, no such trodden emptiness announcing, "Here would meaning go." Or perhaps: here once went meaning. She imagined hunting dogs, tiny as motes of dust, being released and racing up and down the rock, snuffling for meaning's trail. The puppies, the young dogs, of course, think they find it – instead, however, they end up tracking only themselves or each other or something else they imagined. But the old dogs, the wily ones, go more slowly. They look for the already broken path not for where it will lead but because the going is easier. That is all. So beneath her fingers now she imagined just a path for weary, aged dogs – such as Fly had been, before he died. (Niṭil-Kišar had relayed to her her son's message. How did he send it, she wondered? How did he find the strength to put emptiness into clay, to burn it in, to send it through the trackless desert, to will it to his wife who, for whatever reason, then willed it to her, the ancient mother? Why did Niṭil-Kišar wish her to know? "See, your son still feels. See, perhaps he may even feel for you when it is your death which is buried within the emptiness of a message, or within even the emptiness of his own breast.")

Still the babe wailed; still she ignored it. (For it was most probably a vision.) "I am Adad-guppi, mother of Nabû-na'id, king of Bābilim, mayor of the desert and the deserted, worshipper of Sîn, my god, for whose divinity I have always cared." She could not tell if these words were spoken or only in her mind, whether these words belonged to her or the babe, whether these words were words. "In the 16th year of Nabû-apla-uṣur, king of Bābilim, king of the gate (bāb) of the gods (ili), Sîn, the king of the gods, the god, became angry with his city, with his house, with his people. He left. The city, the house, the people, became as ash, as dust. That is when I began to wear dust, that is when I began to wear ash, so as to be the living overlooked as the dead, so as to care for the sanctuary of Sîn as a living ghost, as the ghost of the living. I revered the deity of Sîn, who mistook me for dust, who mistook me for ash. Still, constantly, I beseeched him, Sîn, the king of the gods." She thought of the wailing babe, lying in the dirt, unattended. Am I being beseeched, she wondered? But no, for it was most probably a vision.

"Without fail, unceasingly, I cared for his deity. I was a worshipper of Sîn all my life, on earth and in heaven. Everything fine that was given to me I gave back, I gave up, to Sîn – daily, nightly, monthly, yearly. Never did I end my beseeching. Gazing at him when present, gazing for him when absent, I knelt, I prayed, I was full of humility. 'May you return to your city, your house and your people. May the black-headed people again worship you. To appease you, I will wear no wool, no silver, no gold; to appease you I will anoint myself with no perfume, no oil; to appease you my clothing will be torn sackcloth and my bath will be dust and ash, so that you will overlook me, you will think me among the dead, even while I sing your praises, set firmly in my heart your fame, stand your watch and serve you food.' So I said to the god knowing his back was turned to me, my people, my house, my city; knowing that but always not knowing whether also his ears were plugged."

She looked at the path her fingers had not traced across the Moon-rock; she could almost see the signs she had not written. Where will this stele stand, she mused, at what frontier of the empire, at what crossroads? Where will it stand to perplex a traveler with its blankness?

"From the 20th year of Aššur-bāni-apli, king of Aššur, in which I was born, until the forty-second year of Aššur-bāni-apli, the third year of Aššur-etillu-ili, his son, the twenty-first year of Nabû-apla-uṣur, the forty-third year of Nabû-kudurri-uṣur, the second year of Awil-Marduk, the fourth year of Nergal-šar-uṣur – for ninety-five years I cared for Sîn, king of the gods, and for his sanctuaries, and for all of earth and for all of heaven. Yes, even as a babe, I did this. Like an overlooked beetle, my ash-disguised, dust-disguised, ghost-like life was spent tending to the god who never turned my way, never bent his head toward me, never offered me his hand. And yet possibly, hearing of my deeds, he felt joy, or when the smell of savory food reached his nostrils, when once again his watch was stood by another, when he drifted into peaceful sleep to the sounds of a praiseful lullaby. Surely, whether he knew the cause or not, his wrathful heart was calmed. He considered with favor again the Eḫulḫul, Sîn's house, Sîn's home, located in the midst of Ḫarrānu, his favorite dwelling and my home, whence I have been exiled this last half-century and more. You, Sîn, have made the majority of my life a life of homelessness; and yet always have I served you, like a beetle pushing dung I have served you always."

"But then a day came, you know it well, when you, Sîn, did in fact look upon me. You looked upon your beetle, and with laughter or mischief or cruelty in your heart, you raised my only son, my offspring, to kingship. He whom I called Nabû-na'id, whom I named not for the god of smooth white rock but for the god of the writing hidden in that blankness. It was to him that you delivered kingship of Šumeru and Akkadê, from upper sea to lower sea, all the land to the edge of Muṣur. Perhaps it was this that you began all those years ago with the eclipse in Luddu. Then did I lift my hands to Sîn, the king of the gods, imploring you reverently in prayer: 'Nabû-na'id is my son, my offspring, beloved of my heart however oddly. It was you, Sîn, who summoned him to kingship; it was your own divine speech which uttered his name. Now go by his side. Fell his enemies. Unforget Eḫulḫul, which my son will rebuild and the rites of which he will restore, all for you, if only you accept our invitation to return.' For in a dream, Sîn, king of the gods, you set your hands on me and, leaning close, whispered thus into my ear: 'Through you will I return my godhead to our home in Ḫarrānu, by means of Nabû-na'id, your son. He will unconstruct Eḫulḫul; he will reconstruct Eḫulḫul better than before. He will reconstruct Ḫarrānu better than before. He will bring me and my attendants back to the temple Eḫulḫul, leading me by hand in holy procession.' So you told me in a dream, the first time you had spoken to me, touched me, looked at me, in my half century of homelessness."

"I attended your words, O Sîn! And I have seen them realized – for my son has dug a very deep hole in Ḫarrānu where once stood the Eḫulḫul – very deep and he is still digging! No more will your rites be neglected within the deep hole which is or will be the Eḫulḫul. Likewise has he reconstructed Ḫarrānu, with a gaping hole at its heart. He has led you to your city, to your temple, to your hole in joy and happiness, even as he digs it! And so, what Sîn had never before done, what you had never before granted, for love of me who worshipped Sîn, who beseeched you the king of the gods – you raised my chin with two fingers, you exalted my fame, you gave me long day upon long day, from the reign of Aššur-bāni-apli, king of Aššur, to the reign of my son Nabû-na'id, king of Bābilim, 104 years for the worship of Sîn, alive and well, my eyesight clear, my mind excellent, my hands and feet healthy, my words well chosen, food and drink still agreeable, my flesh vital, my bitter, grief-stained heart now full of joy. I have seen generation upon generation. I have reached a ripe old age – 104 years from birth to death. For I too am called to my home, to my hole."

Had there been an Akītu festival, on this the fourth day: the recitation of the poem "When on high," and the interminable list of names.

(Nabû sat on the ground, still clawing it with his talons. In the background, Sîn, still. A child – the child – wailed, naked, alone, lying in the dirt beside Nabû. Neither god responded. The old woman remained bewildered. "I am having a vision," she thought. "That is so. And yet, what does it matter if it is a vision? The gods will not tend to the baby. It falls to me, then, that I do it; that I lift the child into my arms and offer it my withered breast. Will milk flow? Does a vision baby need milk? How, in fact, will I hold a vision to my chest, how in fact will I give my nipple to its vision lips? But if the gods will not act, then I shall – for the gods, possibly for the child." So she thought but still she did not stir. Unstirring, she was, like the majestic Moon, still and radiantly white. "Go to the babe," a voice did not say, and so she did not hear it. "I am having a vision," she thought again. "That is why as of yet I have not lifted what I know I cannot raise.")

She stood before the quarried desert rock from Teima, the rock she called Moon-rock. She had all of yesterday transformed it into a stele. All of yesterday with her ancient finger she had traced words across its smooth, pathless surface. And yet here it was, still blank, radiantly blank. A strange, almost triumphant grin spread across her face. "See, Sîn," she said aloud. "I too can write inscrutable messages. See, Nabû, I too can deface a rock with scars." And then with her bent, ancient finger, she again traced the surface of the Moon-rock with the tale she cared to tell.

"Does it surprise you, god," she wrote, "that my thoughts now are of my eccentric son, self-exiled in a desert, commanding from afar the digging of bottomless holes while kingdoms crumble and empires rise all about him? It is to him, you know, that I have entrusted your care, Sîn – for it is the task of humans to care for the almost helpless gods, more than it is the task of gods to care for us almost helpless humans. So I have entrusted you, Sîn, to Nabû-na'id, king of Bābilim, my son. As long as he lives, may he not offend you. As long as he lives, may he not forget you. For are not gods as easily forgotten as blank messages? Still, I would have him believe in the possibility of that message which even now my finger traces on this rock which I call your rock. Let him, then, worship you, and appoint for him a protective spirit such as the one you gave me, that allowed me to reach old age in its silent, somber company. For it is not just you whom I and my son have tended. In the 21 years of Nabû-apla-uṣur, king of Bābilim; in the 43 years of Nabû-kudurri-uṣur, king of Bābilim, son of Nabû-apla-uṣur; in the 4 years of Nergal-šar-uṣur, king of Bābilim – while they reigned, for 68 years, I worshipped them, I stood their watch, I fed their ghosts. I caused my son Nabû-na'id to do likewise, to serve Nabû-kudurri-uṣur, son of Nabû-apla-uṣur, and Nergal-šar-uṣur. He was good to them; he made my name excellent before them, and he exalted me as if I were, for each of them, a daughter."

(And Awil-Marduk, she wondered? The king named Marduk-Man? Or the king called Labaši-Marduk, the king whose name begs Marduk to protect him from shame? What kind of service had her son done for those kings? In her life, only the kings whose names invoked Nabû endured any length of time, while the ones named for Marduk were granted only the briefest reigns. Her son had something to do with the brevity of those reigns. It was said that her son masterminded the toppling of Awil-Marduk by Nergal-šar-uṣur. The latter in any event believed that he had. As for Labaši-Marduk, had her son not, in fact, stood that king's watch, more even than for any other king? So well, so thoroughly, did he stand the watch of Labaši-Marduk that, when the time came for a changing of the guard, it was her son who was king. Is that proof of the highest fidelity, to serve a king so greatly as to become the king? Or is it proof of the lowest infidelity, the servant who betrays the master? Do we not need both, however? Does not a new year start with an insurrection, a god or king deposed, either to be restored – and hence the world renewed – or replaced – and hence a world anew? Is this not the *Akītu* festival, wherein a different Marduk-Man plays a role from time immemorial, slaps the king, degrades him – and then is saved by that same king? Did my son, did I, save Awil-Marduk or Labaši-Marduk? But from what? Who would want to be saved as they were saved? ["My son," she said aloud, simply.] Shall I trace this confusion into the rock with my magic finger, she asked herself, or is it better to leave blank the blankness where Awil-Marduk's name and Labaši-Marduk's name might be sought?)

(I shall leave it blank, Sîn. Are not things between us already complicated enough? But I wonder, and perhaps you too have wondered, god, whether this is the reason my son has gone away – to avoid the new year and what it portends, to avoid the new year and what it reminds. Perhaps my son no longer has the strength to stand before any Marduk-Man at all, there to be chastised and blamed, there for his crimes to be cast into the light of the sun for all to see, most harmfully for him to see.)

(She thought of the costumes of the puppets – sometimes dressed as gods, sometimes as kings, sometimes as men – and then she imagined Awil-Marduk, king, facing the Marduk-Man in the *Akītu* festival. They eye each other warily. You are a version of me, each thinks, but then, each wonders, what am I version of? Awkwardly, peripherally, unconsciously mirroring one another, each casts a sidelong glance at their audience of puppets. Am I what they are? each asks himself. Yet, all of this, a tumult and riot in the heart of each, transpires in an instant. It is off script. They have a part to play. They play it. What else is there to do?)

So much did Adad-guppi not trace blankly into blankness, only thinking it, but now she found her finger again poised over the Moon-rock. She did not know what it would write – if, that is, it counts as writing to trace something which, as far as any eye can see, leaves no trace. What path do you yearn for, finger? Where would you take me? What is there left to say? Is it for you to give an account of my death, o finger? You could write – and her finger touched the stone – "In the ninth year of Nabû-na'id, king of Bābilim, I died." The finger paused over the verb, over its inflection. Is it I who died? the finger seemed to ask. Or you? Or she?

Adad-guppi did not wait for the finger to resolve the question.

Had there been an Akītu festival, on this the fifth day: the king and the Marduk-Man face one another.

Nabû sat on the ground but was still. In the background, Sîn, still, always still. The child – naked, alone, lying in the dirt beside Nabû, still – was quiet. Neither god attended it. "Does the child need me anymore?" the old woman wondered. "Has the child died? Did it beseech me for life all this time, and I, unheeding, gave it death? And yet, can visions die?" She strode to the child. "Are you now, belatedly, still-born?" she said to the pathetic creature lying motionless at her feet. "Are you still to be born?" She did not bend to try to pick it up. She did not offer it her withered breast. But tears erupted from her eyes and her face was transformed into a fierce and anguished grimace. She looked up, ferociously, at Sîn. "Why did you not tend this child?" she demanded. "For once you will answer my question!" The god was silent, still, radiant. "Is it I who should have tended the child, neglecting you, neglecting me?" the old woman asked tremulously. "Is this your final taunt, Sîn? That not only have I wasted my life honoring you, but I have neglected a child, wasted a child's life too? And now, even now, after 100 years, still you only speak to me when you deign to. Even now you will not converse with your most faithful follower, the one you made complicit in the death of a baby."

In her mind she corrected herself: "The death of a vision."

There was no reply. Neither god moved; the baby did not move; all were still, all were silent. The old woman wept.

Then at her feet she saw the scratches which the talons of Nabû had torn into the ground.

"This is the child of Sîn and your child," she read the marks as saying. "Its name is Death."

Her heart leapt in terror.

Even as she looked, however, what were signs became just scratches in dirt, already disappearing, already gone. And, peripherally, she saw a third god, almost indistinguishable from shadow, one who never opened his eyes, never parted his lips; forever was he listening with his wide, his perfect ears. But then, like the scratches which may have been signs, he faded and disappeared too.

From the Babylonian Royal Chronicle:

Ninth regnal year: The king lived in Teima; in Akkadê were the prince, his officers and his army. The month of Nisanu arrived but the king did not return to Bābilim. Nabû did not enter the city. Bel did not come out. No god left his sanctuary. There was no Akītu festival. Offerings were still presented, in the Esagila and the Ezida, to Bābilim's gods and to Borsippa's, as if the times were normal. In the month Nisanu, on the fifth day, on what in normal times would have been the fifth day of the Akītu festival, the king's mother died at Dūr-karāšu, which is on a bank of the Purattu, upstream from Sippar. The son of the king and his army were in mourning for three days, but the king ordered that the official mourning of his mother in Akkadê be deferred until the month of Simānu, over which Sîn presides. Also in the month Nisanu, Kuraš, king of Anšan, mustered his army and crossed the Idiqlat below Arbela. In the month Ayyaru, he marched to the country of [illegible]. He slew its king, took his possessions, and stationed his own garrison there.

* * * * *

From the [fragmentary] Assyrian Accounts of Herodotus

...Why the Babylonians did not come to Croesus' aid, despite their alliance, has never been fully explained. Some say it was because Cyrus' invasion into Lydia was too fast and unexpected for Croesus to rally to his side the armies of his allies. Perhaps the Babylonians saw no reason to come, since Croesus so unwisely had already disbanded his own army – what hope could the Babylonians have of saving him, if, far from endeavoring to save himself, he inflicted his own worst wound? On another account, however, the problem was more the fault of the Babylonians than of Croesus. For their king was away; and the relay of messages from Sardis to the king and back again was too confused for quick action. Perhaps Labynetus even wasted valuable time questioning the accuracy of the report he had been given; for it stretched credulity that a king so powerful as Croesus could have his fortunes overturned so quickly, moreover seemingly in contradiction of the oracles. But the third report I have heard is that Labynetus did not come because he was in mourning; some say for his mother, who had lived over 100 years and died in his absence. She was a priestess of their god of the Moon, or else of their god of writing, if they are not the same god; or perhaps she was no priestess, as some say, but instead a private fanatic, one who believed it was for the god to choose his devotees, not for temples and their priests. However, others say that the mourning of Labynetus was not for his mother, though it was around then that she died. They say instead that he was mourning the loss of his dog.

Even Odysseus let fall (or very nearly) a tear at the death of Argos. Yet that is strange, is it not? What was it that Odysseus and Argos shared ever so briefly, when the one was a young husband and father and the other only a puppy, that survived and even was nurtured (is it possible?) over 20 years of absence? That Penelope remained faithful to Odysseus (if she did) is one thing – she who could recall to mind his name, his features, conversations, activities, lovemaking, all that they had shared – but why would a dog remain faithful to a man and to the memory of a man, especially if the dog was probably not much more than a bumbling, clueless puppy (even if a very fast one) when he had first and last known the man? And why would the dog stand out to the man, even after 20 years? I sometimes think that this is a moment when Homer dozes, when he invites us to believe what is simply unbelievable. That faith can exist between man and dog; not only that, but that faith can endure. Even that a man and a dog would truly recognize one another after 20 years.

But they did *hunt together, they* did *kill together. Maybe their friendship was forged in that, in mutual reliance and in blood, in the triumph and desperation of killing and in its complicity. You have seen my blood-drenched, my gore-splattered beard, each says to the other; you have seen what I am capable of. You have seen my delight in killing and, perhaps more rarely, you have seen my remorse. All other forgivenesses are as nothing if we cannot forgive each other, knowing as we do and as no one else does what we each are capable of – even what we each have been. What we each have delightedly been.*

But, to return to our story, why Labynetus mourned a mere dog – if he did (for he was no Odysseus) – and if he did at the expense of the empire of Lydia and at the expense of further empowering Cyrus who would soon gobble up Babylon as well – of that there is no record. As far as I can tell, there is little evidence that dogs are considered of much worth among the Assyrians. Mostly, as here in Greece, the strays are simply rounded up and stoned every now and again, because typically the lives of dogs are for us human beings little more than nuisances. They steal food and bite children and, like certain philosophers, defecate and copulate shamelessly in public. Nuisances, then; though it is a wonder that we men only stone them but do not eat them. I have heard of peoples who eat their old women, but still not their dogs. A mother might die and be eaten but, among these peoples, not their dogs. But what was it in Babylon? Which is more likely, that an eccentric king would mourn the death of his eccentric mother or of his dog – a dog quite possibly eccentric too and likely to have been, like most dogs, a nuisance?

Chapter 12. Moving Statues

Speak to Nabû-na'id the king, thus speaks Bel-šar-uṣur the prince-regent.

Is the white stone from Arabi before which your mother lay when we found her – is this truly to be my object of care? Is not a net closing about us, while you monumentalize a blank rock? Kuraš, king of Anšan, destroyed the kingdom of Luddu and its king, our ally whom we failed to aid. Daily I receive messages from our border, warning of raids and insolence and begging for protection. If you will not go yourself, send me with the army.

Speak to Bel-šar-uṣur, prince-regent of Bābilim and son of its absent king, Nabû-na'id the far-off one, orphan.

What can an army accomplish against insolence? Move the stele to Ḫarrānu. Let it stand before the Eḫulḫul. Also, consult En-nigaldi-Nanna. She understands what there is to preserve, what there is to lose.

Speak to Nabû-na'id the king, thus speaks Bel-šar-uṣur the prince-regent, his son.

My sister orders that a duplicate be made! A duplicate of a blank white rock which you both call a stele! That way, should it some day be a stepping stone, used by the bare feet of men to climb heavenward, yet might its message still be preserved. So speaks En-nigaldi-Nanna. But it is blank! Nor will she tell me if it is the god who commands this or if it is her own heart always mournful for what is lost, for what is irretrievable, for what is already forgotten.

Let me campaign on the frontier before it is too late.

Speak to Bel-šar-uṣur, prince-regent of Bābilim and son of its absent king, Nabû-na'id the far-off one, orphan.

Make the duplicate. Have Nabû-zer-lišir oversee it, if En-nigaldi-Nanna cannot. Raise them both before the Eḫulḫul in Ḫarrānu. Nor should you waste time reminding me that there is no Eḫulḫul in Ḫarrānu, that there is only a hole. As you know, a net is closing about us. We must keep our eye on what is most important. Often this is what is not there.

"What is this exalted mourning my father pretends to offer? He did not return even for her funeral, but now immense rocks must be carted across the empire as blank memorials of his mother? What can be achieved by this?"

Itti-Marduk-balaṭu, enveloped within the smell of his strong perfume, tugged absent-mindedly at his beard. "The House of Egibi does not know," he answered. "We do not understand yet what your father's strategy is." He paused. "Some wonder if he has gone mad like so many of his predecessors. It is no easy task being king."

"Is that what you believe?"

"That it is no easy task being king? Certainly – though it is also no easy task to know who is king."

"No, I mean, do you believe that my father has gone mad?"

Itti-Marduk-balaṭu laughed.

Bel-šar-uṣur abruptly interrupted his laughter. "Do you? I want an answer."

"My house learned long ago never to underestimate your father. We also learned long ago and are still learning that, like his own father, it is not clear for what he is playing. And so the answer is – I don't know. Whether he is mad or not depends on whatever it is that he's playing for."

"Why do you assume he's playing for anything at all? Why do you even assume he's playing? Perhaps he has gotten up, left behind this game you always talk of; and it is we who foolishly await his next move, we who foolishly interpret the moves that he makes as moves in a game he is no longer playing."

Itti-Marduk-balaṭu raised an eyebrow. "Perhaps you are more like your father than I realized," he murmured. "Let me ask you a question. Why did you bring Adad-guppi with you to Dūr-karāšu? I am sure that I wasn't the only one surprised that she died in a fortified camp. And why were you lugging that stone from Arabi with you?"

Bel-šar-uṣur sighed. "Stones. There's more than one. My father commanded that they be brought to Ḫarrānu even before his mother died, even before she took an interest in the one she called the Moon-rock. So I was bringing them; but I was using that journey to the north and west also as an opportunity to inspect and prepare our military camps. I'll do the same once I get to Ḫarrānu. I hear reports that the king of Anšan and his underlings, now that Kirsus has fallen, are nibbling at Ḫilakku and Kue, maybe with designs even on Kinaḫḫi. If we strengthen Ḫarrānu, we can try to deter him. Otherwise, while my father endeavors to bend stones to his will, Kuraš will bend men to his will – and will surround us to the west as well as north and east."

Itti-Marduk-balaṭu frowned. "How strange your father is. All this time that I have been travelling with you, I thought our purpose was the one you now reveal as secondary. I had understood as your father's intent what you now reveal as your own."

"That seems to vex you."

"I do not like having misunderstood." He paused. "You only answered one of my questions. Why did you bring Adad-guppi with you?"

The prince regent gave a harsh laugh. "What choice did I have? She somehow heard I was travelling to Ḫarrānu, and so one morning, on the outskirts of Bābilim, as my army prepared its departure, there she was. 104 years old, arrived on her own strength, without explanation or request. As far as I know, she must have walked, but she did not bother to tell me when I asked. 'I am here,' she said, 'that is all. I am here in order to go to Ḫarrānu.' I realized that I lacked the strength to dissuade her, so I arranged a conveyance for her – at least a woman 100 years old wouldn't have to walk – and brought her with me. Even then, she was not content. Few days passed without her remonstrating with me for my lengthy stays at our various fortifications en route. She found them, as she put it, 'dilatory.' I tried to explain to her that I was safeguarding the empire, that even she would concede this as a responsibility of a prince regent, but she would have none of it. 'There are far more important things to do,' she informed me, 'than to safeguard a mere empire.' I came close to mocking her then, though I held back. I wanted to say – 'What, moving stones and an old woman so they can stand before an immense hole in a backward, mostly-destroyed city – that is more important? What world do you live in, you mad hag?' But of course I said nothing, just turned my back and directed myself at the tasks that I had set myself, tasks that really needed doing."

Itti-Marduk-balaṭu looked interested. "Hmm. I wonder if that's the better question. Not – what game are you playing? but – what world do you live in? Maybe we at the House of Egibi have been asking the wrong question, assuming different games in one world. I will have to think about this."

To Nabû-na'id, king of Bābilim and father, thus the priestess En-nigaldi-Nanna.

I have inspected the stone called Moon-rock and have selected a second very like it, as near a twin of a rock as a rock can have a twin. With my own finger I traced the story of your mother's life, so far as I knew it, onto its surface, into its surface. I do not know if the story I have told resembles the one which she told; nor do I know why she chose her tale or I mine. But I have done my best, father.

To inspect the stone and to impress it with meaning, were I able, I travelled far up the Purattu, such travels as are rarely done by a woman. But I come from a tradition of wandering women, from Adad-guppi who did not fear to walk any of the face of the earth's many aspects; and from my own mother, your wife, Niṭil-Kišar, too. I remembered tales that she told me of her travels with you to Ṣurru. They were much on my mind as I did my duty for you and for my grandmother; in fact, so much were they on my mind that I carved those tales too into the stone. With what right I do not know. But now, those tales and your mother's are woven into each other, sometimes one, sometimes the other on top, interlocking, diverging, returning to one another, never staying. Why have you gone far away, father, and not returned? Why has my mother stayed near and not stirred? What in the desert so calls you? What of her waterworks so calls Niṭil-Kišar? Do you work together or apart, or is this yet another series of tales that I will braid into each other and away from each other, back and forth, on the surface of a perpetually blank stone so like the faceless moon?

(But who can tell what is faceless, father, who can tell what is not? Perhaps the moon is veiled like a virgin, and we mistake the veil for what would be a face. Perhaps the Moon is bearded, and beneath that statuesque impassivity is a face worn with care, suffering, even sympathy. And perhaps when I ran my fingers over the surface of those rocks they felt tickled almost to tears, almost to the threshold of breaking, of cracking into a smile or something tender, they who so rarely feel the play of fingers against their cheeks, their eyelids, their lips. Almost, almost, I soothed them into speech, or at least into expression, whether grin or grimace. Almost, but not quite. Like the god, they are tempted but do not yield. Like all the figurines with which I surround myself and live. Someday I shall cajole at least one of them into motion – the dog figurine with a broken foot, for example. 'Come,' I will say. 'However useless you feel, however ugly, however disabled, come. I am glad to share my life with you.' And then the dog

will hobble over, wagging its crippled rear.)

(I am sorry if my fantasy should remind you too much of Fly's loss.)

Nabû-na'id kicked a stone with his sandaled foot and watched it coast pointlessly through the dry dust of the ground. Time seemed slow and sound muted. No dog investigated anything beside him or in front of him or behind him. No dog wondered why he had kicked a stone, or for that matter, didn't wonder. Fly was not there. He did not really know where Fly was.

My mother has died, he thought to himself, and I am more stricken by the death of a dog. But perhaps I am putting it this way to myself only to exacerbate something, to make myself more hateful in my own eyes. Would I be a man, a tyrant, who does not mourn his own mother? But I do mourn you, mother. It's just that Fly was my companion, and you never were. No, mother, you weren't. You were never my companion. You haunted my life like you haunted Bābilim and the palaces and the temples. You told me stories and lived a story that you left me, among others, to tell. I am not ungrateful. But all of this is different from being my companion. Gubaru has been my companion since childhood; I called him brother, but you denied you had given me one.

(I am rambling, he thought.)

Why did I not return for your burial? Isn't it obvious, mother? Because of the *rēḫātu*. Almost daily I receive rancid meat destined first for the gods – who reject it – then for me. I go through a ceremony of pretending to eat it, even as the maggots writhe and wriggle beneath my nose. But the pretenses of the ceremony aside, I reject it too. Of course I do. Always my gorge rises; and who wants to spend an afternoon picking vomit from his beard? Coarse, I know, mother, coarse. But I did not want to see you, my mother, transformed into *rēẖātu*, flies buzzing about, some of them perhaps born of your own body. Let her be buried, I thought. Let my mother be buried. I do not want her brought before me to be eaten before my eyes.

So it was with Fly, too, mother. I did not wait long to bury him. I did not want his body to bloat in the heat. I did not want a worm to drop from his nose. I did not want to smell his decaying flesh, no more than I wanted to smell yours.

But now I have ordered that the *rēẖātu* not be brought before me. I will no longer look at it. Let the priests do what they will. I am determined. I do not know if it is death which appalls me or life – its careless excess, its egoism, its insouciance. Maggots crawl and nibble their ways across what once were the faces of those I love; they leave these tracks not unlike what you and I might trace in stone; and they rejoice in their good fortune, to be born into plenty. But they are born into the worst and most unthinkable lack, and this makes their joy an atrocity. This and their obliviousness. Atrocities!

With what right, however, do I lament atrocity? What has my life become but an atrocity? I remember a boy who was eager to know animals, who liked to fall into stories, who thought he could find a way to live peacefully with others. He turned to ancient texts and the arcana of the heavens – what harm could come from such esoteric activities? And yet... What has become of that boy, mother? Do you remember him? Did you ever know him? Or am I making him up? Fly may have known this boy more than you did, though he never knew me as a boy, though this boy I describe may in fact never have existed. Still, Fly may have known him better than anyone. But Fly was also at my side when I ordered the annihilation of cities – and it never seemed to bother him. Maybe there is greater continuity between what is peaceful and loving in me, and what is callous, dark, destructive. Maybe a dog understands that better than a man ever could. Or if not a dog, then a fly.

Fly also was a peaceful creature. Yet I saw him eat a living, baby bird once. He swallowed it whole. I listened to its panicked chirps as it fell down his throat. Fly meant no harm, but harm was done. Can I pretend to myself that so too has my life been? I have demolished cities like Fly demolished a baby bird. I meant no harm, but harm was done. Is that excuse available to me?

You, mother, would not shy from devastation, not if it was in the service of your idée fixe – Sîn's return to Ḫarrānu, to a rebuilt Eḫulḫul. (Yes, mother, I am still working on it. I promise. Even though you are dead, I will keep this promise, even if broken a thousand times I will keep it.) Had I killed countless innocents, still you would have deemed it justified in the service of this end. Why was that mother? Is it because the god, the temple, maybe even the city, are so much more important than we fly-like men? Do we buzz around, mucking up the holy meal, the *rēḫātu*, unaware of what we're about, while something great is transpiring all around us – to which we are incidental, less than incidental? Is that how you saw it, mother? Surely, though, you also see that it cuts both ways: maybe we are all as flies, marring ever so slightly a transcendent ceremony; but maybe what would be a transcendent ceremony is really just a happy occasion for flies. And then, as you know, I have more than once wondered whether it wasn't the gods who were most akin to the flies, even more than men; and I don't know if that is a degradation of the gods or an exaltation of the flies. Maybe it is neither, less than neither.

(Your grandchildren are on my mind. Who would have thought that it would be Bel-šar-uṣur who cared for you in your final days, who humored you and brought you with him as he travelled to the north and west? It was he who arranged your funeral and the official period of mourning; and while he wasn't especially imaginative, he wasn't heartless either. I told him to make your place of burial secret. Not even I know. I wonder if anyone else does. Meanwhile, I bequeathed your stone to Ennigaldi-Nanna. I do not doubt she will make something different of it than you would have, or even than you would have wanted; but I think, over time, whatever she decides will intrigue us both. That is, if either of us is still capable of being intrigued.)

I have seen so many beings die, mother. I think to myself that I should die as peripherally as they all did. Because we always die on the periphery, don't we mother? We think we are the center of the world, but we die alone, somewhere in the backdrop of other people's lives. Even those who love us ardently can't keep their eye on us as we die; other concerns intervene, other hopes, if nothing else the warmth of the sun, and plus, how boring, how insufferable, it can be to watch the dying die! Maybe that's what makes dying possible. You look about you and suddenly with the greatest clarity you recognize how peripheral you were in the lives of others – even if you were king! There you are, exhaling your last breaths, sometimes in terror or anguish or resignation or exhaustion or confusion, there you are, other people overseeing you – and overlooking you too – and you realize: I am globally trivial. I have been on the periphery all along. Why not cross?

(These ones to whom I bequeath myself – well, foreseeably, for the most part, they will fail to carry me. Very well.)

Do you notice, mother, how I have forgotten your perspective, and it is my own that I imagine, my own dying, as if I get to cling to the first person all the way to the bitter end? But what would it mean if instead I clung to the second person, held onto your dying rather than my own? The same holds true for you, Fly… And when I die, if only to make amends to each of you for how miserably I have failed to mourn you and to share in your loss and your losing, when I die I will try to die in the second person, as someone else, as someone peripheral even to me. Maybe I will even die in the third person, somewhere in the shadows. If you can die, Fly, and yet the world continues; if you can die, mother, and yet the world continues; then I too can die and let the world continue, mostly unbothered, mostly oblivious, as it has always been and maybe as it should always be.

He kicked again a stone with his sandaled foot and marveled that it was real, that this insignificant, unmeaning act was real, that dust flew up, that there were sounds, that eventually the rock tumbled back into stillness, and all of it was real, all of it, though it did not mean.

To Niṭil-Kišar, my love and friend, thus Nabû-na'id.

You are much on my mind. Our son sometimes writes me with reports about your waterworks, about which he is genuinely befuddled. I suppose I am – not befuddled; in some strange way not even puzzled – but I am waiting *– to see and to understand. Perhaps not even that. I am waiting, Niṭil-Kišar, because I trust you. But what that means, I'm not sure. Partly I think it means that I know there is something within you which will always be a mystery to me. I think to myself, maybe these waterworks are some kind of expression of that. And so I wait, hoping to understand. But I will not be surprised if I don't understand. That does not mean I will regret waiting.*

I spoke earlier today with a person who said that secretly all men think women are witches. It made me laugh, Niṭil-Kišar! Not out of happiness – nearer despair, perhaps, but not out of that either. It demands such gigantic courage for all of us to take even a single step out into the day. We men, I think, bluff that courage. If the required courage is gigantic, then we must be giants – that's the logic of a man. But how do we become giants? It seems to me we invite women to transform us. That's one kind of witchcraft that women do: they aggrandize us, make us equal to the day. But the flip-side is that we men know, or suspect, that it's all an illusion; and who is there better positioned to see through the illusion than the witch who made us? So that's a second kind of witchcraft which women do: they belittle us, or at least threaten us with belittlement. Never in reality having been equal to the day, we begin to suspect that we were equal not even to a single instant of the day. Perhaps we were not. Maybe this is why men are so angry at women.

(You undoubtedly know of the restive spirit of Kuraš, strutting the frontier, fretting his hour which he thinks is a day or a month or a year or forever. I wonder if it has occurred to him that he does not know his own height. He may think he is tall, he may fear that he is short, but surely Kuraš never strides into the world in complete inconfidence of his height. "I must at least have a height," he thinks to himself – but of course he doesn't think this, men like Kuraš do not think such things – "I must at least have a height," he doesn't think to himself, striding confidently into the world. If I meet him someday – likely a sorry day for me – I may ask him how tall he is. "What do you measure yourself against?" I will ask. And he will answer with some standard measure, but if he asks me, I will tell him: "I measure myself against the day." If he has a flicker of life in him, he will ask, "How do you do that?" And I will answer, "I don't know. But probably with the help of women.")

(I wonder, sometimes, how women muster the gigantic courage needed to take a single step into the day. I wonder, even more, how you do, my love, my friend; and our daughter, I wonder about her too. But my mother – she was a case apart. Her courage dwarfs all of our courages. Perhaps she alone of all human beings was equal to the day, if only out of sheer obstinacy, sheer insistence, sheer single-mindedness. But the day she was equal to – there was something so cold about it, so harsh, so unrelenting. It was as hard a day to be equal to as could exist. I am sure I would never wish to be equal to such a day.)

(And our son? Does Bel-šar-uṣur know how much courage he needs to take even a single step into the day? I think he probably does not. He probably just does it, not believing it is courageous at all. But I think I see something in him that for too long I missed, Niṭil-Kišar.

I think I see moments of doubt, moments of uncertainty. I am glad.)

I don't know why I am writing you these things, except that I have been so lonely, so terribly lonely, since Fly died. Gubaru doesn't know what to make of it. After all, has he too not accompanied me on many of my romps, for much longer than Fly ever did? But I will not scratch Gubaru's beard or let him smell my face – and those intimacies matter. They were intimacies I have only ever shared with a dog and – if in a somewhat different way – with children and with you. Have you ever wondered why we can reveal ourselves, let ourselves touch and be touched, only in these particular ways, with these particular beings and no other? Certainly I love Gubaru; certainly he is as true a friend as I have ever had. But what I could do with Fly, the ways I could be and reveal myself to Fly, I can never do with Gubaru.

This will sound strange, Niṭil-Kišar. but I sometimes wonder about the ways women and animals are alike. Both have been disparaged. In some way men are aggrandized on the backs of both – of women and of other animals. Women they use as mirrors; other animals they use as opponents, to vanquish, break and destroy. (Is this really so different from a kind of mirroring?) Maybe the male hatred of animals is related to their anger – is it hatred? – of women. Because this beast knows better than any man what else I truly am. He can smell it. I have to destroy him, the man thinks, because otherwise no one will believe in me, least of all the one I destroy, least of all I the destroyer.

(I write this, but who has destroyed more than me? Well, I suppose, many a king has – but besides that, no ordinary man. Cities lie in ruins because of me. Was I trying to prove something with each of these destructions? Was I, through them, trying to muster the strength to take just one step into the day?)

Oh, Niṭil-Kišar, I miss you, I am lost, I do not know what or why I am writing.

He was lounging on a couch, but he put the tablet down when Gubaru entered. "Are you still writing?" he asked. Nabû-na'id gave a single, terse nod. He did not say "Affairs of state," as if to imply his writing were the business of a king. Gubaru would likely know better. Nor did he say, "I am writing to the love of my life, who chose not to come with me." Gubaru's eyes might express no surprise and yet still ask a question of him. So he simply did not say anything at all.

"The priests are beside themselves," Gubaru began, with a sigh.

"Better priests would wonder at that possibility," Nabû-na'id observed.

"What possibility?"

"The possibility of being beside themselves."

Gubaru looked at him quizzically, then regrouped and continued. "The *rēḫātu* has been piling up, day after day, in the corner of the temple. No one touches it."

"That is not true," Nabû-na'id said. "Flies swarm about it. Maggots writhe on its surface. If gods are flies, if they are maggots, then they are well-pleased."

"Priests do not think gods are flies or maggots. I also do not think that," Gubaru answered stiffly.

"But why, Gubaru?" Nabû-na'id asked earnestly, almost eagerly. "Are not flies wondrous? Who in his wildest dreams could imagine a fly, and yet here they are. They take to the air, which you and I cannot do; not only that, but to do so they transform themselves from worms. And they eat the consecrated meat. Were you or any man other than me to do that, the priests believe you would die; perhaps, to assure themselves of that fact, they would kill you. But the flies eat the meat and are no worse for it. Maybe they are even happy. Maybe they become holy."

"I am supposed to say – flies do not get to be happy, that there is no happiness for flies. Even less so can flies be holy. That's what I'm supposed to say. And we could fall into one of our conversations of old, just as when we were boys. But, Nabû-na'id, though you are my friend as well as my king, though I cherish my memory of our shared childhood, I will not say what I am supposed to say. Instead, let me tell you – let me *warn* you – the priests are beside themselves. You can push them only so far."

"Or what?" Nabû-na'id asked. "I mean that genuinely, Gubaru. Or what?"

"I don't know. But surely you realize that you are challenging not just the foundations of their beliefs, but the very role they play in the world, the authority they have, their sense of importance and meaning. Men will endure that kind of challenge only so long."

Nabû-na'id narrowed his eyes. "Does it bother you, friend, that they are more upset to see their roles challenged than the foundations on which they stand? Does that not strike you as the greatest damnation of all, far beyond any pedantic sacrilege I may happen to commit?"

Gubaru said nothing.

"From my experience of men," Nabû-na'id continued, "they can endure, probably without limit, challenges to what they claim to believe. Because, at bottom, none of us believes what we claim to believe. What we claim to believe is simply what we want to believe or are trying to believe, or, in less interesting cases, what it is convenient for us to pretend to believe. But to want a belief or to try to believe is also to admit that the belief is not yours, that you do not believe. At least not yet. But the trickier thing is whatever it is that men do, in fact, believe – what they believe *without knowing it.* The priests aren't upset because of a seeming sacrilege, the piling up of the *rēḫātu*. Most of them know that the statues' lips never part, that the *rēḫātu* never disappears into the statue. They are perhaps more upset because of the flies, but that is because flies, however weak they are, still cannot be controlled by men. Flies are so weak, and yet we have no power over them! Kill as many as we like and yet still there they are, as many as ever! What does that say of men? But even more than the flies, they are upset because of me. Because, in contrast to the flies, over me they have or are supposed to have power. And yet here they are, swatting at me with the same ineffectualness as at the flies.

"So, Gubaru, what do these men believe? Do you see the question? Do you see that, whatever it is, it can't be what they say it is? Some of their anger at me is not because I contradict their belief. It's because I expose their non-belief. They are angry at me because my actions force them to confront, if nothing else, what they don't believe... and then, somewhere on the tail end of that confrontation, the slippier thing is at best just a suspicion: that what they believed in was never what they said but what they did, the role they played, the complicity each had in the roles everyone else played. They believed in a game – but you're never allowed to admit it, maybe it's not even possible to think it."

Gubaru grimaced, then stroked his beard. "Everything you say may be true. How would I know? I do not understand what men believe versus what they believe they believe. It is too hard for me. But Nabû-na'id, what on earth makes you think it matters? What makes you think it's relevant? The priests may every one of them be liars and scoundrels, and still their anger has consequences. It may grow atop an illusion, and still there it is, real anger. You talk about them role-playing, game-playing. But what role are you playing, what game are you playing? I know better than to ask you what you believe... but whatever it is may not be that different from what these men believe, the ones who resent seeing the *rēḫātu* become a nursery of flies."

Nabû-na'id laughed. "Of maggots, my friend, not flies. They're not even flies." He paused, wringing his hands with growing agitation even though he had just laughed. "Gubaru, I don't know what to say. Ever since we were children, our conversations have always left me realizing how much more honest a man you are, how much better a man you are, than I am. And yet I am king, people look to me to decide what to do with the *rēḫātu*, even though I neither know nor, increasingly, care."

He paused. "I haven't really told you this, Gubaru. But maybe you will understand. I can't stand the sight of the *rēḫātu*. Every time it makes me think of my mother. Flies undoubtedly nibbled her; maggots undoubtedly broke through her skin to see the light of day. They may even now be doing so. And if anyone has ever been holy, if anyone has ever been consecrated to a god! I look at the *rēḫātu* and I don't just feel horror; I feel futility, like my mother wasted her life in pursuit of not just an illusion but a lie – and she bequeathed that to me. How do I say yes to that? How do I say no? And so I say neither, I defer, I tell the men in Ḫarrānu to keep digging, forever and ever, while the only thing I know with certainty – because I *feel* it – is that I cannot stand the *rēḫātu*, not the sight, not the smell, not the idea. And the more the priests pester me, the angrier I feel. Damn them! Because my mother is dead, and Fly is dead, and the animal who was sacrificed is dead – and somehow I am supposed to make it all mean. But I don't know how; I feel the absence of meaning; I lack the strength and the courage and the conviction. I think it doesn't mean – or less than that: it doesn't even not mean. Not even that."

Gubaru said nothing.

"You know what else?" Nabû-na'id's voice was harsh but also strangely plaintive. "I regret, I deeply regret – it hurts me! – that I named Fly 'Fly.'"

"Gather the statues round," he said. "Make a half-circle, like a half-moon. In the middle let there by an altar, made of fragrant wood, wood from the cedar forest. Let the priests know that it was for this and only for this that the wood was brought here from a far distant land. Let them know that men and pack animals died bringing the wood here, for this sole purpose. Let them know that at every half-moon, when in the sky we see an image of our own ceremony, on that night, near when the moon sets, whether in the early evening or late night, we shall pile all the accumulated *rēḫātu* atop the altar; and under the half-sleeping, half-waking moon, beneath the cold, changeless stars, we will set everything ablaze, the fragrant wood, the rancid meat, the maggots, and what flies venture near. The statues – they are not gods, God has no statue – will bask in the warmth and in the savory smell. And you will be there, you will stand watch, you will endure. Tell them that this is what you have decided, and if they do not like it, tell them that this is not a ceremony which you invented but rather one which you found, from far-off days, from a time when God walked with men and there was no need for statues. A time before there were flies."

"Am I dreaming?"

"Does it matter if you are?"

Nabû-na'id thought for a moment, but whatever he thought he kept to himself. "I don't know if it does or not," he finally answered. "I know that if this is a dream, then when I wake up I will feel your loss more, even if I will also be so glad to have seen you."

"Maybe those two things, the sense of loss and the sense of joy, have really always gone together, even if somehow we have mostly not noticed. The Eḫulḫul, hole that it may be for now, is also, as you know, the house of joy in the ancient language of Šumeru."

"Maybe."

A long silence settled between them, neither quite comfortable nor quite uncomfortable. Eventually it was Nabû-na'id who broke it. "It has been a long time since I have heard from you, even longer since I have seen you. Your last letters made me think you were coming here, but you have never arrived."

"Haven't I?"

Nabû-na'id ignored the question. After a moment he said, "I sent a messenger after you. But I have not heard from him either."

The other one chuckled. "I believe he may be under the impression that I am on my way to Ḫarrānu, and so he awaits me there."

"Was that where you were headed?"

"Perhaps, in the end, I didn't know where I was headed, or at least where my end was. The end always comes as a surprise. But, if I was headed to Ḫarrānu, it was not an unworthy destination. In distant days, it was a place of mourning, a place of remembrance. Let me tell you the story: there was a man, one of my forebears. He had three sons. One he loved above all the rest; one he did not love; and then there was the third. The one he loved above all the rest begot three children, two daughters and a son. How he did so, with whom, no one knows. No wife is mentioned. And almost as suddenly as there was a son, the child's father died. The name of the man who died, the son whom the father loved above all, was Ḫarrān. That left the father my ancestor two sons, two granddaughters and a grandson. In order that Ḫarrān share in life, though dead, the father married the son he did not love to one of Ḫarrān's daughters, and the other son to the other daughter. The son whom he did not love begat children with his wife; but the third son's wife was barren. And so Ḫarrān's line persisted only through the line of the unloved son and in the grandson who was but a small boy still.

The old man found this unbearable, that his loved son's existence should depend on his unloved son's. And though the unloved son worked the land with his wife and children and always treated his father and his brother with kindness, still this in no way attenuated the father's grief but exacerbated it. At some point it passed enduring, and the father collected his third son and Ḫarrān's barren daughter and Ḫarrān's son, and together they left Uru, their city, heading west and north. Legend has it that they paid so little attention to the unloved brother that they never told him that they were leaving and that, after they had moved away, they forgot him. But I do not believe that part of the story."

"What guided their travels I cannot say, even if I know. But after some time, the father called an end to them. 'We will settle here,' he said. And the place they settled he called Ḫarrānu, in honor of the son whom he loved, the son who died. That word also came to mean "journey," and so it is both the place where you stop and the going there. Or the going there is the place where you stop, or you have always stopped and gone nowhere. It is where you are digging an endless hole to find the foundation of the house of joy."

Nabû-na'id smiled, a laugh almost escaped his lips. "It sounds like mourning," he said. "Joy's foundation is sorrow obscured. It sounds as well like the journey which you may never end and perhaps have never started."

"Maybe it sounds as well like your journey."

"What do you mean?"

"Why are you here in the desert? Why are you digging a perpetual hole in Ḫarrānu? Why are you not with your wife, your daughter, your son? Why did you not attend the funeral of your mother? What are you doing here, my friend, and when will you leave?"

"Perhaps I am like that father you mention, mourning the

son whom I loved, the son who is lost to me."

"What son would that be?"

A dark cloud raced so quickly across Nabû-na'id's face that no one who saw it could have been sure it had been there. And it was unclear if there was anyone to see it. His jaw clenched, he made no effort to answer.

"Is it the son that you are?" the other one asked.

"Clearly it is not the son that I am. Maybe it is the son I am no longer. Or maybe I never was that son. Are you sure, old man, that this father had three sons? Maybe he had two: one whom he did not love, and then the other. Maybe in his heart he invented the third son, to assuage his grief for not loving the other. Maybe that whole journey, maybe that city which he founded and which was so dear to my mother, maybe they are memorials not to what was but to what never was."

"And if that is the case?"

Nabû-na'id didn't answer.

"And if that is the case," the other continued, "is there any desert in all the wide world which can hide you from it?"

Still Nabû-na'id did not answer. Silence again settled between them.

In his mind, Nabû-na'id was thinking: I have heard versions of this story of yours. You have told them to me before. But you have always emphasized that third son, the one with the barren wife. He did not stay in Ḫarrānu for long. His journey did not end there. He left – you always used to tell me – because his god commanded him to. ("Not his god. The god, the only god," the voice of his old friend interrupted. "My god. Your god.") (Nabû-na'id ignored the interrupting voice.) What was it, he continued to think, that drove that ancient man on? Didn't he also struggle into a desert, periodically digging wells, not knowing for what he searched, just like me? (But I have dug no wells, he admitted.) Could he not endure living in a city memorializing his dead brother? (Did he love that brother like his father loved that son? What if he did not?) Could he not endure living in a city memorializing a brother who never was? Did he regret leaving behind the other brother? Did he strike out into the desert in order to suffer, to be punished, for one or the other of the brothers whom he lost?

("He struck out into the desert," the voice interrupted, "because God commanded him to.")

("How easy it is for you to say that!" Nabû-na'id objected.)

("No, it is not easy for me to say it. It has never been easy for me to say it.")

"Are you sure?" Nabû-na'id said aloud.

But there was no one there.

He closed his eyes.

"When will you leave the desert, old friend?"

(But he knew the voice wasn't there.)

"What are you waiting for?"

(Still he did not believe in the voice.)

"Why have you come?"

(He refused to answer a voice which was not there.)

Gubaru shook him. "Nabû-na'id!" he said for a third time. Nabû-na'id opened his eyes. "What are you doing?" Gubaru asked. Nabû-na'id did not reply. "Have you been sleeping?" Nabû-na'id could not say. He did not know.

He was now dreaming, he was sure of it. A man approached, one who was almost recognizable and yet whom he did not recognize. "Do I know you?" Nabû-na'id asked. The man didn't answer. "What shall I call you?"

The man's eyes shined. "Call me Daniel," he suggested.

"Is that your name?"

"It will do."

"All right," Nabû-na'id said with a sigh. "I will call you Daniel. But that name doesn't sound quite right to me. I don't know why."

The man with the shining eyes laughed. "Can any name really sound right? Whose name is there which can truly be sounded? Might it not be that every name is like God's name, unpronounceable, even secret?"

"I mean something simpler than that," Nabû-na'id replied. "Your name feels wrong. But not every name would."

"Very well," the other man said.

"Can you give an account of why you are here?" the man whom Nabû-na'id reluctantly called Daniel abruptly asked.

"You mean here in this dream? Or here in Teima? Or here in the desert? Or here in the world? What do you mean?"

"Yes," the other man answered.

Nabû-na'id rolled his eyes. "This is tiresome," he muttered.

The man whom Nabû-na'id called Daniel rolled his eyes in response. "Surely you realize that everyone in Bābilim asks that question; that someday there will be men who study the past who will ask that question; perhaps even God's chosen ask that question. Shouldn't you be asking that question too?"

"Why I am here?"

"Yes."

"But which here?"

"All of them."

"Maybe I am losing my mind," Nabû-na'id suggested, speaking through clenched teeth.

"If you are, how will you regain it?"

Nabû-na'id didn't answer.

"More importantly, how will you return, how will you reclaim the life you left behind?"

"I have wondered that too," he said softly. "How do I return to my wife and my daughter? How do I return to a city whose streets are not haunted by my mother?" (Are you sure they are not?) "How do I return when I myself cannot haunt the streets with my dog?" (Maybe you and Fly can only haunt them.) He stopped, then resumed. "To what am I returning? Where have I been? Why?" He looked levelly at the other man. "Do you think these questions are not familiar to me? I somehow exiled myself to the desert. I never knew why. Now the time is coming to unexile myself, and I still don't know why. I'm also not sure how."

* * * * *

A tablet lost in the sand, somewhere between Bābilim and Teima:

To Nabû-na'id, my friend and yes, my love, thus Niṭil-Kišar.

Your letters wind their paths to me – I do not know how long they take, what sights they pass, what conversations they overhear, or how many straggle disoriented into the desert to join bleached bones of forgotten wanderers and of lost messengers. How many of your letters gave up the ghost en route? And can those disembodied ghosts be tracked, can they themselves follow a track, do they dare make a track of their own? Is there even now a chorus of ghosts who, against all odds, made it this far and now wave their hands and strain their voices, hopping up and down, trying – so far futilely – to snatch my attention? They waste their time so long as my attention is on writing you.

Nabû-na'id, my friend, you do not know and have never known the strength of tears. You underestimate the power that the smallest trickle of water has as it wends across the hardest stone. Perhaps it is its own form of writing, and perhaps all of my mysterious waterworks, so befuddling to our son and to you and maybe to all the world, is the best I can do to write my own note, bequeathing it to no messenger but leaving it carved into the very face of the earth. Who will read it? Perhaps no one. There are so few who read lined faces, whether of the earth or our own; so few who see the cracks which mark the quarries of our grief and joy. Do you not know that long ago, after a sudden rainstorm, a mere thread of water stumbled downward from the mountains and obstinately persisted to the sea, resolute in its purpose like a chain of ants – and as easily overlooked. Not only you but a child could overleap that thread of water; it was too small even for a single fish; over and over again, a few pebbles became almost insurmountable obstacles – almost, but never quite. Over and over again, unrelenting, the trickle strained forward. And that thread grew over time, became a modest brook, then a creek, and now what is it but the mighty Purattu? That is the strength of tears – or it can be.

Of course, a time will come when the Purattu re-becomes a creek, then a brook, finally a mere thread of water, and then not even that. It is like a god who enters a cella through a mere crack – expands into the fullness of the room – only to leave again by way of another, mere crack. Our lives ebb and flow with these streams of tears. Our sorrows bring us the wonder of rivers that reflect the sky and house the fish and blanket the pebbles which, for all we know, dance only when submerged and hidden from the gaze of heaven. If we divert a river and bury a king – or a dog – in its bed, and if we fail to see even a single dancing pebble, still we can say nothing about whether pebbles dance, or when, or why.

You, perhaps, will think: Niṭil-Kišar is doing what women do, using her witchcraft to make me equal to the day. But I am not. You are not equal to the day. You never have been. But to say so is no belittling witchcraft either. I have loved you always knowing that the day would overcome you. What then? What becomes of a man mastered by a day?

Perhaps it is only then that he can see. Come home, Nabû-na'id. Come home to me, to your daughter, to your son. Let your tears strengthen the Purattu. You have done enough in the desert, even if you have done nothing at all; whatever trickle has escaped you there – perhaps that *will come to something. But the better hope is to join your tears with mine and with our children's and our city's and our ancestors' and our descendants', from time immemorial to time immemorial, but never for forever. Waterworks have always been the work of women. We do not insist that our tears take their solitary way.*

Come home. I am waiting for you. I have always been waiting for you. I will wait for you. But come home. Come. Just come.

* * * * *

Years passed.

* * * * *

Nabû-na'id had started something new. He sat on the ground, in the dirt, and he wrote – but they were not letters to loved ones nor commands to underlings. He simply wrote what came to mind, what gave expression to his silent, secret struggles. He generally wrote in wax – wax which he would spend an afternoon carving, then melt at night. Always fresh boards awaited him in the morning, as if the travails of the prior days had all been a dream. Perhaps that illusion was not the least of the attractions of these writing projects of his, projects which his officials took to be a sign of debility. But they were Nabû-na'id's attempts to save himself.

Here I stand, oasis-perched overseer of a desert which stretches in all directions around me. Don't be fooled by the date palms; the truth of this place is its rock salt. I have built palaces here and walls; I have taken a small town and turned it into a city worthy of a king. But the truth of the place is its rock salt, even while the date palms sway in the breeze, even while the trickles of water can be heard in the oasis and its canals, even while a king's court buzzes about self-importantly. And who more self-important than I? I am king, overseer of a desert which stretches in all directions around me. This is MY domain, index of MY power: a world where life endures but does not thrive, where creation has wilted into mere survival. But the palaces say otherwise, the courtiers say otherwise. The swaying date palms also lie. The oasis is a lie. My truth, the truth of this place, is the rock salt.

I needn't be here, of course. I could return to Bābilim. There too I am king, or else my son is, or we are. But nominally anyway it is my domain, which stretches from vibrant, throbbing Bābilim all the way to this land of useless striving, where the whole tally of life is simply not to have died. Sheer obstinacy as the measure of life. One lives long, but for what? I am an old man; my mother, who died not long ago, was 104 or 106 or some such – not even she remembered. The goal of her life was to see Sîn return to Ḫarrānu. In one way she did, and in another way she did not. Would she be satisfied with so ambiguous an outcome? Was her life fulfilled if its fulfillment was ambiguity itself? Does it matter anymore? She died, and a kingdom was ordered into grief – if grief can be ordered. But my own grief was and is for my dog Fly. Were I to undertake a heroic journey like Gilgameš's, it would not be to discover eternal life for myself, or even for my mother. It would be in the hope of that dog romping again. I would rather leave him with the loneliness of MY loss, MY absence, MY death – a loss, an absence, a death which I have earned, an erasure which I deserve. No one was so special as to survive me; nor will I be so special. Let death cut me down to size, which is to say to the nothing that my heart acknowledges as its own. But you, Fly – your heart was always greater than mine, your life was worthy of life, but mine is worthy only of death. Or is that the last form my hope takes, that death at least can be earned?

I found inscriptions here, words and names which endure when nothing else does. There was a king of Muṣur, no doubt mighty, who stood his stela here, perhaps more than half a millennium ago. He is gone. I am his kingly heir, but there will be heirs to me as well – heirs as unforeseen as I was to him. But the final heir is already here – not the swaying date palms, but the rock salt. It is the tomb of lost water, the tomb that life left when, not thriving, long ago having ceased from creating, its striving to endure stopped enduring. My inscription left for the ages will be that salt, testimony to the dried-up promise of water and of life. My inscription, then, will be my heir; my text will be its reader.

I know that I shall never leave Teima, though even now I ready my return to Bābilim. I may succeed; my ancient capital, my people, my wife, my children – all may receive me, as they receive the dates and salts we send from here. Will they recognize me as a spice, as an exotic food, as a mineral, perhaps as a fragrance? Or will they think they embrace the man who left? It was never clear to me why I came here; why I, the king of Bābilim, exiled myself to the desert in Arabi. Certainly not for reasons of geopolitical strategy, whatever my court believes. Perhaps not even because of the Moon God who is also a statue, Ṣalmu, Ṣalm, Sîn, salve. Psalm. Something within me cries out, but sounds, not words; I hear only wailing, and I don't know why or to whom. To a god? To a statue? To a lost dog? To my mother, larger than life and gone from it? Or is the wailing an echo of the suffering I have inflicted, gashing through me like steam screaming through a pinprick, like the wind's high-pitched squeal through a tear which very soon will rend the sail? Is the sail rent by the wind or the screech? I would like to call this agony of my heart a psalm, a word my old, lost friend Belet-seri-dannat taught me, but I can't begin to imagine how to transmute a shriek into a song.

Would my return to Bābilim be that transformation? One last gasping grasp for hope, for deliverance, for pardon? I would like to look in my wife's eyes and see her love for me, scarred and deformed though I am; but I am also afraid to look in her eyes and see – something else. To look into her eyes and see this desert once more. To look into her eyes and see my own reflection. To look into her eyes and know that even she, who is far greater than I, far braver, far stronger, cannot love me. And what of my daughter? She is very like her mother and very like me; she has my torments but her mother's life, her mother's aliveness. Will she see me and see a father? Will she see me and see kin, something kindred, possibly even something kind?

I know how her brother will see me – as king. Perhaps even as threat. Why, he must wonder, can't that doddering fool stay forever in the desert, or better, dodder off to death? Kingship is for the strong, for those whose heart is iron and whose eyes can never be blighted. For him, in other words; and I have robbed him of kingship once already. My return means twice. That will not be lost on him, though much else will be. Should I leave him to deal with Anšan, with Kuraš, strong in arm, spirit of the coming age? The outcome is not in doubt, though he doubts it. If I leave him to Kuraš, my son may dodder to death before me. But, like me, he will deserve it.

So what am I hurrying from the desert for? Can I, the great king of Bābilim, truly escape the desert of my own devising? Can I go home? Can I return to a land where once as a boy I played, where friendship opened before me, where thought was still hopeful and feeling throbbed in my heart? Where I was as yet still trickling water and not yet more crystal than liquid?

I remember the days… I remember the days. Gubaru and I would climb a nearby tell, the highest point around, and survey a land that I at least never dreamed would bow to me. We were alike exiles; I, a refugee from Ḫarrānu, full of the tales my mother had told me from that land and people, though I had never known either; and he, like Kuraš, from Anšan. What was that boy doing in Bābilim? I suppose the question could have been asked of either of us. The city then, perhaps as it always has been, was full of foreign peoples. Everywhere one went, one heard exotic languages and saw exotic practices: people invoking native gods with accented tongues, people wearing the costumes of lands they had never seen, people longing for a return to where they had never been. Perhaps those people hummed along on the stories their mothers told them just as I did. Perhaps the customs, the clothes, the gods, even the words which they took to be peculiarly their own had long ago become a species of make-believe, a hybrid of an imagined origin and the actual world they had known, moreover without any of them even beginning to suspect it. Perhaps as I turn my eyes back toward Bābilim, it is under the sway of a similar illusion. It may be best that way for all of us – to long for an origin we don't know and can never reach, to embroider it in our minds and hearts as the home we've never visited. It gives direction to our lives, better than memory because memory can submerge us, memory can drown us, memory can sometimes even be true.

We would climb the tell, Gubaru and I, and look down on the barley as wind rippled through it, look down on the women sitting cross-legged in the dirt grinding grain or else rounding up children, look down on the men driving oxen or donkeys through the fields. Beyond that was the clutter of houses that grew into the city, with its worn paths full of mud-brick debris and the persistent clamor of activity and purpose. Between the fields and the gradual eruption of houses, canals crisscrossed the land, and where they met, children, dogs and pigs would often all splash about, delighting in the relief from the heat, somehow all of the same mind despite their differences in size and shape and custom. I used to marvel at those scenes when I was a boy, watching the children, the dogs and the pigs be all of the same mind. Why cannot that be more often the case? What is it that forbids us from always converging at the water hole, to frolic and delight, to drink and cool? Here I am now at an oasis in the desert, but even I who am king do not dare to splash about in the canals alongside dogs and pigs. Or children. I doubt any of my courtiers even imagines the possibility, for me or themselves. But Fly imagined it; with Fly it was still imaginable, for both of us. Fly did it, and sometimes I did it with him.

I am trying to recede into memory, to sink like a fish in a pond.

I am trying to call back to mind those days when Gubaru and I stood atop the tell and surveyed the knowable world. But no sooner do I start down those paths of memory than I interrupt myself, interposing my present grief on what I would remember. I see in my mind's eye those children, dogs and pigs playing beside the canal – even their clamor would sometimes reach our ears – but I can't help but merge those memories with my memories of Fly. Memories won't stand apart; they flow together like streams and make a sea of themselves, currents braiding this way and that, their places of combination sometimes calm and sometimes turbulent. Maybe the still memories are only in the deepest, coldest waters, but if they are, you have to go through the waves and the froth and the fury of the surface to get to them. And you have to hold your breath, perhaps saving none for the return – pushing deeper with all your strength, as if you wouldn't need some strength and some air to bob back to the surface. We belong to the surface, and yet I want those still memories in the depths where my present sorrows can't merge with what I once beheld, once thought, once felt. Where there is some calm – or so I remember it.

The pigs liked the mud more than the water; perhaps it's not true that pigs, dogs and children were of the same mind. The children were also sometimes very cruel to the dogs and the pigs. And the dogs and the pigs were wary around one another – the cruelties of the children concerned them less than their own possible misunderstandings. The frolicking beside the canals was often more complicated than I've been letting on, more fraught, sometimes even dangerous. But from a distance those tensions weren't always apparent. From a distance – a geographical distance when we were atop the tell, a temporal distance now as I remember or make believe – it's easier to believe in something hopeful. But it works both ways – distances can also obscure hopes. The brief and gentle smile, the kind word, the friendly, playful charge can all be lost or misconstrued from a distance. The dog nips a child and we think it's an attack when it's only a tease. Or what looks like a tease is actually an attack. I'm not sure how good we are at making these distinctions, however far or near in place or time we happen to be.

But let me go back to when Gubaru and I would stand atop the tell, surveying the world beneath; or sit in the dirt, telling stories; or sometimes chase one another, running and then tumbling down the hillside. Those days did indeed exist, even if what I remember is something different; and if I am to return to Bābilim, it seems I must first re-climb that tell – or else dive deeply, dive as deep as I can go, use up all my breath and see if thereby I can gain the stillness.

I have never received one – a letter from a god. Nor have I written a god. But I am aware that such letters exist. Aššur-aḫa-iddina wrote to a god after his father's murder, demanding justice be brought to his patricidal brothers. To some extent it was – the two brothers ended up throneless exiles – though whether the letter had anything to do with that is another matter. I suppose it's not very surprising for a man, even a king, to write a god. There's much that we want from gods. Why one would write a letter rather than pray is the more interesting question. Perhaps in acknowledgment of the obvious absence of the god? After all, Aššur-aḫa-iddina's father had been killed. Where was the god when that happened, when his brothers rose up against their father? Perhaps his father even cried out, but no god answered him, at least in time to save him. Would it have been better had Sîn-aḫḫē-erība written instead? But his son-murderers probably would not have permitted him tablet and stylus, much less a scribe – and then, to which god would he write? How long would they wait for the god to reach his judgment? What would they do while they waited? The names of these men, these kings, even suggests that the gods' penchant for irony would make reliance on their words foolhardy. "Aššur gave me brothers" – whom I had to battle in civil war after two of them killed our father. Quite the gift from Aššur. "Sîn replaced the brothers" – which led those brothers to conspire against and murder the one so named. It is with trepidation that I would dare interpret the word, spoken or written, of a god.

But if kings write gods in acknowledgment of their absence, why do gods write kings? As I noted, such letters do exist. The letters of gods even are sealed with the seal of a god – a cylinder seal which, perhaps, the god wears around his neck or wrist much as we do. Perhaps that question interests me more even than why gods write kings. Why do gods have cylinder seals with which to sign the letters they send? Are the gods not literate? Can they not write their own names? Or is this perhaps the origin of writing, right here before our eyes? An image chosen by the god to represent him. One day it occurs to a man to pronounce the image according to the name of the god. Over time the image simplifies, loses some of its pictorial character – and then one day we see not the seal of the god in lieu of a signature, but the seal of the god as a signature. Meaning arrives: that is his name, not the cylinder he rolled over clay because even he, a god, didn't know any other means to write his name. In the same moment, the absent god becomes present and the fact that he only wrote a letter, though we cried out to him, becomes inexplicable. But at least we have an excuse to overlook that the god's last act was to seal his message shut.

How do I leave the desert?
You just go.
I don't need a reason?
No.
Nothing builds up to it? I just get up and leave?
Just as you got up and arrived.

In the summer we travel at night. I like the strangeness of it all – the flickering light of the torches, the unusual sounds of commotion when usually the world is still, the unfamiliar forms which everything takes in darkness. I like travelling under the stars rather than the sun. It is surprisingly cold, given how hot the days are – and I like that coldness too, because it makes me feel alive and because then the torches don't just illuminate our way. They warm us. I like seeing the sparks fly this way and that, almost like insects drawn to the flame, though the sparks are drawn from it. The emotional feeling of the march is different, too, at night compared to the day. People are more on edge. The animals, too. The dogs usually don't run off, like they do during the day. They stick with the crowd. Everyone sticks with the crowd. After all, you can't really see what you're going towards, or what may be waiting for you. In that way travel at night is more like our lives; it's the daytime which is really illusory. And then the god watching us, Sîn, is sometimes there, sometimes not; sometimes waxing, sometimes waning. We all know how small we are under the distracted gaze of the Moon, but under the Sun we think we're more significant than we are. And moonlight is cooler than sunlight, almost tender in the way it watches you and in the way it doesn't. When the Sun abandons us, we feel the terror; but when the Moon does, we know it's because nothing merits much attention, nothing is great, and everything is small. Even terror. The Moon has seen it all, and prefers sometimes to look elsewhere, at other small things.

There was a time when I felt the excitement and intimacy of night travel, but now I am so much more alone – even though hordes always travel with me now. Once it was me and Gubaru and Niṭil-Kišar; we were on our way to Ṣurru, full of hope and trepidation. I remember how much comfort I took to see the shadows dance across Niṭil-Kišar's face, as the nearby flame flickered; how glad I was that she was there. She gave me courage, to attempt what we were attempting; and she made me laugh and wonder how I could be so lucky. And Gubaru – he is always steady. In the day or in the night, he will put one foot before the other and not think much of it. He trusts. I've never really understood what he trusts, but I understand that he trusts. And now I am thinking of later years, when Fly would dance around my feet on these night marches, his joyful prancing somehow kin to those shadows that once played on Niṭil-Kišar's face. Such lively creatures, Fly and Niṭil-Kišar. And Gubaru, too. But not me. I am not really alive.

But there's the paradox. I am probably closer to the human norm than Niṭil-Kišar or Gubaru. (Dogs are another matter.) Most of us human beings make it from one day to the next by not being alive. When actual death overtakes us, the only change is that we no longer lie to ourselves that we could choose something different. Niṭil-Kišar and Gubaru, on the other hand, found the strength for something else. I wonder if they know it, or if they too think of themselves as secretly dead. I doubt it. It wouldn't occur to Gubaru, and Niṭil-Kišar, probably correctly, would consider it only a mad form of megalomania, a self-aggrandizement disguised as disparagement.

At night, before the march gets on its way, you hear crickets, and you can see the moths swoop towards the torch flames. Sounds echo more at night – clearing of throats, belches, noses being blown, the clatter of armor being put on or pulled off, the snorting and stamping of horses. Those noises happen all the time, but at night you hear them more. It's because the world becomes smaller at night, just as the light of the torches makes the night darker. The periphery is marked more clearly, and its closeness can't be denied. This is our world – as far as the light gleams. Sometimes the Moon shines for us, almost like a prophecy, showing us a bit more of the future and of the past than our torches manage on their own. But sometimes the Moon leaves us to our own devices, to our ball of light with its surrounding wall of blackness – a wall that the light plays a role in making. Our world is the blackness, too, but it's impossible to say how big that blackness is, how far it extends, whether it's the thin shell of our illuminated world or if our illuminated world is a tiny oasis in a cold, vast, perhaps endless, blackness.

I wonder what to make of flowers at night. The bees don't visit them – it is probably too cold for the bees. But perhaps the bees also need the color of the flowers to recognize them. Maybe, though, flowers don't have color at night; maybe it is only the flame or the Sun which gives them color. Sometimes the night air is thick with the scent of flowers, much more so than in the day, even though at night, at least past the boundary of the torch-illumined world, they retreat into a kind of bland colorlessness. It would probably surprise my court as well as my enemies that I, the king of Bābilim, famed for my merciless cruelty, ruminate about the colors of flowers at night, about what flowers are at night versus in the day, about whether something so simple as a flower stays one thing all the time or is secretly many things from one moment to the next. Maybe the bees don't visit the flower at night because the bees, too, are different then. And maybe I am different at night than during the day. Of course there are those moments in one's life when day and night become one; maybe what we reveal of ourselves then is our truest form.

Or maybe those moments are moments of aberration when it is too much to demand that a being be himself. The Moon and the Sun struggle in the sky, night is cast into day, and we men quail and tremble. The decisions we make then should not shape our lives. It is too much to ask. We are creatures of the day, or of the night – but we can't be both, not at once. Have some compassion, then, and permit those crises in our lives to be aberrant rather than revelatory of our secret truths.

But am I only comforting myself into something like forgiveness? Are these the honeyed words of a man desperate for pardon? When Niṭil-Kišar, Gubaru and I set off for Ṣurru, I remember feeling like I could earn my pardon, like my actions to come could somehow compensate for, or even erase, my past deeds. I was full of hope! The actions or inactions which I took long ago on a day which was also a night had set into motion so many extraordinary things – not least, my marriage, my falling in love. Not least the daughter who was born to us. Set into motion as well was my political career, which has culminated in kingship, even if I carry that kingship off into the desert. I never thought that I was being rewarded for what I did – or for what I didn't do – but I did have some hope in my heart that good might yet come of my life, that pardon might take this form.

It seems so different now. I accept that there is no compensation.

That doesn't mean there isn't erasure, however. It may be that I have come to long for erasure because I have ceased to have the courage to long for pardon, all the more when I know, when I accept, that pardon can't be earned. May the time come, then, when all this is erased, when all that has happened is indistinguishable from never having happened at all? Forgiveness – is too much. Too impossible. But forgetting is possible, and a forgetting that forgets the forgetting, and a forgetting that forgets the forgetting's forgetting... An erasure so complete that what ceases to exist ceases to have existed. I almost long for this, but I cannot bear the thought of Niṭ and En-nigaldi and Fly not having existed. It is only a comfort to imagine that I, someday, will have not existed – that I will disappear into a night never bounded by a day. A night which suffocates light and sound and smell, where no torch or star or Moon brings color to a flower. But let there be light elsewhere, flowers with their bees to adorn my loves, my wife, my daughter, my dog. Gubaru too. Let there be light for them and darkness and erasure for me – that is the deal I want to strike, which I guess I will call forgiveness, the paltry forgiveness, its dregs, left to me to earn.

There's a wildness in her eyes which I sometimes hear in her voice and see in her movements. I don't know that I can describe what I see, maybe because I feel it more than I see it. Something barely contained, in fact not contained but overflowing, eyes sparkling and the sparkles pouring out beyond the eyes; laughter in the voice and pouring out beyond the voice; a dance and sway in the step that could never be found in any step or sway of a dance. Eyes, voice and body all somehow laugh, a turbulent rill full of life, full of her. There was a time, early in our courtship, when she loved me wildly. She does not anymore. Something harsher, probably also truer, has entered her gaze of me. She is not without fondness for me, even now; sympathy, too; sometimes gratitude. There's judgment, too. That harshness is what sees me best. It would be easier if it were hatred, but it is not – just something stony, something all-too-clear-sighted, something cold. Harshness. It doesn't fully suppress the wildness in her eyes, voice and movements, it isn't quite strong enough to stifle the laughter which somehow all of her expresses, but it holds them back, dampens them, maybe even suffocates them a little. I would love it if she loved me wildly again, but even then I didn't really believe it, and I would believe it less now. I believe the harshness in her eyes, though. I think her eyes are harsh because she sees me more truly than she once did, more truly than I myself have ever managed. In fact, her harshness knows even that about me – that I don't really dare to see myself truly. I hear it in her voice, too. Something tired. Something which acknowledges that, though she hasn't fully given up on me, she's come close and probably should come even closer, as close as possible.

Gubaru is different. When he looks at me there's such innocence in his gaze, and somehow that innocence colors what he gazes at. Much of what I write and say and think is unintelligible to him, but it doesn't bother him and it doesn't even matter. It isn't that he still sees the boy I once was, the boy that he knew as a boy; it's that he sees with the same innocence he had then, when we were children. It's not an innocence born of inexperience or cluelessness. He has, after all, lived a soldier's life and done a soldier's deeds. Nor is he unaware of suffering, including of the suffering I cause. He has even suffered it. But somehow he can look at me with that innocence of his which is beyond judgment. You'd think innocence requires judgment but for Gubaru it does not. Some would call him simple-minded, but I know that for all my striving I will not ever understand what he understands intuitively. An understanding that he is more than has. He is simple-hearted, not simple-minded, and for all the churnings of my mind I will never manage that simplicity which is a blessing to all. Maybe that's my punishment, which he does not have to bestow or judge because I live it, while he lives something else and better.

Did I come to this desert, or rather to this oasis in the desert, to endure my memories? Were I in Bābilim, my memories would be subtly shaped by a world so often alike to them – that similarity blunts the memories, softens them. But here my daily world is so very different from the world of my memories, it provides them a kind of relief against which they stand out. I can sense them more, run my fingers against their raised edge, feel better their heat or coldness. They become like statues, here in the desert oasis, three-dimensional, something I can walk around, rather than the paintings they are in Bābilim, where you can't even see their backside. But I must return to Bābilim; I must find a way to leave these memories, which, behind my back, conspire together to swarm me, stifle me, end me. Or perhaps they are simply revolting at my attempt to make them into art when what they are is something else, something both more alive and already dead.

What have I been doing in this desert oasis? Campaigning, destroying this city or that, consolidating control over trade routes. Meanwhile my mother has died, has become the ash she bathed in; my dog has died; and my wife, my daughter and my son are all far away in Bābilim. But I stay here in Teima, unmoved, unmoving, and in my mind re-create events which happened long ago. Sometimes my long dead father sits before me; we are in Sardis; conversations that once took place take place again, or perhaps they never took place and yet take place again. Sometimes it is a young version of myself who ambles into my memory and my storytelling. Have I retreated to Teima – have I fled Bābilim – to have it out with all the past versions of myself I can gather? I see them tumbling over each other, pontificating at each other, reviling and creating each other… Why was the desert the necessary backdrop for this cage-fight?

I feel a chuckle rising to the surface, bubbling up through all this sorrow. I remember a conversation long ago with Gubaru, in which I invited him to think that there was a collection of things called Gubarus, and that it was his task to find what was common to them all. But I doubt Gubaru, who has become old like me, has felt summoned to that task. It's I who has been summoned to it, to the task of finding what is common to all the Nabû-na'ids I have been. But in my heart I am not sure that there's anything common to them all. I see at times a Nabû-na'id who is merciless and callous; at other times, a thick-headed, oblivious Nabû-na'id; here a Nabû-na'id who is idealistic, there a Nabû-na'id who is despairing. There is a kindness in that one's smile, something terrifying in that other one's grimace; and yet the smile and the grimace are very nearly the same. Maybe the only thing common to this collection of Nabû-na'ids is not internal to them but external: the name.

And yet Fly loved me; Niṭil-Kišar loved me, and perhaps still does; and it would never occur to Gubaru, my oldest friend, not to love me. What is it that they love? Do they love all the versions of me who, even now, are brawling in my mental courtyard? Do they love some essential version of me? Do they love their idea of me, which may have little to do with any of the brawling Nabû-na'ids? Sometimes I want to shake them and say – what I have become cannot and should not be loved. Bel-šar-uṣur would understand. He cannot and should not love me – and never has. Perhaps it is only a son who knows the empty truth of a father. We shared meals, he and I. The rēḫātu. *It was our task to fill the emptiness within us with the meals of gods – or with the meals of statues. Those statue-gods have nowhere to put the food, no emptiness to fill – and so it fell to us, father and son, the ones who know that their own secret, inmost commonality is this hollowness. Or perhaps it is blankness. I'm not sure I can decide. Anyway, the day came when we stopped attempting even this.*

The funny thing is, Bel-šar-uṣur may know not to love me – or simply does not love me – but he would not understand any of these musings. They would signal only inactivity to him, a pointless paralysis when renown could be won. I wonder if any renown would satisfy him – a renown, for example, which he had not earned; or a renown, whether earned or not, for cruelty; or a renown attached to some deformed and unrecognizable version of his name. What would he think if my deeds were called his, or his were called mine? Would it aggravate him, if our fate were to be each other's indissociable shadow? Would he perhaps recognize in that fate a kernel of truth, a kernel of justice?

(He would not. He is not interested in truth and his conception of justice is confined to a court.)

I've never managed to interest him in reading or writing. In that he is unlike his sister and his mother and me. Perhaps he is more like Gubaru and Fly… two beings for whom he doesn't or didn't have the time of day. He and Gubaru are enemies, and in my heart I think they are right to be enemies. At least I think Gubaru is right to be my son's enemy. But what kind of father does that make me? It's one of those ironies which entrap me: I side with Gubaru because as a father I can imagine the horror of losing a son – even worse, losing a son to violence, maybe purposeful violence. But siding with Gubaru contributes to my own loss of a son. Or maybe whatever happened that day with Kayvon took away both Gubaru's son and mine.

It is horrible for me to think so. I still have a son I can endeavor to retrieve, perhaps even rescue. Gubaru does not. How he might wish to trade places with me!

I am not sure if Fly could read or write. And as for Gubaru – I suspect that Gubaru can read some of the documents which pass before his eyes, but I doubt he would trust himself to write. But that's reading and writing in the narrow sense, the sense that doesn't apply to Fly. What applies to Fly might also apply to Gubaru, and it is actually I of the three of us who struggle with reading and writing only because I too easily fall into their narrowest senses. There may be something that Gubaru and Fly managed to read and write, almost effortlessly, that no matter how hard I strain I will never even approach. Perhaps Bel-šar-uṣur also would appreciate what I cannot – perhaps everyone does but me. Perhaps of all the beings under moon and sun I am, in this peculiar respect, the only illiterate one.

What makes us think there is a category which contains us?

Anzû asked one question over and over: what are you? No matter what anyone said, however, he pitched them off the cliff. Some of the answers may seem ridiculous to us: how can a man be a chicken or a donkey? How can a man be a hat? But I wonder if we need to hear what's ridiculous when a man answers that he is a man. How does Anzû hear that? What, after all, is Anzû? Part lion, part bird? But a lion can't exist as a part, as a fragment. Neither can a bird. And so Anzû can't be part lion, part bird. Nothing comes of parts. What is Anzû, then? The man who answered that he was Anzû – did he get something right? Or is there nothing to get right here, which is why Anzû, whatever he is, pitches everyone off the cliff?

Imagine a man came. Anzû asks his question. The man is at a loss; he does not respond. What will Anzû do? He will pitch him off the cliff.

When I think words I often can't help but spell them. Regularly I see them before I pronounce them or hear them. Somehow what a word is is all confused with the writing of a word. I'm not sure that I can go back. Rather, I am sure that I cannot go back – not by thinking, anyway. Something like that problem is what is at issue here. Whatever we are, it is what escapes words. But we can't escape words. As soon as we think we understand Anzû's question we are lost; the words have caught us, as in a trap. As soon as we think we understand the tale, we are lost, the trap is sprung. All of our understanding comes at the price of not understanding. That's how language works.

Another version of the problem: Who is it who decides from among the categories? Anzû asks his question; something reflects, goes through a list of possibilities, makes its choice. What is that something? The something chooses a chicken, a donkey, a hat or a man. Is the something itself any of those things? Eventually someone will say the something is just the thinking, but is the thinking really any different from those other categories chicken, donkey, hat or man? Whatever we are, it is what escapes words. But we can't escape words. That is what we are too.

What I remember is not the darkness, not the way that day became night in the middle of the day, but instead the coldness. The world became cold. I remember thinking about that coldness because my own act, my own decision, had seemed so cold. A war ended, many lives were undoubtedly spared, and all it took was the lives of strangers and the blindness of the Sun. At least I assume the Sun was blind, because of the darkness that we all fell into, the cold darkness. But I couldn't stare at the Sun to see.

You have to imagine that men, enemies, were grappling even then. As the light waned and the coldness settled, somehow their grappling became more and more absurd. And at some point, on the cusp of actual darkness, they just stood still, looking at each other, these men who had been in the process of killing one another. The coldness and the darkness, the blindness of the Sun, the suspension of justice – somehow it let these men, these strangers, these warriors stop and see something of themselves and of each other. It let them see the absurdity. Maybe it let them see the terror and the bewilderment that each of them felt suddenly expressed in the face of the other. Maybe it let these men mirror each other, just when the Sun's view was blocked by his own reflected light.

Yet we also have to imagine, at that same time, at that very moment, strangers, guests, had been led single file from the palace, led by their hosts, the ones who welcomed them into their homes, led against a wall where, when darkness peaked, but in advance of the still-peaking coldness, their hosts slaughtered them. In one place, the eclipse made strangers see in each other their likenesses; in another place, not far away, it enabled them to see in their likenesses strangers. Or something even worse than strangers – something that enabled men to kill those who had long been their guests, with whom they had broken bread and drunk beer, with whom they had laughed. To do that, strangers had to become something even less than strangers, something with whom all possibility of likeness was lost.

How could these events happen more or less at the same time, more or less in the same place, more or less because of the same extraordinary occurrence? And why is it that the part I played had nothing to do with strangers seeing in each other likenesses? Somehow my prophecy enabled hosts to kill their guests, but it had nothing to do with the warriors on the plain suddenly stopping and recognizing each other.

Why is it that the Moon is parent to the Sun? The Moon, unlike the Sun, waxes and wanes; grows weak; disappears; eventually is reborn. Not so the Sun; it rises and sets, but at no point in its normal life does it grow weak or small or partial. The Sun is so bright that it pains the eye to look at it. The Sun can blind you, as you expect looking upon a god would blind you. But anyone can stare at the Moon, for as long as he likes. No one has been blinded by the Moon – no one, that is, but the Sun. The Moon doesn't warm, though the Sun does. And women grow weak and bleed according to the Moon, not the Sun. So why is the Moon parent to the Sun? Is the Moon an aged Sun, a Sun grown feeble with time? Or is the Moon a Sun which has seen all things, grown cold, grown blighted or else perhaps grown wise? Maybe once the Sun has watched mankind long enough, it will turn its gaze away, let itself shrivel, and become pale. But why then does the Moon, jaded by its sight of us, still come back? It even comes back on schedule, like some enormous celestial ritual that will play for all time. Having done it so often, doing it even now almost mechanically – maybe that is what has cooled its fiery light and turned it into a soft white glow. And parts of the Moon, you can see, are more like ash – those dark blotches where the cooled fire has at last gone out. Maybe the Moon, parent of the Sun, is a dead parent.

Sîn, are you listening? Are these thoughts worthy of your devotee, whether that devotee be a king or a priestess? One of us haunts a temple cella, waiting for the breath of air which ever so slightly precedes and announces your voice; the other of us exiles himself to Arabi, thinking that perhaps there, amidst the white stone, he will at least recognize you. Recognize you from near, not far; hear you; perhaps even embrace you. But beware the embrace of that king: he is the one who uses the proximity of the Moon to slaughter guests. Perhaps you would be better off with his daughter the princess, his daughter the priestess – she who writes notes to long-dead prior priestesses and princesses while assembling an audience of statues.

Or Sîn, maybe these strange folks are not the ones for you! Perhaps it is time for you to bestow your godhead elsewhere, among more sensible people, ones who lead their nations into the future rather than the past, who stand at the origin not the end of empire, the ones whose spirit is of the world to come. But maybe you are too late, Sîn. Maybe those people belong already to the Sun.

* * * * *

He was standing with his father on a tell near Bābilim. It was a place he and Gubaru had frequented regularly in their childhood; and it was the place where they had lost the pukku and the mekkû. "Ah," said Nabû-balaṭsu-iqbi. "This is where you lost tomorrow."

"We have had this conversation before," his son responded. He was old, somehow older than his father, and he realized that in fact he was an age that his father had never lived to see.

"We have had a conversation like this one before," his father corrected. "Already our conversation is differing from the earlier one."

"Why are we here?" Nabû-na'id asked.

"You're more likely to know the answer than I," his father proposed. "This is your dream, not mine."

"Do you still dream?" his son asked.

His father did his strange bark-laugh. "Would it bother you if I admitted that I don't know?"

They were silent until Nabû-na'id repeated his earlier question, but this time in a tone which suggested it was more a question for himself than his father. He looked around the tell and suddenly recognized the time of day was morning. The sun was rising in the east, birds were singing, the morning felt cold but already the splashes of sunlight on him were warming and welcome. A few spiderwebs in waist-high bushes became threads of light, almost like tears in space revealing all the light beneath them, like space was some stifling blanket tossed over light. He slowly surveyed the farther scene – the barley fields beneath them, the canals crisscrossing the fields, already animals toiling with a stick-carrying human at their side, as unseen roosters crowed. As he turned he observed that the crescent moon, almost waned to its fullest, would set before long in the west. The rising sun on one side, the setting, almost waned moon opposite. He looked at his sandaled feet and his dirty toes and then past them, at the dirt, the clay, the dust, the ash. His eyes had been opened long ago to all the sherds.

"Yes," said his father. "The dirt, the clay, the dust and the ash – all of it are the remains of lost writing, of broken sherds and tablets, of messages which disintegrated in a distant past. Imagine the sorrows that gashed their way through the hardening mud or scratched themselves on the sherds; imagine the banal requests for clothing or for updates on chisel manufacture; imagine the joys communicated, the marriages arranged, the births announced, the sales completed. All of it now dirt, clay, dust and ash. There is even a letter which lost its way to you and at every moment slowly gives itself to the sand, a letter which, had you gotten it, would perhaps have brought you home."

Nabû-na'id felt turmoil gusting in his soul – felt anger and sorrow ripping through him – felt a desire to weep and to despair and to die.

"Why are you tormenting me?" he asked his father. "Why must you remind me of all those yesterdays that I accepted as the

compensation for the tomorrows I gave up?"

"Did you give them up?" his father asked.

"Yes," Nabû-na'id answered simply.

"No," his father answered equally simply. "I can't find that lost letter which would have mattered so much to you. But let me show you something, something which perhaps that letter could have shown you too." He didn't wait for an answer. He squatted, saying nothing, and drew his hand through the dirt, leaving behind a trough. Nabû-na'id looked intently at the trough, at the indistinguishable particles, the remains, indeed the ruins, of the past. Dead and crumbled hopes, mistakes, fierce atrocities, all anonymized into dust. But then, to his surprise, he thought he saw slow stirrings, scarcely observable. He was uncertain; he did not know whether to believe his sight. He watched more closely. Yes. Slow stirrings, dirt grains suddenly rolling to the side, something peeking through the ground. It took a still longer time before he could convince himself that out of the gray and brown was emerging a pale green. It was curled up, like a curled-up finger; but then suddenly, like a spring released, it uncurled, and he could see not just a stalk but tiny, infant leaves. The trough his father had drawn was filling with these dirt grain-rolling, pale-green stalks; the slow stirrings were accelerating; the stalks, the spires, were suddenly springing toward the sun, their leaves growing and unfurling, a silent hymn being written rather than sung before his very eyes. Some of the leaves clasped, as if in prayer; the clasp became a bud; the bud flowered. All through the trough flowers of many colors and many shapes rioted into silent song, filled the trough, stretched toward heaven, swayed and danced and perhaps even dreamed. And then slowly they withdrew, withered and wasted, first into rigid brown stalks and crispy, fallen leaves, then to clay and dust, finally returning to the original barren trough his father had drawn in the dirt.

"Do you understand?" Nabû-balaṭsu-iqbi inquired.

"No."

His father bark-laughed. "Oh, my son!" he exclaimed. "You have a trickle of life in you, not just death. You have a trickle of life in you! You have suffered because you have believed in your trickle more than most people have believed in theirs."

Nabû-na'id looked at his father silently.

"Out of broken tablets flowers may bloom," his father said. "And even if your trickle of life barely fills this small trough I have drawn, still it supports those blooming flowers – and then the bees who visit them – and in some way all who the bees go on to visit, all who visit the bees. You didn't just bring death into the world," his father said, laughing, "and you didn't just discover death in the world, either." He clasped his son by his shoulders and looked intently into his eyes, and in turn Nabû-na'id saw not only his father's eyes, but his mother's, and felt her clasping his shoulders as well as his father. A voice very close to his face, his father's or his mother's or the voice of both of them, whispered.

"Nabû," it said, or wrote in the trough, "IS Nisaba. And Nisaba is Nabû." On one side of the bewildered king the moon set; on the other rose the sun. "Sometimes they rise together; sometimes they set together. Often they are out of sync and on rare occasions they cross one another," the voice said or wrote. "But even those rare crossings, those life-changing eclipses, depend on perspective – and what is extraordinary here is ordinary elsewhere."

Nabû-na'id saw Nabû crouching in the dirt and, in near darkness, scribbling with his repulsive long nails; he saw dawn break and, rising out of Nabû, a smiling Nisaba grew like a stalk of barley; he watched the stalk flourish throughout the day and then, as night approached, decline and crouch back into the form of Nabû. Here day was giving way to night; elsewhere night was giving way to day.

A dog barked, and he knew the dog and he knew the bark. Delight flooded his gashed and scarred heart, his rent soul, and Nabû-na'id, now by himself on a tell near Bābilim, smiled. A trickle of water, nothing dramatic, barely observable, seemingly too small to sustain life, stubbornly found its way down the trough-like wrinkles of what for now was a face, though at other times it was and would be other things. Slowly the tell sank into the ground and the barley fields gave way to rising groves of date palms. His tears had become a spring in the Teima oasis. Somehow, Teima lay beneath Bābilim like the light which the spiderwebs revealed beneath space. Or else those threads of light were not lacerations in space revealing what lay beneath it, but instead what tied it all together, hemming the world like a garment. It was a question of perspective, he realized, whether tablets are gouged by signs or sewn by them – sewn or sown.

* * * * *

Read Nabû-zer-lišir, thus writes Nabû-na'id.

I understand that now an immense hole stretches where once stood the Eḫulḫul. Many times now you have written me and worried, "What if I have dug through the foundations? What if I have missed them?" And many times now I have responded: keep digging. Whatever a foundation is, it can't be something you dig through. For years now, there are two white stones, Moon-rocks I call them, which oversee your unending labor as if they were sentinels or prison-guards. Like a messenger sent in search of a ghost, you probably curse your fate – and perhaps my name too.

Stop, scribe. You may stop. I am ordering you to stop. Let us call where you stop our foundation. Let us make it the foundation of the Eḫulḫul. Stop your digging and rebuild the temple, in accordance with the ancient ways, the ancient documents, all that is ancient even if what is ancient still falls short of a beginning. Scribe, we read and we write, do we not? We dig and we build. And sometimes we cannot tell the difference. But today I am telling you the difference. Stop digging; rebuild, build anew, build the Eḫulḫul, the house of joy.

* * * * *

Nabû-na'id was once more planting gardens. It was a source of bewilderment to the courtiers with him in Teima why he spent his time planting gardens. For some of them it recalled to mind the madness of Nabû-kudurri-uṣur, after he had had those extravagant gardens built for his homesick and no-longer-loving wife. But these gardens of Nabû-na'id were by no means extravagant. He built them himself, by hand; he weeded them himself; he seemed to take particular delight that his flowers attracted bees. Gubaru was often with him, talking, although Gubaru took no part in the gardening. He had started these gardens when the dog was still alive; and the dog, old by then, would often sit there in the shade of a date palm, panting and watching him, or else sleeping. The king seemed so glad to garden in the company of that dog, or of his friend Gubaru, even while neither did much to help him. After the dog had died, however, he stopped – but now he was once again planting, often humming to himself as he did so. And of course he talked to the bees and thanked them. "I would like to give these gardens to my people, along with you bees," the king would say. "But I know that I cannot. So maybe I shall, for now, just keep you for myself."

* * * * *

Izdubar sat motionless with the black cat on his lap. Suddenly, before him, at the entryway to the hall was a gray striped cat with mischief in his eyes. This cat was full of life, full of angst, full of trouble. This cat wanted something which Izdubar perhaps could never give him. This cat would ask nonetheless – sometimes moaning for it, sometimes demanding it, sometimes drawing blood for it. "You are a cat more than equal to the day," Izdubar said aloud. The gray cat just stared. And then, to Izdubar's astonishment, the black cat stirred. She lifted her head, perked her ears, looked directly at the gray, striped cat. He returned her gaze. He was more than equal to the day. She raised herself on Izdubar's lap, stretched unhurriedly, groomed her fur – all to Izdubar's astonishment. And then, with no further ado, she jumped from his lap, trotted toward the gray, striped cat, passed him, left. Izdubar and the gray, striped cat stared at one another. "Go on," Izdubar finally said. "I will see what I can do for you. I will give you what I can. And before too long I will follow after you." The gray, striped cat approached, leapt on his lap. For a moment Izdubar thought: I shall be stuck again, afraid to disturb a resting cat, a dead cat. But he was wrong. The gray, striped cat instead climbed onto Izdubar's back, clawing it painfully. He wrapped himself around Izdubar's neck and gently purred, as if to say – I will not wait for you to follow. Come now. And so Izdubar rose.

Chapter 13. Returns

From the Babylonian Royal Chronicle:
Thirteenth regnal year. The king lived in Teima; in Akkadê were the prince, his officers and his army. The month of Nisanu arrived but the king did not return to Bābilim. Nabû did not enter the city. Bel did not come out. No god left his sanctuary. There was no Akītu festival. Offerings were still presented, in the Esagila and the Ezida, to Bābilim's gods and to Borsippa's, as if the times were normal. In the month of Tašrītu, on the 17th day, the king and his court returned from Teima and entered Bābilim...

He would have liked to wander the city incognito, which almost seemed possible given how long he had been away. Perhaps over the last ten years people had forgotten what he looked like. After all, he wasn't an especially remarkable looking man to begin with; what most stood out about him, he imagined, was his stoop. But plenty of men, most of them scribes, were stooped in Bābilim. Were he to dress himself beneath his rank and wander stooped throughout the city, it's likely he'd not merit a second glance or even much of a first. He could weave through crowds, step into shops, listen to the babel of a hundred different languages and breathe the city's odors, spices, sweat and shit all mixed together into something at once pleasant and repugnant. (He thought of the *rēḫātu.*) Most of the people he'd encounter would be too busy with their own projects to pay him the slightest heed. The challenge, however, would be slipping past his own courtiers. They guarded him, not – to his mind anyway – in the mode of protecting him, but rather to prevent his escape. They nipped at his heels, like dogs nip at sheep, driving them somewhere the shepherd directs. But there was no shepherd in his case, or else he was the shepherd; the dogs nipping at the sheep were nipping at the shepherd, with little idea what their own goal was; it's just what they always did, what all the other dogs did too. He was just a king, merely the man who ruled it all, a lone, envied shepherd-sheep herded by an enormous pack of purposeless dogs.

He sighed. His own images made him think of Fly. The men who accompanied him were an obstreperous pack of dogs, while his own dog, his true companion, was gone, was lost forever. Were he to wander the city now, it would be in this awful, newfound nakedness. (And yet Fly had been dead for many years.) Returning to Bābilim brought Fly's absence nearer, made him feel again the sharpness of the edge, of the grief. From now on, whether he wished it or not, Fly's absence would be part of his disguise, as if he had cut off one of his own limbs to better hide his identity.

(Why, he wondered, is it "Fly's absence"? Even absence no longer belongs to Fly. It is the absence of Fly. It is an absent absence. Would that flowers could bloom in your absence, Fly! In it, inside of it! Would that this gash could become the furrow of seeds, this gash in space and in time and in a heart, this absence that is marked all the more pitifully for its not being there. Absent absence. He remembered the threads of light in his dream, the tears which promised a world beneath the one we're in – a world where perhaps Fly romped even now. Tears as rips and gashes, but tears also as the nourishing water born of grief. Those threads, those tears, those rips and gashes, tied it all together, somehow tailored it into a single costume, sewed the broken, wounded skin back into one so it could once again contain and not leak, so that he could again be one of those water bladders the nomads carried as they straggled across deserts without end.)

Oh Fly. Oh Fly, I miss you. (Something within was wailing.) I was so lucky to share a life with you. A life – one life – whose life? Yours or mine or ours? It must have been ours, but what does it mean to share our life now without you? And yet, Fly, it will be our life. I refuse to make it only mine, to accept it only as mine. Even now, I refuse. (Gradually the wailing began to die down.)

He found himself wondering about the others whom he missed, the others whom he had shared a life with. Niṭil-Kišar. Mikum-Nisaba. Unlike Fly, they weren't dead. But, as with Fly, it wasn't clear anymore what it meant to share a life with either of them. Indeed, how many lives were at issue? Was the life he shared with Fly also the life he shared with Niṭil-Kišar or with Mikum-Nisaba? Or were they all different lives and he a different person, depending on whomever he happened then to be sharing life with? Was there a life all by itself anywhere, a life only his own, or was his whole life just a series of lives shared with others, albeit different others and hence different lives? (The wailing suddenly started to rise, to whine into the heights, to flame grief into panic. But abruptly it subsided again. The panic couldn't be endured, it always broke.)

He imagined seeing Niṭil-Kišar in front of him, for the first time in 10 years. How would they react to each other? Would they be shy? Or would it be even worse than that, each of them wondering – is this…? Is this… *him*? Is this… *her*? How embarrassing it would be to embrace someone as your long-absent spouse, only to discover you were embracing the wrong person. But surely they would recognize each other, even after a decade apart. Perhaps in fact they would see each other too clearly – they would see how much each had changed. You've become gray and lost some teeth, he might think. You've become a monster, she might think. And then each of them would grope for a word that let them pretend enough remained the same. A name. Their names.

(Do you love me? Can you still? That was the question he felt hiding in his heart. But he doubted he could ever ask her, just as he doubted he could ever fail to read a negative answer in her eyes. But maybe her eyes and her answers were more delicate than that, more nuanced. Maybe it was a mistake just to read "No" in her gaze, a gaze which while seeing him might never suspect the question being asked of it.)

(Another voice inside of him taunted him. "And you?" it asked. "Do you love her? Do you love her still? If you saw a yes in her gaze rather than the no you expect, how would that affect your own answer? Could you love her, knowing she loved a monster? Could you love her, knowing she didn't love the real you beneath the monster? How different are the real you and the monster, anyway? Are perhaps both terms, the "real you" and the "monster," lies and consolations? Aren't you a little afraid she'll see that, too?")

(Again the wailing nearly flamed into panic, then suddenly broke and was gone.)

They looked warily at each other.

He had changed. He was a physically stronger man than his father, which had long been the case but was all the more pronounced now as the two faced each other, one in his prime or just past it, the other a stooped old man. His hair had grown more gray, which surprised Nabû-na'id, who suddenly realized that he thought of his son always as a boy. But this man was not a boy, was not even especially young. He bore himself with more dignity than when they had last seen each other. He was more confident. A decade had passed of him making decisions, commanding and being obeyed. Perhaps at one point, when he had first started as regent, he had doubted whether anyone would follow his orders. But now he took it for granted. If anything, the challenge he now faced was to recede into the background, to defer to his father and obey rather than command.

Staring at each other, they hadn't yet spoken a word, either of them. How cold we are, thought Nabû-na'id, not without a hint of humor – a father and son separated for a decade who now stand before one another, probably each wishing to be elsewhere. Somehow we're doing it all wrong, failing to be family reunited and failing as well to be king and regent reunited. Falling short of each.

Recognizing this could not go on forever, his son gave a curt nod. "Welcome," he said without much enthusiasm. "Welcome, your majesty." Then, almost as an afterthought: "Father."

They didn't embrace.

"You have done well, Bel-šar-uṣur," Nabû-na'id murmured. His use of his son's name seemed to startle them both. "I have been impressed." Then, in a lower voice, he added, "I am proud of you."

Bel-šar-uṣur showed little reaction. "Much needs to be done," he said brusquely. "Kuraš is only getting stronger. We need to plan our campaigns and strike him while there is still time."

"In the service of what?" Nabû-na'id asked gently.

Contempt flashed across his son's eyes. "Survival," he said. "Our city's. Our empire's. Ours."

"Ah, that," his father responded as if it were a light thing, something almost to be forgotten. "Yes," he added almost to himself, even while in his mind's eye he gazed upon the plain from the perspective of a thousand years, ten thousand years, when no sign of any of this would be found. "Yes," he repeated, "we shall have to give that thought. But there are other things to do too, more important ones than surviving."

"Oh?" his son asked, with contempt and anger again not far beneath the surface. "What is more important than surviving?"

Nabû-na'id grinned. "Living!" he almost barked, for a moment sounding like his own father. He saw a hole being dug, the *Namburbi* ritual, sorrow and grief and graves, the abyss of the Eḫulḫul, and then, out of all of them somehow superimposed, he saw stalks grow, leaves unfurl and flowers riot. "We should celebrate the day to which we are not and will never be equal," he added. "We should have a festival."

"Father, please –" was all Bel-šar-uṣur said.

"Now is the beginning of Sîn's *Akītu* festival in Ḫarrānu. We shall celebrate it here too." Nabû-na'id spoke very simply, his tone matter-of-fact. "In honor of the god. In honor as well of my return." He paused. "Of course, with so little time to prepare, this year's festival will be modest, but it will set the stage for those to come. We can think of it as seed-planting."

Bel-šar-uṣur frowned. "Father, this idea is ill-advised. You have already incurred resentment from the religious establishments for your neglect of our own *Akītu* festival, Bābilim's. And for your belittlement of Marduk. And for your treatment of the *rēḫātu*. Now is not the time for yet another innovation, all the more when we have a serious threat on our borders."

"I understand. But we also have to be careful, my son, not to defer our lives indefinitely, simply so we can survive. We have to live, while we have time."

"Now is not the time."

Nabû-na'id smiled. "Now is never the time to live. It never has been. Still, let us try to live nearer it, or perhaps pretend."

His son took a step forward and then, probably as much to his own surprise as his father's, put his hands on Nabû-na'id's shoulders. "Father, no. Not now. You've been away for a long time. You have an enemy at the gate – and you may have enemies inside the gate, too. To deal with the first you can't provoke the second. Wait, bide your time, or all will be lost."

Nabû-na'id looked earnestly at his son's face, at the mole on the arch of his left cheek – the mark of his mother. Beneath the beard, he knew, was also a chin very like his mother's. But it was hidden, maybe safeguarded. Slowly, he let his eyes drift from the beard and the cheek until they met his son's hazel eyes. "I understand," he said a second time. "I know there is wisdom in your advice. But sometimes wisdom can be found in many different courses of action, even contradictory ones. Please trust that there is wisdom in my own plans, too."

Bel-šar-uṣur still held him by the shoulders. "But there isn't, father. There just isn't. I've been here; you haven't. I can detect the strains and the tremors running through the people and the city. You can't – not yet anyway. You can't neglect the city for a decade and then one day arrive and insist it become something of your choosing. Kings are strong – but not that strong."

"If we had more time, I would agree with you. Like I've already admitted, there is wisdom in what you say. But time is short. Time is very, very short."

Bel-šar-uṣur opened his mouth to speak but closed it again without saying anything. Instead it was his father who spoke. "That mole on your cheek – it's the mark of your mother. A gift she gave you, without of course having much say in the matter. Still it is her mark, as perhaps your hazel eyes are my mark. Everything is stamped with marks from others. We're usually in such a hurry that we don't pay much attention to those marks. We don't try to read them. But there they are, anyway."

His son looked at him quizzically. "Why does it matter?" he asked.

His father smiled – a friendly and sorrowful smile. "Oh, it may not matter," he admitted. "But shouldn't it be celebrated?"

"A gift my mother gave me without having any choice? How

is that even a gift?"

To both of their shocks, Nabû-na'id suddenly embraced him. "Bel-šar-uṣur," he said, his voice thick with emotion, "I am truly glad to see you."

Bel-šar-uṣur didn't respond. He just looked at his father, his gaze stony and bewildered.

Zeriya said that he had noticed it too. The crescent of the Esagila. "How do you understand it?" Nabû-na'id asked.

"I do not understand it," was Zeriya's simple response.

"If we were to ask the priests, what do you think they would say?"

"They at least would claim to understand it."

"But what would they say they understood?"

Zeriya looked at him blankly. "I don't know."

Nabû-na'id continued to stare intently at the crescent on the Esagila. If there were two of them, mirroring each other, then the priests could try to claim them as horns, not as a crescent, he thought. Then we could return to that argument of long ago. But there's only one. The asymmetry would bother the priests. Horns come in pairs. At best they would claim one of the pair had been lost, had eroded away with time. But such an acknowledgment would be dangerous; Nabû-na'id could reply that the erosions of time were a god's message, that loss had meaning. Then they could play that game. But Nabû-na'id wasn't especially interested in that game, because he didn't believe there had been a second horn, and he doubted that any priest would truly believe that either. There, on the Esagila, on Marduk's great temple in Bābilim, was a lone crescent.

It was a mark of something, like the mole on a cheek.

He had looked for her in the palace, but she was not there. He found himself wishing, as often he had before, that they still lived in a private residence – that they still had a house which was their own, rather than a palace which belonged to no one. Or to which they belonged, not so much as people but as royalty. If they still had their house, then he didn't doubt that he would find her there, waiting for him. But where was she to wait in a palace? For whom or for what? A palace was alien to them both, a hardship for each of them. Kings had palaces – not husbands, much less friends. If she waited for him in a palace, it was a king she waited for. So where would she go if she was waiting for something other than a king?

Since it was impossible to imagine that she had not learned of his return, he was originally pained by the thought that she must be avoiding him. But now this new thought had come, that she had gone some place to await his return as something other than a king. Perhaps she was even playing with him, inviting him to play. Or she was teasing him. For a moment he felt like he was in a game with Fly, something lighthearted because, after all, Fly did not think of him as a king and so he didn't have to think of himself as a king either. With Fly he could offer his sleeve, and Fly would attack it, not for a moment considering it the garment of a king. So now the question was, where would Niṭil-Kišar go so that he could offer her his sleeve?

He had no idea.

At another time in his life, he would at this point have wandered aimlessly through the city, perhaps in the company of Fly. It is hard, however, for a king to wander even his own cities aimlessly, and even more for a king just returned from ten years of self-imposed exile. He wouldn't get too many chances to give his attendants the slip, if he managed it at all – and those limited chances ruled out something aimless. He felt trapped, like an insect in amber.

That image struck him, however. An insect incapable of moving, trapped in what resembled fire. Fire that had cooled and become stone; entombing fire. He remembered his first conversation with Niṭil-Kišar, when he had talked about the dying fly, the one fallen on its back, incapable of flight, staring at the sky. He remembered the burning ember she had kicked at him. "Fire inhabits what it burns," she had said – and he had seen it then, the fire somehow inside of the ember, creating bright orange lineaments just beneath the surface not unlike pulsing blood. Not unlike the tears in space which had so moved him in Teima, the webs to which the sunlight stuck like a doomed fly.

Not having been able to wander aimlessly in his city, he realized that he was instead wandering aimlessly in his mind – exploring an image which had occurred to him, he knew not from where. An insect in amber. Amber as stone fire. Sunlight stuck like a doomed fly. To whom or to what did he owe such strange notions? If he and Fly were wandering the city, they would turn left or right, every turn potentially fateful but somehow just happening rather than chosen. So too with these mind images. Perhaps this is how a god speaks to a man, by surprising images and unthought left turns. Perhaps aimless wandering, in space or thought, was a mode of divination, the way the divine speaks with us even if it never occurs to us that what has happened is speech or the divine.

He thought of that dying fly and that dying ember and suddenly he recognized that his aimless wandering had not been without purpose. He knew where she was.

He went.

It was evening, with the sun mostly set, the air already growing cold. Around this time, in this place, they had first met. It was a courtyard in her father's palace. So she was, after all, in a palace – but a palace which she had transformed into something else, beneath the unrecognizing eyes of those who watched, those who even believed themselves to inhabit a palace. Nabû-na'id tried to do something similar. He didn't dismiss his attendants so much as assume that they could not and would not see. In choosing a palace to meet him, she also gave him the veil of kingship under which to hide: she would meet him after all as a king, but somehow, hidden in plain sight, she would meet him as something else as well.

As he stepped into the courtyard, he noticed that there were flowers which trimmed its periphery and adorned its center; flowers even graced the walls in intricate mosaics. He hadn't noticed or didn't remember noticing flowers that first time. The light, then and now, was dim; much of what he saw was in that gray-blue dimness – but still this time the flowers managed to cast off that shroud, or perhaps to shine through it – not untempered by the dimness, but also not stifled or conquered by it. No riot of life, but something calm and enduring and steadfast. He even noticed a few bees, languid, weak, but despite the setting day, despite the cooling evening, not yet given up. Some torches affixed to the wall had been lit and sparks flew from them a bit like buzzing flies. He wondered why there was no god of flowers, no god of bees or flies either – even if gods were also flies.

She sat on the ground near the center. Beside her lay an ember, black with no vein pulsing through it that he could see. She also wore a veil. He smiled – his heart surged within him – he understood the veil to represent not what was hidden but what was shared. But perhaps it was both. Waving his attendants aside, he walked to her, silently sat down beside her and, still without a word, offered her his sleeve. The offer obviously confused her; she started, then paused, then after a moment gently pushed his sleeve away, while turning her head only partially towards him.

"I don't bite sleeves," she whispered.

Nabû-na'id felt very much like the boy he'd been when he'd first met her. He was surprised and even a little delighted by his sense of nervousness, by his uncertainty. "I know," he answered in a low voice. Then, unnecessarily, he added, "I was thinking of Fly, how he could bite my sleeve without me having to be a king."

"It isn't as easy for you and me," she responded slowly.

"No."

They sat side by side in silence. The night grew darker and the flowers on the periphery began to disappear. As the coldness gathered around them, it somehow made the torches feel stronger in their heat, with that heat occasionally reaching them where they sat and then wafting away.

Still with her veiled face turned only partially towards him, he heard her say, even more quietly than before, "Welcome home, poet."

"You wrote me a letter that I never received," Nabû-na'id said, surprised by the words as he spoke them. "My father told me about the letter in a dream."

She bent her head slightly forward, which he took to be a kind of nod – acknowledgement or even encouragement.

"My father showed me blooming flowers. He suggested Nisaba and Nabû were one god, not two." He paused. "But you know that already. Perhaps you've known that all along."

"I don't really know much," she mumbled. "Knowing hasn't been as important to me as it's been to you." She touched his hand, though still not looking fully at him. "It is good that we're here at night," she said, almost in a sigh. "The day is too strong for us, for what we've become, at least now. But we have a night to prepare."

He stared at the *rēḫātu* and then, after a while, broke into a smile. "It's more appetizing when it hasn't travelled hundreds of miles over many days," he observed.

Bel-šar-uṣur raised his eyebrows but didn't return the smile.

"Of course," he muttered distractedly.

"Do you miss it?" his father asked.

"The *rēḫātu*?" The question clearly surprised him. "No."

"It didn't mean anything to you, to eat the meal left over by the gods, to be one of only two human beings in all the world worthy of the gods' scraps?"

Bel-šar-uṣur didn't respond until the priest had shuffled away, leaving the two of them alone with the *rēḫātu*. "Don't play these games!" he said angrily. "Do you think the priests don't hear your mockery, your irony?"

"But I wasn't mocking. I wasn't being ironic." Nabû-na'id responded, taken aback. "I was just curious."

His son gave him a level, disbelieving look. "You and I both know statues don't eat. What we are left with are not the gods' scraps. They're just scraps, in an elaborate theater that no one really believes in and everyone is supposed to pretend to believe in. Play your role and stop causing trouble."

"Ah, there it is. The sneer of cold command" murmured Nabû-na'id. "No one but you could talk to their king that way. You do miss it."

"No!" Bel-šar-uṣur answered angrily. "But I play my part and let the ceremony unfurl without difficulties. Has it not occurred to you that a kingdom may need that?"

"Oh, it's occurred to me. But has it not occurred to you that a kingdom may need a king who genuinely believes and doesn't just pretend to believe?"

His son gave him a mocking look. "Don't tell me that you've become a true believer? I would never believe it." As he said "believe," he almost stopped, as he heard the echo he hadn't intended. But the word's momentum carried it through.

"Which of us is the true believer?" Nabû-na'id wondered seriously and aloud. "You who believe you don't believe, or me who can't believe that he believes? Me, for whom belief is a problem, or you for whom it isn't?"

"Enough of these word games!" Bel-šar-uṣur almost snorted. "Kings have greater responsibilities than word games!"

"How can you tell?" Nabû-na'id asked softly.

His son scoffed but didn't answer. A silence settled between them and over the still untouched *rēḫātu*. Suddenly, Nabû-na'id seemed to remember that he had to eat it, and so he reached forward, took a morsel and began to chew it thoughtfully. All the while he looked at his son, and especially at the mole on the arch of his left cheek. A propos of nothing, he broke the silence and inquired, "Have you ever noticed the crescent on the Esagila?"

His son didn't immediately respond but walked to a window and looked in the direction of the temple. "What of it?" he eventually answered.

"You can't see it from that side," Nabû-na'id observed.

"I'm not looking for it. I know what you're talking about. I've noticed it."

"How do you understand it?"

"I've never tried to."

"Have you ever tried to understand the mole on your left cheek?"

"The mole again? Why are you so obsessed with the mole on my left cheek?"

Nabû-na'id didn't respond but shuffled to the window where his son stood. They were on the second floor of the palace. Beneath them lay a courtyard where various functionaries milled about or hurried through. Beyond that was a wall and a gate and then, the city. Walls and guards could keep ordinary people out, but the smells and the sounds of the city encountered no real impediment. No guard could halt a smell or a sound. Nabû-na'id was glad of their weakness. Not that the sounds and the smells were especially delightful – the creaking of carts, the braying of donkeys, the shouts of vendors or of angered men, the odd laugh; the stench of shit and food mixed bewilderingly with the odor especially of baking bread. But he was glad that no wall had been built, no gate devised, no guard so well-trained, as to keep all this out. This was what tablets decaying and crumbling into dirt sounded like and smelled like; great cities too; and it was as well the sound and smell of the flowers surging forth. The waxing crescent moon could be seen to the west. It would soon set, not long after dusk, Nabû-na'id judged.

"The mole on your cheek is the mark of your mother," he finally said. "I am glad to see that she has left her mark on you."

"You called it a gift the other day."

"Yes," Nabû-na'id agreed. "I did. But maybe it's not a gift. Maybe it's a request, or even a command."

Bel-šar-uṣur rolled his eyes. "It was easier," he said, "when you were in Teima. The land could be governed without irrelevant distractions."

"You mean – you could govern the land without irrelevant distractions."

"We governed it. You and I together."

"Together though apart."

"Yes, but still. I think about different things than you, father. When you were in Teima, you left me to those things and I left you to yours. And it actually worked. But now we're back in each other's presence."

"You mean – in each other's way." Nabû-na'id suggested.

Bel-šar-uṣur frowned. "I didn't say that. But it's harder. You would agree it's harder."

"Of course."

Nabû-na'id again looked out over the city. He was thinking about the collaboration his son had described, a collaboration possible precisely because of absence. It made him think once more of the crescent on the Esagila and of the mole on his son's left cheek. They were all marks – possibly gifts, too – but marks which announced both an absence and something like a collaboration. The mole was a mark of Niṭil-Kišar, even if it wasn't hers to choose to give. And among the things marked by the mole was her absence, the way her son carried beyond her something that was also in some way from her. The crescent on the Esagila seemed that way too. It was the mark, the spire, of Sîn albeit on the temple of Marduk. It announced their collaboration even if they didn't work in each other's presence. And it was always a question, even in the temple of Marduk, which god was present, which absent – or even whether any god wasn't absent. He tried to see the city sprawled out before him in those terms, as a crescent on the Esagila, as a mole on a cheek – but this, what he beheld from the window, was the mark *he* had given his son. Not necessarily a gift; not simply an imposition. Like the noises and the odors. Decay, loss, destruction, and also a riot of flowers. His son carried the city, on his shoulders if not on his cheek, as the mark of his father, as the mark of his father's absence, too. He would have preferred if his mark on his son had only been the hazel eyes.

But what Bel-šar-uṣur carried on his shoulders wasn't quite what his father marked him with; when Bel-šar-uṣur scanned the city, he saw something other than decay, loss, destruction – and almost certainly not the riot of flowers either. He saw instead expectations and duties in the service of political projects which it didn't occur to him to question. Marduk is ascendant in Bābilim; therefore do what's required by Marduk's priests. Kuraš stalks the frontier; therefore fight and destroy him. Whether either of those is true or right – was beside the point. Could there be a more ascendant god than Marduk? Could Marduk in fact be some kind of phantom or puppet? Bel-šar-uṣur didn't care about such questions, in part because it wasn't important to him whether Marduk was puppet or puppet-master, shadow or that which cast it. Play the part – that was his rule. Even if the part goads him and all into a hopeless bloodbath on the frontier. It's the script; follow it. Despite years of not bothering to learn to read, Bel-šar-uṣur nonetheless believed in scripts and in following them. And in parallel, Nabû-na'id thought loosely and wildly, Bel-šar-uṣur has only one mole on his cheek – his mother has two.

He noticed he was growing angry, but he knew it was a foolish anger. You leave a mark – you don't get to determine how it's read. And it's never quite the same mark as any other. Long ago he remembered being frustrated as he learned to read and write, because part of the trick was to look past the sign in front of you and see it with enough blurriness and enough distinctness that it could be recognized. If you didn't blur your vision, you only saw that it was yet another unique sign, in a world full of signs that were only unique. If you didn't force your vision into enough distinctness, you'd miss the crucial feature shared with a collection of other signs which allowed you to say, madly but quite helpfully, that they were all the same. If he was angry at his son right now, it was because what was true of signs impressed in clay was no less true of signs impressed on cheeks – or carried on shoulders.

Sometimes, when he was very tired or used his fingers to put pressure on his eyes, he could make an object he knew to be one appear in his vision instead as two. That was the trick of interpreting signs – creating the illusion of repetition, of doubling, even while what was repeated or doubled could never be repeated or doubled. Niṭil-Kišar could not possibly have two moles on her left cheek. In fact she couldn't even have one – to call it a mole was already to invoke that repetition or doubling upon which the interpretation of signs depends. What she had on her cheeks were not even moles, each too singular to be even a mole. But if this was so, then what was on Bel-šar-uṣur's cheek?

Could it still be the mark of his mother, as the city on his shoulders was the mark of his father? Or was that city crumbling into dust even now, that mole imploding, neither managing even to be marks? Nabû-na'id felt madnesses leaping within him like flames, one madness which insisted that moles mean, another madness which denied there were such things as moles. And yet there was the crescent moon on the Esagila.

Wasn't there?

Was there?

"It is almost as if you wish to be taken for a statue," she commented.

Her father didn't so much as stir. She had been surprised to find him in this cella, alongside statues on benches, shelves and the floor, perched motionless like they were, as of yet without an accompanying tablet. Even his dark gown seemed to have been specially chosen so he could blend in with the diorite statues, like the one of Gudea near which he sat. She strode unhurriedly across the room and stood beside him. Still there was no reaction. Gently she placed her hand on his shoulder. He started.

"Mikum-Nisaba!" he cried in surprise, and then, more questioningly, "Or En-nigaldi-Nanna?"

"Me," was all she replied. "Just me." They stared at each other, she crouching to be closer to his seated height. "Father," she said simply, her hand still resting on his shoulder "I am glad to see you." These bare words seemed almost to melt him, almost to reduce him to tears. She could tell that he believed her and, beyond that, that he was desperate to believe her. (Was she the first to say she was glad to see him? Was she the first to be glad to see him? Fly never said it, but at a reunion he'd frolic gaily about, half-leaping to nip his sleeves, running away to run back even faster, barking happily. Fly, he never doubted, missed him. But all these others, who knew him in so many different ways – could they be glad to see before them the author of eccentric letters, the desert exile, the king?) (Had he missed them? That was a question too.)

He realized he hadn't responded, at least to her. "Mikum-Nisaba," he spoke again, saying the name more confidently this time, clearly choosing it. "I have missed you too." (Had he?) He clumsily patted her hand on his shoulder, looking upward at her face.

"Why have you seated yourself like this, so like a statue, here in my collection?" she asked.

He looked at her blankly for a moment, then blinked. "I was waiting for you. I didn't want to command you into my presence. I just wanted to wait until you came."

"Like Gudea there, waiting for his god? Like me, waiting for mine?"

The old man pointed a trembling finger at a figurine on a nearby bench. "Perhaps like that dog with the broken foot," he suggested. "It's so hard to find one's balance. When it's found, why stir? When it's found, just wait. That's what I was doing."

Mikum-Nisaba smiled and walked to the figurine. "He's surprisingly stable, despite his broken foot," she observed. "I have no trouble balancing him."

"Yes," her father agreed. "Dogs are like that. But men are not. I am not. I am learning in my old age to wait, if I'm lucky enough to be confident in my balance."

"You make yourself sound like some doddering elder. But you're in good shape, at least as good as this dog here." She smiled again.

"I try to learn what dogs have to teach me. There are even days I aspire to be a dog," Nabû-na'id added playfully. "And days when I fear that I am a statue."

"It would be easier for you if you were a statue, wouldn't it?" She looked at him questioningly. "Statues needn't act, and most people doubt that they feel."

"Would you say that of a divine statue, too?" he asked, curious.

His daughter frowned and held his gaze. "A divine statue is made much like a dog statue is made. The rituals we do later, to open the statue's mouth, to feed the statue, to dress or undress the statue, to shepherd the statue into rest and to wake it, don't change the statue, so far as anyone can tell. They change our relationship to the statue. But that suggests that there are many relationships one can have with statues."

Her father slowly looked around the room, at the hundreds of statues and figurines occupying it, from floor to bench to ceiling-aspiring shelves. Few statues stood out for their beauty or perfection; if anything, most stood out for being broken and damaged. Some wore tattered garments; on others the paint had thinned and chipped. Holes lay empty where jewels once served as eyes. Limbs were missing, sometimes whole bodies. Faces seldom were well-preserved.

Mikum-Nisaba picked up the dog figurine and held it in her hands. "I have wondered what accompanying message to give this one," she mentioned. "I often write something brief for each statue, but it's always a question what to write." She chuckled. "For this one, I could simply write, 'This is a dog.' But some might think that's a label when really it's a poem."

"A poem?" he inquired, but she didn't respond. He waited a while, and then repeated matter-of-factly, "A poem."

"Do you understand?" she asked.

He shrugged. "Maybe." She raised an eyebrow and looked at him inquisitively. "Those who think it's a label will believe the name corresponds to the form of the figurine, albeit a broken one. Those who instead read a poem will understand that the brokenness is part of what the poem calls attention to – that at stake in being a dog is what is done with brokenness."

She smiled and nodded encouragingly. "Yes, that's something like what I was thinking."

"I have watched three-legged dogs in barley fields run like the wind, perhaps – once they get going – no whit less fast than four-legged dogs. As far as I can tell, those dogs don't lament their lost limbs. They don't compare themselves to what they consider the proper form of a dog. They are not cowed by a label whose expectation they fail to meet. Their brokenness is no detraction."

"It's doubtful that they consider themselves broken," his daughter added.

"'Broken'" they might ask, not unreasonably, "'with respect to what?' But even that question is of no concern to any dog I've known."

Nabû-na'id sighed, suddenly very tired. "But dogs are not monolithic, Mikum-Nisaba. As you know. Some dogs suffer in ways others do not. Some dogs seem to labor beneath the weight of an idea, even if it is not an idea you and I would recognize."

He sighed again. "When I aspire to be a dog, I must be careful that that not become a form I endeavor to fit. Otherwise I'll just be a poorly made dog, a broken one."

"A label," she added. "You'll just be a label and not a poem."

He still thought about the crescent on the Esagila and the mole on his son's cheek. Were they poems, not labels? A mark could be either, couldn't it? Or was it what was done with a mark, how it was read, that made of it either a label or a poem? What was he to do with the mark on his son's cheek or the mark on the Esagila? He'd rather they be poems than merely claims.

(Kuraš was coming. Would he be fool enough to make of that coming a poem rather than a claim?)

(Hush.)

(Fool!)

(Hush.)
(Fool!)
(Hush.)

Ah, I was wondering when you would come. It is presumably your turn to welcome me to Bābilim. Or, if not to welcome me, at least to acknowledge my return.

She shuffled across the floor, dressed as usual in sack cloth, covered as usual in ash. She didn't raise her head to look at him.

You know, of course, that you have died?

Still she shuffled across the floor, not responding, not looking at him. The room seemed wall-less, expansive, permissive of as much shuffling as she should care to do. Perhaps it wasn't a room. If he looked up, perhaps he would see the sky. But he did not look up, just as she did not look at him.

I read a copy of your autobiography. The actual stele on which it is inscribed is set up in Ḫarrānu, as you would have wished. But I had a copy made and sent to me. If the copy is accurate, then your autobiography was written from beyond the grave.

Still no response.

I wouldn't put it past you.

Still she shuffled, somehow failing to make ground even as she moved incessantly. She shuffled still. He found himself tiring of her antics – everything from her mournful costume (a costume, he reminded himself, of perpetual mourning), to her obstinate silence.

When my father visits me, he condescends to speak, even though he, like you, is dead. He even managed to give me a great gift, a trough or a grave or an immense hole in Ḫarrānu out of which nonetheless flowers bloomed. He managed this despite being dead. But here you are, you who were more alive than he ever was, you who wrote an autobiography from beyond the grave. Yet you won't even look at me.

Ah – he paused. You *wrote* it. I should be more attentive. Maybe I am even confused about father. Maybe what I pretend was speech was in fact writing. He wrote me that trough – or that grave – or that immense hole. Maybe even now you are writing me something too.

(She shuffled – still.)

Shall I get up and see?

(But you did not get up for my funeral. You did not leave Teima. Even now you are not privy to the place of my secret burial.)

What was that mother? Did you say something?

But she did not look up, she did not speak, she did not stop shuffling, and she did not go anywhere.

He decided to rise. He was, for some reason, afraid to look up, afraid to see the sky or to see what was there instead of the sky, or to see that there was nothing there in the sky's stead. Getting up became more difficult if one of its conditions was not risking the sight of the sky, or the sight of what was there in the absence of the sky, or what wasn't there at all. Why that should be was unclear, but so it was. The possibility of an accident loomed – the accident of looking up. He must not. If anything he must overdeterminedly look down, focus on looking down, even as he got up.

Now he was standing beside her. Still she averted her gaze. Still she shuffled nowhere. He was averting his gaze too. He was looking down, not up, not at her either. Looking down at her feet, at the dust at her feet, at the troughs and graves and holes her feet were making, at writing written in the ground by her feet. But it wasn't writing, and it wasn't the ground. It was the crescent moon, lying at her feet in the sky. But no, it was not even that. It was the moon eclipsed, lying at her feet in the sky.

"I have decided."

Bel-šar-uṣur looked exasperated. "What benefit comes from doing this? You'll just alienate everybody. The priesthood will revolt. The government officials will mock you. Everyone will slow-walk your orders or else defy them. And for what? For what?" He pounded the table. "What will be gained?"

"I am the king," Nabû-na'id answered icily. "Not everything I do must be for gain, not everything I do must be understood by others, and not a single thing I do requires anyone else's approval." They glared at each other. "Not even yours," he added angrily.

Bel-šar-uṣur got up, stalked around the room and then, visibly, collected himself. Visibly he calmed himself down. He lowered his voice and spoke slowly. "Father, I understand your devotion…"

"Do you?" his father interrupted. "What makes you confident that what you think you understand is devotion? Maybe it's something else."

Bel-šar-uṣur took a deep breath. "Ok, fine. I don't understand your devotion – or whatever it is. But I'm not opposing it, father. I'm just saying – be politic. We don't need to do this *now*. It can wait. It can wait until you've re-established yourself more strongly here. It can wait until Kuraš has been dealt with. Once that threat is no longer looming, once everyone sees how committed you are to Bābilim…"

"But what I am committed to is not Bābilim," his father stated clearly and distinctly.

His son stood stock still. "What, then, are you committed to?" he asked, speaking slowly and articulating carefully each word.

"Something better. It doesn't have a name."

Bel-šar-uṣur's eyes looked wild. "It doesn't have a name," he quoted almost in a monotone. "It doesn't have a name," he repeated. "You're going to drive all of the elite, probably the commoners too, into the hands of Kuraš. They're going to welcome him with open arms, for something that doesn't have a name. Is that what you want?" Then, suddenly, a startled look spread across his face. "*Is* that what you want?"

Nabû-na'id sighed. "No," he said shortly. "But there are worse outcomes than that, if it comes to it."

"Like what?"

Nabû-na'id didn't answer. He got up abruptly and stalked about the room, unconsciously mirroring what his son had done only moments before. In his mind swirled a confusion about the ground and the sky, about what counted as foundation, about what a human being needed most in order to stand and move in the world, whether something beneath his feet or something above his head. He even wondered sometimes how well he could tell apart feet and heads, grounds and skies. (He thought of Mikum-Nisaba's dog figurine.) But he knew better than to let any of this confusion escape into words, assuming that was even possible; and he knew better than to saddle his son with whatever words he managed. After a long period of silence, he instead simply repeated, "I have decided."

Bel-šar-uṣur stared at him. "The officials won't do it. They'll defy you."

"I know," Nabû-na'id acknowledged, his tone subdued. "I've already thought of that." He paused. "It's why I've also decided to replace them."

Bel-šar-uṣur started. "*All* of them?"

His father smiled grimly. "A lot of them," he said. "The most important ones. I've already made lists."

"You've already made lists," his son repeated numbly.

"Yes, lists. Lists of names, like the lists of names read at the

Akītu festival. I've made lists, and I hear each name, just as I hear your name and my name, not as a label but as a poem. And sometimes not as a label or a poem but just as sounds, not even words." He stared abstractly into space while his son looked helplessly at him.

"But" he added at last, after the lengthy pause, "we'll keep that part to ourselves."

* * * * *

From the [fragmentary] Assyrian Accounts of Herodotus

...It was a signature, he said. But what was a signature?

The court scholars were unprepared for the question. What indeed was a signature? Wasn't it simply the impression rolled into clay from a cylinder seal? On a contract that impression meant agreement – Yes, I have agreed to this arrangement. Yes, I have borne witness to it. But how could a mole on a cheek be a signature? No agreement was required, no witnessing. It just happened. How could what just happened be a signature?

Omens, he said – were they not signatures too? Some people would say the abnormalities of a liver just happened – but did we not say that they signified some kind of agreement, some kind of witnessing?

No, one of the scholars said. They signify a message. A message is not a signature.

Can't it be?

No.

This is what the priests told me had been discussed. They said the king believed everything was a signature, even messages. They said the king even claimed that some messages were not messages and only signatures. They said that this was evidence of the king's madness, that he saw poetry in all things, and signatures in all things, and poetry in signatures, and signatures in poetry. They said he was mad. The crescent moon on their temple, he claimed, was a signature. "Are you saying the temple is the Moon god's?" they asked, incredulous. "No, I am saying only that he signed for it, that he put his mark on it, his signature." "But what does that mean?" the priests demanded. The king supposedly leered at them in some ghastly way and answered enigmatically, "I don't know. Perhaps it doesn't mean. *Perhaps it can only be read." But he was mad, said the priests, and nothing can be made of madness. Madness mistakes meaning or is without it.*

I remember wondering, if nothing can be made of madness, if it mistakes meaning or is without it, why is it so important to all of you priests to insist that your king was mad? They kept repeating that he was mad, everything he said or did they interpreted in terms of madness, every few sentences they reiterated that Labynetus had gone mad. It was – forgive my humor – their signature move. "He was mad," they scrawled across his words and deeds. It was, however qualified, the assent they gave him, the witness they bore to him. It was their poem about their king, how they labeled him. Or else it meant nothing at all.

* * * * *

From the Babylonian Royal Chronicle:
Thirteenth regnal year. The king lived in Teima; in Akkadê were the prince, his officers and his army. The month of Nisanu arrived but the king did not return to Bābilim. Nabû did not enter the city. Bel did not come out. No god left his sanctuary. There was no Akītu festival. Offerings were still presented, in the Esagila and the Ezida, to Bābilim's gods and to Borsippa's, as if the times were normal. In the month of Tašrītu, on the 17th day, the king and his court returned from Teima and entered Bābilim. The king announced that on this day in Ḫarrānu begins the celebration of the Akītu festival of Sîn. He declared that henceforth Bābilim would celebrate it too, in honor of

his return and of a new new year unexpectedly begun. The crescent of the Esagila he declared the mark of Sîn. Marduk's temple for which Ea-Mumma himself in the earliest days laid the plans – this the king declared Sîn's.

* * * * *

He heard hastening steps behind him. But he didn't turn; he waited to be addressed.

"Hi," she said as she caught up with him.

"Hi," he responded.

"What are you doing?"

He was walking and looking at the ground, as dusk gently gathered itself in order to settle later around him. Soon it would strengthen into night. He was also pretending that Fly was with him – or he was conjuring Fly's ghost – or he was broadcasting an open-ended invitation throughout the universe, should Fly be anywhere to receive it. "I'm trying to go on a walk with Fly," he said eventually.

"Oh," she answered. "Can I tag along?"

He smiled weakly. She had avoided affirming Fly's presence or denying it. She had left it open. He stumbled forward. They were in a palace garden, one which her father had commissioned in his futile hope of pleasing his wife. It was one of the few spaces he could walk unhindered by courtiers or guards. And yet he had seldom come here with Fly. With Fly he had often chosen to stumble around in the city, even after he became king, partly because that's what the two of them had always done, partly because the commotion of the city – the people hawking goods, the neighbors bumping into each other, the children playing, the dogs and pigs wandering about with aims all their own – comforted and sometimes fascinated him. But now he was looking at his sandaled feet and at the ground, in a garden out of season and reserved for people like him, uncomforted and unfascinated.

"Yes," he said, "you can tag along." Then, quietly, he added, "I'd love you to tag along." He kicked a stone forward with his foot and watched it tumble ahead.

"It's just a stone," she said, watching it. "Not an ember."

"No, not an ember. And this fly is looking at the dirt and not the heavens."

"They're not unalike, some of the time," she observed.

"No."

"Why so glum?" she asked, at the same time taking hold of his elbow, while the two still walked side by side. He was touched that she so self-assuredly possessed herself of his elbow, as if she had as great a right to it as he. (He had no right to it at all, and yet, there it was, his.)

"Oh, I'm not glum," he answered. "I'm just lonely." (I miss Fly, he thought. Fly was truly my companion, Fly was my true companion.)

They walked together in a comfortable silence, despite his loneliness. She was probably lonely too, but he didn't ask her.

"I've heard," she said after a while, "that you will soon be lonelier."

"Because of my recent decisions? Because I'm alienating the court?"

"Of course."

"That's not a real loneliness, Niț. I will feel less lonely having driven them away than in their company. You know what I mean?"

She nodded but didn't say anything. They walked together in silence, arm in arm, doing several circuits around the garden. Eventually he asked, "Do you think I'm being a fool?"

She laughed. "Of course you're being a fool, but that's probably neither here nor there."

Neither here nor there. Then where?

"Neither here nor there," she repeated, somehow having read his thoughts. "You'll of course wonder – then where?"

This time he laughed. "I don't know where," he admitted. "Being a fool may be irrelevant – in the same way water is irrelevant to fish and air to the rest of us. Air is what we depend on, what we can't be without, and what therefore we have to take for granted. Foolishness may be like that too. But still there's the question where."

Where, for example, was Fly? In the corner of his eye he could almost see him prancing about; he could almost hear his bark, even to the point of not knowing whether he was imagining the sound or not; and then suddenly he fell back in time and heard a younger Niṭil-Kišar laughing, her hair unstreaked by gray, a babe in her arms. Their son, whom Nabû-na'id had held at a distance from his heart even despite the mole on his cheek. So many of their earlier babies had died – why risk loving this one? Even now he held that baby – that grown man – his son – at a distance from his heart, somehow unable to bring him closer. The laughter he heard from his still-young wife was sonorous, musical, almost like bells. But then he drifted back into the present, into the garden where his aged wife pressed his arm, walked in circles beside him and did not laugh.

"How did you dare to love our son, when we had lost all our earlier children?" he asked abruptly.

She furrowed her brow. "If you have to dare," she answered coldly, "it's already too late."

He felt grief swell inside of him, but he knew that he would no more erupt into tears than a stone would weep and so he beat the grief back. He patted the arm locked with his, though the arm had grown stiff with her anger, and answered calmly, "No, Niṭ. Even now, it's not too late." He thought of a seed long forgotten and dormant in exhausted soil. Might it not be biding its time, like the crescent moon on the Esagila, like the mole on his son's cheek? Might it not yet flower? Who was he to say it wouldn't? Who was anyone to say it wouldn't? He wondered what colors this flower might have, at dawn and at dusk and in the shroud of night.

"I haven't given up, Niț," he mumbled, still patting her arm. "It may look like I have, it may look like it – but I haven't. What I do I do just to keep open the hope of not giving up."

She took hold of the hand now absent-mindedly patting her arm and stilled it. They stopped walking. She wrapped her arms around him and held herself closely to him, their faces averted from one another. "Fool," she said sadly into his chest. "My dear, stupid fool." They held one another, he looking to the ground where even now long-forgotten seeds might stir themselves into life, and she after a while twisting her head to see the darkening sky, where stars already were revealing themselves, seeds which flowered as seeds, the brightening stars every night the flowers of the hidden stars at day.

In the early spring on a high mountain tiny flowers bloom, flowers so small and so close to the ground that only the sharp-sighted are likely to see them, or else those who know to look. Sometimes the flowers are so small that, viewing them, one can detect that they have color without really knowing what the color is. To imagine stars as flowers blooming at night is to imagine stars as flowers like these, so small, so distant, that their color is at best an intimation, a suggestion. To whom is the suggestion? Are there even tinier bees which fly about in search of these mountain flowers, bees which will nuzzle the petals and bathe themselves not in ash but in pollen? Do these bees see more clearly the flowers' color? And, in parallel, are there bees for the stars, bees which flit from one star-flower to the next, carrying their load not of ash but of pollen, bringing in this way star-messages from star-flower to star-flower? One is tempted to think that these flowers, whether in the sky or on the ground, never know their own color, just as we also don't know their color; and then one wonders if it is only the bees who know the color, or if even the bees do not know. How easy it is to overlook that in all of this, the bees themselves are unattested! There may be no bees flitting from flower to flower, whether those flowers are on the mountain ground reaching for the sky or in the sky reaching for the mountain ground. And if there are no bees, there may also be no flies, and if no flies, possibly no gods. Who then is there who knows the petals' colors and relays ash or pollen messages from star-flower to star-flower? Or even to that flower which over the course of a month dilates into bloom only to contract, the flower with a heart's rhythm, its waxing diastole and waning systole, pumping emptiness across the heavens, emptiness its own redundant and auxiliary message unadorned, unfettered, unencumbered by ash or pollen or anything... Who is it that relays, to whom is it relayed? Or are all these mistaken images, not signatures but counterfeits of signatures, stars that are not flowers though they look like them, moons that are neither stars nor flowers nor even hearts, though in a certain light or from a certain perspective or during a particular frame of mind they bear likeness to them. Is it all counterfeit, the heavens mirroring the earth, the earth mirroring the heavens, the crescent on the Esagila, the mole on a cheek? A cylinder seal rolling through the universe, leaving behind traces here and there, seemingly attesting to a signer who is not there, not to a witness then but to a no-witness, not to an agreeer but to a no-agreeer. A cylinder seal run amok, a cylinder seal all awhirl, a whirligig forever flattening and inscribing the universe with what we take to be stars or flowers or hearts or moons or even ourselves.

Chapter 14. Tašrītu 17

The city celebrated. However novel, however unorthodox, however opposed the priests, still the city celebrated, still the citizens delighted in the festival. Even now as the celebrations sputtered to a close music could be heard in bursts tumbling and dancing and leaping from the different city quarters, dying down and then re-erupting; and alongside the music, even part of it, was the occasional raucous laugh or a person shouting happily to another. It had been a beautiful, sun-gilded, fall day, with the languid river water meandering unhurriedly through the city, geese and ducks bobbing about, birds chattering in the early morning and now again in the waning day. The food vendors were closing shop but still the smell of their offerings, the crisp, savory meat and the freshly baked bread, wafted through the air, seemingly as inclined to linger as were the river and the slowly departing audience. Time was slow right now, as people cleaned up, departed or mulled about; everything went slow, patiently slow, as if time too were conspiring to draw out these final moments before something more ordinary re-asserted itself. Nabû-na'id had ordered a puppet show, something playful, not steeped in religious lore or in the drama of the other *Akītu* festival, the one properly Bābilim's, the time-honored, orthodox, unopposed one. He had wanted something simpler than that, something more glad, something which made no claim to deeper, much less cosmological, meanings. He wanted this even while knowing that the claim was not his to make or forbid – even while knowing that angered priests and ambitious sycophants even now racked their minds to uncover what they assumed was purposeful significance. And what would they make of the jugglers, dancers and singers whom he had commissioned? Would they suspect that the apostate king wanted to fill the crowds only with wonder and delight, to infect them with their own desire to dance and sing and even juggle? Would they suspect that the apostate king wanted a city which could play *pukku* and *mekkû* as he and Gubaru had done when they were boys long, long ago – before either of them mattered or even dreamed of mattering? The king wanted more than that, however: he wanted a city which could lose its toys without waking from its entrancing dream – a city which could celebrate a new, new year full of faith in all the tomorrows to come and unhaunted by the undiscovered, mostly forgotten, happily forgotten, needfully forgotten yesterdays.

They had done this the year before, but very much at the last minute. He had only had the idea a few days' march from the city, when he had suddenly been struck by the seemingly meaningful coincidence that he was likely to arrive on a day full of significance to Ḫarrānu, to Sîn and to his dead mother. Not only that, but in the month whose name meant "beginning." A second beginning, then; a new beginning – a new, new beginning. Hurried commands had been issued, proclamations made – but they had managed to do little more than declare the holiday, invite people to rest, and open normally closed parts of the palace and temples for awe-struck people to wander through. Still, it had not gone badly, and Nabû-na'id wondered if in some respects it had even been better than this well-planned repetition a year later – if only because the first time had been unexpected, at least in Bābilim. (It was entirely expected in Ḫarrānu.) Expectation and preparation didn't only open new possibilities; they restricted possibilities, too, and took away some of the life of it all. When at last the festival runs seamlessly and as expected, it will be dead, Nabû-na'id mused; and then he smiled and congratulated himself for the brief resurrection he had given the other *Akītu* festival merely by going off script. I will long be blamed for that, he observed to himself, and yet it was the kiss of life I gave that festival. What is resented is precisely that, the kiss of life. What is alive is always threatened with death; make everything dead, even festivals, and there is no longer the threat. Perhaps this partly accounted for the obsessiveness with which the temple officials regulated the celebrations – always with the worry that slight deviations, minor errors, would provoke and even justify a god's vengeance. Since at least retrospectively every festival could be found to have had flaws, the god's vengeance was always, it turned out, provoked and justified. This at least had the consolation of making catastrophe meaningful, even if it seemed also to posit that all would be secure, all would be safe, only when all was dead – when there was script only and no performer, when text never risked being marred by reader.

He was attempting something different, something which risked life and therefore also risked marring. Marring and being marred. Scarring and being scarred, too. There's no life without the possibility of mistake, the possibility of wound, the possibility of wounding. Our faces bear witness to that, if only in the scars which sculpt them. Accepting that, or trying to, he had written much of what was performed in the festival. He had written it and then he had given it over, not unreluctantly, to the interpretation of others. In particular, he had written the script which the puppets performed. Perhaps it was the first such performance in the history of puppetry – a performance of a tale unstrapped to religion or the city or the world, a tale in fact signifying nothing. A blank tale. Could there be such a thing? From the perspective of the puppets, yes: in their amethyst eyes and lapis lazuli ears, all tales were blanks. So, in any event, Nabû-na'id assumed. But from the perspective of the audience – the non-puppet audience? Did that include the flies buzzing overhead, the waterfowl in the nearby river, a passing dog or pig or braying ass? Did it include the sun or the moon or the sky-hidden stars? Or the sky itself? Could it be that blank tales proliferated, that there was more than one blank tale to be told? Or could all of these beings endure blankness no more than human beings could endure it – and as a result did all of them impress meanings wherever they encountered blanknesses, even if that meaning was a fly's or a duck's or a star's, or even the blank sky's? He imagined blanknesses and meanings rippling from the single puppet performance at their center, like waves in a pond in all directions – and he wondered whether blankness and meaning implied each other just as did crest and trough.

But then he wondered whether there was such a thing as a non-puppet audience. Insofar as there was a script, not just the one which the puppets performed but the one which the audience followed, laughing as if on cue, applauding as if on cue, silent and apprehensive as if on cue – was this not at least confusable with puppetry? He had seen so-called automatic puppets, puppets with springs and levers which, when released, jerked the puppet into motion – not unlike the muscles in animals and men. Their strings were inside rather than outside – but strings there were nonetheless. Were any of us different than that? And if not, then what is there but blankness for our amethyst eyes and lapis lazuli ears to perceive? What trouble we all will have gone to, just to misapprehend blankness! Even though the misapprehension torments us too.

What was the tale he had written for the puppets to tell? What was its peculiar flavor of blankness? There had been a puppet, ridiculously overdressed – one might mistake him for a king if one didn't suspect him for a buffoon. Or for a puppet. Or for a collection of rags and wood and string. Calling this a king or a buffoon or even a puppet already muddied the tale's blankness. But so be it. It muddied the blankness and yet also left the blankness completely untouched. Both at once. This puppet – buffoon – king – whatever it was – wandered around the toy city in what appeared to be evening, often in the company of a dog – or a puppet – or a collection of rags and wood and string (and not even that). Let's call it a dog – a dog whom he couldn't control, a dog who frequently knocked him over. Together they were in search of something. Wordlessly, always only through extravagant gestures, the king-buffoon puppet, after having encountered this or that – a piece of pottery, for example or a tablet or a statue – would give expression to his excitement and delight. Arms raised toward the sky, ridiculously dancing a jig, face contorted into masks of pleasure and joy, the king-buffoon would celebrate his discovery, in the process forgetting himself. Meanwhile the dog circled about him, unconcerned by the great discovery, in pursuit of his own discoveries – and in a way the dog seemed to be dancing his own jig, his steps jaunty and exaggerated, his tail wagging almost in unison with the king-buffoon's waving hands, his face asmile with lolling tongue in a way evocative of the king-buffoon's delight-twisted face. Eventually, inevitably, their two dances became entwined, the two dancers nonetheless insensible of one another. For a while the two dances interwove, the corresponding puppets still charmingly oblivious, but eventually interweaving gave way to intersection, then to tripping, then to falling. It was always the king-buffoon who fell; always he fell in such a way that the object whose discovery had so delighted him would break. This was the cue for the audience's silence to flower into laughter, even as dust and fragments from the breakage soiled the costume and person of the king-buffoon, while the dog, initially hurt and mistrustful, gradually accepted that the physical contact had been accidental rather than intentional, meaningless rather than meaningful, and licked first himself clean, then the king-buffoon.

So it went with each discovery – a piece of pottery, a tablet, a dog figurine, a statue of a king's head, a god's statue – until at last the king-buffoon spotted a puppet-moon presiding over the puppet-sky. Puppet-night had fallen; the puppet-stage had tiny flickering flames illuminating it; and the full puppet-moon had only recently risen, in all its serene, untouchable glory. Here at last was something the king-buffoon's clumsiness and self-absorption couldn't destroy. The moon was beyond his reach; he could not hold it, which also meant he could not drop it. All he could do was point. Pointing, his puppet-face contorted with puppet-laughter, puppet-dancing his puppet-jig, he tried to call the puppet-dog's attention to what he pointed at. But the dog kept looking at the pointing finger and not beyond. Frustrated, the king-buffoon would pause his jig and instruct the dog, wordlessly but with ever-more emphatic gestures, trying to guide the dog's eyes down his hand, then finger, then beyond towards whatever it was the finger pointed at. After many a comical misunderstanding, he would at last succeed in getting the dog to look past his finger – but each time, in his preoccupation with making the dog understand, the king-buffoon would forget that the moon was itself moving – and so each time, when the dog at last looked past the finger to what it pointed at, it pointed at where the moon no longer was. Most often it pointed at nothing, at the emptiness of the sky, at the sky's blankness. The king-buffoon, frustration building, would try again; ever more absurd misunderstandings would follow (the audience laughing happily); but always the outcome was the same: the dog would understand only when the finger pointed at where the moon no longer was. Meanwhile, however, as a kind of distraction from the intensity of the farce the king-buffoon was enacting, perhaps as a kind of refuge from it as well, the dog on his own had noticed the moon. He started to howl. The king-buffoon, non-plussed, would hush it (the audience chuckling), would try to capture once more the dog's attention, would once more begin the lesson of showing the dog the moon – the very moon he was already howling at. But always the same mistakes would be made; always the king-buffoon would point elsewhere than where the moon now was, always the dog, distracted by the moon itself, would howl out of tune with the king's attempted demonstration, and always, at the height of their misunderstanding, the crowd would laugh.

Meanwhile, of course, the puppet-moon was making its westward way. Both king-buffoon and dog seemed oblivious to what that portended, and the king-buffoon in particular was unprepared for the eventuality which followed. The moon disappeared. Indeed, it did so behind the backs of the puppets, but in plain view to the audience, all while the king-buffoon was engrossed in his laughable, angry remonstration once more with the uncomprehending, periodically howling dog. Indeed, the dog was just throwing his head back to erupt into yet another howl, the king was just in the process of turning to look at where he pointed, when both stopped short, the howl dying in the throat of the dog and transforming into a comical, sputtering cough, the king's pointing arm dropping abruptly to his side as if the string holding it up had broken. It was as if each had been struck. Where was the moon? Where was the moon? The words were never spoken – the entire performance being mimed – but the meaning of the gestures of both puppets could not be clearer, even though the gestures of the king-buffoon and of the dog were vastly different. The newly-born puppet-day dawned on the puppet-stage with the king-buffoon dashing back and forth, looking first upward for the moon, then looking downward, peering over this edge of the stage then that, even digging into the ground, before looking behind, in or under this or that object – the door of a house, a jar, a puppet-passerby's clothing (in the process hilariously revealing the passerby's nakedness). At one point the king-buffoon jimmied open the dog's mouth to look for the moon, even sticking his own head far inside the mouth to check if the moon was there. To no avail. Meanwhile, the dog stared frantically at the sky, then frantically all about him. He spotted a cream-colored round clay pot in a second story window and started to howl, only to realize his mistake and stop; a fantastically obese, almost spherical woman dressed in white and fully veiled similarly provoked a near-howl, aborted as soon as it sounded; the king-buffoon's round ass as he bent to look for the moon beneath a doormat likewise elicited a near-howl, to the particular delight of the itself-almost-howling audience.

So on the puppet-stage passed an accelerated puppet-day, until suddenly, puppet-night once more falling, the king-buffoon and the dog simultaneously made an exciting discovery: there the moon was, where they had in fact regularly looked, somehow not seeing it: in the eastern puppet-sky! But something was wrong; the full moon was gone. It had somehow become chipped or damaged, even without the king-buffoon tripping over the dog, falling and dropping it; somehow the moon had nonetheless been reduced to this lesser, broken form. The king-buffoon's gestures betrayed his consternation, his confusion, but the dog was unaffected, seemingly just as happy to howl at this, after all, ever-so-slightly lesser, ever-so-slightly broken moon as before at the full one. The king-buffoon, observing what might have been merely the dog's acceptance or complacency, appeared instead to believe that the dog had failed to detect the difference – and so a new comical exchange began, in which the king-buffoon endeavored to call the dog's attention, not to the moon, but to the missing portion of the moon. Many of the same problems repeated themselves, but now in an even harder form: for, if it's difficult to point at what's there, how much more difficult is it to point at what's not? Add to this a further confounding factor: it wasn't clear that the dog in fact didn't detect a difference. Perhaps the dog detected a difference without being bothered by it. Or perhaps for the dog this wasn't the old moon returned in a new, lesser form, but rather a new moon, perhaps even unrelated to what the evening before he had howled at. Perhaps then not a moon; perhaps for the dog never had there been a moon. The comedy of it all relied on this paradox, that the king-buffoon needed the dog to accept that the moons were the same in order to detect that the moons were different. All of his gestures, facial contortions, building frustrations and then erupting angers and finally drooping despairs circled around this paradox which, conceivably, for the dog didn't even exist. And if it didn't exist for the dog, even less did it exist for the puppet-dog.

It must honestly be acknowledged that this new stage of the puppet show elicited less laughter from the audience than the earlier ones. In fact the laughter died away, withered on the vine, gave way to ever longer expanses of silence, to growing disinterest, and to a fading away of the crowds. Plenty of other spectacles attracted their attention, after all, and so the wilting of the crowd seemed harmless rather than judgmental; no boos or jibes were heard. People just dispersed to other things. Even this, perhaps, was on cue, however, as earlier the laughter had been. Only a few remained in the audience for the final act, when the drooping, despairing king-buffoon made one last discovery, alongside the dog. The lesser, broken moon still shone over the puppet-sky, still in the east but advancing toward the west, when the dog noticed something else, something past it. The dog began to howl, much to the irritation of the king-buffoon, who had remained single-mindedly focused on making the dog see what was missing in the moon. This time, however, the dog was peculiarly obstinate in his howls; nothing the king-buffoon did succeeded in redirecting his gaze. Even as the puppet-moon journeyed westward, the puppet-dog's eyes remained fixed to the east; and after an embarrassingly long time, after many a comical, utterly failed attempt to gain the dog's attention, it at last occurred to the king-buffoon to look toward whatever it was which had so riveted the dog. Perhaps in so doing he finally understood that the dog too could point. And indeed, he had not been looking long in the direction towards which the dog stared before the king-buffoon too began to point, all excited and astonished.

But what was it that the dog was howling at? What was it that the king-buffoon pointed towards? Most of the handful of people still watching were at a loss; they looked up and down the stage, bewildered; more and more the gesticulations and then admonishments of the puppets seemed directed specifically at them, the audience members, rather than at each other; and eventually, if only out of awkwardness, perhaps out of boredom, the remnants of the audience just wandered away, thinking the show had lost its thread, had ended, unfortunately, in failure. They shrugged it off, however, most of them in good enough spirits not to let this detract from their enjoyment of the festival. Perhaps there were still jugglers or dancers to see? Perhaps there were some vendors of food who hadn't yet closed their shops? In the end only the two puppets were left, alone on their stage, looking eastward, even while their small puppet-moon was far to the west; they had ceased to gesticulate, had settled into stillness, and sat side-by-side on the stage, watching the enormous blankness of the full moon rise over the waning festival.

Such was Nabu-na'id's blank tale.

She was seated by herself in the center room, near a crackling, sputtering fire, wearing white robes, a white shawl and a white veil. Beside her rested a cup, and he could see in the fire's light the cup's turmeric stains – its colors not unlike the fire's. She had dismissed her attendants and seemed lost in thought. He hesitated whether to disturb her – whether to join her. He kicked the dirt on the floor shyly and eventually cleared his throat.

"Do you want company? You can say no."

She didn't immediately respond, but he knew she had heard him. She was probably trying to decide what her answer was to his question. "You can come," she finally said.

He drew near her. It felt odd to tower over her, so he too sat down, a few feet away, like her simply on the ground. She appeared to wrap the shawl more closely around her.

"Are you cold?"

Again she paused for a long time to consider the question, then answered, "Not really."

They listened to the fire. Occasionally it popped, shooting out sparks in shivering arcs. He could see the wood inhabited by fire, the dark coals glowing red. Perhaps the sparks, once they had tumbled to the floor and cooled, were like the doomed, upside-down fly of long before.

"I watched your puppet show," she eventually volunteered. "You had told me it signified nothing. You had told me it was a blank tale."

"So I understood it," he acknowledged.

"And yet, the central character was very like you."

He laughed. "The dog, you mean?"

Her head swayed a little, perhaps to indicate that her amusement was at best tepid, perhaps for some other reason. He wondered why she was staying veiled, first all by herself in this room, and now in his company. She didn't answer his question for a long time.

"Ok," she finally said. "The dog. But also the king or the fool or the foolish king or the kingly fool. That one and the dog – perhaps they were both very like you."

Something like a smile tore through his face, though whether it expressed humor or sorrow, happiness or anguish, was unclear even to himself. He was trying to accept that unclarity, to let it lurk.

"Can the tale still be blank if the characters are very like you? Can it signify nothing and still signify you?"

He suddenly felt very tired. Where did this tiredness come from? It seemed somehow to be related to how she was dressed, to how she hadn't unveiled, to how her body, behind the white robes and white shawl and white veil, seemed to be facing something other than him. But how could he know? What kind of facing was even at issue? He looked away from the voice coming from the whiteness facing he knew not what. He looked at the turmeric stains in the cup, how the colors flashed in and out of existence depending on how the light and shadows caught them, how the stains became the fire's puppet or just the fire's.

"You don't need me to answer that question," he finally said.

* * * * *

From the [fragmentary] Assyrian Accounts of Herodotus

... learn little regarding the first puppets, who they were, who made them and for what purpose. Elsewhere I have written about the Dionysian rituals performed by the Egyptians, which involve puppets the size of small children. It is on this occasion only that Egyptians will eat swine; only to Dionysus and the Moon will Egyptians sacrifice a pig, which they do in one and the same festival. But this is not because they honor pigs. It is because they consider them unclean. How this makes sense, the Egyptians can explain, for they have an account of why this particular festival requires the sacrifice of swine, and it's not unrelated to the puppets. For, as I wrote in my Histories, these Egyptian puppets are unusual for their proportions: the puppets themselves stand about two feet in height and are worked by strings, but the only part of them which actually moves is the phallus, which

also is almost two feet in size. Thus it is as if the puppet has a puppet, and it is not the puppet proper which moves. An account closer to the truth is rather that the puppet proper moves its own puppet, which is the phallus. But what a curious puppet the phallus is – not unlike a hand puppet, but who is the puppeteer? Is this not the appendage of man least amenable to his own direction? Our comic poets have sometimes even suggested that it is the phallus which moves the man. The Egyptians suspect something similar, especially the women who during the festival carry the puppets and work them. It is the women who make the puppet's puppet rise, nod, and slacken. But then – again – who is puppet, who is puppeteer? As in any Dionysian festival, what is top and what is bottom, who leads and who is led, gets turned upside-down or inside-out. This is part of the explanation of why unclean animals are sacrificed – because in this festival it is uncertain what is clean and what isn't, what the distinction is between dirty and pristine. So it is as well that under the spell of Dionysus an army of women will rout an army of men, and only the maniacal Maenads are sane.

Some have suggested that the puppets of this festival began as thyrsi, others that only the phalluses of the puppets were once thyrsi, and still others that thyrsi began as phalluses. No one has suggested that thyrsi were once puppets, but even this is not inconceivable. Such confusions are common enough; there are similar debates about the crescents – or horns – of Dionysus, as indeed about his origins – he more than any other god having different accounts of his birth, or else perhaps having many different births, and himself being perhaps one and many. Some say he is the child of the Moon, others that that claim is due only to a mere and insignificant accident, the confusion of names – of his real mother Semele and of the Moon goddess Selene. No less dispute plagues the place of his birth – somewhere in the east, certainly, but was it Egypt, or Thrace, or India, or somewhere in between?

Let us say Egypt. My inquiries have shown that almost all the names of gods came to Hellas from foreign lands, and of these, mostly Egypt. On the other hand Aegyptus was a descendant of Io, an Argive impregnated by Zeus, who, having been turned into a heifer, was harassed by a fly all the way to Egypt, where once more she became a human being and bore Zeus' son Epaphus, father to Libya, grandfather to Belus, great-grandfather to Aegyptus, for whom the refuge of his great-great-grandmother was named. Is Egypt ancestor or descendant, then, puppeteer or puppet? Let us say "Egypt," as I have already suggested, but let us not hasten to assume that we know what "Egypt" means. Or even that it means. Perhaps we must come to accept that before meanings come words; before words meant words named – and what were the names but what was sought? Whether what was sought exists, existed, ever will exist, or is beyond any possibility of existence, we cannot say. All we can say is the name, and we give the name. This is the reunion of broken parts, of fragments, which I'm told the Babylonians call algebra and by which a man may prove that he himself is the ghost of his own father. In the beginning is a reunion of broken parts. It is as much to say that there have always been puppets and perhaps have only been puppets, cows the puppets of flies the puppets of gods the puppets of men birthed of cows.

Egypt, then, let us say. The first puppets were Egypt, who they were, who made them, and for what purpose: Egypt.

* * * * *

She found him sitting among the statues.

"Father!" she exclaimed in surprise. "Why are you not in the capital?"

Her father looked up from his seated position on the ground. "Mikum-Nisaba," he said slowly. "I just wanted some time with you and the statues… these puppets who have lost their strings."

She stared at him in silence, then tracked his gaze to the

broken dog figurine – or perhaps the figurine of a broken dog. "Even if we put strings on its limbs," she said, "we could not make that dog run."

"But I see it running already – in my mind's eye. There must be strings somewhere then. Something must make that dog move. A puppeteer, or even just a desire. The rabbit being chased. Who would have thought the rabbit being chased was the puppeteer? How clever."

Mikum-Nisaba pulled a stool over towards her father and sat on it, so that the two of them both were facing more or less the same direction rather than each other. "I am surprised to see you," she observed. "I've heard disturbing things. I've heard Kuraš's kingdom almost surrounds us, except to the south. I've heard that his army is nibbling away our neighbors and our vassals."

"Yes," Nabû-na'id answered glumly. "I've sent Gubaru to Gutium – I need at least someone on that frontier whom I can trust. He stands between Kuraš and us. For now. But, my daughter, do you know what that means?"

She shook her head.

"It means that I am all the lonelier. My dog is dead, my best friend is off to the east, my wife is..." He stopped.

Mikum-Nisaba raised an eyebrow. "My mother is what?" she asked.

He was silent. Then he grumbled, "Occupied."

"You know," opined Mikum-Nisaba – or perhaps it was the high priestess En-nigaldi-Nanna – "it comes across as rather self-indulgent to be focused on your loneliness right now, while your kingdom gasps. You are not the only one who has become lonely in the service of a state. Or a god."

He didn't reply. He just stared at the statue.

She tried another tack. "Why this sudden fascination with puppets? I heard about the performance at Sîn's *Akītu* festival."

Then, somewhat to her own surprise, she added, "Some would say Bābilim had more pressing concerns than a new religious festival which happened to alienate most of the elite and the entire Marduk priesthood."

He continued staring at the statue, but gradually a smile broke across his stony visage. "You sound like your brother. Life is full of surprises." Mikum-Nisaba didn't respond but felt irritated by the comparison.

"Your mother and I are also alike, you know," he suddenly volunteered. "She's occupied with what other people call canals. But I see them for what they are."

"What are they?"

"A kind of writing," he answered. "That's one way of looking at it. But of late I've been musing over another possibility – maybe just the same thing in different words, maybe not."

"What?"

"Her canals, or her writing, or whatever it is – they're the strings by which she is luring a puppet forward, getting it to dance. She has her blank writing, I have mine."

"How will that work?"

"We shall see."

She got up off her stool, strode to the broken dog figurine and picked it up. She held it in her hands, rotating it this way and that to examine it more closely. Eventually she asked, "Am I among the puppets who have lost their strings?"

"How can you be?" he responded. "You just marched across the room and goaded that statue into motion."

"So it turns out I have strings?"

He didn't miss a beat. "If you're a puppet."

"Would I be your puppet then?" She looked up from the figurine and directly at him.

He didn't hold her gaze but instead let his head drop. "Who is to say who is whose puppet?" he muttered. "I'm not sure that conversations have to be puppet shows, but they can become them. Everything can. Maybe when the eclipsed moon set during the morning watch long ago we both briefly glimpsed our master. Wouldn't that be appropriate to the priestess of the Moon? Or maybe it was my desire that there be a puppet master that caused me to read, and to invite you to read, that moonset in the particular way that we did. Is it better for us to be mere puppets, moved by strings, or for us to be alone in the world with no puppet master?"

"Is that an apology?" she wondered aloud. "If it matters, I don't know that consecrating me to Sîn requires one."

"If it matters," he repeated.

"You used to tell me about the man from Uru who set off for Ḫarrānu and then beyond, all at the urging of his god."

"Yes, those were the stories Belet-ṣeri-dannat used to discuss with me, stories which resemble ones my mother told me too." He stopped, then mused aloud, "Now each of them has set off on their own mysterious journey, my mother having died, and Belet-ṣeri-dannat – I don't know what's become of him, beyond what dreams and visions may say."

"Did you know that that man of Uru's father was a statue-maker?"

"I don't think so. How do you know?"

"I found what I think are records of him here in the temple." She paused. "You know, father, I don't just collect statues. I also dawdle in the archives, read long-forgotten tablets. What else am I to do with my time, while I await the god's whisper? Maybe I read the tablets in part to find out how others waited – or how others were whispered to. For example, that man of Uru whom the god sent on his journeys, the one who sacrificed his son rather than his daughter."

"Belet-ṣeri-dannat always insisted that in the end the son wasn't sacrificed."

"If it matters," she responded, echoing herself and him.

"If it matters," he agreed.

"Some of the statues here in this temple – probably not these antiquarian ones which I've collected, though it's possible, but certainly the statues of the gods whom I help feed and clothe and bed – some of those statues may even now be the handwork of that man of Uru's father. His name –" she paused dramatically "– was Teri."

Nabû-na'id perked up. "Teri – like Ilteri?"

"Perhaps."

"One of the names which we say Sîn goes by, when he wishes not to go by Sîn. How curious. No wonder, then, that they left Uru only to settle in Ḫarrānu."

"Do you remember the name of his son? And of the wife of his son?"

"Abu Ram. Šarratu."

"Yes," his daughter said pregnantly.

Nabû-na'id thought for a moment. "The elevated father. The Moon?"

"And what would Šarratu be in Šumeran?" Mikum-Nisaba was enjoying the role of teacher.

"Ningal," her father said slowly. "The wife of Nanna." He paused. "Another name we say is Sîn's."

"Yes," his daughter repeated.

"So you're suggesting that this story Belet-ṣeri-dannat and I discussed is an account of men and women, all named in one way or another for the Moon, for Sîn, migrating from Uru to Ḫarrānu, from one of the two great temples of Sîn to the other. But what does this have to do with the father being a statue-maker?"

"I came across a legend in the archive. There was a man, not named Teri, who was the maker of temple statues. A woman came to make an offering to the statues, but the father wasn't there. His son, not named Abu Ram, for some reason became enraged, drove the woman off, and destroyed all but the biggest statue. In the hands of that statue he placed a stick. When the father returned, he saw, to his amazement, all the destroyed statues, but for the one holding the stick. 'What in god's name happened here?' he asked his son. 'Sîn,' his son said, pointing to the stick-brandishing statue, 'sickened to see flour offered to stone. He destroyed the statues.' 'You mock me!' the father retorted. 'Do statues have will, do they have knowledge, do statues move?' To this it is written that his son replied, 'Father, listen to yourself.'"

"That is the story which I've read. As far as I can tell, it wasn't long after that the father and the son, with their wives and families, set out on their journey, their *ḫarrānu*, to Ḫarrānu. But the ones who journeyed had new names: they named themselves Teri, Abu Ram, Šarratu. I suppose it is not clear whether they named themselves for the god or for the stick-brandishing statue. Whichever it was, they became a new form of it: a god made incarnate, or a statue made mobile – what you might be pleased to call a puppet. Maybe the statue-destroying son was already a version of the god or of the statue."

She fell silent. Her father let his head fall into hands – the posture perhaps indicated grief, perhaps thought. Mikum-Nisaba didn't know. En-nigaldi-Nanna didn't either. She waited. Eventually he spoke.

"If they were puppets," he said, "the string which moved them began with the son's advice to the father to listen to himself. The whisper of the god was his own whisper. And maybe the same is suggested if they were the god made incarnate." He looked at his daughter for a moment, quizzically and yet also with something like a smile in his eyes. "You've become quite the scholar, my dear."

"No, not a scholar," she answered quickly. "I was trying to

understand how to wait, how to listen for whispers or feel the tug of a string. Even a puppet has to learn that."

They sat in silence, neither one moving. Only after a long while did Nabû-na'id inquire, "What whisper did you hear, what tug did you feel, which sent you into the archive?"

To his surprise, a peel of laughter erupted from his daughter Mikum-Nisaba and from the priestess En-nigaldi-Nanna.

"I am archived!" she exclaimed. "Whispers and tugs are the way out of an archive, not the way in!"

* * * * *

They were to escape him, the white one, their relative – his uncle, their father. How he would glower at them through the darkness of night if they were detected! But the whisper had been clear: Return to the land of your fathers, your relatives. Only there will I abide you.

But where was the land of their fathers, their relatives? Ḫarrānu was one such place, and they were already there. To the southeast was Uru – and Uru, too, was one such a place, a land of their fathers, their relatives. Or they could go to the southwest, whence he had come, the land of his father and his grandfather, once they had left the lands, Ḫarrānu, Uru, of their fathers, their relatives. Whichever destination they chose was at once a return towards fathers left behind and a leaving behind of fathers, including this one, the white one who glowered.

This was her question, not his. He seemed not to doubt what the whisper, what the whisperer, meant. She heard ambiguity, but he a destination, he a command. Only there will I abide you. Only there. There. He would go there, and she was to follow. Her sister too, their children and the lambs. But what if he were mistaken, what if the whisperer if there were a whisperer, the whisper if there were not, meant something else, a different land, a different father, a different relative, a different there? How could he not wonder? Had he not once before been too quick to know what darkness concealed?

(She looked at her sister, her angry, unloved sister, her angry, unloved, fertile sister, surrounded by her children, by her lambs. What have I to carry with me, she wondered? For she was barren, no god had taken from her her disgrace, no lamb had been added or offered. It was then that her eyes caught the gleaming statues, statues flickering with the flames, statues of their father's god. No cry wakens me from sleep, no mouth tugs on my breast. I am alone, cold, stony, like those statues; let them be born of me, they are already my children, it is in fact they who whisper us away. Return us, they say, to the land of your fathers, our fathers, your relatives, our relatives. But where is that? It is the land itself; it is the desert, the source of stone, there where no seed, no plant, tosses a psalm at the sun; it is the barren womb. He had not understood, he who had mistaken her sister for her, his brother for himself. And so she took them, she took the statues, she bore them. If the white one should ever find them, if in his glowering light she were asked to stand, she would decline. I am in the way of women, she would say. It is what I bear.)

* * * * *

"Why *him*?" he asked angrily.

"He is my most trusted friend."

"He is a Parsuan!"

"His name is Parsuan – if names belong to any language. But that doesn't make *him* Parsuan. He has lived almost his whole life in the same places where I have lived almost all of mine. Whatever he is, how can I not also be that?"

Bel-šar-uṣur kicked a stool out of his way, then glared at his father. "Gubaru is an oaf and a Parsuan, and you have put him in charge of all that's left standing between us and Kuraš. Are you a fool? Do you not care?"

"Gubaru is not an oaf," his father answered mildly. "He has

extensive experience, most of it at my side, with both military matters and governance. He is a capable, thoughtful man, and above all a man I trust."

"A Parsuan!" his son repeated, almost spat. "You send him, not me, and of course not yourself, all while your empire is crumbling. You say you sent Gubaru because he has experience – but his experience is a fraction of mine. For ten years I was more Bābilim's king than you! And yet you keep me in the city, and you send your childhood sidekick to the frontier, and you yourself go dodder with statues!"

Nabû-na'id gave his son what he hoped was a benign, or at least bland, look. "Ah, you know about that, do you?" he asked calmly. His son didn't answer. "My trip to Uru was no secret, but what I did in the temple was known to few. Do you spy on me?" his father inquired. Again no answer. "Yes, then. Spies," his father stated simply. "I am of course aware that you ruled this land for ten years in my absence, that you were more its ruler than I. I even will grant that you ruled it well. Given my unpopular decisions, given my eccentricities, it's a wonder that powerful cliques haven't tried to return you to the throne."

His son looked at him curiously but still said nothing.

His father continued. "Of course that is to misunderstand the wonder. Those cliques exist, I am well aware. Surely they have approached you."

"Now who has spies?" his son asked tauntingly.

"Oh, they're available to me, but I don't need them. And, for this, I don't use them. Like I said, the wonder is misunderstood. What's wondrous is not that the cliques haven't tried. They must have tried. What's wondrous is that you haven't agreed to their proposal."

Bel-šar-uṣur held his father's gaze, both their faces expressionless. Still he said nothing.

"As you well remember, I came to the throne because the

Egibi house, whom I still pretend are our friends, used you like a tool for their own ends. You were tricked; you were lucky to escape with your life; you were even luckier not to have to become king, right then and there. But it wasn't all luck. Believe it or not, I helped you. Arguably, I saved you. It was not my ambition that put me on the throne in your stead. It was something else."

"Love?" his son said, with a hint of mockery.

His father stifled a laugh, but what came out was almost like a bark, like how his own father had sounded. "I wish I were worthy of that word. Let's settle for something seemingly more ordinary, though that's more appearance than truth. Care."

Bel-šar-uṣur looked away from his father, out the window toward the temple with the horns or the crescents or whatever it was his father wanted to claim they were. "Because of my mole?" he finally asked.

"No."

An uncomfortable silence settled between them while, for some reason, neither could bear to look at the other. Finally Nabû-na'id spoke. "You were tricked once. People have approached you, I assume, to try to trick you again. Perhaps even the same people. It may surprise you, but it doesn't much matter to me. I am instead thankful – more than that, I am *proud* – that you haven't so easily yielded."

"So the wonder is that I haven't been tricked?"

"No," his father answered slowly. "Fifteen years ago, perhaps, that might have been the wonder for me. But I wasn't oblivious to how well you governed when I was in Teima. I know you're not a fool."

"What is the wonder then?" his son asked, his voice harsh.

"Care," his father repeated. "Mine for you, yours for me."

His son continued to look away, out the window. The clamor of courtiers talking in the courtyard below suddenly erupted, then gradually subsided. For some reason, Bel-šar-uṣur calmly walked to the toppled stool and placed it upright again. Then, in a subdued voice he asked, "Why have you kept me here then?"

Nabû-na'id stared at the floor. "It's not that I don't trust you with the frontier, with Gutium," he said, seemingly to the floor. "It's that I know that most of the temple and governmental elite don't trust me. They trust you. They think you have your head screwed on right, while mine is screwed on wrong – or maybe it isn't screwed on at all. I need you here to help keep them all in line. Our enemies are not just outside but inside; not just there" – he gestured vaguely toward the horizon " – but here."

"Have you considered that these elite might not be wrong in their judgments?"

"Which is to say, have I considered that my head is indeed not screwed on right or at all?" He sighed. "Of course I have, more honestly than you might expect. But I have decided that they are mistaken and that I am not." He paused and then finally looked up at his son. "So long as you are near, the Egibi house and their partisans will think they have a hand on the lever of power. They will conspire and contrive, and all, or at least most of their energy will be spent on a dead-end, on something harmless."

"Ah," his son muttered. "So I am a decoy."

"No. You are my strongest defense of the city." Nabû-na'id said each word slowly and deliberately.

"How?"

"The Egibi house – their allies – their ilk –" Nabû-na'id made an awkward, scoffing gesture with his arm, as if he were pawing them away "– they serve their own interest. They will betray us to Kuraš, if that's where they perceive their interest. They will betray me to you, if instead their interest, they think, lies there. I want to encourage them to think their interest lies there."

"Perhaps it does," Bel-šar-uṣur suggested enigmatically.

"Mmmm," his father responded.

"You think I will stand up to them out of loyalty to you?"

"I don't especially want you to stand up to them. Better if they think you aren't."

"Let me correct myself," Bel-šar-uṣur stated, with something like mockery in his voice. "You want me to stand with you, out of loyalty to you."

"Of course I want that. I even oddly expect it. Do it for me, do it for your mother, do it for your sister, do it for the city. Do it for whatever you need to do it for."

"But you trust that I will do it."

"Yes."

"Out of loyalty."

His father walked to the window where not long before his son had stood. He looked at the same temple, at the same horns or crescents or whatever it was he pretended to believe they were. "No," he said at last, his voice determined, even a little shrill. "Out of care."

Speak to Bel-šar-uṣur the prince-regent of Bābilim, thus speaks Itti-Marduk-balaṭu, son of Nabû-aḫḫe-iddina and head of the house of Egibi.

May Šamaš, Marduk, Sîn and Nabû keep you alive and prospering. We are, as you know, a trading house, with business in all lands, friends in all places. We have been entrusted with an important message for you. We seek discreet consultation with you, to better serve the kingdom.

Speak to Gubaru, governor of Gutium, thus speaks Itti-Marduk-balaṭu, son of Nabû-aḫḫe-iddina and head of the house of Egibi.

May Šamaš and Marduk keep you alive and prospering. We are, as you know, a trading house, with business in all lands, friends in all places. We have been entrusted with an important message for you. We seek discreet consultation with you, to better serve the kingdom.

Speak to Kuraš, great king, king of the world, thus speaks Itti-Marduk-balaṭu, son of Nabû-aḫḫe-iddina and head of the house of Egibi.

May the gods keep you alive and prospering. We are, as you know, a trading house, with business in all lands, friends in all places. We have been entrusted with an important message for you. We seek discreet consultation with you, to better serve the kingdom.

Speak to Nabû-na'id, king of Bābilim, king of the four corners, king of the world, thus speaks Itti-Marduk-balaṭu, son of Nabû-aḫḫe-iddina and head of the house of Egibi.

May Sîn and Nabû keep you alive and prospering. We are, as you know, a trading house, with business in all lands, friends in all places. We have been entrusted with an important message for you. We seek discreet consultation with you, to better serve the kingdom.

Itti-Marduk-balaṭu, as usual cocooned within a cloud of perfume, was unconcerned. He studied each tablet briefly, laid each down in a straight line on the table and then easily met his gaze. "Forgeries," he stated. "Given my house's reach and reputation, you can hardly expect me to be shocked that others try to profit from our name."

"The seal impression is one of yours."

"Well, yes. But cylinder seals are easily stolen."

"You did not report one lost."

"I did not know it. Again, who can be surprised? Besides the disruption due to the recent death of my father, our house, as you know, also handles very complex interactions. Some of the work has to be delegated. And with the delegation of the work goes the delegation of my seal." He laughed. "Don't tell me that it's any different in the palace."

Bel-šar-uṣur stared at him for a moment. "As a matter of fact, it is quite different in the palace. The king my father demands scrupulous care of all seals and all tablets. And precisely because your house handles complex interactions, as you say, I find it – surprising – that you don't require similar care. As we both know, a carelessly signed document can lead to great troubles."

"And great triumphs," Itti-Marduk-balaṭu added, almost in a whisper.

"No," Bel-šar-uṣur stated firmly. "Troubles."

Itti-Marduk-balaṭu sighed. "Do you want me to promise to be more careful?" he asked, with a hint of mockery.

For a moment it appeared like Bel-šar-uṣur might strike him or smash his desk. But at the very cusp of explosion he instead smiled.

"Yes," he answered. "I expect you to be more careful. I expect you to be full of care." And then he erupted into laughter.

Itti-Marduk-balaṭu looked at him curiously. "I fail to understand what's so funny," he observed calmly.

"It doesn't matter," Bel-šar-uṣur responded. "I expect you to find the thief of your seal and report to me quickly. I'd like to talk to him."

"It may be hard to find the thief," murmured Itti-Marduk-balaṭu.

"Is anything hard for the House of Egibi?" the crown prince replied, his eyebrows arched, his tone mimicking the hint of mockery which had been directed at him only moments before. "Find him. Find him and bring him to me. I would hate to trouble my father with such matters."

Itti-Marduk-balaṭu didn't respond. He raised himself slowly from his chair and then, still slowly, paced the length of the room. He then turned, slowly retraced his steps, and sat down. "Suppose I can find the thief. What then?"

"We will talk."

Itti-Marduk-balaṭu grinned. "You mean you'll have a discreet consultation, perhaps?"

"Perhaps."

"And you'll ask him about the scribe." They looked at one another.

"Of course. It's clear, as you obviously observed, that the letters were written by the same scribe. I'm sure you would have told me if you had recognized the writing style."

Itti-Marduk-balaṭu looked again at the tablets lined up on the table. "I can make inquiries. About the seal. But to find the scribe, I would need you to leave the tablets behind."

"No. I will leave one tablet behind."

"Leave the one to the governor of Gutium, then."

"Why that one?"

"It's the one that doesn't belong."

"How's that?"

Itti-Marduk-balaṭu lifted his head and looked calmly at Bel-šar-uṣur. "It's the only one not addressed to a king."

"What do you think?"

Nabû-na'id shrugged. "He's testing the waters. He's testing you. Those tablets didn't find their way to you by chance."

"What do you want me to do?"

Nabû-na'id inspected his son closely. "Whatever seems best to you," he answered – frankly or enigmatically.

"Is that all you have to say?"

Nabû-na'id looked weary. "The Eḫulḫul will be finished soon," he said, changing the subject. "My promise is almost kept. Soon I will lead the god by his hand into his long-abandoned city and long-abandoned temple. But what form will this god have when I lead him back? I have been thinking about that."

Bel-šar-uṣur looked exasperated. "Now it's you who's testing the waters," he said. "Now it's you who's testing me."

His father wrinkled his brow. He thought about it for a moment, and then conceded the point. "Maybe I am baiting you, trying to convey how small everything seems to me nowadays, how unworthy of the fight that nonetheless is coming. We may die for all this smallness, you and I... and part of me wants to die for something even smaller. This is where my father and I always differed from the Egibi House. What they see as large, what they see as worthy, he and I always saw as –" he paused, searching for words, "– barely worth re-marking."

His son said nothing.

"And yet," Nabû-na'id continued, "all those terribly small things, all those terrible small things, have nonetheless ended up directing my life, shaping it, shaping me. Even the grandest statue is the work of something small – small gestures, small hands, small men. And I am not even the grandest statue. I am not even that."

His son still said nothing.

"What form should Sîn take when I lead him by his hand back into his temple? Is the white stone from Arabi before which my mother lay – is this truly to be my object of care?" He stopped and became thoughtful. "You wrote that once – do you remember?" he asked his son.

Bel-šar-uṣur looked confused. "No," he admitted, shaking his head.

"You did write it," his father asserted confidently, "even if you don't remember. Or you had it written, anyway. What is to be your object of care? Will it be me your father, or me your king, or me your rival? Will it be my kingdom or even your kingdom? Will it be your own life? Or will it be some stone lying even now somewhere in a desert half-exposed to Sun and Moon – half-exposed and half-buried too?" He gestured vaguely toward the window and toward whatever stretched endlessly beyond the window.

He looked up at his son. "Will my object of care have been a mere stone? That's a question I ask myself all the time."

He stopped, seemingly at a loss for words, and abruptly directed his gaze at the ground.

"These tablets…" his son began.

"Not even stone," his father interrupted. "Dried mud. The Egibi house may finally conclude that I am mad because of my concern for a mere stone, but they are even madder because of their concern for dried mud."

"For what is written in it," Bel-šar-uṣur corrected.

"No. In the end they are concerned with the mud.

"They're trying to bait me into some kind of conspiracy. They probably have baited others already. Maybe Gubaru. Maybe Kuraš."

"Mud," his father repeated. "It's all mud." He paused. "You know, in my mind's eye I see my mother lying before that white stone from Arabi. Of course it was you who saw her, who found her, not me – but still I see her. Maybe I alone see her. And I think that huddled mass, or perhaps what that mass stood for – I think it eclipses the god. She eclipses the god. I think she should have been my object of care, not the stone – and yet it was she who put the stone first. Or the god. If the god isn't stone. Or is." He looked up, his eyes wild like his mother's had been, but not with fanatical belief – with grief, if that's different.

"I think my mother outshone Sîn but never knew it. I think her greatness exceeded his, eclipsed his. But her greatness, bizarrely, *was* her belief in him – him whom she eclipsed. And when you found her lying before that white stone of Arabi, what you saw was an eclipsed moon setting during the morning watch. What mattered wasn't the moon," he said, standing up. "What mattered was what eclipsed it."

The two men stood in silence, looking at each other.

"Do you understand?" Nabû-na'id finally asked, almost timidly.

"No," answered Bel-šar-uṣur curtly.

His father sighed. "It's not surprising. I don't understand either." He paced the room, back and forth, from window to door and back to the window again. "It's why I have been giving thought to the form the god will have when I lead him back to his temple. When I finally accomplish what may be the god's wish but what assuredly was my mother's."

"Does this have anything at all to do with whatever the House of Egibi is up to?" Bel-šar-uṣur asked, his voice tinged both with exasperation and something more tender than that, though who could be sure what it was?

His father laughed sadly. "Yes and no. They, for all their cleverness, will never be able to notice what eclipses the moon. But you know what?"

"What?"

"I am now realizing that you – you do see it. Even if you don't believe in it, or value it, or think much about it. Still, you see it."

"Is that a good thing?"

His father shook his head. "I haven't the slightest idea."

* * * * *

From the [fragmentary] Assyrian Accounts of Herodotus

...controversy, even rebellion. If one faction of the priesthood had always opposed him, now the other faction did as well. For the ceremony returning their god to his temple was deemed sacrilegious. This despite its conformity to the rituals of old in all respects. The king did indeed lead the god's statue by hand to his temple; the god was clothed in garments lined with gold, feasted with the most succulent

meats and richest wines, anointed with the purest oil, all as in times of old; the proper words, I am told, were spoken. But it was the god's statue which the priests objected to. It was as if the statue were unfinished, as if the god were yet being chiseled from the rock, as if the god were not fully formed – that was one interpretation; but another interpretation was that the rock was reclaiming the statue, that what had been finished was now unfinishing – as if the god were yielding his form back to the rock, or the rock were clawing it back, tearing it from the god, ripping it from him. A third interpretation was that rock and god were only fortuitously in relation to one another; that neither came from, nor yielded itself to, the other; that their conjunction in this moment, which partially obscured each, was mere accident, a circumstance, an intersection, wrought only by the ceaseless revolutions of all things.

Perhaps the king dared so strange a representation because the ceremony was so far from the capital. Perhaps he counted on the story not being told. Or perhaps, as others suggest, he had gone mad. His work to rebuild the temple had begun with an excavation of its foundations. But once he set his workers to digging, it seemed he could find no way and no cause to stop. Years passed with the hole only becoming bigger, with the king insisting that the true foundation hadn't yet been found. Men despaired; workers fled; some died in the hole, unable to climb out. And then, suddenly, with no change in the material circumstances of the excavation, with no discovery having been made, for no reason whatsoever that anyone could tell, could articulate, could say in words – suddenly a letter arrived and the digging stopped, and the building or rebuilding began. All of this reminds me of the labyrinth of Deioces of which I have written elsewhere. But the labyrinth of Labynetus was even more subtle than that of Deioces: it was a labyrinth which was only a hole, an emptiness, into which not even a messenger could enter. The escape from this labyrinth was by way of a messenger who did not enter, who arrived at its edge and yelled into the abyss that the time had come to stop. Then the building began; then the temple rose toward the sky; then a return was enabled, then a ceremony and with it a statue was possible. Whether the statue was sacrilegious or not, to my ear, misses the point. It even seems an example of how we men, we creatures of a day, are distracted by the small when the immense hovers over us. For all of this was built on top of a labyrinth which was an abyss. The foundation was a hole. Perhaps the statue's main achievement was to distract all from this horrifying fact. In this way, too, the labyrinth of Labynetus was most subtle. How comforting it would be to find a minotaur instead! Minotaurs can be slain – or buried – or made up. But what to make of heaven and earth when each is an abyss?

Meanwhile Cyrus nibbled at the frontier and internal enemies conspired. If nothing else, Labynetus' decisions seemed to drive them into each others' arms. With a consequence so foreseeable, should we accept that Labynetus failed to foresee it? This would be evidence of his madness, of his monomania, of the idée fixe which drove him. It is not impossible. All of us who have lived into old age have seen instances of such remarkable blindness – have lived those instances as well as seen them – have found ourselves confronting with shock and horror what was always before our noses. Have found our tails in our mouths. This is even, in some ways, the secret of the rebuilt temple I just described, whose horror is its foundation, evident to all, in a hole without bottom.

But the figure of horror which is that temple has other readings too. The temple was destroyed when the Medes and the Babylonians jointly sacked the city. What greater evidence of the god's desertion was there? Cast into destitution thereby was a woman soon to be pregnant with the man who would become Babylon's last native king. That man, Labynetus, some 20 years later, while still a youth, negotiated a peace in the shadow of an eclipse with the Median king, Cyaxares, the very one who had destroyed his mother's homeland and the temple of her god; his reward was to marry the grand-daughter of the Babylonian king who had joined Cyaxares in that enterprise. This led to his own kingship, which in turn enabled him to rebuild the destroyed city and the destroyed temple and to bid the god return, activities which so preoccupied him that his own kingdom in turn fell to Cyrus, Mandane's son, the grandson of Astyages, the great-grandson of Cyaxares. Such a tale may sound almost like a genealogy, but what it describes is the ouroboros, the closed circle which marks a hole and is a labyrinth, the beast who sustains himself only by destroying himself and destroys himself by sustaining himself. It is not impossible, as I have already admitted, that Labynetus failed to perceive all of this, failed to taste his own tail in his own mouth.

Yet, in my Assyrian Accounts, I have found myself returning over and over again to this last, eccentric king, a man who, like me, was concerned with the stories of the past and desired that they (or something) not fade with time, that they (or something) not bleach like bones on a strand, only insensibly to become the sand itself, rounded, softened shards each so like a pebble as to be confused for one. He, like me, feared what such loss would portend. Or is it that he feared that such loss would not portend?

* * * * *

From the Babylonian Royal Chronicle:
16th regnal year. The king returned to Ḫarrānu, once defeated, a river run dry, now reborn, and there led Sîn by his hand to his temple the Eḫulḫul, restored – he said – according to the ancient ways. There was outcry: Marduk in Bābilim, Nabû in Borsippa, Ištar in Uruk, all turned their backs. They looked instead to Parsua.

Chapter 15. Turns

Lugalzagesi saw that the city would fall. Šarru-kēn was upon them. The man was ferocious; fury reigned; from the walls he could see his soldiers die and flee and flee and die. The army of Kiš, not of Uruk, would prevail. His advisors urged him to flight, but already he was bowing his head to the stocks which Šarru-kēn would place on him. Already he was preparing himself to be dragged before Enlil in his temple in Nippur, where he would be accused of atrocity, found guilty, and killed. All because of that tablet, the tablet from the now-dead king of Kiš, which had demanded that he kill the messenger. Kill the messenger, it said, or your city and mine will fall. Kill the messenger he did. But killing the messenger was what led to the cities' falls – it led to the death of Ur-Zababa – already it was leading to his own death.

Was the letter a forgery? Had it not been written by Ur-Zababa? Should he not have trusted it? But he was the son and the priest of Nisaba, she who wrote with a sheaf of barley, she who gave both grain and writing. He had never known Nisaba's gifts to betray. Always they led to life – even if, as in this case, they demanded death. Would his mother and his goddess deceive him? Deceive him into his own destruction? Why?

Or was it not writing which he had received, but something which only looked like writing? Had he been given a counterfeit, a thing which, like writing, seemed to convey meaning though in fact it did not? Was this the work of some other god, a death-writing god rather than a life-writing one? "Mother," he called out from the walls, "was this not your doing? Are you no longer the deity of writing and grain? Are you, like me, falling from grace?"

His mother did not answer. He saw from the walls the plain strewn with battle – he saw how bodies piled up like gashes in the plain, how the land itself was scarred, how those scars superficially resembled the furrows from which grain would sprout. He also heard the cries of agony, panic and rage. Not one articulate word could he make out; what he heard was babel, or rather terror, not language. What he heard was full of feeling but not meaning. Before his eyes the gashed and scarred land became a tablet, a kind of transcript of the chaotic noise, noise made by men willfully and unwilfully, made with their voices and their dying bodies and their weapons, expressing something which no man controlled, no man corralled into meaning, no man planted into life. The land wrote all this, like some faithful scribe charged simply to record the sound, no matter what it said or didn't say. "Is this writing yours?" he asked his goddess, his mother. She did not reply. "Was this writing always possible?" he asked her. "Was this writing somehow underneath that other writing, the writing which inseminates the fields with life? Or is this a new writing which is replacing the old writing, taking it over, conquering it, destroying it?" But his goddess still did not answer; he received no answer from his mother.

* * * * *

Speak to Nabû-na'id, king of Bābilim, king of the four corners, king of the world, thus speaks Itti-Marduk-balaṭu, son of Nabû-aḫḫe-iddina and head of the house of Egibi.

May Sîn and Nabû keep you alive and prospering. Our house has heard disturbing rumors about the governor of Gutium – that Kuraš courts his kinsman. Whether they are true or not, you must find out!

Nabû-na'id stared at the tablet, turned it over several times in his hand, stared at it again. Niṭil-Kišar coughed. "What troubles you?" she asked.

He looked up and smiled at her. "Your cough," he answered. "I am worried how much you have been coughing."

She shrugged. "It's the dust from the riverbeds, from the canals. It's nothing."

"You don't have to oversee it all, you know. What you've envisioned will soon be brought to accomplishment, after all these years."

"All the more reason for me to be especially vigilant now – to avoid failure on the cusp of success."

"What kind of success will it be?" he asked, his tone morose.

She coughed again. "I only plant the seeds. What comes of them – maybe that won't be for me to know."

He walked over to her, wrapped his arms around her, kissed her forehead, and said nothing. She turned her head and let it rest sideways against his chest. "The letter troubles you, not my cough."

"They both trouble me."

"What does the letter say?"

He sighed, then patted the back of her head, drawing his hand through her mostly silver hair. "It says that Gubaru's project too is near its end – near its success. It says that seeds even now are being planted – and warns me what will come of them."

"Gubaru wrote you?" she inquired, murmuring into his chest.

"No." He gently pushed her away and handed her the tablet. She read it, then looked at him quizzically.

"Surely you don't trust the Egibi House more than Gubaru?"

"No," he repeated.

"Then what do you think is coming to fruition?"

He put his hands on her shoulders and held her at arms' length from him. "Everything," he said. "My love, everything. But you and I both know that the fruits are themselves only seeds

– that all that lives are just different stages of seeds, that seeds only lead to seeds and more seeds, that it is only a dream with which a seed consoles himself that he will ever grow into anything other than a seed."

She looked at him with gentle mockery in her eyes. "That," she observed, "is an unnecessarily enigmatic answer."

"Like your canals," he retorted.

"Maybe the two of us can't help but be poets."

He held her glance. "I am glad that we are poets together," he said softly. "Maybe everyone is a poet, maybe there's no option but to be a poet. The difference, then, is if you know it, or even how you yield."

"Mmmm," his wife murmured. "Yielding seems much on your mind, lately." She coughed again.

A look of fear entered his eyes, then fled. "You cough, I yield," he said. "The fruit falls from the tree. What must happen if its seed is to grow? The fruit must decay, rot – in other words, yield. Or it must be taken, eaten, eventually shit. It yields either way. The future approaches. Not the fruit's future, not ours either. What must be done? What can be done?" He pulled her back towards him, wrapped her again in his arms, and held her tightly as if that would keep her from coughing.

"Yield," she whispered.

"Yes," he said. "Yes, that's all." But a tear fell down his face. "I'm ready to yield so much, but I'm not ready to yield everything. Some things, a few, I refuse to yield." He held her even more tightly. "Don't cough," he said. "Please don't cough. Refuse."

She smiled – and coughed – and then, gently, laughed. "You haven't really yielded, if you still think you can refuse," she said lightly. "What will you do about Gubaru?"

"I will go to Gutium and talk with him."

"Let's go together," she said, surprising him. "He is dear to me, too. It may be the last chance we all have to be together."

"And your canals?"

"The failure of the fruit is the success of the seed. Didn't you just make that point?" She arched an eyebrow and only with her eyes laughed at him.

For a moment he felt a surge of happiness – time evaporated – they were as young as when they had gone to Ṣurru together, when they had stumbled together in the cold, dark night under a million stars, when the end of day was at least as exciting as its dawn. "Yes!" he said excitedly. "Yes! Come! Yes!" And then, full of exuberance, full of youth, he kissed her forehead, her eyes, her nose, her cheeks and finally her lips. When their lips met, she kissed too. Yes.

As before, they traveled at night, the two of them and their entourage a cocoon of flickering light and crackling flames within the vast blackness of night, the sounds of their progress amplified within their small band of color, as if the darkness were the walls of a canyon against which sound could only smash and return. He saw that she had grown weaker and that it wasn't just age which weakened her. But he let himself stay within their small sphere of illumination, he chose to avert his gaze from its borders, much like a child wrapped in blankets holds off admitting the coldness of the breaking day. He saw, or thought he saw, that this was what she was doing too, that this was what she wanted. They would lie in bed together, basking in the warmth of blankets and of each other, and pretend that all the birdsong was a nightingale's.

But what they heard was far more often the sounds of crickets or tramping feet or wind racing through hollows than it was the sounds of birds. And when they did in fact lie in bed together, they were in a tent, and their bed was a portable piece spruced up into comfort by an excess of blankets and cushions.

They were now lying side by side, not on the edge of night, but in the throes of day. She had slept fitfully and clearly remained very tired. He ordered water and beer to be brought, and then he just lay on his back beside her, holding her hand. When she stirred and opened her eyes, he offered her the water and the beer. She drank some, mostly the beer, then let herself fall back into the nest of blankets and cushions, which they were lying on top of rather than in.

"Do you remember that story you told me about the bees?" she asked with her eyes closed.

He lifted his head, thought a moment, sifted through memory, and arrived at what he imagined she meant. "You mean the king who brought bees and honey to his people?"

"Yes, that's what I mean."

"I do remember. Why?"

She sighed, still without opening her eyes. "I feel like that's what you and I are doing right now. We are on an expedition into the mountains, in search of we don't know what. But we will know it when we find it, and we will bring it back to our people, and they will have a gift in plain sight that almost everyone will fail to see. But it will still be a gift, it will be something which gives and keeps giving."

He let his head fall onto the cushion beside her, and then he too closed his eyes. "If that exists, I will need your help to find it," he eventually replied.

"Or Gubaru's," she suggested, then added, enigmatically, "or maybe he's the gift."

He turned onto his side and looked at her. "No, you're the gift, Niṭ. You. Those bees which that king brought home to his people were led, not by a king, but by a queen. No one noticed, but that was the truth. It still is the truth."

"If it's the truth," she answered, "somehow a king was still needed to bring the bees and their queen down from the mountain."

"Yes, that king was a kind of escort, like you and I have an escort. That was his proper role."

"And it seems he knew it."

"Yes, it seems he knew it."

"What became of him again?"

He thought for a while, and then offered, "It depends on whom you ask. Some say he was conquered and killed by a stronger, better king. But it's not what I think. I think he became honey and mead – that he flowed through the veins of his people – that he sustained them, not with the recollection of his name but with something better if easily overlooked."

She continued to lie motionless on her back, her eyes closed. "Honey and mead," she murmured, "flowing through the veins… does it matter whose veins they are? Does it have to be his people or our people? Do the honey and mead even have to end up in veins?"

Nabû-na'id lay quietly beside her, then turned onto his back and examined the ceiling of the tent. "I suppose it doesn't matter," he admitted. "But then I wonder what the difference is, between bringing the bees down from the mountain, and just leaving them there, unmolested, letting them make their honey, flow where it will; leaving the honey to ferment into mead, or not, as circumstance dictates. No king will have been needed, then."

"No escort either," she said. "And the same is true of my canals," she added in a soft voice. "The waters will find a path or make one, with or without me escorting them." She finally opened her eyes and stared at the same ceiling her husband was staring at. "It feels like our lives will have been pointless."

"Only if we thought they were ours to give a point to," Nabû-na'id answered. "Only if we thought we were somehow different from the water finding or making a path, or the honey, or the mead, each finding or making its path, whether through veins or canals or just through mud."

"But we did think that."

He was surprised to hear himself laugh. "I suppose we did. But perhaps the water and the honey and the mead tell themselves similar stories. We don't know what stirs them into motion, what motivates them, to what they aspire."

"Whatever it is, though, it's pointless," Niṭil-Kišar said flatly. "The waters rise up into a flood and drown mankind, for no point at all; they fall as desperately needed rain and give us all hope, again for no point at all. They stream down cheeks as tears, all pointlessly."

"Would it be better if the flood waters rose to drown mankind because the gods tired of our noise? Would it be better if the rain fell to sustain our hope and were held back to make us weep? Why are we so dark, my dear? We're at the end of our lives, our sun is very near setting, but here we are resting side by side in the daytime, when as youths we could barely wait for darkness. It makes me wonder if we can really tell the setting sun from the rising one, the day from the night, east from west."

She stared at the tent ceiling. "What is on the other side of this canvas? You might say the brightness of day. What is on the other side of that? You might say the heavens. But what is on the other side of that?"

"Does there have to be another side? Maybe the blueness of the sky is our limitation, not the sky's; maybe what appears to be an end instead reflects the weakness of our sight."

"The same could be said of beginnings."

"Yes, the same could be said of beginnings."

She imagined the water tumbling down from a mountain, finding its way into one of her canals smoothing its path toward the city; and then she wondered where the water in the mountains came from; the sky perhaps; and where did the water in the sky come from? Maybe from the smoothed water in her canals rolling slowly beneath the unrelenting sun.

"We shall see Gubaru tomorrow," she said.

"Yes, I think so."

"We've come full circle," she murmured, "the three of us coming together, going apart, coming together. It's like the tide we observed in Ṣurru. Do you remember? Who would have thought there was an endless sea which breathed, whose chest rose in great day-long heaves, then fell in a lengthy, lingering sigh, water slowly flooding the land and then slowly retreating, back and forth, the grains of sand tumbling up and down the strand, the birds racing the waves…" She closed her eyes and let the image drift away.

"The fishermen told me the tide changes with the Moon. Did you know that?"

She smiled with her eyes closed. "You are your mother's son, always connecting everything back to Sîn."

"Maybe it isn't Sîn who calls forth the breath of the sea, then its release. Maybe it's the other way around. Maybe that endless cycle of water calls forth Sîn, shapes his shape, sculpts the form the Moon takes."

"Maybe," she murmured. He could tell she was starting to fall asleep again.

"Maybe," he continued, "the tides of the sea sculpt his face like tears sculpt ours."

"Mmmm," she said. Her mind was withdrawing into sleep, slowly retreating, tumbling the pebbles of words down the strand, so that they could gather their strength again in dreams before approaching anew the shore. Birds were running up and down along the edge of the waves. They could fly, but almost never did, just like water they could enter the sky but for some reason, for now, they chose not to. Something bobbed just off the shore, on the water's surface, a skiff, which could move back and forth with the tide. It would be nearby when she awakened. It would always stay near the shore, wherever the shore happened to be. It was like Gubaru, yes, Gubaru was like the skiff, Gubaru, not far from shore, wherever the shore happened to be, a skiff which stayed near despite the tide or with it. But she was like the birds, running along the edge of the waves, able to fly but for now not flying, running, but she would fly soon, she would enter the sky, into the blueness, past the clouds, away, like a bird flying ever higher, disappearing into the heights, becoming one with the sky, and then, long afterward, when everything had changed, when everything had been forgotten, the whole sky would come together, scrunch together, condense, would become a small dot which would grow as it neared the earth, not a bird returning, but a single drop, yes, water, a single drop, the whole sky, falling all by itself toward one of her canals, a single drop that would plop into her canals, the whole sky would fall into her canals, would plop, a small splash reflecting for an instant the whole sky above which fell.

When he saw her, a smile broke out across his face. Even his eyes smiled. "I never knew to suspect this surprise," he admitted. They were in a reception room off a courtyard; a warm afternoon breeze every now and then found its way to them through the open doors and windows. Everyone was standing, although there was an embroidered couch, chairs and a table arranged in the room.

"How could it have been a surprise had you known to suspect it?" she answered coyly. They embraced, not like a governor and a queen but like the old friends they were, friends who had travelled great distances together and endured many hardships. For some reason, the memory which immediately bore down on him was from twenty years before, when Nabû-na'id had been imprisoned during the brief reign of Awil-

Marduk. He had seen how distraught she was, how scared – and how angry. Her anger wasn't just directed at Awil-Marduk; it had not taken him long to realize that she was at least as furious with Nabû-na'id. At the time, her anger had confused him; he had not understood why she blamed her husband, all the more given that Nabû-na'id was certainly at that very moment suffering and in grave danger. But now, as an old man, he understood better – or rather, he felt something, something which it surprised him and worried him to recognize as anger, and that feeling substituted for what otherwise might be called understanding.

He turned toward Nabû-na'id. They too embraced. The expression on Nabû-na'id's face was not at all guarded; it was easy to read joy there, joy not only on his own account but on account of how fondly Gubaru and Niṭil-Kišar greeted each other.

He took a step back, for a moment at a loss for words, but then summoned himself to his role as governor. "I am glad to see you both, but I should ask why you have come. The letters I received told me to expect you," he said, looking directly at Nabû-na'id, "but they did not explain the purpose of your trip."

Nabû-na'id waved his hand. "It's like when you, Fly and I took walks to 'inspect the battlements.' It was the veil under which friendship was concealed, even excused. We have come for friendship – and to 'inspect the battlements.'" Nabû-na'id smiled, for a moment somehow looking like a child despite his old body, full beard, gray hair and worn face.

"Friendship may bring you both here," Gubaru answered, "and I am glad for it. But there are also battlements to inspect – and other developments, dangerous ones, which we need to discuss."

A dark look flit across Nabû-na'id's face. "Yes, I imagine so," he said soberly. "But I am thinking of something else. I am thinking of the three of us. I am even thinking further back in time, back when you and I were on the tell and lost the *pukku* and *mekkû*. Do you remember?"

Gubaru, surprised, again felt that small ball of anger far within him. "No," he lied, not knowing why. "I don't remember."

Nabû-na'id laughed. "But you do! I can see it in your face. We lost the *pukku* and *mekkû* – and I, dramatic boy that I was, announced that we had lost tomorrow, though with the gain of yesterday."

"It was perplexing," Gubaru observed, non-committally.

The eager, boyish expression returned to Nabû-na'id's face, again for some reason stirring the ember of anger deep within Gubaru, all while Nabû-na'id's glance darted excitedly between Gubaru and Niṭil-Kišar. Neither of them seemed able to meet his enthusiasm; both instead held back or were held back by some small but powerful sorrow. But something about Nabû-na'id's eagerness, which had, perhaps, a tinge of franticness to it, did not permit him to admit that what was happening among the three of them, what he was bringing forward for the three of them, somehow wasn't shared. Instead, he plunged forward. "I am still that dramatic boy," he declared, "and so I can proclaim that tomorrow, after all, wasn't lost."

Gubaru smiled weakly. "Then I am glad," he said softly.

"Do you understand?"

"No."

Nabû-na'id turned to his wife. "Do you understand, Niṭ?" Somehow he asked the question as much with his eyes as with words.

She looked at him and allowed her head to nod forward exactly once. "You've realized that tomorrow was never yours to lose."

"Exactly!" He was so excited that she desperately wanted to be excited with him and for him, but that small, powerful sorrow weighed her down, as she could see it weighed Gubaru down too. She didn't quite know what it was or where it came from. Perhaps it was the way she recognized that Nabû-na'id was lying to himself – or else was trying to believe something which in his heart he couldn't or didn't yet believe. The sympathy she felt was bitter and verged even on pity, if only because idealism and hypocrisy lie so nigh one another.

Gubaru furrowed his brow. "I am an old man now. Even after all these years most of what you tell me I fail to understand."

Nabû-na'id interrupted him. "It isn't that, I don't think. It's that what it takes me so long to arrive at, wending my way through thoughts and words, you don't need to understand – you feel it instead."

Gubaru shrugged. "Sometimes I wonder if you know what I feel," he said.

Nabû-na'id looked more closely at him, then abruptly turned away. He walked to the open door and looked out on the courtyard. A black bird was hopping on the ground in the shade of a vine, and he watched it. Gubaru and Niṭil-Kišar said nothing but from where they stood further in the room, they too looked out on the courtyard.

"All right, old man," Nabû-na'id said at last, drawing out the last two words, with his back to them both. "Perhaps we shouldn't talk about the tomorrows which don't belong to us. What should we discuss instead?"

Gubaru hesitated and then said, "If we hadn't been friends all of our lives, then our meeting would be between a king and a governor – and even though we've been friends all of our lives, our meeting is still also between a king and a governor. I suppose we should talk –" he stopped and searched for words. "– about where things stand."

"Mmmm," was all the agreement Nabû-na'id could muster, still not facing either of them.

Gubaru suddenly walked forward and put his hand on

Nabû-na'id's shoulder. His face became animated with kindness, making it somehow indistinguishable from all the kind faces of his youth. "My friend," he said, "my dear friend. I am glad to see you. I have missed you." Only then did Nabû-na'id turn and the two men embraced a second time.

"We will talk about where things stand later," Gubaru continued. "But let's have dinner together first, just the three of us. Can it be arranged?"

Nabû-na'id smiled. "Of course it can be arranged. I am, after all, the king of the world." Then he winked at Niṭil-Kišar. "Naturally, I will have to lie, to get my courtiers to leave us along. An 'inspection of battlements' kind of lie. The best kind of lie."

Niṭil-Kišar joined the two of them, put one arm around each, and smiled. "You better hurry up and lie, then," she suggested, "king of the world."

He and Gubaru were alone together in a private courtyard. Evening was giving way to night, and Niṭil-Kišar had left them to go to sleep.

"Is she all right?" Gubaru asked, his voice at once rough and worried.

Nabû-na'id looked at the ground and didn't respond for a long time. Finally, his voice muffled, he answered with a question. "What do you think?"

Gubaru sighed. Had Nabû-na'id looked up he would have seen sorrow grip Gubaru's face, but instead he kept staring fixedly at the ground. Gubaru took a step towards him but stopped. "I am so sorry," he said, helplessly.

Nabû-na'id didn't respond, but his friend could see that he was struggling with something – struggling and losing. Struggling, losing, and not able to bear the loss. Before Gubaru could say anything else, however, Nabû-na'id abruptly changed the subject. "Is he in contact with you, Gubaru?" he asked, looking up.

The old warrior, Nabû-na'id's childhood friend, for a moment looked puzzled, but then his face cleared. He stood motionless for a long time and then, very slowly, nodded.

"What does he want?"

"What do you think? He wants me to betray you. He thinks that because he and I are of the same race and speak, or once spoke, the same language, then I will do it. You can imagine what he has offered me."

"What I imagine Kuraš would think to offer, I doubt you would care to accept," Nabû-na'id said without hesitation.

Gubaru looked at him, his eyes oddly sympathetic. "You would be wrong."

"Ah," whispered Nabû-na'id. He examined his friend with care, somehow gently. "He hasn't offered you riches or power, then. I must stop underestimating him."

"You know then what he has offered me?" Gubaru asked.

Nabû-na'id pursed his lips and nodded. "He must have offered you my son. He must have offered you Bel-šar-uṣur."

"Yes!" Gubaru hissed.

Nabû-na'id sank slowly to the ground and then, as so often he had done before, he sat in the dirt. He rested his head in his hands, propped up on his knees. "Oh, Gubaru," he breathed more than said. "Oh, Gubaru."

For a while Gubaru stood not only in front of him but over him. Neither spoke. But then Gubaru turned and lowered himself to the ground too. They sat side by side in the dirt, their backs to the wall, silent. With his finger Gubaru idly drew in the sand.

A long time passed.

Eventually, Nabû-na'id lifted his head from his hands and looked at the dirt where Gubaru had been drawing. "What have you drawn?" he asked.

Gubaru seemed surprised by the question. He looked at his drawing, and that seemed to surprise him too. "I guess it's Anzû," he said. "The beast you told me about long ago, who knocks men off of cliffs for not knowing what they are."

Nabû-na'id didn't say anything.

"Or maybe," Gubaru continued, "Anzû just knocks them off of cliffs, whether or not they know what they are. Or who they are. I recall that you suggested something like that."

Nabû-na'id sighed. "What did I know, Gubaru? I liked thinking I had some special insight – I liked thinking that then, maybe I still like thinking that now. But what did I know? What have I ever known?" A tear slid down Nabû-na'id's cheek. "Kayvon died because I liked him and because I loved my daughter. I wanted something special for her. I thought I knew what I was doing."

"No," Gubaru said resolutely. "Kayvon didn't die because of something you did. He died because of something your son did."

"Sometimes," Nabû-na'id answered in a strangled voice, "I am not sure which deeds are mine and which are my son's. Maybe we are both Bel-šar-uṣur and there has never been a Nabû-na'id. Maybe I made up a story about Nabû-na'id so I wouldn't always have to be Bel-šar-uṣur. But wouldn't it have been better if I had helped Bel-šar-uṣur make up a story so that he wouldn't always have to be me?"

"As usual, you speak things I don't understand," Gubaru said. "What you say makes no sense to me."

"Just like it made no sense for a man to tell Anzû he was a chicken? Or an Anzû? Or even, possibly a man?"

"Stop it!" barked Gubaru, in a tone he had never used before with Nabû-na'id. "Stop it. Let us just sit here in silence, no more stories, no more words." Then he added, gently, "Just for now."

"While you decide?"

"I have already decided."

Nabû-na'id looked at his hands and at the ground. "Gubaru," he said, speaking so softly that it was hard to hear him. "I want you to change your mind. I want you to say yes. Join Kuraš. Find a way to help the city fall as gently as it can, with as little cost as it can. Just like Niṭil-Kišar has done with the canals."

Gubaru's eyes were wet, but no tears fell. For a long time he didn't respond. Then he said, quietly, "I asked you to be silent, to sit here with me in silence."

"Ah." Nabû-na'id leaned back against the wall, his head cocked toward the sky.

They sat together, side by side, in silence.

Nabû-na'id thought about Lugalzagesi. He thought as well about Šarru-kēn and Kuraš. Were not the latter two very similar? Both came of obscure birth; it was their actions, not their fathers, who revealed their hidden royalty. And he, like Šarru-kēn and Kuraš, was also of unlikely birth: the son of a nobody, or rather a scribe; and his mother's son, too, though what that meant he could not say. Was it his actions which revealed his royalty? Or was it rather this thing between action and passivity, writing and reading, or writing-reading? It was, after all, his ability to read the writing of the heavens which had set him on the path toward kingship; it was moreover his son's inability to read the writing of the house of Egibi which had set him on the actual throne. Šarru-kēn too gained a throne by reading what others could not. And Kuraš? Was he a secret reader too?

But if Nabû-na'id had a hidden kinship with Šarru-kēn and Kuraš, did he not also have a likeness to Lugalzagesi? Was the day not coming when he too would stand on the battlements and see written in gashes and scars across the plain the death-writing? Would he remember on that day to look as well toward Niṭil-Kišar's canal-writing, the life-writing? The first was written in blood and in the bodies of men with weapons as stylus; the second used a sheaf of grain to sweep clear the passage of life-giving water. And it could give passage to something else, maybe also life-giving: ironically, an army. He paused over that irony and wondered once more what the relationship was between death-writing and life-writing, between his namesake Nabû and Lugalzagesi's mother and goddess Nisaba. He wondered as well how to understand his own double-part, the way he was like Lugalzagesi, who delivered men to death because of a message he read and hence was also delivered to death, while also being like Šarru-kēn and perhaps even Kuraš. Can I at once play the role of conquered and conqueror, writer and reader? Was that quite the right comparison? Was the writer conquered, the reader conquering? Or did the writer plant what the reader harvested?

Such odd thoughts I have, mused Nabû-na'id, here in Gutium, a new exile, a new refuge. These thoughts somehow will goad me into my departure for Bābilim, a return to life while simultaneously a heading toward death. Well, Fly is there already, to lead the way; and now my mother; and before them my father and Kayvon and all those children Niṭil-Kišar failed to bear. And yet she is the life-writer! Whereas if I write it is death-writing I do. (But everyone writes, his mother had once said. Does everyone death-write or life-write? Or am I terribly confused to insist on a distinction that even I fail to see clearly?) (And then he thought of his couplings with Niṭil-Kišar, death coupling with life, carrying giving way to miscarrying, still-borns. He thought of his son, whom he had mostly failed, including failing to truly love him; and of his daughter, whom he truly loved and still had mostly failed. How will I have the strength to go back, he wondered, Fly-less, to the very ones whom, however much I have loved, I have not loved enough or loved right or loved well? How will I go back and face the destruction my own love has wrought – or written – and how will I go back and face the creations of that love, too, the other writing it has done? He wanted to weep, even while an internal voice whispered to him that his tears too were life-giving water. But another internal voice observed, coldly: you want to weep. But you do not.)

His thoughts returned to Šarru-kēn and Lugalzagesi. Did they ever want to weep? Were they unable? How should that inability be understood? Perhaps the desire to weep was simply the desire to feel what one didn't – the desire to be a different, presumably a better, person than one was. Perhaps he wanted to weep but did not because in his heart he was without feeling and without conscience. Were Šarru-kēn and Lugalzagesi different? What kind of conscience did each of them have? Some said Šarru-kēn had read the tablet which Ur-Zababa had sent, the tablet with his death sentence. If he had, and if he had consequently manipulated Ur-Zababa's son into being the doomed messenger, then he was complicit in the death of that son, the very man whom Šarru-kēn had also saved and who had shown him not only gratitude but friendship. That was the dark tale told by many in the priesthood, who also saw Šarru-kēn and his heirs as apostates and who therefore were in no hurry to exonerate or like him; but another story neglected that possibility and instead saw in Šarru-kēn only a loyal avenger, unaware of how narrowly he himself had avoided a death contrived by the very ones he avenged. On that account, Šarru-kēn emerged as a puppet, albeit one who ended up through dumb luck following a different script than the one intended. Still, a script-follower, a non-reader who followed a script. A substitute king fantastically become king, *šar pûḫi - šarrum*. The first account was of a more interesting man – and a more frightful one, a human horror of a kind. But there perhaps was something horrible about the second account, too – the way a tool could nonetheless change history and inaugurate a new era, an era of conquest and empire. If we are to plunge into such writhing, blood-soaked transformations, would it not be comforting to imagine the men who drove them also authored them? That they had some idea where they were going, rather than that they too were swept forward by forces they not only did not understand but of which they barely had an inkling? Shouldn't world-historical events require world-historical men?

And what of Lugalzagesi? What kind of conscience did he have, to let himself become the instrument of another's death, merely because he received a tablet requesting that? Shouldn't murder be personal, be the consequence of rage or even of cold calculation? To kill because some signs scratched in mud urged you to do so – wasn't that madness? But here Nabû-na'id's heart sank, as he thought about men who died because of signs which he had read in the sky. Lugalzagesi should have sought a greater reason for the murder asked of him; he should have sent a messenger to Ur-Zababa asking for clarification; or rather he should have gone himself and face-to-face demanded an account. As for himself, Nabû-na'id, what should he have done? Should he have sent a messenger to the heavens – should he have gone himself – and demanded an account? What account do gods owe men? He imagined himself now as Lugalzagesi, standing before Ur-Zababa. What does Ur-Zababa say? He says, the gods have sent messages, they have sent dreams – that is why this man must be killed. Why this messenger must be killed. What response is there to that? Would Nabû-na'id, in the role of Lugalzagesi, say – I will abide no hearsay. I will not act until the god has spoken with *me*. I will accept no substitute. I will await the god's word from my mountain top. That was one possibility. But another was this: Nabû-na'id, acting as Lugalzagesi, would ask instead – should not the divine messenger be killed rather than the human one? Would it not be better to cut us off from the world of gods so that only we are responsible for our choices?

His mind strayed to his daughter, the priestess and human spouse of Sîn. Even though he wondered whether men would be better off severed from the gods, still his own daughter was consecrated to a god; still, he too had felt the promise his mother had extorted from him to rebuild the Eḫulḫul in Ḫarrānu. He had felt it and he had fulfilled it – or declared it fulfilled, anyway. He had gone to Teima in part because somehow there, not only was the statue the god, but the god was a statue – a transitivity nowhere else admitted. He had gone there to wrestle with that, to wrestle with his own devotion and, in connection with that, his own sorrow. But then and now he wondered: Have I committed my beloved daughter to marriage with a statue? Did my brilliant, mad mother mourn her whole life for a mere statue? Was something better possible for either of them?

He had initially wanted Mikum-Nisaba to marry Gubaru's son Kayvon. He had thought something like real friendship would be possible between the two, something like what he imagined he and Niṭil-Kišar had. But perhaps he only imagined that; perhaps human friendship frays and crumbles with time, like mudbrick does, like a baked tablet does. After all, for all the time that he was in Teima, were he and Niṭil-Kišar not estranged – both physically, with vast distances separating them, and emotionally, with even vaster distances? Did he need Teima to give an excuse for that, to make the emotional distance correlate with a physical distance? In contrast, what estrangement is possible with a statue? What fraying, what crumbling?

But he stopped and remembered the statue of Šarru-kēn, the one which required either the restoration or the bestowal of a face. Statues fray. Statues crumble. Statues are even deliberately damaged or thoughtlessly made into fill. There is nothing human which endures. Marriage to a statue is no more promising than marriage to a human being. And the statues that are gods, and the gods that are statues – they also don't endure. Perhaps Adad-guppi recognized that? Perhaps that is why she demanded Eḫulḫul's restoration? He always thought his mother saw further than he – saw deeper – saw the deep. Did she see that the only enduring that's possible, whether for gods or for men, is the enduring through renewal? What crumbles, what frays – renew. Start anew. Let it rise anew, not only restored but different. Even if it is called by the same name, let the name be pronounced differently. Let different signs be used to write it. Let what endures endure by changing. Let the future belong to the future.

He sensed that in these thoughts lay some kind of synthesis of what he called the death-writing and the life-writing. He sensed that somewhere in this tangle of thoughts lay not only his wife's devotion to her canal project, but his daughter's devotion to her collection of statues. Mikum-Nisaba wasn't just creating some mausoleum of the past; she was handing the past over to the future, to do with as it will. She was offering an explanation of the past – not the only possible one, certainly not a complete one, but an explanation in fragments. "Here is an attempt we made. Here is another. We knew not what we strove for; we just attempted; moreover, we mostly failed. But here, take our attempts, claim them in what way you will, learn if you can from them – and don't fail to imagine (but you can only fail to imagine) what will become of your own attempts at some later time."

And Gubaru? He was the least and the most poetic of the figures who made up what he thought of as his family. Gubaru was his brother, the brother he gave himself because neither of his parents had managed it. Gubaru had stayed loyal to him – and more than that, his friend – through all the transformations of his life, whether from nobody-scribe to king of the world. Gubaru had witnessed him bring peace to Ṣurru and desolation to Teima. Gubaru had seen him whisked from prison to throne. Gubaru had known him to weep for a dog and not for his mother. Throughout it all, Gubaru had remained, and had remained his friend. Why? To what was Gubaru faithful? Was his friendship just a measure of his obstinacy, even of his obtuseness? Or did Gubaru remain faithful to something that perhaps really was there, even while he, Nabû-na'id, had lost faith in it? He thought of Gubaru's dedication to Marduk, a god become a corpse-puppet in Nabû-na'id's imagination – and then wondered, am I too a corpse-puppet to whom Gubaru remains dedicated?

But Gubaru was also tempted. What Kuraš had offered him was tempting – or else it was just cruel, as if Kuraš were testing Gubaru's mettle: will you at last avenge your son? Or did you not love him enough? Or even is it that you lack the courage? Nabû-na'id knew Gubaru well enough to know that he would feel the stings of those implications even if the implications themselves never became explicit to him. Those stings, inarticulate, for Gubaru inarticulable, more profoundly challenged Gubaru's faiths and his dedications than any story, any whimsical query, Nabû-na'id had ever thought to tell or to ask. For a second, that observation astounded him: how is it, he demanded of himself, that I have always challenged Gubaru in a language I had every reason to know he couldn't understand? How is it that I never faced those same challenges thrown down otherwise than in that language? Was what I was doing a way for each of us to not confront those questions, Gubaru because he didn't understand the way I posed them, and I because the way I posed them secretly protected me from having truly to understand them? Have I been treating Gubaru as my stooge – all the while being my own stooge too?

Kuraš had done something more direct, maybe more true. He had stung Gubaru, left him to make a choice which he felt rather than tried to think. Perhaps Kuraš was doing that to him, too. Perhaps Kuraš was so discerning, or so undiscerning, as to believe that even he, Nabû-na'id, could be made to feel, as if something could break through all the thoughts and words, as if something could be found underneath that protective crust which, Nabû-na'id suspected, protected nothing – had not even nothing at its center – had no center – was crust protecting crust protecting crust.

* * * * *

From the [fragmentary] Assyrian Accounts of Herodotus

...As Cyrus's grip of the surrounding lands strengthened, as he co-opted the allies and underlings of Labynetus, as vassal state after vassal state switched allegiance, as skirmish after skirmish was lost to the Persians, Labynetus preoccupied himself with the god of the Moon. Indeed, it is as if the royal house were gripped by individual madnesses: Labynetus obsessing over his god, Nitocris over her canals, their daughter over her statues. Courtiers jockeyed for the highest position on a crumbling tower. Priests agonized over liturgical minutiae. All this despite an enemy at the gate, or because of it. The terror which even moderate far-sightedness brought into view was eclipsed by near-sighted fascination, as if the buttons on a garment, being round and bright, could truly rival the sun. All perspective was lost. So it seems, but in making my inquiries, I have repeatedly wondered how perspective can be lost. Perspective, far from being losable, seems inescapable. Some of us bury the dead, because we have perspective; others of us burn them, out of a different perspective; and there are even some who eat their dead. Which of these has lost perspective? Which of these has escaped it? When a king's kingdom totters, is he mad to devote himself to a god – or to his wife – or to his garden? Is it truly clear that any of these are less important than a kingdom, whether tottering or robust and strong? In making my inquiries I have found a plague of perspectives, a plague which, like Midas, converts everything it touches into, not gold, but more

perspectives. All perspective was lost, I wrote – all too optimistically.

This god who claimed the attention of Labynetus – I am uncertain how to explain or merely describe him, about whom all accounts are murky, disguised or unintelligible. In no way does he seem to me an equivalent to Artemis, Selene, Hecate or even Bendis. Indeed we Greeks have not known a god of the Moon, only goddesses. But even had we known a god of the Moon, we have not known this god of the Moon, the one Labynetus exalted, to whom his mother and his daughter both were high priestesses. This was a god who obscured the heavens and shattered the earth; a god who took to himself the offices of the other gods, not unlike Kronos swallowing his children; a god who, being lord of all, became lord of nothing – and yet, without whom, who can do what? So reads an inscription of Labynetus, at least according to the priests who read it for me. But they also tell me that in the inscriptions of his final year Labynetus emphasized not the words of his god, but his god's deeds – deeds, moreover, unknown not only to all mankind but to all the other gods. Unknown deeds which, nonetheless, Labynetus claimed all had seen, though not once had any word, any tablet, recorded them. Even the very monument on which this passage was inscribed was at pains to state, said the priests, that it did not record the god's deeds. Then what deeds did Labynetus have in mind? Every priest whom I asked gave me no answer I could make sense of, apart from understanding that whatever their words meant, what they expressed was contempt, dismissiveness, even hatred. For the king, for his beliefs, perhaps even for this god – I don't know. They say he was a heretic. If so he was a heretic who got under their skin, somehow even generations after he breathed his last. A century, after all, has passed.

There was one man, not a priest but a scribe, who frequently was present as I pursued my inquiries. Though he regularly came, he held back and didn't join with the others in their discussions. Nothing about this man stood out, apart from his silence. He did not dress peculiarly; he was neither outstandingly ugly nor handsome; his face was very like most human faces, to the point even that I can't now call it up in recollection. But one morning he approached me when I was alone in a garden jotting notes. Perhaps he had been watching me for a while; certainly I had not noticed him until he was upon me. He had no need of a translator; he spoke Greek, though with an accent which sometimes amused and sometimes confused me. He pointed at my scroll, which was partially unfurled as I wrote. The day was bright and the parchment, due to its light color, reflected the sunlight, which made my work hard. Often I angled myself between the parchment and the sun so that my shadow protected my eyes and eased my writing. "You ask about the god's deed – every day you ask. I listen to all the different ways your informants articulate their unknowing. The king" – he must have meant Labynetus – "was clear that the deeds were unknown to men. Even to gods." I nodded and waited for him to continue, but after a while it became evident that he had nothing more to say.

"They were unknown to men and to gods," I observed eventually, "and yet your king also said everyone has seen them. I am at a loss what he could have meant. Is there something that you understand that those I have questioned do not?" To my surprise, he laughed – a harsh, almost bitter laugh. Then he pointed at the sky. It took me a surprisingly long time to realize that he was pointing at the waxing crescent moon. It was as if the rich blue sky were camouflaging the moon, somehow hiding its blotchy, broken blankness. But once I had recognized the moon I couldn't fail to see it. I could only be surprised that at first I hadn't. Meanwhile this strange man said nothing. Irritated, turning my gaze from the moon to him, I again interrupted what had become a long silence and stated that I didn't understand. Why was he pointing at the moon? But, instead of answering that question in words, with his arm outstretched, re-drawing my attention to his pointing finger, he slowly drew it away from the moon and rotated it until it settled on and indicated my unfurled scroll. While I was following his finger, I had carelessly allowed my body to shift its

relation to the sun, so that my shadow no longer protected me from the sun's glare when my eyes met and rested on the parchment. For a moment I was dazzled, and I blinked. I squirmed to recast my shadow over the parchment, but all I saw was its mottled paleness and that finger, as if no longer belonging to a man or even a being, pointing.

* * * * *

They were in the palace in Bābilim, in a back room on the second floor overlooking the courtyard. A tapestry hung from the wall, its red, orange and yellow colors evocative of autumn. Three square windows on one wall were the only source of light. Cut flowers in floor vases lined the wall opposite the windows. Bel-šar-uṣur was pacing angrily. A broken tablet lay on the floor.

"You went all that way, and no sooner are you back than he betrays you. Now Kuraš has Gutium. An invasion is inevitable."

"Of course it's inevitable," Nabû-na'id murmured, his voice calm. "It's been inevitable for a long time. We both knew that." He was seated on a chair a few feet from the wall and staring at the broken tablet on the floor. He had barely moved since reading the tablet and then absently letting it fall to the ground.

Bel-šar-uṣur stopped pacing and stared at him, his eyes bulging. "What have we been doing for the last months? Why are we not preparing?" He spoke almost without inflection, articulating each word carefully in a monotone which could not have more effectively conveyed his impatience and ire.

"We are preparing," Nabû-na'id answered, his voice still calm, his gaze still directed at the broken tablet, his body still motionless.

"Oh? How would that be?"

Nabû-na'id sighed and looked up at his son, meeting his gaze. "I have ordered the divine statues to come to the city. Those that can."

“Those that can,” his son repeated, with a hint of disbelief in his tone. “They all can, right now,” he continued, matter-of-factly.

“Some will wait until they cannot.” Nabû-na’id stated simply while returning his gaze to the broken tablet and listening to his son’s heavy, angry breathing. He listened as Bel-šar-uṣur deliberately slowed it, deliberately took charge of himself. Nabû-na’id, though aloof and cold, was impressed with him.

“I concur that cultic matters must be addressed expeditiously,” his son began. “But we also need to plan our defense – or even more wisely, our offense.”

“Mmmm” was all Nabû-na’id offered in response.

“I can lead the army to the north and await him near the royal canal, before he crosses the Idiqlat, probably at Upija, where our wall will drive him. Meanwhile the city has to prepare –” he paused and then almost immediately resumed, “– for a siege.” Unconsciously, Bel-šar-uṣur returned to pacing.

“Mmmm,” Nabû-na’id repeated, almost as if articulating even a single word required too much motion of him.

Bel-šar-uṣur caught himself pacing, stopped and whirled around. “Father, please,” he said urgently. “Stir yourself!”

Again the old king looked up. He visibly shook himself, a bit like a rattled dog composing himself, and then with evident effort forced himself to articulate agreement. “Yes, we must prepare. There are many things to prepare. The statues must come – those that can. Their temples will need to send personnel and supplies. We probably don’t have enough boats; we’ll need to get someone on that right away. And then there’s the festival.”

Bel-šar-uṣur, who had started pacing again, again stopped. “The festival?” he repeated quizzically. A look of bewilderment gave way to a dawning comprehension. “You mean Ḫarrānu’s *Akītu* festival, which we’ve been celebrating here in Bābilim the last few years? Surely we can cancel it, or postpone it, until the danger has passed."

His father surprisingly laughed. "No," he said, but added nothing more.

Bel-šar-uṣur waited for a while and then gave up. "No what?"

"No, the danger won't pass. No, we can't cancel the festival or even postpone it. We will have the festival. It is even good that the statues will be here for the festival – those that can."

Bel-šar-uṣur pursed his lips. For a moment something frantic danced in his eyes, but he quelled it, much as he had done earlier with his breathing. "Father," he said slowly. "You know, as I do, that Kuraš will attack the city. There is a very good chance that he will prevail. There is a very good chance the city will fall. There is a very good chance that you and I will die. We can't afford to be distracted by festivals. We have to focus on what is most important. We have to defend the city and save ourselves."

"Yes," Nabû-na'id answered airily. "Yes, that is what I am thinking too. It will be odd for a statue to float downriver at this unexpected time – those that can anyway. It will discombobulate all who see them – it may even discombobulate the statues. Provisions will have to be sent for them." With a crooked, pained smile, he looked at his son. "Statues, you know, require enormous quantities of food."

"Forget the food for the statues! We will need the food for the city!"

His father continued to smile the crooked, pained smile. "Yes, that's one way of looking at it."

Bel-šar-uṣur slowed his pacing, which had resumed, and gradually came to a stop. "The statues will bring the food," he muttered almost to himself.

"The statues will also be here for the New Year, the end of the old, the beginning of the new, the new beginning. The statues will be here – those that can."

"For your festival? Does it really matter, father?"

"Ah, the festival. Yes, that too. Does it matter? Who can say?" Then he added almost in a whisper, "Without the festival, who can do what?"

"Everything can be done without the festival. Everything, father. The festival is neither here nor there."

"Yes, it is neither here nor there, but that is why everything depends on it."

Something about this last claim broke through Bel-šar-uṣur's attempts at self-control and he suddenly kicked the broken tablet across the room. "Have your festival then," he declared angrily. "I will take the army to Upija, where men will fight for their lives and for this kingdom while you direct a puppet show."

Nabû-na'id turned his head from his son. His glance passed over the pieces of broken tablet but continued until it settled on the middle window. He stared in that direction for a long time and then abruptly gathered himself, rose and walked to it, his gait slow and unsteady like the old man that he was. He then turned and looked at the flowers in the vases lining the opposite wall. "I wonder what it's like to be a cut flower, straining toward the light in this dim room, the sun on the wrong side of the building for much of the day," he said. "I wonder if it's cruel that the vases are against that wall, rather than beside the window. I wonder if the flowers would be better off – happier even – in the courtyard below." He looked thoughtfully at the flowers for a moment, then pivoted and directed his gaze instead at the sunlit courtyard, gently bronzed by the waning day. Then, with his back to his son, he said firmly, "Enough, Bel-šar-uṣur. Stop. We will not prevail. Perhaps we cannot. Just stop."

An expression of astonishment spread across Bel-šar-uṣur's face, though his father couldn't see it. Briefly it was as if he were paralyzed, with that look of astonishment frozen on his face, as if his father's command to stop had worked like a spell and stopped him. But then the ice cracked, rage drove out the astonishment, and his limbs broke free into motion. He strode to his father, put his hands angrily on his father's shoulders, and forcibly turned him around to face him. "Are you just giving up? Are we just to open the gates and lead the Parsuans into our kingdom?" he demanded incredulously, contemptuously. He didn't wait for his father to answer. "Do you not see that they will massacre us whether or not we fight? Kuraš will care as much about you as I care about the flowers. He will not honor your eccentricity with mercy; he won't find you curious or whimsical or refreshing. Why should he? He'll cut you down, assuming some eager soldier doesn't get to you first. And Kuraš will disdain us all the more for having been too cowardly even to defend ourselves." The rage suddenly kindled and took fire. "I am not a coward!" he roared, erupting at his father.

It was now Nabû-na'id's face which betrayed anger and fear and something else which Bel-šar-uṣur couldn't recognize. The two stared at each other, disdain and even hatred in Bel-šar-uṣur's eyes. "No," Nabû-na'id answered harshly, shaking his shoulders free of his son's grasp and stepping back. "No, you are not a coward. A fool, perhaps, but not a coward." He immediately regretted calling his son a fool, but it was too late to call the words back, words uttered in anger when something more deliberate was required. He tried to correct his tone, to make it gentler without being gentle, to make it matter-of-fact. "You are mistaken to think it's cowardly for you to leave, to live your life somewhere else, not as a king's son or as a king, but just as a man. I was wrong to call that foolish, but it is a mistake, a mistake you have made many times in your life. However courageous you are, however courageous you have been, still to live your life on those terms, to let yourself be born anew, would require a new kind of courage you have yet to discover."

"You forget," Bel-šar-uṣur said slowly, with a hint of

contempt, "I AM the son of a king."

"You are the son of a nobody. How much better your life would be if that nobody had never been confused for a king – if that nobody, like every other substitute king before him, had served his time, gone to his fate, and made room for another king, maybe someday even a real one."

"Enough of this! If you are done being king, let me be king, let me rally our people to the victory you've despaired of."

"None of this is worth your life or theirs. Send the troops home to their families and their farms, muster tribute to Kuraš and to all the others like him who will come, let something else, something better, matter."

"What are you saying?" Bel-šar-uṣur almost shouted. "What are you saying?" he repeated, raging. "Do you lack the courage to lead your people to safety or to die trying? Is this just the babel of a feeble man who, despite his long years, is still afraid to die?"

"I've been dying all my life," Nabû-na'id spat out, his voice raised. "Maybe something else was possible, but I never found it." He grabbed his son by his shoulders. "I am telling YOU, you damned fool, to go live, that I WANT YOU TO LIVE." The old man was shaking, his arms and legs and hands. "I want you to live," he said a second time, almost feebly, as if his outburst had taken too much from him.

His son looked at him, unconvinced, suspicious, a little surprised. "It's not on any terms that I will live," he said, once more in control of himself. He detached himself from his father's hands and then added, "I am the son of a king, and I am a king. I will live as the son of a king and as a king, and that's how I will die, too. You can plan your festival, your puppet shows, your statue ceremonies. But I will plan battle." He turned and walked away.

Nabû-na'id looked at the floor, at the broken tablet. He felt hypnotized by it, but he needed to stir himself to say one last thing to Bel-šar-uṣur before it was too late. "Bel-šar-uṣur!" he finally managed to pronounce in a tone of command. His son stopped at the doorway. Nabû-na'id didn't shift his gaze but kept it fixed on the tablet pieces. "Before you go, talk to your mother. Talk to Niṭ. She's not well. But she's wiser than me – wiser than you too. Talk to her before you go."

There was no response from Bel-šar-uṣur, but Nabû-na'id heard him stop, and then, after a moment, heard him leave, heard him walk confidently down the corridor and down the stairs.

She was probably inside, but he didn't knock or try to enter. He just looked at the door. Why his father had sent him here he did not know. Even less did he know why he had come, why he found himself here before her door. He wasn't a little boy anymore; what could his mother give him? Did Nabû-na'id really believe that somehow she would talk him out of defending the city? How would she do that? Crying, begging, threatening? No, it was not possible. He would die either defending the city or because he couldn't live with himself having not even tried. So why was he here? Did he want his mother to give him her blessing? "I am to do what my father won't do – I am off to repel invaders and save Bābilim. Mother, give me your blessing." Something almost laughable struck him about this imagined scene. He doubted that his mother approved of many of his father's decisions, but that didn't mean she approved of his either. He sometimes had this suspicion that both he and his father were trapped in something from which it was unimaginable to either of them that they could escape – even while his mother, bewildered and horrified, saw that escape was all too easy if only they would open their eyes. But they thought their eyes were open; they had no idea how to open already-opened eyes. So she was left to watch them trapped in what was no trap, unable to escape what was easily escaped. This was his suspicion; he sensed it in her attitude toward both of them. But the suspicion gave him no help, no way out, even if it was right before his eyes.

He had also heard the other thing his father had said. "She is not well." He wondered why his father had said it, whether it was his last stab at manipulating him or if instead it expressed some grief and despair which Nabû-na'id couldn't fully contain or conceal. He had never admitted to himself that she wasn't well, but some part of him had long known it. Some part of him even felt angered that his father put it into words and made him have to face it. He hadn't seen his mother for a while, and it occurred to him that perhaps he had even been avoiding seeing her – just so he wouldn't have to admit it. It was a cruel thing to do to her – a cruel thing as well to have to admit to himself. Maybe for that reason he let the thought slip away and be replaced by a surge of anger at his father. Even if she was unwell, Bel-šar-uṣur thought, it still seemed likely to him that she would outlive him – that he, too, would turn out to have been among her miscarriages, among her still-borns.

There the door was. All he had to do was knock. But already in his heart he knew that it was too late – that he wouldn't knock – that he had already seen her for the last time. He was going. But he suddenly realized he wasn't headed north to Upija. Not yet. He would go south first. He hadn't a clear idea why, but he had to do it. He had to do it, oddly, because he had chosen not to knock on his mother's door.

She looked at him coldly, with statues in the dimly lit background. "Why are you here?"

He laughed a shrill laugh and walked past her into the room. "I don't know," he answered truthfully. "I tried to visit our mother and couldn't, so I came here. After this I will go north and lead our armies against Kuraš. Against Gubaru too." He looked at her face, but it was expressionless. "Did you know?" he asked brusquely.

"That Gubaru joined the Parsuans? Yes, I knew. Everyone knows."

He hadn't intended to talk about this, but here they were. "How do you understand it?"

She looked at him coldly a second time, long and hard, then re-entered the room herself. She was wearing a blood-red robe which was somehow startling in the black-and-white world of statues which the room otherwise was – barren of any other decoration, no tapestries, no flowers, the walls uncolored, the floor uncarpeted, though a few of the statues were still painted and a few of them were dressed. Most were barren.

"I have no desire to understand it. That's not my object. I still trust Gubaru. I expect father does too."

Again Bel-šar-uṣur was surprised to hear himself laugh a shrill laugh. "I doubt Kuraš cares who trusts whom. I doubt he especially cares that Gubaru defected. The tide is coming in – it will pound our familiar world and then withdraw, taking much of that world with it. Whether Gubaru, or father, or I myself – whether we end up out to sea or just stranded flotsam on the beach – that's no concern of Kuraš."

"Who would have thought you could be poetic," his sister said sarcastically.

"Yeah, the poetic strain from our father may come out more now, as I face – what's coming." From our mother too, a voice in his head added.

"What's coming has no face," she answered quickly. "Like many of these statues," she added, pointing around the room. He was surprised to see that she was right – surprised and horrified as he followed her gesture from defaced statue to defaced statue. He recognized suddenly that he was afraid. What she said next made him more afraid: "Like you."

He didn't react, almost like he hadn't heard. His not reacting took root, so that after a while he could no longer be sure she had actually said it. Then he heard a voice which apparently was his own. "The death of Kayvon was also poetic," the voice said. "What happened to Kayvon, what I did to Kayvon, was its own awful kind of poetry."

She didn't respond.

"Now I will face his father. Maybe there will be poetry in that too. Or perhaps I will be killed just by some random soldier, no poetry in my death, just a random act, a javelin cast into the air that happens to hit someone, it doesn't really matter who, even if it happens to be me."

"Surely you don't want me to pity you?" she asked, her anger and sarcasm relentless.

For a third time he heard the shrill laugh which was apparently his own. When the laughter stopped, he heard himself say softly, "No."

"What do you want then?" This time there was actually a question hidden in her words.

"I don't know." He looked her in the eyes briefly, then turned away. "I want not to have killed Kayvon. I want to be visiting you in his house and yours, right now, perhaps with a young child in your arms while others of your children approached adulthood, rather than finding you in this cella full of lifeless statues, statues which are neither your children nor your husband."

"They're closer to my brother," she answered. "Most of them faceless, most of them deformations of something which once was purer, something which didn't match our conception of what a thing should be, but still was itself."

"Our mother is unwell," he heard himself say abruptly.

His sister sighed and unceremoniously, in her beautiful

blood-red robe, sat down on the floor, next to a bench on which were placed numerous figurines of dogs, most of them broken. Her head bowed and she looked at her lap. Finally, after a long silence, she said, speaking into her lap, "And yet you did not go to her."

"No, I did go. I stood before her door. I just didn't knock."

"Was she to open the door miraculously? Or was it just to be chance which delivered you from having to rap on the door with your fist and humbly request entrance?"

"Would it have been a miracle or mere chance if she just happened to be home? I could have knocked, and she might not have answered. She could have been out, overseeing the work on the canals. Or she could have been sleeping, undisturbed and undisturbable by knocking."

"When you say she is unwell, what you're really saying is – she's dying. And then, when she is dead, our knocking will not disturb her, or if it does, she will nonetheless be helpless to respond. By not knocking, you treated her as if she were already dead."

He denied the charge. "No," he said. "No." Then he added, "I don't know that she's dying. I was afraid to see that she is. Maybe she isn't."

"Maybe Kayvon isn't dead either, then."

He walked closer to where she was seated, stopping in front of the bench with the broken dog figurines. He picked one up. "I hear you accuse me. I hear you damn me. What else are you to do? But you called it "our knocking," not my knocking. That's something – I'm even grateful for it. And I also see that you have dedicated your time if not your life to preserving faceless statues and broken figurines. Maybe that just means you're mad and your life and your time have all been wasted. That's what I was comfortable thinking even quite recently. But maybe I was wrong and it means something else."

"Oh?" Though seated, with him standing over her, she managed, looking up at him, to hold her chin at a defiant angle. "I suppose you have an idea what?"

For a fourth time he heard a shrill laugh which must have been his own. "I won't ask for what you won't give and for what I can never earn. I will leave and fight at Upija and probably die there. I'm not asking you for pity either. I guess I am only trusting that – perhaps despite yourself – you'll find a place for one more faceless statue, for one more broken figurine."

"Because I'm mad? Because my life and time have been wasted?"

He shook his head, at a loss for words. "It's not a prediction," he finally said. "It's a request." And then, without again looking at her, he strode confidently out of the room, out of the temple – soon he was out of Uru and on his way to Upija.

* * * * *

From the [fragmentary] Assyrian Accounts of Herodotus

…Prior to Babylon's fall, Labynetus ordered – or invited – the divine statues from the surrounding cities to take refuge in Babylon. The scene must have been chaotic: rumors running rampant of Cyrus' impending, unstoppable approach; farmers transformed into soldiers by imperial command and sent off to camps, hamstringing the harvest; and then the temples scurrying to get their charges prepared for a journey as likely as not to become an exile. The rivers became stopped up with boats; there were even boat shortages, with priority being given to the needs of the temples, not only for the conveyance of the statues but of all the necessary cultic materials, especially the divine food. It must have been an extraordinary sight, watching gods in their austere dignity scramble to the capital, round basket boats overloaded with grain scampering after them, their gunwales barely above the water

surface. (I call them round basket boats because they were in fact shaped like round baskets, made from plaited rushes and animal skins and not unlike the baskets some barbarians use to carry material on their heads to this day.) Yet some said that this was all a cynical ruse on the part of Labynetus – and that, some cities perceiving the ruse, they refused or at least did not heed his command. After the earlier forays of the Persians, many areas surrounding Babylon – notably Orekh – were already in famine. How could the king acquire all the necessary supplies to endure what was anticipated to be a long siege? By ordering (or inviting) the statues to take refuge in the capital. So claimed the enemies of the last king, the ones who viewed Labynetus as a heretic or a non-believer. Labynetus had other ends in view for that food than as fodder for statues. But another explanation every now and then reached my ear: that Labynetus did all of this, not to protect the divine statues within impregnable Babylon during the expected siege, nor in order to appropriate the cultic food for the city, but in anticipation of one last New Year's Festival, the new celebration of which he had inaugurated after his return from the desert. The traditional celebration had also brought the divine statues to Babylon; and perhaps Labynetus understood that this mostly unplanned, chaotic assembly of the gods under the shadow of the sword marked a truly new year, or rather a new age, one whose arrival could only fail to be announced, scheduled and choreographed.

I wonder as well how he, and perhaps the Babylonians more generally, understood the inertness of their gods. The traditional New Year's Festival – not the one which Labynetus had instigated after his self-imposed exile, the one deemed impious by so many in the priesthood – celebrated the ascendancy of one god over the rest and, in parallel, the creation of man from mud and divine blood, the blood of a rebel god. But now in this moment of urgency no divine blood could be found. Statues do not bleed. When gods are but bloodless stone, what are men but mud? Perhaps what this unscheduled, unprepared new age ushered in was a new breed of men: not men of gold, or of silver, or of bronze, or even of iron. Not even men of stone, but men of mud. Men who did not spring from the earth, the spawn of dragon teeth, but men shaped out of mud and then left to harden in the sun. What energized them? What force moved their limbs, their lips, even their hearts? Or did they just float, like the gods in their boats, wherever the current took them?

* * * * *

The god-statues had bedrooms. What is more important, after all, than the sleep of the gods? More than once have gods resolved to destroy mankind because their sleep was disturbed. But what was the sleep of a god-statue? Were the god-statue's clothes, their brightly colored linens and silk, changed to prepare for bedtime? Did the god-statue sleep naked or wear pajamas, perhaps wool ones to better fend off the coldness of night? Or were they nestled under blankets? Did the god-statue's eyes close? Did the god-statue dream? Surely the priests wondered about this, talked among themselves about it, offered speculations or else hushed them. Surely there was one who said, "We are the dreams of the gods," and another who corrected him: "No, we are their shadows."

Whether dreams or shadows, the priests' relationships with their god-statue were intimate. It was they who brought the food before the god-statue at mealtime, they who set up the table, they who put out the water bowl for hand-washing, they who drew closed the curtains to afford the god-statue privacy while eating. The musicians played. Incense wafted about. First one course, then a second, curtains swishing open and closed, the clatter of transported dishware, the murmur of servers. After a prescribed time, or perhaps only when the priests' ears no longer strained to hear the meal sounds, the curtains were drawn open, more bowls of water were brought forward for cleaning, and the bread, meat, beer and wine – was any of it touched? – was spirited away. In their invisible forms gods were fed oblations, but as statues they were fed what you and I are fed. Gods are most like us when statues. As statues theirs was no more a repast of smoke than ours could be. And yet how little they ate, how little sustenance is needed to sustain a god and a statue.

Afterwards – sleep. Only the priests of the innermost chambers knew whether they slept in their beds or stood by them; whether they closed their eyes or stared blankly into darkness; whether they snuggled into blankets and snored. Who dared to ask what else god-statues did in the privacy of their chambers? After all, god-statues need water bowls to wash their hands before and after meals; but when else might they need water bowls to clean themselves? The palace had lavatories, complete with drains and sewers; why did the temples have bedrooms and kitchens, reception rooms and family quarters, all for the god-statue, his family and his occasional god-statue guest, and yet not have lavatories for them? Why was it specifically this which was overlooked? Where else has it been overlooked?

Such were Nabû-na'id's impious thoughts as wearily he washed himself, wondering how it was that, even amidst impending loss and disaster, even amidst the licking flames of terror, still man every day defiled himself then cleaned himself, the defilement necessary to live, and the cleaning – was that necessary for life too? Did the washbowls imply that a god-statue too endured a daily defilement as a condition of life, or were those washbowls instead the ironic and mocking evidence that a god-statue doesn't live because there is nothing generated by its self but not by its agency to clean itself of?

"Why are the gods so tired?" Gubaru had asked long ago, while the two of them ambled about a tell, youths still but on the cusp of adulthood. "Why do they long so much for sleep?"

“It’s a good question,” Nabû-na’id had responded, as he stopped to finger the felt of his left shoe until a pebble fell loose. “We are told that the gods created humans to do their work for them, so what is left to tire them out? Or are they tired because humans do their work for them? We feast them, we entertain them, we save them from toil. I wonder if it makes their existences empty, dull. Perhaps that is the allure of their dreams: while we dream of an existence of luxury and ease, perhaps the gods dream of struggle and strife, if only to escape their boredom. Maybe that’s why they get so angry when their sleep is disturbed, why more than once they have brought humankind to the brink of extinction. We have interrupted their struggle and strife; bleary-eyed, half-asleep, or at least not fully wakened, the gods enact on us the struggle and strife they had only dreamed of.”

“Their rest is deserved,” Gubaru had said. “It is to gods that we turn for justice; it is they who hear our prayers; it is they who punish us. They are like our kings, or our kings are like them: they may live in luxury, but that is their reward for the trials only they can endure.”

“The kings, then, are their mirrors, as we are the shadows of gods and slaves are the shadows of us. But Gubaru, why do gods need mirrors? If they are so busy with our prayers and punishments, with our justice, why are kings needed at all? Is the orphan or the widow evidence that a god has lapsed, that he miscalculated or erred or perhaps even didn’t care?”

“Why should the gods care about us?” Gubaru had replied, defiantly.

“If they don’t, why do gods worry about justice, or listen to our prayers, or punish us? Do they do this for all beings? Does the bleating sheep appeal to its god, even as we drag it to the knife-brandishing priest who, moments later, now covered in the sheep’s blood, offers it back to the gods? Why, in the eyes of gods, should we be any different than sheep?"

"We were created for them and of them; the sheep were created for us."

"So the sheep are our shadows, like slaves are our shadows? But don't slaves have divine blood coursing through them to the same degree that you and I do?"

"Their slavery is a punishment imposed on them by the gods, for something they have done."

"How can you be so sure, Gubaru? Doesn't it sometimes seem that their slavery is a punishment imposed on them by men, for being weaker than those men? And perhaps the same is true for the sheep. Their bleating never becomes a prayer because it is men and not gods who hear it."

"Maybe the gods are tired," Nabû-na'id had added, "because it takes such effort not to hear the bleating of sheep."

Waves of men surge forward, clash with waves of men surging from the other side, foam and froth splash into the air, red not white, a roar like boulders crashing, colliding, dragged to and fro by the enormous and furious flood, when all is weaker than water, even stone. Everything then freezes, nothing happens – only men dying and killing, while the line neither advances nor retreats – the moment almost lasts forever. But then a bulge breaks through, covered in blood. The world before it gives way, all is silent, one holds one's breadth waiting, waiting – and then it's there, the cry, the scream, the wail, announcing that what's born is no still-born, what's born is life itself, wriggling, wrinkled, stained in blood, crying, screaming, wailing. Victory, eyes pinched shut, shrieking.

Perhaps that was the birth of Bel-šar-uṣur, birth in battle, battle in birth. It's not clear whether to celebrate or to mourn. Something has broken through – something has broken free.

Now it will have to endure. Now it will have to grow. Now it will have to die, to give way to what breaks through, what breaks free, what breaks it. En-nigaldi-Nanna – something about her is beyond death, like her mother. But Bel-šar-uṣur belongs to death. Like his father.

Is another kind of birth possible? Can a baby yield the warmth and snugness of a mother's womb, the sound of a mother's heart-beat, the effortless feeding, even the breathing done for you – can a baby yield all of that, emerge into the light of day, into the cold, into the world of effort and strain, into the ever-widening separation from what it once was – can a baby yield all of that and not shriek? The baby who takes it all in stoically, without screaming, patient and possibly wise – that baby we assume is dead. Have we ever been wrong?

And what about battle? Is it always a birth? Does something alive always emerge from it, not simply in the mode of escape but as its necessary consequence? Why should life exalt its own destruction, why should horror be its proem, why should it wriggle free at that very moment when all the rest of us long for everything to be over, to be done, to be silent, when we kill just to make it all stop? In the thick of battle, past the terror and the horror lies the coldness that wants the battle to end everything, so there's nothing to go back to and nothing to remember. Otherwise, you just emerge on the other side, eyes pinched shut, shrieking. It may look like a birth, but it's a birth you don't survive – what toddles off is what you are when everything that was once alive in you has died. But maybe that's not unlike the other birth, which delivers a baby to our world. We forget the baby has left a world of its own, and because we forget that, we forget to wonder why.

* * * * *

Gubaru hovered over the fallen man, a sword in his hands, eyes furious. But Bel-šar-uṣur, lying on his back, looked past him, at the endless blue sky. "Look at me," Gubaru demanded. Bel-šar-uṣur didn't stir. "Look at me!" Gubaru almost shouted. Slowly, reluctantly, Bel-šar-uṣur tore his eyes from the sky and settled them on Gubaru. He settled them almost gently. The two men just looked at each other. Then, after a long interval, almost like a cloud blown by the breeze, Bel-šar-uṣur's eyes drifted back to the blue sky.

Gubaru took a step back. "I will not kill you," he said, dropping the sword, his eyes relenting. It didn't appear, however, that Bel-šar-uṣur was listening. He seemed utterly enamored with the sky, utterly enchanted by it. He did not even notice that vigorous old man sinking to the ground.

* * * * *

From the [fragmentary] Assyrian Accounts of Herodotus

...Gobryas killed him and avenged the death of his son.

* * * * *

It was a feast. It was a festival. Everywhere about them was excess, exuberance, excitement. But he did not sense joy, though he couldn't tell if that only meant he himself was not joyous. Along the walls were all the divine statues, richly dressed and ornamented. Niṭ was there, but she was younger and well. Bel-šar-uṣur was there and, surprisingly, was laughing. When did Bel-šar-uṣur ever laugh? (How had he not noticed that his son no longer laughed? What had become of his son? But here he was, laughing.) Mikum-Nisaba was there as well, off to the side, in her blood-red robe, awkwardly conversing with the statues. Gubaru too was there, but somehow he was both an aged man and the young boy from long ago. The glint of his eyes gave expression to his playfulness. (How had he not noticed that Gubaru was no longer playful? But here he was, playful.) Kayvon was present as well, just behind his father, looking towards Mikum-Nisaba's engagement with the statues. Only the distant, worried expression on Kayvon's face mirrored his own feeling that somehow joy was lacking. But then the dog came in, Fly came in, pranced happily about the room, jumped up on people, explored the meats on the table without eating any of them, and then, catching sight or wind of him, Fly approached. He squatted to the ground, Fly smelled his face, Fly happily licked it. And then he too felt joy.

A commotion suddenly broke out at the door. Someone entered, but Nabû-na'id couldn't see who it was. It was almost as if there were a hole in his sight – he could see everything clearly but what was at the center. That he could not see. Shift his gaze, even his posture, however he would, still somehow the center never shifted and never came into sight. What he saw was not nothing – nothing can't be seen. It was more an absence, but an absence he couldn't see. Who's there? he heard himself ask. But the room was so full of excess, exuberance, excitement that at first no one heeded. Who's there? he repeated, louder, and then again a third time. Something broke through; the excess, exuberance and excitement died down – but he had this unsettling feeling that it wasn't actually dying down – it was withdrawing. He could still see, but not hear, Bel-šar-uṣur laughing, but he couldn't catch his eye. Mikum-Nisaba, or rather En-nigaldi-Nanna, was still cavorting with the statues, but far far away. Gubaru was so distant that he couldn't tell whether his eyes still glinted with playfulness. But Kayvon was near, his expression still worried and remote. He could barely see Niṭ, but somehow their gazes met – the distance was impossibly far, but somehow their gazes met. In his peripheral vision, he sensed Fly leaving the room.

Still, someone had entered, someone at the center whom he couldn't see. He was afraid to look, afraid to break the gaze holding him and Niṭ together. The commotion was growing, however; it was almost like a whirlwind had entered the room, though a whirlwind which he couldn't see, a whirlwind which didn't clothe itself in the debris it put to flight, a whirlwind moreover which was soundless, gustless and voiceless. Niṭ was so far away he didn't understand how he could still see her eyes and hold them with his; Mikum-Nisaba had become a tiny figurine alongside the tiny divine statues; Bel-šar-uṣur's distant face was frozen in a grimace which as easily accommodated a scream as a laugh; Gubaru's eyes had tears in them; Fly was gone. Kayvon stood nearby, his expression worried and remote. Still he could not see the center, but somehow he knew who it was. His long-lost friend had returned, Belet-ṣeri-dannat. But he had returned in a form which Nabû-na'id could not understand how he recognized. Marks they were, only marks. Not even writing, just marks. Marks on a wall.

Chapter 16. The Sun

"How curious," the man said out loud. He was looking at the piled earth, at the channels, at the flattened bed where, it seemed likely, water once had lain. The borders of that missing body of water were marked by all the plant life, not yet shriveled and died but making a perimeter around what wasn't there – a perimeter which was inexplicable until it wasn't. It was only in the mind's eye that a lake could be guessed, then seen. They must have diverted water here for some purpose. Then, for presumably a different purpose, they drained it – but only after enough time had passed to ring the missing lake with shrubs and trees. What could their object have been? The answer had to lie with the destination of the channels. They would need to send men to trace them out, to follow them where they led. It would be wise to include an armed guard, in case the enemy lay in wait. He gestured a slave to approach him and, in peremptory fashion, gave the necessary commands. But even as he sent these minor expeditions out, probably at some risk, already he had an inkling of what they would learn. In fact he had two inklings: the channels would lead to the river – what other major source of water was there? And of course the river would lead to the city, to the enormous square with a hundred gates which called all of itself the gate of god. To their quarry, then. They would need to prove that his guess was right – but he considered that a mere formality. It would be so. And then perhaps they could turn the strategy of their enemy against itself; perhaps they could take these defenses – for what else could they have been? – and turn them from strengths into weaknesses. Already a vague idea was glimmering in his mind. He would need to let it settle, let it solidify – and then he would go to Kuraš, tell him what he knew, tell him how that knowledge could be exploited. Kuraš, he thought, would be pleased. Kuraš, he thought, would reward him. Perhaps it would not be necessary to launch a prolonged siege against the most famous city in the world, a city which had had months to prepare. Perhaps something easier and faster was at hand. Kuraš, he thought a second time, would certainly be pleased and reward him.

In the darkness the immense walls of the city loomed more as intimations than realities. Here and there, at corners and more or less equal intervals along the wall, was the glimmer of torches; now and then a sound which might be a watchman's. The soldiers passing beside and then beneath endeavored to be as quiet as possible, but they couldn't help splashing the water they trudged through, all the more because, denying themselves torchlight, they couldn't see where they were going. At any moment, then, a cry of alarm would be sounded and then – what? Who could stumble up the mostly dry riverbed and not expect an ambush, a trap, catastrophe? Perhaps the defenders would wait until everyone was inside, then lower the gates and massacre them. It would be easy enough. There would be no way to defend against it. Did Kuraš not foresee this risk? All the soldiers had faith in him, even to the point that perhaps only a few of them felt the risk they were even then undertaking. But was Kuraš the proper object of faith, or should it instead have been the engineer? (Who trusts his life to an engineer?) It was the engineer, after all, who had convinced Kuraš to attempt this. Kuraš then made a selection of his men for the attempt. But they were the second-finest men. They were very good, but not the best. Didn't that imply that even Kuraš doubted it could be so easy? Here they were trudging up the mostly dry riverbed into what was likely a trap, though if it wasn't, the gain was great. Kuraš had weighed the potential gain against the likely trap and found the balance with his second-finest men. But men in their hearts know when they are second-finest; and that knowledge encumbers them as they trudge toward what their general admits them worthy of.

There was certainly a sky overhead, certainly a million stars. When they had set out, it had been under a full moon (a less-than-ideal circumstance), but now the steep walls on each side of the river prevented the moon from being seen. Certainly no man looked up who, sword drawn, stumbled in the shallows towards a city lying in wait for him. What could this be but a trap? The river had been diverted into the dry lakebed. They timed it as well as they could so that the water levels wouldn't too noticeably drop until darkness had settled – but surely someone would notice the lowering of the river. It cut across the whole city, this immense home to multitudes, this capital, and it took only one man to notice, only one man to raise the alarm, along the entire length of the river's passage.

Somebody slipped, swore, splashed and sank – the noise unimaginably loud in the darkness and amplified all the more by their sheer vulnerability. Everyone stopped, stilling even their breathing. Their pounding hearts would give them away. An archer on the wall above would hear their stuttering hearts and let loose. Or if he did not, it was only to lure them further into the trap. Those really were the only options – and yet, after waiting an interminable time, someone up ahead started moving again, and everyone behind dutifully followed.

For that period when their stuttering, tattle-tale hearts were so loud, when they all were holding themselves frozen in the knee-high water with death imminent from the wall-tops or possibly even from the distant stars, for that period, very subtly, there had been the slightest suggestion of music. For the longest time it wasn't clear – was this their hearts or was it the rhythm and beat of a dance? If it was, from where? Who would be dancing on a night like this, on a night when men born of women marched to their deaths? Men who not only were sons but fathers? Men who, when pierced, would bleed and wail and beg? Who would dare dance when such men risked oblivion because someone told them to? But, as soon as they began moving again, the hints of music disappeared, and with them the questions the music had provoked or even posed. It was easy to believe that the music was only how their imaginations embroidered their panicking hearts.

The men were wet and cold as the darkness of night deepened, like some ever-heavier covering tossed on top of them. They were past the first set of walls now. They had ducked under gates which went several feet beneath the water surface when the river was full – but now, with the water so low, they hovered over the slinking men like the teeth of gaping jaws, for some reason unable to close. The second set of walls, seemingly no less great than the first, now loomed. Where the men were was a kind of no-man's land between the two sets of walls, with ramparts along the riverbanks as well. It was the most dangerous place, the place where armed men could fire down on them from all sides with impunity. And what if the gates they had passed under were suddenly lowered, trapping them like fish in a barrel?

Another man slipped and fell. The clatter was like a command; everyone instantly obeyed and stopped. Pounding hearts stuttered and skipped and, once more, ever-so-faint music was heard, though more clearly this time, music and maybe even the suggestion of stamping feet – the panicking hearts of the invaders like a frivolous melody twirling above the beat, the only real thing, the only solid thing, the foundation of it all – but was it the beat or the panicking hearts? And then, again, after an interminable interval, after every man among them had lived and died a thousand times, some anonymous person near the front made the decision to start moving again, and everyone followed. As soon as they began to move, the faint music, if it even existed, disappeared.

The comical part was when they had passed beneath the second wall, when they had achieved their goal and were inside the city. Only then did everyone realize that no one had expected to get this far – that no one had expected to survive, much less succeed – and yet here they were, still undetected, past both the outer and the inner city walls. The comedy was that no one now knew what to do. Had enemies fired upon them from a wall, it would have given direction to their cause, hopeless though it had suddenly become. They would have known where to throw their spears – up! – and where to surge in flight – backwards! – even while they would also have known that their doom was inevitable. But now their plight was, apparently, victory. This surprisingly paralyzed them. Where exactly should they climb out of the riverbed? Once out, where should they go? They would want to open the major city gates, the ones overlying not water but roads – but where exactly were those, and what was the best strategy to approach them? Presumably they could take one or two before the alarm was given and the city roused itself to its internal threat – but then the question was, which one or two should they take? The answer was obvious – open the gates nearest their own lurking army. What was not obvious was which gates those were.

Now that they had climbed up from the riverbed, the waning gibbous moon hung over them, still not yet at its zenith. It shone over an eerily empty city. After a while the soldiers made no effort even to hide themselves. They let themselves cluster together and mill about; they even whispered to one another, all while the moon cast their shadows along the vacant streets and against the houses which lined them, some as many as four stories high. Behind the houses was the wall they had crossed beneath. There a few flames could still be seen, signaling guards who at this point were either asleep or looking the wrong way. Those flames were the only signs of active human life, though – perhaps because this part of the city was so deserted – the glowing eyes, or the slinking bodies, or just the moon-shadows of dogs, cats and pigs were seen. Some of the dogs even barked, but no one cared, not even, after a while, the invaders.

In the opposite direction from the wall they had crossed under was the shadow of an immense building, some kind of pyramid or tower, far off in what was presumably the city center. Somehow the sight of it made clear the dubious music they thought they might have heard earlier – the sight of it made the music cross over into reality from what might have been a dream – a crossing over which had occurred more or less in lockstep with the men crossing under. The city was celebrating something; a festival was underway; and whatever this was had drained all the people from the city's edges to its heart, not unlike the man-made lake which the invaders had used to drain the river. It was puzzling that a festival would be underway, especially so soon after a catastrophic battle, a battle in which this city's army had been decimated and its leader killed. What was there to celebrate? How could these people give themselves to song and dance when their annihilation was at hand? Not only at hand, but inside. The enemy was no longer at the gate. The enemy was within. The enemy had arrived with the life-giving waters, the very waters which – though the invaders could not have known this – had carried many of the god-statues into the sanctuary of the city in the days and weeks before. Now that the enemy was here, strolling the city's vacant streets, all that had to be done now was one last opening, once the right gate was found, so that this small bolus of death which was already inside could metastasize and overcome the whole body of this empty, celebrating city.

Most of the enemy set off in search of that gate, but one man was somehow drawn or lured toward the music and the dancing and the moon-shadow of the towering pyramid. He had no idea what it was that compelled him, but he found himself alone in the abandoned city walking toward the hovering colossus at its center where songs were being sung and dances danced. His comrades went some other way – he had no idea where. He was soaked from the waist down. At some point during his solitary wandering through the empty city he had dropped his sword and his shield. His armor perhaps would distinguish him as a foreigner but this was a city where foreigners, even foreigners in armor, were familiar. Even as the right gate was found, even as more enemy soldiers poured into the city, even as a few defenders were slain in their sleep, mercifully, or less mercifully in hopeless panic, this soldier wandered alone toward the city's heart, towards the city's celebration. But of what?

It seemed he wandered all night; it seemed, for the longest time, that the center could not be approached, that no distance between him and the tower could ever be covered. And then, suddenly, it was; suddenly he was in the midst of it all, plazas lined with torches, warm not only from the flames but from the revelers, all crowded together, some drunk, some singing, some shouting, a chaos of delight or despair. The invader could make no sense of any of it. Everyone seemed as isolated as him – no more struck by a wanderer-conqueror in their midst than they would have been by a prophet or a king or a mobile god or even a beast. He saw gigantic, richly dressed statues near the immense tower, lined up in some kind of order; he saw what must be priests scuttling around them and driving away carousers who approached too near or too boisterously; he saw half-gnawed meats and breads tossed on the ground for daring, darting dogs to dash at. Here and there a few jugglers were juggling half-heartedly, but no one paid attention. Bands of musicians sawed and plucked and blew away at their music, not only unheeded but even themselves unheeding, their tunes often jarring with the competing tunes of other bands, similarly negligent, set up almost on top of them. He passed a raised platform encircled by torches where puppet figures lay abandoned – some kind of animal, some kind of man, and a pale sphere – all tumbled together in a small pile. His overwhelming sense was of ominous magic: that the city was enchanted, that all these beings were somehow spellbound, at once both alive and dead, the city so crowded here in its center somehow at the same time the mirror image of its vacant periphery.

The man realized suddenly that the night was growing darker. At first he didn't understand why, since there were flickering torches in all directions. The growing darkness somehow seemed of a piece with the ominous magic that he sensed, as well as with his intuition that even now the city gates, lifted or swung open, were full of his swarming comrades, the city's conquerors. This conjunction of events in his mind briefly satisfied him, but then he shook himself and remembered that growing darkness needed some other kind of cause. He more deliberately inspected the world where he found himself, a world at once fantastical and oddly familiar. What he was looking for, in this case, was the familiar disguised beneath the fantastical. It took him a long time before he found it – before he thought to look west. Only then did he realize that the darkness came from the setting crescent moon – a moon which seemed even then to be waning – a waning sliver which, at the instant of its disappearance, set new.

Looking west, watching on the distant horizon the last vestiges of the setting, self-erasing, born anew moon, he observed one other sorry sight which once more he did not understand. There in the foreground, with the moon evaporating behind him, was just a weeping old man, seated on a throne, unattended, ignored, alone.

The writing was in the sand; she could see it rolling through the arroyo's sand like a trickle of water modestly announcing a torrent to come from the mountains. Insects clambered out of the way, just as they would were it flooding water – though that water were to us but a trickle. Floods too are matters of perspective; or even this dry flood of writing, which stymied and panicked insects who knew the danger of water but not of writing, or who saw no relevant distinction between water and writing, or who perhaps in both cases scrambled in fear not from the water or the writing but from whatever invisibly guided water and writing. Can writing drown an ant just as water does? Is that also a matter of perspective, not the ant's but rather – who is not an ant when writing overtakes them?

She had a vision of that long-ago dying fly alongside that long-ago dying ember; she had a vision of her dying son and dying husband alongside the dying fly and dying ember. At first she saw them all in gruesome detail, side by side by side by side – each one staring helplessly at the sky. She saw their faces, her husband's, her son's, the fly's, even the ember's. But despite herself she was pulling away, hovering higher and higher above them, so that first their faces all together became indistinct and then indistinguishable; then their bodies; then that against which their bodies lay. All of it was sand – they too were sand – and she herself, what was she but sky?

The question could not linger; her attention was redrawn to the writing in the sand. Water plus sand makes mud; mud is the medium of writing. But what did writing plus sand make? And whose writing was it? She herself had inscribed great channels throughout the land – but did that make the channels her writing? Didn't the channels belong at least as much to what flowed through them, whether that was water or writing or wind-blown, tumbling sand, or even the clambering insects who themselves flowed to escape whatever flowed?

From so high aloft she saw the river – that was writing – but whose? She saw the roads stretching from mountains to seas – that was writing – but whose? She saw ziggurats, pyramids, towers, even gigantic statues, and they all became mountains, and then they became anthills, and then they became the smooth surfaces of lakes or seas. Writing in stone lasts a long time; in clay, if it's baked, a long time; in sand – less long. In water, not long at all. But from the sky they were all the same.

Grief sobbed through her. Grief for her son, who was dead; grief for her husband, who perhaps had never lived; grief for her daughter, whose life was a statue's; grief even for Gubaru, whose great heart had finally yielded and become stone. All of them were down there. How was it then that she alone soared in the cold heavens where the eyes of the dead peered always with longing and with wonder? Somehow she knew the answer could only lie, was even then lying, in the writing in the sand; and she mustered all her powers to try to concentrate on what that writing wrote, even if she should never know who wrote it – whether gentle Nisaba or malevolent Nabû, whether her husband or herself, whether Atraḫasīs or Zisudris or Gilgameš or Izdubar or Lugalzagesi or Ur-Zababa or Šarru-kēn or Kubaba or Sîn or the innumerable names of Marduk. With all her strength she gathered herself, diffused across the endless blue sky, with all her strength she concentrated herself into that single drop which, lens-like, would magnify the writing into readability, into something scrutable – but the wind too was gathering its strength, was opposing her efforts to consolidate herself – she heard the winds howl, then the clap of thunder, but no, not a clap, the thunder was growling, the thunder was barking, the howling wind, the barking, growling thunder – she recognized it all, how familiar, how dear, not threatening but joyful, lifeful, playful, she was being called above all to play, to play above all, she was being called to Fly. And so she let herself go. She let herself go. To Fly.

* * * * *

From the [fragmentary] Assyrian Accounts of Herodotus

...Some say he was taken at Hippar, others at Barsip. The first city is sacred to their god of the Sun; it is also where Xisuthros buried his tablets to protect them from the flood. Indeed the city's name is related to their word for writing, for it is there that writing was buried. But this may account for the confusion with Barsip, since the latter city is sacred to their god of writing, whom I have heard called Nebo but whom the Egyptians call Theuth, though they also identify him with their Sun-god Horus. Hippar is to the north, Barsip to the south. It would be better if Barsip were in the east, where the sun rises and writing is born, and Hippar in the west, where the sun sets and writing is buried. But it is not so; it is north-south, not east-west, because the logic of the stories we write is not the logic of the earth, even an earth full of buried tablets themselves made of earth and full of stories.

* * * * *

Kuraš and Nabû-na'id examined one another. Kuraš was considerably younger than Nabû-na'id, energetic and, though physically small, still imposing. He was wearing armor, leather boots and a stunning purple cloak, while Nabû-na'id was dressed in his familiar robes and stood with his familiar hunch. "You must know who I am," Kuraš declared haughtily in Akkadian.

"You are the ŠU king, the omen of Gilgameš," Nabû-na'id almost whispered. "And also, like me, *šar pûḫi*" he added, yet more quietly.

"What?" Kuraš asked impatiently, leaning forward.

"Yes," Nabû-na'id answered more clearly. "I know how you are called and even possibly who you are." For a while neither spoke, Kuraš taken aback by this qualified answer. Eventually

Nabû-na'id broke the silence. "Your name – does it refer to the Sun?" he asked, switching to Parsuan.

Kuraš smiled. "I had heard you were a scholar. You're the first defeated king to address me in my own tongue." He paused. "As for my name, perhaps it does refer to the Sun. So indeed some say." Then he murmured, "Does it matter to you what my name refers to, other than me?"

Nabû-na'id shrugged. "Why not? My unusual path to kingship began, without my even suspecting it, with an eclipse of the Sun. That eclipse ended a war between Manda and Luddu, both of which," he observed drily, "are now vassals of yours. For a time the Moon blocked the sight of the Sun. But perhaps now, at last, that eclipse is over."

Kuraš bowed his head slightly. "So it would seem." He paused, and then added, "I know quite a lot about that battle. I am, in some ways, its child – or the child of the peace which followed."

Nabû-na'id looked Kuraš in his gold-glinted eyes, not so much holding as demanding his conqueror's gaze. "It would surprise you, perhaps, but I am relieved if the eclipse is finally over. However harsh the light of the Sun, its distortions of the world are the distortions we are familiar with, ones which the miserable race of men knows how to do something with."

"Ah, the miserable race of men. Perhaps you would feel differently about men had your side prevailed."

"No," answered Nabû-na'id, "I would not."

Kuraš sniffed meaningfully. "Why has the city yielded so easily? I expected that a siege of many months would be required."

"You must have caught us with our guard down. Who could have foreseen that you would use the canals?"

Kuraš looked at him quizzically. "It's like you left the door open," he said. "It makes me suspicious, as you would be too, after my years of experience. Why would you do that? To deliver the miserable race of men to their Sun?"

"I have –" He stopped, almost choked. Then, nearly in a sob, he continued. "I had a friend. She taught me that writing abounds, that the earth is scarred with writing." Tears streamed down his weary face, but he refused to stop speaking even though he was unable to stop crying. "The scarring of the earth is not only its disfigurement," he insisted, his eyes wild. "It may be what gives the earth, or even you and me, as much of a face as any of us manages to have. She reminded me to see in writing life rather than death, or rather to read in writing life as well as death." He stopped again. "But she died!" he gasped.

Kuraš gave him a bemused, not unsympathetic look. "I have no idea what you're talking about," he admitted, his voice soothing, "but I am not unfeeling either. Was this your famous wife?"

Nabû-na'id didn't respond directly. "A lot of people died at Upija," he observed. "I have heard my son died there. And yet, in my heart, I never have thought Bābilim would prevail. What did they die for, if I have never thought that?" There was urgency, almost panic in his voice. "What did my son die for?"

"I am sure he died bravely," Kuraš commented, again not without sympathy. "I'm sure a father could be proud of his death."

"I have no desire to be proud of his death," Nabû-na'id almost spat. "He probably had that desire, perhaps even to his last moment. I hope, or I think I hope, that it outlasted his last moment."

"Mmmm," Kuraš murmured, nodding his head.

"We were prepared for a siege," Nabû-na'id acknowledged, abruptly changing the subject. "We brought many of the gods to the city, and we have even now a great supply of food, for them and for us. You'd be astonished," he added, "how much food the statues of gods require."

"Would I?"

Nabû-na'id grimaced. "It's a time of festival," he stated. "Not so much in Bābilim as in another city, far to the west. Perhaps you were surprised that our city was in celebrations even as your army encircled it. Perhaps you were as surprised by that as you were by the easy entrance into the city through the canals. A writing which swipes clear impediments, a writing which leaves life as well as death to be read."

"Again, I must admit that I do not follow you," Kuraš said with some delicacy. "Perhaps your meaning would be clearer if we weren't speaking Parsuan."

"You would be wise not to follow me, in whatever language."

"Why is that?"

"Why should the Sun follow the Moon?" Nabû-na'id answered enigmatically. "Why wane? Yours is the glory of day. When the Moon is present in the daytime, it is rare, ominously rare, that you fail to outshine it. And who worries about the setting of the Sun at mid-day?"

"You mean to remind me that I too will die?"

"I mean to remind you that it is rare for the Sun to die at any time other than the end of day. But the Moon dies at any time, all the time." The men stared at each other silently. "How good it will be for my people," Nabû-na'id said at last, "to once more be under the reign of the Sun, Šamaš, god as well of justice, rather than under the cold light of the Moon, Sîn. It seems to help people to believe the Sun sets only at a proper time, that death comes only at the end. It seems to help them –" he paused, and then said almost fiercely, "— live."

Kuraš shrugged. "People live with or without help, believing or not believing." He was tiring of this interview, which was unlike any other he had had with a conquered king.

He had expected haughtiness or begging, not eccentric ramblings. He didn't even sense courage in the ramblings.

"I have a request," Nabû-na'id suddenly announced.

"Oh?"

"If Gubaru is with you, may I see him?"

"The traitor?"

Nabû-na'id examined him questioningly. "Are you unaware that we are childhood friends?"

Kuraš suddenly laughed. "Maybe I had heard that, but I didn't believe it."

"May I see him?"

Kuraš looked him in the eye. "I would have no objection, were it possible. But he is not with me."

Nabû-na'id looked at the ground.

"Do you want to know where he is?" Kuraš inquired, almost teasingly.

Nabû-na'id continued looking at the ground. "He is where I will follow," he finally mumbled. "With the *pukku* and *mekkû*."

"What is this *pukku* and *mekkû*?" Kuraš asked, growing impatient.

Nabû-na'id looked up. "Just something we lost long ago. Something we gave up. Something yet to be found."

"Didn't you just say your friend Gubaru had found them?"

"No. If anything, they found him."

Kuraš laughed again. "You are a very strange fellow!" he announced. "Were you like this when you brokered the peace with my great-grandfather, at that battle with the eclipse you mentioned a moment ago? Did your ramblings make more sense then? Or have you just become old?" Nabû-na'id didn't answer, so Kuraš continued, "What ever shall I do with you?" Again Nabû-na'id held silent. "Shall I put you to death? Or shall I let you live?"

"It isn't in your power to let me live. No one had managed

that throughout my long life."

For a second time Kuraš looked at him quizzically. Then abruptly, harshly, he laughed. "We shall see what is in my power."

The proclamation Kuraš issued was well-received by the priesthood, the functionaries and the Egibi House, among others. Each accepted in the proclamation that part of it which served their ends; and, on receipt of that, they happily served Kuraš's. The stories they disseminated to the commoners – but also, perhaps unwittingly, among themselves – such that the commoners were not the only credulous ones – were tales of retribution or of mercy. Kuraš, they said, was a divinely-appointed avenger, come to punish the previous king for a host of misdeeds. That king had been a usurper, murderer of the rightful heir and hence rightfully murdered. He had been an apostate, a heretic who denied the primacy of Marduk and instituted his own perverse devotions. He had misled his city, his nation and his people, bringing them to evil, an evil expressed inwardly by the wickedness of their hearts and outwardly by the conquest of their kingdom. No greater sign of this was there than his irreverent festival, his lunatic festival, his moon lunacy – and the true god's meaning, in delivering the city to its enemies while in the throes of its profane celebrations, could not have been clearer. But the old king, the usurper, the fanatic, was also a bookworm, a scholar lost in the maze of his own pedantic trifles, an antiquarian who could not distinguish the brightening of dawn from the darkening of dusk. And he was doddering, too, weak of body and of mind, kindly dealt with by Kuraš, who mercifully spared him both the burden of rulership and the indignity of deposition. The old king, murdered on some accounts, killed in battle or put to death or dead of a broken heart or from a cough or after tripping, was on other accounts exiled to the dreary life of an administrator, a scribe's life, the life proper to this man who stumbled into kingship with a stylus rather than a scepter. The old king toiled away at his administrative arcana in some far-off province, dutifully sending monthly reports of grain rations and annotating them with evidence of past yields when the world was richer or poorer, full of bounty or neglect, all while his underlings snickered behind his back and his supervisors filed his reports away unread. An old man likes to be kept busy; it gives a life meaning. Perhaps he continued in his odd moon worship, in his *Namburbi* rituals for the tending of the dead. Who else was there for him to tend? His wife was dead – his best friend – his son – even his dog. But nonetheless the old fellow, full of self-importance, hunched over tablets throughout the day, reading them and writing them, as if somehow he still mattered – as if any of it mattered. He belonged in a museum, among the statues. He was, however, a peculiar, moving statue – not all of him, to be sure, but his hands gripping stylus and tablet and his tablet-focused eyes, the rest of him lying still.

* * * * *

From the [fragmentary] Assyrian Accounts of Herodotus

...the history of Assyria. But it was the maze of Deioces again, he who by twists and turns forbore Cyrus whose great-grandfather by twists and turns Labynetus placated with a marriage which generated by twists and turns the mother of Cyrus who overthrew by twists and turns the father of his mother and overthrew as well, by twists and turns, the man, Labynetus, who negotiated the union which, by twists and turns, led to him. Who cannot get lost, who cannot be dizzied, by all this which happened not in some subterranean, torch-lit world, some edifice of walls corners and door frames, but under the vigilant

and blinding gaze of the sun? For the maze of Deioces was held together by a name – his, even if it was as it is now no longer his own. The name marked the absence which united the whole. But this maze, this history of what I call Assyria, is held together by an absence not even marked by a name. An unmarked, unmarking absence. An absent absence. What it is I could not say.

Cyrus, as is well known, drained the river and thus gained entrance to the city. But he uncovered another entrance in the revealed riverbed, whose pebbles, long dancing unobserved beneath the waters, froze to stillness when squinting in the light of the sun. It was a tomb, it was a gateway to the dead, that he uncovered – and presumably this tomb or entrance or hole was also discovered by Nitocris when she preceded him in this toil. Perhaps it was even this tomb which became the principal object of her work, so many years in the making, otherwise to so little effect. For the canal project of Nitocris was the work of more than a decade, a duration which is hard to understand when a very similar labor was accomplished by Cyrus in weeks. So some other work must have been at stake, even if the king her husband, Labynetus, was unaware of it. Indeed what Cyrus and before him Nitocris discovered was the tomb of a great king who had sought eternal life and failed, and yet who brought word of a destroyed world back to our own, and who then left this and his story inscribed in tablets buried in the walls of his city, to be revealed only when those walls fell – almost as if, as with Nitocris' own tomb, the story were the goad for a defilement, or rather its reward, its fruit. So, anyway, I am told by the priests; I have not read the story and could not read it – if it exists at all. I do not even know the king's name, though some say he became the god of the dead, even as he had been king of the living. Perhaps this king or god is the one we know as Rhadamanthus, who ordained that when men swear oaths they must swear by animals or not at all. For to swear by the Sun is to swear by what never changes, what never shows judgment; to swear by the Moon is to swear by what always changes, but always in the same way, and hence, like the Sun, what never shows judgment. Every other god is between the Sun and the Moon, between one way of never showing judgment and another. So to swear by the gods is no option. But to swear by men is not either, because men don't show but make a show of judgment. That leaves the animals – or even the plants and the trees. Beings which the mud can bear, who thrive or wilt in accordance with judgment.

You might think I pestered the priests to tell me this story they say was left in a king's ruins. Am I not an excavator of stories, their seeker, their re-teller? Am I not a channel-digger too? But I did not. I eyed its possibility warily. I carefully circumscribed it, looked at it from this angle and that, and was vigilant lest in error I awaken it. I felt it teasing me closer, taunting me closer. I felt the temptation and the danger and at the very moment when I was already yielding I took to flight. My history of Assyria is the trail of breadcrumbs I left myself in the pretense or hope that it could unwind me from a labyrinth, should that be needed – but suddenly I realized that such a fistful of crumbs becomes a false courage and is itself what flatters the wanderer deeper into the maze. So I dashed the crumbs to the ground, where they lay like stars at night, and I fled, not following because not trusting the trail promised either by crumbs or by stars, but just fleeing, madly fleeing, blindly fleeing. Perhaps in this regard I was not unlike Nitocris, discoverer, I think, of this gateway to the dead, who knew the allure of the dead, who was tempted by it, but who instead returned the waters to their channels and herself took to flight. Her less-wise husband clawed the dirt, much as their god Nebo, mute and malevolent, is said to claw the dirt, the king believing that the marks reveal a meaning or express one, and the god not believing. Just so do we see marks on the Moon, blots, whose meaning we strive to comprehend even while, before our eyes, their pale dominion checks the light.

* * * * *

Somehow the tablets found their way to her. At first she received them greedily, her heart yearning for what the tablets claimed. She, who forever awaited the visit of a god, would settle for the mere message of a man, all the more now that she alone endured. But her initial enthusiasm subsided; doubts crept in; and she wondered if she wasn't just the plaything of some cruel potentate mocking her loneliness and her loss. If her father had taught her anything, it was to read – which above all was to resist the temptation of accepting as present what the mark always announced as absent. In other words, no one reads by the light of the word "day" – but that is also the only light by which to read. She received them, then, the tablets, and she strove to read them (always failing), and, exhausted, even lonelier now, she set them aside next to the statues.

She had no idea what this region Karmanā was like, and only the vaguest of ideas where it was. These letters, purportedly of her father, though carved in mud, were short on dirt – their author didn't make any effort to describe the place he was in, or how the people dressed or acted, or what languages they spoke. Perhaps he was surrounded by mountains and midgets – but it apparently didn't occur to him to say so. Perhaps he was in another desert, there to govern nomadic herders who hadn't the least notion they were being governed. Perhaps it rained without respite in Karmanā, perhaps it was a cloud-covered place where Sun, Moon and Sky were at best theoretical abstractions. But where this author lived was in his head – or better, in his words – and all of these other things, insofar as they weren't words or escaped words, escaped him.

But, she could imagine the author pointing out, when you say "insofar as they weren't words or escaped words," how far exactly is that? If the author were her father, he would look at her with his wild, hazel eyes and yet with a steady gaze, the latter all the more infuriating just for being steady, and she would want to shake him and scream at him, "Let there be something besides words!" He would probably shrug, concede the point, then irritate her further by observing that letters did, after all, limit him to words. And he would probably also wonder whether it was possible to live in words. Perhaps, he would say, your anger is because all I can give you is words – I can't even stay alive in them. Perhaps, he would say, you're mad at this tablet, which is all of me that's there. And it isn't alive, even if it's all of me that's there.

Perhaps, she conceded.

Just as with every other death, no one can do your reading for you. (But she didn't know whose thought this was.)

(This is not a land of midgets, nor a land of perpetual rain. In some respects it is not unlike Teima – a steppe with oases where date palms flourish. But oranges flourish here too, which was not true in Teima. And the wine! But what most interests me is that their canals are underground. It makes me think of your mother. And it makes me think of the difference between a writing impressed on a surface and a writing burrowed through the surface – the latter not unlike the way insects gnaw a nut, leaving their traces or their writing, if that is what it is, only to be discovered when the nut is cracked open. Ah, but I see your brow furrowing, your anger rising. Even when I attempt to give you dirt, I end up back at writing. I would sigh if I could mark it in clay for you.)

(Of course the tablet in your hand isn't saying any of this. How could it? The tablet couldn't have anticipated that you would criticize my writing for its want of dirt. And so what is this dialogue between you and me, for which the tablet in your hand is inspiration rather than transcript?)

(Oh father, she thought.)

(Yes?)

She walked to one of the shelves where she had gathered many of her broken dog figurines. There was one especially dear to her, the one with the broken foot. She held it in her hand, almost pet it. Oh father, she thought a second time. I hope you've found a dog.

But then, as if waking from a dream, she returned to the question – who was the author of these letters? Perhaps they were in fact letters from her father, a governor now in a far-off land; or perhaps, if this was different, they were messages transmitted across the old-world-devastating, new-world-originating flood; or perhaps, if this was different, they were even letters he sent her from beyond the grave. Or perhaps they were not letters of his at all – if that was different. She found herself believing each and all of these possibilities.

So she let the letters accumulate. She placed one atop the next, she built a tower whose bricks were tablets, whose name she made Bābilim, in whose shadow lurked the dog figurines, eclipsed by a spire of signs.

She wrote no other reply.

www.ingramcontent.com/pod-product-compliance
Lightning Source LLC
Chambersburg PA
CBHW022346020726
47500CB00002B/153
* 9 7 9 8 9 9 0 8 4 5 2 0 6 *